Cassandra's Crossing

A William Langdon Novel

By
Stephen Fredrick

Copyright Page

Published by Stephen A. Fredrick, Author

First Printing, September 2011

For my wife, Shelly
My real life Sandy Langdon

Chapter One

It started with a phone call.

I was working in my office on a report due to the client by the following morning. There was a backlog of upcoming work filling up my inbox and our little private detective agency was humming along better than it had been at any time during the past five years. Clients were lining up and best of all, paying their bills on time. Professionally, I was happy as the proverbial clam.

Outside, the dog days of summer had settled upon New Orleans with a vengeance and the combination of the heat and humidity was slowly steaming the city. I could feel the outside radiating into my office on Magazine Street even though I had the plantation shutters closed and the air conditioning was working overtime. People's tempers were flaring as they always do during the summer months in Louisiana and divorces were on the rise. To a private investigation firm which primarily works for plaintiffs attorneys, that was a good thing.

I had also fallen victim of the recent divorce boom, but mine had nothing whatever to do with the heat, humidity, or my temper, but rather my temperament, which was something I've been working on. I had nobody to blame but myself for my failure. My ex-wife, Sandy, remains my business partner, and we get along well given the nature of my stupidity which caused her to cut me loose from the husband role. When we had married, she told me there was one unforgivable sin, and one night in the presence of a former client by the name of Vanessa Lafontaine, I broke it. Dumbest thing I ever did, up to that point, but as they say, I'm still a relatively young man.

Anyway, since I've already mentioned her and because she'll play an integral part in this story, I may as well briefly introduce my ex-wife to you. As I said, her name is Sandy. Not Sandra, but Sandy; I've seen her birth certificate and I've met her parents, so I could swear in a court of law that these two people named their daughter Sandy Beach.

Absolutely true. Google it if you don't believe me. Beach is an actual surname. This particular branch of the family tree first arrived in north America in 1635 when Richard Beach landed in Cambridge, Massachusetts and settled in Boston two years later. Sandy's parents, amateur genealogists, have traced the lineage back to around 1254 in jolly old England. In over seven hundred years not one parent had the guts to play on the name until Joseph and Angela brought Sandy into the world. Funny, to be sure, but twisted all the same, don't you think?

When we divorced, she refused to take back her maiden name. Who could really blame her? What woman in her mid-40's wants to go back to the jabs and jibes of being Sandy Beach? I'll never forget the first day of high school in Mr. Hansen's sophomore World History class when the school nurse knocked on the door and announced she was 'looking for a Sandy Beach'. I laughed with the rest of my classmates, but it was in that instant I also conceived the idea for a punchline which took nearly two years to bring to fruition.

Sandy and I started dating - the first time - during the summer break between our junior and senior years. After returning to school in September, I loved answering the question of 'What did you do over the summer?' with the practiced and wryly delivered, 'Well, I spent a lot of time on a Sandy Beach'. My friends and I thought it hilarious. Sandy not so much. She broke up with me the first time around Thanksgiving during our senior year - she said I was 'too irreverent about everything' - and after that we drifted apart.

After high school, Sandy bounced around a bit and wound up married to some loser named Bobby Rhodes from Altoona, Iowa. Fortunately, that match made on a bar stool lasted only eighteen months before she saw the light and dumped him. For Sandy, it was an awakening on many fronts and she changed back to being Sandy Beach, enrolled in college, earned her law degree at the University of Wisconsin in Madison and then moved to Chicago as a new associate for a personal injury firm which handled the cases of those killed or injured in aviation accidents.

I ran into her again one day, literally, in the lobby of the Cook County Courthouse about eleven years ago. She was heading out and I was going in and neither of us was watching where we were walking. After I picked her up from the floor and we recognized each other, I asked her to let me make up for my clumsiness by buying her lunch at a nearby deli. That's the second time we started dating, but it turned out to be equally as fruitless for us as the first go.

See, that was a tough time for me because I was going through some professional issues as a detective on the Chicago Police force. I had lost a partner in a highly publicized and controversial gun battle with a group of drug runners which took place one night in a warehouse on the west side of the city. When the smoke had cleared, I was the only person to walk out of the place, and there were unsubstantiated rumors that several of the bad guys had tried to surrender, only to be given their last rights rather than their civil rights.

The press, which had always praised my work over the years jumped on what they saw as a good story and turned on me. They began peddling headlines which labeled me a vigilante cop after some people in the department who weren't even there began suggesting I had executed the last two bad guys that night. I guess anything that sells papers and ad time is fair game to media slugs. At least that's my opinion. Anyway, as the stories continued and the speculation raged, the brass began taking heat from both the public and their bosses downtown, and the brass doesn't like taking heat. So, in the middle of the night, I wound up being offered two choices: early medical retirement or early medical retirement. Thus ended my tenure with the Chicago PD.

The timing for Sandy and myself had been terrible. She was a rising star on the road to making partner in her firm, and I was a falling one feeling the heat to get out of the city. In the end we parted friends, and I not only left the city but the whole country for the Cayman Islands, taking a job offer from a former partner who had a bar in one of the resort areas down there. Sandy and I promised each other we'd stay in touch, and for a time we did, but you know how that kind of thing usually works.

Then, one day about seven years ago, guess who's on the other side of my bar ordering a strawberry margarita? Yep, Sandy Beach was in the Caymans on a short vacation and she decided to look me up. By this time, I was a full partner in the bar and had bought a small place out on Spiny Point on Little Cayman. I was a happy expat living abroad, but there was a gap in my life and as it turned out Sandy fit it nicely. That's the third time we started dating and this time it took, until that night where I screwed up with Vanessa Lafontaine.

Sandy took a leave of absence from her firm, moved in with me, and we married on the beach one morning about six months later. Over the last six and one half years, she's been Sandy Langdon. She didn't change it back after the divorce, and frankly, I'm in no hurry for her to be changing it to anything else anytime soon.

So, back to the phone call.

"Did you get a name?" I asked over the intercom.

"She said her name was Mrs. Cassandra Yeats-Thomason." Pause, then: "You know, Cassie Yeats."

Sandy obviously had recognized the caller's name as a long-ago flame of mine because there was a certain pleasured twist in her voice over the intercom as she announced the lady behind blinking light was 'requesting an immediate appointment to see me regarding a personal matter about which she refused to speak about with some menial functionary and would only discuss with me in person'.

Cassie Yeats. Shit.

"Did you get that?" Sandy said with more than a hint of mischief in her voice.

By the way, never tell a current love any more about your exes than you are prepared to live with being reminded of for the rest of your life. That's a rule; but, it's one I violated in the matter of Willy Langdon and Cassie Yeats one night shortly after Sandy and I began dating the second time. We had been reminiscing about 'back in the day' while drinking margaritas at a small Mexican joint on the city's north side and I told her about me and Cassie Yeats. Well, part of the story, anyway. By the way, here's another rule, or rather a few words to the wise which should be codified as law: 'Tequila is evil'.

Of course I had heard the name when Sandy announced it the first time. At the shock of hearing the words Cassie Yeats come out of the speaker, I had pushed myself back into my chair and started to rock a bit as I eyed the blinking light on the phone and pondered a response.   See, Cassie Yeats was the only person in my entire life whom I had been afraid of, she had been my first love, and had ripped open my heart in front of our classmates when she turned on her heel one day and walked away from me. Cassie Yeats was the one unfinished chapter in my life and I wasn't certain I had an interest in reopening it to close it.

The fingers of my left hand massaged the point of my chin. I glanced again at the phone.   Behind the annoying little light relentlessly blinking away was someone I had thought of often over the years, but whose voice I had not heard in three decades. The last time I did hear that voice, the words it sent forth in my direction were less than pleasant. I wasn't so sure I wanted to cross that bridge over those dark and roiling waters back to the age of fourteen - nearly fifteen - without some type of preparation.   Hence, the rocking, and the chin massaging. Yeah, okay, I hope it's clear that Cassie Yeats still scared me.

I took another moment to think.

My eyes darted over my desk. The Owens case report was only half done and due by the morning. There were several unreturned calls to the attorney representing Marcia LeRoux, the next client whose husband's life I was about to dissect for purposes of their pending divorce. And I had that thing for Sammy which I had been dodging since Memorial Day.

A response formed in my head: I was just too busy.

I smiled at my brilliance of finally being able to use what was usually a lie - but was this time the absolute truth - as an excuse to avoid seeing Cassie Yeats again.   It was now my turn to turn and walk away. The decision seemed right. It felt good, too. The old adage is correct, revenge is indeed a dish best served cold.

Leaning forward, I put my elbows on my work pile, took a deep breath and responded to my ever-patient partner and ex-wife.

"Sandy, would you please deliver a message?"

There was no response, but I knew she was still there because I could hear her talk radio in the background. She had the timing down perfectly, because just as I was taking a breath ask again, she calmly replied.

"I'm not doing your dirty work."

God, she could be annoying when she wanted to be. What was even more annoying right now is I knew she wanted to be. Arguing, I had learned long ago, would do me little good in moving her, so I swallowed a bit of my pride and tried a softer approach.

"Please, Sandy?" I said plaintively through gritted teeth. I glanced again at the flashing light silently hoping the delay had caused Cassie to hang up. It hadn't. She was still there, blinking and blinking and blinking.

Sandy didn't answer, but a few seconds later I noted the light had stopped flashing and through the still active intercom I heard Sandy say, 'I'm sorry Mrs. Thomason, but Mr. Langdon cannot see you today as he has other more pressing matters previously scheduled'.

I sighed in relief. I was in the clear. Cassie Yeats would recede back into deep memory and I waited to see the phone line light go dark.

Then I heard, 'But he'll be more than happy to have you come by at 1:30 tomorrow afternoon'.

A pause, then, 'Well, you're very welcome. We look forward to seeing you tomorrow. Good-bye now'. The phone line turned as dark as my rapidly souring mood.

"How was that, Otto?" Sandy then asked over the intercom.

I counted to ten. Then did it again. Then again because she had called me Otto and has refused to tell me why. She started doing it right after I confessed to the Vanessa Lafontaine situation and I hated her having a secret from me.

"Great, just great," I finally told her.

I heard the intercom click off.

I tried to resign myself to tomorrow's meeting. Of course, I knew Sandy would, in the end, be proved correct in her decision to bring Cassie Yeats back into my life. I trusted her. She always did have good instincts about what was best for me, and for our business. I still had a right to be upset though, didn't I?

Five minutes earlier, I had been happy as that clam of legend. Now my guts were churning and my head felt like it was going to explode. I looked at the files spread across my desk. I glared at the wall behind which sat Sandy. I thought about Cassie Yeats coming back into my life tomorrow afternoon for the first time in thirty years.

Then, I asked myself what would any normal, red-blooded American male in the same situation do? Yep. And that's exactly what this one did. I blew off writing my final report to the client, sneaked out the back door to my office and headed to my favorite watering hole up on St. Charles Avenue to down a few.

Walking into the coolness of the tavern from the blistering heat of the mid-afternoon sure felt good. Molly, the owner after taking over for her retiring father, knew me over the last year or so, since shortly after the Vanessa Lafontaine situation, and I've become a regular. She stood at the bar behind what looked like a mountain of bottles of various sizes and shapes, each filled with a brown nectar I recognized as the ever mellow bourbons of the world. As luck would have it, she was just about to launch her annual Bourbon Tasting event and said she needed a guinea pig. It was a role for which she had come to learn I was well suited. However, as she looked into my eyes at that moment, I think she understood in that seasoned tavern owner's way, it was a job for which I was also very highly motivated.

She lined up some shot glasses, looked me in the eye again, tilted her head as if she was rethinking the whole arrangement, and then admonished me that this was for taste testing purposes only.   I agreed.   She poured out a small sample of the first bottle and I pounded it back. It was a routine which was to be repeated many times as we worked through the bottles. I did the best I could to give her the feedback she needed. After all, regardless of *my* current need, a deal's a deal.

Somewhere around the tenth or twelfth sample, I decided that I needed some music, so I wandered toward the juke box and started a rotation of 1970s classics, starting with Gerry Rafferty's *Baker Street*. When I was done lining up the tunes, I took a sidetrack to the head and then retook my seat to continue tasting.

The next few tasted good, as I recall, but by the time darkness had fallen and the tourists started taking over the joint - and the jukebox - each successive sample was tasting much the same. I think Sandy may have checked on me by calling and talking to Molly somewhere along the line because Molly became less interested in my critiques and the portions she poured became more generous.

Around midnight, Kelli - 'Kelli with an i' as she likes to tell everyone - poured me into a cab, gave the driver a twenty from my wallet along with my address before kissing my cheek and telling me to take care. I vaguely remember a poorly executed attempt to pull her into the cab with me, a move she deftly sidestepped. Regardless,

I knew there would be no reason to feel embarrassed next time I saw Kelli. While it's never a moniker I have ever pursued, sometimes it's good to be a regular.

The cabbie must have followed directions well, because this morning I awoke on my couch next to a grease-soaked bag containing my duck sandwich which I had paid to have delivered to the bar from Juanita's. Even cold, it was a great sandwich and this morning it would be my breakfast. I fumbled for the remote I knew would be close by and clicked on the TV.

It was to be another real scorcher in Southern Louisiana today, the weatherman said. As I munched my sandwich and washed it down with Advil and an ice-cold Coke, I could feel the heat already soaking through the walls of my living room. Hell, you don't need a meteorology degree to tell people it would be hot and sticky in New Orleans in July. I could prognosticate that little gem, and I hadn't even stuck my head outside yet.

By the time I walked into my office at ten, Sandy was already at her desk out front - she preferred being out there to her office next to mine - and she wore an evil little smile. It was a look I was becoming to know well. Since we were no longer husband and wife, I doubted it had anything to do with her being disappointed in me for yesterday afternoon and night, and more likely due to the fact she was going to take pleasure in busting my balls all day.

"Let me guess..." she began.

I glared at her and she stopped short. I never used to glare at her, and I don't like doing it. She did nothing wrong, but I'm not fond of having my balls busted. Especially when I'm hungover.

"Don't even start, Sandy."

"Mr. Owens called this morning," she said.

Aw, shit. The client whose report I had blown off yesterday afternoon. This could be bad, I thought.

"What did you tell him?"

"Nothing."

"Come on, Sandy," I said in the best exasperated hangover voice I could muster. "As much as I normally enjoy semantics games with you, I'm in no mood to play those games this morning."

She smiled, left me dangling a few moments longer.

"Like I said, I told him nothing. He wanted to thank you for all the hard work in completing and sending over the report you emailed to him last evening. Oh, and he wanted me to tell you how amazed he was at your ability to summarize so many details into such a concise, cohesive narrative, or words to that effect."

"You finished the report?"

"I felt bad about the Cassie Yeats thing and how I sandbagged you. So, yeah, I pulled your ass out of the fire because of guilt and for the good of *our* business. Nothing more. Don't expect you can go out drinking and I'll be there to save your bacon from the frying pan next time."

She leaned back in her chair and crossed her arms across her perfect bosom. It was then I noticed she was wearing one of her push-up bras and a nicely revealing flowered dress. Somehow I knew her legs under the desk would be freshly waxed and tucked into size 7 open-toed pumps with a four-inch heel, her favorite dress-up shoes. She wore that kind of look of self-satisfaction on her face.

"I know I've been sinking into a bottle far too often over the last year, Sandy. I truly appreciate your standing by me."

"Can I have a raise?" she asked.

"No," I said and I turned to go into my office.

A moment later, I opened the door and stuck out my head.

"Really, thanks for saving my ass again, Sandy."

"No problem, Otto."

Someday I'm going to find out why she calls me that.

Promptly at two p.m., and half an hour late by the way, I heard the door open to our outer office. Exactly three-seconds later the air conditioning came on to beat back that real scorcher we were having and announce the arrival of Cassie Yeats back into my life.

The intercom buzzed. My stomach flipped, then flopped; that's something that probably happens when your first love comes back into your life after three decades, I thought. All this was new to me. I started to reach for the intercom and noticed my hands were sweating. I wiped them on my pants and then reached again. I pushed the button.

"Send her in, Sandy."

Sure, everyone talks about going back to 'the day' if they could know then what they know now, and many of us want a second chance to do some things over. Some people want a second chance to do most things over. Don't let anyone kid you, being fourteen pretty much sucked and reliving one of the most painful memories of your life at forty-five pretty much sucks too.

Over the previous four hours I had been massaging my slowly receding hangover with Advil, Coke, and multiple trips through my 1970s classics on my iPod, and my mind had played and replayed dozens of scenarios of what was about to happen.

I finally convinced myself this meeting was going to be a totally professional matter, but had a hard time convincing my ego which was holding out for her running into my arms while sobbing 'I'm sorry, I love you' over and over followed by the two of us falling into some sort of passionate fumbling about right there on my office floor.

Earlier this afternoon, I even imagined her as that nearly fifteen-year-old girl wearing those ubiquitous, formfitting, hip-hugging bell-bottom jeans, loose fitting peasant blouse, and of course that glistening and very fragrant strawberry lip gloss of the early 1970s teen fashion. Maybe I was over-thinking this whole thing.

Moments later, there was a light double tap on my door immediately followed by its opening. I held my breath, and Cassie Yeats took two very fluid steps inside my office doorway. She was neither a time-stopped teenager nor the love-starved femme fatale of my musings, but rather a full-grown, adult woman dressed to the nines; and wearing something which smelled to be more French than from the Jelly Belly factory.

She definitely had what we call in New Orleans, *lagniappe*: something extra. She was confident, classy, and refined; and that summary was all conveyed in a mere few seconds in her presence. Something told me the hoped-for resolution to one of the few unfinished chapters in the book of my life was not going to have an ending written for it today.

No doubt about it. Mrs. Cassandra Yeats-Thomason had entered my life. Cassie Yeats was long gone.

Chapter Two

She closed my door, paused - Sandy would say posed - about twenty feet from me, and waited. The girl Cassie Yeats may indeed forever remain a gauzed photo in my memory, but the woman Cassandra Yeats-Thomason obviously wanted me to take a few updated, crystal-clear mental images. Never one to disoblige a lady - well, not lately anyway - I pushed the iPod to the side of my desk, sat back in my chair, put my hands behind my head and started looking her over. Head to toe, and over again. She definitely looked good.

Even handicapped by a residual hangover, I gave her my best *Who me?* face. Those of you who have seen it know what I'm talking about; it's the look you always say makes me appear adorable. From recollection, it's the face I used to make Cassie fall for me the first time around.

I noted her smile was fixed and affected as she stood there, like she was giving me what she thought I wanted, but wasn't real happy about doing it.

Even so, I continued soaking her in. Her body was tanned and sculpted, the visible difference being the sculptor now had more good stuff to work with than back in the day. As a teen, Cassie had nice, ah, attributes, shall we say, but I noted God sure knew how to put together a woman.

The last time I saw Cassie Yeats, she had been outfitted in bell-bottomed jeans and peasant blouse, her hair was just above shoulder length, blow-dried and lightly curled, she wore little to no makeup and unflattering, brown moccasins. Thirty years had created quite the contrast.

Cassandra Yeats-Thomason entered my office wearing an obviously expensive, formfitting, light, silk dress in a once-again-fashionable pattern reminiscent of those from the 1970s. The dress did indeed hug her contours, ended about four inches above her knees, and on top exposed a tasteful touch of cleavage. I had no doubt the tag inside carried some fancy foreign boutique name and cost many times what its cheap, imported counterpart would have thirty years ago.

Anything she wore underneath the dress was either so fine it didn't telegraph or it simply did not exist. Her legs were bare, and at least six inches longer than they used to be. The little pudginess her teenaged legs had carried had been stretched and shaped into a prime version of a woman's gams. They ended in shapely feet disappearing into finely crafted, plum-colored Mary Janes which sported four inch heels and looked like some designer - Wang or Choo or God-knows-who - had put his or her name inside them while charging Cassandra a thousand bucks a pop for the privilege.

Don't paint me wrong here, it was my time with Sandy which had an impact on how I recognized and acknowledged items of fashion.

Cassie's deep brown eyes caught the light and I saw their viridescent flecks flash. I remembered how even as a teen her eyes could capture my imagination. She still wore little make up, save some jet black eye liner and a light brown shadow. The rest of her beauty was revealed in the natural glow of her skin accented by a medium tan. Her hair was a little longer than she used to wear it, now falling about her shoulders, was finely feathered and coiffed, and it still carried those faint auburn highlights in a thick sea of chestnut.

Apparently, Cassandra possessed the same minimal level of patience for which Cassie had been well-known, because midway through my second visual trip, she sighed, affected a slight pout, and changed her stance slightly. I knew my time was up.

So, I stood, hiked my Dockers a bit onto my developing middle-aged belly and moved around my desk toward her. Unsure whether it would be more appropriate to shake her hand or give her a hug, I decided to follow her lead, but be cooly prepared for either possibility. The net result was I closed the physical distance between us in some odd posture combination which had my right hand extended low for a handshake and my left arm thrown open above shoulder height like I was coming for a hug. I must have looked as ridiculous as I felt, because she started to grin broadly, then squared her feet and opened her arms to welcome the hug.

We momentarily enjoyed a long-denied closeness, or at least I did. Up close, she smelled even better than she looked. Then, there was a tactile silkiness and warmth of her dress and body underneath. She felt good.

Then, as quickly as she had welcomed the embrace, she just stopped hugging, and gently pushed me back. She had her hands on either side of my abdomen, with her palms in perfect blocking position to fend off any attempted Take Two.

I took the not-so-subtle hint, removed my arms from her shoulders and took two steps back. My eyes sought out hers. She deftly sidestepped my gaze. Whatever her purpose for coming to see me, my ego told me she obviously wasn't ready for searching eyes.

My head screamed 'say something!'.

"It's been a long time," I said.

Oh, good one Shakespeare.

"Has it?" she asked and a faint smile flickered across her face, then was gone. On her timetable, as always, her eyes now sought out mine. When our eyes met, I saw a coldness within her, then, an instant later, she warmed. She had always been a mercurial chameleon, but over the years Cassie had obviously acquired a few tricks.

After a mini-eternity of uncomfortableness, she allowed me to take one of her hands in mine and I led her to a guest chair by my desk. I motioned for her to sit, then I took the adjacent guest chair, eschewing the much larger, and more comfortable, judge's chair behind my desk in a show of informality. You know, the old friend treatment.

As I sat, our knees nearly touched, and in another of her fluid moves, she crossed left leg over her right and eliminated any further potential of physical contact. I thought that two can play that game and flipped my right ankle on top of my left knee and slid back in my chair.

In her lap, she held a small Chanel purse. I recognized the logo on the clasp. The color perfectly matched her shoes. Around her neck she wore a double loop of diamonds on a simple chain. I had never seen anything quite like the pendent. The loops were separate yet linked, like magician's rings.   In each ear, she wore a single diamond stud.   On her left hand, she wore a platinum wedding band studded with diamonds and a separate engagement ring which featured about a four-karat, square-cut, yellow diamond.   Even in the limited light of my office, her jewels flashed every time she moved. On her right hand, she wore a large amethyst ring, more of as a fashion statement to match her purse and shoes than anything else.

She glanced around my office.   Something in her look conveyed a level of reluctant acceptance.   So I made a show of looking around as well.   Seemed okay to me.

My office is relatively spacious; about thirty feet in each direction. I've got a burgundy leather couch and chairs set around a sitting area with a unique glass coffee table held up by a bronze casting of a bear on his back; a small conference area with a table which accommodates six; and my work area with two guest chairs in blue leather in front of the large, antique mahogany desk sporting a well-worn leather inlay.   A bank of plantation shutters runs along two walls of windows, and are invariably closed.   During the summer it's against the sun and heat.   In the winter, it's to isolate me from the numbingly desolate view of this part of Magazine Street.   Sandy loves to open them in the morning to let the world in, as she puts it. When I come in, I slap them shut.

One of the remaining walls is lined with bookshelves and of course, there's a wet bar tastefully hidden behind the one packed with leather bound classics.   I was beginning to wish I had started the day not with a duck sandwich and Coke, but rather a little of the hair of the dog.   I had decided it wouldn't do to show weakness to Cassie, so I had eschewed that thought a couple of hours ago.   I looked at her now, measured her patience, and decided it was time we got down to business.

"You called this meeting," I said, hoping to start the conversation.

She ignored the opening and seemed to be collecting her thoughts.

"I take it you're not here to talk about old times," I said, trying another opening.

"I'm here to hire you," she said, almost defiantly, and locked her eyes upon mine.   "As far as old times go, for now let's just allow the past to stay in the past, shall we?"

Cassie was never a girl of many words, and it was obvious from her demeanor, that she was a woman quite acclimated to not needing many to get what she wanted.

I had done a quick internet search on her this morning. She could more than pay my fees; in fact she and her husband were part of that often-maligned, rarified ultra-rich class. Not that her husband, Gregory Albert Thomason, had been any whiz-bang moneymaking genius. His family money went back several generations and he was the product of trust funds and inheritances which all funneled his way because he was the last Thomason heir. So, even though Cassie Yeats came from fairly common, middle-class stock, she had married well.

The couple was said to be a bit reclusive, but when your wealth is measured in ten figures to the left of the decimal point, you can do pretty much whatever you want in this world.

No, fees wouldn't be a problem. The problem was I was rapidly growing a ginormous dislike of her. Cassie Yeats had been a fiery, amusing, fun, witty, down-to-earth girl. The woman with the matching shoes and purse sitting across from me was an obnoxious, unapologetic, self-centered, spoiled bitch.

Then she started to cry; I mean real, liquid tears. My eyes darted around the office, even though I knew there wasn't a box of Kleenex within fifty feet. She reached into her purse and pulled out a lacy handkerchief and deftly dabbed her eyes and the two short trails on her cheeks. Then, as quickly as it began, it was over. She regained her composure before I had completed my visual sweep of the office for the box of Kleenex I knew didn't exist.

"Willy..." she began. "I need your help."

"Nobody has called me Willy in years," I said. It had been her pet name for me. As an adult, almost everyone called me William, except for Sandy, who, for some reason, has been referring to me as Otto ever since the Vanessa Lafontaine situation.

Cassie replaced the handkerchief into her purse.

"Before you begin, Cassie, I agreed to see you, but, I'm really not accepting new clients right now. My schedule..."

"I know," she interrupted. "She," with a head motion toward the outer office through the wall, "She, told me yesterday you were booked solid. Then within a moment or two changed her tune and said you'd be happy to see me. So, which is it, Willy?"

"You refused to share with Sandy the reason for wanting an appointment with me. I agreed to see you today more or less as a favor because you're an old friend. I really cannot take on any new cases at the moment, and, frankly, Cassie, given our history, believe I may not be the best person to serve your interests."

I could almost hear her mind counting off the pause.

"As for our history and my best interests, I'll sign anything you wish which will release you from any claim I could make. I want the best. I've done my research. You're the best, Willy. I want you. Period."

This was indeed a woman used to getting her own way, just as Cassie had been capable of doing years ago, albeit using slightly different tactics.

I made the decision to at least hear her out.

"Why don't you tell me what you need, Cassie."

Like turning off a light switch, as soon as I agreed to at least hear her out, the change in her demeanor was instantaneous. No more feigning. No additional pretexts. No phony histrionics. Nothing but the whole unvarnished story - or so I thought - flowed from her over the next half hour. In fact, she explained her needs without theatrics and with such a flat affect that I almost found it hard to believe hers was a cheating husband case. Most times, a scorned woman is very emotional about her story and not at all shy about her desire for revenge against the bastard who had dared to shred her heart; not to mention having stolen her youth, and crushing her dreams, and ruining her body with HIS children, and blah, blah, blah.

No, Cassie was flat, unemotional in the telling. Until, that is, the story worked its way around to the money issue and The Prenup. Then she seemed to muster a little bit of emotion.

I maintained a prepared speech for my female clients in her position and usually punctuated that speech with cliches such as 'you can't squeeze blood from a turnip' or 'men aren't all the same, really' and always concluded my talk with the sage advice given to me by my mother when I divorced my first wife, 'the best revenge is living well going forward' to help defuse the emotion and bring them back to reality.

However, with the cash promised by this particular prenuptial agreement - as Cassie described the document - there would be no issue whatever of Cassie being able to live very, very, very well. I briefly wondered what would motivate a man to sign something so obviously punitive in the event he strayed from the marital bed, but when I considered the whole of Cassandra Yeats-Thomason I had my answer.

Therefore, I saved my speech for the next *real* grieving soon-to-be ex-wife and rose with her to escort Cassie out. There was no small talk on the short walk to my office door and she offered no second hug when we arrived there. I opened it and watched her walk out of our front lobby without giving Sandy even so much as a sideways glance.

When I could no longer see her in the hallway, I gave Sandy a smile and shoulder shrug and then went back into my office and closed the door.

I stood there and stared at the backside of the mahogany slab. Again, Cassie had turned the tables on me and gotten her way. For a few moments, I felt like that insecure ninth grader standing alone amongst a swirl of fallen leaves again. How in God's name could she still do that to me?

Cassandra walked with a purpose through the outer office, down the hall and out the front door. She knew Willy and his receptionist, Sandy or whatever, could see her until she disappeared down the stairs and she intended to use that time to her best advantage. So, she walked with a purpose.

She glided down the stairs and out the doors onto the street. The heat hit her in the face like a wave of nausea. She hated the southern subtropical climate, especially in the summer; and she loathed the state of Louisiana in particular. She found it an inbred cesspool of insidious decay and felt since most of it had been hewn from a fetid, malarial swamp created by the downwash from the rest of the continent, she believed it should go back to being just that. She despised the humidity, the heat, the bugs, the people - especially the idiots enamored with the mouldering decrepitude who referred to it as 'old southern charm'. Most of all, she hated that damn relentless sun which scorched the hide from anything not fortunate enough to carry with it a little shade and relentlessly seared what was left to the barest bone.

The limousine waited at the curb; it's engine, and air conditioning, left running on her order. The driver was watchful, and mindful of his tip, so he beat her to the rear door and held it open. He nodded his head in deference and she looked right past him and moved inside without comment or compliment. It wasn't until she settled into the soft, cool leather that she again smiled. This time, the smile was not affected, but genuine, and crafted specifically for the man holding a glass for her.

The man waiting inside the back of the limousine handed her the tumbler of iced lemonade, then changed positions to the back seat alongside her. He was younger than she, maybe mid-thirties, but looked even younger than that. His smile was bright white and seemed to jump forth from his deeply tanned face. His shirt and pants were of fine silk: off white pants and two-toned gray and black shirt. Sunglasses were perched on top of his head. Cassandra noticed he had removed his shoes and he flipped his bare feet onto the side seat and crossed his ankles. Even the sight of his feet turned her on, and he said nothing as her eyes moved up his body slowly because he knew what she was feeling, and thinking.

"How did it go?" he asked as her eyes finally met his.

"Better than expected. He's still carrying a torch," she said. Her fingertips traced on his bare arm. "That will be useful as things unfold."

He pushed a button on the overhead and said, "Back to the hotel, driver." They could see the chauffeur beyond the privacy divider nod in response.

"The hotel?" She asked, her fingertips moving further up his arm and under his sleeve. "I thought we were catching flights back to Dallas."

He smiled and took a sip of his club soda on ice.

She read his mind, then purred and curled up to him.

The driver glanced into the rear view mirror. He enjoyed that his passengers thought the glass was one-way. He slowed to just under the speed limit to enjoy the show.

"Dammit," I said to myself as I stood staring at the backside of my office door.

"Did you say something?" Sandy hollered from her desk.

Her question, I knew, was rhetorical.

Because I knew her so well, and she knew me equally so or better, her query had signaled two things: One, she knew to leave me alone for a while; and, Two, I knew I would have at most thirty minutes before curiosity got the best of her and she came in to ask about the reasons for Cassie Yeats' blast from the past.

Being the executive type, I made the decision to put those thirty minutes to good use. First, a glass of bourbon over ice would help salve the reopened thirty-year-old wound. Next, I needed to sort through what I had just heard; and while Sandy's allotted thirty minutes would not nearly be enough for that, the nine hour airline flight I was now seeing in my near future should just about do of it.

I pulled my eyes from the stained and lacquered mahogany slab that is my door, and without turning my head moved them to the left. There, just a few steps away, behind the dozens of leather-bound classics was hidden the object of my current desire. Were someone glancing around my office, they'd never guess a bottle of Kentucky's finest, and most anything liquid, distilled, and aged I or my guests would desire to imbibe, was hidden behind row upon row of the classic works of Melville and Twain and Plato, even de Tocqueville - all of which I've read several times, by the way.

The architect had designed the hidden wet bar for the building's previous owner, a real estate firm whose broker had loved to party after five o'clock. Eight hours a day it was work, work, work, but come happy hour, it became Mardi Gras in the office. Sandy and I picked up the building from his widow after he created a new off-ramp on the bridge going over Lake Pontchartrain one night. The wet bar was so well hidden, I hadn't even known it existed until the agent revealed it on the day we closed escrow.

I took those few steps one at a time, placed each hand on a different bookshelf at just the right spot to release the hidden latches, pulled the two doors open to expose the bar, grabbed a glass from the shelf then opened the coolest little gizmo ever advertised on late night television, the Ice Butler. Twenty-four hours a day, three hundred sixty-five days a year - and the additional day each leap year - this little gadget continuously supplied fresh, crystal clear ice cubes to it's little reservoir. No old ice, no clumps, just individual, perfectly shaped, dice-sized cubes, each one the perfect size for not bruising the bourbon.

I removed the Butler's cover, grabbed a handful of cubes and then spilled them into the glass before adding a splash - okay, maybe a little more than a splash - of my favorite adult libation, Jim Beam's

Kentucky Straight Bourbon.   Even given my occasional foray into taste testing for Molly, I'm really a simple, white label kind of guy.

I walked over to my desk, sank into the comfort of my judge's chair and tossed my legs up onto the work files scattered about its highly polished leather and wood top.   I left the bar doors open, knowing that I'd be back, and that Sandy would most likely agree to join me in about twenty-six minutes.   It was cool in the office; the sun fought its way through the cracks and seams of the closed plantation shutters and cast an intricate pattern of shadow and light across the room.   I took that first drink, held the glass up to an errant ray of light and admired the caramel color reflected through cut crystal. Cheap bourbon in an expensive glass.   I smiled.   Quite the contrast to some of the expensive stuff I drank from cheap shot glasses last night.

The warmth flowed down my throat.   I closed my eyes, pictured Cassie in my mind.   Thirty years of my life flashed by, little glimpses of battles won and lost, joys and sorrows, love and heartbreak.   Until yesterday, I had always likened my life to the famous Jim Morrison quote: 'The strangest life I've ever known'.

With the dawning of today, however, and the arrival of Cassie Yeats back into my world, my life had definitely moved to the other side of the looking glass.   I took a second sip of bourbon and dispatched it to follow the first, down the throat, to the stomach and quickly to the brain, then contemplated the quantum leap in strangeness my life had taken.

Since we're going to be sharing this drink - and the next twenty-two minutes or so - just between the two of us, perhaps we should use the time wisely and get to know one another.   Well, the conversation is going to be a bit one-sided, so why don't I just tell you a little about the world-famous William Langdon and my little investigative agency headquartered in perhaps the best city in the New World, New Orleans.

For those of you who don't know, running an investigative agency makes me what some people call a Private Detective.   My preference is the less formal and somewhat 1940s handle of *Private Dick*, and not for the reasons you may be thinking.   It's just that I have always felt that I had been born thirty or forty years too late with the most exciting parts of the twentieth century having taken place before I was born.

I mean, who could compare two world wars, a first-inning skirmish against the domino theory of Communist expansion in Korea, the invention and domestication of the automobile and the airplane, the envisioning of the space race, 'the bomb', movies going from silent silver and black events hand-cranked in a nickelodeon to full color, wide screen spectaculars, to the likes of Watergate and oral sex from an overweight Jewish intern in the Oval Office, global warming scares, coming ice age scares, a drugged out generation of the nonjudgmental who went on to screw up the next three or four generations, and one despotic leader - here and abroad - after another? Sure, the second half transitioned us from rock and roll to rock, but is that really enough to redeem half a century? From my perspective, I missed everything good, and caught most of the bad of the twentieth century.

Perhaps I am an anachronism in my time. I possess a sense of right and wrong painted in black and white, not shades of gray. I drive an Escalade, even the two blocks to my favorite restaurant. I love my kids, even though they may still carry a bit of a grudge toward me for the way I treated their mother, my first wife. I eat too much. I drink too much, especially during the last year. I judge too severely, some say. I've got a very long fuse, but once it's lit, be somewhere else. Life has forged and hardened me on the outside, although there's still a soft center in there if anyone can find it. The last person to do so was Sandy, and I am happy she still knows the way. You may feel free to consider me however you wish as you get to know me better. That's your right. After all, I'm telling the story, but it's playing inside *your* mind.

My background story is easy to capture in five or six paragraphs, so bear with me. I'm a Midwestern boy. I grew up in a small town of less than fifty-thousand people and the minute I graduated from high school, I took off for the glitz and glitter of, wait for it, Chicago. I wanted something more exciting for my life than drudging through an existence laboring at the local manufacturing plant or dairy, but Chicago was hardly the welcoming Mecca I had envisioned. I've heard similar recounted stories about people who chased the golden lure of California only to discover the lure was a tarnished hunk of brass. From my experience, every place you live is just a place to live once you've done all the cool, touristy stuff.

After a couple years of bouncing around at odd jobs, I was accepted into the Chicago police academy, skated through the training, and less than a year after I was hired, hit the streets as a rookie patrolman.   Five years later, I made detective and began working the seedy drug underworld.

Watching justice play out during the 1980s in Chicago was like sitting through a silent-film version of someone trying to herd cats. We'd build a case, arrest the bad guys, put them in jail and before the paperwork was done, some smart, corrupt lawyer would come along and convince the equally corrupt judge to let the bad guys out. Chicago justice has never really had locked doors with bars on the portals, but back then it had revolving doors, and the bad guys held the keys.

I witnessed some of my contemporaries start taking bribes; being on the take was a time-honored way of padding the pay in many big city police forces. Or even those in smaller towns. How else do you explain brothels operating right out in the open in places like Cedar Rapids, Iowa?

I watched from a sea of blue-clad mourners as others were buried because they were stupid, unlucky, or just refused to play along. Cops were tuning up defendants, many times, more to elicit a bigger payoff than for any other reason.   Drug profits were so prodigious in those days, even bigger payoffs didn't the impact the drug runners' bottom line very much.

So, to stay sane, you either got used to it and went along, or you didn't. I was the type who didn't and after a few years I began to take it personally against those who did. It started eating my insides, destroyed my first marriage and alienated me from my kids. Eventually, my trigger finger got itchier, my fuse shorter, and my career ended nine years later after a meeting downtown.

I was mustered out with what they termed a 'medical early retirement'. The CPD was suffering a lot of public black eyes at the time, so the brass had no desire to prosecute a cop for a couple questionable shootings of drug runners if they could just get him gone without much fuss.   Behind the scenes, the press was already labeling me the midwest's Dirty Harry and was rumored to be pulling together enough allegations of blue line vigilanteism to get a federal special prosecutor named, or at least that's what the bosses told me when they offered me my two choices. My agreement to choose retirement combined with some late-night, high level, back room talks to the powers-that-be in the media closed down further stories about slime balls meeting an early demise at the hand of an overzealous cop and I left Chicago.

Frankly, I was glad to leave. I had been getting very close to transitioning into a functioning alcoholic. My kids weren't speaking to me. I was living in a room rented by the week in some cheap hotel downtown, just down the hall from a local radio personality suffering similar marital woes at the time, by the way. My ex-wife was threatening to take me back to court to grab a bigger part of my pension. So, what did I do? I called an ex-partner who had done the routine thirty-and-out cop retirement and had bought a bar in the Caymans and had been wanting me to come down and work with him. He had an extra room in his condo, a new young wife from Venezuela, and a job for me if I wanted it. I did, and it was the lifeline which eventually lead me to reconnecting with Sandy and the best time of my life. Until I blew it, that is.

During the next six years, I sobered up to the point I could handle being sociable with a drink on occasion - I know that flies in the face of the twelve-step cure, but it works for me - became a partner in the bar, bought a little house out on Snipe Point on Little Cayman, and, as I said, rediscovered Sandy Beach, who was down in the islands on a vacation. I also began to slowly patch up the relationships with my daughters. I had recovered my soul and was beginning to be happy again.

Sandy and I seemed to skip over our ill-fated reunion in Chicago just before I left town and to pick up where we left off in high school. We pursued a whirlwind rekindling enhanced by fourteen tropical days and nights. Eventually, the time came for her to leave and instead of going, she had decided to give us a longer chance. She took an extended leave of absence from her law firm, moved in with me and eventually we got married one morning on the beach.

After a while, the sometimes claustrophobic island life got to her and it was my turn to make a decision. I gave back my share of the bar to my partner and we landed in New Orleans to make a new start. We formed the Langdon Agency as equal partners and with her legal background and my cop background made inroads with local lawyers representing jilted women, and sometimes men. Six months in, we bought this building from the off-ramp building real estate broker, took over the top floor for William Langdon Investigations, drank two bottles of cheap champagne, and made love on my leather couch.

I did keep the Snipe Point house, and the considerable nest egg I had built with earnings from the bar and medical disability pension payments, so I didn't need the money I would have received for selling back half the bar. That's why I merely returned Ben's favor of taking me in at my lowest point, and signed my half over to him and his wife.

A knock came on my office door. I glanced at my cell phone on my desk - I refuse to wear a watch - thirty minutes to the tick. I smiled. For some reason it felt warm inside to know Sandy so well. The door opened and she walked in. She really looked good today, even better than most days. Sandy was both the first and last beautiful woman to take my breath away today and it wasn't even five o'clock. It must have been five someplace, because Sandy headed for the bar, grabbed a glass and some ice, looked around for the bottle which now was on my desk, came over, poured herself one and topped me off. She toasted me in the air, winked and took a sip.

"I locked the office," she said, taking a seat on the couch, slipping off her shoes and tucking her feet under her skirt. She patted the other end of the tufted leather.

"Come on, Otto. Talk to me."

Cassandra exited the bathroom wrapped in a big white terry cloth robe, her hair wrapped in a matching towel. She flopped down next to the man who was lying on the now-destroyed bed covered only by a sheet across his midsection.

"That was way better than catching a flight," she said as she moved up to kiss him. "But, my love, we had better catch the six o'clock to Dallas."

He groaned in disagreement, started to slide his hand into her robe. She rolled away deftly and was on her feet an instant later. She reached down and pulled the sheet away, exposing his erection.

"Captain, your rudder is definitely impressive, but you had better save your strength. We've got a long flight home tonight."

"I'll let Jason fly. I already told him and Bev to be ready to leave at 10:30. We'll be in Kahului by midnight local. The chopper will be waiting and have you home shortly after." He grabbed the end of the sheet she still held and pulled, surprising her and landing her next to him. As his hands moved to open the robe, hers moved to his rudder.

"I guess we'll be catching the eight?" she asked as she submitted to his touch.

"You're just about right on that," he said, his expression playful.

His eyes drew her into him as her body drew him into her.

I set the bottle on the coffee table, walked over to the Ice Butler and pulled another handful of little cubes for my glass, then went and took a seat at the opposite end of the couch from my partner and ex-wife. I took a long draw of the chilling bourbon, turned myself toward her with one leg on the seat and one hand balancing my drink on the back of the couch.

Sandy waited, safely tucked into the other corner of the couch. Sadly, from my perspective, not a bit of her legs were visible under the draped skirt. Her drink was cradled in both hands near her lap. She clicked a nail against the glass. I noted the fresh French manicure. Sometime yesterday, after completing the report, she had found time for a manicure, and, I assume, a pedicure to match. I dragged my mind from her cute little toes and began to bring her up to speed on my meeting with Cassie.

"Cassie has hired us to do some investigation on a matter related to her marriage." I pointed to the overstuffed envelope on my desk. "That's our retainer."

Sandy glanced over. "Well, if those are singles, I'd say there's about five hundred bucks in there. Not much of a retainer."

I smiled.

"Hundreds. Your count is right on, though, five hundred of them, fifty-thousand dollars, nonrefundable and charged off against future billings at our normal rates, plus expenses, of course."

"Who do you have to kill?" Sandy asked with a nervous laugh.

Fifty-thousand dollars was at the time about one-sixth of our annual revenues.

"Nobody, just track down a handful of women and document some suspected infidelities on the husband's part which will purportedly trigger some tough penalty language in their prenuptial agreement."

Sandy looked as if she had something just aching to get out, so I let her talk.

"You know, Otto, I did some Goggling of Mr. and Mrs. Thomason while she was in with you. They've had a long-term marriage, about twenty years give or take. He's reportedly got more money than God, mostly from inheritances, family trusts and the hard-built fortunes of five generations of ancestors passed down to the family's only living heir. Mr. Gregory Thomason doesn't appear to be very entrepreneurial, or particularly driven toward anything but leisure, it appears. His early years were stereotypical for a trust fund kid: bending expensive cars and chasing cheap women. Then, he meets and marries Cassandra Yeats. He's about five years older than her, a licensed pilot and experienced yachtsman. A bit of a media recluse is what they report, or perhaps since the couple moved to Maui as their principle residence after his father died about fifteen years ago, he simply flies under the media radar."

"And Cassie?" I asked.

"As for Mrs. Thomason, she spends much of her time being philanthropic with the family money, sitting at the head of a variety of charitable causes ranging from 'Save The Whales' to women's rescue missions around the country, but mostly from a distance through intermediaries who take the headlines and public adulation. Pardon the pun, but Cassie's role is more titular than anything.

"The couple have houses around the world, but spend most of their time in Maui at a custom-built spread on the southern coast. These are members of the world's richest people club."

Sandy delivered the synopsis from memory, but I know she's assembled a pile of specific data and has it stored and ready to be printed.

"So, Mrs. Thomason is done with the mister, but isn't too keen on simply taking her fair share?", Sandy smirked while asking the rhetorical question. 'Of course not' is the answer she knew was coming.

See, one thing Sandy was not when we split was greedy. In fact, she's openly judgmental about greedy women and I often think she'd be happier if we worked for more of the aggrieved men in divorce situations, but how we do our business is just the way the world currently turns. One attribute amongst many positives about Sandy is she is one of the fairest people you'll ever come across, and I think, is why it bothers her so much when she perceives people being unfairly greedy or malicious. 'Stuff happens in life, but move on with living', would be her motto, were she to have one.

Besides being unwaveringly fair, Sandy is one of the most discerning people I have ever met. She's able to gain insights into a person's real character and motives which I often overlook because I'm more focused in painting the whole picture before I judge it. Often she will see problems looming and have worked out a number of potential solutions long before I even realize an issue exists.

"Otto?" she asked to bring me back from my thoughts. "I said, so, Cassie wants as much as she can take him for?"

"Yeah," I said, shaking my head to clear it. "I think she's a believer in the axiom of what's mine is mine and what's his is at least half mine."

I could see Sandy stewing on the concept of Cassie's greed. Sandy has a process for handling information. First she stews, then she chews, then she tells you exactly what she thinks. She doesn't believe in shading her commentary once she puts her opinion forward.

"What makes her think he's been cheating?" she asked, taking a sip from her drink. "Sometimes a man can keep that kind of thing secret for years." She tossed me one of her disappointed looks. "Others have a hard time hiding the existence of the indiscretion for more than a few hours."

I definitely got the shot, it hit directly in the center of my heart. The Vanessa Lafontaine indiscretion, hell, call it what it was, a single, deplorable act of cheating on my part which I wasn't able to just tuck away in the vault and never let happen again. I had to come clean to Sandy. I was so torn with guilt that I had thought it would be best if I kept no secrets from her and so in order to return to a slate clean, I told her. Telling her had been the second biggest mistake of my life.

"I guess that's why God created divorce courts," she said.

My face must have displayed an appropriate level of supplication, because she took another sip of her drink and stopped talking. Sandy's neither mean nor vindictive, but sometimes her verbal filter fails and her brain lets words just tumble out her mouth.

"According to Cassie, she discovered a list of women's names and other information in his desk," I said.

"Snooping?" Sandy asked, again rhetorically, or so I hoped.

She hated snooping almost as much as she hated greed and dishonesty. In Sandy's world, you trusted, or you didn't. If you did, life was good. If you didn't, what's the point?

I rolled my eyes and shrugged my shoulders. I knew Sandy's view on the issue, so what's the point in deepening her annoyance with our new client? She noted my hesitation, and like any good lawyer, left the question going unanswered speak for itself and moved on.

"Did she give you a copy of the prenup?" she asked.

"No, she did not." I wasn't sure we'd be reviewing the document or even if was necessary we be given the opportunity. As far as I was concerned, our role was to investigate the allegations and present the client with a report, not litigate the issues. I was certain there would be any number of lawyers hired on both sides who would be eager to get their firms in on the billable hours on this one. Sandy always wanted as much information as she could lay her hands on, however, hence the question.

"Okay, so I take it we are supposed to track down these women and expect they'll just admit to the affairs?" Sandy obviously knew that wasn't going to happen. She was chewing on the case now. "Or are we going to try to do this forensically, tie together a bunch of circumstantial evidence like matching schedules?"

"You know there's nothing more difficult to tie down than a past affair," I observed. "However, Cassie believes there may be one or more affairs ongoing right now that can be more easily proved."

Sandy made a sour face like she had just chewed a piece of sand in our oyster of case. I could tell she was curious about where the pearl would be in this whole exercise.

"Did she give you a copy of her list?"

I also could sense Sandy was already becoming a bit skeptical of my handling of the preliminaries here. That assessment wasn't going to get better with my next response.

"Nope," I said. No pearl here, I thought.

Sandy stared at me.

I sighed.

It was time to put the rest of the cards onto the table before she leaned forward and smacked me in the forehead with the palm of her hand.

"Cassie wants me to come to Maui and meet her husband, gauge him a bit, and then do some snooping around on the island. She said she'll provide the list, and perhaps the prenup when I get there and then we can hit the ground running."

"So I would guess we're headed for Maui?"

I drained the rest of my drink just in case the smack to the forehead was still in my future.

"Well, me is," I said.

Cassandra exited the bathroom this time fully dressed. The Captain rolled out of bed and walked in after her and jumped into the shower. She watched him step inside the glassed enclosure and ached to strip down again and join him, but more imperative tasks were calling. Like Gregory had always told her, 'Cassandra, there are important things in life and things in life which are imperative. You, my dear, are always important, but sometimes I have to forego the important and give attention of the imperative things in my life first'.

"I'll see you in Dallas," she said above the running water and blew him a kiss through the glass.

He knew that meant she was leaving and they'd be traveling separately and as strangers from this point until she boarded her husband's G-550 jet which Captain Dan would command on the flight tonight from Dallas Love Field to Kahului, Maui.

He heard the hotel room door close and felt the air pressure bump in his ears. Dan snickered and continued soaping and rinsing his toned, tanned body. He enjoyed having Cassie as his, and all that having her promised for *his* future, but there was something extraordinarily evil about screwing her while she set about to screw over Gregory, and that really gave him a kick.

Seventeen floors below, Cassandra entered yet another limousine for the ride out to the Louis Armstrong New Orleans International Airport. She would check in, sit in First Class on the short trip to Dallas / Fort Worth International, be greeted by a driver and ushered into another limo at the curb on the Arrivals loop to take her across the field to the General Aviation ramp and a waiting Jet Ranger helicopter which would then whisk her across the city to Dallas Love field where Gregory's jet was parked and waiting.

Captain Dan caught a Southwest Airlines cattle-car flight leaving at 8:20 p.m. directly to Love Field and arrived to find Jason and Bev had everything prepared and ready for the trip home. Being the captain had its privileges.

When Cassie and Dan next saw each other, he was in uniform seated in the left seat of the cockpit, his face illuminated by indirect lighting and the soft, multicolored glow of CRT instruments. He watched the Jet Ranger land fifty feet from the steps of the Gulfstream jet and out the corner of his eye, savored the view as Cassie exited and walked to the waiting jet. He already had the number two engine running - the one on the right side of the aircraft's tail - and would turn number one when they closed the door. Cassie could feel the subtle vibration of the running engine as she stepped from the tarmac to the jet's stairs and observed Dan as she climbed aboard, feeling another vibration within herself. At the top of the stairs, she accepted Bev's greeting, turned right down the center aisle and found her favorite, oversize, reclining leather seat.

The open cabin door warning light extinguished on the CCAS display, meaning Jason had secured the portal, and Dan accepted the 'all clear' signal from the ramp attendant then punched the button on the overhead to start the number one engine. In the back, Bev brought Mrs. Thomason a glass of ice-cold lemonade, then returned to strap herself into a jump seat in the galley area. As Jason strapped into the right seat in the cockpit, Dan was acknowledging the taxi clearance from Ground Control and began the $45 million dollar jet rolling across the ramp toward the blue-lighted taxiway.

Four minutes later, the jet accelerated down the runway and leapt into the night sky, climbing rapidly to its cruising altitude of 44,000 feet while turning west toward a point in space just south of Los Angeles where they'd leave the bright lights of the coastline behind and head out over the deep, dark Pacific.

In the cockpit, Jason handled the flying chores while Captain Dan fantasized about this jet, and everything inside it, someday belonging to him. He had two paths to the fruition of his dream, and regardless of which way things worked out with Cassie's plan, he'd be on easy street the rest of his life. He smiled and stared into the inky blackness of the Mojave desert passing by underneath and contemplated the contrast of this dead, dark wasteland to the life and lights of Las Vegas in the distance out Jason's side window. As they moved further west, he could see the glow of Los Angeles appear in the distance on the horizon and it reminded him of the promise of a new dawn in his life.

In the back, under subdued lighting, Cassandra absently picked at the crab salad Bev had brought after takeoff and thought about the fuse she had lit in New Orleans with the hiring of William Langdon. She prayed to God her plan worked as she had envisioned it, but then realized God would never entertain sanctioning of such a plan, and especially not from the woman she had become over the last two decades. It was upon the realization that no divine help would be forthcoming that Cassie decided that rather than rely on anyone or anything else, she'd fully embrace Destiny and make her plan work by shear force of her own will.

The decision to maintain control in her own hands buoyed her spirits and the next bit of crab was the sweetest she had ever tasted.

Chapter Three

The Hawaiian Islands are the most remote spot on the face of the earth. You cannot get further from any continent or large land mass on the planet than when you are standing on one of the eight islands which make up the United States' fiftieth member.

Actually, those eight islands poking out of the middle of the Pacific Ocean are only a small part of the land formation known as the Hawaiian-Emperor seamount chain. They are the most visible portion of an archipelago the Hawaiians refer to as the Mokupuni o Hawai'i, which formed through volcanic activity over a single undersea hotspot and that extends northwest some fifteen hundred miles from the island of Hawai'i which currently sits on top of the hotspot.

The island of Hawai'i, more commonly referred to as The Big Island - aptly so since it is currently Hawaii's largest island - was formed over millions of years by five volcanos, three of which are still active. Of those three active volcanos, only Kilauea is currently erupting, and has been since 1983, each year adding acres of landmass to the island. Mauna Loa, or the Long Mountain, is also considered an active volcano, but has not erupted since 1984 and Hualalai on the west side of the island hasn't erupted in over two hundred years.

The Big Island contains the only active volcanic activity in the United States. While each of the other islands and undersea mounts in the Hawaiian chain is volcanic in origin, because each has moved off the hotspot there is as much danger of a volcanic eruption occurring on any of the other islands as there is in Kansas City.

At some point in the earth's history, each of the islands was located on the hotspot, which is, in simplest terms, nothing more than a hole in the earth's crust which exposes the molten magma layer to the floor of the Pacific. The entire island chain moves several inches each year along the surface of the earth, and as the islands age and move, wind and water erosion slowly eat away at them until eventually each in turn is reclaimed by the sea. Several million years from now, the islands currently known as Hawaii will be underwater somewhere closer to the shores of Japan, long ago having been replaced by new islands.

In fact, the newest Hawaiian-Emperor chain island is already forming under the sea and has been named Loihi. Centered approximately twenty-two miles southeast of the Big Island, Loihi has already risen two miles off the sea floor and is just one mile from breaking through on the surface. In another thirty or forty-thousand years, Loihi will have emerged from the depths to be the newest Hawaiian Island.

Maui is the second largest of the current Hawaiian Islands - bigger than Oahu, home of Honolulu and Pearl Harbor - at a little under 730 square miles. Scientists believe Maui was once much larger and included above-sea-level connections to the neighboring islands of Moloka'i and Lana'i to the west and northwest and perhaps even the uninhabited island of Kaho'olawe to the southwest since they all share the same undersea mount. The channels between these islands are relatively shallow, only two to three hundred feet, whereas the depth of the open ocean to the north and east of Maui drops rapidly to over twenty-thousand feet.

The Big Island lies to the south of Maui across the thirty-mile-wide Alenuihaha Channel. On a good day, when the trade winds are not blowing full force, you can see Upolu Point on the Big Island from the shoreline at Kipahulu on Maui. However, due to the normally strong trade winds funneling through the channel between the ten-thousand foot high Haleakala Mountain on Maui and the nearly thirteen-thousand foot Mauna Kea on The Big Island which relentlessly churn the waters and raise a wall of heavy mist that can rise several thousand feet into the air, there are very few good days in the Alenuihaha Channel.

While the Alenuihaha Channel (locals call it the 'I'll End You Ha Ha' Channel) has allowed for crossings by as fragile a system as standup paddle boarding - essentially surfing with a long paddle for propulsion - its roiling waters and soaring mists have claimed any number of larger vessels over the centuries. Locals warn anyone away from challenging what some refer to as the most dangerous channel crossing in the world in anything but a large, well equipped boat.

What was being launched into the Alenuihaha from a narrow strip of fist-sized, erosion smoothed, black lava rocks sheltered within a small cove west of Kipahulu that evening was well-equipped, but a very long way from being considered large. In fact, the craft had been designed to hold only one person, and not comfortably.

Moving the small boat along the piles of the constantly shifting, smoothed lava rocks was not an easy task and getting it afloat safely, even with the protection of the tiny cove, was a physical and logistical challenge, especially when done by one person. The man launching the boat was well-motivated, however, and well-practiced, having done this numerous times before.

With a lunging pull, he scooted the craft another few feet closer to the water and wondered how much longer he could physically do this kind of work since he had turned fifty over the past winter. While he usually had some assistance, such as it was, tonight's launch was required to be a solo operation.

He paused to look up at the full moon which had clawed its way to the top of Haleakala behind him and judged the time to be nearing eight p.m. One more lunging pull moved the nose of the boat to just touch the water. The depth dropped rapidly just offshore, so once the boat made it to the end of the stony beach, it would float free. The man was breathing hard, partly from the tremendous physical exertion and partly because of the excitement he felt at nearing the conclusion to yet another reconciliation.

The man moved to the rear of the craft. One last shove, he knew, and the water would float the boat and its one reluctant passenger. After that, the small motor would be started and the boat would move slowly into the channel. While the day had been one of the channel's worst, tonight's forecast had called for lessening swells and calmer winds, evidence of which he was already observing.

He took comfort knowing tonight would be the perfect opportunity to launch the craft and its precious cargo. He opened a peephole in the larger cargo hatch for one last check of the equipment and passenger, then closed and secured the small plastic cover. Then he gave the boat that one last shove and it, and its lone occupant, floated out about twelve feet offshore before the engine started and it began to move off under its own power.

In contrast to the relatively shallow waters separating Maui and its neighbors to the west, because The Big Island occupies a different undersea mount, there is a very deep canyon about midway between the two islands. The target tonight was a spot a bit southwest of the direct line to Upolu Point - a total distance of about sixteen miles. The depth at the target, according to his chart, was 1,286 fathoms, or just over 7,700 feet. The boat would find the exact spot without further input by using the onboard GPS navigation equipment.

The motor surged and the craft accelerated to a speed of about fifteen knots. The trip to the chosen spot, were he able to maintain this speed, would be roughly an hour. He looked up at the moon again. He had plenty of time.

From inside the tiny control room, located within a natural formation in the mountain known as a lava tube, he confirmed the autopilot had taken proper control of the boat's helm. The preprogrammed coordinates had been locked into the navigation computer an hour before he began the transfer and launch process. Four weatherized cameras captured and transmitted back to his base station time-coordinated views on the small boat. One was located on the exterior bow and was rotatable three hundred and sixty degrees, the others inside of the control room, cargo compartment, and the cramped engine compartment also could be remote controlled to a lesser extent. The last of these cameras was currently focused on the two golf-ball sized objects on the floor near the stern drain plug. Along with the High Definition 1080p video content, the interior cameras sent back stereo sound as well.

Even with the diminishing swells, the ride was not comfortable for the boat's occupant. The bow of the small craft rose and fell with gut-wrenching regularity; first it would climb the face of the wave, run off the back of the swell and drop into the trough, the next swell would break over the bow and the pattern would repeat. Regardless of comfort, or the lack thereof, he maintained the speed of fifteen knots. The woman's contentment was not the first concern.

Just under fifty-five minutes after launching, the GPS display signaled arrival at the desired coordinates. He motored another thirty-seconds and switched off the engine. He confirmed all four cameras were being recorded and then he activated the onboard sounding equipment and was rewarded with a water depth reading of 7,689 feet. Very close to perfect. He smiled, moved his face closer to the display focused on the occupant of the boat's cargo compartment. All looked well, at least from his perspective high and dry in the small workshop. He was certain the perspective of the woman was not quite so rosy. Sadly, he thought, her viewpoint was about to get a lot worse.

Without taking his eyes off the monitor which showed the beyond panicked face of a young woman with bobbed blonde hair which aggravatingly - again from his perspective - kept falling across her eyes, the man toggled a switch on the control panel. As fast as the radio command traveled the fifteen or so miles between control panel and the boat, the light in the woman's compartment went off and the camera switched to night vision mode after only a moment's delay. Again the cargo was fully visible, though now in an eerie green glow. The woman's eyes were wide and he could see her fruitless struggle against the restraints in the small compartment growing more frantic by the moment. The man was always entranced by the eyes as they transitioned from human to the eerie greenish white under night vision camera. The change reminded him of an almost-animal quality, like confused prey caught in headlights.

He kissed his fingertips and then used them to touch her cheek on the monitor. With his other hand, he moved to the safety cover from the next switch, lifted the cover and toggled the switch. A look of sadness moved over his face which only he witnessed in the reflection on the screen in the semi-darkened workshop. A camera mounted in his little room recorded his finger flipping the switch but did not capture the wide grin of victory which quickly replaced the momentary mocking sadness on his face.

A subtle click originated from the boat's engine room compartment and was heard on his workshop speakers, followed immediately by the muffled sound of a small explosion, then a second in close succession. The woman flinched, her eyes grew even wider and more panicked. The man turned on the lights in the boat's compartment. It always gave him a thrill to watch as their eyes took some comfort in the return of the light.

The man knew it would take a full two or three minutes for the cargo compartment to flood once it began, so small and precise were the two holes punctured in the hull by the two shaped charges of plastique. He now could see water slowly flowing into the cargo compartment, just a hint at first as the engine compartment was designed to flood before spilling the ocean water over a bulkhead and onto the passenger's feet.

He momentarily wondered how it felt to form from utter confusion the realization that the cold water splashing onto their feet would soon engulf them, then deprive them of the ability to breathe as they struggled impotently against their restraints and confines.

He had seen his mother panic and then succumb, almost peacefully he thought, the last time he watched her go under, just before her lifeless body sank into the depths of that lake when he was seven. He concluded, like the question as to proof of the existence of Heaven, or Hell for that matter - one needed both for either to exist, or at least that's what he had been taught as a youth - this too was a question only those who had experienced the sensations and emotions could impart. Sadly, they were dead, and nobody could speak with the dead, he concluded again.

The cameras recorded every moment; they were watertight as was their power source, so he could witness every detail of what was happening on the boat until the building pressure overwhelmed the seals about one-hundred feet below the surface. He remained intently focused on the monitor with a mix of childlike curiosity and monstrous pleasure which now played in his reflection on the glass.

Within seven minutes of the explosions, just over an hour from launch, it was over. The cameras lost power, and the small craft settled the rest of the way to the bottom, some seven thousand feet below, unwitnessed.

It would never resurface.

Janet Hopkins was now physically gone forever. He had released her from her admitted wrongdoing; they all admitted their wrongdoing in the end. Once they did, once they surrendered to him, he released them. It was a simple calculus, really, he thought. By this time tomorrow, he knew, she would officially and forever merely be listed as missing, the ultimate answer to the riddle known only by him. And one other.

His work completed, the man stood straight, stretched his back and left the workshop. He closed the door but did not lock it. There was no need, he knew. He moved his head side to side, cracking his neck and releasing a bit of tension. He moved to the foot of the walkway and began his ascent to the surface. He would take a shower, perhaps grab a cold beer from the fridge and handful of beef jerky from the pantry.

It was time to await the return of his wife.

Just after midnight, the man stepped onto his home's large south-facing lanai, the one overlooking the calming waters of the channel which now concealed the body of Janet Hopkins. He wore pajamas and a light robe, the polished marble tiles cool under his bare feet. He was fresh from the shower, his body scrubbed clean for the next stages of the ritual.

The channel was lit with moonlight, the large whitish orb had descended from its apex in the northwestern sky and was now reflecting sunlight from far over the horizon onto the endlessly changing surface on the water. Regardless of the peacefulness and beauty of the scene, she was late, and his hands gripped the railing with a viciousness reserved for those who made him wait. Then, in the distance to the west he detected the sound of still, quiet air being whipped by helicopter blades. She had apparently told the pilot to take the route along the Hana coast tonight. He'd speak to him tomorrow.

He turned and walked back into the master bedroom, his hands formed into balled fists. He'd speak to her tonight.

The French-made helicopter settled gently onto the lighted concrete pad less than fifty feet from the house. The strobe lights on the top and belly of the aircraft cast flashes of red across the grounds. The pilot reduced the power to ground idle and the large rotor blades adjusted to a flat pitch which minimized the downdraft and allowed for a safe exit of the craft's lone passenger. An attendant jumped out and opened the rear door for Cassandra. She carried the small shopping bags from Dallas with her. The rest of her purchases from this mainland trip would be delivered to the house by car in the morning.

Cassandra crossed the stone pathway from the helipad to the house and walked into the side entrance to their expansive two story home. When the attendant had re-boarded and closed the door, the pilot increased power and lifted off, peeling away to the west and the short flight back to the airport. The noise and generated wind was short lived, and through the window of the garage entry door Cassandra watched momentarily as the helicopter dropped out of sight beyond the cliff and skimmed just above the surface of the Alenuihaha Channel.

She glanced at her watch. From the time the wheels had left the runway in Dallas, to the time Cassandra walked into her house was just over eight hours. She walked through the garage and into the kitchen, down the west wing hallway to the rotunda foyer and up the staircase. Low-intensity, floor-level lights on sensors illuminated as she entered each room and then turned themselves off after she left. At the head of the stairs she glanced right toward her husband's master suite and noted the light coming from under the door. She turned left, and as she took the first few steps down the hallway, she heard him open his door behind her.

"I was hoping you would stay in here tonight, Cassandra" he said, more of an order than a request.

She heard the familiar and frightening implication in her husband's voice and Cassandra well recognized the tone, which was simultaneously concerning and confusing to her tonight. Twenty years of learning, and understanding his moods and routines had prepared her for these moments, and she clearly understood the consequences of noncompliance. She took a deep breath and slowly turned around. Gregory stood there in his bedroom doorway with the light behind him brighter than the low-intensity movement lighting in the hallway and though she couldn't quite make out the expression on his face, she knew from history what it was; and what it meant.

"I'm really tired," she said, attempting an excuse which she knew had little chance of succeeding. "It's been a very draining day, Gregory, what with seeing my stepfather and all." She knew he had a better illuminated view of her face, so she did her best to maintain a non-threatening, yet strong and deliberate expression.

"That wasn't a request, my dear" he said and he turned and walked into what he liked to refer to as The Master's Suite.

Cassandra set her bags down on a side table in the hallway and followed him into his room. As she entered, she changed her demeanor and she willed herself to become docile while maintaining her dignity and honor. She could not let him see her surrender her will. She could surrender her body to his uses, but could not let him see her weaken. She called the affectation her passive resistance, and her mind raced to other things as he began. She knew which events usually precipitated this behavior of his, yet she had no knowledge of this particular predicate incident. Was there one? Had he changed his pattern for some reason? Had he indulged while she was gone? She knew there would be evidence if he had, and with her plans underway, she had to know if this was simply a repeat of so many times before, or if there was a dangerous escalation in his behavior taking place. After all, she thought, in his world, she herself was now a wrongdoer. Were he to discover her indiscretions, it could be very dangerous indeed for her, regardless of whatever else was going on.

She was naked now, lying on the floor on her back, stripped by him with the viciousness and anger brought on by what she knew was his own self-loathing. Her arms were loosely to her sides and he was kneeling on her wrists when his hands moved to her throat. She did not outwardly resist, and her eyes held not fear, but resolve. Resolve to not be broken, resolve to survive. As his hands tightened around her neck and she began to feel her brain go fuzzy, for the second time tonight she silently sent forth a prayer for herself. A small, non-challenging smile came to her face as she again realized the futility of that kind of act. As his grip tightened still more around her neck and she slipped further into the embrace of the darkness, she actually hoped there was no God.

After it was over and he had collapsed into a deep sleep, Cassandra slipped from his bed, collected the remnants of her torn clothing, and while mentally overruling the physical desire to wince at nearly every movement, padded across the carpeting to the door. She took one last look over her shoulder to confirm he was still asleep, then moved through the portal into the hallway, finally closing the door quietly behind her. She walked toward her room on the far end of the opposite wing of the house, the marble tile mercifully cool against her feet, and once there, opened the door and entered her master suite. She did not collect her shopping bags from the hallway table. They could wait until morning.

Once inside her bedroom, she locked the door and went to the bath to inspect her body, although Gregory rarely left any visible marks. She sat on the side of the tub and ran a hot bath. Cassandra knew she would be sore for several days, but on the other hand, she knew she also had at least that number during which he would leave her alone, physically. Gregory, she knew, would be apologetic in the morning without acknowledging his actions. He would be loving, and caring, and giving. It was his attempt to fool himself into believing he had done nothing but exercised his husbandly prerogative. Within a week, she knew, he will have completely blocked the events of tonight from his memory. At least that's the pattern she had been used to. Should something else be at play, she shuddered at the thought that she could expect almost anything from him.

He may erase tonight's events from his memory, but not from his diary - that assemblage of legal pads which she found hidden in his desk years ago in New York and which he had later forced her to recopy into what he now called his Journals. His writings were cryptic and as self-deluding as should be his post-event actions again this time, yet she was well-practiced in knowing how to decipher them. It had been several months since the last time he had her transcribe his writings into the second large, red, leather-bound book, and she knew there would be more about tonight to be transferred later, when he was ready. She toyed with the thought of checking his writing pads tonight for some answers, but knew should he awaken and catch her, he may very well kill her this close in time to the event she suspected. No, she thought as she sunk into the tub, it will be best to wait. The coming dawn would bring Saturday, she realized, and that meant he'd be gone for the day.

The woman currently known as Janet Hopkins claimed her checked bag from the carousel and exited the baggage claim area. She had passed through Customs and Immigration in Vancouver when her flight from the United States had landed there. She was wearing navy shorts, sandals, a white tank top under a long-sleeved, button-down, light blue shirt, floppy hat, and, even though it was shortly before midnight, sunglasses. It was early morning by the time she climbed into a taxi at the Montreal-Trudeau Airport. Half an hour later, the cab pulled up to a nondescript, u-shaped, brick apartment building on Saint Catherine Street, it's only distinctive feature setting it apart from scores of others being a glassed central staircase which squared the building.

The woman could have easily taken the Green Line One metro train which would have dropped her at the Beaudry station from which she could have walked the few remaining blocks, but that would have meant more people would see her in the well-lit subway car.   No, a dark cab exiting directly onto a dark street was the preferred method of arrival at Janet's apartment.

Janet Hopkins' apartment was located in a district of the city known as *Le Village*, an area now populated mostly by members of the Montreal gay community.   Formerly a poor, working-class neighborhood, gays and lesbians began concentrating to the area in the 1970s and 1980s in an attempt to escape persecution and ill-treatment they would still experience in those days even in enlightened, liberal minded Montreal.   From then, the area survived a colorful history with periods of expansion and expulsion of gay businesses taking place, but persistence and numbers finally won the day and the area developed the personality of Le Village as it was currently.

Janet hadn't necessarily wanted to move into Le Village when she had arrived from Calgary six years ago, but after finding more than enough discrimination still lingering around the city, she soon gravitated there.   While the woman currently impersonating her had never meet the real Janet Hopkins, there was a sadness in her heart as she began the last items of her assigned tasks, which was to make it appear to anyone who would come looking that Janet had returned safe and sound from her conference in Hawaii.

Using Janet's apartment key to let herself into the building and then into the first floor apartment, the woman next donned a pair of light-blue nitrile gloves before touching anything once inside.   She flicked the switch next to the entry door and a light went on in the kitchen area as did a lamp on a small desk in the street side corner. The woman looked around.   The apartment was small; an 'efficiency' is what the one combination room plus bath would be called in the United States.   She wondered momentarily to herself if they called it something different in Canada.   It didn't matter.

She wheeled the single suitcase over to the Murphy bed, pulled down the mattress and tossed the suitcase on top of the multicolored comforter. A few minutes later, she had the clean laundry put away and had stuffed the dirty items into an already overflowing - and ill-smelling - laundry hamper in the bathroom. She unpacked the jewelry and makeup pouches and stowed things in the bathroom cabinet and multi-drawer jewelry box which sat on a dresser under the large front window down the wall from the desk.

Next, she removed a small duffel from inside the suitcase and tossed it onto the other side of the mattress. Finally, the woman pulled off the computer generated tags used to check and track the luggage on its trip and tossed them into the garbage pail under the sink in the tiny kitchen area before stuffing the empty suitcase into a space in the corner of the small closet. She pulled the mirrored doors closed and studied her reflection.

"Not bad," she said to herself. "I do look better as a brunette or red head, but being a blonde isn't too bad."

Next, she looked into the mini-fridge where she found an English muffin and some orange marmalade. She split and then toasted one side of the muffin, spread on some of the goopy orange confection, tore off about a quarter of the disk, laid it onto a paper towel on the countertop and then stuffed the rest down the garbage disposal. The woman decided she would leave the uneaten muffin and the paper towel on the counter for whomever eventually found it. She wondered if they had roaches the size of VW's here like they did back home. It didn't matter. She wouldn't be back.

Turning her attention to the bed, she rumpled the sheets then tossed them open as if someone had been in there, slept, got up and left without remaking or stowing the bed. Given the general disarray of the rest of the place, the woman had no doubt anyone looking for Janet over the next days would consider the disheveled look all that out of the ordinary.

The woman took one last look around the small space. Satisfied she had done exactly as he had instructed, and had left nothing of herself behind, the woman currently known as Janet Hopkins pulled out a change of clothes and new wig from the small duffel and repacked it with the sunglasses, hat, shorts, tank top, shirt, and sandals she had worn in. She pulled off the wig and now the blonde, who bore a striking resemblance to the real Janet Hopkins, stood before the mirrored closet doors and looked into the eyes of a brunette who bore little likeness to the woman whose identity she had temporarily co-opted.

Finally, she removed and slung a small purse over her shoulder. She pulled out the new passport and other documents just to make sure everything was there and in order. The brunette turned out the lights, opened the door, locked it from the outside, removed the nitrile gloves and walked out into the early morning street to blend in with the bar crowd spilling out onto the sidewalks around the corner. She passed a dumpster in a small alley behind a bar and restaurant and tossed the duffel and gloves inside. He had told her to bring it all back, but she was not going to risk going through U.S. security and customs and immigration with the identity and clothing of a dead Canadian woman. She would tell him she had lost the items. What did it matter?

This time she did walk the couple of blocks to the Beaudry station and took the train back to the airport.

She looked at her watch. It was early Saturday morning in Montreal and it would be almost twenty-four hours before she'd be back home, certainly exhausted, albeit considerably richer.

Chapter Four

To keep the peace, I had promised Sandy a small consolation prize after telling her she wasn't going to Maui with me. We agreed I'd take her for breakfast at Brennans followed by a day of shopping at Canal Place, some of the antique stores on Royal Street in the French Quarter, and the Riverwalk. Sandy being Sandy and me being me, she had also successfully negotiated a late lunch at The Commander's Palace in the Garden District and an evening on Bourbon Street after dinner at Antoine's, possibly one of the most expensive and unarguably one of the oldest restaurants in New Orleans, in addition to two nights at the Hotel Monteleone in The Quarter. In return, she agreed to make my airline and hotel reservations for my trip to Maui for the coming Monday, and complete the research for a briefing book on the case.

So, at just past eight thirty on Saturday morning, I was cooling my heels in the bar area of Brennans, having just ordered a Creole Bloody Mary for Sandy and a Sloe Screw for myself. I know it's metaphorical, and that's on purpose, but the Sloe Screw also has orange juice in it, so I felt quite comfortable making a statement while also maintaining the breakfast theme. I had considered ordering the Long Slow Comfortable Screw Against The Wall, but felt a four-shot drink this early, even on a Saturday in New Orleans, may have been a bit tacky. Besides, while I may have felt temporarily put upon by the deal we had struck, Sandy always more than made up for any concessions she wrangled out of me; and, after all, it was half her company too.

Sandy had obviously stopped in the rest room to fluff and freshen up because she had called my cell as the limo approached the restaurant - yeah, she talked me into getting a limo for the outing as well - and asked that I order her the Bloody Mary with spicy green bean garnish. That was ten minutes ago. Hence, the cooling of my heels part. Knowing this could be one very long day, I hadn't yet touched my drink. I was pacing myself. The maitre'd maintained a watchful eye and I wondered if Sandy had pre-tipped the man because he seemed excessively solicitous for so early on a Saturday, even for Brennans.

Sandy has always been what people called a natural beauty, even during high school. She had bloomed at just the right time and always managed to turn the heads of the boys, and now men. She is normally satisfied with being just naturally attractive, and is not usually a woman who sought to draw too much attention to herself merely for her looks. Rather, she's the kind of woman who can pull her hair into a ponytail, put on some jeans and a sweater and be ready to go just about anywhere, and look good doing it. When she did want to look her best, as she did yesterday when Cassie had come for her appointment, she could knock your socks off.

When she had entered the professional world, she always felt maintaining that natural beauty concept gave her credibility. While working at the law firm, she had been very aware of the axiom which stated first impressions are the hardest to change. She had wanted nobody to even give a thought that she had risen to her position by way of any means other than talent and hard work. So, she had always worn modest business suits with conservative length skirts and sensible heels to the office or court. Her natural glow meant she needed little enhancement and thus she never wore much more than a little powder and some light eye makeup.

In our office, Sandy dresses like the partner she is and rarely goes overboard with her hair or makeup. That's why it shocked me yesterday when I came in. She had obviously felt competitive for some reason with the return of Cassie Yeats and I don't think I had ever seen her so done up, yet at the same time so naturally beautiful.

Then she entered the Brennans bar area and surprised me yet again. The black and white polka dot dress she wore was simple, yet, with the addition of a single element: a wide, black-patent-leather belt, her outfit became compellingly elegant. The dress's bodice was formed and tight to her curves while below the belt, the skirt portion flowed as she moved. Her legs were bare and she was wearing black, heeled sandals that many women would find difficult to manage, but in which she moved with an appealing fluidity. My ex-wife had so many attractive parts moving at the same time, I wasn't sure where to look; neither was the maitre'd, I noticed, nor were the bartender and the men and one of the women at the other end of the bar. By the time my look got to her hair and makeup, she was next to me, the subtle scent of her perfume making its arrival half a second before her. Sandy's eyes sparkled, and when she smiled at me and kissed my cheek, I almost slipped from my perch.

"Good morning, darling," she said.

I moved her drink closer to her. She picked it up, stirred it with the bean, then held it to toast. Suddenly, my joke of the Sloe Screw seemed too clever by half, but I picked it up anyway and lightly clinked my glass to hers.

"To the most beautiful ex-wife I've ever seen," I said.

I sipped. Sandy did as well.

"I'm starving," she said.

I signaled to the maitre'd and he was instantly at our side. Sandy set her drink on the bar knowing someone would bring it to the table, but since I have always been very uncomfortable with people over-waiting on me, that someone turned out to be me. Sandy fell in behind the maitre'd and I was only too happy to pull up the rear of our little procession through the bar and into the restaurant area.

"You know, I don't think you ever took me here while we were married," Sandy said over her shoulder.

Her hair bounced slightly as she moved and I could have closed my eyes and followed by the trail of perfume alone. Under the dress, her hips were dancing in that hauntingly enticing way and I mentally kicked myself for being so stupid to give her up for a few minutes of phony passion with the likes of Vanessa Lafontaine. Now, don't go judging me as merely some stereotype of a shallow male interested in nothing but the body and appearance of a woman. Sandy's got so much more to offer than just physical looks to any man lucky enough to attract her attention, so what I am saying is a man would really have to be a total moron to let her get away.

As we turned a corner, Sandy glanced over her shoulder at the drinks in my grasp.

"You know, Otto, I didn't notice it at the bar, but the Sloe Screw as your drink of choice, cute."   She paused and then with a conspiratorial hint, continued.   "For what I have in planned for the weekend, the Long Slow Comfortable Screw Against The Wall may have been a more appropriate choice, if it's a statement you were meaning to make." Her eyes sparkled playfully.

"I thought about it," I said. "It just seemed a bit over the top."

"You may rethink that decision when you get your credit card bill at the end of the month," she teased.

Eyes in the restaurant followed us, or rather, her. It made me feel good, the attention, but thinking about it, in the eyes of the gawkers, I could have just been some slightly balding, overweight doofus schlepping her drink to the table. Then, her comment about me not ever bringing her here hit the pit of my stomach. She was right. I had never brought her here; or done other things with her that perhaps I should have. I felt even more the failure at Husband 101.

We arrived at what may have been the best spot in the house, a table for two set in front of an arched window overlooking the courtyard dining area. Outside the magnolias were still blooming in a mass of verdant, tropical foliage along the aging red brick walls. Because of the heat of the summer, the area was devoid of diners.

I pulled the chair and held it for Sandy, beating the obviously off put maitre'd by half a second. Smiling at him, I moved to my side of the table and took my seat. He did have the final laugh, however. While looking at me, more than at her, he fluffed out her napkin and placed it delicately across my ex-wife's lap. He then stood straight, thanked us, and handed us off to Luella, our waitress.

In contrast to the maitre'd's overzealous stuffiness, Luella couldn't have been more easy going and pleasant. She gave us a bit of the tourist's spiel, until she found out we were both residents of the city and then the treatment became more home team.   Luella was tall, black, had a quick and easy smile, and, we found out later, a laugh that lit up the room.

We waved off another drink while we perused the menus, but I noted that Luella had left the wine list behind. Having never been here, with Sandy or anyone, I was to learn from Luella upon her return a few minutes later, that it's traditional to have wine with breakfast at Brennans. I asked her whose tradition that would be and she just smiled and said, 'Sugar, welcome to the Big Easy'. She then touched my shoulder and said she'd be back in a minute if I had any real questions.

My eyes ran down the menu. I never realized there were that many ways to stage poached eggs.

"I never realized there were this many ways to stage poached eggs," I said to Sandy.

"You've lead a sheltered life, Mr. Langdon," she said, her eyes peering at me over the menu.

That was it. I loved looking at Sandy, even all the way back in high school when I'd sit and just stare at her across the room. I leaned back in my seat, brought the fingers of my right hand up to my chin and watched her going over the menu. I don't think she had any idea how much I watched her, not for how she looked, but how amazed at everything about her I always was. She must have sensed me watching, because she stopped reading the menu, lowered it to the table and looked back.

"What?" She self-consciously smoothed her skirt, checked the degree of cleavage she was showing.

It wasn't too much.

"Just watching you."

"Geeze, Otto, get a grip." Then she added, "You're way too transparent, you know." Finally, she gave me a smile, which meant her comment to me was well intended.

"Transparent?" I closed my menu lying on the table and sat forward, moving my elbows from the arms of my chair to the table. "How so, Sandy?"

I reached for my drink and drained a healthy portion. Since I was starting to see the bottom of my glass, I was beginning to reconsider the second drink decision.

"I've known you for most of your life, right?" she said.

"On and off. Mostly off."

She closed her menu, sat back. Her body shifted slightly and I heard her cross her legs under the table. She reached for the spicy bean in her drink, let it drip off, and then held it horizontally in front of her.

I stared at the bean. I got the metaphor.

She bit the bean in half with exposed teeth and carelessly tossed the remaining half back into the Bloody Mary.

"Sometimes," she began, and then her eyes drifted toward what I heard was an approaching Luella. "Sometimes, my dear ex-husband and partner, you need to realize who you're dealing with when you're dealing with me."

Luella arrived at the table and thankfully derailed my witty, yet slightly sarcastic, retort.

"Any questions on the menu, folks?"

I looked to Sandy.

"Do you mind if I order for us?" I asked her.

Sandy shook her head just enough to relay the message that she'd not only not mind, but would enjoy my display of gallantry.

"No questions, Luella, my dear," I began, my eyes locking onto Sandy's. "My lovely companion will begin with the strawberries with double cream, then the Eggs Nouvelle Orleans and wrap it up with the Crepes Fitzgerald.   A full circle if you will, strawberries to strawberries."

Luella nodded. Sandy maintained her lock on my eyes.

"And for the gentleman?" Luella asked.

"Oh, I'm going to skip the appetizer and dessert, because I am certain I will end up sharing my date's portions as it will all be just too much for my lady friend's figure, and have the Oysters Benedict. Oh, and please bring a bottle of a decent vintage of the Gewurztraminer."

"Excellent, I'll get that going right away."

"No rush, Luella," I said. "She's got a whole day of shopping on my credit card ahead, so I figure the longer I keep her here and out of the stores at Canal Place, the better off I will be the next time my statement arrives in the mail."

Luella looked at me like I was pulling her leg, but then she noticed Sandy was looking at her and nodding, a big smirk on her face.   It must have been some female-to-female conspiracy move, because Luella disappeared as quickly as she had appeared.

"Why do I have a feeling she's going to set a land speed record getting us out and you to the stores?" I said to Sandy.

"It's a woman thing." Sandy smiled and said, "How did you know what I wanted?"

I again looked Sandy in the eye and drained the last of my Sloe Screw.

"Sometimes, my dear ex-wife and partner, you need to remember who you are dealing with when you are dealing with me."

She lifted her glass and toasted the air.

"Touche'." She drained the rest of her drink and said, "So, tell me the whole story of you and Cassie Yeats."

I thought for a moment, or two. Long ago, I had made a rule against providing full disclosure to a current lover about any previous lover, and had violated it before with Sandy by telling her snippets of the story of my first love, Cassie Yeats.

As a young man, full of vim and vigor - back in Wisconsin they would say piss and vinegar - I learned the hard way on a couple of occasions that women didn't really want to know about old lovers, even if they did ask. I also learned very early on that they could lay out stories on their own experiences - true or not, it didn't really matter - which would wilt a man's body and whither his soul. In fact, I learned that particular lesson first from Cassie Yeats.

Sandy sat waiting patiently. Her eyes were gentle and nonjudgmental. I concluded my longstanding rule wouldn't necessarily apply in this case for three reasons. First, Sandy was no longer my current lover. Second, the official title of lover had never been attained by Cassie Yeats. Lastly, Sandy and I had already played the little game of 'tell me about your first puppy love'. That's how Sandy had even known the name Cassie Yeats.

The strawberries and double cream arrived and after Luella again left us alone, Sandy offered me one. Scientists will tell you that odors are the carriers of the deepest and most intense memories. There is no science, however, which can confine and define the elements of a boy's first love, or his first broken heart for that matter. The smell of the fresh berries, even under the drape of the thick, sweet cream took me back to when I first met the chestnut haired girl with the bewitching eyes, and the cheap strawberry balm on her lips.

I inhaled deeply of the aroma as I chewed and swallowed the slice of the delectable red jewel while I considered my next move. The wine arrived and Luella and I played the game of smell the cork, swirl the wine, take a sniff, then a small aerated sip, swish it around, and then smile and say, 'that's just fine, thank you'. I really had no idea what I was doing, but unless the wine should taste like vinegar, or in the case of Gewurztraminer some old German woman's feet, I had predetermined that whatever she poured for me would be just fine.

After a clink of our glasses, Sandy and I each downed some wine. She continued on the strawberries and offered me a chance at seconds. I declined. I had decided, given the totality of the last couple of days, Sandy deserved the full background on our newest client. I had a story to tell, and so I began at the beginning.

"I was fourteen. Just turned, actually." I could feel my mind wanting to take me back, and I let it. "It was a warm summer evening in mid-August, just after dinner. A couple friends and I were going to hang out at what, in a couple short weeks, was going to be our Junior High School for a year. Maybe we'd throw a ball around, hang out, share a cigarette if Freddy had managed to sneak one from his sister's purse. By this summer, we'd grown too strong for whacking golf balls like we had done for years in the sports yard at the school. The neighbors had started complaining after some of our shots started crossing the street and banging around on their front porches."

"You must have been a much better golfer back then to have hit a house. I've watched you golf and you couldn't hit a barn, now," Sandy teased and then absently slid another cream-covered strawberry into her mouth.

"If you're going to toss rocks from the peanut gallery, this is going to take a very, very long time."

Sandy shrugged at me and then signaled with her fork bearing yet another piece of berry that she would try to do better and I should go on.

"Well, we were hanging around the school building. I grew up a block away and we had been playing there for years, so we knew every nook and cranny of the place. I remember Jeff had a tennis ball we were throwing at each other. Catch was a kid's game, trying to bean your buddy in the nuts with a tennis ball was a young buck's pastime."

Sandy looked a bit perplexed at the remark, so I explained.

"Young males in the animal kingdom with an overabundance of testosterone will buck horns for social standing, but since we didn't have horns and physical fighting could quickly get out of hand, we substituted with things like tennis balls."

She nodded, rolled her eyes just a bit and gave me the 'must be a guy thing' smile.

"Well, anyway, somewhere during the goofing around, a gaggle of girls wandered by. Being pubescent teenage boys we did what pubescent teenage boys do, and we left the ball, and my ball-busting, tag-along little brother who had shown up just to annoy the crap out of us behind and started following the girls.

"I remember there were four of them. Two brunettes, one blonde, and one fat chick; it was your typical gaggle of teenage girls."

I laughed. Sandy kicked me on the shin. I took it like a man.

"The three of us and the four of them fell into chatting, and eventually some coy introductions were made, which led to us boys doing a little good-natured sparring for alpha male status. Not that we understood it all, but the sequence of events just seemed to come naturally. I was painfully shy back then, still in my Catholic grade school shell really. And these were public school girls, as alien to my cloistered upbringing as hearing someone order broiled walleye at the local tavern's Friday night Perch Fry.

"There was Katie, the blonde. She was short, about five-foot-three and while not officially the fat chick of the group, she did carry a bit of baby chub. Perhaps it was because she was a year younger than the rest of the girls, but I rather suspect she had a chubby gene pool and a fat future. Katie had thick blonde hair which went halfway down her back, green eyes that I would find twinkled when she laughed, wore bell-bottomed jeans and granny top, and possessed a shy smile.

"The taller brunette with the shoulder length hair and glasses was Lydia. I'm sure it was a familial name going back to some old grandmother somewhere, and she told us the name meant 'noble kind', but Lydia never lived up to her name and she turned out to be quite an ignoble soul.

It would be her basement hang out that we'd eventually frequent, listening to bubble gum records on a small record player. You know, the ones back then by Donny Osmond and the Jackson Five - before Michael grew up and got weird. The door to the room would be locked, lights would go out, the music would go on, perhaps a strobe or lava lamp or some incense would spice up the atmosphere, and the three or four couples invited for that night would pair off and scatter about the floor and start necking.

"The fat girl was giggly and happy. Her name was Mary. She obviously was on a sugar high that night but Mary Campbell was perhaps the nicest and easiest to talk to of the group. She had yet to develop that stereotypical nasty attitude honed by years of rejection and ridicule which often saddles heavy adults."

"Real nice, Mr. Sensitive," Sandy interrupted again.

"Just a lot bumps along life's experience road, my sweet. I had to learn a thing or two about people along the way."

She speared the last strawberry and as she chewed told me to go on and called me Dr. Phil. I think it was a good-natured insult, and frankly I prefer Otto if given the choice, but I followed directions and went on.

"Finally, there was Cassie. Her hair was short for the time, above the shoulder, thick, the color of autumn chestnuts, and, I would find out, smelled of flowers. Her eyes were brown, with flecks of green, vulnerable and intimidating at the same time. With the retrospection available through the intervening years, I think now her eyes hinted at a wisdom beyond her years."

I said the last of that sentence with a tone of revelation because I realized I had never detected that in her eyes thirty years ago, but yet is was a part of my memory. It made me think, and I filed the conclusion away for further consideration when I had the time.

"She wore the same type of jeans, moccasins, and granny blouse outfit as the other girls, but she filled out the uniform much better. Cassie was rounded in the right places, soft and pliable in all the others. Her legs were shorter than they are now. I guess she grew into the rest of her body over the years.

"Our eyes met that night and even in my inexperience I believe we both felt a spark inside, but as it turned out she was already involved with someone. So, I turned my attention to Katie and got my first invitation into the basement make-out room just as the sun was setting. I'm not sure if Jeff and Freddie went along that night or if they were edged out of the group by a pair of older guys who showed up."

Luella brought our breakfast entrees and I dug into my Oysters Benedict with a renewed hunger. Across the table, Sandy slowly savored her poached eggs framed with lump crab meat and brandy-cream sauce. On the table between us Luella set a mini-loaf of fresh, hot, crusty French bread - another tradition of the Big Easy and Brennans - and an assortment of country fresh jams. I was in hog heaven.

I chewed another big portion of perfectly fried oysters, washed it down with some wine and then continued the story.

"Back then, we would measure relationships in days or weeks. After that, for one reason or another, the pairing would seem to just evaporate into the ether. We would sting for a bit, and then like a bee collecting pollen, move on to the next flower."

"Not me. Bob and I lasted from our freshman through our junior years," Sandy injected.

"Yeah, and then I found you during the summer after and part of our senior year." I pointed my empty fork at her like a stinger. "Buzz Buzz."

She went to kick my shin again, but this time I was ready and deftly dodged the assault.

"Well, one morning shortly after school started, I had a visit at my locker from Lydia who said that Cassie had dumped her beau and was curious in knowing if I'd have an interest in dating her." I caught Sandy's eye and winked. "I guess she like-liked me."

Luella must have been monitoring us, because moments after we each finished our breakfast entrees, she showed up to ask if everything had been okay and we both nodded our compliments. Before leaving, she topped off both our glasses, revealed that the bottle was now a dead soldier, and asked if we would like another or something else. We begged off the additional wine, and a few moments later she appeared with Sandy's dessert crepes, set them between us and removed the used dishes.

We shared the dessert for a bit, and then I let Sandy finish them off while I went on with the story.

"I passed a message back through Lydia that I was definitely interested and I would love to walk Cassie home that day. I guess I like-liked her too.

"With each passing class my anticipation grew. Finally, as the last bell sounded, I bounded from Mr. Carroll's English class, down the stairs and up the hall to my locker to drop my books. Well, guess who was waiting for me?"

"Let me guess," Sandy said and then looked skyward. "Cassie Yeats, in all her teenaged glory."

"Nope," I said, a bit of pleasure at Sandy's wrong assumption in my voice. I sat back in my chair, pushed it away a bit and put my left ankle on my right knee. "Her ex-boyfriend, Tim whats-his-name. And he wasn't a very happy camper. I thought it was going to come to blows, but you know me, I reasoned with him, dazzled him with my brilliance..."

"Please, I'm still eating here," my ex-wife interjected.

"Okay, okay. Suffice it to say, I talked my way out of the confrontation. Two minutes later, I was standing at the flag pole out front on Union Avenue watching Cassie come strolling out the ancient bronze doors." I paused, caught Luella's eye and motioned for the check. "I'd like to say it was love at *that* first sight, but it really wasn't."

Sandy gave me a look over the top of her wine glass.

"Because you had met her a month earlier, but had been concentrating your efforts on working through her friends up to this point in your schooldays pattern of two-week romances?"

Properly stung back for my bees hopping from flower to flower remark, I paid the check and we left the restaurant. Sandy's little jab would go unanswered, for the moment.

The sky to the west was just beginning to reveal the promise of the new day. Saturday was when Gregory played golf at The Plantation, but that was hours from now and why was the frigging phone ringing?

Gregory rolled over, noted that Cassandra had left his bed sometime during the night. His only smile thus far into his day came at the remembering of the encounter he had enjoyed with his wife just a few short hours ago. Then his hand reached for the telephone.

"Yeah?" he said, picking up the receiver.

"Greg, Keoki Keaweaheulu here. Howzit, brah?" the voice said, dripping with phony courtesy and thick with the local Hawaiian accent.

"You know it's Gregory," he snarled. "What the hell do you want?"

"I thought we had an agreement on these late night chopper flights onto your property," Keoki said.

Gregory always marveled at how these Hawaiians could fall into and out of their clipped pidgin whenever they wanted to. But Keoki was correct, the pair had indeed hammered out a deal after Keoki had used his connections to stall the Maui County Board's approval of the zoning variance for the installation of the helipad on the Thomason's newly acquired land.

"You were to not fly in or out over my property after sunset."

Even with the concession on the limitations of the operations over his property, Keoki had extracted a two-hundred-fifty thousand dollar payment to himself and another equal amount for the County of Maui just so Gregory could obtain the variance and have the privilege of installing the helipad on his own land. Such was the politics of the place.

"So what do you want?" Gregory asked, already knowing that Cassandra's little late night arrival had breached the agreement and now required a five-thousand dollar penalty be paid.

"Da cash, Brah," Keoki said simply. "Keoki run out beer. Could use da cash today. No want call my Bruddah."

Gregory chafed at that last comment. The money was a drop in the bucket to him, but it's that damn gloating this old bastard does which really rubbed Gregory the wrong way. However, he also understood how Maui worked, and money is meaningless if you don't have the right connections. It's an island run by relationships, and Keoki Keaweaheulu had more than he did.

It also didn't help that Gregory and Cassandra are haole - white visitors - who have no roots to island power. It doesn't even matter that he and Cassandra are kama'aina, meaning they had lived on the island for years, they were still considered outsiders because nobody has ever welcomed them with the affectionate titles of Uncle and Auntie, and that simple act of acceptance and aloha was more powerful in island society than all of Gregory's money.

"You know, I just call you to complain and then I call my Bruddah on da County Board to do da same. Then I think, no, can wait until noon for da cash, then call if no here."

'Go fuck yourself' was what Gregory wanted to say to the man, but the last thing he needed was attention from the government. Instead, he simply agreed to have the money to him by noon and hung up the phone.

A moment later, he was pounding on Cassandra's locked door. Even being of slight build and a little under five-feet-nine, when riled, Gregory could present a frightening front, especially to his wife, and those whom he collected for atonement. He pounded again and called her name.

Cassandra roused herself and leapt out of bed at the second set of fists on her door. She winced in pain as her deeply bruised thighs brushed against each other. She realized from the tone of the calling that the faster she responded the easier things would go for her. She opened the door a crack and he shoved it wide open, sending her sliding on her behind across the polished marble floor. The rage in his eyes terrified her, but it was what he held in his hand that made her scream. There was nobody to hear her.

Sandy is a prolific shopper. She never needed my money, having made more than enough during her years of private practice and when she sold her partnership back to the firm, but she sure seemed to enjoy spending my money when she got the chance.

We had finished our breakfast, and even though the limo had been waiting, we decided - well, Sandy decided for us - to walk the few blocks from the restaurant up Royal Street so she could do some window shopping at some of the antique shops she would want to visit later. At Canal we turned left and walked toward the river. Beyond the levee, I could see the upper rows of containers loaded onto a seagoing vessel slide by, headed down river to the Gulf.

The limo had been instructed to wait for us in the small Canal Place parking lot off Wells Street. Packages, and the two of us would be there, eventually, the driver was advised. He didn't seem to care. His meter would continue to run, as would the engine and air conditioning.

Sandy and I arrived at the Shops at Canal Place shortly after they opened. Saks was Sandy's first stop. I longed for a big screen television and lounge chair while she shopped, but part of our agreement was that we would spend the day together; so as clerks brought box upon box of shoes by Chanel and Gucci and Prada and Louis Vuitton, I decided I would use the time to continue my story of Cassie Yeats.

Sandy modeled a peek-toe, leopard print pump with the perfect heel which nicely lifted and rounded everything from her calf to her butt when I, seated on a spare one of those shoe clerk benches, restarted the tale.

"My first real chance to be alone with Cassie was the day we met out front of our school. I watched her approach. Even though back then she was six inches shorter than she is now, she still seemed almost liquid in her movements, and when she saw me, she bounced down the stairs with happiness. She mesmerized me with her eyes the first time I had seen them, but she sealed the deal that day with almost everything else she possessed. It was the first day we really talked to one another, and I quickly felt more comfortable with her than with anyone else I knew.

"It was early September and the days had been getting noticeably shorter and the nights noticeably cooler, however, this particular afternoon was sunny and warm. There wasn't a cloud in the sky and the light breeze carried an array of soft fragrances." At least, that's how I remembered it.

Sandy was turning around, looking at herself in the multiple mirrors and throwing a glance or two my way. I smiled and gave her the thumbs up. I imagined that simple gesture may have just cost me five hundred dollars, although I later found out it was eight hundred. I also later learned she had returned them and found a similar pair on sale at the Metairie Mall that made her legs look just as good for less than one hundred bucks. That's my Sandy.

Sandy came and sat next to me while the clerk hustled in back for another stack of boxes. She still appeared to be interested, so I continued.

"Like I said, I found Cassie as easy to talk to as she was to look at. She listened intently to my stories of youthful bravado and I believed she thought I could jump buildings in a single bound. At least that's the way she could make a boy feel just by the way she looked at you when you told her things. She laughed easily, and you know me, I love to make a lady laugh.

"After about six blocks of walking, I found the courage to hold her hand. It was soft and warm and welcoming. The butterflies which had been bouncing around in my stomach took perch. They would be replaced by pterodactyls bouncing around in there before the first time I tried to kiss her."

Sandy laughed.

"Do you mean you weren't always so suave and debonaire?" she teased, nudging me in the side with her elbow.

"Oh, I was always suave and debonaire," I teased.   "The problem was, back then it was more pronounced *swave* and *deboner*."

We shared another little laugh.

Sandy pointed out the boxes she wanted, I flipped out my American Express, and the clerk hustled off again, this time to the cash register.

"How about we check out the fall lines?" Sandy said. "I hear the Armani Collezioni collection this year is to die for."

"I thought he did suits," I said. "I don't need any suits."

"Good, because I'm talking about the women's line. Let's go."

I signed for the shoes, asked they be delivered to the limo occupied by Armand outside, was assured by the clerk that she would see to it, double checked that I had my AMEX card back and jogged to catch up to Sandy. As I closed the distance, I slowed to a walk at a speed which would get me there eventually.

Walking behind Sandy was almost as good as having her on my arm.   She knew I was back there and understood I was looking. Sandy never missed a trick. I have always had the knack for getting gorgeous, talented, intelligent women to fall in love with me. Someday, I'm going to learn how to keep one.

As I caught up to her by the escalator, she said, "So, how long did it take you to settle those pterodactyls in your belly so you could kiss Cassie?"

"Not as long as I thought it might, but much longer than you may think. Remember, you've known me as a man. Cassie knew me as a boy." Maybe that's why she had such an impact upon me, and still does, I thought. "Anyway, it turns out Cassie was quite receptive to any of my advances. It was like she was just waiting for me to muster up the courage, because she never rebuffed one of my rookie moves."

"Who could resist you?" Sandy said, never turning to look at me. "I remember that head of hair you had back then. You were always so tall, people could see you coming all the way down the hall, and that hairy chest you would display out the top of your shirt you always wore undone an extra button." Her eyes focused on a distant memory. She smiled.

"Yeah, I hit six-foot-six by the time I was fifteen and never grew another inch.   Vertically, that is."   I rubbed my fingers over my thinning crop of head toppers.   "As for those flowing locks of yesteryear, well, what the Good Lord giveth, the Good Lord taketh away." I pulled open my shirt collar and looked down my chest. "That's still there. The problem is some of it's shifting to my back." I shrugged.

Sandy took a left at the top of the escalator, and I stayed by her side. By this time, the little buzz brought on by the drink and wine had begun to subside, so I was hoping we'd be offered a glass of champagne somewhere along the way. Saks didn't disappoint, and as we entered the land of high couture on the second floor we were greeted by a leggy saleswoman with two bubbly flutes. They also had some big, comfortable chairs. I guessed the combination was designed to lubricate the customer's wallet and keep him or her from falling too far when they signed the tab. What did I care, though? There wasn't anything I wouldn't do for Sandy, even if she wasn't my wife anymore. She never took advantage like many people do, and she was always fun to be around no matter what we were doing.

I decided to just enjoy the ride, keep the light buzz going with free champagne, and drift back in time with my story. Each time Sandy came out, I'd watch her preen and turn for me and check out her reflection on the six mirrors in this rather private nook, then I'd wrinkle my nose, all the time inserting snippets of the saga of Cassie Yeats.

"By the time we were going steady," I said, "the relationship was already breaking records. Heck, we had made it into early October. One month. Double my previous long.

"She even met my mother. Another first. To my chagrin, mom wasn't as enchanted by her as I was. You know mom, Sandy. She picks up on subtle things like you do, and she had noticed the age in Cassie's eyes and had attributed it to something mom wouldn't share with her fourteen year old son. Instead, she had just suggested, strongly, that I find someone else. In perhaps my first act of young adult defiance, maybe my first act of any kind of defiance when it came to mom since I was three, I continued to date Cassie.

"One night, I was assigned to watch my siblings while mom went to play cards with her Bridge Club. I had gone out right after dinner to get Cassie so she could hang out with me at my house for the evening, and we arrived back just as mom was leaving. We sat on the stairs in the back hallway while my brother and sister peeked at us from the kitchen door. Mom called me into the kitchen to issue a warning about remembering my responsibilities and then hinted at not letting myself get into trouble. Whatever, I thought, and I went back out to sit with Cassie on the steps.

"Mom gave me a mindful look as she left. Hormones were raging inside me, I recall, and as I sat there with Cassie all warm and fragrant and willing, I wondered just what mom had meant about getting into trouble. I mean, what kind of trouble could two teenagers get themselves into? We had been necking for weeks now, and I had been making some consistent moves to second base. I was slowly expanding my man credentials, I guess, and I was having a ball. Trouble? What trouble?

"Being younger siblings, my brother and sister continued to be a real pain that night, paying me back for all the gags I had pulled on them. They spied on us from inside the kitchen door, making kissing noises and giggling. So, I took Cassie downstairs to show her our basement. It wasn't as fancy as Lydia's little make out den, but it did have one thing that even a darkened room at Lydia's didn't: complete privacy. As I led her down, I think we both knew what may happen that night. My heart was beating inside my chest so hard that I thought she could surely feel it when I gave her a hug."

Sandy finished spinning in a gorgeous business suit, I got a look at the price tag at a distance - at least the eyes aren't failing with the hairline - gave her a thumb's down and poured myself a refill from the bottomless bottle in the ice bucket on the table next to my chair. A few minutes later, she came out wearing her own clothes, having passed on everything from both Italy and France, and said one word, 'Coach'. We headed for the Coach store.

Thankfully, the handbag maker's establishment was much smaller than Saks and thus afforded less opportunity to excessive shopping. The problem was it didn't have any chairs for me, nor any free champagne, so as Sandy began to browse, I told her I would hit the little toy store we had passed en route. Not only could I engage in a little shopping for an adult toy or two, but my sister - yeah, the pain in the rump sister of kissing noises fame - had just announced she and her husband were expecting a new arrival in January and I could indulge in picking up a few cuddly things for my new niece or nephew.

To save some time, and since I was beginning to wear off my breakfast and was getting hungry again, I told Sandy I'd meet her in an hour at the limo and we'd head to The Commander's Palace in the Garden District for our late lunch.

I walked out into the common area, down the pavilion and into the World's Best Toys. I could feel my eyes grow bigger, and I whispered, 'Cool, remote control airplanes. Wow, and way cool kites.' Boys never really grow up, I thought to myself. I felt for my wallet. I had left my AMEX with Sandy, but still had the comfort of my VISA.

Cassandra moved slowly. The changes in her husband's long-practiced routine of recovery were beginning to frighten her. She was now certain he had indulged while she was on the mainland. What she wasn't certain of, however, was how things went, and what may have gone so wrong to cause the pattern of post-coping this time to be so much more violent. She descended the steps one at a time to the main level, using the handrail for support. Remembering her pledge to take matters under her own control, she willed her concern and fear be transformed into a firm resolve. She would burn him down, and risk the consequences. All of them. There was no turning back now. By the time she crossed the tile of the main floor, she was already walking straighter and with less pain.

After his rage-filled attack on her, Gregory had gone out for his Saturday routine. The helicopter had picked him up three hours earlier and she knew he'd golf the Plantation course, have several drinks in the clubhouse bar and then grab dinner in Lahaina before returning home around nine p.m. Years ago, she would have accompanied him on these weekly excursions, but as of about a year ago, he had begun to leave her behind.

At the bottom of the stairs, she went left down the hall, past the theater and billiard rooms toward his private office. The west wing was Gregory's domain on the ground level, but the office was the only room he kept locked; he held the only key. She had discovered his key left behind one day several years ago and had made a copy which she kept hidden in a small notch underneath the top of a side table along the wall in the hallway. She hadn't used it since before her mainland trip when she had last checked his diary and sneaked into the lava tube. She hoped he hadn't changed the lock while she was gone. There was exterior access if she used a ladder and the window was left unlocked, but for any number of reasons that would be a dangerous last resort. Besides, he rarely opened the windows to the office.

Cassandra approached the hallway table. It was a heavy, hand-carved, contemporary piece she had found in a small gallery on the northern end of the island which specialized in creating unique sculptures or furniture pieces from driftwood washed ashore or naturally fallen trees from the rainforest. The artisans' claim to fame was their stated belief they are merely tools releasing the form nature has already placed within the media. She became such a fan after first visiting the gallery, that she had also commissioned other works in bronze and stone, including the large alabaster nude which was the focal point of the fountain in their front drive. She had often wondered how nature had locked the voluptuous woman who had an uncanny resemblance to her inside the rock.

She kneeled down, slowly, reached under the top and moved her hand to the little crevice Mother Nature had secreted into the original eucalyptus log. Her body turned cold as her hand touched the key's bow - the part one holds to turn the lock - sticking out of the notch. She had always tucked the key away bow first, leaving the lighter pointed blade portion of the key protruding from the niche. Cassandra could feel her heartbeat pounding in her ears as her mind raced to the last time she had used the key.

Had she broken her own routine and accidentally placed the key in backwards? Had Gregory somehow discovered the key and that was perhaps part of the reason for the changes in his behavior? Was there some other explanation? With her hand still just touching the key, she debated the options. She could leave the key untouched, and if Gregory had indeed found it and replaced it backwards, avoid his further wrath. Or, she could use the key and perhaps obtain more answers to her burning questions. She forced herself to calm down and think rationally. She had already committed to the end game of this nightmare. It would only be a matter of a few short weeks, or less, until she could work herself free of Gregory, his manipulations, and his wrath. Cassandra closed her eyes, gripped the key and slid it out. She winced as she stood up, stared at the small brushed brass object in her hand. In that instant, the key became a metaphor for the unlocking of the rest of her life; tears welled in her eyes as she realized that tiny object's significance.

She turned and faced the closed office door, then with a purposeful stride which belied the pain took the dozen steps to reach the portal. She resolved to be extraordinarily conscious of anything she would touch, or move, or manipulate when she entered the office. Gregory was obsessive about his personal belongings, and compulsive about how he placed them, how he would arrange them in order. She knew were she not careful, it would allow him to know she had been inside his private space.

She slid the key into the lock. Her hands were sweating and trembling. Her stomach was flipping and flopping. She wiped her hands on the back of her shorts. Gripping the key lightly, she attempted to turn it to the left. There was a slight resistance, but to her relief, the lock's tumblers operated successfully and she slowly turned the knob, pushed the door open and moved tentatively inside.

The Commander's Palace was located in an expansive, old Victorian two-story painted aqua blue and white. The architecture, complete with turrets, columns and gingerbread would be an oddity in any other setting, but in the Garden District of New Orleans, it was a conformist landmark, and a place of world-renowned, culinary excellence.

The restaurant's founding by Emile Commander dates to 1880, a time when the Garden District was home for the last days of the former President of the Confederacy, Jefferson Davis, and frequented by notables such as Mark Twain.

In contrast to Vieux Carre, or the French Quarter of New Orleans, which at the time served as home for a majority Creole population, the postbellum era of the 1880s brought an influx of Anglo-Saxon *Americans* - as the Creole's called them - to New Orleans and these Americans wanted a residential section of their own. Thus was forged the character of the Garden District. The area had been initially developed several decades earlier when several plantations were subdivided beginning in the 1830s and the area was annexed to the city of New Orleans in 1852.

Bounded today by St. Charles Avenue to the north, 1st Street to the west, Toldedano Street to the west and Magazine Street to the south, the Garden District is an area of expensive, large, Greek Revival style homes, huge, old oak trees which provide acres of shade and all variety of lush and verdant tropical plantings. Our office building happens to be located on the wrong side of Magazine Street - the side which is more characteristic of cheap, shotgun-style homes on small lots overgrown with crabgrass. There's also not much shade on the working class side of Magazine Street.

Our limo arrived at the Washington Street entrance to the restaurant. Even though the drive from Canal Place had taken about twenty minutes, Sandy was still smiling and shaking her head at my purchase of a couple of kites when she exited the limo. I thought they were really cool, though.

As we walked toward the striped awning which marked the entrance, I glanced across the street to the bleached white plaster and brick walls of Lafayette Cemetery Number One. I have always been fascinated by the cemeteries of New Orleans, and this particular location had been established in 1788 by the city of Lafayette before being absorbed by New Orleans. It now stands as the first planned, aboveground cemetery in the city and the site has served as locations for several movies and books.

Local author Anne Rice used Lafayette Number 1 in many of her novels, and the movie *Double Jeopardy* filmed a scene there, even though they referred to the place as Lafayette Cemetery Number 3. For you factoid geeks, there is no Lafayette Number 3 in New Orleans.

By far, my favorite of New Orleans' Cities of the Dead has to be Saint Louis Cemetery Number 1 located on Basin Street in the French Quarter. It's the oldest of the remaining cemeteries in the city, having been opened for business in 1789 by the Catholic church. It also has a filmography, being the location used for the LSD-enhanced scenes with the two hookers from Bourbon Street in the movie *Easy Rider*.

Saint Louis Number 1 is also the resting place of many early, local notables, including the Voodoo priestess Marie Laveau and her daughter, Marie Laveau II. Their ghosts are reputed to haunt the grounds, and believers will tell tales about the rituals of St. John's Eve - the evening of June 23, the day before the celebration of the Feast of St. John the Baptist - when the pair come to life and lead their followers in a wild, celebratory orgy.

"That reminds me we missed the orgy over at the Laveau place again," I said.

"What?" Sandy turned, then offered me a wry smile when she saw my thumb hoisted toward the cemetery. "Well, there's always's next year, if you can find a date."

"Who brings a date to an orgy?" I asked.

Sandy just shook her head and refused to play the game further. I know what she was thinking, though: 'Sometimes you're such an incorrigible brat, William'. Or Otto as I am now known to her.

We ducked inside the shaded relative coolness of the restaurant's covered back area and waited at the small podium for the hostess to return. Even being covered, the outside area was excessively warm and like the courtyard of Brennans, devoid of diners. Another couple followed us in, and to Sandy's chagrin I spoke loudly enough to include them in my continuing discussion of cemetery legends.

"Hey, did you know that if you stand in front of Marie Laveau's grave, turn three times and then knock three times, your wish will be granted," I said.

"Doesn't work," Sandy said. "I tried it."

"What did you wish for?" I asked. "Because I did it and my wish comes true every time I come here."

Sandy refused to bite, but the woman behind us did.

"Excuse me," the woman said. "What did you wish for?"

"Twenty-five cent martinis with my lunch," I said, turning to face the couple. I smiled and arched my eyebrows, a la Groucho Marx.

The young woman hostess arrived just then, verified our reservation, and asked us to follow her to the front dining room. Before we departed the podium, I completed my little game.

"Do you have twenty-five cent martinis with lunch?" I asked our hostess for the benefit of the next couple.

"In fact, we do, sir," she said with a smile.

Over my shoulder, I winked at the woman and then walked off in trail of Sandy and the hostess.

"How many times are you going to pull that one?" Sandy asked when we had passed out of earshot.

"As long as they still have twenty-five cent martinis with lunch," I said as we wove our way through to our table.

"Has anyone ever told you you're still a ten year old?"

"Only everyone."

We arrived at our table in the front dining room. Bright yellow walls adorned with murals above a painted gloss white wainscot was the decorating theme in this particular room. The carpet was rich and thick underfoot and the air was filled with an inviting blend of aromas. Sandy and I had our third anniversary dinner in here. That had been a wonderful evening, and night.

For the second time today, I pulled out the chair for Sandy and she sat. The hostess removed the napkin from Sandy's wine glass and draped it across her lap. Then she did the same for me.

We ordered identical lunches: turtle soup, blackened fresh Gulf fish, and crab-boiled summer vegetables. I had discovered shopping could really work up the appetite. On the drink side, we both passed on anything with alcohol and settled for iced tea, sweetened for me and unsweetened for Sandy.

A loaf of fresh, hot, crusty French bread arrive moments after our lunch order departed with our waiter. Sandy cut the end for me - she knows I love the contrast of the crusty cone filled with soft, airy bread - and then a slice for herself. She's more of a soft inside lady, being not a huge fan of excessively crusty things, except for me, that is. I dug my knife into some softened butter and applied it to the bread.

"So, you and Cassie had finally worked things up to what could have been *the moment*? Kinda young, weren't you?"

"We were young," I said after I pondered her question while chewing a bite of my bread. After all, I have three daughters and a father's view of this kind of teenage behavior is a lot different from my perspective as a hormone-driven teenage boy. "Too young, I would say today. But can you really forget the lure of that age? Can you honestly not remember how it felt to be straining at the bit to grow up, wanting to grab everything life had waiting for you?"

"Oh, I remember the grabbing. As a girl, I played defense."

"Some played better than others, as I recall."

"By the time you and I got together before our senior year," she lectured, driving the point home with the bread knife pointed in my direction. "We had each gotten fairly good at our respective roles, as I recall."

"I'm not talking about just the physical stuff here," I pled my point like a defense attorney left with nothing in his quiver but the arrow labeled *Emotional Plea*. "Where's your sense of romance, Sandy? I'm talking about the heart. The feelings which washed over you in waves at that age. The happiness, the fear, the longing, and the trepidation of the sting of loss. It was a time where you could fall in love on a Friday afternoon, spend all day Saturday pining, and be shaking your head in wonder on Monday morning what the big deal had been."

I could see Sandy was a bit skeptical with my lame attempt at verbalizing the emotions and feelings of pubescence. She came from a slightly different perspective, having spent the majority of junior high and high school tethered to what's his name. She didn't suffer the bimonthly patterns of pleasure and pain we mere mortal boys had to endure.

Then I saw her eyes lit like her brain had captured an idea, you know, the *Eureka!* moment.

"Cassie Yeats was your first true love, wasn't she? We're not talking puppy love here." Sandy's eyes examined me across the starched and immaculate expanse of white table cloth. "I had thought it was just an old fling from the past when she called and I busted your balls by making the appointment. There was something in the way you were handling it; something in the manner in which you ran from it and then embraced it. It all makes sense now."

How could I respond? They say you never forget your first car, your first time - as unmemorable as that may have been - or your first love. My first car was a 1968 Mustang convertible, my first time was, well, that's still a state secret, and yes, my first love was Cassie Yeats. So I said the only thing I could think to say.

"I plead the Fifth, your honor."

"Never made judge, remember?" She offered me the other end of the loaf, I nodded and she sliced it off. "I was just a lowly practitioner at the Bar. We'll take up whether you can hide from me behind your constitutional rights another time, but knowing what I know now puts a whole new light on the story. So, tell me more about what happened that night in your basement when your mother was out playing cards and your brother and sister had given up pestering you in favor watching something a little less funny on TV. What was that show? *Laugh In?*"

I took the second end, buttered it. Bought some time and gave her a whimsical grimace face, like a nonverbal expression of 'ha-ha'.

"So, mom had just left, having given me an irritated look as her departing remark," I restarted.

"And yes, the monsters who *are* my siblings had grown tired of tormenting us in favor of the lame jokes and low-budget skits of *Laugh In*, most of which they were too young to understand. Cassie and I were standing in the darkest room in the basement. In the furnace room, there's one small double-pane window on each end wall which lets in just a hint of light from the streetlight over the nearby intersection. In the center, sat an ancient coal-burning furnace converted to gas to heat the house sprouting hot air pipes the size of barrels into the first-floor rafters. It was far from anything romantic in either ambience or decor.

"But it was the best place in the basement for me to hear the television and my brother and sister bouncing around in the room above us. The coast was clear. I pulled her close and we stood there, kissing in the dark. My hands began to move over the somewhat familiar parts of her body. As before, she was more than willing to let me satisfy my curiosity and expand my knowledge base of girls' mysteries. There was something which seemed different from the previous make out sessions, however. To me, Cassie was reacting strangely, more responsive perhaps, and making little sounds I hadn't heard before."

Sandy stared at me from the other side of the table. It was her *move along* look. Since I was already past the bluest part of the story, I just continued the narrative.

"I was about to conquer new ground, nervous as hell but sure eager enough, when, WHAM! the lights came on and I heard fast-moving, adult footsteps coming down the stairs. We were busted. Standing together in the now illuminated basement, fully clothed thank goodness, although I seem to recall Cassie's shirt looked like she had two sets of bulges, one real and just above a set of empty shells. And, the top button of her hip huggers may have been undone. That part's a bit foggy."

Sandy was now grinning, almost relishing my misfortune.

"My mind raced for something to say. Something which would salvage me with both mom and Cassie. My fourteen years of life experience left me splashing around the excuse pool but coming up empty handed.

"I imagine she would have yelled, 'out of the car long hair' had she been hip to the then-popular song - and had we been in a car -

but she certainly knew the 'you're coming with me' line. Oo-wee, yes she did."

There was nothing to do but laugh. So we did. Me because of the absurdity of the moment when viewed from thirty years later, and Sandy, because she found glee in my getting busted by my mother. The two of them see eye-to-eye on the human being who is me.

Just then, the turtle soup arrived. Sandy and I each accepted some fresh ground black pepper and then picked up our soup spoon. The creamy concoction was perfectly seasoned, and hot, but not too hot. The turtle meat was succulent and sweet, not gamey like it can be sometimes. Between spoonfuls, Sandy let me off the hook, just a little.

"So, your mom caught you," she said. "Big deal."

"It was a big deal," I said, taking another big scoop of the soup and holding the spoon just above the bowl to allow it to drip clear before bringing it to my mouth. "I just didn't realize quite how big until a few days later."

Cassandra closed Gregory's office door behind herself, pocketed the key and twisted the lock. Her thinking was even if he did come home unexpectedly, she'd have time to figure a way out of the room without him seeing her. She looked around, took a quick mental picture of every detail, but nothing appeared to be new or out of place.

The room was roughly forty feet long and twenty feet wide, long enough to reveal the existence of the subtle arc of the wings of the home. The midday light filtered in through floor-to-ceiling tinted windows which mimicked the appearance of the lanai doors in other locations on the house's south exposure and reflected off the polished marble floor. Unlike the rest of the house, where Cassandra's airy and light decorating tastes carried the day, this room was dark and somber in comparison.

She backed into the corner against the closed door and took a longer look around the room. The stuffed trophies of safaris past started back with lifeless eyes from perches on every wall. Wood panels hewn from Koa logs from the island of Kauai filled in areas not taken up by book shelves and stuffed heads. The shelves were jammed with books of all sorts. Of course, she knew they were merely show trophies too, having never been read by the room's usual occupant.

The marble on the floor was a dark and intricate matrix of green and black with a touch of ivory. Gregory said the tile, which had come from a quarry in India, had the appearance of the color of money. A large, thick, Persian rug in green and accents of black, beige, saffron, and burgundy anchored an intimate seating area with an oversized, tufted leather couch and two similarly designed chairs separated by a pair of heavy, antique brass floor lamps with cut glass Tiffany shades. A coffee table made from antique wood and brass and leather claddings with a look much like an oversize pirate's treasure chest with a flat top took up much of the large, open center area.

On the opposite side of the room from the seating area rested an enormous desk made of black walnut. The leather inlaid top was polished and immaculate. Two desk-sized replicas of the Tiffany floor lamps guarded the outside corners. The remainder of the top was barren, devoid of even a fingerprint.

Cassandra padded across the tile, avoiding another Persian area rug - this one more black than green and lacking the accent colors of the other - so not to leave any footprints in the deep wool pile, and around to the back side of the desk. The custom-made leather chair was an illusionist's miracle, fitting every inch of Gregory's smallish frame and at the same time giving the seated occupant the projected vision of a much larger man.

The chair stood guardian to an open area which could nearly fit a normal size desk between the two drawer pedestals. It was inside that open area that Cassandra had discovered the hidden compartment on another day when she had been snooping inside the office and had to seek momentary refuge under the desk when Gregory had returned unexpectedly.

She rolled the chair aside just enough to allow her to crawl inside the cavernous area. Shocks of pain accented each movement as she lowered herself to the floor, but she willed herself to ignore all but the worst of them.

In the very back of the area, which sits opposite the front of the cabinet and was virtually undetectable without a tape measure to match inside and outside dimensions, was the door to the hidden compartment. She pushed against the moulding on the top of the baseboard and a moment later the hidden door popped open revealing a four-segment area with each compartment measuring roughly fifteen inches wide by twelve inches high and about four inches deep. A horizontal leather strap ran across each compartment about midway up.

On the left side, one compartment held a small box which contained, by her count one day, one-point-five million dollars in cash. The one below held a black-lacquered box filled with rings, pendants, necklaces, earrings, and other jewelry. Many of the items were family heirlooms and included broaches carved in all manner of fine and rare media which had been worn by previous generations of women in the Thomason clan.

On the right side, the upper compartment contained two, one-inch thick, leather bound journals. The bottom right compartment held half a dozen legal pads behind which were two, well-worn and aged Cuban cigar boxes resting one on top of the other and each encircled by individual rubber bands. In keeping with the theme of the rest of the office, each cigar box held more trophies. To Gregory, perhaps the highest prized trophies in the room.

She carefully extracted the closest legal pad and flipped the sheets to the last completed page. Cassandra began to read the recently penned notes. The page was titled like all the rest, but this particular title bore two words she did not recognize: JANET HOPKINS. Her blood ran colder and colder as she read his words and then seemed to freeze in her veins as she finally arrived at the date, for which she needed no calendar to calculate because it was yesterday, written underneath Gregory's inked monogram.

Replacing the pad, she reached around the stack and removed the uppermost cigar box and slipped off the rubber band, being extremely careful not to break it, and with trembling hands, lifted hinged the top. An assortment of small, sealed envelopes filled the box and contained baubles and dozens of paper and laminated items slightly larger than business cards. She sorted through the envelopes until she discovered the latest numbered item. Carefully, she slit the seal with her fingernail and inside found in a protective wrapper which warned the document contained an RF identification chip a Canadian driver's license issued in the name of Janet Hopkins. She stared into the eyes of the blonde woman.

Suddenly she felt sick to her stomach. This woman had been in her house as recently as yesterday. She was the same height and build as the others, according to the ID, but she had bobbed blonde hair, and that was way out of character for Gregory. Janet Hopkins was gone now, of that fact Cassandra was certain. She made a mental note of the name and listed place of residence: Montreal, just in case she decided to turn this one over to Willy along with the handful of others from further back.

She resealed the envelope, replaced it into the cigar box, closed it and reinstalled the rubber band, making sure it lined up perfectly where it had been, and put the box back into the compartment. She made sure it all looked just like it had when she opened it, and then closed the door. She had started to crawl out of the space when she froze. Cassandra knew she had made a mistake and she silently cursed herself for her carelessness. She turned around and repeated the movement needed to reopen the compartment and then flipped the cigar box over, the way it had been when she opened the hidden niche.

Out from under the desk, she stretched and laid on the cool tile. She rested her bruised and battered body and fought to calm her frenzied brain. Cassandra checked her watch. It was already after two p.m.. She was glad she had dropped that cash off to Keoki as Gregory had told her to do before she began snooping in his office. She had no idea how long this all would take, or what she would find. She pulled herself up, replaced the chair exactly where it had been, then walked over to the room's northeast corner and reached inside the side moulding of the bookshelf. The irony of the title of the book she needed to slightly displace to reach the latch had always made her chuckle, but not today. Today, Jules Vern's '20,000 Leagues Under the Sea' didn't hold the same degree of mirth for her.

Pushing the small buttons in order by feel, she entered the code to release the latches and then the bookshelf released from the wall and she slowly pulled it open. The subtle smell of the ocean entered the office.

On the other side of the island, a short distance up the mountain in Kapalua and overlooking the island of Molokai across the Pailolo Channel from the seventeenth tee, something in Gregory's pocket began to vibrate.

Pulling out his cell phone, he was not totally surprised to see a photograph of his wife, the south wall of his office in the background, but still he felt the rage begin to seethe deep down inside. He had installed the new security camera during the last two weeks because his suspicions of his wife had been growing and he had too much to lose. So, while she was off-island visiting her stepfather in the hospice in Dallas and doing some shopping, he had spent time putting in the additional security equipment himself. He tucked the phone back into his pocket and looked out over the fairway. He began to grit and grind his teeth.

He watched his caddy impatiently shifting from foot to foot over on the cart path. Gregory had the sudden urge to pummel the man to death with his driver. It was an urge quickly overcome when he realized the caddy was thirty years his junior and half again larger a man than was he. The caddy was also Hawaiian, and although they were an outwardly sedate people by nature, Gregory had never really wanted to find out what they could be capable of if roused. He'd seen some of the war clubs this man's ancestors had crafted and used and those were some fairly effective looking weapons. Not just deadly, but vicious.

Instead, he addressed his ball, transferred his anger into thrust and slapped an impressive drive, down the center-right of the fairway and into the narrow neck which takes the gully out of play, about three hundred yards out.

As he watched the ball trickle to a stop on the manicured surface, he tossed the club to the caddy and started down the hill. Walking along the fairway, the big Hawaiian following behind, Gregory smirked as he personalized and mangled the old adage under his breath, 'Well, my dear, perhaps curiosity will kill the Cass after all.'

After consuming over three-thousand calories during breakfast and lunch - when you added in the alcohol and a couple of iced teas - Sandy decided the dinner an Antoine's had indeed been insult added to injury and canceled the reservation. 'On one condition', she had said, 'I get a raincheck for when you get back from Maui'. Never one to be able to refuse her much of anything, I agreed.

So, having closed the antique shops on Royal Street back in the French Quarter we treated our feet to a couple block limo ride to the Hotel Monteleone where Sandy had reserved for us a two-bedroom suite for the weekend.   I was familiar with some of the accommodations at the Monteleone because I had done surveillance on some political guests of the opposition party during the last gubernatorial election in Louisiana, and they are nothing, if not luxurious. The accommodations, not the politicos.

As we approached the entrance, Sandy told the driver he was done for the day and to add a hundred dollar bonus to his regular tip and charges and to have his office send the bill around to our office on Monday. I rolled my eyes, glad I would be in Maui by then and wouldn't have to see the invoice amount until I got back.

The limousine stopped in front of the Vieux Carre's alabaster landmark that is the Hotel Monteleone and a doorman waited while our driver ran around the back and opened the door for Sandy and myself. Then, the hotel employee did his job, greeted us, opened the door to the right of the highly polished brass revolving door set in the center of the entrance and summoned a bellman to collect our luggage for our two-night stay, plus our packages accumulated during today's shopping spree.

As we passed through the entryway and into the parqueted marble and cut glass encrusted lobby, I caught the departing bellman by the sleeve.

"Be especially careful of the kites, son. I have an important experiment planned for later, if it storms."

I made a show of looking up toward the ceiling of the lobby. He did the same. His unengaged expression went even more blank, then he smiled as he got the joke and was out the door.

"Will you ever grow up?" Sandy asked.

"Nah," I replied, "But won't he be shocked when he sees I really did bring kites."

I stood in the lobby while Sandy checked us in. Even after saving on dinner - for now, that is - I had no interest in learning what the room was going to cost us, I mean me. So I stood for a few minutes admiring the ten-foot high, antique grandfather clock which stands as a quietly ticking sentry in the center of the lobby and then sauntered about, trying to look like I wasn't impressed by the history and opulence.

A few minutes later, we entered the elevator, then exited on the designated floor and were ushered down the richly carpeted and elegantly decorated hallway by yet another bellman. I began to think about how this kind of thing was just more routine in the life of Cassandra Yeats-Thomason. Not bad for a couple of midwestern small town kids. The main difference being, she owned this kind of life, I was just renting.

The plaque on the doorway announced our set of rooms as the Tennessee Williams Suite and I wondered if the people at American Express were considering giving little old William Langdon a call right about now. The bellman gave us a brief history of the association between the Monteleone and the famed playwright and author best known for little ditties such as *A Streetcar Named Desire* and *Cat On a Hot Tin Roof*. From the story being related, Tennessee often stayed at the Monteleone until he bought for himself a mansion in the French Quarter. We entered into the parlor area, which was drenched in shades of gold and ivory and was bigger than my office, and then were shown to each of the two bedrooms.

After a few minutes of orientation and a plea that we don't hesitate to call him personally should we be needing anything, a knock at the door heralded the arrival of the other bellman with our luggage and packages which the pair quickly dispatched to each bedroom. I sent the two on their way with a twenty dollar tip for each of them and then wondered if I had either under or over tipped. I guessed I would find out on the highly unlikely even I had to call Brock in need of anything. Somewhere during all this interaction and activity, Sandy had disappeared.

Then, I heard her running a bath on her bedroom side of the suite so I sneaked into mine to jump up and down on the bed before she caught me. I didn't do that, although I wanted to. Rather, I found the mini-bar and poured a couple small bottles of Bourbon over some mini-bar ice cubes and wondered if Tennessee Williams had ever jumped on the bed in this room.

Six hours later, Sandy and I stood at the intersection of Bourbon and Bienville streets under the flickering gaslight outside the Old Absinthe House bar, having eschewed an elegant dinner at Antoine's so we could buy a couple of hot dogs from a guy with a cart shaped like a big plastic hot dog. Something seemed a bit unbalanced in that equation, but after a night on Bourbon Street, it worked.

After cleaning up and dressing down from our day, we had spent the evening drinking beer and watered-down Hurricanes, walking up and down Bourbon Street, at times pausing to listen to the various genres of music waft from the establishments and turning down, mostly, the street hawkers employed out front to shame people into coming in for a couple of drinks. 'After all, you're enjoying the music for free, and we all have to eat', they'd say.

The night still held much of the day's heat, and the humidity continued to climb until the tops of the taller buildings downtown disappeared into the lowering clouds. We could see the normally nondescript gray office towers on the far side of Canal Street morphing into enticingly artistic patterns of gauzy lights in the mist.

Our dogs purchased and dressed in ketchup, mustard, and onions for me, and ketchup and relish for Sandy, we grabbed our *Go* cups of reasonably cold beer courtesy of the gentleman in the little kiosk between regular establishments and started walking down Bienville in the direction of the river. At the next intersection on Royal Street, we turned right and continued half a block down to the hotel.

Under the watchful eye of the night doorman who hadn't yet been on duty when we had arrived hours earlier, we ambled past about fifty feet, sat on the curb and consumed our late dinner. Finished, we tucked the napkins and wrappers into the empty plastic cups and walked back to the Monteleone. Casting a gaze of suspicion, the doorman eventually let us into the lobby, where other watchful gazes tracked our steps to the elevator.

As the brass-clad elevator doors, polished to the shine of mirrors closed behind us, Sandy kissed me. It wasn't a seduction kiss, or on the other end of the scale, a sisterly kiss. It was a right-down-the-middle kiss. And it caught me totally off guard.

"I just want you to know that I care about you, Otto," she said as she backed away.

I smiled, because I saw she needed me to smile at her.

The doors opened before I could say anything and we walked, me in stunned silence, down the hall to our door. I thought she may have been a little embarrassed because she didn't say anything more. I know she was a little drunk. But, then, so was I.

She had her key out first, slipped it into the door and was inside the room just ahead of my outstretched hand. In the middle of the parlor she paused and I caught her.

I took her in my arms and kissed her back. Not a seduction kiss and definitely not the kind she'd have gotten from that dimwit brother of hers. Then I let her go.

"I care about you, too, Sandy."

I left her standing there and turned to go into my room. When I turned to close my door, I noted she wore a look of total confusion on her face which I was certain mimicked the expression I must have displayed in the elevator.

I closed the door to my room and I could swear I heard her whisper something.

Sandy stood there and watched him close his door.

"Yeah, well I'm also still madly in love with you, Will," she whispered. Sandy then went to her room and closed the door. As she leaned against its backside, she said to herself, 'I just hope you find what you're looking for'.

Chapter Five

Cassandra opened the stainless steel door beyond the bookcase and lights came on in the passageway descending to the lava tube. The custom-built, stainless steel walkway zigzagged for a total length of approximately six hundred feet through the rock as the shaft descended to a concrete pad one-hundred-thirteen feet below. She slid on the pair of cheap, orange flip-flops - on the islands they were called slippers - she had stuffed in her pockets before leaving her room and started to descend along the narrow path.

Lava tubes are natural formations in the rock which allowed for hot lava to escape to the surface during volcanic eruptions. They can stretch for miles, the longest recorded lava tube being from the Big Island's Mauna Loa 1859 flow which runs over thirty miles through the mountain to the ocean. Most lava tubes are singular tunnels which run horizontally, or nearly so, but the one on the property bought by she and Gregory consisted of a main shaft about a mile in length, which exited the bluff just above sea level at the ocean and rose as it dead-ended about a hundred feet below the surface inside the mountain. A branch connected to the surface of the bluff where the house was located and it was down this vertical anomaly that Cassandra moved toward the main shaft.

Gregory had hired workers from Indonesia to build the original structures supplemental to the lava tube: the walkway, the entry and exit structures, and several concrete pads and enclosures in the sea level segment. Along with the confidentiality agreement he had them sign, he had paid them well enough to ensure their silence about what they had done and where.

When they had built the home, Gregory had also insisted on using an architect and contractors from Europe to design and build it. The entire house structure was prefabricated offsite and then shipped to the islands for final assembly and finishes. No local labor was used in the construction, and only a handful of local businesses profited from the construction. Cassandra knew it was just one of the reasons the locals don't really care for Gregory. There were many others.

As she moved along the walkway, which took about six minutes to traverse at normal speed going downhill, her mind was racing ahead. The last time she had ventured down here on her own had been before she left the island for the recent trip to Dallas. The reason she had given Gregory for the trip was that her stepfather had been doing poorly and she had wanted to spend some time with him in case he was failing for the last time. Even though she had spent some time with him, watching him slowly succumb to the cancer, the trip had been much, much more.

On Cassandra's last trip down here, Gregory had four of his little boats. She now suspected she would find three, given the new name in his journal. She had been surprised by two things when she had read the name Janet Hopkins. First, that he had concluded the events so quickly. Second, that he had broken his own protocols. Was his addiction escalating? Was he becoming unpredictable, even to her? Was she in any personal danger? She felt the throbbing of the deep bruising he had inflicted last night and again this morning. The revisiting in the morning was unusual, but given the issue with their neighbor, Keoki, and how much Gregory despised having anything to do with the old Hawaiian, could be not wholly attributable to changes in his normal routine of recovery. As the temperature warmed and the humidity rose the further she descended, she was surprised that a cold sweat had formed on her forehead. In totality, Cassandra was scared.

She hoped she had not made her move too late.

About the same time as Cassandra was asking herself those silent questions, Gregory was sinking his par putt on eighteen. He had played the course today in seventy-four honest strokes. Not his best, but still very respectable. As he had walked to the eighteenth tee, he called the hangar and told them that there was a change in plans and that he wanted to be picked up early. He had made a second call as well, apologizing for having to miss the drinks and dinner. His jilted guest had been disappointed, there being so much exciting news to be discussed between the two, but there had been no prying as to the reason for the sudden cancellation. It was all right. She'd merely turn around on the ferry back to Molokai when it docked in Lahaina, she had said.

Gregory tipped the big Hawaiian caddy at the clubhouse. He could see the chopper approaching in the distance to the south. By the time he walked to his car, he knew they would be setting down. He drove the car along the meandering Plantation Estates Drive out to the Honoapiilani Highway. The stop he made there was barely legal, and some tourists honked their horn as he accelerated through the left onto the highway toward the Kapalua Airport. The drive normally took eleven minutes to cover the five miles, but on this trip Gregory made it in seven.

He left the car running in the lane in front of the support building and headed directly to the idling helicopter. The folks knew him here and he had no issues passing onto the ramp south of the clay-colored main terminal building. On the way he passed one of his people who had ridden in and would drive his yellow Corvette back to the hangar in Kahului.

"Just take me home," Gregory told the pilot as he climbed into the back seat of the chopper and put on headphones. Remembering the five-thousand dollars last night had cost him, he added, "And take the west side route this time." He leaned back and buckled in, then helped himself to a cold bottle of water from the cooler on the floor by his seat.

The pilot pulled up on the collective causing the angle of attack on the main rotor blades to increase, the engine RPM accelerated automatically with the demand for more power and the helicopter rose into the air. He pushed the cyclic forward which pitched the nose down and the blue and white chopper accelerated down the hill toward the ocean. Being a pilot himself, Gregory understood the thrill of making that downhill move and didn't begrudge his pilot performing the maneuver. He merely sat back and thought of what to do about Cassandra; and when.

As they turned south down the coastline, Gregory could see the Molokai Princess pulling out of the harbor at Lahaina. On the aft deck, he thought he could see her. He smiled.

Cassandra was at the vestibule for the lower doorway, the one which connected the walkway to the main lava tube at sea level. Made of poured, reinforced concrete, the vestibules sealed the vertical rise on each end. She knew the lower door was never locked. In fact, there was no lock at all on the door. Anyone entering the shaft had only two methods of egress, from behind the bookcase, or down here at sea level. The waves and strong currents offshore mostly eliminated the potential for anyone entering the tube from sea level. Even if they did, Gregory had said on multiple occasions, 'Where would they go?'

She pushed open the door. The main chamber was large for a lava tube, about ninety feet across and ten feet high. The walls were black, rough, and variably porous, yet the floor in this area of the tube had been smoothed by a layer of concrete. The vestibule doorway opens facing the sea and sits about two hundred feet distant. As it heads to the ocean, the tube narrows horizontally, so by the time it exits to the sea, the opening is roughly circular. Its dimensions constrict as the tube heads back into the mountain as well. Cassandra felt another wave of nausea sweep through her as she recalled how Gregory had once compared the geometry of the tube to a snake after it had swallowed a rabbit.

At the closed end of the lava tube, there was a small crevice which extended to the surface, but after trying several times to climb it, Gregory had concluded it was a maze which nobody would dare attempt to penetrate. He felt good, since the land it would have broken through to sunshine in was owned by Keoki Keaweaheulu.

Between the seaside mouth at the edge of the cliff and the water, stood an area of stony beach, roughly sixty feet wide and thirty feet deep. The rocks which constitute the beach are roughly the size of flattened tennis balls which had been smoothed by eons of wave action.

Along the wall to the left of the vestibule there were three blockhouses made of concrete block with a poured concrete roof. Each house was roughly ten feet by ten feet by eight feet high and was separated from the next by about five feet of open space.

Mechanical equipment attached to each compartment sat in the open space. Power had originally been supplied from the house line, but in the last six years Gregory had gone green and installed a large photovoltaic system which now powered both house and subterranean chamber. They sold back the excess power to Maui Electric, although had it not been for times of emergency, Gregory would have preferred to be totally off the grid, she knew.

In the center of the area, there was a larger blockhouse, about thirty by thirty and eight feet high. More support equipment sat alongside this structure as well. Even though the normal temperature could be relatively comfortable this close to the opening, there was no real air movement through the closed tube and humidity would build to uncomfortable levels. Depending upon the day, the ambient conditions inside the tube could be cool and clammy or hot and muggy; today was a typical summer hot and muggy day in the tube. Cassandra shivered from the sudden trickle of sweat which ran down the small of her back.

As the door to the surface moved to close behind her, she quickly stopped the transit by grabbing the door knob to make sure it moved freely in her hand. Sometimes, she thought, there's no knowing what kind of changes Gregory would make in his subterranean world, and a sudden shock of that realization sparked a shot of fear to her heart. Thankfully, the knob did twist freely, but to not risk being found trapped down here, she took off her slippers and wedged them into the opening to prevent the door from fully closing. Satisfied she would not be trapped, Cassandra walked barefoot and began her exploration.

The helicopter cruised offshore and after passing what some people would call the chin of Maui, just west of Ma'alaea and its harbor, the pilot banked and made a direct line for Cape Kina'u, just north of La Perouse Bay at the end of Makena. There he would turn eastbound along the south shore of the island toward the house.

Gregory always enjoyed the water route away from shore. Somehow he found it calmed him. Water had always been a draw to him. It cleansed, quenched, was beautiful to look at in both its reflected colors and endless motion, and hid your secrets. He never understood people who would move to the desert. To him, those types lacked imagination. Only the dead are drawn to the desert, the living are drawn to the water, he would say.   The irony of that thought just now as they made the turn to the west and transited above the Alenuihaha Channel made him smile.

First, Cassandra checked the small block houses.   Each of the doors were locked.   She stood on her tiptoes and cupped her hands over the dark glass porthole.   Nothing.   Empty.   Then she checked the large room, the one Gregory used as his work room and to house his electronics, computer equipment, tapes and DVDs.   That door he never locked, although he could, from the inside with a thumb latch. There was no key that could unlock that door from the outside. Inside there was nothing out of sorts that she could detect.   The equipment was all off, except for the mechanicals, the air conditioning and dehumidification units Gregory always kept running.

She then walked down the tube toward the seaside entrance.   She saw three covered boats sitting on wheeled carts.   The fourth cart was in place, but empty of its load.   She exited to the beach area and could discern the plowed pattern in the stones which revealed a keel had been dragged through them recently.   She looked out into the channel as the waves lapped gently at the shore.

Suddenly, she felt her heart leap into her throat as she heard a helicopter approaching from the west.   Too low for the tourist variety, she thought, but way too early for Gregory to return from his day. Having not brought sunglasses along, she shielded her eyes from the sun slowly moving downhill from its midday apex and strained her eyes. She stood there motionless for several moments, but when she saw a glint of blue and white she began to run for the walkway door.

Barely breaking stride, she snatched her slippers and threw open the door.   Her heart was already threatening to beat its way out of her chest from the combination of fear and exertion, and she had a long way to go.   The clock was ticking and she did the mental math as her legs churned against the cushioned walkway.   It took six minutes down at normal pace and about ten minutes going uphill, she wondered how much she could cut off the time if she could maintain this pace.   Then, of course, she had to get out of his office, and get herself someplace where Gregory wouldn't have endless questions over her being sweaty and out of breath.   Perhaps to the exercise room, she thought. Would he buy the fact she was working out when he knew exactly how sore her body would be today?

She did the math over and over as she continued pushing against the strain of the climb and time wasn't working out in her favor. When she had spotted the helicopter, it had been perhaps three minutes out. Give a minute for landing and exiting. A leisurely walk into the house, another two minutes, perhaps. That's six.

Her mind raced, how long had she been running? Three minutes? She was just over halfway up the walkway. She was never going to make it. My God, she thought, could her heart take any more pounding? She pushed on even though it was becoming increasingly clear to her there was no way she was going to make it. He couldn't catch her in here. With the wildly erratic state of mind he displayed since she had returned, she could not risk him catching her in his sanctuary. For the third time in two days, she sent forth a prayer into the ether.

Gregory jumped from the chopper and jogged to the house. He used the same side entrance which Cassandra had used last night. Once inside the house, he stopped and listened. There was no sound at all. Not unusual in the house of twenty-one rooms totaling sixteen thousand square feet on two floors, but at least he knew she wasn't rattling around in the kitchen or playing her music loud in the gym. He headed for his office, through the kitchen, the west wing hallway, across the rotunda and central foyer where he paused and listened again, and then down the east wing hallway, past her precious eucalyptus side table.

He pulled his key from his pocket and slid it slowly into the lock on his office door. As quietly as he could, he turned the lock, and twisted the knob. He paused and listened again. Nothing. Slowly he pushed the door open. The sun was lower in the west than when Cassandra had been in here, yet he could still see every corner. His eyes swept the room. Then they stopped on the center of his desk.

His mind replayed the snippet of the scene in *Cape Fear* - the remake - when Robert De Niro's character called out for Nick Nolte's character after beating away three would-be toughs sent to rough him up. As he quietly moved toward the desk, he called out for her, "Cassandra, would you be here? Could you be here?"

Cassandra was running out of steam.   She was about three quarters of the way to the surface.   She realized she would never make it as she approached the final turn, the last straight run to the door behind the bookcase.   She was about to take that turn at a brisk walking pace, when she heard the door open at the top of the stairs. She felt the air pressure shift and it sucked the breath out of her. Her mind raced and her eyes searched for anyplace to hide.   There was no place.   Cassandra heard his steps start down the walkway. She had no choice, so she turned around and started back down as quickly and quietly as she could.

Gregory had not found her underneath his desk, so now he was headed down the walkway of the lava tube. Of course, he knew she could be in her room or somewhere else in the house.   How interesting would it be if he found her down below? His lips curled into an evil smile at the thought.   He approached the first turn, stopped and listened.   There was a rattle below, a small bit of lava had fallen onto the walkway. He thought of repeating his Cape Fear line into the abyss, but that moment of playfulness had passed and he simply continued walking: and listening.

Midway through the second straight run, he found the fallen rock lying in the middle of the walkway. He looked around, studied the crevices of the walls and ceiling.   Then he kicked the rock off the walkway.

Cassandra watched him search the crevices where the rock had stopped rolling downhill. She had found and tucked herself into a small alcove uphill of the spot where he now stood in the rocky passageway.   Had he been coming up the walkway instead of heading down, she would have had no cover and he would have surely seen her.   As he disappeared around the next turn and thankfully never looked back, she began to breathe for the first time in what seemed like minutes and minutes.   Perhaps God was answering one of her prayers.

Gregory walked out the door and into the sea level tube. He stood and looked around, then bent down and picked up something he knew should not be there. He slapped the item against his hand and walked around the area. He could feel the rage again building within him. It always started deep inside. In his gut. He could clearly recall his temper tantrums of early childhood and how they would begin in the same place. Psychiatrists had told his mother that his tantrums were the frustrated manifestations of his sense of a loss of control. While he would enjoy jumping up and down and cursing in an adult version of a child's tantrum, fifty years of living - even this type of privileged living - had taught him that to bring any situation to the next chapter, he needed to maintain control. So he stifled the impulse and walked to his control room.

Cassandra could feel the air pressure shift again. Slowly, she slipped out of her hiding space and continued up the walkway. Her feet were raw from clinging to the rough alcove. She looked back and was relieved to not see any blood on the walkway. After taking a few steps, she remembered her slippers and went to pull them from her pocket. She stopped dead when her hands returned holding only one of the pair. She looked around the walkway, went down to the last switchback and saw nothing lying on the last run. She knew it wasn't in the nook in which she had hidden, but looked anyway. Out of time again, she headed back up to the entrance, stepped through to the office and closed the bookcase, just has it had been when she arrived at the top. She padded toward the door, noticed that Gregory's desk chair had been rolled away from the desk.

She searched her nearly frazzled memory. Had she not replaced it when she first went down? Had Gregory moved it when he came in? Fear gripped her. If she had left it out of place and he had noticed it, he would have known she had been there. If he had moved it out of place, he either had been looking for her or was changing his habit of being fastidious about his surroundings. He never would leave it out had he simply sat there and done something at the desk. Should she put it back into place? Should she leave it? She was frozen in place, locked in indecision and fear. She felt like she was ten again, and her stepfather...

Gregory started back up the walkway to his office. In his left hand, the item he had retrieved from the bottom; his right hand a tightly balled fist. His rational mind fought his irrational thoughts. Unlike his wife, Gregory was rarely crippled by indecision. He had decided to spend the night in his office. To avoid losing his temper with her, he would avoid his wife altogether. Yes, he thought, that would be best. For tonight.

That night, Cassandra cowered in her room. She had locked the door to the hallway and all three sets of lanai doors. She not been able to sleep. She heard nothing of Gregory. When the sun had begun to rise on Sunday morning, she showered and decided to get out of the house, to drive toward Hana, perhaps stop in at the Palapalo Ho'omau Church to light a candle and meditate.

The limestone coral church had been built by early white missionaries in 1857 and it's churchyard was the final resting place of famed aviator Charles Lindbergh. In the past, she had found comfort during confusing and stressful times by sitting in the cool, green and white building with the crude stained glass window of Jesus in white robe and Hawaiian-design yellow and red overcoat. She couldn't remember if they had a Sunday service anymore, but something inside her hoped they did.

She made a quick call on her cell phone.

When she was dressed and ready to go, she put an ear to her door. Still nothing. She had thought of going around on the lanai and see if she could see Gregory in his room, asleep. She dared not risk rousing him if he were. If she could avoid him for at least the morning, she was fairly sure he would be over the worst of what she feared.

When she opened her door, she stopped dead. Laying at the foot of her door, was her missing orange slipper.

Chapter Six

I awoke hungry and to the smell of bacon and eggs wafting under my door. In the parlor separating our rooms, I could hear Sandy moving about quietly. I looked for my pants, pulled them on and went to find the source of those delicious aromas. Don't let anyone kid you, a hot dog and a beer sitting on the curb at midnight makes for a decent snack, but it doesn't satisfy like a big dinner at Antoine's.

"Good morning," I said as I opened the door.

Sandy stood arranging items on the room service table in a floor length robe made of sheer black tulle over a tasteful black nightie that ended mid-thigh. Don't let anyone kid you, waking to find your ex-wife standing there in sheer robe with a black nightie underneath is great way to start the morning. I felt something stir inside, or rather outside. Hunger can take many forms, but I quickly decided I'd feed my stomach rather than make a fool of myself by putting a sober move on Sandy.

"Good morning," she responded. "I figured after yesterday's hectic schedule, we could both use some quiet, down time."

I moved toward the table. I was starving, and I do love bacon.

Sandy pulled the covers from the platters, and I mean platters, to reveal piles of bacon, eggs over easy, white toast - none of that healthy whole grain crap - and breakfast potatoes with onions and peppers. It was a meal fit for a working class king, and I was very grateful for the effort and the results.

I sat, dug in and stuffed a slice of bacon into my mouth. Perfectly done, firm yet with a chew left in it. A few moments more on the grill and it would have been bacon bits, a few moments less, and the rubbery fat would have overwhelmed the meat.

"Don't stand on ceremony," Sandy teased, watching me chewing like a ravenous animal. She took a chair opposite me.

As I took a sniff of what appeared to be tomato juice, she read my mind.

"Don't worry, it's virgin today. No booze on Sunday."

I added a little salt and pepper to the top of the juice and let it float there. Never mix the salt and pepper in, you lose the taste. Just let it float and coat your upper lip as you drink down the glass. Best way in the world to drink virgin tomato juice.

Sandy slid an egg off the platter onto her plate and a ladylike helping of bacon and potatoes. I was dunking my first yoke with a piece of white toast.

"So, how did it end between you and Cassie," Sandy asked. "Certainly not in the basement with your mother dragging you out by your ear."

I swallowed my toast.

"Are we still on that subject?"

"Yeah, until we get to the end."

"Well, Cassie and I were breaking Junior High School records for remaining together. I think we had passed seven or eight weeks and Halloween was approaching. I asked her to the movies on the Friday night before, a special double-feature horror production which promised to draw a ton of kids eager for a little 'here, move closer and I'll protect you' action.

"So we go and it's us and a few of her friends who didn't have steadies. It was a typical teenage event at the old Sheboygan Theater and jam packed with kids. When the lights went out, many of us didn't see much of the movies. A fella needs to get creative when he's sitting with his best gal and her friends are sitting right next to them. We both got more than a little worked up.

"After the movies, the five of us walked home, the three solo girls up front and Cassie and I behind, arm in arm. It was cold for the season, maybe forties that night. Well, to move it all along, we ditched her friends and soon found ourselves behind her garage. We were freezing, but making our own heat, until her old man turns on the porch light and hollers for her out the back door. She froze at that instant, literally turned to ice in my arms. Then, before I knew what was happening, I was standing there all alone, her wet goodnight kiss on my cheek, evaporating in the wind."

Sandy was studying me while I continued the story. Something in her demeanor had changed. Call it the ex-cop in me, or the ex-husband, but while I could not put my finger on exactly what had taken her off guard, I knew something had.

"What?" I asked, my eyes searching hers. "You wanted the whole unvarnished tale. Believe me, we are way past the worst of the sexy parts. From here on, it's all G-rated."

She hesitated, poked her fork around her potatoes. Her eyes would not meet mine.

"No, it's not that. Please finish."

"The next afternoon, I ran into Cassie's friend, Lydia. She had been one of the singles with us at the movies the night before. She said to me, 'I guess you're getting serious about Cassie'. I said, 'Yeah, I guess I am'.

"Lydia then began to relate a story about Tim and Cassie; how they had gone all the way in a sleeping bag in Lydia's basement. I felt like my heart had been ripped out. Eight years of Catholic grade school had instilled in me the virtue of being virtuous. Even though Cassie and I had done some exploring, and she was not the first girl I had done that with, nor I was certain, I was not the first guy she had done that with, fooling around was way different from 'going all the way'. You crossed a line when you did that. It was a line you could never recross in the other direction, especially girls. It changed my view of Cassie."

"That's a fairly stern, puritanical viewpoint, Otto, and frankly, a bit misogynistic," Sandy interjected. "I was never raised that way, so I guess I don't understand it, but I accept what you're telling me. From my perspective, what's happened before, is before. It can't be changed."

"True, from the perspective of today, or even from the perspective of having just a couple more years of living under my belt than I had the day Lydia burst my bubble, I could have changed my view. I never got that chance.

"On Monday, I approached Cassie on the steps outside our Junior High School. It was a cold day, and it was early. The doors were locked and a crowd of kids had gathered like always. I pulled her to the edge of the crowd, and said to her, 'I heard about you and

Tim and the sleeping bag'. Her face turned pale and at that instant I knew. She then asked who had told me and I lied to protect Lydia. I told her Tim had given me the lowdown. She said to me, 'So what?'. I was incredulous. How could she be so cavalier about the whole thing? Didn't she understand how this changed things between us?"

Sandy's eyes were judgmental when she looked at me this time.

"Would it have been any different had she lost her virginity to you in your furnace room?" she asked.

"At the age of fourteen, um, yeah. Today, who cares? Then, it was a big thing. Cassie's attitude was annoying me. Between her lack of remorse and my fourteen year old brain trying to contend with such an adult issue, I started to see red. So, I said to her in my best sarcastic voice, 'Well, how was it?'"

"Oh boy," Sandy said. She was sitting back, drinking her orange juice.

"Yeah, oh boy. Cassie's eyes teared up and she said the worst thing she could have ever said, 'It was great!'. I called her a slut. Some of our schoolmates heard and turned to look. I noted their open-mouth stares in my peripheral vision. My eyes were focused on Cassie's challenging and unrepentant expression.

"I have often wondered why she didn't slap me that day. Instead, an instant after my verbal dart had pierced her heart, her face fell and she simply turned on her heels and walked away without saying another word. Not a single word. Why? I've always wondered that."

Sandy shrugged her shoulders.

"Anyway, a week later, she transferred to a private school out of state, or at least that was the story. It had been rumored she was sent somewhere to have a child, but I never knew that for certain.

"Until two days ago, I haven't had the chance to speak to her again. The end."

Sandy just stared at me.

"That's it? That's the Cassie Yeats story?"

"Were you expecting more?"

"Kind of," she said. "From the way you've been carrying on."

"It may not seem like such a big deal today, but back then, and to that point in my life, the Cassie Yeats story was the hugest and most confusing series of experiences that had happened to me. Furthermore, there had never been any closure."

"There's no such thing as closure, Otto," Sandy said, a bit too callously for how vulnerable and empty I was feeling. "It's a cruel hoax played on grieving people by fringe professionals who should know better."

I know I sounded defensive. Sandy's lack of empathy added to my need to be so, even though I understood her loathing for the term *closure*. Over the past twenty-four hours, I had shared the details of a very painful time of my early life, a story to which I had never had the chance to type the words, *The End*.

"I guess it's still an issue for me because I never had the opportunity for resolution. You know me, Sandy. I like things cut and dried and packaged and put away. I hate loose ends, and Cassie Yeats was, *is* the sole piece of my life's unfinished business."

"So, we're taking this case because you're still nursing a pubescent crush after thirty years?"

What could I say? There was a portion of truth to it.

After retrieving her lost slipper from where Gregory had obviously left it outside her bedroom door, Cassandra had quickly retreated back into her room and locked the door. She resisted the immediate urge to call someone. What good would it do her? They were so remote out here in the middle of nowhere that it would take at least an hour for someone of authority to arrive, and while their closest neighbor, Keoki Keaweaheulu, was only a few hundred feet up the mountain, he hated them. Although, if push came to shove, she thought the old Hawaiian would probably take her side over Gregory's since she was certain he hated her husband beyond almost anything short of, Kiapolo, the devil. There would be no deliveries, maid, pool service or other workmen coming around as her husband had always insisted he wanted total privacy from employees or services on at least one day each week. She sat on the edge of her bed and thought through her options.

She couldn't just hide in her room. If he wanted to get to her, there were any number of ways he could do that, and it was important to her plans they remain connected. She had information to provide Willy and would need to be available to him for several days after he arrived tomorrow afternoon before turning him loose like a French pig in search of the elusive truffle. Could a truffle be elusive, she thought. At some point she would have to interact with

Gregory, if only to gauge his mood before she arranged to place Willy and him into the pit like two agitated, fighting roosters.   In addition, she had already arranged the day that she had no intention of foregoing.   Cassandra decided she had to just suck it up and rely on the skills she learned as a young girl on how to manage life on the fly.

Cassandra unlocked her door, opened it, exited the relative safety of her room and closed the door as quietly as she possibly could. She then tiptoed along the hallway, and crept down the stairs.   She grabbed a bottle of water from the kitchen before heading to the garage.   At that point, she relaxed a bit because she knew if Gregory had wanted to see her this morning, he would have already been standing behind a corner waiting for her.   He had always enjoyed giving her little frights; in the beginning it was to hear her squeal and then playfully chastise him, but over the years it has gotten to be an increasingly obnoxious behavior.   The larger problem for Cassandra at this point was he was truly giving her some serious scares since she had returned.

For a while last night, she had considered leaving the island again; just getting out of Dodge, as the saying goes, to give Gregory time to get over his issues.   Then, the more she pondered her next move, she realized he hadn't just changed in the last two weeks.   He had been changing slowly over the last several years and she now felt like a fool for not having seen it.   Each shift in his moods, each high and each low, had been so subtle and she had been too close.   It was like watching someone approach you in a dark room lit only by a strobe light.   One moment they were across the room, and seemingly the next instant they were standing right next to you, and you had never seen them move.

Standing in the garage, looking over her half dozen options, Cassandra decided to take the Jeep today.   She'd be heading toward Kipahulu and the four-wheel-drive would come in handy if the road turned treacherous because of rain blowing around the mountain from the windward side, or if she decided to take a side trip off the beaten path.

She slid into the driver's seat of the Jeep, locked all the doors, started the engine and then backed out of the garage.   She turned the vehicle around and headed up the driveway to the main road.   In contrast to the touristy and heavily traveled road to Hana along the eastern shore of the island, the road on the south shore was a combination of bad paved road, bad gravel road and really bad, one-lane gravel road. But it was your only option along the south shore between the points where the paved road ended as it was the only connection between east and west on this side of the island.

Outside the gate at the end of the driveway, she turned right and pointed the Jeep to the east. Up the hill she saw Keoki Keaweaheulu sitting on his porch nursing a beer. He tossed her a shaka - the friendly two-finger wave which translates to 'hang loose' - with his right hand and hoisted a can of what she imagined was a Sunday morning beer in mock salute with the other. She guessed five thousand dollars for doing nothing but antagonizing Gregory would keep him in Red Stripe for a while. She gave him a small wave back, being, even after all these years, still uncomfortable with the shaka.

This first stretch of road toward the east was bad gravel and joined almost immediately with really bad, one-lane gravel. Gregory had made an offer to the County that he'd pay to pave the road to connect one side to the other, but that offer went nowhere. Maui can be a strange place. An island community where even Oprah Winfrey gets landlocked by her neighbors refusing to sell her anymore land on the Hana side. At least that's the way the story played on the coconut wireless. Rumor had it, that's the reason she built the OW Ranch on the other side of Haleakala near Ulapalakua.

Cassie decided the slow drive would do her mind and body some good. She rolled down the window, powered back the sun roof, turned on the Sirius and tuned in some classic rock. The wind tousled her hair and the sunshine felt wonderful on her face. She could already feel herself relax. Although the road itself wasn't much to write home about, the view ranged from spectacular to breathtaking. The top of the mountain to her left was clear this morning, even though in the distance she could see some lower clouds stacked up by the trade winds on the windward face around Hana. To her right, the wind-whipped ocean disappeared over the horizon. Shortly, the road began a series of switchbacks which took her to from one gorgeous ocean overlook to another by way of a short couple of inside turns at the edge of the increasing forest. She became lost in the scenery and her thoughts.

Almost sooner than expected, Cassie approached the turn off to the church, which she knew from memory because it was unmarked except for a small sign for a horse riding stable. She braked the Jeep and cautiously navigated the ninety-degree right downhill turn toward the ocean onto a hard-packed, one-lane roadway seemingly hacked out of the jungle foliage. A few moments later, when the road forked, she followed the drive to the left, then pulled up under a large banyan tree and parked. Roots sprouting from the major boughs of the tree hung just above her head outside the sunroof as they grew slowly earthward in their search for water and nutrients. It was as if the ancient guardian was reaching down for her soul. She shuddered at the thought of this beautiful and peaceful place turning frightful in the shadows after nightfall. There was only one other car there, a lemon yellow Mustang convertible, an obvious rental. It was empty, and she could not see its occupants in the graveyard or on the grounds beyond.

She sat for a moment and savored the overwhelming silence, then grabbed her water bottle from the center console and exited the Jeep. She walked around the back of the vehicle and through the stacked lava rock fence. Already feeling the peace of the place, Cassie stepped lightly from pad to pad which lead through the grass to the small entry and pulled open the ancient wood door of the green and white Palapalo Ho'omau Church.

The coolness greeted her the instant she opened the door and she stepped inside. About half a dozen rows of green wooden benches sat on each side of a center aisle. The polished plank floors stretched to the white pulpit and the elevated choir loft behind. Elevated wasn't really the right word, it was just an area behind the pulpit raised by about four or five steps. So raised, rather than elevated.

A lone crucifix was mounted on the wall behind the choir area. Over the center aisle hung two chandeliers designed for candles, and single-candle sconces were mounted in between each opening on the long walls - three windows mauka, or mountain side, and two windows and the side entry makai, or ocean side. The lone hint to modern times was a single fluorescent light fixture mounted in the center of the ceiling.

Following Hawaiian custom, Cassie kicked off her sandals and padded up the center aisle bare footed. She wondered how many local and visiting worshipers over the generations had walked this floor, polishing the planks with the soles of their feet. At the front pew, she sat down. She stared at the wooden cross on the wall, a lonely, unadorned pairing of two brown pieces of wood on the pristine, glossy white wall.   Cassie had been raised Lutheran; Cassandra was an agnostic.   She would have loved to soothe her troubled soul by declaring herself an atheist, but even given the events and thoughts of the last few days, she could not bring herself to the point of totally disavowing a God she had grown up praying to and believing in.   Nor could she disavow the sins she had committed over the last two decades and the ones which she continued to add to her burden.   She discovered she may need something more than her own will to survive this.

She hoped He was indeed a loving and forgiving God.

She bowed her head.

Gregory heard her leave.   He had indeed spent the night inside his office as he planned, venturing out but once around midnight to place her slipper outside her room.   He had put his ear to her door and thought he could hear her breathing inside.   He had seen her earlier sitting with her back to the door, not sleeping, but rather with a look of deep thought and wonder on her face.   Good, he had thought.

Before returning to his office, he stopped by the garage and walked across the immaculate floor in bare feet.   He selected a three-quarter-inch open end wrench from the red Snap-On tool chest sitting on its cart along the back wall.   Then, standing in front of their six vehicles, he pointed the wrench at each in turn while going through a single rendition of Eeny, meeny, miny, mo, coming to the end lyrics of 'you are it!' and landing on the fire engine red Jeep.

Dropping to one knee at the right rear tire, he reached around and the wrench found home.   With a slight tug, the coupler broke loose.   Putting just a little back pressure on the wrench, he snugged the coupler, but not quite enough to restore the seal.   He wiped the wrench on a shop towel and then replaced it and closed the toolbox drawer.

He didn't sleep much through the night, but instead watched Cassandra's activities on his closed circuit system.   Like the still camera he had installed on the bookcase access to the lava tube, his wife had no idea he had rigged a dozen cameras throughout the house while she was gone on her latest trip to visit her precious stepfather; each of the cameras routed into his office and his subterranean control room.

The flat screen television on which he watched golf tournaments and football games in his office was tied into the system through his computers. He could view one, several, or all the cameras' live or recorded feed at one time by use of the remote control.

This morning, after he heard her leaving, he again left his office and walked through the kitchen to the garage. He grinned as he stood at the empty spot where the Jeep had been. He turned and grabbed a shop rag, then wiped up the quarter-size spot of amber liquid where the vehicle's right rear tire had been. He tossed the rag into the garbage can.

Before returning to the office, he snatched an orange from the refrigerator in the kitchen and pulled a paper towel from the dispenser on the counter. He glanced at the kitchen wall clock which stood at exactly nine a.m.

Back in his locked office a few moments later, he turned on the television and found the Golf Channel on the satellite feed where they were in the middle of broadcasting the final round of the Canadian Open. He turned to look out one of his lanai doors over the channel and laughed out loud at the irony.

Sandy and I spent that Sunday relaxing in our suite, except for the several hour diversion to the hotel's pool in the early afternoon followed by a short walk to the Gumbo Shop on St. Peter Street (the Gumbo Shop closest to the river for those of you who may come looking) for a hearty late lunch of Blackened Fish appetizer, some fresh French bread and a big bowl of File Gumbo with Chicken and Sausage which would surely hold us both through until morning.

Upon returning to the rooms, I broached a situation with Sandy which I knew had been on her mind.

"Don't worry about me in this thing," I said.

She was sitting curled into the corner of one of the couches holding one of the embroidered throw pillows in her lap, obviously deep in thought, her open laptop untouched on the coffee table.

I walked over to her and sat in the adjacent chair.

"I mean, I will certainly be able to maintain my professional countenance in working through this case. This isn't about bringing closure to a pubescent love affair, as you put it."

I could tell she wasn't buying it.

"See, Sandy, Cassie Yeats was the first girl, first person in my life really, with whom I could talk about anything. We would talk for hours about everything from music to school to our dreams about the future. We were, for that eight or ten weeks, closer than any two humans could be. There was nothing we couldn't share with each other. To this day, I cannot understand how she couldn't speak to me about that simple inquiry into her past."

"Simple for you, maybe," Sandy interjected. "Things are a bit more complicated for us girls. By the way, in your childishly superior judgment, you *did* refer to her in public as a slut. Not that I'm taking her side in this, Otto, but just how did you expect her to react to that?"

I opened my arms and sat forward in the chair.

"It's simple, Sandy, because I truly believed Cassie and I could talk about anything. Why would she not talk to me? Why would she just walk away and never make a move to clarify the situation?"

Sandy thought about those questions for a minute. I could see her mind mulling things over. Then I saw her face transition to the acceptance of an idea.

"Otto, there's no telling why Cassie reacted the way she did way back when. It could have been any number of things, from PMS to perhaps she just wasn't as enamored of you anymore and this was a simple path to end it." She saw my face not wanting to accept that answer, so she added, "That's all in the past, you can't chase it. Let it go."

"I don't want to let it go," I said. "I need to know what it was that caused her to change almost overnight."

A moment passed.

"Perhaps you don't want to know," she said.

Then Sandy posed the question that my ego wouldn't allow me to ask myself.

"Did you ask her why you?" Sandy asked. "I mean, with her financial means and connections, she could have hired any mega-firm she wanted. Why come to you? Doesn't that strike you as a bit odd? It does me."

"I did ask her, as a matter of fact." Actually, I hadn't, so I assembled this little white lie for Sandy from snippets of things Cassie had said and my own assumptions. "She had recognized my name on some news reports years ago from Chicago, and then again from that incident down in Thibodaux a year ago. She had used another P.I. to ensure she tracked me all the way to back home before she decided to come to me for help. To make sure it was really me."

"Yeah, but, why you?" Sandy continued with heavy emphasis on both the *why* and the *you*.

"I think it's because she feels she can trust me."

"Trust you?" She stared at me with incredulity on her face. It was a look like you'd give the used car salesman when he tells you the Corvette you're looking at was only driven to and from church on Sundays by a little, old gray haired granny. Then she added the zinger: "Because you felt her up back in the ninth grade?"

A quickly stifled smile flashed on my face. I hoped she hadn't seen it, but knowing my ex-wife, she had, and it would cost me in ball busting somewhere down the line.

This wasn't going well. Sandy wasn't buying it, and I was beginning to doubt my real motivations here. As I've said, I trust Sandy's judgment more than anyone's, and if she's not on board, then my red warning flags should be flying and they're not. I'm still running around this thing on yellow. Okay, maybe half yellow, half red.

"There's something not right here, Otto." She was pulling the pillow closer and shaking her head. Her gaze remained straight ahead and unfocused like she was trying to figure it out. "I just think you had better be very, very careful." She turned and captured my eyes with hers; it was her 'Hey, I'm serious here look' and then added: "About everything." Her eyebrows arched in emphasis.

"I'm always careful," I said, trying to be cute with the implied double entendre. When she didn't seem amused, I added some meat to the bone. "Plus, I'm planning on bringing Willie and Sam with me."

"Well, that makes me feel better."

Willie and Sam are my 10 mm SIG Sauer P229 semiautomatic and the .38 revolver snub nose back-up piece. Normally, Willie fits in the small of my back, while Sam is positioned in an ankle holster. That system works great with my normal attire of sports jacket and slacks, but I had been wondering how they would accessorize with island casual. I had decided Willie would easily still be concealable by an untucked Aloha shirt, but I still hadn't figured out what I'd do with Sam if I were wearing shorts. I wasn't real comfortable not having Sam on my person, because while Willie had protected me many times over the years, it was Sam which saved my life that night in the warehouse.

"I figured you would," she said. "I've already sent over paperwork to the Maui Police Department requesting they honor your concealed carry permit. Probably a good thing. As it turns out, they haven't granted but two concealed carry permits in the last twenty years, and those were ex-MPD guys."

I hadn't thought about that being a possible problem. As an ex-cop, I can tell you that it's better to ask permission than to beg forgiveness on this issue. After all, Maui wasn't Louisiana, where every Bubba and his brothers had some kind of weapon on them or in their truck. I'm sure the Tourist Bureau on Maui wasn't too keen on possible shoot outs between the visitors.

I yawned. It had been a long few days. Tomorrow would be an early rise for the flights to Maui.

"You're thinking something, else. Spill it."

I watched her wheels spin. Later she would tell me why she hadn't been ready to spill the beans quite yet, but that didn't help me at this point.

"Let me sleep on it," she said. "Maybe I'll tell you in the morning before you go."

Rising, I stretched.

"Speaking of morning, six a.m. comes awfully early and it's getting late." I bent down to kiss her on the top of her head. "Good night."

I walked to my room and turned to look at her as I started to close the door. I could see her mind still working. When she got into this mode, she would work and rework the problem until she had it figured out. The problem was, I'm not sure she had all the data in this particular case. Hell, something told me I didn't either, but I wasn't really listening anymore.

"Don't stay up all night," I said as I closed the door.

Cassie spent an hour or so inside the church before wandering outside. She walked through the graveyard makai of the building and then over to the Lindbergh grave. Along the fence line at the bluff, she read the recently repainted inscription on the white arch with the heart at the apex which proclaimed the memorial to be 'In Loving Memory of Our Dad, Herman Nelson, Jr.'. She had always wondered about the back story on this particular marker, but never enough to really research it. According to the memorial, the man had died in 1994, months before his forty-first birthday. That's really all she knew. Leaning on the fence and looking out over the channel, Cassandra could smell the ocean. The wind had picked up a bit and the waves were churning at the coast from the south. The Alenuihaha was working itself into a frenzy. Her mind momentarily touched on the thought of Janet Hopkins of Montreal, Canada. She dismissed it.

She walked over to the Kipahulu Overlook, moving along the wooden fence which shielded the inland private property from tourists wandering out to take in the view on the public access. At the end of the grassy strip was a chain link fence which shielded these tourists from stupidly tumbling off the bluff's edge. She put her hands on the top of the fence and threw her gaze over the edge.

The craggy shoreline of the island's south shore was being pounded by the increasing south surf, spray from every collision of sea to shore flying up twenty or thirty feet onto the bluff. The small islets of lava which poked above sea level offshore were being swamped. A building gray mist was working its way onshore. Across the small cove, she could make out the lone house built on the flat plain back from the bluff. The house's solitary state had always reminded her of their home further to the west. She wondered if the people who had ventured here to build a house away from everyone else also had secrets.

Cassie didn't hear the approaching footsteps, so lost in the view and her thoughts she was. She didn't even sense his presence behind her until his hands grabbed her hips. She let loose a scream they could have heard in Hana and spun in one fluid motion to face the man with the palm of her left hand poised to drive his nasal bone deep into his brain while her right leg coiled to drive his nuts up there an instant later.

"Whoa, baby," Captain Dan said, while he reflexively moved to protect both his face and his testicles.

Cassie nearly collapsed in his arms as the adrenaline rush was immediately recalled until it was needed next time. She let her body fall against him. He was laughing as he held her. She didn't know whether to hug him back or raise her knee and send him another message.

"Goddammit, Dan," she howled, deciding on some middle ground. "You know I've dealt with that crap for twenty years. Don't ever sneak up on me again."

"I'm sorry, baby," he said. "I couldn't resist. You looked absolutely delicious standing there."

He gave her a repentant smile, but she already had forgiven him. Such was new love.

Her heartbeat returned to normal and she snuggled against his chest. He felt good to her. He smelled so naturally like himself. His arms were around her, pulling her close. She didn't need her sixth sense to feel something else coming up between them. She smiled to herself and then gazed up into his deep blue eyes.

"What about the Mustang?" she asked, but knowing what his answer would be.

"What Mustang?"

"There was a yellow Mustang parked out by the church when I got here," she said. She felt herself melting into his eyes, and melting somewhere else too.

He made a show of looking around.

"Nobody here but you and me, babe."

She could feel his gentle guiding. Cassie turned her back on him and grabbed the top rail of the fence again. This time, she wasn't looking at the view or thinking of the house and the possible secrets it contained. She was lost in thoughts of him. His hands slid over her breasts, down over her hips again, over her outer thighs, down to the hem of her dress which he lifted up over her butt; his fingers slid her panties to one side. She closed her eyes and wondered if he was, in reality, part magician as an instant later, his hot, hard, thick manhood was at her door. A moment later, he was inside her.

When it was over, they walked hand in hand back toward the churchyard. The Mustang was indeed gone. It was just now being replaced by a small Maui Tours bus which pulled in, parked, and disgorged its cargo of about sixteen Japanese tourists. Cassie could see they each had a camera and smiled to herself that they would have indeed returned home with some interesting shots from their vacation had the driver been a tad earlier.

Dan and Cassie walked to a short section of fallen log which made a perfect bench for the two of them to sit and talk. She told him a bit about the escalation of Gregory's mood shifts. She knew it would be unwise to tell Dan everything, even though some marital confidences had been shared over the past six months since they had acted upon what each found out was a mutual desire. Cassie knew Dan was a calm and cool personality - that must come with being a pilot - but no one knows what Dan may do if he knew what she had endured on Friday night and Saturday morning. And there were other things he'd *never* know as well, she resolved.

So, after the brief mention, she changed the subject to the activities of the coming week. Cassie told him she would be tied up with Willy for a few days, but would also have time for some stolen moments with him since some of the meetings with Willy would take place in Kihei where he was going to stay. The Four Seasons was just down the road from where she had recommended he acquire accommodations, and the Four Seasons had been a favorite playground for her and Dan. She knew Dan enjoyed the perks of the place.

It was then Dan told her that Gregory had scheduled a flight to San Francisco for the morning, returning on Wednesday. She was momentarily uplifted a bit when she thought Gregory might captain the jet himself with Jason, leaving Dan behind, but Dan quickly said the entire crew was scheduled to go. Gregory was apparently going to ride in the back on this trip. He had also told Dan to plan on a 'plus one' when filing the souls on board count on the flight plan with the FAA, but he kept that detail from her.

Cassie's mind worked ahead a bit. A couple of days free of the need to be tied to the house or forced to make excuses to Gregory may just work to her advantage and she shared that thought with Dan. She considered the advantages of being able to spend more time massaging things, figuratively, not literally, with Willy. After all, she thought, he is obviously still carrying a torch for her and what better way to manipulate a man than give him a smile, laugh at his jokes, and touch his arm occasionally?

The pair turned in unison at the sudden chattering coming from around the corner of the church. The group of Japanese visitors had apparently finished their little tour and were very animated as they pointed to the LCD displays on their cameras, showing each other captured images of what they had all just seen. Soon after, they were aboard their bus and headed out the drive.

"I guess it's about that time we head out as well," Dan said. He looked at the sun and then his watch. "After all, I've got at least three hours back to Kahului and I hate driving that road from Hana after dark."

"Go the other way," she said. "Straighter, and you can follow me."

"Not in my BMW, baby," he said.

"I take my Beamer on that road all the time," Cassie challenged.

"I don't have your money, baby," he said, while thinking that eventually he would. "I have to think about resale value."

She feigned a pout. He thought it was most likely a routine she had used nearly all her life, and then he noticed some new wrinkles around her mouth.

He stood, extended his hand to Cassie, who took hold and stood up as well. They walked to her Jeep where Dan opened her door. His eyes scanned the perimeter of the area. He had learned long ago that it was prudent to be vigilant when dating another man's woman. He noticed nothing.

Cassandra touched his chin with her fingertips and moved it toward her. His eyes followed.

"Have a safe trip," she said.

"Driving home tonight or tomorrow?"

His smile lit up and his eyes sparkled at her.

"How about both?" she teased. She slipped her arms around his waist and hugged him close. He rested his chin on the top of her head, and hugged her back.

Down the road, just before the fork where Cassie had turned left to the church a couple of hours earlier, and behind a layer of dense foliage, a digital camera equipped with telephoto lens collected photos to its memory. The woman behind the camera smiled as she thought to herself these may not be as interesting as the ones she captured earlier at the outlook, but would certainly help to punctuate the story.

A few minutes later, Dan watched Cassie drive away and head the Jeep toward the fork in the road. As she made the right turn onto the drive segment which connected to the main road and disappeared from view, his eyes flashed back to something he thought he saw for an instant in the foliage. His eyes strained, but whatever had caused the movement or reflection or whatever it was his eyes had noted was now gone. He turned and began to walk to his BMW when he noticed something wet on the ground where Cassie's Jeep had been parked. Dan bent over and touched the three-inch diameter puddle on the packed gravel. He rubbed the liquid between his fingers. It was obviously petroleum based and slightly slippery. He carefully sniffed it and detected a slight odor which he couldn't immediately place. Given the traffic which came and went here, he made no connection between the spill and Cassie's brand new Jeep.

After again checking his watch, he slid into the soft leather seat of his pride and joy, and began his drive back to Kahului.

He paid no attention to the small scooter which pulled out onto the road shortly after.

Cassie drove west toward home. Her mind was flooded with thoughts. The fuse had been lit, the players were in place, each step had been calculated. Her plan had a long way to go, but it would all work out in the end, she told herself. She only hoped that she had the *time* for it to play out.

Her Jeep approached the first switchback. She gently applied the brakes to slow to a prudent speed going into the blind turn and sounded her horn. She'd seen all sorts of drivers on these roads over the years, from timid tourists to careless tourists, to reckless locals who loved to scare the hell out of them all.

As she came out the backside of the turn, she was able to clearly see both legs of the U which made up this particular switchback. Each terminus of the U was an overlook several hundred feet above the ocean, while the bottom represented the low point nearer sea level. They were all different, some higher, some lower, some with waterfalls or streams spanned by bridges. There was no traffic anywhere on this particular switchback.

She rolled down the incline, out her window on the driver's side was a steep, heavily foliaged ridge down to the stream, on the right side, a near vertical barren hillside. She looked through the sunroof toward the top of the ridge and remembered the time she had been driving this road and had felt something hit her in the head. Whatever it was had startled her and hurt like hell. A while later she had noted a small piece of red lava rock the size of a dried pea on the passenger seat. As she recalled the event, she took note of rocks the size of bowling balls protruding from the clay-type hillside like raisins sticking out of an oatmeal cookie and pushed the button on the console to close the sunroof.

Her vehicle picked up speed moving downhill and she again applied the brakes. They felt a little soft, or maybe it was her imagination, because they worked just fine and the Jeep slowed again normally. At the bottom, she traversed the small bridge with the date 1931 cast into the crumbling railing and started up the other side.

Just as she arrived at the start of this second switchback, she heard what sounded like a semi's air horn and took note of a trio of locals in a jacked-up dark blue Ford pick up truck with huge off-road tires skid around the top of the U she had just completed. The truck threw gravel from all four churning tires as it roared down the incline toward the bridge behind her.

With nowhere to get out of their way up where she was, Cassie pulled the Jeep around the outside corner and decided she'd wait for them to pass her at the bottom of the next hill. She could see a small siding just before the next old, crumbling bridge. She rounded the corner and headed the Jeep down the hill. Again, her vehicle began to pick up speed. Her foot moved to the brake pedal and to her horror it moved all the way to the floor without resistance and definitely without effect as gravity began pulling the Jeep faster and faster downhill. She could hear the air horn blaring several hundred yards behind her as the locals rounded the outbound turn. Her vehicle was accelerating rapidly. She pumped the brakes and in her increasing panic she forgot everything she had learned to do in this type of emergency, especially the use of the cable-operated parking brake. Her hands tightly gripped the steering wheel as her racing mind began to calculate how to best navigate the turn at the bottom of the hill, hopefully transit the bridge and then let gravity slow and stop the vehicle as the road again headed uphill on the outbound leg. She glanced momentarily into the rear view mirror and saw the blue monster truck falling further behind as even the locals inside must have thought her crazy for that kind of speed down the hill.

The bottom was coming up fast. She didn't take note of how fast she was traveling but as she began to try to steer through the turn, she realized it was too fast. Her tires slid on the loose gravel, she heard herself scream, and then in a series of disorienting pitches and impacts the Jeep's passenger side slammed into the side of the hill, bounced off, and then headed for the bridge abutment, its direction altered by the mountain but its momentum barely affected.

As the now out-of-control Jeep challenged the well-aged concrete railing, it was the concrete which relented and the Jeep tumbled off the side of the bridge into the small stream about twenty feet below. What had been moments before a new, shiny red Jeep came to rest upside down in a crumpled heap, its air bags already deflating, and its sole occupant hanging inverted from her seat belt as the stream waters ran through the shattered windows.

Cassie struggled to find the seat belt release when suddenly there were voices surrounding her and several hands on her body. She couldn't make out what the voices were saying, but the hands and arms connected to them were strong and they unfastened the seat belt and pulled her from the wreck. A couple of minutes later, she was standing with two locals at the edge of the bridge looking down at the underside of her SUV. A third local was clambering up the hillside holding her purse.

Cassandra fished into her purse with shaking hands. The bag was wet on the outside but the phone came out dry. She pushed the buttons for 911 but the immediate, rapid beeping told her there was no cell signal in the gully area.

"What da mattah lady, you lolo? Why you go so fast?" the shortest of the four said to her.

They were all looking at her like they were thinking his lolo moniker fit.

"My brakes," she said in quavering voice. Then with more confidence, "My brakes failed." Her composure returned quicker than she would have thought, and she added an answer to his first question, "And no, I'm not crazy."

Knowing it would be a long time before any police or wrecker would be able to reach the area, she asked the group if they'd consider taking her home and then when they hesitated and started mumbling about this interfering with their plans for the evening, she quickly added that she'd pay them and pulled a couple hundreds from her wallet which she saw from their faces was plenty to buy their inconvenience.

Gregory was in the kitchen making himself a sandwich of piled-high Italian meats and cheese on some thickly sliced, multigrain bread from Stillwell's in Wailuku.   About a dozen pepperoncini garnished his plate, and an ice cold can of Miller Genuine Draft was beginning to sweat on the counter inches away. He had just finished slicing the sandwich in half when through the open kitchen window he heard unmufflered exhaust way too loud to be coming from the road two hundred yards away. His fist gripped the knife firmly as he walked to the garage and peered out the window.

What he saw was a group of locals in a swamp buggy, it's huge off-road tires leaving black rubber marks on his pristine white, stamped concrete drive. One of the men climbed out of the truck, reached his hand inside and then Gregory saw his wife being hoisted down to the ground. She reached into her purse, pulled out some bills and gave them to the young Hawaiian.   Then she looked directly at Gregory.

Cassie said something to the men in the truck and then flashed them the shaka - having received instruction from the Hawaiians on how to quickly make the gesture during the drive home - as they drove out, leaving more black marks on Gregory's driveway.   She turned and began walking toward the house, entering through the side door of the garage. Gregory watched the truck pull out onto the main road where they stopped for a moment before heading back toward the east.   After they drove off, Gregory could see that old fucker Keoki staring down from his porch and shaking his head.

Cassandra passed by the fronts of now five cars in six stalls and Gregory met her near the door to the kitchen.

"What happened?" he asked. "Where's the Jeep?"

"I had an accident on the way back from Kipahulu.   Coming down the hill, the brakes failed and I wound up going off a bridge."

His face remained as if cast in stone.

"I take it those were your heroes of the day?"

"They were right behind me, dragged me out of the car and agreed to bring me home."

"And the Jeep?"

She could feel the need to walk on eggshells.   His eyes were boring holes right through her.   It was then she noticed the knife in the fist of his left hand.   She looked from his eyes to the knife and back again.   On the third trip, his eyes seemed to relax, and his body language became less threatening. He looked down at the knife in his hand.

"Oh, this?" he said chuckling. "I was making a sandwich when I heard you pull up."

To Cassandra, the only way to describe his change in demeanor was to equate it to a light bulb which had experienced a power surge and was suddenly illuminating so brightly it threatened to burn itself out, and then someone turned an unseen power control and it reverted to a normal glow.

"I think the Jeep is totaled. It's upside down in a stream, twenty feet below the roadway. I called the police on the way home, once I got a signal a little closer to home. I also called Bill Anders from the dealership at home and he said he'd get it all taken care of in the morning for us."

They walked into the kitchen together. Cassandra let Gregory lead the way. She really didn't want to turn her back on him.

"Do you want half a sandwich?" he asked. "How about a cold beer?"

Cassandra said she needed a soak in a hot bath, and maybe she'd get something later. She walked toward the central foyer.

"The most important thing is that you're all right," he called from the kitchen.

"I'm fine," she said. "Thanks."

The truth was she was even more sore now than she had been. She moved carefully up the stairs, walked down the hall to her bedroom, locked the door, slid out of her clothes and ran the bath. She poured some peach foaming bath salts into the water flow and a few minutes later sunk her aching body into the frothy warmth. She wrung out a washcloth and placed it over her eyes as she sunk to her chin and reclined in the oversize tub.

A few minutes later, she took the washcloth from her eyes and put it into the water to refresh the cloth and a cold chill ran down her spine. There, on the edge of the tub, was a plate with half a sandwich and a sweating can of Bud Lite next to it.

There was no sign of Gregory having been there other than the items left behind and she had never heard a thing; and that, she thought, was the creepiest part of the entire incident.

Chapter Seven

On Monday morning, Sandy and I checked out of the hotel early. A limo was waiting out front and took us to the airport. Even at six a.m., the sun and heat were conspiring to tear the paint off buildings. I felt bad about leaving Sandy to deal with the lingering heat and humidity when I was headed for paradise.

I had told Sandy there was no reason for her to make the trek out to the airport with me, but she said she wanted to see me off. Before we left the hotel, I confirmed with the airline that my weapons would be approved for travel on the flight. They were unloaded and locked in portable gun cases in one of my checked bags. A box of hollow point ammunition for each caliber was in a separate locked box in a second suitcase.

Sandy had confirmed receipt of the sent copy of my Louisiana Concealed Carry Permit and P.I. license with the Maui Police Department in Wailuku, which is the county seat. She had held back any mention of me being a retired cop from Chicago. I've found that information sometimes antagonizes people and I usually play telling people of my cop past by ear.

Just to be friendly, I planned stop in with the MPD and give them a courtesy call, then gauge whether to mention being a retired member of the brotherhood. Experience has taught me that it pays to let the local cops know if I'm in the area on business and meet at least one management type in person, even when the case has nothing to do with any criminal matter. After all, why risk an hour in cuffs in the back of a cruiser when some neighbor calls about a strange guy sitting in a car parked down the street while the beat cop sorts it all out, when a little preplanning gives me a name to give him when he first approaches? Cops are cops everywhere.

Traffic out of the city on I-10 toward the airport was fairly light and we progressed quickly. Of course, the inbound lanes were already starting to jam up with commuters. The haze on the horizon confirmed what I had felt when I stepped from the air conditioned lobby: It was going to be one of those short-tempered summer days in southern Louisiana.

Sandy removed a black two-inch binder from her briefcase and handed it to me.

"Just a little bit of background and other information I threw together for you. Some light reading on the flight."

"I flipped through what I estimated was about two-hundred pages split between half a dozen tabbed dividers. These were labeled: 'Cassandra Yeats-Thomason', 'Gregory Allen Thomason', 'Maui Info', 'Legal', 'Contact List', and 'Miscellaneous'. In the front was a three-page document which had all my flight, car rental, and lodging information, including confirmation numbers and after-hours contacts. Typical Sandy. I don't know what I'd do without her.

"Thanks," I said. "When did you have the time?"

"In between." She gave an 'it was nothing wave' and looked out the window.

I closed the binder and went to slide it into my computer bag. It was then that I noticed in the little plastic memo holder on the spine, just under our imprinted company name and logo, she had inserted a white tab with the typed words *Operation Puppy Love*.

I nudged her in the ribs.

"Cute," I said from behind a wry smile as I pointed to the label.

"I thought you'd like it," she said from behind a huge grin.

The limo took the airport ramp and exited I-10. Louis Armstrong International Airport in New Orleans was an aging throwback. Landlocked to prevent further expansion, it would be forever relegated to the short haul, domestic flight market. The only reason I think it gets to use the 'international' label was a flight or two to Canada or Mexico each week.

Even driving into the terminal area was outdated. Instead of the dedicated, sweeping drives off the connecting highway right into the terminal, rental car, or parking ramp areas of most modern airports, in New Orleans we do it the hard way, exiting the highway to take surface roads to the airport entrance.

I checked the time on my cell phone as the limo turned onto Airline Drive: 6:45. My flight was scheduled to depart at 7:42 a.m., so I had just under an hour. Barring any delays at check-in or security, I figured I'd arrive at the gate just in time to walk onto the airplane.

Sandy was chattering away with last minute reminders. She handed me a little USB device for my computer about the size of a thumb drive. I rotated it in my fingers.

"Cellular internet connection for your computer," she said. "I wasn't certain about access everywhere you'd be going, so I picked it up for you on Friday. Just plug it into your USB slot and launch your browser." She noted my quizzical look. "Don't worry, Otto. It couldn't be easier."

I slipped the gizmo into my jacket pocket.

We drove up and stopped at the United departures area. Porters milled around a desk with the United logo. The driver jumped out and popped the trunk before coming to open the rear passenger door.

I stepped out. Sandy followed. The chauffeur had my two suitcases on the curb, inquired if there is anything else going with me, I told him nope, and he closed the trunk. I slid my computer bag strap over my shoulder, patted my pockets to make sure I had my wallet, tickets, cell phone. I handed Sandy my keys.

"Would you drop off my kites?" I ask with a wink and smile.

A cop, cranky because he's got airport detail, eyed us and sent the unspoken message, 'Move it along'. I nod to one of the porters, ask if he'll go to the check-in counter with me. He tosses both bags onto a hand cart and waits for me.

Sandy tucked my keys into her purse.

"No problem." Then, "Thanks for a great weekend, Otto."

"One day you're gonna tell me where you picked up that nickname for me," I said. She has refused to divulge the meaning since the first time she referred to me as Otto after the divorce. "Thank you for everything, Sandy."

She changed the subject and ticked off several alternatives for saying good-bye.

"Good luck. Be safe. Have a good flight. Don't forget to write."

We hugged, and before she released me, she whispered in my ear.

"And be careful of Cassie. There's something not right there; I just can't put my finger on exactly what."

I let her go. The cop was starting to waddle over. I tossed my head in his direction and Sandy took note. My face sent the dual message of 'Trouble's coming, we better wrap it up' and 'Thank God they put the slow, fat ones on airport detail'. She smiled back, getting both messages.

"I'll call you when I get in and settled tonight," I said over my shoulder.

Sandy slipped into the limo and it drove off just ahead of the impatient cop.

Half an hour later, I was seated in First Class scanning the emergency briefing card for the Airbus A-320 which would take us to Denver. There, I'd change planes to San Francisco and finally from there directly to Kahului, Maui. The itinerary said I'd arrive at 3:42 p.m. local time, a total of about thirteen hours of traveling after adding in the five hour time difference. I tucked the safety card away, pulled out Sandy's briefing book and sipped on a glass of orange juice.

I flipped to the section titled 'Cassandra Yeats-Thomason' and began to read.

"Yes, I'd like to report a possible missing person," the female caller said into the phone. The caller was tall, broad of shoulder, had short, spiked platinum blonde hair and deep green eyes, and she stood alone in the middle of Janet Hopkins' apartment.

An hour later, there was a knock at the apartment door, which the tall woman had left slightly ajar. When she opened it fully, there stood one of Montreal's finest, probably all of twenty years old.

"Êtes-vous la femme qui fait état d'une personne manquante possible?" he asked.

"Actually, I'm more comfortable in English. But, yes, I reported the possible missing person."

He smiled. Had her doors swung that way, she would definitely have found him attractive; but they didn't. She asked him to come in.

Before entering, he wiped his feet on the mat at the door and then removed his hat as he entered the room. His eyes scanned the small apartment.

"Who would it be that you are making the report on?" he asked while opening a report book and pulling a pen from his shirt pocket.

"My girlfriend, Janet Hopkins."

Over the next several minutes, she gave him all the statistical details: Height: 1.7 meters, about 5'6", Weight: 65 kilos, about 142 pounds, Hair: Short, about top of the neck, a Bob cut blonde, strawberry blonde to be exact, Race: Caucasian.

"What would be your relationship to Miss Hopkins?" he asked without looking up from the report.

"Girlfriend," she said.

His left eye peered up at her.

"We're lovers, is that better?"

He went back to writing.

"Name?"

"I told you, Janet Hopkins."

"No, your name."

"Oh, sorry. Marcy, Marcy Simon."

"Are you from Montreal, Miss Simon?"

"No, Calgary. I moved here about seven years ago." Then she added, "I heard there may be a little more cosmopolitan tolerance here than out west. I'm originally from Detroit."

"American?" he asked, like it would make a difference.

"No," she said. "Full Canadian citizenship now."

He nodded as he wrote.

"I don't judge, Miss Simon. The lifestyle, I mean. I'm just doing my job." He looked up and gave her another smile. "When's the last time you saw, Miss Hopkins?"

"About two weeks ago."

"Two weeks? Why are you just calling us now?"

Marcy exhaled with obvious frustration.

"This is going to take a long time if you keep repeating my answers as questions. How about I just give you a statement and then we'll fill in the blanks?"

Over the next ten minutes, Marcy filled him in. How she had taken Janet to the airport two weeks ago Sunday when she left for a ten-day medical seminar in Hawaii. They had communicated by way of email, phone, and text several times a day. About a four days ago, the phone calls stopped and she just heard from Janet by way of emails and texts. The purported explanation was she was exhausted and just needed some time to relax. On Friday morning, every form of communication stopped after the text that said she was headed for the airport. She was to return to Montreal late Friday night.

Marcy explained she had been in Calgary for her brother's wedding over the weekend and just returned to Montreal this morning. She came to Janet's place to see her, knowing she would be off until going back to work on Wednesday.

No, Marcy didn't live here, just had things here because she would stay for several days at a time. She told the officer how she had come, found evidence like the suitcase, the luggage tags in the trash, the bed rumpled and stuff put away, meaning Janet had returned. That's where it got strange.

"See, Janet's a neat freak. She would never leave the bed unmade."

He looked up, one eyebrow arched.

"That's it?"

"No," she said as she opened the top left drawer in the dresser and pointed inside.

"Underwear?" he asked.

"These on top are Janet's panties and bras."

"So?"

"This is my underwear drawer," she said. "Janet's underwear drawer is upper right. She wouldn't do this."

"Maybe she made a mistake."

Marcy gave him the 'Really?' look.

Not being an expert at women's underpants, he tried another line of questions.

"Have you tried to call her? Maybe she went out."

Marcy replied with the escalated 'Are you kidding me?' look. Irritated because he was refusing to hear her, Marcy marched past him to the countertop and pointed at the half eaten English muffin with a glop of dried out marmalade on top.

"Maybe she was full, or forgot it when she went out."

"No, that's not it. Janet HATES marmalade."

Gregory was downstairs early on Monday morning. He was dressed in travel attire with a jacket draped over his left arm. He carried a single suitcase in his right hand and had his computer bag slung over his left shoulder. He was surprised to find his wife already down there.

Cassandra stood at the grill in a white, mid-length, gauze, tube-top dress and bare feet, flipping some French toast. She had poured two glasses of orange juice which stood in insulated glassed on the marble-topped island behind her. He could see through the open lanai doors that she had also set two places at the umbrellaed table.

"Expecting someone for breakfast?" he asked.

"I thought you might like something to eat before you left. I know you love my French toast."

He eyed her.

"You haven't made breakfast for me in years."

"Things need to change, Gregory," she pleaded. "I thought you'd like this."

"Actually, I would like it." He looked at his watch. "I just wish you had told me about your surprise earlier. I would have made time."

She pointed the black nylon pancake turner at him. "You have all the time you want to have, Gregory." She put her left hand on her hip. "It's your airplane, for God's sake."

He smiled at her. It took all her concentration to mask the cold shudder as it raced down her spine.

"I guess I can make some time since you went to all this trouble. What with everything you went through yesterday."

He set his suitcase down on the floor, laid his jacket and computer bag on the island countertop. Then he grabbed both glasses of orange juice and headed to the lanai. She was right behind him with two plates, each containing two pieces of thick, hot, French toast topped with a sprinkling of powdered sugar. The maple syrup was already on the table.

Gregory pulled out her chair. He used all his concentration to mask the look of disgust which he felt.

Ten minutes later, the helicopter landed and idled on the concrete pad. Gregory wiped his mouth, finished his orange juice, kissed his wife on the top of her head, wiped his mouth again with the back of his hand, and thanked her for breakfast. He grabbed his things from the kitchen and made his way to the chopper.

Cassandra disgustedly pushed her half-eaten breakfast toward the center of the table, sat back in her chair, crossed her legs, and watched the blue and white helicopter turn to the west and skim along the channel before climbing. She liked the pilot, but at that moment she really wished the damn thing would drop into the sea.

Inside the helicopter, Gregory asked the pilot if he had make the pickup on Molokai this morning.

"Yes, sir," the pilot replied. "Miss Shea is waiting at the hangar."

"Good. Thank you."

Gregory rendered a silent belch. The bitch had used too much cinnamon, he thought to himself. He dry swallowed a Prilosec he pulled from the pocket of his computer bag.

Cassandra left the dishes and breakfast mess for the maid. Physically, she was tender and sore this morning, but her spirit was buoyed by the fact Gregory was gone for a few days and that Willy was en route. She went upstairs much easier with the lighter mood to help with the pains. In her room, she flipped open her MacBook Pro and navigated to the United Air Lines site. She could see the flight from New Orleans to Denver had arrived on time and that the flight to San Francisco was about one hour out.

Just out of curiosity, she went to www.flightstatus.com and plugged in the tail number of their jet. After a few seconds of searching the FAA and international databases, a flight plan indeed came up for a trip this morning from OGG to SFO. She clicked the details button and looked over the filed document. She was about to click it closed when an item caught her eye. Why would there be listed a crew of 3 and 2 passengers? Who else was going to San Francisco with Gregory? That part would be easy to find out.

She smirked and dialed Dan's cell.

When she hung up, she considered it would be fairly simple to discover who this Jennifer Shea from Molokai was. She'd just add her name to the list she'd give Willy later today. What really had her curious was the description of the woman Dan had offered. Where in the world had Gregory found her twenty-five year old doppelganger with a bit of an east Texas drawl? She closed down her computer. She'd work on that later. Time was ticking away.

Cassandra stripped off her dress and jumped into the shower. As the water cascaded over her body, she was almost surprised to find she was feeling giddy over spending some real time with Willy. She felt thirty years younger and her stomach flip-flopped with a real sense of anticipation she hadn't felt in almost as long. Wrapping herself in the oversize, Egyptian cotton towel, she found her excitement growing.

She padded across the cool marble into her closet. As much as she had anguished over selecting what she had worn to his office last week, today's choice was easy. Cassie knew just what she'd wear to meet Willy this afternoon.

The wrecker pulled the Jeep from the stream bed and the police stopped traffic while the recovery took place. Cassandra had been lucky she went off that side of the bridge where the drop was only about twenty feet. Had she gone off the other side in this particular switchback, the drop would have been over one hundred feet followed by a steep roll to the ocean.

Everyone involved in the recovery also knew that had not the locals seen the accident and had she been injured or knocked out, it could be possible that nobody would have found her for days. It had happened before on these remote roads. A couple of years ago, an elderly couple had disappeared from the road to Hana on New Year's Eve and they still hadn't found the vehicle or its occupants. There are many areas on the island of Maui that are still wild and inaccessible right off the beaten path.

The crew rolled the Jeep onto its wheels once they had it on the roadway. Before they loaded it onto the tilt bed truck for the trip back to the dealership, one of the cops asked if he could look at the brake fluid reservoir. The mechanic sent out pried open the mangled hood. They both looked.

"Got a screwdriver?" the cop asked.

The mechanic slipped one out of his pocket and opened the brake reservoir. They both looked inside. It was bone dry.

"Do you see any evidence it leaked out?" asked the cop.

The mechanic looked around the engine compartment and checked the underside of the hood for any residue and found nothing.

"It looked sealed to me, and I don't see any residual brake fluid spill inside the engine compartment." He looked toward the underside of the Jeep. "I would guess it was a line leak."

"Considering the statements we got from the driver and the guys in the truck behind her, it sounds like it there was a little warning, but then all of a sudden, nothing," the cop said.

"Could have been a slow leak or a catastrophic line failure all at once," the mechanic speculated. "Although with all stainless steel lines and connections, on a new vehicle it's fairly rare. We'll check it over when we get it back to the shop."

"Mm-huh." The cop gave the mechanic his card. "If you find anything unusual, give me a call."

The United Air Lines Boeing 767-300 operating as Flight 494 headed for Kahului, Maui, was climbing through 17,000 feet on its way to its initial cruising altitude of 36,000 feet and had just turned southwest out of San Francisco International Airport when it passed within five miles horizontally of N100GT, the Gulfstream 550 business jet carrying Gregory and company into San Francisco.

In seat 2A of the First Class section of the United jet, William read his briefing book about the reclusive billionaire, Gregory Albert Thomason.

In a custom-fitted, cream-colored, leather chair in the luxurious cabin of the G550 business jet, Gregory was reclining with his feet up, tapping on a keyboard. Across the aisle sat his guest, Jennifer Shea. She split her time by reading an *In Style* magazine and looking out the window. Gregory had almost fallen over when he met her in the hangar's lounge area and saw she was wearing a white, gauze, tube-top dress and heeled espadrilles for the trip. She was definitely her mother's child in so many ways, he thought.

After she was dressed and had finished her hair and makeup, Cassandra pulled some papers from her safe, copies of documents she had made for Willy. She hand wrote the names of Janet Hopkins and Jennifer Shea onto the bottom of the printed list of women's names and the associated city from which they came. She hesitated and then decided it would be best for her plan if she did not include the location information for Janet and Jennifer as she had with the others. No, she thought, they are too fresh, too new. It would be best to have him struggle for a while.

She tucked the list into a manila envelope with the other information she had prepared for him and then wedged the package into her purse. She forced herself into a pair of heeled sandals even though the pain in her legs demanded flats, then left her room and glided down the stairs in practice of masking her sore body from Willy. Mind over matter, she told herself. Of course, even if he did notice, she could blame it all on the accident yesterday, she thought.

Cassandra left the house in the white Cadillac Escalade just before noon. At the top of the drive, she turned left, taking the route around the west side of the island, through Ulapalakua and past Kula before the long downhill drive between Pukalani and Makawao into Kahului. She knew the drive would take about ninety minutes, or about half what the normal tourists took to make the drive with all the photo stops. She noted that Keoki was not out on his porch this morning.

As she rounded the turn just outside of Kula, her cell phone rang. Even though it was against the law in Hawaii to use a hand-held cell phone while driving, she answered the call.

"Cassandra?" the voice said. "It's Bill Anders."

"Yes, Bill. Hang on a moment while I stop." She pulled to the side of the road and stopped. "What can you tell me?"

"Well, we collected the Jeep this morning early. MPD met my people on scene. It arrived back to our facilities about thirty minutes ago and I've had the chance to give it the quick once over. Your thought last night that the vehicle would be unrepairable is correct. It's a total loss. I've already spoken to your insurance agent and told him we'd certify it unsalvageable, even for parts."

"Well, it is what it is I guess."

"The wrecker crew and our mechanic on the scene tell me you were one lucky lady. Had you gone off the other side of the bridge, they may never have found you. The drop would have killed you and the vegetation would have swallowed you and the vehicle."

Cassandra pondered that thought for a couple of moments. She remembered the elderly couple that they still hadn't found.

"Anyway, I've got good news and some not so good news," Bill said. He hesitated a few beats before continuing as if he were weighing his words. "And there is something I want to talk to you about in person."

"It's been an interesting few days, so what's the good news?"

"The good news is I have a brand new, next model year, similarly equipped Jeep that just came in. I can have it dropped at your house tomorrow."

"And the not so good news?"

"It's not red, and I know you loved your red Jeep. It's black."

"That's not so bad, I can deal with that. Let's do it. You know how to handle it all."

"Sure thing. I'll take care of everything for you."

"And the issue you would prefer we handle face-to-face?" She listened again and could hear him struggling with the words.

"I'd really rather speak to you in person. Will you be coming to Kahului in the next week or so?"

"In fact, I'll be there in about half an hour. I'll stop by the dealership."

"Good, I'll see you then." Then he added, "Since you're coming in anyway, would you prefer to look at the new Jeep before I get it prepped and the paperwork going?"

"No, go ahead and wrap it up." She clicked off and pulled back onto the road. A wave of foreboding washed over her as she replayed Bill's words regarding an issue he could only discuss face-to-face. She had her suspicions, but she again adopted the fatalist's position of it is what it is.

She turned up the volume of the radio and could now see into the valley. The airport was visible near the northeast shoreline and she again thought about Willy coming in soon. Her spirits buoyed as she considered this whole twenty year nightmare being on its way to a conclusion. A few minutes later, the Escalade started the descent from upcountry and she smiled as she was reminded of the old saying, 'It's all downhill from here'.

I'm not a big fan of airline travel. Even First Class seats are not a good fit for my six-foot-six frame. Were I to have a swimmer's build and weigh in at what the government charts say, around two-hundred-ten pounds, I'd still be hard pressed to be comfortable, but with my frame more akin to a football defensive end at two-hundred-sixty pounds, I'm squeezed from every side. So, by halfway through this third - and longest - flight of the day, I'm getting a little cranky.

I'm restless. I open my window shade. There's nothing to see out over the middle of the crossing but hazy glare. I can't even see the seven miles down to the Pacific. I re-close the shade as the woman across the aisle gives me a dirty look because the light is apparently causing issues with the grainy projection of the entertainment. I've already seen both movies in the theaters that they're playing and they weren't that great. We've eaten the reheated lunch, and an hour from now they've said they're going to stuff a snack down our gullets. So, I guess we'll all walk off the plane bloated and irritable, except of course for the poor bastards stuck in coach who are fighting over bags of pretzels and stale box lunches. They'll just start their vacations being merely irritable. Great way to start your holiday, I thought. No wonder people call a journey to Hawaii the trip of a lifetime. Who'd want to go through this twice?

Okay, so I imagine I should back off a bit on the complaining. After all, I am getting a fat paycheck to go to paradise, spend time catching up with my first love while helping her to eviscerate her cheating husband. Should be a relatively easy job. I'm figuring a week to ten days to complete Operation Puppy Love. How bad could it be?

I shift in my seat. The petulant teenager in shredded jeans and black T-shirt sporting the name of some band I've never heard of that they plopped into the seat next to me has thankfully been sleeping since shortly after take off. Mom and dad behind us had been trying to drain the champagne supply since we boarded and now have been contentedly snoring for about an hour after the blending of ethanol and thinner atmosphere hit critical mass in their brains. I pity them the hangover they are going to start their vacation with. I smiled to myself and thought, bloated, irritable *and* hungover, now that's way to start a vacation.

Sandy's binder was in the seat back in front of me. She had done a typically excellent Sandy job of assembling the background data on Mr. and Mrs. Gregory Thomason. She had also uncovered some interesting information on Cassie that even I hadn't known. I decide that rather than stare at the back of the gent's head in front of me, I pull out the binder, push the button on my armrest to turn on my reading light, and catch a glimpse in my peripheral vision of the lady across the aisle leaning forward again to give me a dirty look. Did she just 'tsk' her tongue? Who still 'tsks' their tongue?

I flipped open the binder to the section on Gregory Albert Thomason IV and reread Sandy's synopsis pages:

GREGORY ALBERT THOMASON -
CURRENT AGE: 52, born October 30, city and state of New York.
MARITAL STATUS: One marriage of record found, to Cassandra Yeats on August 17, twenty years ago.
RESIDENCE: Spends almost all of his time on Maui, in a large, custom-built, seaside home on the south shore of the island. Reportedly owns homes or apartments in New York (Park Avenue apartment), California (San Francisco house), Wyoming (17,000 acre ranch).
CHILDREN: None known.
MOTHER: Angela Michelle Thomason, nee Ruis, deceased. Drowned at the family vacation home in upstate New York when Gregory was seven years old. Gregory was the only reported witness to the event.
FATHER: Albert Harold Thomason, deceased. Heart attack in his New York office sixteen years ago. Personally credited for taking the family fortune from millions to billions.
SIBLINGS: None.
EARLY YEARS: According to articles (included herein), had a very close relationship with his mother. After her death, was raised by a series of caretakers and surrogates. Father traveled extensively on business, and the two grew further apart. At the age of ten, was enrolled in the first of several boarding / preparatory schools. While most scholastic records are sealed, the frequency of school changes could indicate disciplinary or behavioral issues.
TEENAGE YEARS: Attended three preparatory schools through the high school years. Abbotsford Military Academy pulled him through the junior and senior years. Rumor of sexual relationship with a female instructor during his junior year when he was seventeen. Press reports of the time indicate shortly after the affair was discovered by school officials, the woman turned up missing. A police report was filed, but the woman was never located to be

charged.   DOT records indicate a number of moving violations, including a sixty-day suspension of privileges when seventeen.

EARLY ADULTHOOD: Graduated with a Bachelor of Arts degree from Columbia University at age twenty-two. Moved into a suite of rooms in the family's downtown New York hotel for most of his twenties. Displayed no interest in the family business and there is no evidence he ever held any type of job. Numerous articles on partying lifestyle, crashed cars, and a trail of women: rich, famous, and not-so-much.

MARRIAGE: At age 29, meets and marries Cassandra Yeats after a very short courtship. The couple continues residence in New York City for first four years of the marriage. After the death of his father, Gregory buys land on Maui and builds their current home. No children.

PROFESSIONAL LIFE: As discussed previous, no evidence of ever having gainful employment.

FINANCIAL: After the death of his father, reportedly transferred ALL family holdings into a charitable trust which reportedly lists himself and his wife as Trustees and then over time, again reportedly, liquidated the holdings to stockholders, management teams, and other investors.   Uncertain as to current investments or holdings - personally or through the Trust - however, according to the Wall Street Journal article around the time of the sell off, it was speculated the value in cash was in the neighborhood of twenty-four billion dollars (That's a very nice neighborhood - S).

MISCELLANEOUS: Became a licensed pilot at age 35, currently holds valid U.S. FAA Commercial pilot license with instrument and multiengine land and sea ratings as well as a helicopter rating. Holds type ratings in Citation 500 series, Learjet 45, Gulfstream III, and Gulfstream 550 jet aircraft.   Holds a valid FAA Class I Medical certificate. Owns an executive hangar at the Kahului Airport which houses currently a Gulfstream 550 business jet (N100GT - White with blue stripes) and Eurocopter EC-130 executive transport helicopter (N111GT - Blue with white stripes).

ASSESSMENT: This guy dropped off the radar screen shortly after marrying Cassandra even better than did Howard Hughes. Perhaps it was the fact he liquidated the business holdings and since he wasn't making the social scene anymore, there wasn't anything interesting to write. While we can compile a decent record of stereotypical spoiled rich kid behavior through his twenties (yeah, were he a Kennedy), he's very much a mystery over the course of his marriage. Holds a valid Hawaii driver's license with no record of violations. There was nothing in the official records on Hawaii - civil or criminal - other than routine recordings on the property purchase in the Land Court in Honolulu, associated building permits and covenants of development with the County of Maui, and a sealed agreement with a neighbor by the name of Keoki Keaweaheulu (I was unable to get any information on this last document - S). On the personal scene, it's as if this guy cleaned up his life when he met and married Cassandra.

I again skimmed the clippings which followed, page after page of articles and photos through his first twenty-nine years of life, then as if someone flipped a switch, nothing beginning about twenty-one years ago. The last article Sandy had included contained a series of photos taken apparently outside a New York City club which showed Gregory punching some guy in the mouth and the guy going down. In the background of one of the photos was an obviously dismayed Cassie Yeats. According to the article, the assaulted man had been a longtime friend who, according to witnesses, had merely referred to Gregory by the informal Greg immediately before the first punch was thrown.

I put that tidbit into memory as I may use it if and when I come across Mr. Thomason. I've found in all my interrogations over the years, that people usually are most vulnerable to slipping up under two scenarios. First, if you come back to them with 'just one more question' after they think you've finished and are walking away, a la Peter Falk's character Columbo. Second, when they are out-of-control angry; and if Gregory would deck an old friend for merely referring to him by the informal of his given name, it was an obvious trigger.

Flipping the tab on the next section, I reread the summary Sandy put together on Cassie.

CASSANDRA YEATS-THOMASON -
CURRENT AGE: 45, born January 31, Monroe, Wisconsin.
MARITAL STATUS: Two marriages of record found: First, to Robert Zimmerman when Cassie was twenty and which lasted a

total of three months before annulment on grounds of, get this, bigamy (him, not her). Current to Gregory Albert Thomason, twenty, nearly twenty-one years ago.

RESIDENCE: Maui, Hawaii.

CHILDREN: None known.

MOTHER: Janice Susan Yeats, nee Colmes, living, aged 67, retired from Wal-Mart. Currently lives with youngest daughter in Fort Worth, Texas.

FATHER: Raymond James Yeats, living, aged 75, retired union electrician. Currently resides in a Dallas hospice facility. Stage four liver cancer.

NOTE: THE FATHER ON CASSANDRA'S BIRTH CERTIFICATE IS LISTED AS UNKNOWN.   THE BIRTH PRECEDED THE MARRIAGE OF JANICE AND RAYMOND BY THREE YEARS. COURT RECORDS SHOW RAYMOND LEGALLY ADOPTED CASSANDRA WHEN SHE WAS FIVE.

SIBLINGS: Three: two brothers, one sister. Raymond, Jr., 40, married (X3) and a Professional Engineer living in New London, Connecticut. Jack, 38, divorced (X1), and works in a manufacturing plant in Xenia, Ohio. Lynn, 34, single, and collects Social Security disability payments, living in Fort Worth, Texas. Cassandra has a total of 6 nieces and 1 nephew resultant of the various couplings.

EARLY YEARS: Records of Cassandra's early life are sparse. Janice was listed on welfare rolls in several states before she landed in Wisconsin shortly before Cassandra was born. Following the mother's marriage to Raymond, the family still appeared to be itinerant, but within the state of Wisconsin. Raymond eventually landed a fairly stable electrician job with a local contractor in Chippewa Falls, WI so for a while, they stayed put. As you know, just before Thanksgiving when Cassandra was in the ninth grade, the family relocated to Augusta, Georgia.

TEENAGE YEARS: Just as in her early years, there is a hole or two in the record of Cassandra's time as a teenager. Shortly after moving to Augusta, she failed to register for the remainder of the ninth grade. She resurfaced the next fall, registered in the tenth grade at the Lucy C. Laney High School in Augusta, from which she graduates on time three years later. Grades were good, about a 3.25 GPA while at Laney, which was good enough to win her a scholarship from the United Brotherhood of Electrical Workers

(UBEW) to Georgia State University. The only extracurricular activity I found for her in high school was band. Cassandra played the clarinet, maybe still does.

EARLY ADULTHOOD: Graduated in four years with a Bachelor of Art and Design degree from the College of Arts and Sciences at Georgia State. Maintained a 3.5 GPA over four years. Following graduation, moved to New York City to pursue a career in advertising until she meets Gregory Thomason at age 25 (He's 30 at the time).

MARRIAGE: No children. Twenty year plus duration. No significant events uncovered.

PROFESSIONAL LIFE: Three years of low level advertising jobs post college graduation at various second-tier firms in New York. Has not held gainful employment since marriage (Why would she?). It is rumored that Cassandra is the driving force behind the Charitable Trust, but she maintains a very low profile and there are no published reports of her actual involvement.

FINANCIAL: Hawaii is an equitable distribution state in the event of divorce, which is supposedly why we are all here. What does the prenup say and will it be validated by the Court?

MISCELLANEOUS: Holds a valid and current FAA Commercial Pilot's license with instrument and multiengine land ratings which she obtained about the same time as Gregory was licensed. Holds a current Class 2 FAA medical. Airport scuttlebutt is she and Gregory will sometimes crew the jet on trips and leave the professionals behind. Cassandra is not viewed as having a close relationship with her adoptive father and natural mother, however, FAA records indicate N100GT has had several flight plans filed in the last two months between Maui (KOGG) and Dallas Love Field (KDAL), including during the time when she showed up at our office. There was no FAA flight plan for any flights between Dallas and New Orleans airports during the time the plane was in Dallas and a contact at the Fixed Base Operator (FBO) at Love reports the plane was there the entire time this last trip (Keeping things 'under the radar' from hubby? - S).

ASSESSMENT: As I will have told you before you left, be careful. There's something not right here with this woman. My female senses are going off big time. Why would she come find you after all these years for this assignment? Don't flatter yourself, Otto, this woman isn't after any rekindling of a long lost love.   She's a manipulator, and a good one. She has all the resources in the world at her fingertips and could hire the best lawyers and investigators. This is a divorce action and yet she didn't give you the name of her attorney? That's odd, isn't it? Why you? I just cannot figure it out, but I will.

There was appended a short list of articles including some on the courtship and wedding, which was surprisingly low key given the Thomason family name.   After Gregory and Cassandra moved to Maui, they appeared to have lived a normal, private life, albeit one with private jets, helicopters, and a multimillion dollar oceanfront home on what many people consider to be the world's best island.

Sandy was right, something was not adding up. I kept doing the math, and one plus one kept coming up three.

Chapter Eight

In Montreal's Le Village, people watch each other's back. There's a familial sense in the community. Yet it's also a closed society to the outside, which is a phenomenon seen repeated within the gay communities around the world. While a growing segment of western society accepts the gay lifestyle, many still do not. Marcy had to admit to herself, the police would still treat a missing lesbian as a second-class crime. She hated carrying around this type of paranoia added to an already full-blown persecution complex, but she had been conditioned by decades of discrimination and curious looks.

Marcy sat on Janet's bed after the young officer left with his Missing Person Report. She had signed it as 'friend'. A canary-colored carbonless copy of the report lay on the bed next to her. He had supplied all the to-be-expected calming platitudes: 'she'll be fine', 'most likely she'll be home anytime', 'don't worry, we'll do everything we can', and the final 'please call me if you have any updates or questions, here's my card'.

When she asked him if anyone else, perhaps a detective, would be around to do a follow-up or if they would want to try to collect any evidence, he had stared at her for a moment before responding that he saw no evidence of foul play and would report the same. Nothing indicated a struggle or other forcible removal of Janet from the premises. A few pairs of underwear put in the wrong drawer? Maybe she thought she'd try the marmalade for a change. No, he would be her contact, no detectives would be sent. They would put Janet's picture and information on their Missing Persons website, and

Marcy realized that would most likely be the end of it unless Janet showed up, alive or dead.

Marcy navigated to the Montreal Police Department's Missing Persons website on her laptop. There was a list of over two-hundred persons reported missing on the site, some going back over a decade. Her blood ran cold, and then hot. They'd never do much of anything to find one missing lesbian from Le Village, she concluded. So Marcy started to make a mental list of things she could to do to pick up on Janet's trail. Number one on the list was to call an acquaintance who she remembered had an office in the security department at the Trudeau International Airport. Before she could do that, however, she'd have to call his boyfriend, Craig, for the number.

Cassandra stood with Bill Anders in the car dealership's back lot looking at the crumpled remains of her pretty red Jeep. Mechanics were taking turns gawking out the shop door in their direction. She was fairly certain they had seen worse wrecks come in, so she was also confident she knew what they were looking at, especially since the wind kept teasingly whipping at her dress. If she had to admit it, she would say she did indeed look especially good today, and she never had much of a problem with men looking her over.

The problem was the asphalt was hot and the heat was coming right through the thin soles of her shoes. She was eager to get out of there. She glanced at her watch, Willy's flight would arrive within half an hour. She wanted to be waiting for him. Why waste this outfit on a bunch of gawking grease monkeys, she thought.

"What am I looking at, Bill," she said with a touch of urgency.

"Well, the brake fluid reservoir was empty," he said.

She sensed some hesitation in his voice, there obviously was another shoe to drop.

"And?"

"There is only one way for that to happen, a leak. We checked our records and during the last servicing, there was no evidence of any leak and the reservoir was full." He hesitated again. "The cops asked us to give the brake system a good going over since they noted the same thing at the site."

"Get to the bottom line, Bill." Cassandra was losing her patience.

"Well, it didn't take a good going over to find it." He pointed to the vehicle. "Inside the right rear tire we found fluid, giving strong evidence of the leak. Fluid spray, very little each application of the brake pedal, most likely, and we'd estimate about twenty to thirty miles of driving in your neck of the woods and the reservoir would be empty. Less than that on the road from your place to Kipahulu because of more frequent applications of the brakes."

"And?"

Bill bent down, maneuvered to a place behind the rear tire and motioned for her to join him down there. She waved her hands over her white dress and shoes.

"Really?"

Bill nodded. "I think you need to see this."

Cassie sent forth an exasperated sigh. She wouldn't do this for just anyone, but she had known Bill and Jill Anders for all of her fifteen years on Maui. In fact, Jill was one of her best friends on the island. The three of them served on the Board for the Maui Arts & Cultural Center, and doing so gave the girls an excuse to get together for an overnight in Wailea once a month. Gregory didn't like either one of them, and Cassie believed the feeling to be reciprocated, at least that's what Jill had told her.

Gathering her skirt a bit, she squatted behind him and looked where Bill was pointing. All she saw at first was the oily coating on everything in the area, then Bill told her to take a close look at the blue fitting at the end of the stainless steel line.

She saw marks, small cuts into the metal.

"And?"

"Cassandra, somebody intentionally loosened the fitting just enough to allow for a tiny bit of fluid to be released from the system each time you applied the brake." He paused and looked around before speaking in a low tone. "This was not an accident."

She stood up. She could taste the bile in the back of her throat. To her, and most likely to Bill, it was an easy guess who did it. She realized the act of loosening the brake line fit with his other recent behavior, to be sure. The question was why. She pulled her sunglasses off the top of her head and put them on, then brushed her dress smooth as then she began walking toward the building.

Bill caught up to her. When he did, she told her old friend a lie, and then posed a question to him.

"What are you going to tell the police?"

He looked at her but could not make out her eyes behind the deeply tinted lenses. When she lowered the glasses and peered over the top, he quickly was reminded that he and Jill were not just friends, but Cassandra had saved Bill's hide about five years ago and never divulged the existence of the favor to Jill. He owed her one.

"If you promise me you'll be careful," he said. "Then, I'll tell the cops we found a bad fitting. That it was an accident."

She stopped just outside the back entrance to the showroom, he opened the door for her. This was a shortcut back to the Escalade and at the door to the main lot she stopped and gave him a quick peck on the cheek.

"Not to worry, Bill. I will be careful."

"Promise?"

"Promise."

She walked toward her SUV, used the remote to unlock the doors and tossed Bill a wave over her shoulder. He watched her drive out of the lot.

As far as I was concerned, they could not have started the descent a moment too soon. My butt was sore, I was cranky, and my middle-aged feet were swollen. The kid next to me had awoken just in time for the snack service and promptly spilled an entire glass of Coke onto the tray and onto my aforementioned middle-aged feet. Mom and dad were still snoring behind us. I remembered that I hate airline travel.

Finally, out the window I saw something coming into view. From studying the map Sandy had put into the binder, I recognized the taller Haleakala Mountain on the left side of the airplane. The road to Hana lay along that eastern coast - it didn't look so bad from up here. We overflew the valley between the two mountains, touched the shoreline on the other side and I felt the plane settle with the addition of flaps and slats as we began to slow for landing. The plane banked to the right, and I could see in the distance the islands of Lanai and Molokai to the west of Maui.

The flight attendants roused mom and pop in the seats behind me. From the noises they made I concluded they don't feel so good. I thought of spoiling their mood even further by telling them what a putz they have created between them, but decided against it. They probably already knew.

The landing gear went down with a thump as we made another turn to the right, now headed back the way we had come. More flaps, more slowing down. The bumps and turbulence-induced surges increased the lower we settled. I remembered the pilot saying something about winds in Kahului gusting from the northeast at thirty to forty miles per hour. Let's see how Chuck Yeager handles the landing, I thought. I was betting against him, and the lower we got and the more severe the bumps became, the tighter I gripped my armrests.

Well, maybe I do have to be more trusting in other people, because less than a minute later we rolled onto the runway on Maui. The nose wheel came down just after I heard and felt the application of a big dose of reverse thrust as the runway rushed past. I didn't see the postage stamp of an airport when we first flew over, so I had no idea how important that reverse thrust was. The roar from the engines subsided and brakes were firmly applied. At the end of the runway, and I do mean end, we turned left and taxied to the terminal. I looked across the airplane out the right side windows and saw the white capes of crashing waves seemingly just off the airport property.

Before the plane stopped at the gate, I had my seatbelt off, my cell phone on - one message from Sandy - and am out of my seat, over the putz, and past everyone headed forward to the one door they're going to use to let everyone off. I waited for the flight attendant to get the thing opened, stepping from foot to foot like the proverbial race horse on an errand.

Cassie stood about twenty feet back from the base of the stairway where people have to wait for arrivals on Maui. She hadn't told Willy she would meet him, but thought it would be another way to keep him off balance. She was surprised by the feeling of butterflies in her stomach, but even more so by the physical sensations which accompanied them. For now, she had decided to merely enjoy the butterflies and worry about everything else later.

Other people waited with her, including the hired lei greeters, and they have all given her the eye. She smiled when she considered that she was wearing at least twenty-thousand dollars worth of jewelry on both wrists and thousand dollar Guieseppe Zanotti heeled sandals on her feet, and all to accessorize a dress she had found online for under one-hundred dollars. What an amazing look that hundred dollars had bought. Her sunglasses were on top of her head, her hair was loose and glowing. Fingers and toes were both done in a fresh French polish. In her left hand, she held a tea leaf lei she had bought from a vendor in the baggage claim area at the airport.

Suddenly, there he was, at the top of the stairs, talking on the phone and obviously not expecting to see her. Then he did. She smiled and she felt her eyes sparkle and saw he did the same.

I answered a call from Sandy and was talking to her as I walked through the concourse. Nothing new at the office, she told me, just checking in to make sure I arrived on time. She must have been tracking the flight online, because my phone had rung before I could even retrieve her voicemail message. A guy wearing a government uniform and sitting on a bar stool, pointed to the left and I made the turn, then saw the stairs headed down to baggage claim.

As I emerged from the walkway at the top of the stairs, I saw her. She looked like a chestnut haired angel dressed in a white halter top dress which hugged her midriff and then flowed outward from her hips to her ankles. She wore white heeled sandals, and as she moved a leg I saw the dress was slit almost all the way to the hip. Our eyes met. She smiled. I smiled. It felt good.

I jogged down the steps - thirty-six of them - and was greeted with a hug, a lei, and a kiss on each cheek.

"Aloha nui loa," she said as she placed the lei around my neck and kissed the second cheek. She stood back and then explained the greeting. "It means 'with much love'."

"I didn't expect to see you here," I said, and I bent forward and placed a kiss on her cheek.

"I couldn't wait to see you, so I came over to this side of the mountain to surprise you. I also thought we might have dinner once you get settled in."

I looked at my cell phone, it was about three-thirty in the afternoon even though to me it felt much later.

"That sounds great," I said.

"Come on, let's collect your bags and get your rental car."

Cassie slipped her arm through mine and we walked through the short hallway and into a large open area with the spinning carousels in process of dumping suitcases, golf clubs, boxes, and even a cooler sealed with duct tape from the holds of planes from the mainland and other islands.

We stood off to the side of the United carousel and waited for my bags to show up at the claim office in the corner. We shared some small talk, which thankfully came easier than it had in my office just three days ago. A woman in uniform pulling a small cart carrying my two bags showed up. Together we verified the arrival of Willie and Sam to the island and I signed for the bags and firearms. Then, piggy backing one bag on the other, Cassie and I rolled out of the terminal and into a partly cloudy and windy Maui afternoon. To the left, I could see a rain shrouded craggy mountain which Cassie confirmed was the West Maui Mountain. On the other side, she said, was the world-famous Ka'anapali beach with numerous, huge resort hotels. It's the place all the rookies go, she told me.

"I'm staying Wailea where you suggested," I said, pronouncing it '*way-lee-ah*'.

Cassie laughed.

"It's pronounced '*why-lay-ah*'. Say it your way and everyone you meet will know you're a rookie."

I laughed.

"I haven't been a rookie since that night in my basement," I said.

Cassie rolled her eyes.

"Come on you old pro," she said, and pointed across the parking lot. "Rental car area is across the way. I'll drive you over in my car, then you can follow me to your condo."

She led me across the double drive and into a crowded parking lot, down three rows to her white Escalade, pushed a button on the remote as we approached and the back door flipped open. I tossed my bags inside, and went to open and hold the driver's door for her. My mother raised a gentleman, but I really wanted a chance to see how that slit in the dress would fall open as she climbed into the SUV. I wasn't disappointed. I closed the door, walked around and slid into the oversize comfort of the leather passenger seat. Cassie paid the fee and we headed over to the rental car lot.

Because I had been so quick getting off the plane, and my luggage had special handling due to the presence of Willie and Sam,

I beat the rush to the rental car counter. Ten minutes after I walked in, we were headed out in tandem, an Escalade followed by my rented Jeep Grand Cherokee. My rental had two thousand miles on the odometer, a leather interior almost as plush as the Escalade and still smelled new. I remained glued to Cassie's rear bumper - no pun intended - and we drove through Kahului, past Costco, Wal-Mart and Home Depot and then out into the country toward Kihei and Wailea.

I remembered from my reading that Kihei was the city and Wailea was a planned development area on the south end of town designed to be an upscale area of luxury homes and condominiums, golf courses, shops and restaurants. The Palms at Wailea, I had learned from a brochure page Sandy had printed for me, was a complex of one-hundred-fifty-two condos in twenty-two, two-story buildings scattered over seventeen acres of tropical plants and green space plus one palm tree planted for every condo. That's a lot of palm trees, I thought.

About half an hour after leaving the airport, we drove through a concrete gate dripping with red flowered plantings on top and to a little cul de sac where the front desk was located. I checked in, drove back out toward the gate but took the left just short of leaving the property, and pulled into a parking spot near my condo. I locked the Jeep and then walked over to where Cassie had parked down the row. She again pushed the button on her remote and I retrieved my bags.

My temporary home on the island was a first floor condominium in building number one. The buildings of the complex have a southwestern feel, with thick walls, adobe tile roofs, and sweeping archways, all painted in a light cream with small green accent panels and awnings. I opened the door to the unit and walked inside, followed by Cassie. She left the door open, said something about island living, and then opened the windows and doors to let the air flow through in all four directions.

"Hey," I said. "Why isn't is as windy here as at the airport?"

She pointed at the mountain rising into the mist to the east and said that it blocks most of the trade winds. In Wailea, they get just enough breeze to move the air, not blow your socks off. She also said some of the best beaches in the world were within walking distance of my doorstep. Wailea, it seems, got many of the best parts of the island.

"And," she said, "Kihei gets only about eight inches of rain each year. So almost every day is the same here. Partly cloudy and eighties during the day, dropping off to the sixties or seventies at night. The ocean temperature is always within a couple of degrees of eighty as well."

"Then how come everything is so lush and green if they don't get the rain?"

"Irrigation, my man. Without it, Kihei withers and dries. You remember what you saw up the hill to the left on the highway: the scrub grass, cactuses, and stunted keawe trees?"

"Yeah. In Louisiana, we get more than our share of natural wetness for our plants. We don't need irrigation."

"Well, you get many things in Louisiana we don't get here, but that's what Kihei would look like without lots and lots of water from the other side of the mountain where they get over three-hundred-sixty inches of rain every year. You're in one of the driest spots on the planet, less than fifteen miles from one of the wettest. You'll find Maui to be an island filled with all sorts of contradictions and contrasts."

"I did a little bit of reading," I said with a bit of pride.

"Careful of books on Hawaii. Just when you think you have this place figured out, something surprises you."

"Is that so?" I wheeled my bags into the master suite area, kept the windows closed in there and turned on the air conditioner and ceiling fan. "I'm going to take a shower," I called. "Plane-scuzzy, you know."

I turned and Cassie was at the bedroom door.

"I'll pour us a drink and meet you on the lanai when you're done."

"Lanai?" I said. "You mean the porch?"

She shook her head to mock me.

"Are you still a bourbon man?" she asked.

"Always. How did you know?"

She smiled, pushed me back into the room and started to close the door.

"You may be the private investigator here, but give me some credit too."

I dropped my clothes on the way to the shower and remembered Sandy's admonitions.   Contradictions and contrasts?   I would say. Things could indeed surprise you on Maui, I thought.

Gregory and the mysterious Jennifer Shea were checked into separate Tower suites in the Fairmont Hotel in San Francisco. Located on Nob Hill just a couple of blocks from Fisherman's Wharf, this newer tower of the hotel was built with a more contemporary theme than the original Fairmont, and affords some of the most breathtaking views of San Francisco.

Gregory stood looking out over the bay. He checked his watch. It was seven o'clock and the sun was starting its downhill slide; he knew it was to set today in San Francisco at about eight-thirty. That's about an hour and a half later than on Maui, he thought. He and Jennifer were going to Alfred's Steak House with reservations for eight o'clock.   After that they were scheduled to meet John McCormick, the owner of a small art gallery to discuss the final details for the upcoming show.

It would be Jennifer's first major exhibition and Gregory had noted she had been almost too excited to sit still during the flight. Her mother was the same way when she fixated on some upcoming event.   It was all he could do to keep his composure.   There were times during the flight over when he would have loved to have slapped her.

The first time he met Jennifer Shea, it was an *accidental* meeting two years ago at a very small gallery in downtown Chicago where she was working and getting a bit of wall space to display a few of her own works.   The girl had an abundance of talent, he had to admit.   Like anything in the artsy-fartsy world, it's not how good you are, but how lucky and connected you are.   Gregory often lamented to Cassandra that he was certain there were far better singers, actors, dancers, and artists undiscovered out there than anything presented to us these days as so-called superstars.   It's all a matter of who got tapped by fate, he would say.

So, he had discovered Jennifer Shea, and although Gregory had few connections in art circles, he had all the money in the world to help Fate make her a success, should he wish it.   For now, he did.

In his opinion, Jennifer had an uncanny knack for being able to capture not just the image, but the emotion of her scenes.   She could attract the viewer's eyes to the most complex and compelling locus in a painting. There were times when Gregory could get lost in her works as he searched for the meaning. She would laugh and say, 'I just paint what I see, Gregory, I leave it up to the beholder to find the meaning'.

He sipped some deeply chilled Polish U'Luvka vodka from a small glass as he stared out the window. The hotel staff knew what he liked, and his room had been stocked with a special mini freezer, a silver ice bucket ringed by a dozen or so of the special legless crystal glasses held upright by a chromed wire rack. Gregory believed if you poured too much of the liquid at one time, or let it sit around, you lost the power of the nectar, so he adhered to the original intent of the maker and treated his glass as bottomless, refilling as he drank and never allowing the glass to be completely drained until he was finished.

Cassandra felt he had been sucked in by the historical story of the brew, he knew. To hear the makers of today tell it, she always said, leads one to believe U'Luvka has magical powers. However, when Gregory drank it, he did feel it bestowed the powers of the ages upon him; and, besides, he did love to tell the story. Who wouldn't love a story that started with the words 'Legend has it...'? He always used those words.

There came a knock at his door. He walked across the suite to open it, then stood back and held the door. Jennifer stepped in. She was dressed in the black with white accents, sleeveless, mid-length evening dress he had ordered delivered to her room for the occasion. She smiled and walked past him into his suite. Standing in the center of the living room, she turned for him. He was taken back many years to the time he'd last seen such striking beauty in a single package. Jennifer's movements were fluid, elegant, feminine; and she was gorgeous. As had been her mother.

"Perfect," he said. "Breathtaking, my dear."

"You know I feel a little fake in this. It's not me."

He turned and looked at her. For an instant, his look froze her, he smiled and the look was gone. Then he waved it all away.

"You know it's all about image, my dear." He motioned to the vodka, the bottle's long twisted neck sticking out of the ice bucket. "Care to join me?" He pulled the bottle's bulb bottom free from the ice. It glistened and dripped.

She stared at it, mesmerized. It's simple beauty drew her artist's eye. She saw there was no label, just an odd icon etched into the teardrop.

"What is it?"

"It's delicious," he said. "A light, sipping vodka, from Poland." He freed one of the glasses from the wire rack, pulled the cork from the bottle and poured her half a glass. The etched crystal caught the rays from the sun, which had begun to turn from gold to orange, and reflected them through the clear liquid. He passed her the glass, and refilled his own. Jennifer noted the lack of a flat bottom to the glasses, meaning she would have to hold it or it would spill if she tried to set it down.

"The bottle is a meant to represent the synergy between the physical forms of man and woman," Gregory told her, his eyes holding an impish twinkle. "The logo on the bottle's neck is a traditional alchemists icon which combines the glyphs for man, woman, spirit, and soul. When the four glyphs are assembled like this, the symbol is said to draw forth from the gods a uniquely human experience of friendship and fellowship."

He sipped. Encouraged her to do the same. She took a sip, her mouth suddenly overwhelmed by the complex combination of flavors and aromas.

"It's wonderful," she said.

"I'm glad you like it." He took another sip of the icy liquid, savored the heat of it going down. "Legend has it, that in 1603, King Sigismund III of Poland wanted something special to serve to his Royal Court. So, he commissioned an alchemist by the name of Michael Sendivogius to develop a vodka of the finest purity and quality which could be enjoyed all night long, leaving nothing but pleasant memories the next day. The result, which you are now sampling for the first time, became known as 'Sendivogius' unfathomable spell'.

"See, my dear, alchemy is all about transformation, and every transformation is a balance between opposites: light and dark, negative and positive, and that most potent of all transformative oppositions, the sensual dance of man and woman, which is ultimately the dance of life itself.

"Even the glass designed for the drink is form and function blended to perfection. Since it cannot be put down, it is considered to have no bottom.   It was said, such a gregarious host was King Sigismund III, that he never wanted his guests to go home.   Being invited to party with his Royal Court was considered to be a one-way ticket.   You arrived, your glass was always full, you couldn't put it down, and you were eventually carried out.

"It was also during this time, four-hundred years ago, when the tradition of breaking vodka glasses began.   It was said, people would shout 'I've had enough' and toss their glass into the fireplace."

He lifted his glass again.   This time the sunlight poured through the crystal and reflected in Jennifer's deep brown eyes and energized their green flecks.   He saw her mother again, and his eyes dampened.   He looked away from her image toward the falling sun.   When he spoke a moment later, it was more to himself than to her.

"It's the dance of the universe.   A mystery to God Himself."

He drained his glass and turned to face her again.

"Drink up.   We'll get our evening started."   He looked into her eyes and asked, "Excited?"

"You bet, Gregory," she said.   "It's the chance of a lifetime and I owe it all to you."   She downed the liquid remaining in her glass and then set it into the wire rack.

On the way out the door, she grabbed the gauzy black shoulder wrap off the chair back and draped it over her arm.   Gregory fixed his tie, put on his jacket and followed her out.

I climbed out of the shower feeling so much better than I had a few minutes before.   It's amazing the amount of grime you can gather onto yourself while riding in an airliner for ten hours.   I grabbed the towel off the counter, dried off and then wrapped it around my waist.   I could see through the glass doors a beautiful view to the ocean and Cassie's moving shadow.   I rubbed the stubble of my beard, then reviewed the look in the mirror and decided the growth gave me a rather raffish look, so I determined not to change that with a quick shave.

I got dressed in a pair of off-white, linen pants and a medium-blue, silk aloha shirt Sandy had bought for me on Saturday. Grabbing a pair of loafers from the open suitcase on the bed, I headed out to join Cassie on the patio...I mean, lanai.

I found her relaxing on a chaise lounge, her shoes lying on the tile alongside.   She had a tall glass of iced pale liquid in her hand

and was watching the palms swaying gently in the greenway. The afternoon sun was shining brightly above the horizon to the west and Cassie had her sunglasses on. I stepped from the living area onto the lanai and noted there was waiting for me on a little table between the chaise lounge chairs a low tumbler half filled with what I hoped was indeed iced Jim Beam.

I picked up the glass, hoisted a toast toward Cassie and then took a healthy sip. The bourbon was cold going in but warmed up quickly as it went down.

"Beautiful view," I said.

"It's relaxing," Cassie commented. "My house has fantastic views from hundred-foot-high lava bluffs directly to the water, but the ocean on the south shore is much different from here. It's wilder, more foreboding." She sipped her drink.

"I'm going to guess lemonade," I said.

"You'd be correct," she said, hoisting her glass back in my direction in a silent toast. "Twelve years sober." She returned her gaze to the greenway. "It's a long, long story."

Feeling a touch of guilt, I pointed to the glass in my hand and asked, "You don't mind if I..."

"Oh, heavens no," she said as if it were a practiced response to the social inquiry of those who would indulge in adult beverages in her abstaining presence. "I have no compulsion to force my choices onto someone else or judge anyone for theirs. Let's just say I indulged in a lifetime of drinking during a very short period of my life, so I figure I'm done with it."

Momentarily somewhat uncomfortable, I looked at my cell phone, hoping for a change of subject. The time was closing on five p.m. on the island, but the sun appeared to be too low on the horizon to match the time. Back in New Orleans this time of year, the sun would be up for nearly four more hours, but I would have been surprised if this sun would stay above water for another two or so.

"It looks like sunset comes earlier here than on the mainland," I said.

"You've never been to Hawaii?"

"No, never." I took another healthy sip of the bourbon. The effect was almost immediate; that little sense of a lightening of the mood. "I'm more of a Caribbean kind of guy."

"I guess having a house in the Caymans will do that to you." She looked at me and then went back to watching the waves roll.

So, she had done some homework.

"I think you have me at a bit of a disadvantage, Cassie." I sat down on the other chaise lounge, put my feet up. "I'm usually the one who knows more than the client."

"This situation is important to me, Willy." She turned to look at me and lifted her sunglasses onto the top of her head. "I needed to know that you were the right person to help me. I don't need just any old P.I., I need a friend who cares."

I looked into her eyes, something I could do for hours back in the day. My gut told me she was being open with me, at least with that explanation.

"Why don't you tell me what else you know about me, and then from that point forward, I'll be the P.I. Okay?" I have always cherished my privacy, which, may seem a bit ironic given my choice of professions. Perhaps it was a result of seeing people's lives spilled open for dissection and not ever wanting my life to fall under such scrutiny. I even hated it when the press would include any kind of information on my life or background in their reporting of the public cases I handled.

Cassie returned her sunglasses to their useful position.

"As I told you in your office, I had seen your name in the papers over the years, mainly when you were working for the Chicago Police Department. You achieved a certain amount of, ah, celebrity."

"I'd rather call it notoriety," I said. "I think there's a difference. In some circles I was considered more a notorious than celebrated character, especially at the end of my career with CPD."

Never turning her head or again revealing her eyes, she continued.

"There were some unanswered questions about how you left the department, but oddly very little reporting after a hailstorm following the Hernandez situation."

Hailstorm, I thought, more like a shit storm.

She paused.

I didn't respond. During my time as a cop, I often found it useful just to let a person talk and see where they wanted the conversation to go and what they'd reveal on their own. People hate conversational silence and will usually fill the void with something, if you have enough patience to wait them out.

The silence went on for over a minute. An eternity of discomfort in conversational lulls. It may be what some longterm lovers consider comfortable silence, but to most of the rest of us, it's quite the opposite.

Finally, Cassie continued.

"From what I read, there were rumors you shot those people after they had thrown down their guns and surrendered."

She threw out the bait. I could see her eyes looking toward me without turning her head.

I didn't bite, and continued to stare down the greenway.

"Of course, it was all speculation," she continued and opened the door for me. "Because your partner was killed almost immediately when the two of you went in, and you were the only person who came out of that warehouse alive."

It had been a long time since I had been forced to face that night outside of nightmares. I drained the remainder of my bourbon, looked for the bottle and spotting it on the counter near the window to the kitchen area, got up and poured a solid refill. I walked back to the lounge chair and sat on the foot of it, leaning forward and resting my elbows on my knees, my back to Cassie on the other chair.

I sensed she was watching me. It was now my long-lost friend who waited out the silence. I heard the tinkling of ice in her glass as she took a drink. I took another deep swallow from my glass, and as the bourbon slid down and the ethanol it contained pulsed into my brain, I decided I should tell her my story, hoping she'd eventually finish hers during our time together.

So, over the next hour or so, as the sun fell toward the Pacific, and set the sky ablaze in brilliant gold which later gave way to smears of orange and purple and left only a gauzy memory of light in the wake of its departing, I told her about that night when two brothers went into a warehouse and only one walked out. As I relived the events, I began to re-experience the same closeness Cassie and I had shared so long ago, when we could tell each other anything. I realized during the telling that I was including details which Sandy didn't even know; details no other living person knew. The level of my candor in the full telling to Cassie shocked me, but in doing so I was filled with the sense of finally shedding a weighty burden; and an old familiarity had been renewed.   Such was the nature of what Cassie and I had shared during those precious eight weeks of our fifteenth autumn.

Sometime during the telling, she had moved to sit behind me and as I described the emotion of seeing my partner go down and the callous, angry looks of men who didn't even merit the shining of his shoes, she started to gently stroke my back.   I was aware of the warmth of her closeness, sensed the subtle lure of her perfume, and felt the urge to turn to her.   I was exhausted, a little buzzed, hungry, but most of all felt vulnerable with my soul fully exposed to her, which had been something I had promised myself I would not do this time around.

Fortunately, I was now equipped with three times the life experience, so I stood up, walked over to the bourbon bottle, and set down the glass next to it.   I turned to look at her as she sat there alone.   Sometime during my story she had removed her sunglasses. In the low glow of the remaining sunlight, I could see a softness in her eyes; and something else, a sadness.   Or did I just imagine that last part?

"I'm hungry," I said, searching her face for any clue of her emotions, but finding nothing on display.   "Is there anyplace nearby where we could get something to eat?"

"Actually, I was planning on a quiet dinner at a place just down the road."   She stood up, slipped on her shoes, tossed her hair and walked into the condo.   She suggested I close and lock the doors to keep out the critters of both the four and two legged variety.

Grabbing her purse from the dining area table, she tossed in her sunglasses and pulled out her keys.   I followed after securing the doors, grabbed my blazer from the chair back, and we walked into the parking lot.

"I'll drive," she said.   "We've got some fairly unforgiving drinking and driving laws here, and it wouldn't do much for your attitude toward our little slice of paradise if you wound up sitting in the drunk tank on your first night on the island."

I obediently took the passenger seat in her Escalade, fastened my seat belt because the car rental lady had mentioned this was yet another of the unforgiving rules in paradise, and silently took inventory of my spilled guts.   I wondered if Cassie again had lured me into a place I didn't want to be.   Suddenly, I felt like the big, old

Mississippi River catfish who succumbs to a bait that was just too tempting.

"I think you'll like this restaurant. They have great local fish dishes. It's just a mile or so down the road in the Grand Wailea Hotel," she said as we headed out the gate we had entered a few hours earlier. "Let's see if I can teach you the name of the restaurant before we get there." Her eyes were playful as she glanced across the interior toward me. She told me it was named for the Hawaii State Fish.

I must be a slow learner when it comes to foreign languages, because we were laughing uncontrollably by the time the valet took the vehicle a few minutes later. We finally settled on me just calling the restaurant by its local short name of 'Humu's' which Cassie pronounced as 'who-moos'.

Arm in arm, we wandered through the open lobby, downstairs to an outdoor, torch-lit, undulating walkway bordered with verdant tropical plantings and the ambience reinforced by the wafting soft sound of small waterfalls, and eventually found our way to the restaurant. She held herself close on my arm, and had I imbibed in a second refill back at the condo, I may have tried a kiss.

Humuhumunukunukuapua'a is housed in a pitched, thatch-roofed replica of a large open-walled Hawaiian lodge in the middle of a man-made lagoon. After crossing a small bridge, we met with the hostess who directed us to a table for two in a far corner overlooking a statue of a spear fisherman and an outrigger canoe. In the spilled light of the restaurant, I could see giant goldfish swimming around, most likely picking up anything diners would drop. Cassie told me they were Koi, expensive imports from Japan, a member of the carp family, and not on the menu.

We each ordered some kind of locally caught fish they called 'Ono' which in Hawaiian Cassie said means 'delicious', in a crust of macadamia nuts for the entree and I decided on a Coke to go with Cassie's lemonade.

When we were again alone, Cassie reopened her discussion of things William.

"The charter papers on your firm names two partners in the 'Langdon Partnership LLC'," she said. "They confirm your receptionist is, or was, a partner in the firm."

"Yes, Sandy is my partner," I said.   "We opened the firm together."

"Yet she serves the role of your receptionist?"

"You must remember that even though New Orleans is a cosmopolitan city, it's still the old south in very many ways."

"Meaning?"

"Meaning, that people still hold certain provincial preconceptions down there, and a woman principal in our line of work will sometimes cause potential clients to go elsewhere.   Old families of the south still view being private investigators as a man's purview.   Hell, to many people, and not just down south, we're barely better than Peeping Toms, and ladies do not peep. Southerners have more of a reverence for the concepts of ladyhood and the traditional female role."

"I know all about the female roles in the deep south," she said with a hint of acid on her tongue.   "Ladies may not peep, William, but they certainly are not averse to the fine art of gossip, innuendo, social shunning, and character assassination."

This was obviously a topic which went right through to nerve, so I took note.   She continued without any comment from me beyond unblinking eyes.

"So, to appease the hypocrisy of Southern social morays you stick her out front on display instead of in her own office?"

"Not at all," I said, calmly.   "Sandy spent years in an office at a law firm and she prefers the open air of the main office area.   She does have an office, but doesn't really like working in there.   She's an attorney, you know."

"Yes, I do know that."

"Sandy is a genius at doing research and ferreting out information from the most difficult and unlikely of sources.   I'm more of a hand's on field guy.   We have a symbiotic relationship."

She didn't respond.

"That means our talents compliment each other so we both thrive."

Boy did she respond to that.

"I know what symbiosis is, I'm not fucking stupid."

Message received.   Anytime a woman reacted with that degree of ferocity to a simple explanation meant she had spent many years with someone or groups of someones telling her she's stupid.   There was a flicker of fire in her eyes and I thought I best move on to something else. So, I added a complimentary start to the next words out of my mouth.

"As I'm seeing your research has been very thorough, you must already know Sandy does exactly as she pleases. Without apology. I could no more *stick* her someplace than I could stop the sun from setting tonight."

She seemed to consider that; and then to recover from the implication she didn't know what symbiotic meant. A fish jumped in the lagoon, the splash apparently a good punctuation for that part of the conversation.

"Did you ever think she agreed to the arrangement because she wanted to keep a third wheel from intruding into your little ex-wife and ex-husband world?"

"She's been doing it since we established the business, and then we were still married," I said. "We only divorced in the last year."

"Ah, the Vanessa Lafontaine problem," she said, stabbing a piece of asparagus from her plate.

I was flabbergasted. Nobody should know of that except for Sandy and myself, well, and Vanessa Lafontaine. Then she waved off the statement just as quickly as she had thrown it out there. Cassie changed subjects and shifted tones like a woman with an agenda. I'd seen the tactic when interviewing witnesses or appearing in court and facing cross-examination by defense attorneys over the years. They plant the seed to make a point but don't want you getting a chance to comment on or ask why. Like the events of this night, it's often much later when one realizes exactly what someone's point was when they put it out there.

"The main reason I asked is not to embarrass or judge your relationship, Willy," she continued. "Rather, I wondered if you told Sandy everything about your cases; or can you maintain the confidences of your clients?"

Was her intention really that simple, I wondered.

"I hold no secrets from Sandy," I said. "On the other hand, I do not necessarily tell her everything." I put down my fork and wiped my mouth to give her the distinct impression that I was coming clean here before I continued. "See, Cassie, even though in a court of law the theory is 'the truth, the whole truth, and nothing but the truth', in the real world of a business partnership, unlike how it should be in

a marriage, sometimes what's not directly asked for isn't offered."
After a moment for that to sink in, I added, "Why does it matter?"

"It matters, Willy, because even though I may seem to be a woman of the world, I am still a small town girl who regards her privacy and reputation."

Was that a statement or a warning, I wondered.

"Besides, the reception area felt a little chilly that day I came to your office."

Her eyes looked into mine and reflected the candlelight.

"I don't think the woman likes me," she said, a mischievous look in her eyes and a pout on her lips.

'Oh, boy', was my only thought.

After dinner, and a little light conversation unrelated to business, the past, the present or the future, we retraced our steps and Cassie dropped me off at my rented condo. She drove to the dead end, thereby avoiding the uncertainties of pulling into a parking spot and shutting down the engine. Instead, she just left the thing running and offered a friendly hug across the center console.

We agreed to meet at a little place in mid-Kihei called Stella Blues at ten in the morning for breakfast. She apologized for making me the center of the discussions tonight and then promised we'd discuss her case over breakfast. I watched her drive out the gate.

The full moon was casting light and shadow over the parking lot and the imagery reminded me very much of dealing with Cassie Yeats-Thomason.

Chapter Nine

In the crew hotel near the airport in San Francisco, Captain Dan sat on the edge of his bed. His head ached, and his mouth felt like one of his socks had spent the night in there. Knowing they'd have today free, he and Jason and Bev had gone out on the town last night. His blurry eyes tried unsuccessfully to focus on the red numerals displayed on the bedside clock and he hoped the call to his cell phone which he had missed a moment ago wasn't from Gregory with a change of plans.

Before he attempted another look at the clock or the phone, he decided to take a leak and walked to the bathroom. He stood there on a towel he had thrown down for his shower last night and aimed by sound more than anything. He wondered if he was still legally drunk. When he finished he found his eyes were able to focus on the bedside clock which he now read as 5:32 a.m. He sat back down on the side of the bed and opened his phone. The call had come from Cassie.

Partially relieved, partially pissed off, he returned the call. After all, even though he was screwing her, she was still the boss, technically. She answered on the first ring.

"Good morning," she cooed. "I am in our special suite at the Four Seasons and woke up in the middle of the night thinking of you. I had to call. I know it's early."

"It's awfully early, Hon," he said through a raspy voice.

"I'm sorry, baby," she said, a deflated tone in her voice. "I just wanted to hear your voice. Willy got in and I'm more convinced than ever I have made the right choice here."

"That's great, Cassie," he said. "Honey, can we talk about this later? We had a down day planned for today and were out late last night. I'm really not focusing very well right now."

There was a moment or two of dead silence. Dan wondered if he had pissed her off and was just about to say something sweet when she responded.

"Of course we can, baby," she said. "I love you."

The three words slugged him in the gut. He knew he didn't share the emotion, but would never tell her that.

"Love you, too," he said, purposely omitting the 'I'. He knew she'd never pick up on the difference in meaning.

"I'll call you later," she said. "Get some rest and dream of me. Bye."

"Okay."

He closed the phone, rubbed his face and rolled back onto the bed. He set the phone on the nightstand next to a small stack of photos. Rolling fully onto the bed, he threw his arm over the lump curled up on the other side.

"Who was that?"

"Nobody," he said. "Go back to sleep."

Sandy called me at seven o'clock Tuesday morning. I had been awake for an hour and was sitting up in bed watching the awakening of the greenway and ocean below as the sun poked above the mountain behind me. The palm trees cast long shadows which darkened and defined as the sun rose, and the greens, blues, and browns of the scene seemed to come alive moment by moment. The ocean was richer and bluer than the evening before, the palm fronds greener and displayed more definition, and the sky was clean and deeply dimensioned with scattered tones of blue.

Some kind of obnoxious bird had been announcing the awakening for about the same time I had been watching. It had been the birds' repeated, loud, and rhythmic *kila kila kila* and a respondent *ka-tee-tar ka-tee-tar ka-tee-tar* screeching which had served as my alarm clock just after sunrise. As beautiful as the dawning day was, my interrupted dreams had been kinda cool, too.

I left out a few discretionary details in briefing Sandy on my initial island meeting with Cassie, deferring some of the news to an update to follow after our breakfast meeting. I could tell Sandy was chomping at the bit to get going on the research. She told me she spent yesterday cleaning up a few things on some of our other cases which were winding down so she'd be free to focus on Operation Puppy Love. I thanked her for the reminder.

After we hung up, I wandered to the kitchen, hoping Sandy had remembered to have someone stock the place with a few necessities: Coke, OJ, chips and dip, fruit, bread, lunchmeat, and anchovy-stuffed olives. In my world, a man can survive on those items alone, if necessary. The bottle of bourbon and my glass were still outside the kitchen window on the extended countertop and I retrieved them. The fridge had indeed been stocked up and I grabbed a Coke and a banana from the pantry and turned on the television to catch up on a few national stories. I found a chair and plopped down, put my feet up on the ottoman and consumed my mini-breakfast while reinforcing through cable news my opinion we're all pretty much doomed.

Marcy spent that Monday night in Janet's apartment, hoping against a growing concern that something had happened to her friend and lover. She was up early, having slept little, showered and headed out to the metro station to take the train to the airport to meet Craig's boyfriend Kevin at the security office. She had made certain before leaving that she had a copy of Janet's travel itinerary and conference schedule, even thought Kevin said he wouldn't need it to do some searching of the security recordings.

Kevin, she learned, also knew someone from the security department at the STM, the entity which ran the public transit systems in Montreal. He promised Marcy he'd ask his friends for any recordings they may have for about two hours after the flight arrival to see if they could spot Janet and any potential threats.

It was hot and muggy when she left the apartment building. The sun was filtering through a haze which had been clinging to the city for the last week. A cold front was promised to move through today, bringing with it cleansing thunderstorms followed by a cooling to the low 30s C - 80s in Fahrenheit - for the rest of the week. Marcy still had a hard time with the conversions as her Detroit-schooled brain still defaulted to US measurements. Janet had always enjoyed watching Marcy struggle with the conversions. 'Just reset your brain,

Marcy,' she had joked. 'You're Canadian now.' Marcy felt a pain deep inside her as the memory played.

Marcy didn't feel like a Canadian, though. She still had way too much Detroit in her, although she didn't know why. Growing up as what she knew she was had always been a struggle, a daily fight against kids who made fun of the way she chose her style of dress or hairstyle. Growing up as a lesbian was for Marcy a daily humiliation exacerbated by the knowing looks of adults who wanted to shield their daughters from her. In the end, she was content in her skin, and she had long ago realized the entirety of her youth experience had mostly served to provide her with an enormous amount of fight in her spirit.

She walked to the metro station and caught the train out to the airport. A trickle of sweat ran down her back and gave her an immediate chill when she entered the air conditioned car. The chill took her back to the feeling she had in speaking with Janet's parents last evening. While they had outwardly accepted their daughter's life choices, there was a definite coolness in their tone toward Marcy, who felt they blamed her for their daughter being missing. Marcy had told them she'd be in touch when she heard anything and asked they do the same. They had agreed, but Marcy wasn't sure they would.

The train rumbled to a stop at the Montreal Airport and brought Marcy's thoughts back to the present tasks at hand. As she exited the car, she opened her cell phone and called Kevin to let him know she had arrived. He answered on the first ring and the two agreed to meet outside the Burger King in the north Atrium area of the terminal.

Since the Burger King was outside of the secured area, she would have easy access, and once accompanied by Kevin there'd be no issue where she went on the airport grounds. Several minutes later, Marcy stood looking up and down the concourse just outside the fast food joint. The smells coming from the restaurant turned her stomach. She hadn't eaten in almost twenty-four hours, but the thought of purging her hunger with fast food was almost too much to bear.

She watched Kevin approach and when he arrived, he gave her a hug. He was a small man, about two centimeters shorter and weighing twenty kilos less than Marcy, in his mid-thirties, he wore his brown hair short and made no attempts to mask either the touch of gray at the sideburns or the distinct thinning on the top. He had penetrating blue eyes and an easy smile. While she and Janet were closer to Craig, Kevin had jumped at the opportunity to help the friend of a friend.

"Before we start this," he said. "I want you to know that you can call me anytime for anything. Consider me like family."

Marcy felt her eyes start to sting. Her mouth moved, but nothing came out.

Kevin took her hand and led her through the terminal to his office. They must have looked like quite the pair. Marcy didn't give a shit.

I arrived at Stella Blues a little before ten, figuring I could grab a private table and wait for Cassie, who was always late. To my surprise, I saw her Escalade parked out front and found her seated at a table in the back corner of the restaurant. The crowd was light. I figured July wasn't prime time for tourists on the island, and any locals who patronize the place for breakfast had surely already come and gone.

Cassie waved to me, but remained seated as I approached. I was momentarily confused on how to personalize the greeting, but she solved that problem by offering a hand for the shaking.

"Good morning," she said. "Did you sleep well?"

I pulled out a chair across from her and sat down.

"I did," I said. "Until those damn birds went off around sunrise."

"Ah, the grey francolins," Cassie said with a laugh. "I should have warned you. I heard them too at the Four Seasons."

"So, that's what they're called, francolins?" I said. "They look like small quail. Their screeching reminds me of peacocks. For a little bird, they sure make a big racket."

"From what I understand, they are prolific breeders and have taken over parts of the island. We don't have them where I live, or I'm sure Gregory would be out with his 12-gauge. The species isn't endemic - that means native to the island - so even with the large feral cat population, they don't have any natural predators here. They can be annoying, but I understand they mainly squawk early in the morning and then usually go silent for the rest of the day."

I let her little vocabulary jab go unanswered. I figured I deserved it and now we'd be even in the ten dollar words battle.

"So that's why I didn't hear them yesterday, I suppose."

Tiring quickly of the bird talk, I let my eyes wash over Cassie. Her hair framed her face this morning and her makeup was barely perceptible and perfect. She wore a bright orange loose-fitting top with puffed short sleeves and those pants that go just below the knee, and cork wedge, white sandals.

As I planned to stop in at the police headquarters in Wailuku after our meeting to make an introduction and ensure all the t's were crossed and i's were dotted on the concealed carry issue, I had dressed in business attire, including a jacket. While Cassie blended in, I realized quickly that I stood out like a sore thumb. If I was going to blend, I was going to have to go a little more island.

Willie and Sam were secure in their locked cases stashed in the spare tire area of the Jeep. There was no need to risk a confrontation with local law enforcement at this point.

The waitress came and we each ordered a breakfast special which came with rice, but we both opted for potatoes instead. I asked for a Coke and Cassie waved off anything more than the carafe of coffee which had arrived before I did.

"Shall we start while we wait?" I asked.

Cassie nodded and reached into her purse.

I opened my notebook - the old fashioned kind which operates with pen and paper - and Cassie handed over a single page of folded paper. I unfolded the sheet and noted there were four computer printed women's names adjacent to the names of cities from around the country. Printed in blue ink at the bottom of the page were two other names: Janet Hopkins and Jennifer Shea. Neither had a city associated with their name like did the others.

"Okay," I said. "Tell me about the list. These are women you believe Gregory has had a relationship with which may violate the provisions of your prenuptial agreement?"

Cassie looked uncomfortable, almost as if she was regretting turning over the list to me. There was something else there as well, I could feel it. I just needed to draw it out of her.

"Yes," she said. Her eyes looked past my left shoulder. Mindlessly, she refilled her almost-full coffee cup from the carafe.

She added a touch of cream from a little white plastic container and took a sip. Her eyes still were avoiding mine.

"Cassie, if you're at all reconsidering this, we haven't gone too far to stop right here and now. I can pack up and go home, wire you the deposit."

It's not unusual for a spouse to have second thoughts when push came to shove in these matters, especially in long-term marriages like Cassie and Gregory's. Even given the popularity of the so-called no-fault divorce in a majority of states these days, meaning neither party has to prove anything beyond it was truly their signature on the affidavit which stated the marriage was irretrievably broken, when it came to equitable distribution states like Hawaii sometimes it was profitable to prove harm.

While Louisiana accepts no-fault divorces if the parties have lived separate and apart for 180 days, it still allows for divorce actions to be charged for fault. The problem which some of my clients have digesting is the news that regardless of fault, Louisiana remains a community property state meaning the assets of the marriage will be split evenly between the parties, regardless of who could be judged as the wrongdoer. Fortunately, for my business anyway, a surprising number of clients still choose to blacken the reputation of a wayward spouse regardless of the final financial resolution.

Cassie seemed to consider my offer to stop now without harm, but then took in a deep breath which appeared to physically infuse her with a resolve.

"No," she said. "Let's do this."

I sought out her eyes, which now were focused on her lap. I reached across the table, and in a move I'd never try on a client without a mutual history, placed two fingertips under her chin and gently raised her head. Her eyes followed and eventually looked into mine. They were turning red and moist.

"You can trust me on this, Cassie," I said. I removed my fingers from her chin and wondered how she would react, but her eyes remained locked on mine. "You can say stop at any time."

"What about sharing things with your partner?" she asked.

"Sandy will be working with me on this," I said. "That's how we work. There is nobody better at research than her."

"Can you keep her at arm's length on what you uncover? This is all very embarrassing to me and I don't think she likes me." She gave me the doe eyes treatment.

"Sandy doesn't even know you, Cassie."

Cassie reached for my hand.

"Just promise me you'll use your discretion with what you share with her."

I pondered her request and how I could make it work.

"That I can do."

Having defused a touchy situation, I decided to move the conversation forward.

"Can you tell me anything about these women?" I asked.

"Other than what you have there, no."

"How did you get these?"

"I pulled them from his diary."

"His diary? Was there nothing else associated? No writings? No dates? No details?"

"Nothing."

For some reason, at that instant I decided to start counting Cassie's lies. Foregoing any others I may have suspected since she walked into my office four days ago, that was number one.

"Can I see the diaries?" I inquired. "Perhaps there is something there that I could discern from other writings."

"Impossible," she said with a strongly implied finality. "Too risky to remove them."

"Okay," I responded. I decided it was best not to push her on them at this point. Later, there may be a way for me to get my hands on them. "What about these two names without associated cities?"

"Those are new."

"How new?"

"Janet Hopkins, apparently while I was gone to Dallas and came to see you. Jennifer Shea I learned about yesterday. She's currently in San Francisco with my husband."

"So, Jennifer Shea lives in San Francisco?" I scribbled a few notes in my book.

"I don't know, she flew out of Kahului yesterday with Gregory on our plane."

"How did you find this out?"

She didn't respond.

"Moving on to Janet Hopkins, then. Tell me what you know about her."

"I saw her name in his diary on Saturday when he was golfing." A look of genuine fear fell upon her face. "He almost caught me and that's why there is no way I can allow you to see his diaries."

"Do you check his diaries on a regular basis?" I wondered if this was just coincidence or if she suspected something.

"No."

Cheating husbands, or wives for that matter, very often will have telltale behaviors when cheating. Contrary to what would be common sense, men will often have an increased libido with their wives at the same time they are cavorting with a lover. That behavior is less common with women, who mostly prefer one lover at a time. Rather, women become more self-involved, taking an intense interest in their grooming and appearance and indulge in more self-pampering.

"Just a coincidence then, or did something lead you to check?"

She blushed; that's an unconscious physiological reaction. However, I was convinced the fidgeting she did accompanying it was feigned.

"I had reason to suspect. So I checked."

"What was that reason?"

She glared at me across the table.

"Just what is this?" she asked with an indignant affect. "Who are you investigating? Me or my husband?"

I returned her glare with my best non-threatening look.

"I have to ask these questions, Cassie. It's my investigative style."

Her eyes softened a bit. For the second time in five minutes, she reached across the table and touched my hand. I was beginning to sense a pattern here.

"I'm sorry," she said. "It's just embarrassing." She leaned forward to close the distance and quickly checked the area. "Gregory was sexually aggressive when I arrived home. Let me say, brutally so. We're not sleeping in the same bed anymore. In fact, it's been several years since we have routinely shared a bed." She removed her hand from mine and resumed her posture.

"So, you've noticed this pattern of his before? You've associated it with an adulterous event in the past? That's how you came to check his diary the day after, on Saturday?" I looked down and started writing another note. I was giving her the chance to lie to me again.

"Yes," she said. "I had noted the behavior before. For some reason, it was far worse this time."

"Just how did you ascertain the correlation with previous incidents if there were no dates associated with these women's names in the diary?" I looked up from my note.

I waited. She knew she was trapped. She fidgeted.

"I will look again," she said finally. "I still will not risk you going through his diaries."

Then she played her trump card.

"I think he tried to kill me on Sunday, Willy," she said in a low, matter-of-fact tone. "I rolled my Jeep off a bridge because my brakes failed. Before I picked you up yesterday, I saw the evidence of sabotage at the dealership. The owner's a friend, so he's not going to say anything to the police who are classifying it as an accident. I truly believe Gregory loosened one of my brake lines."

I sat back and watched her eyes and thought about how that fit into the equation and what I may have to do to protect my client from physical harm.

Gregory ate breakfast in his room on Tuesday morning. Eggs sunny side up, sausage, hash browns, wheat toast, grapefruit juice, and coffee. He watched the rising sun glinting off the multiple angles of the pyramidal TransAmerica building, outside of Seattle's Space Needle, probably the most universally recognizable structure on the west coast.

As he leafed through the San Francisco Chronicle, he sipped his coffee and then was probing his tongue over a small speck of sausage which had lodged between a pair of molars when a knock came from the door. It was a soft, tentative knock. He folded the newspaper, dropped it on the room service table, and walked to the door while dislodging the errant bit of sausage with a fingernail. He loathed the thought of swallowing food he picked from his teeth, so once it was free, he spit it out onto the floor. It wasn't something he'd do at home, but people do all sorts of things in hotel rooms they wouldn't do at home, he thought.

At the door, he playfully asked who it was.

"Gregory," came the response. "It's me, Jennifer."

He opened the door. She stood there, waited. He invited her in. She walked past him into the room. He was in his pajamas, slippers and a robe, not an uncomfortable manner of dress given their relationship. She was wearing a lightweight dress and the ugliest pair of Birkenstocks Gregory had ever seen. Of course, he thought as he followed her into the room, that's assuming there are variations in the ugliness scale of that particular brand.

Gregory invited her to have a seat on the couch. He returned the chair by the room service table.

"Have you had breakfast yet?" he asked. "We can order you something if you haven't."

"Yes, I went down to the coffee shop this morning." She was smiling broadly. "I was so excited after our meeting with Mr. McCormick, I couldn't get much sleep last night; so finally, I just gave up and went out early to get something to eat."

"You should be excited," he said. "It's a very big deal to have your first dedicated exhibition."

"I don't think I could have done it without your help," she said. "People have told me for years that my work was good, but I never came close to interesting a gallery in doing an exhibition of my work before you came along."

"Your art speaks for itself. You've earned every bit of the acclaim and success you're going to receive." He pointed to the paper. "Have you seen the Chronicle this morning?"

"No," she said.

"Take a look." He smiled at her. Watched her move to grab the newspaper. "I think you'll like what you see in the Entertainment Section."

Jennifer squealed when she saw the full-color, two-page advertisement in the newspaper. She looked at Gregory with a mix of puzzlement and excitement.

"But how? We just met with Mr. McCormick last evening. How could they get this into this morning's paper?"

"Never underestimate your sponsor, my dear. I had great faith things would work out last night so I ordered the ad a week ago, with Mr. McCormick's permission, of course. It's going to run in various forms for the next two weeks."

Her eyes filled with tears. She looked at the ad, held it up. Her pride was overflowing, then a look of sad realization took hold.

"I just wish my mom and dad could have shared this," Jennifer said. "I mean, I know they were my adoptive parents, but they were the only mom and dad I ever knew."

"I'm sure they know," he said as he headed for the bathroom. "I'm going to take a shower and get ready for the day. I think you deserve a day of shopping. My treat. I'll meet you down in the lobby in, say, half an hour?"

She nodded to him. That thought made it a bit better.

Jennifer didn't know what to say as she watched the bathroom door close behind him. How could this be happening to her? It's as though Gregory Thomason was her Fairy Godfather. She grabbed the newspaper and headed back to her room, pinching herself on the arm to make sure she wasn't dreaming as she nearly floated down the hall.

The electronic security system of the Montreal public transportation system, of which the airport was a part, consisted of a complex matrix consisting of thousands of still and video cameras linked to an array of digital, and a dwindling number of older, analog storage devices. After a series of upgrades, there was hardly a nook or a cranny of the public transportation system which was not electronically surveilled. The captured data was date and time stamped along with the location and identification number of the camera. Because of the huge amount of storage required each day, the data was maintained for thirty days before being overwritten.

Marcy and Kevin sat at a table in a small conference room in the airport security office. On the wall was a large flat-screen monitor on which Kevin was displaying various recordings of security files from last Friday evening going into early Saturday morning. The room was darkened to maximize the clarity of the video.

Kevin had already confirmed with an airport contact at the airline that Janet Hopkins had indeed completed the flight itinerary from Maui to Montreal as originally ticketed. Her final flight arrived on-time and parked at Gate 4 shortly before midnight. That information certainly helped Kevin cull through the mountains of captured and stored security video. Had he not been able to confirm her travels, spotting one person out of the tens of thousands which passed through the airport on a daily basis would be like finding the proverbial needle in a haystack.

Currently, the pair was watching video captured of the gate area where the aircraft had parked. Kevin started the playback at the time of arrival. Through the windows of the terminal, they could see the nose of the Airbus A320 appear and stop. The several minutes of time before the deplaning commenced would pass slowly in real time playback, so Kevin pushed the fast forward button on the remote control. As the door was opened to the jetway, Kevin resumed normal play and Marcy leaned forward in her chair.

People passed out of the jetway, were held full faced in this particular camera point of view momentarily and then disappeared off camera. Marcy anticipated the First Class cabin would come out first. From the boarding pass she found in the apartment garbage can, she knew Janet had been assigned seat 23A near the rear of the airplane and would most likely be one of the last to deplane, yet she studied the face of every passenger.

Kevin told her that once they spotted Janet, they should be able to move camera by camera as long as she stayed in or near the airport proper or the STM, the public transportation system. Because the system was designed to monitor as large an area as possible from each camera location, most cameras in the system were ceiling mounted and fixed. While some cameras in the system were controllable in real time by operators, there were way too many of the electronic eyes for humans to effectively monitor and that's why the majority of the system relied on fixed views and archived data so that people could to go back and find video of any reported events, so long as they were reported within the thirty days before the data was overwritten.

People exited the jetway in small groups. The video from above caught a short glimpse of each of the faces just beyond the doorway. As they walked out of frame, the tops of their heads was the last image captured. The flow of people would ebb and then pick up again and then Marcy's heart sank as the crew exited the jetway and the gate agent closed the door.

"That's it?" she asked Kevin. "I never saw her. Are you sure this is the right gate? The right flight?" She couldn't believe it. She never saw Janet get off the plane.

"Let's look at it again," Kevin said as he pushed another button on the remote which jumped them back to the time the first person walked through the jetway door. Seeing Marcy's obvious anxiety, he said, "Don't worry, we'll find her."

While he couldn't change the point of view of the camera, he could manipulate the data a bit by zooming in or out, stopping at a particular frame or moving frame by frame through the data. This particular camera was programmed to capture the activity in what most people would consider normal video at about thirty frames per second, meaning that every second of data consisted of thirty separate still images. He knew, but the public didn't, that depending on the location of the camera and the criticality of the need for monitoring, system frame rates varied from one per second to one-hundred-twenty per second.

Unlike the first running at normal speed, this time through Kevin focused more on each group coming through the door. He would slow things down, zoom in on any women who were of the approximate shape or build of Janet Hopkins. This time, about a two-thirds of the way through, Marcy grabbed his hand and said stop.

She pointed at the woman in the floppy brimmed hat and asked him to zoom in on her. Kevin manipulated the remote to slowly loop through the images from the instant the woman appeared until she disappeared. She was blonde. Her hair was about the length of Janet's. The hat was one of those cheap, off-white, tightly knitted, floppy hats people often picked up in tropical climes to keep the sun off their face and from this particular vantage point, it completely prevented a clear view of her face. The woman's hands were in her pants pockets and she wore running shoes, so Marcy could not see either to help identify Janet. Marcy pushed herself out of her chair and moved closer to the monitor. Kevin zoomed in as much as he could before the image began to pixelate. He backed her up a frame at a time, zoomed in on different parts of her body.

"That's Janet," Marcy said. "I'm sure of it. While I've never seen the hat, the rest of the clothes I recognize."

"Well, that hat is going to make her easy to track as she moves along," Kevin said. Then he added, "Are you certain?"

"As certain as I can be," she said. "Can we see the next camera, I'd like to be able to see more of her face."

Kevin pulled out a tablet with a touch screen and tapped a few command icons. A crosshair appeared on the big screen and Marcy could see the same image repeated on the tablet. Using a fine-point stylus he pulled from a storage spot on the device, he encircled the floppy hat.

"This hat is distinctive," he explained. "The computer will make some searches and move us from camera to camera based on the shape of the hat and the timestamp of the previous contiguous camera location. We may have to fine tune it a bit as we go along, but this automatic function works slick. Most times we'll use a face for tracking, but it also works with unique shapes or patterns on clothing."

He tapped a few more times on the tablet. On the screen, the frozen image changed slightly and a row of smaller icons appeared on the bottom. Marcy could see these smaller icons were images in miniature of a woman in a floppy brimmed hat.

"What the system is doing is finding the first-in-time frame of captured video after the timestamp of the image we selected as identifying Janet. It's placing each camera location in sequence. Should it lose tracking, or if the system detects a gap in sequential coverage which has camera locations in the geographic area between the two confirmed track points, we'll get an icon with a red question mark in sequence. That allows us humans to interface with the system and make some decisions the computer feels uncomfortable making."

Marcy could tell this was hugely exiting to Kevin. He was grinning from ear to ear as he explained it to her. Boys and their toys, she thought to herself.

"That is amazing," she said. "Remind me never to pick my nose in public any more."

Kevin looked at her and then saw she was kidding and they both laughed.

"I could tell you some stories," he said. "You should come to our next Christmas party when we do our own little blooper reel."

He saw her face fall at the thought of Christmas and put it into context with the invitation offered in the singular.

"I mean, you and Janet, of course," he said.

Marcy touched his hand. It felt small and fragile in her grip. She smiled and nodded. No words were needed to tell him it was okay and that he should just keep working. They both looked up to the screen.

The addition of smaller icons stopped at ten and then a cursor appeared to the right of the last of the ten. Marcy looked at Kevin.

"Don't worry, the system defaults at ten possible cameras to not overtax the computers. We can add up to one hundred locations in a single event track, but we need to confirm each computer find as correct before it will add another in sequence."

He tapped the first miniature and it expanded and replaced the first camera shot on the main part of the screen. The confirmed first camera shot took a spot as a mini-icon on the upper left of the monitor. He played the second set captured images, this one from the concourse behind Janet. This segment offered about seven-seconds of the woman in the hat. About all the pair got from that segment was a confirmation of the hair color and style.

"That sure looks like Janet," Marcy said. "Next?"

Video captured her picking up her suitcases at baggage claim. Marcy asked Kevin to zoom in on the ring finger of her right hand. She identified the jewelry as something the two of them shared and showed Kevin hers.

"It certainly looks identical," he said. "Where did you get them?"

"Cancun, last Christmas." Tears misted Marcy's eyes, and before she could wipe them away, one tumbled down a cheek. "It was a sign of our commitment."

Kevin touched her shoulder.

"No need to explain," he said.

They went through segments which tracked Janet into the bathroom in the baggage claim area. Marcy was surprised there was coverage in the main area of the women's room which captured Janet entering a stall and then exiting a few minutes later.

"Janet hates using airplane toilets," Marcy observed with a chuckle. "The bathroom is always her first stop after the plane lands and her last stop before boarding."

So far none of the cameras captured more than a glimpse of a portion of her face and right hand. Kevin zoomed and sharpened each frame as much as possible and Marcy moved around the room trying to get the best view, but they had not one frame of Janet's full face.

"That frigging hat sure is a pain in the ass," Marcy said with an edge of frustration.

"Well, if she goes into the Metro, we'll have a better chance," Kevin tried to reassure her. "Lower camera angles." He tapped a few times on the touch screen. "Let's just get as far as we can and then take each of the segments through frame by frame. Not only will it help us to see if we get a complete face shot of Janet, but we'll be able to see if there's anyone who's paying an inordinate amount of attention to her."

"Do you think someone could have snatched her and we could see it?" she asked.

"Well, let's put it this way, we're the only people to see this footage since it was recorded four days ago. It's captured and stored, and unless someone is monitoring in real time or we get a call to go over some particular camera footage, nobody ever sees this stuff but the computers."

Marcy's anticipation in seeing something happen and anger at the thought of someone snatching Janet each increased. Her heartburn smacked her in the chest like being pierced by a hot poker. Then, the cameras caught Janet walking through the lobby and the next in sequence was at the cab stand.

"Aw, crap," Kevin said. "It looks like she took a cab."

The pair watched Janet hail and get into a cab. The driver put her luggage into the trunk and drove off into the night.

"That's it?" Marcy asked. "We lose her?"

Kevin sat thinking for a moment before responding.

"Some cabs have cameras. Plus, I think I can pick up a traffic camera at the intersection down from her apartment building." He mentally calculated the travel time at that hour of the night. "What do you think, Marcy? That time of night, a cab from the airport to Janet's doorstep. About twenty-five minutes?"

Marcy thought for a moment before replying.

"Sounds about right, maybe a little more."

Kevin tapped a few times on the tablet and the screen on the wall went black.

"Hey," Marcy exclaimed. "The video's gone."

"Don't worry, honey," Kevin salved her as he continued to tap away. "I sent the sequences to burn on a DVD in my office. We haven't lost anything."

"So what are you doing?"

"As I said, I think I can access the traffic cameras in the area of Janet's apartment building at about the time we think she arrived home that night." He made a few final taps and then waited.

A few moments went by and then the screen segmented into four equal parts, each one showing a different view of the front of Janet's apartment building. It was dark, and Marcy noted the time was about twenty minutes after the cab had pulled away from the terminal.

"Since we know we're watching for a cab, let's speed this up a bit and watch for it," Kevin said. He tapped a few times more and the screen shots played at about four times normal speed. People came and went, cars passed by, traffic lights changed.

Then, at about thirty minutes after the cab left the airport, it appeared coming around the corner and pulling to a stop in front of Janet's building. They watched as Janet exited the cab, paid the driver, grabbed her bags and went inside. Then they played it again focusing on each frame from each of the three cameras which caught images of the cab and the woman. The fourth had no images of Janet. They had no more luck at getting a clear shot of her face with this video as they had in the airport, but neither did they see anyone accost her or pay inordinate attention to her before she entered the building.

"Well, we can say she got home all right," Kevin said. "That's something."

"Can we get an identification off the cab?"

"Of course, I've already made a note of it. You know it's odd, we got more full face shots of the cab driver than we did of Janet. It's almost like she was keeping her face hidden on purpose."

"She did, didn't she? You noticed that too?" Marcy looked at him with questions written on her face. "Why would she do that on purpose?"

On a pure hunch, Kevin ran the footage forward about an hour at ten times speed. For the next six minutes he and Marcy watched intently for any movement at the apartment entrance. Nothing. Then, just as he was about to stop the playback, there was a shadow inside the glass door and a moment later it opened and a brunette woman stepped out onto the stoop, looked both ways, then descended the steps to the sidewalk. She turned left, walked to the corner and turned left again. She carried a small duffel bag and a purse over her shoulder.

"Zoom onto her face," Marcy said.

Kevin complied and then put the woman's face on full screen. He watched Marcy look at the woman hard, but her face showed no recognition.

"Do you know her?" he asked. "Have you seen her around the apartment?"

Marcy's eyes remained locked on the image and she shook her head slowly. Kevin tapped some commands and the screen went black again.

"I'd think your next stop is the cab company," he said. "Let's go get your DVDs and the cab information in my office."

They left the conference room. As they walked down the hall and he observed Marcy's slumped posture, Kevin thought about the pain she was feeling and how so many people refused to believe there was more emotion than biology to their lifestyle. When he thought about how the world viewed them he got angry. Both right and left were wrong, he thought.

The right thought being gay was a choice and that one could cure a person of the affliction, while the left wanted every gay person to be an example of something they didn't understand. In his experience, most people within their community just wanted what every human being wanted, the freedom to live their own life.

He gently put his hand on Marcy's back. He could see the tears had returned.

Chapter Ten

I was late. I pulled into the parking lot and wheeled the Jeep into a spot at the Maui police headquarters building off Kamehameha Avenue between Wailuku and Kahului. I had stopped at the county building in Wailuku thinking that was the location of the MPD administrative offices and was redirected down the road by a lovely Hawaiian woman named Angel. Making the error cost me about fifteen minutes and I jogged into the reception area of the building and told the uniformed female officer at the front desk that I was late for my appointment with the Deputy Chief.

Nervously pacing in the lobby area, I remembered that I had forgotten the binder which held my paperwork for the firearms permitting. I was just about to tell the desk officer that I'd be right back when a door opened and out walked the uniformed Deputy Chief. He wore three stars on the epaulets of his impeccably pressed black uniform, appeared to be of Japanese descent, stood about five foot six, had short salt and pepper hair and a quick and gregarious smile. His dark brown eyes gave me the quick once over. Cop's eyes. A cop's cop, I thought, not a political puke. Good.

"Mr. Langdon?" he said. He extended a hand. "I see you've discovered Maui time."

I reached to shake his hand and began to fumble with an apology for my tardiness. He waved the apology away with his left hand away while giving my hand a firm grip with his right.

"No worries," he added with a smile. "We all fall prey to it. Heck, if the surf is up, I sometimes have trouble filling all my squad cars for a few hours."

"I want to thank you for seeing me, Chief," I said. "Should I call you Chief?"

"Whatever you're comfortable with, Mr. Langdon," he said, releasing my hand. "Even though your office didn't tell me in their transmittal, I understand from my own inquiries that you're retired Chicago PD, so if you're more comfortable with the formal, that's fine. Otherwise, if you want to fit in on the island, call me Tom."

A cop's cop all right.

"And you please call me William, or any version of it you're most comfortable with. Since I've been off the force for years and don't miss the formality of brass, Tom it is. I apologize for the oversight in providing my full history. You know how it is, sometimes it's better to talk between cops face-to-face."

He nodded and waved it away.

"Care to come into my office, Will?" he asked.

I made motion to the parking lot.

"I left my paperwork in the car," I replied. "I can get them in a..."

"Don't worry about it. I've got everything I need in the office. Your assistant is quite efficient. She called to confirm this morning."

"Sandy is my partner," I said. "And, yes, she is very efficient."

"Oh, I'm sorry, I just assumed."

This time it was my chance to wave it off.

"No worries," I mimicked with a smile.

He motioned me through the door with him. As we passed the inside desk area, I was handed a Visitor badge and I clipped it on my jacket.

"How do you like the new Jeep," he asked. "I've got the last body style, but I understand the new ones ride almost as well as a Cadillac Escalade."

"Someone told me it was a small island," I said, wondering how he knew these details. "I guess they were right."

He flashed me a knowing smile. We walked into his office and he offered me a seat in front of his desk. We both sat.

"It is indeed a small island, Will. Can I offer you something? Water, coffee?"

"No, thank you. I just came from breakfast and I'm good."

He flipped open a file, but something told me he already had every detail in memory.

"I don't know what kind of case you're working, Will. I don't want to know so long as you tell me that it has nothing to do with any active police investigation."

He looked up from the file.

I shook my head.

He looked back to the file.

"You realize this isn't Chicago, not even New Orleans. This is Maui. I doubt sincerely you're going to need a gun here, and certainly not two, but you're a professional, an ex-cop, trained and licensed to carry and you know best what you need."

He looked up from the file again.

This time I nodded.

He looked me in the eye. He was sizing me up, trusting his experience, his training, and his gut rather than anything that was written in the file.

"I'm going to approve your carry permit for Maui County," he said as he scribbled his signature in the file. "You realize it's no good if you venture outside of our jurisdiction which includes this island, Lanai and Molokai. If you need to travel to Kauai, the Big Island, or Oahu, just check with me first and I'll help smooth the path. I'm not guaranteeing anything, mind you, each department has its own protocols. Ironically, you'll probably find Kauai tougher to get permission than Oahu."

He slid his card across the desktop and I took it.

"You can call me anytime, Will." He stood and our meeting was over.

"Thank you, Tom." I got up as well, tucked his card into my wallet, and followed him out of his office.

"Any questions?" he asked as we made our way back out to the lobby.

"Not at this time," I said.

"How long will you be with us?"

"As lovely as your little piece of paradise is, Tom, I'm not planning on an extended stay to get this thing done."

I handed back my Visitor badge and we prepared to part ways in the lobby. He shook my hand again and offered good luck and some final words of wisdom.

"Just remember this is a small island community, Will. It's a closed community which welcomes outsiders while at the same time holding them at a distance. Don't expect to be treated like a local. People will be friendly, but suspicious until they get to know you."

"I'll remember that, Tom. Thanks again for your help."

I walked out to the Jeep. The summer sun was hot, but the weather was pleasant with a breeze and temperature in the mid-eighties. Unlike New Orleans in July when you could wring water directly from the air, the humidity level here seemed to be about sixty-percent and very comfortable. No wonder they called this paradise.

I tossed my jacket into the back seat and reconsidered my wardrobe. Perhaps I did need to try to fit in a bit if I was going to go around asking questions. Before getting in, I decided rather than strap on Willie and Sam in the parking lot of police headquarters, it would be better to do that back at the condo. As I drove to Wailea, I dialed Sandy.

Sandy had been waiting for his call and made some quick notes of the names and locations being relayed by William on the phone. When she looked at the sparse information, she let out a sigh.

"Any timeframe, or just sometime during the last fifty years?" she asked in a sarcastic tone.

"Not at this time. I asked Cassie to check for more details and she said she would. It would be great if she would agree to turn over the diaries, but she seems quite concerned about doing that at this point."

William looked over and changed lanes to get out of the way of a jacked up pick up truck with huge off-road tires which was coming up fast. As the truck passed, he saw a bumper sticker that proclaimed the owner as being 'Maui Built' and out the window the passenger threw him a hand gesture.

"I think some guy just flipped me off for moving out of the lane so they could pass. What an asshole."

Sandy let out a laugh.

"I hope you didn't flip him off," she said.

"No, his friend was going too fast. They were gone before it hit me." There was a pause, then, "Okay, what's the joke?"

"Otto, did the gesture include an extended thumb?"

"Ah, yeah."

"The other finger wasn't his F U finger, it was his pinky. He was tossing you a shaka. It's an island greeting meaning 'hang loose', but it's also used as a 'thanks, brah'. I wrote you a note about it in the briefing book."

"I guess I didn't get that far," William said.

Sandy heard his embarrassment come through the phone.

"I have a feeling I'm going to miss the United States," he said.

"Ah, Otto, Hawaii *is* a state." She laughed again. "If you can keep from starting an international incident, why don't we finish this up so I can get some work done tonight."

Sandy looked at her notes, repeated the names and spelling:

Jessi Bollenbeck	Augusta, GA
Michelle Wirtz	Orlando, FL
Tammy Boeldt	Cheyenne, WY
Randi Janzen	Des Moines, IA
Janet Hopkins	?
Jennifer Shea	?

"Our boy certainly spreads it around," she said.

"I'm not sure what's going on," he told her, balancing his duty to Sandy with his promise he made Cassie.

What Sandy heard in his voice more than in his words was a bit of frustration wrapped in uncertainty.

"What does that mean?" She sensed there was something he wanted to tell her, but she also knew him well enough to know when to push and when not to. She thought a simple question was all that was needed at this point, but she made a mental note regarding his comment.

"Nothing," he said. "I'm just getting a lay of the land here." In the back of his brain, there began a little red flash so small it was currently easy for him to ignore. "I'm home," he said. "I'll talk to you later. Let me know if you come up with anything."

"Gotcha," she said. "Be careful."

They hung up. She slid the phone across the desk. Sandy sat back in her chair. While she was finishing up with William she had done a quick search for Janet Hopkins on a popular social networking site and had come up with over two-hundred-fifty names.

"This could be interesting," she said to herself.

My next call went to Cassie's cell phone. She picked up on the first ring.

"Aloha, Willy," she said. "How did things go at the MPD?"

"Just peachy," I told her.

"So, now you're armed and dangerous?"

"I'll never tell," I said. I never did. The only people who ever knew for certain if I was carrying were my partners.

She floated the question with what I perceived to be a bit of flirtation mixed with a large dose of curiosity. I wondered to myself, of all of them she had been showing me, which was the real face of Cassie? Was she the flirtatious girl? Was she the cool business woman? Was she the injured and abused wife? It seemed almost every interaction with her revealed a bit of a new personality or affectation, and she could obviously morph from one persona to the next with such seamlessness that I decided to start a mental diary of my own.

"Where are you now?"

"I'm leaving my masseuse in Haiku," she said. "Why?"

"Because I want to see you. I've got more questions and I would like to take a look at some of your other documents." Sure, I could do it over the phone, but after catching her in her first definite lie, I wanted to see Cassie's eyes when I asked my questions.

She paused, enough to make me wonder what excuse she'd use.

"Um, can it wait until tomorrow?" she asked. "I've already planned to get home this afternoon. I'm stopping by the airport and having the chopper take me back to the house. I'd like to do some snooping around for more information for you, and Gregory won't be back until tomorrow evening."

"I've passed the names and information on to Sandy," I said. "She's probably neck deep in researching these people by now."

A tick passed. Then a tock.

"Sandy?" she asked.

I could hear in her voice no more flirtation, but rather an irritation. Man, this woman could change moods quicker than anyone I knew.

"Um, I thought we had agreed you wouldn't share things with her."

"No," I said. "If you recall, I told you that I would hold back my findings, but I also told you that I would share information for research purposes."

Another tick. Another tock.

"Whatever, Willy," she said. "I don't want to argue with you. Why don't you come to the house tomorrow? Drop by late-morning, we'll have lunch, and I'll share whatever I turn up. Promise."

"Sandy included a map with driving directions from Google, so I'm thinking the drive will take me about two hours since I have to loop back to Kahului before heading south."

I was now sitting in the condo, trying to figure a way to strap Sam to my ankle while wearing shorts.

"Sandy, eh? Isn't there anything she doesn't do for you?"

"She's my right hand, Cassie."

"Yeah, I know, symbiosis. See you tomorrow."

The phone went dead in my ear. I looked at the screen and confirmed that she was indeed gone, flipped the phone closed and tossed it onto the couch next to a loaded Willie.

A knock came at the door. I tossed both Willie and Sam along with the boxes of ammunition and the two clips I had filled for Willie into a coffee table and closed the lid.

I walked over by the window to see if there were any strange cars in the parking lot. A red Honda convertible was parked at the end of the row, not in a spot but pulled in where I had seen 'Car Wash Only' stenciled on the asphalt.

"Who is it?" I asked.

"It's the owner of 102. You're parked in my spot."

I opened the door and found a slightly irritated, balding man about two inches shorter than me but about twenty pounds heavier. He wore shorts, a sleeveless T-shirt, and the ugliest pair of shoes I'd ever seen. In fact, they weren't even shoes, more like something Bullwinkle would wear: brown, bulbous toed scuffs with no heel. When he saw me, his irritation lessened. Except when a college tournament is in town, I'm always the tallest guy in the elevator back home. I imagine from his demeanor before I opened the door that this guy, whose parking spot I obviously have violated, is used to the same experience.

"I don't want to be a prick," he said. "It's just that our parking spots are marked here."

I didn't want to be a prick either.   I looked over and saw a woman getting some things out of the trunk.

"I'm really sorry," I said. "I was on the phone when I came back and must have just made a mistake."

The woman approached us; the stairs to their unit were adjacent to my door.   She was about five-eight with shoulder length, light brown hair and was carrying a couple of Wal-Mart bags. When she stopped and raised her sunglasses, I saw she had gorgeous deep blue eyes.

"Hi," she said. "We live up stairs."

"Hi," I said. "I kind of assumed so. I'm really sorry for parking in the wrong spot."

"No worries," she said.   She nodded toward her husband. "Sometimes the big guy gets a little overly protective. I usually park in that spot and I come home from work after nine at night many times and Steve doesn't like it if I have to park farther from the door."

"Well," I said. "I don't blame him one bit for being protective. I'm the same way."

The man was shifting from one foot to the other, obviously uncomfortable. I stuck out my hand.

"William," I said.

He shook my hand firmly.

"Steve," he replied. "But Shelly already told you that."

I put out my hand to Shelly.

"I guess that makes you Shelly," I said. "You two live here?"

"Yep, forty years of Wisconsin winters was enough for me," Steve said.

"You're from Wisconsin?" I said. "I was born and raised there. I live in New Orleans now, and I'll second you on that midwest winters stuff."

"New Orleans?" Shelly repeated.   "We love New Orleans!   I think it's Steve's favorite place on the mainland."

"Is that right?" I asked. "It's a great city, but I came to live there in a very around about way, through Chicago and then the Cayman Islands."

"We just made a beeline from Chippewa Falls to here," Steve said.   "Bought this place, sold everything, got a ride to the airport and here we are. Eight years now."

"Are you here on vacation with the family?" Shelly asked. "I thought we saw your wife on the lanai last evening."

"No, I'm here on business. I'm alone."

The next question would undoubtedly be 'What business are you in?' so I reached into my pocket, pulled out the rental car keys and made a move to come outside and move the Jeep.

"Well, let me move that Jeep out of your way," I said.

Shelly started up the stairs.

"Nice to meet you, William," she called.

Steve and I walked over the parking spots and swapped them out. As we walked back, I again apologized for making the mistake and again I was told 'no worries'.

"Hey, why don't you come up around six for a beer?" Steve asked. "We can trade some stories about Wisconsin winters and New Orleans food."

I looked at my cell phone. It was about two thirty. Since I had nothing on the agenda for the evening beyond perhaps a pizza and some online research and television, I accepted.

"Sounds good," I said. "You like Corona?"

"We do."

"I'll run out and get some."

"That'll be great. I've got some fresh Maui limes in the fridge," he said as he started up the steps. "See you around six."

Gregory made two calls. The first was to Captain Dan with instructions to have the jet ready to go back to Maui at noon on Wednesday. The second was to the owner of the company installing the surveillance equipment in the Molokai house to make certain they would be done and gone long before Jennifer returned.

Satisfied with the results of both calls, he returned to running on the treadmill in the hotel's work out room. Next would be weights, finishing with a little pounding away at the light bag. A good sweat was what he was craving now.

He smiled as he ran. Going out for a day of shopping with Jennifer had been an invigorating experience. He was finding that just being around her thrilled him on so many levels. She possessed so much of her mother, her real mother, not the Shea's with whom she had no genetic connection.

Gregory had some knowledge of her adoptive parents, Bruce and Elisa Shea of College Station, Texas, but beyond the fact they both perished in a house fire last year, he had little further interest in who or what they were. The fire had been a minor expense paid to an illegal whose current address was a shallow hole in the west Texas desert. That second little job had cost a little more.

"Eh, it's only money," he said to nobody.

Upstairs in her room, Jennifer sat curled up in a chair. She was mesmerized by the sight out her window of the Golden Gate Bridge's deep red iron oxide frame melding with today's sunset of deep reds and oranges. It was times like these that she really missed her mom and dad. They both had sacrificed so much for her to chase her dreams, and now that they were coming true, the ache of them not being able to see it, to share it with her, was almost unbearable. A tear ran down her cheek, hooked the corner of her mouth. She tasted the saltiness, felt the pain deep inside her chest. Suffering the pain was how she endured it; and she never denied it when it came. For Jennifer, feeling the hole in her soul meant she was fully alive, and being fully alive was the greatest testament she could give to the memory of her mom and dad.

Then she thought of her biological parents and felt a pang of guilt run through her even though she knew her mom and dad would never feel threatened or lessened by her consideration of her bio-parents. Her mom had sat her down when she was twelve and they had a long conversation about her being adopted. She had reminded Jennifer how her coming to them had been their choice and a gift from God. Her mom had said over and over how very much they loved her and wanted her. She had also told Jennifer that they would never stand in the way, and would render every assistance should she wish to locate and reach out to her bio-parents. Until recently, however, the idea of finding them had never been more than a fleeting thought.

During her teen years, Jennifer had suffered the pangs and anxieties of any maturing human female. Through every issue, mom and dad were there for her. Upon reaching adulthood, she realized her mom had executed one of the most difficult adoptive parent and child talks leaving Jennifer informed, comforted, and feeling nothing but safe. She also came to understand that while she was a genetic product of two strangers to her, the person she had become had been the result of the years of love and care from mom and dad, Bruce and Elisa Shea.

Her boundaries of thought on this subject were always framed by her mutually exclusive concepts of mom and dad and the bio-parents. Naturally, there was a curiosity about her bio-mom and bio-dad. She wondered who her bio-mom was, where she was now. Was she still alive? What circumstances had caused her to give Jennifer up for adoption? Had the bio-mom considered the polar alternatives of keeping the child or of terminating the pregnancy before deciding on adoption?

Then there were the genetic traits and talents. Did Jennifer look like her bio-mom or bio-dad? Whose eyes did she share? What had their heritage been? Did she get her artistic talents from her bio-mom or bio-dad? Was it a gift directly from God? Who was her bio-dad? Was he in love with her bio-mom when they had created her? Did something happen to cause a change in their life plan? Did he even know about her existence? The questions could make you crazy, she thought.

The lights had come on on the bridge, their original placement and design obviously more for artistic display than for safety or function. The entirety of the architecture was the epitome of art deco design on the west coast, while the engineering had proven itself almost miraculous over time. The Golden Gate Bridge stood as the ultimate testament to the successful blending of form and function.

The sun had slipped silently below the horizon, leaving behind the memory of the light and heralding the promise of the dark. She looked around the room at the remains of her day. Clothes, art supplies of every imaginable type, shoes, and even the basics of life not so readily available on Molokai were all piled in the corner, waiting the carts which would haul them to the limousine and then to the jet tomorrow morning. Gregory had been so very generous with her today, like he had been with everything since taking her under his wing.

When he had first walked into the art gallery on Michigan Avenue in Chicago at which she had been laboring to sell other people's art just under a year ago, she had just returned to work after her parents' funeral and attending to all of life's duties and responsibilities people leave behind. She was still numb, operating in a state she described to her friends and relatives as like observing the world from underwater.

Fellow artists told her to use the pain, and express herself through her art.   She had tried that methodology, but the only emotion she captured on the canvas was pain wrapped in emptiness, and nobody wanted to hang that on their walls. So she had stopped painting altogether. Her life was in limbo. She found no excitement in selling the works of others and was having little success in persuading her boss to allow her more than a sliver of wall space on which to display some of her earlier paintings. 'If I do it for you, honey, I'll have to do it for everybody,' he had told her.

She was still young, just nearing her twenty-eighth birthday at the time, and she understood that many artists don't catch on with the public until later in life, but that didn't make the waiting any easier. Jennifer had always been impatient while waiting for life to catch up with her aspirations and dreams. She never lacked for attention and adulation amongst family and friends, but Jennifer Shea wanted the world to know her name. It seemed to her that for her whole life she had wanted to leave a mark which would last forever.

So just before Gregory had walked into her life, she had been slowly drowning, watching the world from underwater, unable to breathe sometimes when the pain became nearly unbearable, and she was beginning to see no hope, no future.

To Jennifer's perspective almost a year ago, the only life she saw was in a past now turned to ashes.   Her friends told her it was normal grieving, assured her that she'd get over it in time.   They would be there for her, they had said, yet she quickly realized they had their own lives into which she hated to intrude, so in the middle of the night when the pain was the worst, she wrestled the demons alone.

Then, one Friday evening last August - it was the third day of the month, and what would have been her father's fifty-third birthday - Gregory had entered her world.   Her new life had begun with a simple, serendipitous meeting.

She was behind the counter in the front section of the gallery, occupying herself with the repeated rearranging of the bottles of cheap wine and equally cheap glasses. She was simply trying to get through the rest of yet another very painful day since losing her mom and dad. The nameless red and white varieties were offered with numbing sameness to lookie loos and patrons alike. Of course, the gallery did stock some chilled Cristal and cut crystal flutes for the real big spenders or repeat clients, but the scuttlebutt from her coworkers was none of them had been around for weeks.

She first saw him out on Michigan Avenue through the deeply tinted glass doors of the entryway as he exited the rear of an unremarkable black Lincoln Town Car. One of the interesting peripheral tidbits she had learned while dealing with people who spent tens of thousands of dollars or more to hang a colorful piece of canvas on their walls is that those who have smaller means but a huge need to impress pull up in sixty-foot Hummers with a spa on the roof, while those who have no such lacking self-image issues don't.

She had once met a multibillionaire who was hosting the opening of a small gallery in one of his resorts. People came dressed for the occasion in competitive cocktail party attire as they all tried to outdo one another, and yet along the back wall there stood the owner in jeans and a well aged flannel shirt with the tails hanging out. Gregory had been like that.

Upon entering the gallery, he had walked directly to her like a man on a mission. Often that demeanor meant the client had been in there before, knew what they wanted and already had a contact person. Were that salesperson working that day, she'd lose any opportunity at a commission, were they not, she might get half. Not that she really cared on this particular evening, but that was the behavior he displayed.

Gregory Thomason is far from a remarkable or notable physical presence. He's not very tall - in her heels that evening Jennifer had been several inches taller - wore his thinning reddish-blond hair short, walked with a slight limp, yet had the most incredibly piercing eyes she had ever seen. They were the color of grey slate with flecks of blue and as he approached her she could feel them look right into her soul.

Jennifer had always been fascinated by people's eyes. After all, they are the windows to the soul, as someone had once said, and as an artist she enjoyed seeing how correct she could be in predicting what type of person someone was just by the color of their eyes.

Gregory's eyes possessed a fluidity which she equated with water, and their subtle gray color with deep blue flecks warned her immediately this man was as changeable as the weather and endowed with a deep mysticism and wisdom.   She understood instinctively that just as water nurtured life itself, it can also engulf, suffocate, even kill. The axiom that still waters run deep played in her mind and reminded her that the most dangerous waters often appeared placid while being capable of wielding an unstoppable power.   When he looked at her, she had felt drawn, yet a primal warning had also stirred deep within her.

Then he had spoken her name, softly and with an intimacy which stirred her on an unconsciousness level, as if someone was gently rousing her from a dream. He had reached out with his hand, and from the depths of her sunken heart, she subconsciously understood he was there to pull her back to the world of the living.

Yet, in reality his offer of pulling her back to the living world was more akin to a ripping, a tearing away from everything she had known, to be replaced seemingly overnight by everything she had ever dreamed.

So she had surrendered herself to his whirlwind of change. Whether the reasons for her releasing suspicions and fears to the winds like so much chaff in her life had to do with the loss of her mom and dad or merely the unlimited horizons offered by Gregory or a combination of the two, she didn't care.   Stepping from one stone in life to the next in order had provided her security over her twenty-eight years, but sudden death and the serendipity of a new encounter had taught her the undeniable lesson that life is fleeting and its future is neither predestined nor guaranteed.   Indeed, meeting Gregory had offered her wings to soar above the stepping stones, and she took to flight without hesitation.

A month after meeting Gregory, to the wide-eyed disbelief of people who knew her, and in total disregard of the words of caution from her family and friends, she had given up her small apartment, her job at the gallery, sold her car and belongings, and moved to a house Gregory had provided on the west side of the island of Molokai, in Hawaii.

Gregory had never made any inappropriate moves on her. While she did occasionally catch him looking at her with something undefinable in his eyes, she never interpreted his looks as threatening to her safety or well-being. He seemed to be exactly as he presented himself, an older mentor and benefactor who was merely interested in assisting her dreams to come true.

He had sent the jet for her on Labor Day weekend a year ago. On Monday morning, it sat waiting for her, along with the welcoming crew, at the Signature Aviation terminal at Midway Airport in Chicago. Jennifer had said her good-byes, and as devoid of caution as Alice had been when she stepped through the looking glass, Jennifer had left the world she had long known behind.

Gregory had met her at the airport when they landed in Kahului, Maui. He whisked her to the helicopter and then piloted them across the channel to Molokai. He flew her past the four-thousand-foot-high waterfalls which dot the cliffs along the north shore of the island and hovered close enough to several that the windshield filled with spray. Along the west side of the island, he flew low just offshore of what he told her was one of the longest white sand beaches in the state of Hawaii. Then, at the foot of Papohaku Beach, right where the craggy, jet-black lava claws into the azure waters of the Pacific, he pointed to the house.

It all had taken her breath away, such was the beauty of the place and the grandness of the gift it was to become. Gregory circled the grounds once and then set the helicopter down on a small paved pad inland of the house, not far from the large covered portico with stone columns and timbered and planked cathedral ceiling. He walked her along that path to the portico which heralded the main entrance to the home, and that's when he told her it was all hers, purchased by him in her name. A gift. She had been flabbergasted and laughed at the thought. She shook her head in disbelief.

The home itself was situated on a lushly landscaped and grassed terrace, to the inland side natural grasses and a forest of keawe trees protected the property from onlookers, to the ocean side, a natural lava wall upon which the ocean lashed repeatedly stood as silent sentry. A single, meandering roadway of compacted, crushed clay-colored rock connected the home with the main road and the rest of the island. The private drive met the public road on the other side of matching stone-piers upon which were mounted an ornate two-piece wrought copper gate.

Gregory had handed her a single key connected to a carved wooden fob by a finely woven gold chain and motioned her to the double koa wood doors with upper panels of glass etched with dolphins leaping from the surf. Through the windows Jennifer could see a short hallway which spilled into a larger central room in which a wall of glass revealed the shoreline and ocean beyond.

She inserted the key into the lock and twisted, then used the thumb latch to release and open the door. Gregory reminded her of the Hawaiian custom to leave ones shoes at the entryway, and she slipped out of her sandals. Her feet were greeted by the smooth coolness of polished marble. She turned to see him smiling at her. Whether reflecting the ocean in the distance, or if it was some internal mechanism, his eyes showed more blue than grey at that moment, and were smiling back at her.

She walked through the house with him following. He let her explore at her own pace, and in a route of her design. He neither led nor guided. The entry hallway spilled into a large great room which consisted of kitchen, dining and living areas. The theme of the portico spilled inside with each room finished in fieldstone walls in hues of mauve, black and gray with charcoal mortar or areas of contrasting ivory plaster. Heavy timbers and planks framed the high, open, and angled ceilings, while immaculate glass panels and doors provided spectacular, unobstructed views toward the water.

Through a set of doors and a short hallway to the right lead to the master suite. Gregory told her the suite alone was over twelve-hundred square feet. It had been his one spoken input during that first trip through the place. She had thought to herself that the suite was nearly as big as the modest home she had grown up in, and twice the size of her apartment in downtown Chicago. The master suite contained its own bathroom with whirlpool tub and walk-in shower, his and hers sinks along a wall of mirrors, a pair of huge cedar-lined, walk-in closets and the bedroom area. One wall of the bedroom consisted of a massive stone fireplace, with inset bookshelves made of a wood she didn't recognize; the bold and contrasting streaks of deep golds and light ambers fought for her attention, drew her in.

Outside the master suite in the grassed area between house and ocean was a swimming pool and sunken hot tub. A dolphin cast in bronze and streaked with various shades of aged patina spouted a steady stream of salt water which cascaded into the pool at one end.

Down the other hallway off the great room lead to an assortment of smaller guest rooms and on the end, almost as an afterthought to the other architecture, a large studio which spilled out onto a covered lanai. The studio was equipped with all manners of paints, easels, canvasses, and supplies. Mounted on false walls were many of her previous works, unsold. In one corner, stacked and almost hidden, were the dark pieces she had done since her parents died.

She and Gregory had walked out the sliding glass doors onto the lanai. She continued alone to the grass beyond. Jennifer had stood there in her bare feet and felt as if the world was spinning with her as its axis. The entirety of it all was overwhelming.

"What a marvelous place to work," she said to him.

He smiled.

"Do you really like it?" he asked.

"I adore it," she replied, the feeling of the world's spinning almost engulfing her.

"It really is yours, Jennifer" he told her. "You are the titled owner. Free and clear."

She turned to him, a look of astonishment on her face.

"What do you mean? I thought you were joking earlier. I could never accept something like this."

"Call it an investment in the future of an artist in whom I believe." He reached into the breast pocket of his jacket, pulled out a small packet of papers and handed them to her. "Besides, there's no need for you to accept anything. According to the state of Hawaii, you own it. Here's the title."

She had accepted the papers that day, uncertain what else she could do in the face of his offering. Later, she found the other documents on the property in the house's safe and checked on the state's website. It was indeed her house. She could keep it, sell it, heck, even give it away to a family of Martians if she wished, and nobody could do a thing about it.

Over the last year, almost, she had come to look upon Gregory with growing affection. Not an affection born of a physical attraction, after all, he was old enough to be her father, nor one based in intellectual commonality because the two rarely conversed on any subject beyond the realm of her art, but rather with a foundation on a deeply spiritual level. He seemed to know her heart, understand her soul.

Like the time this past spring when her mind had turned to thoughts of tulips in remembrance of her mom's approaching birthday and later that day he had arrived unannounced with dozens of her mom's favorite flowers in huge vases which decorated the entire house for the next week.

Then, before she would have to endure the sadness and dark memories as the flowers dried and lost their beauty, they had disappeared while she walked the beach one afternoon, only to be replaced by an impeccably faceted, reflective crystal in the main hall which she learned caught both the sunrises and sunsets and threw brilliant colors about the room. He had left a note: 'So your world never knows anything but joy, fondly, Gregory'.

A smile formed on her face as she revisited her memories, and as full darkness fell upon San Francisco, she drifted off to sleep.

Chapter Eleven

Dawn broke in the east first on Wednesday in Montreal. Marcy had been up most of the night going over frame by frame of the surveillance video obtained from Kevin. He and Craig had brought Chinese food by last night around seven - vegetable fried rice and Kung Pau shrimp - to make sure she was eating and to check up on her. They also brought some staples, bread, cheese, lunchmeat, orange juice, milk, and eggs.

Kevin had left her another DVD which tracked the brunette woman all the way to the airport last Saturday morning. While they had lost track of her after she boarded the 7:20 a.m. flight to Chicago on JAZZ - a regional carrier affiliated with Air Canada - he told Marcy he'd keep working on getting some cooperation from people he knew in the U.S.

In addition, Kevin had pulled some strings at the airport with JAZZ. The woman's name was shown on the flight manifest as Tamra Sommers of Burlington, Vermont. The only way they had been able to figure that out was because she was the only female of the eleven passengers.

Marcy knew Kevin had gone out on a limb for her in this and she told him how much she really appreciated his help. It had made her cry when she told him she'd keep his name out of it and he had responded, 'Heck, Marcy, if it helps get Janet back safe, post my name on a billboard'.

Marcy stood and stretched. She rubbed her eyes, then moved to the window and parted the blinds. The sun was coming up and casting long shadows in the street. She went back to the computer desk, took another look at the sheet of photos which comprised the best captured surveillance camera images of Tamra Sommers and clicked print. When it got a little later, she'd canvass the building to see who knew the woman. She glanced at the clock on the microwave which showed 5:47. Given the comings and goings she'd heard since she'd been staying with Janet, she figured 6:30 would be a good time to begin checking with the other seventeen apartments. Then, she'd go to the cab company to speak to the driver who had brought Janet home. According to the dispatcher with whom she'd spoken, the driver would be ending his shift around 9 a.m.

Marcy padded to the shower, set her coffee cup on the kitchen counter as she passed. She stripped out of the clothes she had now been wearing for nearly twenty-four hours and tossed them onto the top of the clothes hamper in the corner. The last thing to come off were her panties which landed on top of the rest. She really needed to feel the sting of the hot water, but figured she'd start with a good dose of cold just to wake herself up. Her body told her she'd need to get some sleep sometime soon. She knew she couldn't do Janet any good with just a few catnaps each night. After the cab company, she promised herself.

As the cold water cascaded over her tired body, she began to feel a little more awake. She washed her body, scrubbed her face and rinsed. She felt clean, invigorated. Then, she reached for the hot water tap and as she began to feel the heat stinging against her chilled skin, she stopped dead. Had their been an animator handy, he would have drawn an illuminated lightbulb over her head.

She hopped out of the shower, nearly fell as the rug slipped under her momentum and raced to the laundry hopper. Carefully, she removed her clothes from the top of the pile and looked inside. She could see the clothes which the surveillance cameras had caught Janet wearing. She already had found the hat on the rack next to the door. She pulled the items out one by one. Underneath were other vacation clothes and business attire for the conference, obviously the soiled items which had been in her luggage. There were none of Janet's panties in the hamper. Janet always wore panties. There were bras mixed in with the dirty clothes, but no panties.

Marcy reassembled the pile in the order which it had come out of the hamper. The vacation clothes were a jumble, not necessarily in order, just like you'd expect dirty laundry to come out of a suitcase when one returned from a trip. She then looked at the clothes Janet had worn home. Shirt at the bottom, tank top, pants on top, just like someone would undress were they standing at the hamper. No bra, no panties.

Even with her sleep-deprived brain, the conclusion was as clear as a train light bearing down on her in a tunnel. Janet had never come home. The woman who had come home had undressed from Janet's clothes, except she kept on her bra and panties as she redressed in her own clothes. That's why there were no undergarments on top of the laundry pile. She looked across the room and saw the photos of the woman known as Tamra Sommers of Burlington, Vermont on the computer screen. Marcy's lips curled into a snarl.

"All right, bitch," she said. "Just who the fuck are you? And what did you do with Janet?"

Sandy decided to work from home this morning. She had been awakened by William's call around three a.m. and couldn't get back to sleep. Apparently, he and his newfound island friends who lived upstairs from his condo had a wonderful time sharing stories about Wisconsin back in the day. She assumed they had each taken a shot every time one of them said the phrase, 'back in the day', because William had been three sheets to the wind when he had called her just before turning in around ten p.m. Maui time. She thought about returning the middle of the night favor, but even with the five hours time difference it still wasn't the middle of the night for William.

So, she grabbed her MacBook Pro off the desk, poured herself a cup of coffee in the kitchen and plopped down on the couch. She took a sip of the coffee, burned the roof of her mouth, added that to her list of reasons that today was going to be a bad one, fired up the computer and logged into the office's system. From here, she'd have access to every digital document stored on the office servers.

Sandy downloaded her research documents associated with Operation Puppy Love and synched the files so that if she made a change in one location, the other location would be updated automatically. She smiled to herself. She loved her Apple products and never had been able to understand much of the world's slavish adherence to everything Microsoft and PC. It gave her immense satisfaction every time she heard a friend had tossed a new laptop after a year or was going to spend the weekend, 'updating and upgrading my system'. What was it she had seen Jim Morrison yelling to a crowd one time? Oh yeah, 'You're all a bunch of slaves'.

She launched the Safari web browser and typed 'Jessi Bollenbeck Augusta Georgia' into a Google search line. She knew Google would try iterations of the first name which began with the Jessi, meaning they'd include Jessica or Jessie. The search return came up almost instantaneously with meaningless results which had one or two of the words scattered in the found document, but nothing with every word in proper sequence. She tried adding quotation marks around the name to force Google to only locate any documents which had the name in order, but then nothing at all came up. She then removed the city and state from the search and still nothing. According to Google, Jessi Bollenbeck didn't exist anywhere on the internet.

Sandy next checked the Bollenbeck surname in the Augusta, Georgia area. That produced some results, and Sandy made notes to follow up with these people to see if they had ever heard of a relative with the first name of Jessi.

She went through the rest of the names which had associated cities and found similar results. Then as if going from famine to feast, when she typed in the name Janet Hopkins Google found over 23,600,000 web pages which mentioned the name. Sandy ran her fingers through her hair.

"Well, let's see how my luck runs with Jennifer Shea," she said to herself as she typed in the name. She laughed to herself when Google returned only 11,900,000 results. "Getting closer," she said.

Sandy took another sip of her coffee. By this time it had cooled enough to be drinkable. She shifted positions on the couch, threw her legs up and got comfortable. She made a gesture of interlacing her fingers and then cracking them as a mocking challenge to Google and the internet.

"Time for some power snooping through some back doors," she said and her fingers started flying across the keyboard.

Jennifer awoke to a gentle knocking on her door. She flinched as her eyes opened to behold the light of the new day. A second knock was followed by someone announcing, 'Bellman, ma'am'. She had obviously slept the night away curled up in the chair. She stretched away the knots as she walked to the door, looked through the peephole and then opened up for the bellman.

"Come to collect your items so we can package them up for your flight home, ma'am," he said as he wheeled two carts into the room.

"Did Mr. Thomason arrange this?" she asked.

"Yes, ma'am," he replied. "We're to have this all ready to go to the airport by 11 a.m."

She looked at her watch. Just after 8:30.

The phone on the nightstand rang and she walked over to pick it up.

"Hello," she said.

"Good morning, Jennifer," came the response from Gregory. "How are you this fine morning?"

"I'm good, Gregory," she said with another stretch. Over her shoulder she watched the bellman collecting bags and boxes onto the carts. "The bellman woke me up. I must have slept for twelve hours curled up in a chair."

"In a chair?" he asked with a laugh. "You let that wonderful bed go to waste?"

"The last thing I remember was watching the sunset and thinking about mom and dad, wishing they could see all you've done for me, and then the knock on the door a few minutes ago. I'm not even sure I dreamed."

"I stopped by your room last evening, thought you might like to take a walk down along Fisherman's Wharf. I knocked but had no response. I know it's been a hectic and full couple of days, so I understand why you didn't respond."

"I'm so sorry," she said. "I would have loved to take in the evening air along the Wharf."

"No worries," he replied. "How about some breakfast downstairs? Let the bellman do his job, we'll fly out around noon."

"Sounds great, I am kind of hungry." She looked around the room, gauged her time. "Let me jump into the shower and I'll meet you downstairs in about twenty minutes."

"Perfect. I'll see you then."

The phone went dead, and Jennifer looked around the room one more time.

"See that small black suitcase there?" she asked while pointing to her bag on the little stand.

The bellman nodded.

"Just leave that bag alone. I'll pack it when I'm done and bring it down myself." She thought briefly about the next sentence. "I'm going to get ready, just let yourself out when you're done, please."

She grabbed a few items of clothing out of her suitcase, jogged to the bathroom, closed and locked the door. She looked into the mirror, tousled her hair, realized she really was hungry and decided to wait to wash it until she got home tonight, then turned on the shower and stepped in.

I was up on Wednesday around eight. I had outsmarted the francolins by closing up last night and running the air conditioning. Even their hoots and screeches were apparently no match for the concrete walls and thermopane windows at The Palms.

Last evening with the neighbors had been like old home week. It turns out the folks living upstairs had come from Wisconsin and in true Badger fashion, we had spent the better part of the evening toasting all the good things from our youth. Truth be told, we finished the Corona I had brought and made a significant dent into a bottle of Jim Beam my hosts had supplied. I remembered calling Sandy to wish her good night after I negotiated the two-dozen stairs down to my condo and that she sounded as if I had awakened her from a deep sleep. So, it was with a bit of trepidation that I pushed the speed dial on my cell phone this morning. Sandy picked up on the first ring.

"Hey, Otto," she chirped. "How are you feeling this morning?"

Having just rolled over into life a few minutes ago, I wasn't really sure yet exactly how I was feeling, however, never being one to show weakness, I adopted her cheery tone.

"I'm great!" Then feeling a bit of guilt, I added, "Sorry I woke you up last night. I'm just not used to this time difference."

"I guess that was it," she said. "The time difference."

My foggy brain calculated this wasn't going to be a good road to travel since she so clearly had me outgunned this morning, so I changed roads.

"Anything on the research end?" I asked.

"Sure," she replied. "Just nothing good."

"Meaning?"

"Meaning I have almost zilch coming up through regular channels on the first four women and millions of possible hits on the last two. Now, what that says to me is one of two possible scenarios. One, perhaps Cassandra has given you bad information, either on purpose or by accident; or, two, the timeframe of the first four women is pre-internet."

"Pre-internet?"

"Yeah, like they just haven't been around with those names since documents began being digitized and placed on servers. Take a look at any search results you get and you're going to notice that the further back in time you go, the fewer documents you're going to find because people just aren't putting them online in a searchable format. Sure, I can get all the old clippings I want by way of converted microfilm archives from places like the major newspapers and magazines, but they aren't indexed like modern documents. Rather they're pictures of the article. Finding them depends on the keywords inserted by the person who puts the item up, rather than searching the document for the words themselves."

I thought about that concept for a moment and it made sense. Many times, Sandy had been able to provide me with print outs of stories going back the last fifteen years or so, but further back they always looked like clippings.

"I get it," I said. "You're one hell of a researcher, Sandy, I know you'll get to the bottom of it all."

"Oh, I've already started to hit the back doors," she said. "I'll track these people down if they ever existed. There isn't a rock they could hide under that I couldn't find them. It will just be easier if you can get me more information."

"I'm heading to Cassie's house after I clean up. She invited me for lunch and promised she'd do more digging before I got there. I'll get what I can."

"I know you will, Otto." Sandy paused. "The problem is the client, I fear. She's going to put this out in dribs and drabs for some reason. I'm telling you she's not being one hundred percent straight with us. She wants something, but is not telling us what her true purpose is." She paused. "Maybe if you felt her up again."

Sandy laughed in that real gut busting way. I finally realized how it felt to be on the other side of the 'on a Sandy Beach' line. It did make me smile, though.

I had no other answers for her as to Cassie's motives or her dribs and drabs, so we concluded the call and clicked off. But Sandy had planted the seed again.

I wandered to the kitchen, grabbed a Coke and then came back for some Advil out of my shaving kit, and downed half a dozen pills with a long draw from the can. I showered, shaved, and then pulled on a pair of khaki cargo shorts I bought on the beer run yesterday afternoon. I decided I could wear Willie in the back of my waistband and that I'd leave Sam in the glovebox. With the addition of a T-shirt that read 'Surf Like Moon, With Aloha' on the back, I looked as 'island' as I could possibly get for a white boy from Wisconsin.

I left the condo about nine, and figured I'd be at Cassie's place around eleven. On the walk out, I saw Steve and Shelly in swimsuits and loaded down with a cooler and a couple of bags, obviously headed for the beach.

"Howzit, brah?" Steve said, tossing me what I now knew was a friendly hand gesture.

I tried to return the greeting, but an operator error made it look like I was either saluting Ozzy Osborne or cheering on the Texas Longhorns.

Shelly laughed.

"I've always told Steve he was the whitest guy in Hawaii," she said. "That's until today, William. You are now officially the whitest guy in Hawaii."

"I'm not sure that's a compliment," I said.

"Depends on how you look at it," Steve replied. "I take it the same as if someone called me the coolest violinist on the school football team." He laughed and added, "Stop by later if you aren't doing anything. Shelly's working tonight and I'm going to grab a pizza and catch the game."

"I may just do that," I said. I opened the door to the Jeep. "If I'm back in time, that is. Don't wait on me."

They waved, got into their Honda Pilot and drove off.

On the way through Kahului, I pulled into the Krispy Kreme drive-thru and ordered a half dozen glazed for the trip. Between the Coke and the sugary wheels - and the Advil - I was going to blow this hangover away long before I got to Cassie's place. Either that or I was going to lapse into a hyperglycemic shock.

After Kahului, I headed up Haleakala toward Kula, passing in between Pukalani and Makawao about twenty-five-hundred-feet up and continued along the Kula Highway. The view from this far up the mountain was spectacular. Whiffs of eucalyptus blew in through the open windows and vents.

Before leaving Kula behind, I had stopped at a little green roadside shack with a sign that said, Kula Farms and advertised fresh strawberries. I remembered that Cassie had loved the little red gems dipped in an odd combination of sour cream and brown sugar, so I picked up a couple of quarts.

Shortly after the road turned east at the southwest corner of the island, it changed from a normal, if not meandering, two-lane asphalt paved road with a center stripe painted by some guy who spent more time watching the scenery than the roadway, into a mix of bad paved road and bad gravel road. My progress dropped to about fifteen miles per hour. Any faster and I would have badly bruised my berries, and I'm not talking about the ones I had bought for Cassie.

Finally, heading up yet another blind rise, the GPS changed from counting down in tenths of a mile to hundreds of feet. The little red dot moved along the electronic road and indicated I'd shortly come upon the driveway for the Thomason estate. At the top of the hill, I spotted the hard-to-miss compound off toward the ocean. Since the road was barely wide enough for one car and one bicycle to pass each other without sideswiping or one running off into sawgrass and lava rocks, I risked death or serious injury by stopping on the roadway and taking note of the compound's layout.

Even at this distance, I could tell the house was large for what I've seen on the island. The main house consisted of a center rotunda and two wings which curved gently toward the ocean from the center point, giving the whole structure the look of a giant parenthesis. I would have pulled out my binoculars from the duffel on the seat which held Sam and other items, but everything was of such a grand scale that it was all clearly discernible with the naked eye.

On the inland side of the house was a tennis court, off to the right on the same side was a small circular area of concrete stained the same reddish clay color found naturally on the island and which I assumed was the helipad. There was a golf green closer to the ocean on that side of the house. Finally, on the ocean side, was a large lanai with scattered furniture and in-ground pool with integral hot tub. On one end of the pool area was a smallish structure which could have been a sauna. The entire compound was lush green grass and tropical plantings and a fountain adorned the center of the circular drive at the house. I counted six garage doors on the very end of the west wing. The paved drive extended to the garage area.

On the roof of both wings, barely visible but recognizable as to what they were, sat row upon row of photovoltaic panels. I guesstimated from the square footage there was enough to power that size house several times over. With the satellite dishes east of the house, it was clearly possible for the place to be totally off-the-grid.

In the center of the drive, near the fountain, I saw Cassie's white Escalade parked like she had driven in and entered the home through the large entry doors in the rotunda. I wondered why she didn't just pull it into the garage, but then remembered that she had told me she was flying back on the helicopter and someone must have driven the Escalade home sometime last night.

Up the hill about fifty feet off the road, in contrast to the mansion below, sat a small, green, wooden shack with corrugated metal roof and white trimmed windows and door. On the porch sat a lone elderly Hawaiian man who was watching me closely. I nodded at him, and he just stared.

I took my foot off the brake and drove up to the main gate. As I approached, the gate swung open. I was certain that function wasn't automatic, given the remoteness of the house and the valuables it most likely contained, so it must mean the property has a very well concealed security surveillance system and that Cassie saw me coming. The absence of visible cameras made me wonder what other security and anti-intruder devices Gregory had installed on the property. Given his wealth, he could have systems which rivaled anything the Secret Service might install at the White House, and given his obvious penchant for privacy, most likely did.

I pulled the Jeep through the gate and drove down toward the house. I wondered why I suddenly envisioned the image of a fly cautiously testing the edge of a large spider's web. I know what Cassie had told me about Gregory and his temper, but there was a growing sense inside me that like much of the arachnid world, this lair may contain a female of the species far more dangerous than the male.

I pulled up behind the Escalade and got out and stretched, I checked the position of Willie in the small of my back. Pulling the keys, I locked the door. Call that just another cop habit.

The front door opened and Cassie walked out a few steps wearing a canary yellow dress with elastic bodice. She was barefoot and I could see her toenail polish matched her dress. If you're thinking of old men and their yellowed and thickened toenails that are always in dire need of clipping, don't.

"You made it," she said. She held open her arms just like she had at the airport and I accepted a hug. My arms went high and hers went low. She patted my waistband and said, "Glad to see you're packing."

"Do you frisk all of your guests?" I asked.

Her mouth formed a mock pout and then she smiled.

"It's good to see you again," she said and then motioned for me to come in.

I dropped my flip-flops at the outside of the doorway and stepped barefoot onto the cool, polished marble.

"I see you have a neighbor," I said, pointing up the hill.

She closed the door, then said, "That's Keoki. Gregory bought this parcel of land from him years ago when he needed money to send his kids off-island to college. He had said the island world of his ancestors was dying and he had wanted his keiki to broaden their horizons. His family owned this entire ahupua'a, the wedge of land from the sea to the mountaintop, since the days of Kamehameha. See, Hawaiians would divide the land that way so each family had access to everything it needed to thrive, from fish in the sea to breadfruit, lumber, and hunting lands up the mountain."

"He doesn't seem too friendly," I opined. "I nodded to him and all he did was stare back at me."

"Frankly, I think part of him died when he divided up the kuleana, the land, and his keiki left. I can't remember the last time I noticed one of them visiting him."

"You sure are tossing around the native terms today," I said. "Just because I may be dressed like a native, doesn't mean I am one." I smiled.

"You're dressed like a tourist," she said. "You have to get a little more grungy to be considered dressing like a native."

"I'll work on it," I said. "Seriously, though, why the native speak today?"

"Since you mentioned seeing Keoki, you may as well understand him a bit. He's really not such a bad guy if you take the time to get to know him." A thought triggered a wicked smile. "Besides, he absolutely despises Gregory."

"Well, that's something," I joked.

"He may have been sizing you up a bit. All he seems to do, day and night, is sit on that porch of his and watch the land. He knows everyone who routinely comes and goes here, and we have few solitary guests stopping by. So, that, and given the fact he must know Gregory is gone, might have him wondering if you may be my new back door man."

"What happened to the old one?" I half-joked.

"You don't want to know," she said with a laugh.

I fully hoped she was half joking.

"Come on in," she said, taking my hand.

We walked down the hall toward the center of the rotunda, which was open to the roof level. In something akin to the Bellagio in Las Vegas, large, blown glass flowers populated the center of the ceiling area. Cassie told me they were backlit by natural light during the day and variable intensity xenon lights at night. Two sweeping staircases lined the perimeter on each side of the rotunda and merged into a balcony walkway which connected to each wing on the second floor. We passed under the walkway and into a semicircle of openness. Floor to ceiling, frameless glass panels soared the entire forty feet and provided for a panoramic view of the ocean which was spectacular, even though the distance we could see today was limited by fog and mist over the channel.

"There are days when we can see the Big Island," she said, releasing my hand and allowing me to take it all in.

"Absolutely spectacular, Cassie," I said, then pulled my gaze to the rotunda itself. This half of the circle was set up as a cozy living area. Nothing sat in front of the glass. A large leather couch, and I mean large, sat with its back to the foyer. A very soft, and very plush arctic white area rug in the shape of the semicircle provided the foundation for the seating area, which included an oversize coffee table made from what Cassie told me was African Blackwood. The focal point of the area was obviously the view.

I noticed there was a silver tray with a glass pitcher of orange juice and what from the visible top I recognized as a bottle of Cristal on ice. Two cut crystal flutes flanked the mimosa ingredients and a platter of assorted fruits and cheese was set out adjacent on the coffee table.

"The strawberries," I said.

"Strawberries?" she asked.

"Yeah, I stopped and bought some strawberries at the Kula Farms stand on the way because I remember you used to like them." I started toward the door. "They're in the car, I'll just be a sec."

A minute later, I was back, strawberries in hand. Cassie smiled at the thought and gestured to the fruit tray.

"I had someone stop at the fruit stand in Kula yesterday when they brought the car back. This is truly thoughtful, though, Willy."

"That's right, you flew back on the helicopter yesterday afternoon. Given the road, I think that's quite the perk."

"It is." She took the two cartons of strawberries from me, her hands gently brushing mine as she did. She walked off toward the west wing, in the direction of what I assumed was the kitchen and returned a moment later. "There, shall we sit?"

We each took a seat on the expansive couch. I had never in my life felt leather so soft and supple. The construction of the couch just swallowed my body while providing just the right amount of support. Cassie pulled her feet up onto the couch and tossed her dress to cover them. She asked if I'd do the honors, gesturing to the champagne and OJ.

I reached for the Cristal, noted the vintage was the same as the year of our birth, and asked her if it was mere coincidence.

"Of course not," she said. "I don't believe in coincidences."

"Funny," I said. "Neither do I."

She wouldn't look me in the eye the next moment, instead focused her gaze out over the water. She came back to the present and suggested we have a drink and something to nibble on.

"Make mine virgin, if you don't mind," she said.

So, I popped the cork and poured my flute about seventy-five percent full, then added a splash of orange juice. Hers I filled with OJ. I picked up both flutes and offered her one.

"What should we toast to?" Cassie asked. "Coincidences?"

Her eyes were playful. Dangerous.

"How can we drink to something neither of us believe in?" I asked.

"Well, we already toasted old friends the other night," she said.

My mouth felt suddenly dry and my heart began to pound in my chest at the thought. I offered it anyway.

"How about to first loves?" I said.

Cassie smiled and her brown eyes twinkled at me. She extended her glass to mine.

"To first loves," she said, giving my glass a solid clink.

"First loves," I replied.

We both drank.

Gregory and Jennifer arrived in the limousine at the ramp side of the Signature operation at the San Francisco International Airport. The Gulfstream jet awaited them, a red carpet extended along the tarmac from the aircraft's stairs outward. The limo driver obviously had done this before and he brought the vehicle around, placing the rear right door of the limo at the edge of the red carpet. His passenger's shoes would not touch hot asphalt.

As he brought the vehicle to a stop, he popped the trunk lid and Signature's employees began moving the bags and boxes from the trunk to the aircraft's luggage compartment in the rear belly area. More boxes and bags had filled the passenger area of the car and those were hustled into the rear of the jet's main cabin.

Jennifer made a reach for the door handle and Gregory touched her knee.

"It's what they live for, my dear," he said. "They think it affects their tip. Who are we to begrudge them the pleasure of serving?"

She sat back in the seat, impatiently waited out the moments for the driver to appear outside the door and open it. When he did, Jennifer extended her hand and the driver assisted her out onto the red carpet. The jet's APU was running and powering the electrical and air conditioning systems onboard. Jennifer waved up at Bev waiting at the cabin door.

Gregory followed her out of the limo and thanked the driver for his wonderful service. The driver grinned broadly.

"Thank you, sir," he said.

Gregory took Jennifer by the elbow and escorted her to the stairs. The two ascended toward the cabin door, Jennifer drawing looks of the ramp workers loading the plane and the limo driver. Gregory watched them gawk out of the corner of his eye.

"Yes, she is spectacular," he said under his breath.

"Did you say something, Gregory?" Jennifer asked.

"I said the day is spectacular," he lied.

"Oh," she said, looking around at the clear blue sky. "Yes, it is one of God's good ones."

The wheels of the jet left runway 28L at exactly 12:02 p.m. Pacific Daylight Time headed southwest.

Although Gregory didn't know it, at that very moment on Maui, at 9:02 a.m., Hawaii Standard Time, Cassandra was luxuriating and pampering herself in her bath. William Langdon, a name Gregory had heard, but a man whom he had never met, was saying good-bye to his new friends from upstairs and leaving Wailea.

The display on the front cabin wall estimated arrival in Maui at 1:48 local time. Gregory would be home by shortly after 2:00 p.m. He smiled.

Bev arrived with two tall glasses of club soda with twists of lime and lemon peel. She set down napkins monogramed with the jet's tail number, N100GT and placed the glasses in the center of each.

Even though they had just eaten breakfast a couple of hours ago, Gregory asked Bev what was on the menu for lunch. When she replied by telling him they had an assortment of his favorite sushi and sashimi, he smiled again.

"Wonderful," he said. Then he looked at Jennifer and said, "Could life get any better?"

"I don't think it could, Gregory," she replied. Out her window she watched the Golden Gate pass behind them as the Gulfstream climbed into the clear, blue sky. She could see for miles up the coast, an unusual feat in normally foggy San Francisco.

"Spectacular," she said to herself.

Before she dressed after her shower, Marcy found the card for the young officer who had taken her missing person's report two days ago. She called the cell number, surmising that were he in or out of the station, or even not working, that his cellular phone would be the most successful method of reaching him.

She punched in the numbers on her cell, put the phone on speaker, set it on the counter and toweled off. After five rings, the call went to the officer's voicemail. Marcy left a message, asking him to call her and telling him that she had further information for his report. She added the statement that the additional information lead her to suspect there was a person or persons involved in much more than a simple missing person, hoping that may cause him to return her call with more urgency. She left her name and contact number again at the end before hanging up.

Marcy dressed, pulled off the copies of the sheet of photos from the printer. She took one, found a marker and wrote on the top, "Do You Know Her?" and added her cell phone number. She searched a couple of drawers before finding some tape and then went and hung the page over the mailboxes in the entryway.

Then it was time to start banging on doors, she thought. The first door she knocked upon was for the apartment right next to Janet's located to the left rear of the building. It belonged to the building manager and his wife. Marcy had spoken to him briefly on Monday morning after the officer had left. He had not seen Janet on Saturday, but had heard her rustling around early that morning. Marcy usually tried to avoid his wife.

In this particular building, which had originally been built in the late 1940s to function as a small department store, there were three floors of five apartments each and a top floor which had three units, each floor arranged in the shape of a U around the center stairwell. Janet's unit was on the raised ground floor in the front. The stairwell sat at the front of the building and was glassed on the exterior wall. It was the only way up or down. The building had a security door on the front, but no surveillance cameras. Marcy had suggested the addition of some to the manager yesterday when she'd bumped into him and all he had said was that he'd take it up with the owner.

Marcy heard someone approaching the door inside the apartment and then that someone could be heard fumbling with locks and chain. Marcy hoped it was the manager and not his wife. When the door opened, to Marcy's chagrin, it was indeed the manager's wife, Carol. The woman was short, about 1.5 meters - just under five feet - in her late 50s but looked much older, with tight gray curls framing a yellowed and craggy face that Marcy thought had never been attractive. The woman smoked like a chimney, swore like a sailor, and according to rumors, drank like a fish. Every time Marcy had run into her, the woman had been most unfriendly.

This morning Carol was dressed in a well-worn cotton nightgown which ended just above bony knees and a burgundy terry cloth bathrobe which hung open. A pair of reading glasses dangling from an ancient silver chain nestled against her tiny bosom. She carried a mug of coffee and had a lit cigarette perched between her lips. The ash tumbled to the floor when she spoke.

"Jesus, do you know what time it is?" She glared at Marcy. "Hell, lady, you ain't even a tenant here. What the hell do you want?" She cocked her hip in a gesture of defiance and put one arm up on the edge of the door. The cigarette's ember glowed orange as Carol took a draw. She seemed to have swallowed the smoke because Marcy didn't see it come out.

The riddle of the disappearing smoke gave Marcy a moment to consider her response, so she swallowed the first words that fell into the back of her throat and affixed to her face her best attempt at a non-combative smile.

"I'm so sorry to bother you so early," Marcy said. "I assume your husband has told you that Janet has gone missing and that I'm staying there until I can find her."

Carol's demeanor softened just a touch.

"Oh, yeah, Janet," she said as her eyes moved to the apartment door. "Nice girl, quiet." Her gaze returned to Marcy and it returned as a glare. "Not like the rest of your kind."

Marcy moved her right hand to the small of her back and made a fist so tight that even her close-cropped nails dug deeply into her palm.

She raised the page of photos of the mystery brunette with her left hand high enough so Carol couldn't help but have a look.

"This woman was spotted leaving the building about an hour after Janet supposedly came home."

"Supposedly?" Carol finally released the dose of smoke from somewhere deep inside and blew it past Marcy. "What the hell you mean, *supposedly?* We heard her. She was quiet, considerate, but we still heard her movin' around in there." Carol kicked at the doorway with one of a pair of feet clad in fuzzy pink scuffs. "The didn't do nobody no favors when they built these walls so thin, eh."

Carol removed her hand from the door, reached for the paper and snatched it from Marcy's grasp. She shifted the cigarette to one corner of her mouth in some sort of magical no-hands method, then fumbled with her glasses and placed them onto her nose, slightly crumpling the paper in the process. The lenses were so smudged and filthy Marcy wondered how the woman's vision could have possibly been improved by wearing them.

"Who is this?" Carol asked. She turned the page toward Marcy. "Where'd you get this pictures?" The last word came out sounding like 'pitchers'.

"I pulled those frames from video surveillance footage I obtained from a friend of mine."

"This first one looks like it was taken right outside the building."

"It was, early Saturday morning."

"Who took the picture?" Carol looked confused.

Marcy wondered if the woman was really this dumb, still drunk, or just so unaware that she didn't know that these days, when a person is in public, there was usually an electronic eye watching.

"There are cameras mounted on most traffic signals these days. That particular photo was taken from the camera on the corner." Marcy watched as Carol looked quickly off to the left of the building. "The others were captured at the Metro station, on the train, and at the airport." Marcy noted in amazement as Carol obviously became self-aware and absently pulled her robe closed. "Do you know the woman in the pictures, Mrs. Stuts? Have you seen her around the building before?"

"Nope, never seen her." She offered Marcy the page back.

"Could I ask your husband?" Marcy inquired, taking the paper from Carol and smoothing it onto the others in her hand.

"I don't care," Carol said, and moved to close the door. "He's in the basement."

Marcy stood there and watched the door close and then heard the locks and chain being reset. She shook her head and wondered how Ernie, whom she found very friendly and personable, could tolerate being around such a troll. She turned to go down to the basement and show the photos to the manager.

Marcy found Ernie inside a large, wire-walled area which took up about one-third of the basement and was used for general storage and Ernie's workshop. He was sweeping up wood shavings from a door he had planed. The rest of the basement area was divided into locked storage areas for each apartment. As she walked through the basement, overhead lights came on automatically. Since they usually stayed illuminated for at least half an hour once made active, she estimated Ernie had been down here a while. She didn't blame him.

"Hey, Marcy," he greeted her. "Any word on Janet?"

"Good morning, Ernie," Marcy said with a genuine smile on her face. "Nothing yet, but I've got some leads to check up on. I just spoke with your wife to see if she could identify a woman caught by surveillance cameras leaving the building about an hour after Janet was dropped off early Saturday." Her eyes moved upward to look through the ceiling and her brow furrowed.

Ernie gave out an understanding laugh, leaned his broom against a workbench. The door he had been planing rested on two saw horses in the center of the open floor area. She could smell the wood, and the turpentine in the stained rag covering a small can sitting on the door.

"Let's see the pictures," he said. "Hey, why don't you hang a copy in the lobby near the mailboxes? Make sure everyone in the building will see them, including the postman."

"Great minds, Ernie," Marcy quipped. "Already done." She handed a fresh copy to him.

Ernie looked at his hands to make sure they were clean, wiped them on his pants anyway and then took the paper. He held the page under the light. Marcy watched him carefully. He was the complete opposite of his wife. Ernie was tall, just under two meters and possessed a body much like Ichabod Crane. Age, and what Marcy assumed must have felt like two lifetimes of nagging had stooped his shoulders slightly and harvested much of his salt and pepper hair. His face was thin and ruddy, his blue eyes were clear and his Adams apple moved up and down while his mouth remained in perpetual motion. Janet had once joked that his mouth was always moving because it was how he tolerated never being able to talk much around Carol. He started to shake his head and rubbed his chin with his free hand.

"Sorry, honey," he said, handing back the paper. "She obviously doesn't live here or I'd know. I've never seen her around the building or with any of the other tenants."

Marcy lightly bit the inside of her cheek. She wondered whether she should mention her evolving theory to Ernie before she gave it to the police. She decided she could trust this man.

"Ernie, I am coming to believe, from things I have found and not found around the apartment, that someone, possibly this woman, had been in there and may have something to do with Janet's disappearance." She watched his face for a reaction.

Ernie's mouth began its nervous gymnastics again.

"Have you spoken to the police about your suspicions?"

"I put in a call to the man-child they sent to take the original report," she said. "Left a voicemail. Haven't heard back yet."

"Well, listen," he said. "Do you have an extra copy of that sheet of pictures? I've got a couple of friends in the Police Department who work downtown. What we called 'brass' in the army. Maybe they can get someone else to look into things."

Marcy handed the sheet back to him with an extra copy.

"No promises, mind you." Ernie looked at the pages, seemed to be thinking. "I'll give it a try, though."

Marcy thanked him and gave him a hug, not just for his help, but because she needed one. He seemed to sense that, so he hugged back. She left the basement and went about knocking on the doors of the other apartments. Nobody in the building had seen the woman on Saturday or knew her. At the three apartments where nobody answered the door, she wrote a note asking if they'd contact her if they knew the woman and then slipped a folded copy of the paper between the door and jamb.

Before leaving for the taxi garage, she stopped in the apartment and grabbed her purse. The screensaver was displaying new photos from a folder labeled Maui Trip which Marcy had discovered had been placed on the computer shortly after the time Janet had arrived home. She must have downloaded her camera as part of her unpacking from the trip, Marcy had assumed. She grabbed her keys and purse from the desk just as a photo displayed showing a smiling Janet at some sort of cocktail reception. The sun was setting over the ocean beyond and a black hulled catamaran sailed under power just off shore. Marcy touched Janet's face on the screen with her fingertips. She could feel a connection and she smiled. An instant later, the picture pixelated and morphed to another photo of the same scene only without Janet and Marcy's heart tore a little more.

Jennifer tucked her feet under herself in the oversized leather seat. Before she had met Gregory, she had never flown on, or even been inside a private jet like this. Most of the time, she flew coach with the occasional upgrade to business class if she had the miles. There was no tucking your feet up under yourself in a coach airline seat. She looked over at Gregory. She felt like being talkative on the flight. Not just about her art, which was the only subject which seemed to interest Gregory most times, but about 'Why her?'. He seemed to be in exceptional spirits this afternoon, so she thought she'd broach a subject which he usually waved off as mere mentorship or sponsorship. Not that she begrudged the philanthropy and all he had done for her, but she was from a blue collar family and these types of things just didn't happen to people from College Station, Texas.

She picked at her sushi and sashimi. It was all the highest quality, from what she knew of the delicacy, but she had never developed much of a taste. For her dollar, a good Texas barbecue with brisket and sausage, corn on the cob, potato salad, all washed down with ice-cold Lone Star was about as good as it got. Add watermelon or a hefty slice of pecan pie for desert and she'd know she was home. Now that was food for the soul.

Across the aisle, Gregory was devouring his servings with relish, occasionally glancing over to her and asking if everything was to her liking. She had replied it was delicious, but that she wasn't all that hungry after the big breakfast.

"The suzuki is excellent today," he said, gesturing with his chopsticks to the white and reddish sea bass on a ball of rice.

"I'm still at the California Roll stage, I guess," she joked. "You're right, it's all delicious, Gregory. I wish I were more hungry, but with the excitement of the upcoming show and all, food doesn't seem a priority right now."

"Everything's going to be just fine, Jen," he said. "You've got nearly a year of fantastic work stocked up, plus the stuff you had done before we met, so we'll get it crated up and flown to Mr. McCormick's place in plenty of time. He'll take it from there. The show is going to be a great success." He stuffed another piece of nigiri sushi into his mouth. "Leave it all up to me. You're the talent, I'm the detail guy."

Jennifer smiled. Bev was up in the cockpit with the pilots, so she decided now would be a good time to again see if she could coax from Gregory the story of 'Why her?'. Jennifer decided to take less of a direct route and used a slight diversion before posing the question directly.

"You know the line from the movie *Trading Places* when Eddie Murphy in the role of the street hustler from the ghetto gets into the limo with the two old rich guys?" She immediately regretted the use of the word 'old' in the question, so she continued quickly before he'd have a chance to latch onto it in comparison to their relationship. "You know, when they are offering him a job, a bank account, a house complete with butler and his own limousine? Then, he turns to them and says, 'This kind of thing happens to me every week'."

Gregory stopped chewing, looked straight ahead. His face had gone blank and he seemed to be deep in thought, almost like a computer which had been fed confusing data. Then just as quickly as he had stopped, he resumed chewing, swallowed, washed it down with a long draw from his glass of Japanese beer. Putting down his chopsticks, he pivoted his chair to face her across the aisle.

"Ah, the 'Why you?' question again?"

Jennifer knew that line usually meant in the next breath he'd wave her off with platitudes of liking her work, wanting to help a struggling artist, his lifelong wish he had talent rather than money, blah, blah, blah, and then he'd close with the routine question back to her, 'Why does it matter?'. This time, though, by setting down his chopsticks and turning his chair, she felt he may actually tell her something new. She studied his face in hopeful anticipation he would finally open up to her.

Gregory looked into her eyes. He seemed to be searching for words. Jennifer held her breath, anxious for him to speak, but frightened he may again close her off if she pushed. So she waited.

"I knew your mother," he said. He cocked his head, looked her up and down. "You know you look exactly like she did when she was your age?"

Jennifer naturally thought of her mom. Elisa Shea had been shorter than her by six or seven inches, had blue eyes where Jennifer's were brown with green flecks, and naturally blonde hair to her thick chestnut locks. No matter how much she worked at it, her mom possessed the physical profile of a pear, both from the back and from the side and waddled a bit when she walked, while Jennifer was lithe, curvy, and amply endowed. Mom wore a perpetual smile; Jennifer's face was most often neutral and she tended to ration her radiant smiles to deserving occasions. Then it hit her like one of the giant waves which heralded a strong storm front. He was talking about knowing her bio-mom.

She frantically looked up the aisle toward the galley, hoping to see Bev had returned to derail this particular story, but the entire crew remained behind the cockpit door. Suddenly, what had seemed like an opportunity, now made her feel quite vulnerable. A thousand questions raced through her head.

Gregory watched her reaction. He smiled at her.

"You must have a million questions," he said, pivoting his seat back and picking up his chopsticks.

"At...at least thousand," she replied nervously.

Gregory selected a piece of the sashimi from the plate, dipped an end into the soy sauce and devoured it as eagerly as a shark would have consumed the entire fish.

He didn't look at her. Normally that would have made her uncomfortable. All her life people looked at you when they talked to you. Oddly, right now him not making eye contact made her feel more at ease.

"Fire away," he said, finishing his beer and pushing away his plate. "I think it's time you know the whole story."

On the lanai, with a bottle of Pinot Noir from a northern California winery I had never heard of - but which had produced a wonderful vintage - upside down in the ice bucket and the crumbs of grilled Norwegian salmon, mango chutney and herbed risotto on our plates, Cassie and I experienced our first truly uncomfortable silence in thirty years.

Fortunately, the view was indeed spectacular and I used the moment to look out across the roiling channel to collect my thoughts. I had just asked her about the rumor of why she left school. She had responded only that she had quickly lost contact with her old friends and had never heard the rumor. I could tell she was lying and as her glistening brown eyes searched my face, it was clear my expression announced that conclusion to her. So, perhaps she too was using the moment to collect her thoughts.

After the mimosas and wine with lunch, I felt a little buzzed. I could feel the ocean mist occasionally touch my face. It was momentarily cool as it evaporated and left behind a layer of salt which I could taste on my lips and feel as it dried and constricted my skin.

So I had broached the question, figuring we'd have plenty of time to go over the additional information she had gathered and for me to try to persuade her to let me see the journals. As I watched her out of the corner of my eye, I recalled her stubbornness, or perhaps it would be better described as willfulness. Even though I could get Cassie to go along with just about anything I wanted back in the day, given enough lobbying, I always knew when she did relent, it was not because of my persistence but merely because she had decided it was what she wanted too.

"Cassie?" I asked.

She looked at me. There was a mist in her eyes, and it had nothing to do with the occasional breeze from the ocean.

"What?" she responded in a defiant tone.

"There's something you are refusing to tell me about how it all ended," I said, cupping my hands around hers. I could sense a crack in the palace walls, but I had to remind myself that she was now a woman used to getting her way without question, not a nearly fifteen-year-old girl who was still unsure of herself. So, I appealed to the woman. "Don't you think it's about time?"

She paused, then she must have determined it was indeed time.

"You had no right to ask me about Tim. What happened before you and I was none of your business." I felt her pulling back her hands just a bit, but not enough to really pull them free of mine. "By what right do you think you could judge me?"

Her eyes were accusing, defiant. Then they softened and I could only infer she saw something inside my eyes which took her back in time, and as I looked even deeper into her gaze, I saw something else too. Regret.

"Why didn't you come after me?" she asked. "Why didn't you call me? Why were you not at my house that night, tossing pebbles against my bedroom window?"

"Frankly, the way I felt, it would have been rocks, not pebbles."

I smiled, just a bit, then continued the metaphor.

"Would you have come out onto the balcony and called 'Wherefore art thou?'."

"I had no illusions of being Juliet, Willy. You broke my heart. I thought we had been closer than that."

"Sorry," I said. "Bad joke. So had I. I thought we could talk about anything. You just shut me out."

She waved it off as if to say, 'it's been a long time'.

"To answer both your unasked questions, I was, in reality, still a virgin on that day. The entire story Tim had been peddling around school about he and I being intimate in a sleeping bag down in Lydia's basement make-out room was a total fabrication. A lie."

I smiled a little at that, and took the bait.

"I know what a fabrication is," I said. I patted her hands, then released them. She looked disappointed at the disconnecting.

"Tim sold the story fairly well," I said. "I was hurt. No, as a fourteen-year-old boy who had just come out of Catholic grade school, I was devastated." As I heard the words tumble out of my mouth, I wondered to myself how it was possible for a such pubescent petulance to linger for three decades.

Cassie's face broke into a huge grin.

"You should have opened your eyes, Willy. There were no bigger group of sluts than the ones who came out of that Catholic grade school with you."

My mouth fell agape.

"Would it have made it any better had I lost my virginity to *you* that night your mother caught us at your house? That's a bit hypocritical, don't you think?" She sat back and cinched up the light shoulder wrap she had put on before we came outside. Her body language was challenging and her line of thinking matched exactly what Sandy had verbalized on the same subject. Interesting, I thought.

I had no response which came immediately to mind that would make me look less the hypocrite, so I fell back on humor and my legendary adorableness to deflect the question.

"I plead the Fifth, Your Honor."

"Well, I won't let you down today. I'll close the chapter for you."

I sat back, tossed my left ankle onto my right knee, wiped my mouth with the cloth napkin, dropped it onto the table, and waited.

Cassie scooted her chair back from the table, got up and took a couple of steps toward the water. She took a moment, and then returned to her seat and began her story.

"I said I was a virgin on that day, the day you and I had that blow up on the school steps. That's the God's honest truth. The other truths are that I was in love with you - or at least how I understood love at that age - and that you broke my heart.

"When I went home that afternoon, my mother gave me the news we were moving again. My stepfather had taken a job in Georgia, and we would be gone in less than two weeks. The heaviness in my heart was unbearable. Not only had I lost you, but I knew I would never have the chance to get you back.

"About a week later, I was procrastinating in my packing and moping in my room. My mother had gone to get more packing boxes. My stepfather came in and sat on my bed."

My heart sank, I could see the light of the train coming at me in the tunnel.

Cassie again pulled the wrap around herself. She folded her arms into a self-hug. When she turned to look at me, there were tears streaming down her face.

"He raped me, Willy. My stepfather raped me."

I came out of my chair and moved to her. She buried her face in my Surf Like Moon T-shirt and sobbed. I held her and stroked her hair.

"Oh, Cassie, I'm so very sorry." My blood boiled. Had the man not been at Death's door already, I knew I'd have surely killed him. "You don't need to go on. What a child I was."

She pulled herself away, looked me in the eyes. Her eyes were swollen, her make-up smeared.

"No," she said. "I want to get this off my chest. No other living soul other than my mother knows what I am going to tell you. Even she doesn't know the full truth."

I continued to hold her in my arms. She was shivering, whether from the occasional cool spray or from emotion, I couldn't be certain. She looked up at me and continued. Her eyes plead for understanding.

"I became pregnant from the rape. After I left, the one person I kept in touch with, for a while anyway, was Lydia, and when I found out I was pregnant, she was the only person other than my mother whom I told. I assume now that she was the source of the rumor you told me about earlier. Bitch.

"Well, my mother assumed the child was yours and I made no comment to her to the contrary. My stepfather also believed the paternity fell upon your shoulders until one night when he came into my room again and I told him three things: that you were not the father, that I had been a virgin on the day he raped me, and if he ever touched me again, I'd kill him.

"Before I began showing, my mother pulled me out of school and sent me to live with a longtime friend who lived in Sulphur, Louisiana until I had the baby. When the baby was born, it was taken from me and sent to foster parents in Texas. I was only able to catch a glimpse of my daughter before she was gone forever."

Tears streamed down her cheeks.

"Through all the years," she said. "I lived the lie that it was our baby girl I had given up to adoption. My stepfather never touched me again and I only visit him as a favor to my mother, although I do get some kind of perverse pleasure in watching him slowly die in pain. My mother never broached the subject of the child after I returned home and had she ever suspected the truth of who the father was - and I don't think she did - she never said anything to me."

She pulled me close to her, held me tightly.

"Please don't hate me," she said. "I'm so sorry."

I hugged her back, then released her just a bit. I put two fingers under her chin, could feel the tears collecting there, and gently lifted her face. Her eyes were downcast, but then followed.

"I could never hate you, Cassie, and you have no reason to apologize to me," I said with genuine affection in my voice. "Truth be told, I have always loved you."

"Truth be told, Willy," she said. "I've always loved you, too.

I kissed her gently. And, she kissed me back.

Chapter Twelve

Jennifer's brain settled on the obvious first question. She stared across the aisle. Gregory's eyes were still looking straight ahead, as if he were willing Bev to come back to clear the dishes and bring him another glass of Soporo beer.

"You said 'knew', that you 'knew my mother'," she said. Her heart had been pounding in anticipation since Gregory first spoke the words. Now that she had verbalized the question, she felt like she was standing on thin, clear ice in the middle of a bottomless lake and it had just cracked under her tread. She licked her lips and took a deep breath before continuing. "That implies one of two things to me. One, that the two of you have lost contact, or..." she closed her eyes and felt herself taking another tentative step on the ice. "...or, two, she's dead."

She envisioned spiderweb cracks running in every direction from her footstep. The next words from his mouth meant that either she'd eventually walk onto the far shore were her bio-mom be alive, or experience the pain should the ice give way and dump her into the numbingly cold water should she be dead. Her mind was already swimming.

Gregory said nothing. He just stared straight ahead. His face telegraphed he was deep in thought.

"Gregory?"

"I was just thinking, my dear," he said, placing the index finger of his left hand on his lips, and then removing it to accentuate the verbalization of his current quandary. "Would it serve the telling better to let you ask me questions, or just let the story unfold naturally." He returned his finger to his lips and pondered.

Jennifer's mind was barely treading water. She had never seen this side of Gregory. He had always been open and honest with her, about everything. Or had he? But this drama, this intrigue to such a simple set of facts. Who was this man? Why would he wish to torment her like this?

Yet, she never had any real interest - before the death of her parents - in learning the identity of her bio-mom, or where she was, or even if she were still alive. So why did the thought of Gregory having any knowledge which could fill in the blanks and lead her to her bio-mom stir so deeply within her? Jennifer knew who her mother was. She knew who her father was. Any acknowledgment that someone other than Bruce and Elisa Shea had any hand in who she was, what she was, and who she became seemed to Jennifer an affront to their memory. Now her mother was dead. Her father was dead. Her only roots had returned to the clay from whence they had come. She suddenly felt a longing for a link. It was only natural to want a link to the rest of humanity. Wasn't it? Of course it was.

"Is my bio-mom alive or dead?" she asked again, with emphasis.

Gregory removed the fingertip from his lips, held it again to make a point as he spoke.

"Why, Jennifer, one never starts a story at the end." He looked at her and his eyes were dead. "How much fun would it be to go through the process of reading an entire book if the author inserted the last page as the first page? The reader would feel cheated. You don't want to feel cheated, do you?"

Jennifer's eyes moved to the trip display on the cockpit bulkhead. The screen showed the map of the world with the airplane's current position marked along a red line which indicated the routing as programmed into the jet's navigation computer, as Captain Dan had explained to her on the flight to San Francisco. They were currently 1,184 miles from Maui, flying at an altitude of 46,000 feet with a groundspeed of 550 miles per hour. The estimated remaining time was counting down from two hours and seven minutes.

She looked at Gregory, who was now watching her, waiting for her answer. She resolved to give him two hours and seven minutes to satisfy her with the story or she was walking away from him, art show be damned. She applied a smile to her face.

"I had a friend in college who would read the last page of a book before she started reading from the beginning," Jennifer said in a nonchalant tone. "She said it was just in case she died before she finished, so she wouldn't have to spend eternity not knowing how it turned out."

Gregory seemed amused by the anecdote.

"I always thought her practice was weird, so, please, tell the story in any fashion you wish. I have no desire to feel cheated," she said.

Gregory's eyes changed. Jennifer thought they now reminded her of the look her old cat Brutus' eyes contained when the mouse he had found decided it was time to stop playing dead and make a run for it. A look of playful surprise. Though the look of a predator, still. Her blood chilled and the joy of the last two days evaporated into a sense of fear.

Gregory arose from his seat and walked to the cockpit door, opened it, spoke a few words and then returned to his seat. He was followed closely by Bev whose face was flushed. She removed the plates and other lunch items from their tables, took them to the galley and returned with a fresh glass of beer for Gregory. He took a sip, then looked out the big oval window next to his seat for a moment. Then he began, looking straight ahead and speaking to no one at the front of the plane, not across the aisle to her.

"I first met your bio-mom, as you call her, about twenty-two years ago in New York. Of course, I didn't know she was anyone's mom, bio or otherwise, at the time. To the world paying any attention, she was merely a party girl; one of thousands of the anonymous creatures whose existence served but one purpose to men like me. However, I could tell immediately your mom was different from the rest of the chattering gaggle because she captured not just my momentary attention, but my imagination. I believe you could say she was 'my type' and that first caught my eye. It was more than that, she intrigued me, and that's what held me to her.

"You see, Jennifer, when one is living life one high at a time, rudderless, unmotivated, everything is empty, the world becomes devoid of substance. I was drowning in a sea of excess but I was smart enough, or aware enough, to know I was going to wind up dead in my room someday soon if nothing changed. Your bio-mom held the promise of substance in an empty existence. There was something in her eyes that I wanted. A spark. The trailhead to a path back to the surface, to the land of the living.

"At that point in my life, I was hanging out in clubs, living in my family's hotel on 5th Avenue near Central Park in Manhattan. My father was still alive and running the family businesses. I never had much interest in the businesses, never had the drive for anything but the perks of wealth. I didn't care how the money was made, only that it was freely available to subsidize my every whim. My father tolerated my indifference toward the business just as he had tolerated everything else I did after the day my mother died. He also indulged me every wish, again from that very day forward. Surely, he took note of my lifestyle, yet so long as I didn't fatally embarrass the family name in the eyes of his contemporaries, he said or did little to derail it.

"I have always attributed my father's indulgences were resultant of the guilt he felt over the fact he was absent from the family on the day my mother died. That weekend was to have been a family time, yet he had crammed one more business meeting into his schedule before the start of the Labor Day holiday and had sent mother and I to the lake house early. I was seven years old that summer. When we arrived, mother had taken me for a swim. I loved to swim, took naturally to the water. Even at seven, I was a strong swimmer, having won numerous competitions, several against swimmers far older than myself, at our natatorium in the city.

"The Friday before Labor Day weekend was sunny and warm in upstate New York, though the spring-fed lake remained a little chilly even following a long, hot summer. After an hour or so of swimming and splashing around with mother, she told me it was time to get out for lunch. I swam for the dock. I thought she was right behind me, but when I climbed the ladder and turned around, I saw her about twenty feet away, struggling, flailing, choking, gasping and I simply stood there in fascination until she finally slid beneath the water and into the depths. Anyway..."

Jennifer could see a new wetness in his eyes. His hand left hand trembled slightly and he steadied it on the arm of his seat. He drained a hearty draw from his glass, waved to Bev for a refill with his right.

"Would you like anything more to drink, my dear?" he asked when she arrived with a new glass filled with amber and foam.

"No, thank you," she replied and then watched Bev walk back to the galley. "Please, go on, Gregory."

"Ah, yes, where was I? Oh, I remember. There were many clubs in Manhattan back then, just like there are now, I would imagine, although I've given up frequenting them for years now. I hear stories and see things on the internet and it appears things were different then than they are now. We would snort lines of coke from tabletops right in the open, have sex anyplace we could find a dark corner or even talk some chick into blowing us right at the table if we felt the urge. Nobody screwed with us. We were rich. It was all the debauchery we could handle without any of the consequences, at least none of the earthly variety. Nobody carried a video camera in their phones as they do today, and the club security kept out the rabble, so inside the club, whatever we did remained only rumor.

"One night, I was heading into Studio 54 on West 54th Street with a group of friends. 'Studio' was one of the hottest places going at the time and one of the founding four partners was a friend of mine - you'll have to guess which one - so we were treated especially well there. Over its prime run, after a few fitful starts and stops, Studio 54 was IT, the center of The Scene. Some media type labeled the place a 'modern-day Gomorrah' which merely intensified everyone's desire to go and be seen there. It was where the rich, the beautiful, and real celebrities hung out when in Manhattan.

"We poured out of our limo and headed for the entrance when I spotted your mother standing in the regular line with a group of her friends. She was breathtaking and I suspected the bouncers would let her in, but her friends were ordinary club types and there wasn't a snowball's chance they'd get through the doors. Your mother, though, was H - O - T, HOT, wearing a silver sequined mini-dress that barely covered her ass, and matching five-inch heels, and I immediately wanted her."

Gregory again looked across the aisle at Jennifer. His eyes moved over her from top to bottom.

"You know, you could be your bio-mom's double at her age. Her almond-shaped, deep brown eyes had a bit more green and a bit less gold flecks than do yours, but other than that you could be twins separated in time. You even wear your hair much like she did.

"Well, I grabbed her by the hand and pulled her over the rope line and she walked in with me, leaving her friends behind without a peep of protest. An hour later, we were doing lines of coke at our table on one of the balconies. We partied all night, finally leaving around 4 a.m., and she came home with me. That was Sunday morning, and by Monday morning she was gone. No note, no good-bye, no nothing. That wasn't unusual back then - right before AIDS arrived and scared the shit out of most of us - and I usually just moved on to the next one. Your mother was under my skin. Like I said, she was definitely my type *and* she intrigued me.

"A week went by and I didn't see or hear from her and it was frankly driving me nuts. I asked around, watched for her at Studio 54 and other clubs, greased the palms of every bouncer in the city. Of course, how were they going to pick her out of the crowds with just a description? I described her as about five-foot-eight, chestnut shoulder-length hair, gorgeous brown eyes with green flecks, a smile that would light up Broadway and a body that would close down 42nd Street. Your mom had a body that just would not quit."

"42nd Street?" Jennifer asked.

"Oh, I forgot you're too young to remember the old 42nd Street in Manhattan when it was the center of the skin trade in the city. The section of 42nd near Times Square was an area lined with grind house theaters, peep shows, adult book stores, and street walkers. Of course, that strata of society, along with those who patronize their services, all gathered in one place tend to attract other unsavory types like pick pockets, pimps, and muggers, which lead one contemporary comedian to quip, 'They call it forty-second street because you're not safe if you spend more than forty-seconds on it'.

"Eventually, but mainly by accident rather than through perseverance, I was able to track her down to her work. She was then employed in the art department of a small advertising company headquartered in Brooklyn. I think her title was something like Associate Graphic Designer, but what she truly aspired to be was an artist. I've seen some of her paintings and I know where you get your talent, Jennifer. Your mother was very good. Almost as good as you. She could have made it as a freelance artist, had she only been blessed with a benevolent benefactor as you are.

"So, one day, I just showed up at the advertising company's offices and then realized I didn't even know her last name. I gave the first name and described her to the receptionist who immediately knew who I was talking about.   She buzzed your mother's cubicle and told a rather surprised woman that she had a guest in the lobby.

"Your mom walked into the lobby dressed in a very conservative business suit, skirt down past her knees, two-inch pumps, her hair up in a bun and wearing hardly any makeup.   When she saw me she stopped dead in her tracks.   Her gorgeous eyes darted back and forth, the only external indication of the fight or flight conflict playing itself out in her head.

"Eventually, she walked over and greeted me in a totally professional manner, which belied our hot weekend of sex, drugs, and rock and roll together.   I asked if she'd like to grab a cup of coffee in the lobby and she agreed.   I think her consent partially had to do with eliminating a possible embarrassing situation from the eyes and ears of her coworkers, but who knows?   Now, this was long before a Starbucks sat on every corner, so we just went down to the cafeteria and got ourselves a cup of Joe.

"Shortly after, we became an item.   We were seen all over town. Not just nightclubs, but she dragged me to art galleries, the theater, the symphony, and once to the ballet.   She was teaching me the finer things in life, and my father's money was making it possible.   On Christmas, I took her home to meet my father.   On New Year's Eve, at Studio 54, with a four karat diamond ring in my pocket, I was ready to make a commitment to her.   I wanted the New Year to ring in on a happy note.

"Your mother was supposed to meet me at the club that night, but instead she sent a letter with a friend of mine.   In the pages, amongst the apologies and promises of further explanation when she returned, she told me about you.   It was the first time she had even hinted you existed.   I was shocked, to say the least.   She said she was going to try to find you."

Gregory reached into his pants pocket and pulled out his phone which Jennifer could tell was vibrating.   The jet was equipped with a cellular receiver which linked through the satellite communications system.   Because his system crossed between satellite and cellular technologies, the jet acted like a mobile cellular tower which linked any cell phones on board to the ground-based system.

He looked at the phone, tapped the screen a couple of times.   His face contorted into a cross between a grimace and anger and he got out of his seat. He headed to the back of the plane and the sleeping compartment. Jennifer could hear him cursing under his breath.

"Gregory?" Jennifer asked. "Is everything all right?"

He stopped and turned to her.

"Nothing for you to worry your sweet little head about, my dear. Nothing at all. However, I do need to take care of this."

Jennifer's mind raced. Was this it? Was this all he was going to tell her? She returned to her initial inquiry.

"What about my question?"

"What was the question?" he asked. "Ah, yes, is your mother alive or dead?"

"Yes," she said. As she felt the jet nose over to begin it's descent, he gave the answer, or so she thought.

"I would say, the answer would be yes, my dear," he said, his eyes a copy of Brutus' when he had finished toying with his prey and had cornered the mouse for the final moment. "I believe you could be meeting your bio-mom very soon."

He went into the bedroom of the jet and closed the door.

Inside the compartment Gregory erupted into a barely controlled rage and threw the phone onto the bed, where it promptly vibrated again. He picked up the phone and watched a second image download. Sensing a headache coming on, he laid on the bed and picked up the intercom to the cockpit.

"Yes, sir," Captain Dan said.

"Call ahead and have the chopper ready for immediate departure when I arrive," Gregory ordered. "Arrange to have one of the charter companies take Ms. Shea to Molokai. Get her off the aircraft immediately after we land."

"Yes, sir."

"Oh, and tell operations I won't be needing the chopper pilot." Gregory turned his head to look out the window but could see nothing but a blinding white haze this far out. "I'll fly myself."

He hung up the inter-phone and then again scrolled through the two images which had just arrived on his cell phone.

"I don't know what kind of game you are playing at, my dear," he hissed. "I can assure you, however, it's a dangerous one."

I felt Cassie release her hug almost immediately after our kiss and I let her go.   Her eyes avoided mine and a moment later she disappeared into the house, leaving me standing on the lanai alone with my thoughts. Any buzz I had achieved had gone and was being replaced by a headache. I rubbed my temples. What the hell was I doing? What the hell was she doing?

I pushed my hands into the remains of the cold water in the ice bucket, then rubbed them onto my face. It felt good, but I needed some Advil. I walked through the doors and into the house. I called her name. No response. I wandered through the kitchen area, peered into several rooms in that wing of the house and then into the rotunda. I went by the stairs and called up. Still no response. I looked down the east wing of the house. All the doors were closed except for the one on the end which was slightly ajar. A brass key was in the lock.

Walking down the hallway in search of her, I felt like an intruder. Two or three times I almost turned around to go back to the areas of the home I had been invited into and wait for Cassie to return. I listened for any activity as I passed each closed door. Through the sliver of light coming through the cracked door at the end of the hall, I observed several flashes of moving shadow. The polite friend part of me wanted to call out. The investigator part of me won out, however, so I lightened my tread and approached as quietly as possible for me.

At the doorway, I peered through the crack of an opening and into what appeared to be a large office or library. I couldn't see the entire room but I could hear activity at the far end. Carefully and slowly I pushed the door a little further open. Finally, I could see Cassie standing behind a large desk, leafing through a book.   I wondered if that was one of Gregory's journals she had told me about. Was this Gregory's private office? Is that why the key in the lock?

I backed off a couple of steps from the door and thought. The house was large, but she should have heard me calling from the other wing or the rotunda with this door open. I had, after all, used what my mother called my outside voice. So, did she want me to come and find her? If she did, she would expect me to walk in and find her with the journals.   If she didn't, and I gave her too much warning, she would tuck them away and I'd lose my chance to go through them for more information.

My decision made, I did three things concurrently. I knocked, I called her name, and I pushed the door fully open. Cassie still stood behind the desk. Two books lay there, one of them open. She looked at me. Did I detect a wry little smile before the painting on of a mask of surprise?

"I'm sorry," I said. "I wasn't sure if you were okay. Plus, I could really use some Advil, if you have them."

I closed the distance between us, maintaining eye contact with her. She looked down at the books, then back up at me. With an absent move, she closed the open book.

"I know we've got Advil," she said. "I find that's the only thing that works for me when I get a headache."

I was now directly opposite her at the desk. She stacked the books one on top of the other.

"I suspect those are the journals?" I asked as I moved around the side of the desk and stood next to her. Her right hand was flat on the top of the uppermost book. "May I take a look?"

"I'd rather you didn't," she said.

It was a halfhearted protest, in my judgment. I could have easily just pulled one away, but this was the client, regardless of what personal interplay was going on at that point, so I didn't make a move for them. If she wanted to play cat and mouse games, I guess it was her prerogative.

So, instead, I walked behind her, moved over to a window at that end of the room, moved aside the shear and looked outside. The topography of the land sloped away from this side of the house and I noted there was no lanai outside. I also noted the windows not only carried the nearly invisible state-of-the-art alarm sensors as did the rest of the exterior doors and windows I had observed in the place, but an additional system.

I turned to walk back toward Cassie and noted something unusual under the desk. From that far back I could make out an open wooden panel with a storage area containing four segments. One of the segments was empty, one held some legal pads behind which sat what appeared to be old cigar boxes stored on their ends, and two contained black lacquer boxes of some type.

Cassie hadn't turned around, yet I had caught her watching me out of the corner of my eye when I was looking out the window. I was beginning to know just what a mouse felt like.

"Willy, I just can't let you go through Gregory's journals," she said. "I told you that I'd look for additional information for you and I did." Cassie paused, then added, "Last night, I did."

"So why the cat and mouse, Cassie?" I asked. I was now standing directly behind her. Close enough to feel her breathe. Close enough for her to feel me breathe. I placed my right hand on top of her hand, my fingers slipping between hers. Neither of us moved or breathed for a long moment.

"Willy, don't," she pleaded. "It just isn't right. I'm still married to Gregory and regardless of what you may think my feelings are for you - and I'm not saying you'd be right or wrong at this point - I just cannot break my vows to him."

I looked over her shoulder. I could see her heartbeat in the artery along the side of her slender, tanned neck. I could see her subtle curves transforming into not-so-subtle curves and then disappearing inside her dress. Her bare shoulders were no more than an inch away from my chest. I could smell her perfume mixed with her musk. It was enough to drive me mad, were I to let it. I wondered if she were feeling the same urges, if her senses were overloading as mine were. The one thing I couldn't see were her eyes. I slid my hand back from hers, my fingertips gently caressing the back of her hand as I withdrew. She drew in a quick, short breath.

"All right, Cassie," I said. "You're the boss." I walked around the front of the desk and waited. I tossed my hands plaintively out to each side. "Your move."

Then, turning my back on her, I walked out of the office and down the hall. I knew she'd follow when she placed the books back in their hiding place. The question was 'Where was the office key was hidden?' I surmised it had to be a hidden single key since there was no fob attached and it was not one of a group of keys on a ring. People are people, and they normally will hide a single key somewhere near the lock it opens. As I approached the end of the hallway, about to pass into the rotunda, I heard the door close and the lock being turned. A moment later, I turned and looked over my shoulder to see Cassie crouched under a hallway table, obviously slipping the key back into its little nook. I turned my head away and continued walking before she noticed I had been watching.

"Willy," she called to me.

I turned and watched her walk toward me. I always loved to watch her walk. When she'd walk away from you in those tight hip hugger jeans... Well, anyway, she walked toward me.

"I've got the additional information and papers for you up in my room." She turned right at the rotunda and headed for the stairway on the east side. "Come on up. I'll show you the rest of the house as long as you're here."

I followed her up the stairs. First, she took me to the west wing, noting it was essentially Gregory's side of the house on this level. He had an impressive gym set up next to a large master suite that I assumed once was their shared bedroom.

"I take it Gregory works out," I said, lifting a forty pound free weight from the rack and doing a few quick curls.

"He's got a routine," she said looking around absently. "Cardio, weights, Taijiquan, Pa-Kua, he tries to keep in shape."

"Excuse me, did you say Pa-Kua? What's that?" I had heard of Taijiquan or more colloquially Tai Chi, but not Pa-Kua.

"Yes, Pa-Kua," she said. "From what I understand, it's some sort of advanced Chinese boxing technique. It took Gregory six months to find someone who would even agree to teach him the fundamentals and another couple of years practicing the techniques before he went back to be judged by The Master, as he called him." As she spoke the words, she looked half interested and half not. "Another one of Gregory's obsessions."

"Went back?" I asked. "Went back where?"

"To China," she said. "That's where they practice the discipline and he wanted to be judged by the best."

I left the gym with her and she gave me the tour of the other various functional rooms on the second level. Apart from his and hers master suites, the upper floor was personally designed specialty rooms of various sorts: sewing room for her, multimedia room, gym for her, gym for him, an art studio for her, a small library, an office for her. A lanai ran the span of each wing, ending at the rotunda. At each master suite, the lanai wrapped part of the outside perimeter as well.

We entered her master suite, a near twin to his, and located opposite, at the far end of the east wing. The bedroom was large - very large, actually - with a king size canopy bed, a cozy sitting area with a couple of chairs and a small table, another desk area, a scattering of small tables, a dresser, and an armoire. I wondered who she entertained in here but then let the question go unasked. Besides, big houses need lots of stuff just to fill them up. On the table in the seating area was a thick hardcover book. I picked it up, read the cover: Ayn Rand's *Atlas Shrugged*. A bookmark was inserted about halfway through.

"How are you finding the book," I asked.

"Heavy," she said with a laugh. "Seriously, though, I've tried getting through it several times and this time I promised myself I wouldn't give up until I did. Gregory suggested it to me years ago. Someone had introduced him to it years earlier and he found it fascinating. So far, to me, it's a story about an assortment of dysfunctional people running an antiquated railroad, in a time where nobody much cares about anything."

I set the book down.

"Have you read it?" she asked.

"Me? No, I'd use it for a doorstop just because of its size. Besides, I've never been much on reading books which could give you a hernia." I had tried reading *Atlas Shrugged* when I lived in the Caymans, but found Ayn Rand's writing tedious. Her metaphors are contradictory and confusing, at least in my opinion, and she liked to change subjects and perspectives from paragraph to paragraph which I found odd. I thought that if Cassie had made it halfway, there would be nothing gained in deflating her desire to finish it this time through so I let her off the hook. "I'm more of a classics and modern thriller kind of guy. I find the easily discernible good guy versus bad guy of Jack Higgins my favorite fun reading."

If she knew Jack Higgins, she let the comment pass. Just as well, I thought. I walked over to the bed and sat on one side of a padded bench which spanned the foot. I watched Cassie's back and then looked out over the channel. The wind had picked up and the fog bank was now much closer to shore. While it was apparent the wind was whipping, I was amazed there was no sound of it inside the house. I started watching Cassie again. Her hair fell softly onto her bare shoulders, a bit of a natural wave giving it bounce as she moved. I closed my eyes and recalled how good it smelled.

Cassie continued shuffling papers in her desk. Finally, she pulled out a manila envelope, stuffed about a quarter inch of documents inside, came over and handed it to me, then sat down on the other end of the bench. A very respectable distance was maintained between us.

"I was able to find more information on the names I gave you," she said. "I also thought I'd give you the prenuptial agreement which lays out the items of proof of adultery we need to show in order for it to apply. No sense us missing anything when we could just as easily get it all assembled at once. I don't intend on giving Gregory another chance."

I took the envelope, hefted it and judged it to contain about fifty pages. Ah, something else for Sandy to go over, I thought.

"Speaking of giving Gregory a second chance," I said, recalling what she had told me about the Jeep's brakes. "Are you sure you want to be staying here during all this?"

"Oh, no," she said, vigorously shaking her head. "Gregory would suspect something was wrong and that would make things very difficult for both of us. It's best to keep things the way they are. Fewer questions."

"I'd feel better if you took some precautions," I said, placing my hand onto hers.

She responded only with a knowing smile.

Marcy's meeting at the taxi company was disappointing. The cabbie remembered a lone woman fare from the airport to Le Village, but he had paid little attention after she had seemed uninterested in any type of conversation. There were no cameras in the cab, she also discovered. About the only thing of substance the driver did recall was that the woman had paid him in U.S. currency. A fifty dollar bill, and had told him to keep the change. Marcy thought it was a handsome tip indeed for a fare of about $20.00 Canadian. Janet wasn't cheap, but she never threw her money about in such a fashion. Why did she pay the driver in U.S. currency when she must have had more than adequate funds in Canadian dollars?

As she rode the Metro train back to Janet's apartment and stared at nothing out the window, Marcy mulled the information which had been assembled thus far. She was becoming increasingly convinced of one central fact: Janet had never come home.

The official documentation completely overruled her conclusion, however. The airline ticket in the name of Janet Hopkins had been used, and U.S. airport and airline security procedures, being at least as stringent as the policies enforced in Canada, meant the woman had obviously checked through with a valid photo I.D. in the name of Janet Hopkins. Once the flight from Maui landed in Vancouver, Janet had entered the Canadian system and that meant passing through immigration and customs before boarding the flight to Montreal. So, the photo I.D. had to have been a valid Canadian passport in the name of Janet Hopkins. That meant either the impostor was physically indistinguishable from Janet to trained security and immigration personnel, which would be high risk, or more likely, fraudulent documents were used.

"Who has that kind of ability? To forge a Canadian passport? Why would anyone go to all that trouble just to replace Janet?" Marcy asked herself.

Her phone vibrated in her bag and she pulled it out and checked the caller identification which indicated the call was coming from a blocked number. Marcy pushed the answer button, even though she normally didn't take these types of calls.

"Hello?" she said. She listened for a moment and then her eyes lit as the caller's name registered. "Yes, Officer, thank you for getting back to me." Another listening moment. "I'm sorry to bother you on your day off."

Marcy explained her suspicions to him. She told him about the mysterious woman nobody at the apartment building could identify. She treaded carefully on the surveillance tape information because the last thing she wanted to do was get Kevin into trouble. By the time she got to the minor details of the cab fare paid in U.S. dollars, the excessive tip, and then closed with the absence of panties in the dirty laundry, she could tell she was losing him.

"Ms. Simon," he said with obvious forced patience. "We checked with immigration, right? We checked with the airline. Both have records which confirm a Ms. Janet Hopkins checked in for the flight, travelled on the tickets, was processed through immigration, and arrived safely home in Montreal along with 156 other passengers and crew. The taxi company records confirm a single woman matching her description was transported from the airport to Ms. Hopkins' home address. The driver told me personally that he watched the woman use a key to enter the lobby of the building."

"I know," she replied. "Many of those facts I have also confirmed, and I have other resources I've checked."

"Other resources?" he asked. "What are you playing at, Ms. Simon?"

"I'm trying to find my friend, Janet Hopkins," she said with an indignant tone. "Just as I hope you people are."

"There is no reason to become annoyed with me, Ms. Simon. This is an open police investigation and we don't welcome meddlers. If you have information, we'd appreciate if you'd simply pass the tips to us for follow up."

Marcy rolled her eyes. *Functionaries*, she thought. They're the same in every country.

She spoke in a calmer tone.

"I'm not interfering, Officer, I'm merely keeping my eyes open. I called you so I could report some anomalies I have discovered and expected not a lecture, but that you'd take note of these issues."

He promised her he'd include the details of their conversation in a follow up report in the morning. She asked if he would like to come and pick up the dirty laundry for possible DNA testing. He hung up the phone on her.

Marcy looked at the dead phone in her hand.

"I guess it really was your day off, eh?" she said before sliding the phone back into her purse. A plan was quickly forming in her mind.

The Gulfstream jet touched down smoothly and rolled to the end of the runway before taxiing to the Thomason hangar at the edge of the field. Gregory could see the helicopter waiting on the ramp. All the 'Remove Before Flight' ribbons were absent meaning they had indeed readied the chopper for flight as he had instructed.

Gregory waited until he saw Jennifer being hustled toward an idling car which would take her to one of the charter companies and then exited the bedroom compartment, exited the jet and jogged to the chopper.

He strapped in, put on the headset, switched the electrical system to battery and pushed the starter button. When the turbine spun to 15%, he added fuel and the engine caught. As the whine of the jet engine increased, the main rotor started to slowly turn, coming up to speed a few moments later.

Gregory scanned the gauges. Electrical - on line. Hydraulics - on line. Fuel and oil pressures in the green. He flipped the switch to power the avionics and depressed the mic switch on the cyclic.

"Maui tower, helicopter triple-one-golf-tango, at the Thomason ramp, request departure from here and flight to the west at five hundred."

"Helicopter triple-one-golf-tango, Maui tower, cleared as requested. Proceed south until crossing the Hana Highway before turning west. We have a United seven-six-seven departing runway zero-two at this time. Caution wake turbulence."

"Roger, triple-one-golf-tango, wilco. I have the seven-six-seven in sight." Gregory raised the collective, increasing power to the engine and lifting the helicopter from the ramp. He moved the cyclic slightly forward and to the right. The chopper responded crisply with the inputs and climbed out over the hangar. By the time he was over the Hana Highway, the helicopter was level at five-hundred feet. Gregory banked to the right and accelerated across the valley toward the far shore.

Gregory knew there would be some site seeing choppers in the air, so he maintained a careful watch. He made a call to the tower to advise he was exiting the airport area to the west at five hundred feet and would be continuing along the shoreline to the Thomason heliport. At north Kihei, he turned south and continued past Wailea and Makena before cutting the corner just short of Le Perouse Bay headed for home. Off to the right, he saw the fog over the channel. As he got closer to home, he could see the line of roiling mist had moved nearer to shore. He hoped the heliport would be clear so there'd be no delays. He couldn't wait to see his wife.

Our first indication that someone had arrived at the house was the sound of a door slamming and a loud calling voice.

"Cassandra, I'm home," came the call from downstairs. "Where are you, sweetie?"

I watched the color drain out of Cassie's face. She pulled her hand from mine and jumped up from the bench.

"Oh my God, it's Gregory," she said. Her eyes darted around the room.

I sat and watched her for a moment and then stood up. I slid the envelope into the back of my cargo shorts, just inside of Willie and pulled my T-shirt back down. I doubted Gregory was going to hug me, so I figured I'd get by with the bulky concealment.

"Relax, Cassie," I said. "Let's just go downstairs and greet your husband. I'm just an old friend whom you happened to run into at The Shops at Wailea and decided to invite out for a friendly lunch and tour of the house."

Her eyes calmed and her face flushed. She touched my cheek.

"My hero," she said, looking into my eyes.

We exited the room, walked down the hall, descended the staircase to the main floor and found Gregory curiously investigating the two empty champagne flutes and bottle of Cristal in the same condition. There was still a half carafe of OJ though and a scattering of fruit and drying cheese were he hungry or thirsty.

Cassie took the lead across the rotunda tile into the front room area. Gregory turned as he heard her approaching. When he saw me, he smiled, but not the friendly type.

"I didn't know you'd be entertaining gentleman callers while I was away, my dear," he said, his voice dripping with feigned congeniality. "Perhaps I should have called first. I do hope I didn't interrupt anything."

Cassie moved to give him a chaste welcome home hug and kiss on the cheek.

"Darling, this is an old friend of mine from junior high school, Willy Langdon," she said, spreading her arms to complete the welcome circle.

I extended my hand and stepped close to Gregory.

"William Langdon," I said. "You must be Greg. I've heard so much about you. It's a pleasure to meet you."

I saw the flash of anger in his eyes which he quickly extinguished. He smiled again and I noted his perfect white teeth. He shook my hand. He had a strong grip, but a small, soft hand with delicate fingers, and he held the shake way too short of a time. I thought he must suffer from some sort of social awkwardness or perhaps just when it came to other men in his home. After all, like all unexpected returning husbands who find their wife on the second floor with another man, he must have wondered just where my hands had been.

"I prefer to go by Gregory, Bill," he said. He wiped his hand on his slacks.

Solid return, buddy.

"I prefer William, myself, although in junior high Cassie called me Willy. With a 'Y'," I added.

Gregory looked at me curiously, and then again at the champagne and hors d'oeuvres leftovers. I caught him toss an irritated look at Cassie.

"I didn't mean to interrupt the party," he said. He moved around the couch, grabbed a handful of grapes from the tray and began eating them one by one.

Cassie followed and sat on the couch, just where she had sat with me. I moved around and sat down myself, just a little more distant from Cassie than where I had planted my behind before. Gregory walked over to the windows and looked out over the channel. The fog was beginning to move across the lawn. I couldn't even see water beyond the cliff's edge anymore.

"Don't be ridiculous, darling," Cassie said. "I ran into Willy at The Shops the other day. He's here on vacation." She smiled nervously at his back. "You can imagine my surprise after all these years."

Gregory turned and stared through me.

"You must not have changed a bit to be recognized by my wife in such a random place after thirty years."

I smiled, pushed my right hand through my hair and then patted my belly.

"Seriously, I haven't changed a bit, Gregory," I said. "I look just the same today as I did in my junior high school I.D. photo. We Langdons age early, then just stop. I know it sounds weird, but it's true." I wondered if he picked up on the sarcasm.

Before he could respond, I let him off the hook.

"Seriously, though, it was I who recognized Cassie. I was sitting on the edge of that fountain they have there, licking an ice cream cone from Lappert's: white chocolate macadamia nut in a chocolate lined waffle cone." I patted my stomach again and grinned. "Then, out of nowhere, zing, Cassie walks through."

I smiled at Cassie. She seemed to be holding her breath. In a minute I figured she'll turn blue, so I resolved to continue to a quick ending. Besides, Gregory wore a look of being a little bored, along with his thinly veiled hostility.

"I would recognize her anywhere." I reached out and patted her hand and from the look which darted from her beautiful brown eyes, I thought she was going to turn to stone. "You know we dated way back when? I'm certain she's told you all about me."

"Sorry, no," Gregory said. "Cassandra has been fairly tight lipped about people she knew before we met. We have an unspoken agreement that what happened before we met is in the past. Washed down the river and out to sea, if you will; to our way of thinking, the past is just so much flotsam and jetsam to be avoided." He walked over and sat on the arm of the couch next to Cassie and rubbed his hand over her shoulders. "Isn't that right, dear?"

I wondered if Cassie felt like a ping-pong ball caught in a match between arch rivals.

"Present company excepted, of course," she said. Then she pulled her hand from my grip and used it to brush the hair off her shoulders, knocking Gregory's touch from there as well.

Interesting, I thought.

"Well, we were an item for about eight weeks," I said. "That was a lifetime back in the day."

"We are about to celebrate our twenty-first anniversary," Gregory said. "I think I have you beat on that point, William."

"You most certainly do, Gregory. I envy you. You're a lucky man."

"Uh, huh," he said and then got off the arm of the couch, walked toward the kitchen.

Cassie watched him walk off and then mouthed to me, 'What the hell are you doing?'. Then, as he was gone from the room, she continued in a low tone. "He's going to go crazy and I'm going to pay the price after you leave."

I shook my head and explained to her that he won't dare do a thing to her because he now knows I am around.

"He's a coward at his core, Cassie. I could see that in his eyes and I could feel it in his handshake. I wanted him to know you mean something to me. I'm an unknown to him, and therefore dangerous. He understands that if he did anything to you, I'd find out about it and that's the last thing he would want."

Gregory came back from the kitchen carrying a can of Coke, popped the top and retook his seat on the arm of the couch. He took a swig from the can, stifled a belch.

"So, what brings you to Maui, William? Business or pleasure?" he asked.

"A little bit of both," I replied. "I guess most of the world would call it a working vacation."

"Are you staying in Wailea?" he asked.

"Sure am. Beautiful there."

"Yes, I'd say all of Maui is beautiful, but there are some parts and some things on the island which are prettier than others. It's all a matter of personal taste, but I'm partial to the south shore myself." He took another swig of the Coke.

I stole a glance at Cassie.

"Well, you are right there, Gregory."

"At one of the resort hotels?"

"No, I went the condo route this trip," I said.

"This trip?" he asked. "Have you been to Maui before?"

"No, first time. I would like to come back here though. So I imagine my comment meant that I hoped for more trips here."

"Many plush condos in Wailea," he said.

"Well, the place I'm at is certainly a reasonable facsimile of plush."

"Which condo complex is that?"

"Palms at Wailea, I think they call it."

"On vacation from what?" he asked.

"Excuse me?" I said.

"What do you do for a living?" he restated. "What are you on vacation from?"

"Oh, I guess you could call me a research analyst."

"I could call you that," he said. "What would you call what you do?"

There was no sense lying to him. A simple Google search for me would bring him to our website.

"I'm a private detective, Gregory."

He smirked.

"Ah, one of those guys who creep around at night and go through people's garbage cans? Or are you more of the Magnum

P.I. kind of private detectives, you know, the type who go around rescuing damsels in distress every week?"

"I've done the digging through garbage at times. I found my flip-flops that way." I smiled and pointed down the hall toward the front door. "As far as types go, I think I'm more of a cross between Jim Rockford and Lieutenant Columbo, although technically, Columbo was still a *real* detective."

"Interesting," he said, but asked for no explanation.

I could tell he was as amused by my flip-flop quip as I was with his damsel in distress remark.

He rose from his seat and kissed Cassie on the top of the head.

"Well, I'm going to tend to some things in my office," he said. "It's been an interesting few days. I think you'll find the story interesting, too, my dear. We'll talk later."

He offered his hand to me.

I rose to shake it.

"William," he said. "It was a pleasure making your acquaintance."

His grip was just as firm as before, but he held it longer, and made eye contact. For an instant I doubted part of my earlier assessment of him.

"Same here, Greg."

He intensified his grip. He obviously carried a great deal of strength in those seemingly soft hands.

"I mean Gregory," I said. After all, it's his house, so why not let him be the alpha male?

We released our grip. I resisted the urge to rub my right hand.

"I hope this won't be the last time we see you," he said. With the hand which held his Coke, he gestured to my T-shirt. "I see you've already been quite a comfort to my wife."

I looked down and saw the smears of eye make-up on my chest. Oops, I thought. I put a smile on my face.

"I guess that depends on Cassie, but I hope not as well," I said.

Gregory left us and headed for the east wing.

When he was gone, Cassie was on her feet.

"Regardless of what you think about what's at Gregory's core, Willy, that was stupid," she said. "He's a dangerous man." She looked toward the hallway. "I think it's best you go for now. I'll be in touch soon."

Cassie escorted me to the front door. I risked giving her a good-bye hug, slipped on my flip-flops and headed out into the afternoon. The helicopter Gregory arrived in sat on the helipad. I could hear the tinking of the metal as the engine cooled. I made a note to myself about the soundproofing in that house, should I ever get the chance to be back there. Something was telling me I would.

As I maneuvered up the driveway, I pulled the manila envelope and Willie from my waistband. The envelope I tossed onto the passenger seat and I stuck Willie and the holster in the center console. My eyes searched for the surveillance cameras and evidence of other trespassing alarm systems. They were well hidden, but I did pick up a couple of camera locations and what could have very well been evidence of what I call a 'trembler system'. That's the same kind of intruder monitoring system which the government uses at high security installations to determine if anyone is walking across the ground.

Years ago, I was doing some employee background checks at a nuclear power plant and while being escorted out by one of the security guards, a large egret landed inside the fence about one hundred feet away. We hadn't taken three steps when he got a radio call to check out a possible intruder. It was my first experience with what the guard called their trembler system.

The guard told me that if he told me more about it, he'd have to kill me. I bribed him with a story about the buxom blonde receptionist's former life. I told him if it got out, I'd have to kill him and then added that I was fairly certain of the two of us, I was the only one who had done it before. We promised each other complete silence, shared the information, and to this day neither of us has been forced to kill the other.

The gate opened automatically as I approached. As I crested the small rise just before the main road, I noted the old Hawaiian gentleman from the porch earlier was now leaning against a piled lava rock wall just on the other side of the road. He had a beer in his hand and another can dangling from a six-pack ring hung over his fingers. He gave me a wave and I pulled over and rolled down the passenger window.

"Hi there," I said through the window as he made his way close to the Jeep.

"Howzit?" he said with a strong accent.

"It's good," I replied. "How's it with you?" Well, so far so good with understanding the natives. I guessed it may get harder.

"Is good, brah," he said. He rested his arms and the one beer on the window sill. The beer in the six-pack ring bumped against the outside of the door. "Whatchoo do at dat place?" he asked, gesturing with his beer toward Cassie's house.

"Just visiting an old friend," I said.

He closed one eye and looked at me with a disbelieving squint. Then he finished off the beer and tossed the empty can back behind him. Next, he reached inside with a gnarled and meaty hand and offered a shake. After a triple change positioning of our hands, we finished the complex shake ritual, he let go of my confused hand and then opened the last beer. A spew of pressurized foam spat droplets on the envelope.

"And dat asshole come home early, yeah" he said. "Not good for make visit?" He laughed.

"You must be Keoki," I said. "Cassie told me a little about you. I heard you didn't like Gregory much."

"You live Maui?" he asked.

"No, just visiting," I said.

"You must like make visit, yeah?" He laughed. "Yeah, my name Keoki Moke Kekipi Keaweaheulu and no, I do not like him."

I couldn't follow the name much past Keoki. It must have been why Cassie only used his first name.

"I hope it's okay that I call you Keoki," I said.

"Sure, brah, what your name?"

"William," I said. "William Langdon. I'm from New Orleans."

That brought a smile.

"My youngest boy take me there one time. New Orleans." He took a sip of the beer. "He work at da university in Baton Rouge. Work wit fish." He shook his head. "I told him you go all dat way to work wit fish. We got plenty fish right here. Dis no place for keiki no more. Not da same aina I grow up. Now all visitors and haole from da mainland."

"It sounds like you enjoyed your visit," I said. "Does your son still work at LSU? The university?"

He nodded slowly. His eyes went distant and got moist. I took that as a yes.

"How many kids do you have?" I asked.

"Six keiki," he said. "All da mainland now. Dis no place for keiki no more." He took a long draw on the beer.

I figured this was not a happy topic of conversation for him, so I decided to change the subject. Keoki beat me to it, although I'm not sure the subject matter he selected was any less painful to him.

"You know, dis land in my family many, many years. Before Kamehameha come. Many ancestors fight dis land. Some die dis ahupua'a. Still, Keoki need sell it to dat haole. Dat Gregory. For da keiki."

"From what Cassie said, you only did it for your keiki, to give them a better life."

He snorted at that.

"Da pilialo, da wife, she a good person. Most time. But Gregory, me no like." He drained the last of the beer and tossed the can and still attached six-pack ring behind him. "Yeah, Keoki do it for da keiki. Now Keoki never see da keiki. Keiki never come back to da aina."

He stood up straight, looked up and down the main road.

"Almost time for da mailman," he said and he turned to go. "You enjoy da aina, Malihini,"

"Malihini?" I asked.

"Visitor, Malihini," he said. "Mo bettah den William."

I watched him walk up his driveway. He picked up the cans and carried them along. I felt bad for Keoki. After a few moments, I heard a vehicle approaching from the east. I looked into the rear view mirror and a mail truck almost fly over the last rise. I saw I was stopped in front of the mailbox and then fully understood the blaring horn. Rolling up the window, I started to drive off on the bad gravel road. About thirty-seconds later, the mail truck passed me going up the next hill. The driver tossed me a big smile and a shaka just before his truck tossed gravel on the Jeep's windshield.

When I got back to good paved road, I pulled out my cell phone and called Sandy's cell. With the five hour time difference, she was certainly not still at the office. She answered on the third ring.

"Hey, Otto," she said. "How's the island life? Is it all coming back to you?"

"Coming back to me?" I said. "This is a whole different world than the Cayman's, Sandy. That was like living in a slightly more casual British Isle. This place is something else, an alien world."

"Can you hear that?" Sandy asked.

I didn't need to. I could envision her rubbing the tips of her index finger and thumb together.

"Yeah, I know," I said. "It's the world's smallest violin, and it's playing just for me."

"You got it, Otto."

"So, how's the digging going?" I asked. "Making any progress?"

"Not much. About like I told you this morning. So, I'm taking a road trip. You caught me in Atlanta. I'm en route to Augusta, Georgia to do things the old fashioned way. You know, microfilm and dusty courthouse records."

"Well, Cassie gave me a smattering of information this afternoon. I also had the lovely opportunity of meeting Mr. Thomason."

"How was that?"

"Everything I imagined it would be," I said. "He's an interesting individual."

"I imagine you put him on notice."

"You mean, *notice notice?*"

Sandy always said I used my size as an intimidation device. Combine that with my insight and ability to subtly let people know that I understand them, perhaps better than they understand themselves, and you have the *notice notice*.

"Never mind," she said. "I'm sure you have it all under control over there. They're doing final call on my flight, Otto. I'll call you when I get settled in."

"Fly safe, Sandy. I'll scan these documents in when I get back to the condo and email them to you. Maybe they'll lighten the load."

"What, and rob me of the joy of paging through dusty, musty records and going blind scrolling though miles of microfilm?"

"Okay, if you'd rather do it the hard way, I'll just go to the pool when I get back."

"If you don't send that additional information, I'll walk there and find you." She laughed. I loved to hear Sandy laugh. "I'll talk to you later, Otto."

"See ya."

Jennifer called a friend from her cell phone on the ride over to the charter company's lobby. She didn't want to go back to Molokai alone, to that big empty house.   Not tonight, not after Gregory's partial revelation about her bio-mom.   So she called her friend, and he agreed to come to the airport and fly home with her.

She killed time by wandering around the little trinket store, browsing the T-shirts and other memorabilia the charter company sold to their tourist clients.   Every fifteen minutes or so, another group would wander out to a waiting chopper, and a returning group would be funneled into the store.

"Excuse me, Miss Shea," the operations manager said.   "We're ready anytime you are."   He was in his late fifties, had dandruff on his aloha shirt from his greasy black hair and she could smell his sour breath from five feet away.   His name tag said, Charles.

"I'm going to have a guest," she said.   "He'll be here shortly.   I would imagine he can leave his car in your lot."

"Certainly, Miss Shea.   Just ask him to leave his license plate number with the desk and let Amy know when you're ready to go."

He walked away.   Jennifer watched him go.   He was watching one of the younger female tourists in shorts and tank top.   She might have been fifteen, if that.   Jennifer rolled her eyes.   Amy caught the move and smiled at her.

"Takes all kinds to make an island," Jennifer said.

"Aw, Charlie's okay," Amy said.   "Just likes looking, is all."

Just then Jennifer saw Alex walk through the door.   He carried a small duffle bag.   When he saw Jennifer his eyes lit up and he smiled broadly.

"Thanks for coming, Alex," Jennifer said as she threw her arms around him.

"Wouldn't miss it for the world, Jenny," he said.   Even though he was about the same height, he picked her up with his hug.   She bent her legs and let him hold her up.   "It's been way too long, kiddo." He put her down.   "Thank you for calling."

Amy wrote down Alex's car and license information, handed each of them a yellow inflatable vest and called the ramp to have someone come in and take them out.

The Eco-Star helicopter was idling nearby.   The ramp worker ensured Jennifer and Alex had correctly donned the lightweight, modern, FAA-approved version of what World War II Navy fliers had called the *Mae West*.   He then led them to the helicopter where they took the two front seats next to the pilot.   There, he assisted them in fastening the four-point seat harness and handed each of them a headset. He gave the pilot a thumbs up and closed the door.

"Welcome aboard," the pilot said. "I'm Brian. If you see me talking and can't hear me, please just wait because I'm on the radio with air traffic control. Any time you wish to speak to me, just push that button on your headset cord."

Jennifer thought this Brian guy was quite handsome. Seated, she guessed him about six feet tall, thin, but not bony, he had a head of thick, auburn hair, and an easy smile of straight, white teeth. He wore aviator sunglasses. She hoped she'd get the chance to see his eyes. He was chewing gum, and when she watched him speak to the tower and then give a thumbs up to the watching ramp worker, she felt an excitement in her stomach she hadn't felt in quite a while.

Alex bumped her in the ribs with his elbow. She turned to see him smiling at her. He raised his eyebrows at her. She returned the smile.

Brian increased the power and lifted the chopper into a ground taxi a few feet off the ground. Once clear of the ramp, he dipped the nose forward steeply and accelerated rapidly while initiating a gradual climb. It's the departure technique he loved performing for the tourists, and it always got some great ooh's and ah's on the video cameras focused inside the cabin. Jennifer's stomach jumped inside her, and the thrill of the ride stirred something else inside her that she hadn't felt in quite a while.

The helicopter flew north, around the West Maui Mountain, climbed to two-thousand feet before leaving Maui around Kapalua to cross the channel to Molokai. Brian told them he'd fly close along the north shore of Molokai and bring them in over the beach. A moving map display, a smaller version of what's in Gregory's jet, showed the progress. Because of the screen's size, it only displayed the detailed topography and landmarks within a few miles of the helicopter. As the chopper flew over the channel, the display showed all blue. It took about five minutes for the shoreline of Molokai to show up like an approaching squall on the screen.

Jennifer chatted with both Alex and Brian on the flight over. She had decided to keep the private stuff to herself until she and Alex were at the house, but making small talk seemed easy with the pair of men with whom she shared the flight. When she got home, maybe she'd have Alex make a pitcher of his famous strawberry margaritas. She hoped she had some frozen strawberries in the fridge.

She did learn Brian had been born and raised in California. Monterrey to be exact. He was 35, never married, and since he paid more attention to her than Alex, she concluded he wasn't gay.

Brian navigated the chopper offshore of the beach, then circled the property before setting down on the small, paved heliport Gregory had installed when he bought the house for her.

"Care to come in for a while?" Jennifer asked the pilot. "I'm thinking of having Alex whip up a batch of his special strawberry margaritas, if I have any frozen strawberries, that is."

"A batch or two," chimed Alex.

"Well, I'd have to pass on the margaritas, but I'd take something else cold," Brian said as he shut down the engine and flipped off the switches. "I'd love a tour of your home."

They all piled out and walked the path to the portico. Jennifer unlocked the door and then disarmed the alarm. Everybody shed their shoes at the entry, Hawaiian style.

Alex dropped his duffle at the corner of the hallway then headed for the kitchen area of the great room.

"Strawberry margaritas coming up," he said. "What can I get for you, Brian?"

"Eh, bottle of water, carbonated if you got it, would be great. Thanks," Brian called after him.

When he entered the great room and got a gander at the view, Brian let out a low whistle. He walked up to the oversize lanai doors with glass sidelights. The architect had designed the ocean side wall of the home with as few solid pieces of structure as possible, creating from room to room an almost continuous panoramic view of the ocean beyond. Waves crashed against the craggy, black lava point and sprayed white foam against a deep blue sky.

"Now, that's the billion dollar view," he said. "This sure beats looking over my neighbor's brush pile he calls natural landscaping to get a peak of the valley."

Jennifer walked up and stood beside him, but a foot closer to the glass. Standing next to him, she confirmed the estimation of his height had been right on, maybe an inch or two short. She balanced on one foot, crooked the other leg and rested her foot on curled up toes, knowing the pose gave him a look at her legs and butt. She heard Alex moving around the kitchen area behind them, but mostly she heard her heart beating with an excitement she hadn't felt in over a year. She could feel other parts of her body also responding with a heat she hadn't felt in far longer than that.

After a minute's pause - which was more than enough at this point, she thought - she turned to Brian and asked if he'd like a tour of the rest of the house. He flipped his aviator glasses onto the top of his head and said he'd love to see it. That was the first time she got a look at his deep blue eyes. Deep blue didn't even describe them fully, they were the velvety azure of the morning ocean. When he smiled at her, dimples appeared in his cheeks and little crinkles in tanned skin framed his eyes.

Alex walked up holding an opened bottle of club soda and an oversized glass of ice with a pinched wedge of lime settled on top of the cubes.

"How's this?" he asked Brian with a smile. "I didn't know how you took it, so I covered both bases."

"That's perfect, Alex," he said, taking both and draining the bottle into the glass. "Thank you."

Alex took back the empty bottle and walked back to the kitchen.

"Strawberry margaritas coming up," he said. "You've got a whole bag of frozen strawberries, Jenny. We could go through the weekend without heading to town, if the tequila holds out, that is."

"Go easy on the salt," she called after him. "If the tequila runs dry, we'll just have to find a friendly pilot to fly us another bottle." She gave Brian a playful smile.

"I'm a phone call away," he said. "Lead the way on the tour anytime you're ready."

Jennifer decided to take him on the tour of the functional wing first, the guest rooms, office, her studio.

When they walked into the studio, Brian immediately walked up to her favorite piece: a slightly gauzy portrait done in acrylic of a mother in a flowing white dress standing slightly bent over an uncertain toddler testing the sand and edges of waves with her toes. Jennifer had somehow been able to capture the dichotic emotions of the mother in paint: the pride in a daughter's first tentative steps toward self-reliance and the pain in knowing someday she'd have to fully let go of the life she had created.

While the images of both the mother and daughter were idealized for the piece, looking at it reminded Jennifer of how her mom had always encouraged her to stand on her own two feet while Jennifer understood instinctively should she stumble her mother was right there behind her to catch her before the fall.

She now watched as Brian soaked in the painting from seven or eight feet back. She observed his body language carefully. A man with a sensitive nature understood the painting. Alex got it. Gregory never had seen the allure and told her so on a number of occasions. He disagreed that Jennifer was planning on this work being the centerpiece of her upcoming exhibition in San Francisco. Fortunately, Mr. McCormick had broken the tie when he saw the photograph of the painting. Mr. McCormick got it too.

Brian turned to her.

"You painted this?" he asked.

"Yes," she said. "What do you think?"

"I think of my mother," he said. "Once when she visited, I bought her a small sculpture of a mother humpback whale pushing a newborn calf to the surface. I think the piece was entitled, *A Mother's Love*. I had told her at the time it epitomized all she had ever done for me, supporting my every dream while subordinating her own. I remember how her eyes lit up when I told her how I felt, what she had meant to me as I grew up. Your painting brings back all those warm memories."

Jennifer wiped away a tear which had formed in the corner of her eye. All this talk of mothers today was getting to her. She wondered where Alex was with the margaritas, when almost on cue, he walked in holding two heavy glasses with green stems filled with frosty red goodness.

"Yours is the one with the light salt," he said, holding it out to her. He noticed Brian was looking at the mother portrait and walked up to him.

"Isn't that fantastic? Jenny is so talented."

"It's captivating," Brian said. Then, he moved around the displays and looked at her other works. Seascapes, sunsets, and an oddly dark piece showing two empty chairs on a patio overlooking a lake scene. They were all wonderfully done, but he saw nothing else displayed which had the heartwarming effect of the first one. The paintings were done in a variety of mediums, from water color to acrylic to oil.   The were good, great, gallery class to be sure, but some of the work in the corner lacked a soulfulness and left him unsatisfied.

"You're a wonderful talent, Jennifer," he said to her.   "While I could never afford the original, if you ever have lithographs made of the mother portrait, put me down for one for my mom."

"I'll do that," she said.   Somehow she could see past the mask he put up and understood what he felt about some of the rest of her work.   She agreed, much of it was soulless.   Everything she had done since her parents died was good, but much of it lacked emotion.   She wondered if people attending her premier show would see what Brian obviously did.   She suddenly wanted to get out of her studio. "Care to see the rest of the place?" she asked Brian.

The pair toured the rest of the house after Alex excused himself at the great room and exited to the poolside patio where he stretched out on a teak chaise lounge chair sporting green and white striped cushions.   Fifteen minutes later, they joined him at poolside.   Jennifer stretched out on another lounger while Brian sat astride a third.

The trio watched the waves.   The setting was idyllic, yet like her artwork, a clash of contrasts, quiet and peaceful on one hand and wild and dangerous on the other.   That dichotomy in her art and in her life was something Jennifer had always sensed on an unconscious level.   She felt the contrasts again as she sat with her old and new friend.   This was home, but not her home.   Something told her she didn't belong here, yet how could she pass up such an opportunity? She pushed the thoughts from her mind.   She saw Brian making movements like he was getting antsy to get back.

"You've got a lovely home, Jennifer," Brian said to her.   He drained the last of his club soda.   "I've enjoyed the tour and spending time with you, but I better get going or my boss will have a fit.   The last guy who took too long getting back had the Coast Guard sent out looking for him."

"I'll walk you out," she said as she stood.   She walked him as far as the front door, watched him put on his shoes and then gave him a hug, Hawaiian style.   "Thank you, Brian," she said and then added, "Now that you know where the place is, don't be a stranger."

"I'd love to come back sometime," he said.   He reset his sunglasses in place, gave a wave and walked toward his helicopter.

Jennifer watched him get into the chopper and then returned inside and closed the door. By the time she made it back out to the patio, she could hear the whine of the jet engine and the whop-whop of the blades. She sat down again and found a topped off margarita on the adjacent table. The noise of the helicopter was deafening for an instant as Brian climbed over the house then fell off into the distance as he banked eastward offshore of the beach. Jennifer watched him disappear and silently wished he really would take her up on the offer of coming back. Suddenly, even with Alex sitting right next to her, she became aware of an immense loneliness inside her.

"Earth to Jenny," Alex said.

That brought a smile from her. She snapped back to the moment, the place she usually preferred to inhabit, but the place she found the most difficult to remain since a year ago. While Gregory pushed her toward the future, and memories drew her to the past, Alex always centered her on what was important, the moment. That's one reason she loved him.

There were many others. She had run into him, literally, at the Maui Arts and Cultural Center shortly after she came to the islands. Gregory was having some work completed on the house before she moved in, so she had stayed on Maui in a condo he rented for her in Makena. This particular evening, she had gone to the movie *Kinky Boots*, about a group of Brits who save a foundering shoe factory by changing the lines from conventional shoes to marketing high-end boots to transvestite clientele. As she came around the corner by the balcony restroom, bam, she ran right into Alex.

She wasn't sure which of the two took the worst of the unexpected encounter since they were of about equal height, with Alex perhaps carrying an extra ten pounds. He wore his hair closely cropped, possessed fetching green eyes, an easy smile, and delicate features. Jennifer immediately thought he would make an attractive woman. They fell into an easy conversation after all the 'excuse me' and 'are you all right' stuff was done. Since it turned out he was at the movie alone as well, they decided to sit together for the show. So started the friendship.

"So tell me about San Francisco; then, tell me what's got you all frazzled today. After that, if there's still time, we can talk about your obvious infatuation with the helicopter guy," he said. He sipped his margarita, then crunched a larger piece of ice he found in his glass.

Jennifer loved the honesty and openness she found in Alex's eyes. They were soulful, and from the moment they started talking when they met, she knew she could trust him with any secret. Of course, she could immediately tell he was gay. He just carried himself that way. Not that she would ever judge him, but she hadn't grown up around that community down in College Station. She was certain gays were there, but they were just more underground in Texas than they had been in New York, Chicago, and, she had learned, Hawaii.

"San Francisco was fantastic," she said. "That was the first trip for me in Gregory's jet since he sent it for me to bring me here almost a year ago. What a wonderful way to travel."

"The perks of the super rich," he said. "Who am I to comment on your sponsor, or whatever he's become for you."

"Stop it, Alex," she mock scolded. "Gregory is my benefactor, that's all. There's nothing physical between us and I cannot ever imagine there would be." She shuddered inside. "He's a married man, and an investor and mentor. My art is merely one of his investments."

"Maybe so," Alex replied. "Just don't be so naive as to not believe he may have additional ideas for his return on investment, honey." He thought carefully about his next words before letting them spill out. "I've seen the way he looks at you when you're not looking. It's beyond covetousness, it's almost like ownership."

"Ew, that's so gross, Alex. He's old enough to be my dad and so totally not even my type, even if he wasn't married. You know I go for the taller ones."

"So I saw," he said. "I take it we'll be working topics backwards and starting with your new friend, Brian."

"You have a problem with that," she chided.

"If we're starting there, I had better make another batch of margaritas. I think it's going to be a long evening."

He got up and headed for one of the great hall doors.

"Come on, honey," he said. "You can at least give me a hand in the kitchen. Got any chips and salsa anywhere?"

I arrived back at my condo late in the afternoon. There were about three hours of sunlight left, I guessed, so I decided to go for a dip in the pool before getting back down to work. My head had cleared during the drive back, but there was a lingering headache and I hoped some time in the pool and hot tub and the handful of Advil I popped before changing into my suit would take care of that.

Sandy had bought me some kind of new swimming suit they called 'board shorts', no doubt the latest style. They hung to my knees and consisted of several patterns of orange flowers and geometric designs sewn together in what I found was an all-too-tight-in-the-ass combined with a my-balls-are-going-numb cut, so I took them off, tossed them back into the suitcase and slipped on a pair of wonderfully loose, old gym shorts I had brought along. They looked close to the kind of swimsuit that I would have worn back when I would go swimming as a kid, so what the hell?

I pulled a beach towel out of the drawer under the bed, grabbed the key off the dining area table and a bottle of water from the fridge and was just about to leave the condo. As an afterthought, I grabbed the envelope Cassie had provided me. After slipping on my flip-flops at the door, I walked the short distance to the pool. I was kinda digging this laid back Hawaiian style.

There were a handful of families with kids hanging out by the pool, so I selected an out-of-the-way lounge chair in the shade of several massive palm trees, put down my towel and tossed the envelope, keys and water onto an adjacent table. I kicked off my flip-flops and tip-toed across the overheated concrete deck to the water. The pool felt great, had been warmed by the sun to a perfect temperature and was of the salt water type, so no chlorine up the nose. I swam/walked to the far side and rested my arms on the concrete edge after splashing some water up there to cool it down a bit. I looked down the hill to the ocean, over the babbling manmade brook with white flowered lily pads and koi in the small pools.

I thought about Cassie and our day together. Her final words had haunted me on the drive back and continued to do so as I relaxed in the pool. There are times when my mouth, and big man's ego, have gotten me into trouble before, but usually I suffered the consequences of the words or actions I'd taken. This time, had I put Cassie into a difficult situation? Or worse?

'Regardless of what you think about what's at Gregory's core, Willy, that was stupid,' she had said. 'He's a dangerous man.'

A *dangerous* man?   I wondered what caused her to use that wording.   When an abused woman speaks of her husband, in my experience, she rarely uses the adjective 'dangerous'.   She'll typically use some other more personal adjective like 'cruel' or 'heartless' - I've even heard 'evil' a time or two - or they relay information about how he treats them, such as being mentally or physically abusive.   Even with what Gregory had allegedly done to the brake line on her Jeep, the descriptive was unusual.   Dangerous?   That's more of an overarching term, going beyond the familial situation.   So, what makes Gregory Thomason dangerous?

I closed my eyes, rested my chin on my crossed arms.   The pool felt good, and there was a slight breeze which cooled my head and shoulders as the water evaporated.   I removed my sunglasses, dipped my hands in the water and rubbed them over my face and head. There was an immediate cooling effect.   It felt wonderful.   I put my glasses back on and returned my chin to resting on my arms.   I felt myself dozing off.

Suddenly, something hit me hard in the back, definitely rousing me from my dozing.

"Sorry, mister," came the call from the other end of the pool.

I turned around to find a hard, plastic football floating in the water a couple of feet away.   I looked toward the called apology and saw a group of teenagers hanging out.   I wondered where they had came from.   Some of them were choking down laughter.   Several appeared like they were wondering what I was going to do.   There didn't seem to be one in particular claiming the toss and for certain in today's society weren't any adults coming in and scolding their behavior.   Typical, I thought.

"A little help?" one of the girls called.

I didn't take her for the anonymous thrower, so I grabbed the football from the water and lofted it over.   My back stung.   Someone had thrown the ball with some force.   Then it struck me.   How Gregory could be described by his wife as being *dangerous*.   She wasn't speaking about his activities toward her or chastising me for focusing his wrath in her direction, she was warning me that Gregory was someone who not only could, but would lash out at anyone, and at anytime.   She was warning me for my sake.

His money provided him with both the sword and the shield.   I'd never see it coming.   Even if I figured out where it had come from, who would do anything? This man could buy and sell anyone on the island, with the possible exception of Oprah, of course. Which meant he also could lash out through hired intermediaries.

I had dealt with drug dealers who worked like that back in Chicago. They'd smile at me as if saying, 'Yeah, I did that, so what?' Even if I did assemble enough evidence to get the D.A. to charge them, they were walking out faster than I could line them up to walk in. It's what led me to do some of the things I did, including that night in the warehouse. I'm not proud of any of it, but it's like my mother had told me a long time ago, 'Right is Right'.

I swam/walked over to the steps and got out of the pool. My lingering headache had been replaced by a throbbing, steady pain in the middle of my back. I thought briefly of soaking it out in the hot tub but then discarded the idea. I spread my towel over the lounge chair, deciding to let the air dry and cool me naturally, sat down and gulped down half a bottle of water. After drying my hands on the exposed edges of the towel, I opened Cassie's envelope and began to read through the papers.

The first page contained the same computer generated list she had given me that first day, but with some significant additional information. The were timeframes listed next to each name, albeit in a very broad range. Regardless, it would help Sandy narrow down her searches.

Next to the name of Janet Hopkins, she had written 'Canada' and 'recently'.

There were also physical descriptions which reminded me of the data collected on a driver's license. All six women were described as being between five-seven and five nine, weights between one-hundred-twenty and one-hundred-forty pounds, brown hair and brown eyes. Their ages were listed as between twenty-five and thirty-five. Apparently, Gregory had a type, and interestingly enough, from Sandy's background data and my own observations, both Cassie and his mommy fit the pattern. Cassie had been twenty-five when she married Gregory, and mommy had drowned at the age of thirty-five, when Gregory was seven.

After the revised first page, came the prenuptial agreement. It was a perfunctory ten-page, double-spaced document written in fairly common language. My first thought was that either Gregory or Cassie had drafted the agreement, rather than putting it out for an attorney for either writing or review. Even from my layperson's perspective, there appeared to be holes in the language you could drive a Mack truck through. Sandy would be able to apply an expert's eye and provide an opinion. It had been signed and witnessed and included a Notary's Seal, but there was no indication it had been filed in any Court.

Along with the amateurish content and construction of what should have been a very legalese document given the amount of money which was at stake, there was something that just didn't fit. I reviewed it again, and then a third time, but couldn't put my finger on it. Knowing how my brain processes stuff, I set it aside and moved to the remaining pages.

The remaining thirty-six pages contained photocopies of what appeared to be journal pages. Whether they came from the books I had caught Cassie with, I couldn't be certain. Regardless of where they came from, they were eye-opening. From the odd androgynous script, I had to assume they were written by Gregory. There was no accompanying identification of the pages in the package.

As I read through them, it became clear that while they were assembled in sequence, there were not contiguous; there were obvious gaps. It was clear they were written at different times with different inks, maybe over years, and in addition, the language used by the writer subtly changed from section to section and there were included occasional, passing references to certain historical or cultural events which could be used to time-stamp the particular passages. I quickly realized it was going to take more than a cursory reading to put everything in these pages into context.

I knew I could dump the journal pages on Sandy's plate and she'd gladly tear thought them, but with the traveling now and doing research to identify and locate the women, and the added peripheral task of legally evaluating the prenuptial agreement, I concluded she already had enough to do.

Perhaps these journal excerpts were of those things Cassie would have preferred I hold back from my partner. Or would I be able to send them off to her and ask her to ignore them? Knowing Sandy, it would be difficult for her to not spend time on the journal pages and I really needed to locate these women quickly. While I had agreed to withhold some conclusions from Sandy if I thought it was in the best interest of the client, these weren't conclusions, this was information.

I pondered the pros and cons for a while, then gathered my stuff and walked back to the condo. By the time I arrived back, I knew what I would do.

Chapter Thirteen

I set myself up at the dining room table with my laptop, scanner, Sandy's briefing book, and the information obtained today from Cassie. I scanned the documents from the envelope in three separate files and emailed two of them to Sandy. A few minutes later, my cell phone vibrated on the table. It was Sandy.

"Hey, Otto," she said. "I thought there were like fifty pages of documents you were going to send me. These two files you just emailed are less than a dozen, total." She paused and I knew what was coming next. "Are you holding out on me?"

"For now, yes, I am."

There was a silence on the line as she digested both that I was holding out on her and that I had so readily admitted it. I gave her a moment and then added some justification.

"You've got enough on your plate right now, Sandy. There is a thirty-six page document which I scanned but did not send. In an abundance of caution, I did upload it to the office server, but I would appreciate your leaving it unread at this point." The image of God casually telling Adam to mention to Eve not to sample any of those ripe, red apples hanging at eye height from that one particular tree popped into my head. I hoped Sandy respected the request better than had Eve.

"I can't think of a single time you've ever held information from me, Otto. Frankly, I don't like it."

She paused, and for Sandy that meant she was either thinking or weighing her words. I hoped it was the former. Sandy is smart and logical. If she thinks about it clearly, she'll understand there's a reason I had decided what I had. The problem was, she knew there was a personal component to this case and that could lead her to believe I wasn't thinking clearly.

"I'll respect your judgment," she said. "For now."

"Thank you, Sandy," I said. "I think it's best you stay focused on tracking down these women. I'll work this other document. I've got the time right now."

"I'm at the Holiday Inn Express in Augusta," she said. "It's close to downtown and the courthouse and newspaper offices where they keep the archives. I can start at either place at nine in the morning, but since the courthouse closes at five and the newspaper people told me they were there until midnight, I think I'll hit the courthouse first."

"That's probably the smart play if you want to get out of Augusta in the shortest time," I said, silently relieved she adopted the change of subjects so readily.

"These date ranges will help narrow things down a bit," she said. "I should be able to track Jessi Bollenbeck tomorrow, if she was ever here in Augusta. Hey, you remember who else spent time in Augusta years ago?"

"I read your briefing book, Sandy," I said. "I know it's where Cassie's family relocated to when she left junior high. Remember the two situations are separated by nearly two decades. I can't envision a tie-in."

"Frankly, neither can I. Just remember that neither you nor I are fond of the idea of coincidence."

"Cassie made a point of telling me that she doesn't believe in coincidences either." I pondered the coincidence for a moment.

"Listen, Otto, it's getting late here, I didn't get much sleep after your wake-up call last night and I want to be fresh in the morning. I'll go over the prenup when I get the chance, but I'm going to focus on finding this Bollenbeck woman. It would be great if she could shine enough light on things to save me trips to Orlando, Cheyenne, and Des Moines."

"Sorry about that, Sandy," I said, knowing she had not mentioned it to obtain another apology. Then I changed subjects to the other cities. "Not exactly glamor destinations, eh?" I laughed. "Good night, Sandy. Don't let the bed bugs bite."

"Thanks, a lot, Otto," she said sarcastically. "I've already been itching just sitting on the bedspread." She laughed and so did I because we both knew Sandy would never sit on a hotel comforter without a biohazard suit. "Good night to you, too, Otto."

We both clicked off and I set upon rereading the journal pages. I assumed that Cassie had placed them in some degree of chronological order, and from the contents of the first page in the package, I again assumed this first contiguous section of photocopies of eleven handwritten pages to be the very beginning of the journal or journals. The handwriting was precise, never faltering, printed margin-to-margin without hyphenation or any detectable alteration of spacing. It was evidence of an obviously disciplined and logical mind, or a psychopath, I thought. The printing flowed in a letter-by-letter script normally associated with a feminine manner, but it also possessed masculine qualities of blocked printing. There were no erasures which I could detect from the photocopy. Again, indicating a careful, thoughtful, and purposeful writer. It began:

"As the famous opening words of Charles Dickens spoken in the character of David Copperfield were penned, 'To begin my life with the beginning of my life, I record that I was born (as I have been informed and believe) on a Friday, at twelve o'clock at night.', I too record that not only was I born, but blessed by Providence the glory of being reborn at the age of seven years when I witnessed the death of my mother.

"I write these words from a distance of years, as did Master Dickens, but mine - and perhaps his, although I have no way of determining - have become clarified by the relentless ticks of time and not wanting them to dull with the issuance of any further, thus I have decided to place them in this journal of my life.

"My friends feel it is feminine to write down words of feeling or emotion in a diary, and often scoff girlfriends for doing such recording, but what could be more masculine than recording for posterity the actions taken by a strong man leading his life?

"As the fictional David Copperfield, who lost his father six months before his birth, my mother had told me my father became lost from us to the family business during her pregnancy when he had been forced to take over the responsibilities upon the untimely death of his father. It was the manner of the times. It will never by my way.

"Ironically, when Copperfield was seven years of age, his mother remarried, thus entering into a transformation which forged the future life of her son, David.

My mother died when I was seven years of age and not only did the event forge my future, but I was allowed to watch it happen.   I WATCHED IT HAPPEN!!!

"*I am an excellent swimmer, and was even at that age.   I'd had lessons and moved through the water like a fish.   I was small and wiry, but I was strong.   I could have saved her, yet I remained fixed to the dock, dripping and beginning to shiver in the early autumn air of upstate New York, but frozen not of temperature, but of fascination.*

"*She looked into my eyes from a distance of twenty feet.   There were no words I could discern which came from her contorted mouth at the bottom of her contorted face.   She bore a mask sculpted from a point beyond fear, I am certain it was indeed forged by the incredible heat and pressure of panic.   (I write that assessment not from the vantage of a seven year old, but as a near adult.)*

"*As she went under the first time - the first time of my seeing, anyway - her eyes rolled in her head.   She flailed and clawed her way back to the surface and her eyes refocused on mine.   Perhaps refocused is too passive a word.   Her eyes screamed to mine.   Yes, that's more like it was.   Then, there was something else which crept into her eyes which I will call the dying ember of resignation.*

"*God, (and I use that word from the perspective of a committed atheist and humanist) how I hated her for giving up so easily.   That hatred of her weakness on display was perhaps the catalyst which sealed her doom.   Once added to the substance of my soul (again, IF I believed in such a thing) the resultant chemical reaction was irrevocable.   What I experienced next was a sensation of heat; glowing, brilliant, blazing heat.   I began these writings with the disapproval of recorded feelings or emotions, therefore I describe this change as an event, a momentous, masculine event.*

"*So I watched as she went under for the second time, in a state of near exhaustion as determined by me through her less-than-exuberant return to the surface.   She gulped a breath of air, appeared to try to speak, yet I heard nothing and I witnessed as her forged mask of panic melted then into sadness.*

"*Unlike fictional writings on the events of drowning, she did not go down for the third time and stay below the surface, nor the fourth, or the fifth.   With each return to the air, she was weaker, more resigned.   Somehow I knew, on her sixth journey below the surface, it would be the time the depths would indeed claim her. On that last excursion, her eyes held mine, and through the clarity of the lake I perceived the instant her life left her body.   I recall that instant as sharply and clearly as the edge of cut class, and I recall it was the first time, but far from the last - even at the year of this writing - I stood on that dock with a full, powerful erection.*"

I sat back in my chair, the pages still in my hand. The imagery was haunting, the impact of the words on my psyche grew by an order of magnitude during the second reading. Gregory Thomason was indeed an individual to regard with caution. I wondered what kind of man could equate such a traumatic event to sexual arousal, but then I'd never worked sexual crimes.

Over the years, however, I had read the case reports of numerous, horrific sex crimes. I listened to recordings of confessions and interrogations of more than a few deviant perpetrators. I participated in several questioning sessions with scumbag drug dealers whom I regarded to be some of the sickest individuals on the face of the planet, and yet none, not one, ever sent such chills through my spine as had the reading of these words from Gregory's pen.

Picking up the phone, I considered calling Sandy and discussing this section, at least, with her. I glanced at the clock on the upper right of the computer screen and decided against it. No, I alone would live with the nightmares Gregory's words would bring tonight. Sandy deserved her rest. Regrettably, I'd already been the source of too many sleepless nights for her.

In Janet's bed in Montreal, Marcy lay awake, staring at the ceiling again into the wee hours. She was physically exhausted, yet her mind would not shut down long enough for her to get some sleep. She considered taking something to coax her body to rest, but her experiences with sleeping pills were not positive ones. She often found the sleep they brought invoked strange and distressing dreams and less than satisfactory rest while leaving behind a chemical hangover the next day. So, Marcy began a self-relaxation technique she had learned at a massage therapy seminar she attended with a former lover several years ago.

The technique was simple. One began by selecting a comfortable position, Marcy chose to lie on her back with her arms at her side. The next step involved the dual objective of relaxing the body while refocusing the brain on rest, and was accomplished by consciously redirecting the mind's energy toward the visualization of individual parts of the body falling asleep.

As the instructor had demonstrated to the group, Marcy began at her extremities and worked her way to her core. She envisioned her fingers and toes relaxing, then her hands and feet, her lower arms and legs, her upper arms, her upper legs, her shoulders, her torso, and finally her brain. The key point was to remain focused solely on the relaxation. If one let their mind wander, or allowed it to focus on something other than the task assigned to it consciously, it would not work. At the conference, the practice session had ended with several participants snoring quietly on the padded mats, but had only brought her to a level of anxious relaxation. Tonight, however, Marcy was begging for rest and by the time she had placed her shoulders into relaxation, she drifted off to sleep.

Dreams stayed away, at first. When they did come, they were happy ones, for a while. When they turned darker, they remained with her until morning. She startled awake to the muffled street sounds and a blazing, midmorning sun searching out every shadow in the city, including those lingering in the apartment. She sat up in bed, shocked by the fact she had been sleeping at all and next by the lateness of morning judging from the amount of light spilling through the blinds. She looked at her watch. Ten o'clock. She had been sleeping for nine hours.

She swung her legs over the edge of the bed, rested her elbows on her legs and rubbed her face. The dreams, although evaporating rapidly from memory, were still fresh enough to cause her some anguish. She had seen Janet. Marcy had tried to get to her, but Janet was too far away to touch. Janet did not reach for her with anything but her eyes; Marcy could see her hands had been bound. She was in a confined space. Janet was clearly frightened in the dream. Alone. Facing her fate. Then her eyes reacted to a sound or a touch or a sight, Marcy had been unable to determine, and she had tried to scream but nothing could come out because her mouth too was bound by gray duct tape. Her eyes had looked directly into Marcy's, and then she was gone.

Just as God created the night to salve the wounds of the day, He created morning to erase the night. As she sat on the edge of the bed they had shared, that's exactly how it worked. In moments, as much as she concentrated, as hard as she tried, the dreams were now gone, evaporated into the ether. Though she would not accept it in her heart, in her mind Marcy realized that Janet was gone too. She arose slowly from the bed and walked to the bathroom. Turning on the faucet, she bent over and splashed cool water on her face. When she stood to face the woman in the mirror, she knew what she needed to do next.

She needed to track down Tamra Sommers or whoever that bitch was who left here the night Janet didn't come home and the first place to start was Burlington, Vermont. Marcy didn't need to verbalize what would come next because the eyes of the woman looking back at her from the mirror told her what she would do when she found the woman. She would make the woman talk, and then she would kill her.

I had spent a couple of hours after coming back from the pool working through the journal pages. Trying to make sense of them was a difficult task, but putting them in some semblance of context was a bit easier. I had nailed down a number of timeframes based on references to external events such as the death of his father, his fifth wedding anniversary, the election of Bill Clinton, and the purchase of the land for his house on Maui.

The whole of the situation in this case was beginning to seem like putting together a single-color puzzle, and because of Cassie's obvious games, one made up of pulled teeth.

From what I could discern, there were a total of seven more noncontiguous events described in the remaining twenty-five pages of photocopied handwriting. The shortest event took a half-page to describe, the longest, eight pages. Each was told through the eye of a desirous, covetous and yet, self-righteous man. Each described meeting a different woman. None mentioned a name, but I was able to make some guesses based on Cassie's date ranges. The most disturbing of these was a three-page description of an event which linked to Cassie and his fifth wedding anniversary.

"The first time I laid eyes upon her was as I drove along south Kihei Road. She wore the female costume of the island, a bikini. Some women played to vanity by wearing a shirt over the top, some women conceded to gravity with a wrap around the bottom. Often, the ones who neither played nor conceded were the ones who should have done both. She was different, though. She was perfect, or nearly so.

"Her bikini was the color of the building she was exploring, a deep teal blue, and it covered her in a very enticing fashion. As I drove by the first time, she was standing at a shave ice concession along the roadway. When she stood on her

tiptoes and bent over to point out something behind the counter, I was hooked.   I had to have her.

"Minutes later, after I had parked in the back and wandered forward, I rediscovered her modeling an ankle bracelet for herself in a small mirror held low by a male concessionaire.   I think he was enjoying the view as much as was I, but he'd never have her like I would.   That I knew for certain.

"I complimented her selection and told her that I'd gladly buy it for her would she merely honor me with her name.   When I heard her voice, it was obvious she was from the Midwest, perhaps Chicago.   Surprise, but if later I didn't discover I was correct!   More talk, and a few trinkets later, and I had elicited additional valuable information from her.   It's so easy when people are on vacation and off-guard, to find out exactly what you need to know about them.   A smile, a friendly manner, an aloha shirt of quality and an air of class are all one needs.   Fortunately, I possess this all, and so much more.

"With this one, the finding was so much serendipity: the simple act of picking up a bauble or two for Cassandra in honor our fifth anniversary, and then the idea to drive back by way of the uninhibited tourist populated south Kihei Road rather than the highway.   Unlike the others, there was no need for planning, no hours of researching, no fantasy or anticipation.   I merely spotted her and determined she was of the type I like; and once found and desired, the getting and the keeping followed suit quite nicely.   Ah, yes, quite nicely indeed."

There was no woman from Chicago or the immediate area on the list of six women Cassie had provided me.   I made a note to question her about this particular woman and then try to track her down.   After all, given Cassie's stated intent and my role in this entire situation, there was no need for her to not wish further buttressing of her position.   If Sandy was going to have to endure a trip to Des Moines, a stop in Chicago would no doubt be a welcome diversion.   I know she'd love the chance to see our old friend, Teddy.

I was beginning to think about dinner when a knock came on the door.   I got up, walked to the door and found Steve standing there with a pizza.   He reminded me Shelly was working late and he'd gone to get a pizza before settling in and watching a rebroadcast of the baseball All Star game.   He wondered if I would like to join him upstairs for some dinner and baseball.   While I'm not much of a baseball fan - all that spitting, twitching, and junk adjusting - I remember that Sandy had told me I needed more male friends and so I accepted the invitation.   I replaced Cassie's papers in the envelope, tucked them into the safe, and went up to Steve and Shelly's place. The door was open, but I knocked anyway.

"Come on in, William," he called from one of the couches. "Help yourself to some pizza. If you want a Coke or a beer, help yourself in the fridge."

I walked in, grabbed a couple of slices from the box and a can of Coke and took up a spot on the other couch. The national anthem was just wrapping up and they were introducing the starting lineups. Baseball is the perfect sporting event to have on when you mainly want to have a conversation with someone. Which, after reading Gregory's journal pages, was exactly what I needed to do. A normal, down home conversation with another guy from Wisconsin was just what the doctor would order had he known what I had spent the last few hours doing. I popped the top on the Coke, took a sip, then added a bite of pizza.

"Not bad," I said. "Although I do miss the old pizzeria style, thin crust with just a hint of bite-back, not much sauce and loaded with cheese and pepperoni. You know the kind, with that orange grease that seems to float on top as time goes by."

"I know exactly what you're talking about," Steve said with a smile and the most animation I'd seen out of him since I accidentally parked in his spot. "This is the best we have on the island. Two things they do lousy here, pizza and fried chicken." A nostalgic look took over his face. "There was a pizza place when I was growing up, an old family joint founded in the late-40's by Italian immigrants. They made just the kind of pizza you're describing. I can picture it; hell, I can almost smell and taste it. We'd go there on Friday nights after dances at the YMCA or wind up there after a night of cruising the main drag."

"Oh, yeah, cruising," I said. "I always thought I was born out of my era, but we still had some great cruising back in the day. Maybe not the idealized, out-of-the-movie kind, but we sure had fun."

"So, how's the big case going?" he said. "Making any progress with your old sweetie?"

I stopped mid-chew and stared across the room at him.

"How do you know this?" I asked.

He pointed at the open lanai doors.

"We heard you out there the night you came in," he said. "Now, don't get mad, we weren't listening on purpose, but voices carry here more than you'd believe."

"Why didn't you say something last night?" I asked.

"Eh, Shelly made me promise not to say anything," Steve said a little sheepishly. "That didn't include tonight, though." His sheepishness vanished and was replaced by something Sandy accused me of being, a goat. "I'm just curious. It comes from living on this island, after a few years, you start craving adventure. Otherwise, every day is the same old same old."

"The case is making progress," I said. "You realize I can't really go into details. Confidentiality, you understand." I took another bite of pizza, asked who he thought would win the game, and hoped he would drop this line of conversation.

"Eh, who really cares," he said. "Bunch of overpaid, pampered, prima donnas, but it's the middle of the summer and nothing else is on, so..." His voice trailed off on the baseball theme and then came back to the original topic. "And the lady?"

"Long story, Steve," I said. "Way long story."

He pointed his pizza at the television.

"Hey, we got three hours," he said and then he looked toward the microwave clock in the kitchen. "An hour and a half until Shelly gets home. I've got nothing but time."

So I told him the redacted, sanitized version. No names, no locations, nothing which could lead him to know exactly who the lady in question was. It felt good to let it out to a guy, and get some male feedback. We also talked about endless summers, kids we grew up with and had drifted away from over the years, high school buddies, cars, and girls. Around nine-thirty, Shelly came home and I excused myself. It was midway through the sixth inning. I told them that since I was getting older, I would be taking my seventh inning stretch a little early. They both laughed. I laughed.

When I went to bed, I dreamed of baseball, and summers playing kids' games, and Friday nights in a small town, and greasy pizza, and old friends. It was the most relaxed I had felt in a long time. I slept like a baby. The therapy worked.

Chapter Fourteen

Cassie awoke after a restless night to the vibrations of heavy rock bass bouncing around inside the house. Even with her door closed, and locked, she could hear Gregory's most aggressive work out music reverberating from his gym. There were years when she would sit and watch him work out, getting turned on by his physical aggressiveness. Those days were long gone.

When she unlocked and opened her bedroom door, she could hear the music better - some 80's heavy metal group, a hair band, she thought - and she could hear the banging and sounds of equipment being operated down the hall. She crept downstairs and out to the garage. She looked underneath the little red BMW convertible and then climbed in, backed out, dropped the top and windows in honor of another gorgeous Maui morning, and drove up the driveway. As she approached the closed gate, she accelerated slightly in anticipation of the gate opening automatically, then had to brake hard to stop when it didn't.

She approached the control box set off to the left side of the roadway, guessing there was something wrong with the automatic sensors and she'd have to operate the gate controls manually. She inched up on the box and reached out her hand.

"Where are you going, my dear?" came Gregory's voice from the intercom on the box.

Cassie nearly jumped out of her skin. Her heart was in her throat and she croaked out a weak response.

"I didn't get that, sweetie," he said. "I thought we'd have brunch on the lanai. You seem to be into that kind of things these days."

Cassie collected herself.

"I've got hair and nail appointments today, Gregory" she lied. Now she would have to make some. "I heard you were working out hard this morning and know you don't like to be disturbed when you're working out hard. I left a note."

"Oh, yes, the note," he hissed. "Just where did you leave that note?"

She summoned her strength.

"Gregory, open the gate," she said. "I'll be home later this afternoon."

"All right, my sweet," he said. "Have a wonderful day. By the way, I may not be home until later myself. I've got some unfinished business on Molokai that I want to take care of before it gets stale."

Cassie heard an electronic beeping over the speaker and the gate began to open. She didn't hesitate. She slammed the little car in gear and tore out of the drive, spitting pieces of gravel off the bad unpaved road as she turned west. On the closed-circuit monitor, Gregory watched her go, then noticed Keoki sitting on his porch shaking his head and laughing.

When she was clear of the house, she made a call. It was answered on the first ring.

"Hi, it's me," she said.

"Hi, me," came the response. "It's me as well. What a coincidence."

"I don't believe in coincidences," Cassie said. "Where are you?"

"Waiting for you, my love," Captain Dan said. "When will you be here? I had a lousy night. I need to see you."

"A lousy night?" she asked. "What was wrong?"

"The largest problem was I was alone," he said. "I missed you."

"I've got to make appointments at the spa for hair and nails," she said. "Gregory caught me leaving this morning and I had to make up an excuse on the fly." She laughed at the unintended pun.

"So less time for you and me?" he said, a little hint of disappointment in his voice. "I was so hoping to ravish you all day."

Cassie sucked in a breath of anticipation.

"Oh, we'll have more than enough time for that," she said. "Gregory has some business on Molokai and said he won't be home until late. I may just have to stay over tonight."

"Stay over?" he asked. "That would be great." He made a bit of a face and shrugged his shoulders as in a 'What can I do?' gesture.

"Well, let me make these appointments before they get booked up and I have to buy someone out," Cassie said. "I'll see you in a couple hours."

"Drive safe," he said.

"I love you," she said.

"Love you," he said, and then clicked his phone closed.

"So, you're going to be busy tonight?" the woman in his room said to him. "I thought we'd have a couple of nights together." She sat on the corner of the bed, her back to him.

He teased her with his foot. Tried to tickle her and get her to laugh. She resisted, moved further away.

"I'll call you later," Captain Dan said. "What can I do? You know, she's your boss, too, Bev. We've got a sweet gig here, and it's only going to get sweeter."

"I know," Bev said with a pout. "Can I help it I get a little jealous when I hear you tell her you love her?"

He sat up, moved over to her, took her chin in his fingertips and made her look at him.

"I've never told her 'I love you'," he said. "I say 'Love you' whenever she says it to me. There's a difference."

"Not to a woman, Dan." She got up, walked toward the door, stopped and turned to him. He now sat on the corner of the bed, naked. "You're a player. I've always known that. I've accepted it." She pointed a finger at him. "Just let me find out that you've been playing me," she said and her finger moved lower in it's point. "And I'll cut off your rudder."

She walked out the door and let it close behind her.

Dan got up and walked to the bathroom.

"What is it with women and rudder metaphors to a pilot?" he said to the mirror. He turned on the shower and walked under the cascading spray.

Cassie cruised along the upper road near the Ulapalakua Winery, her hair blowing in the wind. The sun felt warm on her exposed skin. She slowed for the speed bump in the road and then continued on. She hated that she could see the Four Seasons Hotel three-thousand-feet directly down the mountain and had instead to navigate the nearly forty mile horseshoe-shaped drive through Kahului and back to Wailea. It would be another hour before she could feel Dan's arms around her. She felt the tingle of excitement and tamped it down with a deep breath.

She had determined she'd check in with Willy, but lie to him about where she was and what her plans for the day were. After all, she thought, it's none of his damn business what I do or where I go. His job is to do what I tell him to do, and she felt no pangs of guilt for leading him on. She learned fairly early on in life that when you wanted something from a male, the most effective way to get it was to appeal to his ego and tease him with the promise of interest. It always worked.

She flipped open her cell phone and called Willy's number.

I was up and giving some thought to spending more time with Gregory's journal entries when my cell phone vibrated and danced on the table. I had expected a call from Sandy, it being early afternoon in Augusta, but the display indicated it was Cassie's cell phone calling.

"Hi, Cassie," I said.

"Good morning, Willy," she chirped.

"You seem in good spirits this morning."

"Do I?" she asked. "It's just a beautiful day."

"Anything you want to tell me?" I asked. Over the last days, I had been becoming re-familiarized with her mercurial mood swings, but given yesterday's interaction with Gregory and Cassie's expressed concern when she sent me on my way blended with the content of the journal pages she had given me, this swing seemed hyper-mercurial. "It sounds like you're driving with the windows open."

"Top down, Willy, top down."

"So, not the Escalade or the new Jeep, eh?"

"I took the BMW convertible today," she said. "I wanted to feel the sun on my face and the wind in my hair." She looked down at the hem of her skirt which also was being tossed by the burbling wind. Even that felt delicious to her this morning.

"Are you heading this way, today," I asked. I wanted to spend some time going over the diary pages with her face-to-face. That way, it would be harder for her to lie to me.

"Not today, Willy," she lied. "I have some appointments. I don't look this good at our age without a little bit of help, you know. By the way, that reminds me that I need to make a call and add a facial to my treatments."

"Well, I'm finding these excerpts from Gregory's journals to be quite interesting. Creepy, really. I'm also understanding what you said about him being a dangerous man and I do have some concern for your personal safety."

"Aw, that's sweet, Willy. You are forgetting I've been married to him for more than twenty years and I'm still walking around. I can handle Gregory. Trust me."

"I do trust you, Cassie," I replied. "If I didn't trust you, I wouldn't be working for you. I have to say it again that there's something in these pages which leads me to conclude you could be the one who's in danger should he suspect what is going on here."

"Oh Willy," she said in a mocking tone, and then her brain clicked in a different direction. "Listen, Willy, I have to call on that facial. How about we get together tomorrow for lunch?"

"That's fine, where and when."

"How about I call you in the morning. I'm frankly not sure how the rest of today and this evening are going to play out. Bye, Willy."

She clicked off before I could respond. I laid the phone on the table and when I did, it vibrated again. This time it was Sandy.

"Hey, Otto, how are things in paradise?"

"Like someone just told me, it's a beautiful day."

"Any luck in Augusta," I asked.

"Yes, and no," Sandy said. "Before you snap, no, we're not going to play twenty questions. I'll just tell you what I found."

Sandy knew how I hated pulling information from her. Everyone else? Yeah, it was a fun game to me. With her, it proved to be pure pain, mainly because she's smarter than I am. So, I let her continue.

"I did locate the only Jessi Bollenbeck on record in the Augusta area during the timeframe you provided, but you have to remember that it was a long time ago and the trail is cold. I was able to determine she voted only once, in the 1980 presidential election. I pulled the address she used with voter registration, but the house she rented had been bought and torn down with a group of others when a developer wanted to put up a strip mall and apartment buildings. I tracked down a phone number for the old landlord by using property records, but his son answered and told me his father has been dead for about ten years and the son had no recollection of Jessi Bollenbeck.

"There was no birth certificate on record at the courthouse, so she must have moved here from somewhere else.   No marriage license on file, and no certificates of birth issued to children she may have borne. Bottom line is, she's not around Augusta anymore, and there's no family or forwarding information on record.

"I put in an information request with city and county law enforcement. I met with their public information officers and they seem helpful, but since this woman was in Gregory's alleged harem so long ago, they too are going to be hampered by the fact their digital records do not go back that far. They each promised to call me one way or another within the next day or two, though. I used my best helpless southern belle act with the city cop, but the county's representative was a woman, so I just was pleasant and professional, then I told her that my boss was a real dick and was pressuring me." Sandy laughed out loud. "I think we made the sister connection."

I rolled my eyes. Were all females such manipulators when it came to men, and women, I wondered.

"So, what's next? The newspaper records?"

"No," she said. "I went to law enforcement after the courthouse and making some phone calls the utility companies. I've got my feelers out here and so I'm on my way to the airport to catch a flight to Atlanta and then down to Orlando."

"Good choice," I said. "Given the other options."

"Yeah, I figure if it's necessary, I'll do Des Moines and then Cheyenne. I have placed some calls up there though, got through to some pleasant sounding people. Hopefully, I won't have to go to either place personally. Did you know it's four flights from down here to Cheyenne, and if I miss the early afternoon flight, I'm destined to spend the night in Minneapolis?"

"What about this Janet Hopkins woman from Canada?" I asked. "The notes from yesterday said she was recent. Have you put out any feelers north of the border?"

"Not yet, but yeah, I meant to ask you about that note. Did Cassie have an estimated time other than 'recently'?"

"I didn't ask her." I felt really stupid at that moment. "I'll find out."

"When you get the chance, Otto," she said. "So, what's on *your* agenda today? Beach blanket bingo and then a hukilau and bonfire on the beach followed by some stolen smooches and gropes behind the sand dunes?"

"Real mature, Sandy," I scolded mockingly while swallowing my guffaw and simultaneously wondering how it was I had ever let her go. Yeah, I remembered, but what a fool I had been to not have fought harder. She made me laugh. She made me feel good. I loved our banter. "Aren't you combining 60's beach movies? Wasn't *Beach Blanket Bingo* with Frankie and Annette, while the hukilau song was done by Elvis in *Blue Hawaii*?"

"Leave it to you to know the details, movie freak. Do you want to recite some lines for me?"

"Nah, not in the mood, baby doll."

"There!" she shouted. "You just did it."

"Did what?" I said, shamelessly feigning innocence.

"You incorporated a movie line into the conversation."

"Oh, the 'baby doll' reference?"

"Yeah."

"I guess all I can say is 'Thank you, thank you very much,' the end of that in my best imitation Elvis. I think I heard her rolling her eyes. Can you hear someone rolling their eyes on the phone?

"On that note, this Elvis has left the building," she said. "I'm at the car rental lot at the Augusta airport. I'll call you tonight from Orlando."

"Travel safe, Sandy," I said.

"Oh, Otto," she hollered into the phone. "One more thing."

"Yeah, I'm still here."

"Keep the sand out of your cell phone," she said. "And any other sensitive areas."

She clicked off. I smiled.

Jennifer and Alex were up early. They met around the coffee pot in the kitchen area. The remains of strawberry margaritas stuck to the sides of the blender and glasses sitting in the sink. The bottle of tequila, fresh from distillery boot camp at the start of the drinking, lay on its side on the back counter, now a dead soldier.

She pulled out some eggs, sausage, and bagels from the refrigerator, tossed two skillets onto the stovetop, fired the burners and started breakfast.

"So have you decided if you're going to press Gregory further on the identity of your bio-mom?" Alex asked. "Last night you weren't sure if you really cared to find out."

"After sleeping on it, I think I'll make an inquiry, but not push him. He's obviously playing at something, and with the exhibition coming up and all that stress, I don't care to play along at this moment. Scrambled or over easy?"

"Over easy," he said. He went to slice the bagels, slid each half into the toaster and went to the fridge. "You want jam?"

"Yes, please," she said. "Just not strawberry, if you don't mind."

"Looks like you have blackberry preserves. Is that a distant enough relative?"

She nodded at him over her shoulder. He got down plates and pulled out some silverware while she tended the sausage.

"Aw, darn it," she said.

"What's the matter, Jenny?"

"I forgot I have hash browns. Do you want hash browns?" She looked at him with the spatula in her hand. "I'd have to start them now and turn down the sausage."

"Hold the hash browns today," he said. "I don't need the carbs on top of yesterday."

They both heard the approaching helicopter at the same time.

"Brian, you think?" Alex asked.

Jennifer shook her head.

"He didn't strike me as the dropping by unannounced type," she said. "At least not at this point."

Alex walked over to the doors and walked out on the lanai, Jennifer watched him through the glass as he searched the sky.

"It's not Brian," he said when he returned. "Helicopter is different. Still blue with a white stripe, but different."

"Gregory," Jennifer said. "I wonder what he wants."

"Should I make myself scarce?" Alex asked. "I don't think he likes me."

Jennifer smiled broadly.

"You're my friend, and legally, this is my house, so no, I don't want you to make yourself scarce. You said over easy, right?"

"Yep, over easy."

They listened as the helicopter landed outside and heard the engine winding down.   A few minutes later Gregory wandered around the ocean side onto the lanai. He let himself in. Jennifer thought to herself she would have to start locking the doors.

"Good morning," he said.   His eyes darted to Alex who was sitting at the counter near the stovetop.   Gregory felt a rush of disgust as he took note that Alex wore nothing but pajama bottoms. "I didn't know you had company."

"Why would you?" Jennifer challenged.

"Why, I wouldn't," he lied. He had tested the new cameras and sound system overnight and found them quite adequate. His eyes moved about the room to see if he could detect their installation. He could not.

"I asked Alex to come over yesterday when we got back.   I needed someone to talk to."

"Very understandable indeed, Jennifer," Gregory said.   "I apologize we didn't get to finish our conversation yesterday afternoon, but as you know, something came up."

"It must have been important for you not to say good-bye," she said to him. "I felt like an interloper on the plane when we landed, hustled out so I didn't make eye contact with the Lord of the Jet."

"Oh, come now, Jennifer," Gregory said, taking a stool one down from Alex. "You know I can get distracted. I apologize. I've come this morning to make amends and answer any questions you may have." He had other reasons, but not for airing in mixed company. "That coffee smells great."

"Would you like a cup," Alex asked, starting to rise.

"Ah, never mind," Gregory said to him.   "I'll get it. You stay comfortable." He walked around the counter and pulled a cup from the cabinet, filled it from the carafe and returned to his seat.

"You want some eggs, Gregory?" Jennifer asked. She slid Alex's pair onto a plate, added some sausages and half a bagel before sliding it across to him. "I can make more. It's really no trouble."

"If you don't mind," he said. "Sunny side up, a couple of those delicious smelling sausages and half a bagel would be very much appreciated indeed."

She whipped up the breakfast. The men ate sitting on the far side of the island. Jennifer stood, held her plate and leaned against the back counter.

Gregory let out a laugh which startled Alex and Jennifer.

"Isn't it ironic," he started. "That people have huge houses with all sorts of rooms, and yet regardless of their station in life, they spend so much time clustered around the kitchen counter?"

"People are people," Alex said to him.

Gregory looked at him and contemplated his remark. He wondered if Alex was implying something beyond the limits of Gregory's observation. Uncertain, he changed the subject.

"Jennifer, if you don't mind, I'd love to finish the conversation with you regarding your bio-mom. Shall we adjourn to the lanai? It's a beautiful day."

"Sure," she said. Then to Alex, "Do you mind?"

"Not at all," Alex said, sliding off his stool and starting to gather the breakfast dishes. "I'll get the kitchen cleaned up and then hit the shower." He looked into Jennifer's eyes to make sure that was what she wished for him to do.

"You're the best, Alex," she said. Her eyes told him the same thing. Then to Gregory, "More coffee?"

"Please," he said, offering his cup.

Jennifer refilled both their mugs and together they walked out to the lanai.

Alex watched as they took up chairs at the teak table with the green and white striped umbrella. He efficiently cleaned up the kitchen, loaded the dishwasher and wiped down the counters. He thought of the line Gregory had said to him on another occasion when the three of them were at the house, 'Someday, Alex, you're going to make someone a wonderful wife'. Alex remembered the laugh that followed. The joke at his expense had cost Gregory. Alex smiled when he thought about how much that remark had cost Gregory.

Alex finished up. On the way to his room, he tossed the dishrag and towels from the kitchen into the wash machine in the laundry room. From his duffle he pulled out a clean pair of underwear, a fresh shirt and pair of shorts. His shaving kit was already laid out in the bathroom, he studied himself in the mirror. He dropped his pajama bottoms onto the floor, shaved, then showered. When he was done, he dressed, and wandered back toward the great hall.

Jennifer and Gregory appeared to be finishing up. She looked to be crying, and Gregory patted her leg. Alex refilled his coffee, stood with his back to the counter so he could observe outside.

A moment later, Jennifer came in, gave Alex a pained smile and then walked down the hallway to her room without saying a word. Gregory followed, carrying both coffee cups.

"Is she okay?" Alex asked him.

Gregory placed the two cups into the sink. He placed both palms onto the counter and leaned forward. He stared into the sink, refused to turn toward Alex.

"You tell me," Gregory said to him. "What went on here last night?"

"She filled me in on the details of the San Francisco trip and the upcoming show. She's really excited. She told me the story about her bio-mom, as far as you got with it, I would imagine. She'll tell me more later. Then there's the unexpected situation."

Gregory looked up, then his eyes shifted toward Alex.

"What unexpected situation?" he asked, never turning his head. He really didn't like looking at Alex unless he had to. His lifestyle repulsed Gregory. For the life of him, he could not understand why men would prefer other men when women looked so appealing.

"The charter pilot, Brian something. There was a spark."

"Oh, is that all?" Gregory asked. "Brian you said? Did you get a last name?"

"No, but he lives in Makawao. Seems like a decent guy."

"Okay," Gregory said, straightening up and stretching his back. "I'm going to go. Are you staying the night?"

"I've got no plans, I can stay on the clock if you want."

Gregory looked down the hallway toward the Jennifer's master suite. The door was closed.

"I'd think that would be a good idea," he said to Alex.

"What did you tell her about her bio-mom?" Alex asked. "The truth?"

Gregory finally looked at him. His eyebrow arched.

"The truth?" Gregory asked. "What would you know about the truth?"

"I have my opinions," Alex said. "By the way, as of yesterday, my account still hasn't received the second payment for this Montreal thing."

"It'll be there today," Gregory promised. "Don't worry about it. Have I ever let you down?"

"Not so far, Gregory, not so far."

Marcy could have easily made the ninety-four mile drive from Montreal to Burlington, Vermont. She didn't for two reasons. One practical, one theoretical. On the practical side, she had no car and none of her close friends did either. On the theoretical end, she didn't really believe that this would be the end of the trail and wanted to be unencumbered so she could follow any possible leads.

So she booked the same routing as had the mystery woman, Tamra Sommers. She flew through Chicago and then to Burlington, meaning to relocate ninety-four miles on the globe, she had traveled nearly twenty times that distance.

Marcy rented a car at the airport in Burlington, Vermont. She had a home address for Tamra Sommers. The rental clerk asked if she could provide any maps or directions and Marcy declined. She didn't want any connections to be made should this Tamra Sommers person turn out to be the one who impersonated Janet.

On her way out to the parking lot, Marcy stopped at a phone booth and ripped the map section from inside the small book. Just to be certain, she double checked the listed home address and phone number for the woman.

At the car, she unzipped her checked bag and removed a small pouch. She opened the pouch and checked the contents. She slipped the collapsable buck knife with four-inch blade and its sheath inside the waistline of her jeans. She pulled her shirt over the top, closed the suitcase and tossed it into the trunk.

Burlington was not a big city, but it did hold the distinction of being Vermont's largest with a population of around forty-two thousand. Located along the shores of Lake Champlain, which forms part of the border between the United States and Canada, Burlington was a typical sleepy New England town with a history which dates to its founding in 1783. Because of it's location on the lake and following the completion of the Champlain, Erie, and Chambly canals in the early nineteenth century, Burlington became an important center of trade and port of entry for the burgeoning new country.

Marcy had never visited the city, but had been to the shores of Lake Champlain on the Canadian side on several occasions over the years.

She sat in the driver's seat and pulled out the map pages she had ripped from the phone book. She located the home address for Tamra Sommers on one of the pages and then pieced the map pages together. She saw the best way to go would be on Kennedy Drive west out of the airport, then exit north on Shelbourne Road, back east on Prospect Parkway to Crescent Road going north again, then a right on Woodcrest Lane to the house. She estimated the trip would take less than twenty minutes.

Even though she had the air conditioner running in the car, her hands were sweating. Marcy had never been a confrontational person, and as far back as she could remember, had never physically assaulted anyone, much less with a weapon like a knife. She wiped her hands on her jeans, put the car into gear and drove toward the airport exit. A minute later she was moving west on Kennedy Drive. Ten minutes later, she had pulled the car to the side of the road on Crescent. She felt sick to her stomach. She started to cry.

Marcy wondered just what it was she thought she was doing. She wasn't a police officer. Who did she think she was embarking on such a wild goose chase? Some kind of Cagney or Lacey? What would she really do if she had to confront this Tamra woman? Would the woman lie? Would she fight? What was the limit to which Marcy would go on this quest? It was all so clear sitting in Janet's apartment in Montreal. The closer she got to this Sommers woman the cloudier the whole situation became. The fact that Janet was possibly gone forever was beginning to hit home. Marcy wished she were back at the apartment, curled up in the bed they had shared. At least there Marcy could still smell her, see her things, sense her presence. What was she doing here? She wiped tears from her eyes.

Suddenly there was a knock on her window. She turned to face an elderly man looking concerned.

"Are you all right, Miss?" he said through the glass.

Marcy rolled down the window. He stood there, in long charcoal gray pants and plaid shirt in tones of burgundy and gold buttoned to the neck with an old gray sweater obviously worn against the heat of mid-July. On his feet he wore bright white running shoes; Nike's from the swoosh on the side. In his gnarled and wrinkled hand he held the end of a well-worn leash tethering a cranky-looking, brown and white Chihuahua.

"I'm sorry, but I said are you all right, Miss?" he said as she looked him over. "It's not often we have an obviously distraught, attractive, young woman stopped by the side of the road up here." The Chihuahua yipped. "Hush, Isabella," he scolded.

Marcy half smiled at him.

"Isabella was my late wife's dog," he explained. "She named her for the queen who sent Columbus on his journey." His look took on a conspiratorial tone and he leaned a bit closer to the window. "There are times I wouldn't mind sending Isabella on a little journey of her own." He restored the distance and his eyes were moist. "But, she's the last tie to my dear departed wife."

Marcy's tears dried up and she sensed a genuineness in the man on the other side of her car door. He reminded her of her grandfather, so she gave him a big smile.

"I'm okay," she said. "It's just been a very difficult week."

"Thomas Kincaid," the man said, and he offered his free right hand through the window. "Not the painting with light gentleman, I couldn't draw a straight line with a ruler and two days to do it." He gestured to the dog who was now sitting alongside her master's feet and observing Marcy. "Of course, you've met Isabella."

Marcy shook his hand gently, it was cool and smooth to the touch, but the strength of his grip surprised her.

"Pleasure to meet you, Mr. Kincaid," she said. "My name is Marcy."

"Please call me Thomas, Marcy," he offered. "Mr. Kincaid was my father, and he's long, long gone. He fought with Teddy Roosevelt in Puerto Rico. San Juan Hill. You must have read about it in school. The second World War was my turn. I wish we didn't need to send young men, and women these days, to fight and die for arguments between their governments. Don't you agree, Marcy?"

She didn't know how to react. Thomas spoke in quick disconnected clips in some sort of stream of consciousness. Marcy wondered if this was what happened to people who had nobody to listen to them anymore.

"I do agree about the waste of war, Thomas," she said.

"Your accent, my dear, I can't quite place it."

"I was born and raised in Detroit, but I've been living in Montreal for a while." She thought a moment. "Perhaps I've picked up a blend," she said.

"I can hear the Montreal, the Quebec Province," he said, tapping his hear with one finger. "We get your people down here all the time. Just across the border, you know. Almost neighbors, as it were." He paused a moment. "Nope, it was the Detroit which was eluding me. Midwest. Detroit Tigers. I'm a huge baseball fan, but the Red Sox. Never been a fan of the Tigers. Do you like baseball, Marcy?"

"Ah, never been much of a sports fan," she said.

"Sure, Canada. You're most likely a hockey fanatic. We've got many of them around here too. No professional teams. After all, this is Vermont. No professional teams of any kind in Vermont."

Marcy could feel her mouth agape and consciously closed it.

"What brings you to Burlington, Marcy?" he inquired. "I see you've got a rental car. Did you fly in this morning?"

"I'm looking for someone who lives near here," she said, and then immediately regretted letting the information slip out. She'd left a trail. Then, she thought, would anybody take this chatterbox seriously?

"Well, I know everyone around here. I grew up right down there, the white house with red trim." He pointed down the road ahead of the car.

Marcy leaned out the window to get a better view.

"Lived there my whole life, ninety years this November. My father and grandfather built the house. Of course, that was after Old Teddy was done with him."

Marcy made a quick decision. She could either tell Thomas she had made a mistake and this was the wrong neighborhood, but if he saw her back there later, he'd remember her all the more clearly. She could be honest with him and hope he'd forget her. She decided on the latter approach.

"I'm looking for Tamra Sommers," she said.

"Tamra Sommers?" he repeated to her. "Are you a friend of hers?"

"Friend of a friend, I guess you could say," she lied.

"Are you a reporter, Marcy?" He cocked his head slightly. His welcoming face slid behind a mask of distrustfulness. "Haven't you people done enough to poor Tamra?" His mask transformed to contempt.

"No, no, Mister...I mean Thomas, I am not from the media." She wondered what he was talking about. "I had just hoped to speak with her, that's all."

"Friend of a friend, you say?" His face had slid back to being skeptical. "Then you should know. Tamra Sommers hasn't spoken to anyone in three years, she can't." He started to move around the front of the car toward the passenger side.

Marcy called out after him, wondered what he was doing. When he reached the passenger door he opened it, Isabella hopped in and got on the seat next to her and Thomas followed. She stared at him in disbelief.

"Let's just settle this thing once and for all, young lady," he said. "Pull around the corner, you know the house if you're a friend of a friend. I'll take you to Tamra Sommers."

Marcy put the car in gear. What else could she do? She turned right at the corner, looked for house numbers on the mailboxes, spotted the number she had memorized and pulled into the drive. She pulled up next to a large blue van with handicapped plates, put the car into park and turned off the ignition.

Thomas had his door open and quicker than Marcy had thought possible, he and Isabella were on the way to the front door. He paused at the porch steps and waved back at her.

"Well, come on, Missy."

Marcy got out of the car and followed him. Thomas climbed the stairs one at a time, Isabella waited at the top of the stoop. Thomas rang the bell, straightened up as best he could, fixed his collar and ran a hand through his full head of snow white hair.

The inner door opened and in its place moved a woman in her late seventies, with white hair to match Thomas'. When she saw him through the screen, she smiled and welcomed him.

"Tom, what a surprise," she said in a friendly, lilting voice. "And Isabella too. Hello, Isabella."

The dog reacted by wagging its tale. Marcy took the two for friends.

"What brings you here, Tom?" the woman asked. She looked past him toward Marcy and her face grew unwelcoming. "Who's that, Tom. You know we don't want..."

"Says she's a friend of a friend of Tamra's. I ran into her around the corner sitting in her car and crying. Says her name is Marcy and claims to be from Montreal, although her accent says something different."

The woman looked Marcy over from top to bottom.

"Reporter?" the woman said to Marcy.

"No, Ma'am," Marcy replied. "I'm not a reporter and I'm not here to cause any trouble for anyone." Marcy took a deep breath to steady her nerves. She could feel the tears and emotions returning and the last thing she needed to do was to lose it in front of strangers. "I have to confess I did tell a lie to Thomas." She looked at him. "I'm sorry, Thomas." She began to tear up despite the deep breath.

Thomas and the woman watched her.

"White lie or black lie?" he said to her.

"Excuse me?

"Was it a white lie or a black lie?" he repeated. "A little one or a big one?"

"I don't know, a little one, I guess." She wasn't sure what he wanted from her, so she expounded. "I am not a friend of a friend of Tamra's. I don't even know anyone who has ever known her. My..." She looked at them, adjusted her next words to fit the generation to whom she was speaking. "My friend has gone missing and my only clue to the trail led me to Tamra Sommers. I'm sorry I lied. I didn't know what else to do, so I'm here."

The woman opened the screen door. She walked out onto the stoop, past Thomas and a hopping Isabella, down the steps and over to Marcy. She looked her in the eye and took Marcy's hands in hers.

"Your friend was more than a friend, wasn't she?" the woman asked.

Her eyes were careworn and surrounded by thick wrinkles speckled with age. They searched Marcy's eyes.

"Yes," Marcy admitted. "Her name was Janet Hopkins, and she was, is very special to me."

The woman turned and looked at Thomas. He shrugged. She then spoke to Marcy.

"Would you like to come in, dear? You can tell us what's going on, we'll have some tea, and you can meet Tamra if you wish."

"I'd like that," Marcy said.

The woman took her hand and led her to the porch.

"Thomas," she said. "Go on in and put the teapot to boil. We'll find something for Isabella to nibble on."

The four of them went inside.

Over tea and some stale, store-bought cookies, the state of which didn't seem to bother Isabella any, Marcy laid out the story of Janet's disappearance and how she had been lead to a woman named Tamra Sommers.

Thomas and the old woman, whom Marcy learned was named Annabelle Wheaton and went by the familiar Belle, sat around the kitchen table topped with a flowery vinyl table cloth. Belle was Tamra Sommers' maternal grandmother and while Marcy told the story, she sat and listened patiently. Occasionally, the two elders would exchange glances and nods. When Marcy spoke of Janet, Belle patted her on her hands.

When Marcy finished, Belle relayed Tamra's story. She told of the accident which had claimed eleven souls from the church group, including Tamra's parents, three years ago. Tamra was the only survivor of the late night crash which occurred as the group was returning from a weekend retreat. Tamra's father had been driving the accident vehicle, which was second in line of a three-van convoy, when he apparently fell asleep at the wheel. The van left the highway, clipped a guardrail, flipped and catapulted into a bridge abutment. The roof of the van was peeled off like the lid of a sardine can. The vehicle's gas tank ruptured and fire consumed the remains of both the van and its occupants. Eleven died on the spot. Tamra was found an hour later, thrown from the impact point to an area of deep grass on the other side of the overpass. Her body was broken. She was unconscious. Doctors soon discovered she was paralyzed from the neck down and had suffered severe brain trauma. Belle's eyes misted with the retelling and Marcy reached and patted her hands.

The media descended upon the small town of Burlington and scoured and exposed the lives of every victim, including Tamra. They invaded her privacy, sneaked into her hospital room and took photos. Reporters stirred up neighbor against neighbor. People in the media called it a miracle inside of a tragedy, yet were not shy about blaming both the dead driver and 'these unsupervised church groups running around and placing people at risk'. Then they left the misery, distrust, and battles staged but not fought behind to sort themselves out while they moved on to the next big story. It was that type of salacious and vicious press coverage which had caused such distrust of media types.

After the stories were told, Belle took Marcy to meet Tamra. The young woman, twenty-eight years old now, was a misshapen figure under the sheet on the hospital bed set up in a bedroom next to Belle's. The respirator, located off to one side, cycled, pumping oxygen into her lungs through a tube placed into her throat. Tamra's face was contorted, one of her eyes was open, vacant.

An overweight nurse in blue scrubs and black Crocs sat in a chair next to the bed and read a magazine. When Belle and Marcy entered the room, the nurse put a finger to her lips, indicating the two should be quiet. She rose from her chair and tended momentarily to Tamra, wiping her mouth with a damp cloth, smoothing her hair with a soft hand.

Marcy's stomach flopped and she felt the urge to vomit, a reaction brought on not by Tamra's condition, but by the thought of someone using this poor girl's name as a cover to Janet's abduction. She wanted to flee, to get away. Then something took hold inside her and the bile which moments before made her ill, now fueled a burning anger and forged her resolve to get to the bottom of this, wherever the trail may take her and no matter how long it took.

When the pair returned to the kitchen, they found Thomas feeding another cookie to Isabella.

"Thomas, you're going to make that dog fat," Belle scolded.

"Or kill her with all the preservatives they put into those cookies," Marcy added.

The three shared a smile. Isabella danced on her hind legs and was rewarded with another piece of cookie.

Belle sat down in her chair. The look on her face suggested some deep thought was making its way through her brain. She reached out and touched Thomas on his knee.

"Thomas," she said. "Marcy has quite the little mystery on her hands, doesn't she."

Thomas dropped the last of the cookie onto the floor and Isabella inhaled it, then looked for more. Thomas waved his hand and she sat, waited. He eyed Marcy.

"Sure sounds like it," he said. "From the look on your face, Belle, you've got some idea in your head. What is it?"

"You've always enjoyed mysteries and detective stories."

"I still do."

"And you used to manage the airport. You have a lot of contacts with the airlines and the people in the federal government."

"A long time ago," he said.

"You only retired ten years ago when the airport committee forced you out," she said. "Besides, to old farts like us, ten years is not a long time." She winked at Marcy.

"Okay, so?" he said.

Belle and Marcy watched him think, and each bore witness to the light bulb which came on as he arrived at a conclusion.

"Oh, yes," he said, wagging a finger at Belle. "Of course, I'll do it."

Sandy worked her way through a pile of records books in the small review room off the County Clerk's office in the Orange County Courthouse in Orlando. To her, Florida meant three things: Disneyland, orange juice, and rocket launches, and it wasn't her favorite place to be. There were too many old people driving around with their blinkers going for what the world joked was the signal for the 'eventual left'. The weather was too hot, it stormed too much, and the bugs got way too big and aggressive. She really didn't want to be there any longer than necessary.

Since she understood it could take days to obtain old information which may not be digitized, she had checked in early this morning with the Orange County Sheriff's Office and Orlando Police Department and asked them to do records checks on Michelle Wirtz similar to those she had sought in Augusta going back to the time listed on Cassie's information.

So far in her manual searching, as in Augusta with Jessi Bollenbeck, Sandy was able to determine that a Michelle Wirtz did indeed at one time live in Orlando, but hadn't been in the area for years. Unlike the public filings dead ends she met with related to Jessi in Augusta, there was a divorce case filed with Michelle as the

Petitioner in Orange County. She had requested particulars from the Clerk of Courts office and had been told she would be able to view the records on microfilm in the afternoon after an assistant clerk retrieved them from the vault. At least there was a glimmer of a trail in Orlando, she thought as she stacked another book onto the already reviewed pile.

Even though the sign on the wall clearly stated that all cellular phones were to be turned off while in the records review room, Sandy had merely turned hers to vibrate. About two hours into her searching, vibrate it did. She removed the phone from her purse and checked the caller I.D. on the display. She looked around to see if anyone was watching and then answered the call.

Sandy grabbed her pad and pen and began frantically scribbling notes as the caller dictated. The information had also been sent through email, he said, along with copies of documents, photos, and other data. It appeared the checkered flag went to the Augusta Police Department's Public Information Officer and Sandy told him so and thanked him profusely for all his help. His only response was that he was glad to help and requested that if there was any information her investigation turned up which could help the Augusta P.D., that she give them a call.

She agreed and closed the phone. Then, as she looked over the notes, Sandy slid her chair back and walked to the hallway where she knew she could use her cell phone and hit the speed dial for William.

I was going through the journal pages again, looking for anything which could be categorized to one particular woman or which may help illuminate any other issues which may be plaguing my new best buddy, when my phone vibrated and then echoed Sandy's special ringtone. I picked up the call.

"Is it still good morning?" I teased.

"It's good afternoon here," she responded, and then provided an editorial comment: "It's hot and sticky outside, and with state budget cuts by the new governor - whom, by the way, I am hearing many not-so-nice things about - it's hot and sticky inside, too.

I know Sandy was not one for hot and sticky, it makes her cranky. Then why do we live in subtropical New Orleans? You can ask her, but you'd get the same response I do, 'Because I love the city, not where it's located'. I could hear that edge to her voice, but mixed with a touch of excitement, so I subtly focused her on the second emotion.

"I'm certain you didn't call me to gripe about Florida's new governor's penny pinching, so give."

Subtle or not, the nudge worked and she said nothing more about the discomfort of being in Orlando, but rather relayed the information she had just received from the Augusta P.D. I reached across the table, woke my laptop, checked my email and found a newly arrived message sent to our general office email which forwarded to both of our private accounts. The header indicated the missive arrived with a dozen attached files.

"I'll go through the documents after we hang up," I said. "Just from what you're telling me, this could be an interesting development in the big picture. It certainly isn't going to help Cassie's claim under the prenuptial, though, if we can't help prove adulterous behavior by Gregory because we can't locate the woman."

"Well, we still have five other names, including the Hopkins and Shea women. Oh, and speaking of the prenup, I reviewed the scanned file you sent me last evening and think there's a problem."

"Problem?" I asked. "You mean because it's so poorly drafted?"

"Well, yeah, there's that. I think it would take Gregory about thirty-seconds in the yellow pages to find any number of brand new lawyers who could slice the document to ribbons in short order."

"So, you don't think it would hold up?"

"Not in a million years, Otto. The language is almost juvenile. The largest issue, however, is that it's *not* a prenup."

"You've already said that."

"No, you don't get it. The document was signed five years after Gregory and Cassie were married. You can't un-ring the bell, Otto. They were already married, so at best it's some kind of performance contract, but it's not a prenuptial agreement. Since they were already married, and from what I could gather, had already established residency in Hawaii, it will be Hawaii law which will guide any rulings on the document and the subsequent division of assets. The agreement may not even be enforceable as a performance contract. This whole exercise as she has designed it could be for naught. I'm not up to speed on Hawaii law, but I do have a friend from law school who lives on Oahu if you think we should seek advice."

As Sandy explained, I thought about our role in the investigation, the proffered reasons we were hired. Cassie said she had provided me a copy of the prenup so we could determine any specifics we'd need to prove her case, not so that we could assess the validity of the document. We were hired to provide our client with information pertaining to alleged marital infidelity, not to provide her with divorce settlement advice. When Sandy finished speaking, I bounced these thoughts off her and asked, if in the overall picture, she'd come to the same conclusions.

"Of course," she said. "I agree with you one hundred percent. We're not acting as her divorce lawyers. We're her investigators. What she does with the report is her business and if it's useless, an attorney in the jurisdiction will tell her." She paused a moment. "No, I'm not going to tell you we need to back off. Our role is clearly defined and legally defensible, should it ever come to that."

"Then you agree that we'll continue to assemble the information we're hired to provide our client and let Cassie worry about how it's used?"

"Again, yes, we continue to do our job," she said with a bit of impatience. "I couldn't care less if Cassie leaves her marriage with one billion dollars or twenty-billion dollars. My life will be affected not one iota either way." Sandy paused before continuing in a different direction. "I do have a question for you, and that's my repeated WHY?"

"Why?" I asked. "What do you mean?"

"Yes, why did she give us this document at all? All I know about her is what you've told me, what I've observed and what I have read. It's clear she's not a stupid woman, nor is she naive. There's nothing in the document which defines or specifies the elements which must be proven under the agreement for the adultery clause to come alive. She must understand the primary idea of a prenuptial is that it's executed before the nuptials, before the wedding. Just like ours was. So, with Hawaii's no-fault divorce laws and their equitable distribution of marital assets scheme which will be more than fair to her given the tenancy and term of the marriage added to the fact that she really doesn't need to prove anything beyond the bare existence of adulterous behavior on Gregory's part under the agreement, assuming, of course, the document is real and valid, then it leads me back to the question of WHY?"

"Maybe she didn't realize timing was an issue. Perhaps she didn't understand what was required under the document. She's not an attorney, Sandy. Then again, neither am I."

"Don't be blinded by the past, Otto," Sandy warned. "Just don't do it. Of course she knew what she was doing. She can certainly understand the content of the prenup, or whatever you want to call that document. A tenth grader could understand it."

I could hear her tapping her front teeth with the end of her pen. I hate that nervous tick of hers, especially over the phone. She tells me it helps her think. In reality, I think she does it so everyone else around her loses focus and *can't* think. That way, when whatever is being formulated in her brain moves from vapor to solid form and she states it, she is the most brilliant person in the room; or, maybe I'm wrong.

"Why are we there? No, why are *you* there?" Sandy asked rhetorically. "There's a reason for it all, Otto. Don't delude yourself that it's because you're the best investigative mind in the world." Even if I do, she thought but didn't add. "No, Cassandra Yeats-Thomason has a reason for wanting YOU involved, Otto. I just don't know what it is. Yet."

"Maybe it's because I'm cute and adorable and she couldn't get me out of her mind for three decades," I offered, even though I knew I was taking a risk of ticking her off.

I heard Sandy roll her eyes. I wish someone could tell me how I could hear that, but perhaps it has something to do with the fact Sandy always includes a loud, exasperated exhalation with the action.

"Keep telling yourself that, Otto," she said. "I have the feeling you're going to get hurt, if you do. Badly." She closed her phone.

The line went dead on my end.

I closed my phone and turned my attention to the laptop. I read through the email from the Public Relations Officer from the Augusta PD. From the preliminary niceties, Sandy had definitely made an impression. Apart from the opening, he proved to be a man of few words. A Sergeant Friday type, just the facts, ma'am.

Jessi Bollenbeck had been the subject of an open missing person's investigation for over twenty years. At the time she went missing, she had been thirty years old, which would have made her fifty now were she still alive somewhere, something I doubted.

Her physical description was becoming hauntingly familiar, five-foot-seven, one hundred twenty-five pounds, shoulder length brown hair, brown eyes. Unmarried, no children. Definitely Gregory's type. She reportedly went missing from a grocery store parking lot in Augusta where her car had been found abandoned. There were few leads of merit through the investigation and the trail quickly ran cold.

I clicked on the first .pdf file attached to the email and up popped a single-page, Missing Person flyer with Jessi's smiling face in the center. She was a beautiful girl. Now gone twenty years.

A slightly redacted case file broken down into a number of .pdf documents was included and comprised the majority of the remaining attachments. Lastly, there were some contemporary clippings from the Augusta Chronicle and photos of the abandoned vehicle and surrounding area.

Nobody claimed her vehicle. There had been no move by any living relatives to have Jessi Bollenbeck declared dead in absentia after the commonly accepted seven-year waiting period. No living relatives had been found in the Augusta area.

I read through the police reports. After finding the vehicle abandoned in the grocery store parking lot - the store manager had noticed it parked in the same spot for three consecutive days and made the report per store policy - the police impounded and searched the car. They identified the owner as being one Jessi Bollenbeck and a pair of uniformed officers went to her house to check on the woman. There had been no exterior surveillance at the grocery store, and none at all in the area of the woman's home.

Once at Jessi's house and having been unable to raise anyone inside, officers obtained permission from their superiors to enter the premises on the belief that a woman who was already known to be missing may be possibly injured, or worse, inside. A search was conducted and they found no evidence of struggle or unusual activity having taken place there.

A suitcase was located in one of the bedrooms with luggage claim checks still attached. Because the suitcase was located outside of storage which officers concluded may indicate current use, the tags were removed and then taken to the airline ticket counter at the

Augusta airport for purposes of identification and verification. The airline confirmed the tags had been issued by them at the JFK International Airport in New York for transit to Augusta four days prior. From all available records, the luggage was claimed normally by its owner on Sunday evening after the flight arrived from Atlanta. The flight had arrived twenty minutes late at 10:17 p.m. due to weather delays.

An answering machine was located in the front hallway. The unit used full-sized cassette tapes for both outgoing and incoming messages and it's message light was flashing. The messages were played by detectives who had been dispatched to back up the uniforms. The only messages were from an employer looking for Jessi on Monday, Tuesday and Wednesday. Both tapes were collected by detectives.

Detectives had questioned neighbors as a follow up to the preliminary investigation done by the uniformed officers. They all reported Jessi to be a quiet, single woman who kept to herself and created no problems. As far as the neighbors knew, she had no routine callers. While he had seen her come and go with a young man or two over the term of her tenancy, they knew of nobody by name, and none recently. She had leased the house just under two years earlier and had recently told the owner she would like to renew for another year. Photocopies of the rental forms were collected for handwriting exemplars.

A criminal records check had been conducted by clerical staff and no records of arrests or other contact between Jessi and the Augusta P.D. were discovered. The vehicle had been tagged for overtime parking on a downtown street fourteen months earlier and the fine had been paid on time, in cash.

Crime scene investigators collected fingerprints from toiletry items found in the bathroom and believed to belong to the missing woman. They were filed to expedite identification in case any unidentified body was located. Gruesome, but necessary.

Detectives went to Jessi's employer, name redacted, and interviewed her manager and several people who were identified as being friendly with the missing woman. They were able to confirm Jessi had taken a trip to New York for an extended weekend. She had left work after completing her shift the Wednesday before, was to have flown to New York on Thursday morning and to return on

Sunday evening.   It was a schedule which detectives had already confirmed. Jessi had been aboard her scheduled flights. She was to have returned to work on Monday morning, two days before the car being reported abandoned, hence the phone messages as her supervisor checked on her absence.

Statistically, even though missing persons cases have increased six-fold over the twenty years since Jessi went missing - back then of the roughly 150,000 people who were reported missing in the United States - the vast majority were run aways and more than half were male. To the surprise of many, only a tiny fraction of people gone missing are stereotypical abductions or kidnappings by strangers. Many people simply walk out of their lives, but most times they resurface, especially during an intervening twenty years.   From this side of the investigation, in this ex-cop's humble opinion, it could be concluded that one explanation for the disappearance of Jessi Bollenbeck could indeed be foul play.

It appeared to me that Augusta P.D. had conducted more than a thorough, routine investigation.   Given the absence of any evidence of a crime, such as blood at a scene, they had gone way above and beyond the normal process.   They used all available resources to advertise the missing person and processed any tips as they came in. Flags were requested with federal authorities on tax records, social security account activity, and any other database which she may use. Her bank accounts were identified and watched for any activity.

Detectives investigated any angle they could think of, but over time, the tips stopped coming and people were assigned to other cases. The world kept turning. After several years, the file was sent to Records for safekeeping and to make room for other, fresher cases. Since the disappearance of Jessi Bollenbeck was still considered OPEN, it meant that she hadn't turned up - alive or dead - in over twenty years.

I was about to file the documents electronically over the internet into our case database stored on a server at the office, and back them up on my laptop, when a light went off in my head. I reached for the journal pages. Sure enough, there it was, on two pages.

"People leave their lives behind in New York City all the time and it is an august occasion for no person other than the one leaving.   There is never any planned fanfare at the departure. Leaving a life behind is as though a thief were slipping away in the night. People plan it that way. My friend and I have proven

that people not only can leave their life behind, but, like the hole left after one removes one's finger from a cup of water, can do so while ensuring absolutely no trace of their physicality is left behind.

"To be certain, there will be lingering memories and worldly trappings to be dealt with by functionaries in coveralls and uniforms, but the memories will fade with time and the trappings will be re-consumed by those who follow. There will also be unanswered questions, but who can speak for the person who leaves their life?

"Today, a woman left her life behind. Will these words be all that speaks of her in the annals of time?"

I looked at the writing which I had read repeatedly without context since yesterday evening. Was this connection merely a coincidence or was it my imagination? Were the other sections going to tie to the five other women? Did Cassie understand which segments of Gregory's journals she was handing over to me? Was Sandy correct? Am I here for some unstated purpose?

I picked up my cell phone, found Cassie's cell number in the recent calls and hit the redial key. In the speaker, the phone rang and rang but went unanswered. I tapped the end key to disconnect when the voice mail message began to play.

I considered whether I should share this information with Sandy but then decided against it. I wanted to speak with Cassie first. Until I could reach her, I decided to go through the remaining journal pages and see if I could spot any other clues, now that I knew how to look.

Gregory landed at the Kahului Airport, turned the helicopter over to the maintenance staff and drove his Corvette out the hangar's side door. He took the bypass and connected with the Mokulele highway at the sugar mill. He made the left turn and drove toward Wailea.

Jennifer walked out of her room about an hour after Gregory had left. She found Alex outside by the pool reading a paperback.

"Hey," she said.

"Hey," he replied. He set the open book on his thigh. "So?"

"I'm sorry for being a baby," she said.

"Oh, stop it, Jenny. You're my friend, probably my best friend. You never have to apologize to me, ever."

She touched his arm, took the seat next to him.

"I'm going to ask again," he said. "So?"

"So, according to Gregory, my bio-mom is alive."

"Well, that's good news." He watched her as she thought about it. "Well, isn't it, Jenny?"

"Yeah, I guess so," she said unconvincingly. "See, I just don't know if I have the right to impose myself into her life after thirty years, even if I wanted to meet her. I'm really not sure I do."

"I think you need some time to think about it," he said. "This isn't a decision you make in an hour, Jenny."

Jennifer got up and walked around by the pool steps. She stuck her toe into the water, then placed both feet onto the top step and sat on the pool's edge.

"See, it's not just the shock of her seeing me after all these years that has me worried. It's the other memories which may hurt her." She appeared to be searching for words, or thoughts, or both. "See, Gregory said my bio-dad is also alive."

"All the better," Alex chirped, then he watched in horror as she seemed to collapse into herself. He got up off the chair and went to sit beside her. Fucking Gregory, he thought. Alex put his arm around her and she fell against him. "What is it, Jenny? What in God's name is it?"

She was crying. Not sobbing, just shedding tears.

"Oh, Alex, it's so awful," she said, using he hands to wipe away the tears. "My bio-mom had me when she was fifteen years old."

"Honey, that kind of thing happens all the time," he consoled. "You are lucky she loved you enough to give you to people who could raise you in an adult and intact family. Your parents are Bruce and Elisa Shea and they loved you with all their hearts as their own."

"I know they did, and I love them. No, it gets worse." She leaned away from him as if she felt dirty. "My bio-mom was impregnated as a result of a rape." Her face took on a distant look. "A rape, Alex. My mother was raped and impregnated, became pregnant with me through one of the most horrible, degrading, despicable torments which a woman can endure."

Alex was speechless. Gregory had indeed told her the truth. Most of it anyway.

She stood up, walked away across the grass toward the lava point. Her hair blew in the wind. When she reached the edge of the grass she stopped, threw her arms into the air and stretched. She twisted and bent herself, slowly, effortlessly, with the fluidity of a martial artist. He knew what she was doing: exorcising the bad thoughts from her chakra and soon she would pull herself into the meditating pose and soothe her mind, body, and soul.

Alex went back to reading his book. His job was to watch over her, and he could do that just as well while enjoying some Baldacci.

Chapter Fifteen

I was outside on the lanai speaking on the cell again with Sandy when I heard the knock at the condo door. Having left the door open to allow a cross breeze through the unit, and figuring this was a drop by from my upstairs neighbor, I hollered for him to come on in and continued my conversation. Imagine my surprise when I turned around and saw Gregory standing in my entryway, about to walk down the three steps into my living and dining areas where at the time on the dining table were strewn dozens of photocopies of his journal pages.

Snapping the phone closed in mid-sentence, I moved quickly across the room to meet his advance. Not knowing what he'd seen from his vantage point and may have recognized laying on the table, and not wanting to unnecessarily draw his attention to anything there by reenacting a scene from some TV sitcom with wild scooping and covering, I staunched his advance by bounding up the three steps to meet him and offer a friendly handshake.

"Well, this is indeed a surprise," I said. "When you said 'don't be a stranger' yesterday, I never assumed you'd be the one exercising the prerogative to drop on by."

"Is this a bad time?" he asked, again releasing my hand from a strong-handed grip. "I was in the neighborhood and thought I'd see if you were home."

"How did you know which unit I was in?" I asked.

"I saw your Jeep parked out there," he said, gesturing toward the parking lot area. "I remembered your license plate number and voila, I found you. Easy as that."

"Can I offer you anything to drink?" I asked. I decided I could do a quick pulling together of the papers on my way to the kitchen, so I walked back down the steps and paused at the chair I was using at the dining table and interposed my bulk between his view and the scattered pages. I closed my computer.

Gregory took one step down and then paused.

"You know," he said glancing down the hall and rescinding the step. "If you don't mind, I really could use your bathroom. Then I'd take a bottle of water, if you have it."

"Sure, it's right there," I said, directing him to the guest bathroom. "When you're done, come on out to the lanai. There's a cool breeze out there."

He walked down the hall, went into the guest bathroom and closed the door. I moved quickly to assemble the papers on the table into a single stack and was just about to shove that stack into my computer bag when the bathroom door opened and he stuck out his head.

"You know, there's no toilet paper on the holder," he said.

I turned and saw him smiling at me. I stood there frozen, his journal pages in my hand.

"Under the sink," I said.

He smiled and closed the door again. I stuffed the papers into my computer bag and then put the bag on the seat of one of the chairs at the table. I grabbed two bottles of water from the refrigerator and walked out to the lanai.

A couple of minutes later, Gregory came out, took his water and twisted off the top.

"Did I catch you in the middle of the working part of your working vacation there?" he asked, nodding toward the dining table inside.

"Just balancing the checkbook," I said.

"Ah," he replied. He took a long drink and looked down the greenway toward the ocean. "I have people for that."

"You have people for many things, I would imagine."

"I do," he said. "Though perhaps far fewer than you suspect. I rather prefer my privacy and solitude. It's one of the reasons I choose to live where I do. You realize we don't have any live-in staff, even though the lower west wing was originally designed for staff quarters. I reluctantly gave in to Cassandra and the architect's wishes on that point. In fifteen years there, I've never employed any onsite staff; but they felt it best to be prepared for down-the-road or resale. Resale, hell. I'll burn it down and leave the hulk sitting there just to spite that prick neighbor of mine."

I noted his right hand ball into a fist, then relax a moment later.

"You mean Keoki?" I asked fully knowing the answer.

"Yes, William, Keoki. The elderly Hawaiian gentleman you spoke with after you left my home yesterday."

I knew my feeling of being watched was correct yesterday. This neighbor was obviously a hot button for him and since the last thing I wanted to deal with was an agitated Gregory, I routed the conversation back to the mainline track.

"So, no staff at all? How do you manage to keep the place up to such an obviously high standard?"

"People clean, stock, and maintain the home when I'm not there. It's how I prefer it." He looked at his watch. "I suspect your luncheon dishes from yesterday's tête-à-tête are being cleaned and put away as we speak."

"That must make it hard to be Cassie?" I said, ignoring for now the implication. "I mean, coping with your desire for solitude and privacy."

"Ah, no, William. See, Cassandra is an integral component of my life of privacy and solitude," he replied, gave me a look out the corner of his eye. "We are a team, her and I. We have been since we met. In everything."

I wondered if Gregory had any idea that the other member of his team was intending to go free agent soon. I took a seat, and since I thought this little drop by may last a while, offered another to Gregory. He accepted. I decided to probe into this team concept a little more.

"You know, I was a little surprised to see you each had your own bedroom suite," I said. "Perhaps that all goes to the other components of your life of privacy and solitude to which Cassie isn't an integral component."

I saw his lips curl into a hint of a smile, his right cheek dimpled. Then it was gone.

"I had almost forgotten where I discovered you two yesterday afternoon," he said. "Thank you for the reminder that my wife had invited you to her bedroom and had obviously showed you the private portions of our home."

"Gregory, I want you to understand that nothing was happening between Cassie and myself other than two old friends reconnecting."

"Ah, yes, but see, William, it's the *reconnecting* that's at the heart of the unspoken issue here, isn't it?"

"Unspoken issue?" I asked, genuinely befuddled. "I guess you've lost me on that one, Gregory. Nothing was happening between Cassie and I when you came home yesterday other than a tour of your home."

"You know you're not the first, don't you?" he said in a petulant tone.

"The first what?" Where was this guy going now?

"The first purported old beau she's run into," he said. "It's amazing how many people from my wife's past wander around Maui and miraculously happen upon her. I've lost count over the years."

"I had no idea Cassie had been so popular on the dating scene," I said. "Of course, I have been out of that circle for a very long time."

"When did you date her again?" he asked.

"Freshman year of high school," I said. "Only for about eight or ten weeks. No big deal."

"No big deal?" he asked with a tone of incredulity. "No big deal? Why it was during my freshman year of high school when the girl who was the second love to break my heart tore my world apart." His eyes focused on something in the distance, he sat forward in the chair momentarily, then settled back, tossed one leg over the other. "I don't know about you, William, but those years of a boy's transition to manhood were a fairly big deal to me. Why, I remember more details, feelings, and emotions of those years than I do about most of the other years of my life."

"Your second love to break your heart?" I asked. "Who was your first?"

"The first love to break my heart?" he asked, turning his head toward me and really looking at me for the first time since he walked in.

I nodded.

"Why, my mother, of course."

He stared me down, didn't blink.

"Well, they do say that every boy's first love is his mother," I replied. "Though there's a difference between a boy's love for his mother and the love for a woman, right, Gregory?"

"Is there?" He asked. "A mother is a boy's ideal, William. She is the first vision of womanhood to which a boy is exposed. It is her body which creates him from the essence of herself and the castoff of the male. It is her voice he first hears in her womb. It is her loving embrace he feels first when he emerges into the world. It is from her hand or from her breast he first takes nourishment as a separate being. She is there for his first steps, his first words. When he skins his knee, to whom does he run? Father? I think not. No, William, he runs to his mother. She is there for him. Always. It is her to whom he can turn with his problems. She always listens. Always helps. Always, William. Does a father do that? Again I think not. A mother never judges a son. Oh, she may judge a daughter - quite harshly at times - but a son, never. It's the purest form of love in the universe. When that love falters, when the son discovers his mother to not be perfect, well, let's just say that is something which can never be recovered. It can never be restored. How could anyone ever believe it could be restored? Can you answer me that, William?"

Boy, talk about grabbing the mommy lure and running out the line. I sat with the conversational drag set light and watched him strip the reel. Then, as the core became visible, figuratively speaking, I thought it was an appropriate time for him to feel the sting of the hook, so I tightened the drag and snapped the rod back strongly.

"No unconditional love in your world, Gregory?"

"Unconditional love?" he asked.

"Yeah, like the love from parents to their children, and vice versa. Surely you've heard of unconditional love." Let's see how much fight he puts up in before giving me a detailed look inside the real Gregory Thomason.

He thought about that for a moment before responding. I watched him like I used to observe suspects during questioning. See, observation of the unconscious reactions is as important as listening to what the suspect says. Hell, more important since most of them are lying every time they open their mouths. It's the main reason police started videotaping interviews. For years, suspects would merely be observed by other cops, mostly through one-way glass, but crooks would know they were there and would sometimes be able to consciously affect their unconscious reactions. Get them comfortable in a windowless room with a well concealed video camera, though, and they'd let down their guard.

Yet, I could discern no tell in Gregory as he spoke. His posture was relaxed, his arms open and resting on the arms of the chair. His hands remained still. Even as he described the virtues of motherhood, he remained physically relaxed, much in contrast to the clipped recital he provided. Then his hand balled to a fist, and instantly relaxed. Something inside triggered a stress response and was promptly overridden.

"When I was growing up, William, love from my father was meted out by the spoonful and only when I behaved the way he desired. As for mother, well, that's a bit more complicated. No, to answer your question, I do not believe in unconditional love. It's a lie."

"So, your mother was the first to break your heart?" I asked. Given what I had read about the circumstances of his mother's death in the journal pages, I was getting curious to hear it from his own lips. Gregory instead rerouted the conversation to a whole new track.

"Why did you leave the Chicago PD?" he asked. "The stories in the press were not very clear, but alluded to some problems met with during a drug bust and a resultant bureaucratic blunderbuss downtown."

Ah, the true reason of the visit is revealed. Obviously, Gregory had done some quick research, or had it done.

"I decided it was time," I said, hoping that would end it but knowing that was a futile hope. So, I tossed out a smoke grenade. "Blunderbuss?"

"In the figurative sense of the word," he said.

"Gregory, why did you come to see me today?" I asked.

He ignored the question.

"The newspapers did say you were the only one to walk out of that warehouse," he stated. "The only living witness to what had originally been described in some media as the worst bloodbath under one roof in Chicago since the St. Valentine's Day Massacre."

Fucking Sun-Times. Yeah, I remembered the article and the two-hundred-point front page headline. Gregory was now watching me like I was the suspect again.

"Then the whole story just faded away, faster than the smile on the face of the pizza delivery guy who receives a quarter tip," he said. "I'm not so curious what deal was worked out behind the scenes, because that's easy to discern. What I am very curious about is what did happen inside that warehouse."

I stared at him, didn't answer. We had come to the point in the interview process when the suspect decides he wants a lawyer, what we called 'clamming up'. Then I decided to confront him, give him my version of the suspect's 'Why me?' question.

"I didn't know my life was of such an interest to you, Gregory."

He set his water on the floor and stood up.

"I'm just wondering why my life is of such an interest to you, William," he said before he rose and prepared to walk out. "Thank you for the water and conversation. It was my pleasure, but I must run now." He turned to go and then returned to looking at me. "I'll say so long, William, because something tells me this isn't good-bye."

He walked through the condo and paused at the front door. He pointed at the now empty dining room table.

"Good luck balancing your checkbook," he said. "Sometimes things just don't add up the way you'd think they should and that can be very frustrating." He gave me a knowing grin. "From what my people tell me, anyway."

He walked out. I heard him start his car and watched through the dining area window as he drove out the main gate. When he hit the street, he left a rubbery calling card on the asphalt.

Gregory wheeled the Corvette around the drive and parked. A valet greeted him, handed him a ticket for the parking and drove the car away as Gregory walked toward the open lobby of the Four Seasons Hotel in Wailea. He was quite familiar with the property and knew exactly how to get to the spa on the lower level. He walked with a purpose. Several hotel employees recognized him, but they also recognized the look in his eyes so they just kept walking.

At the spa reception desk he was told he could currently find his wife at the Orchid Salon next to the fitness center. He walked into the salon, past the receptionist and into the work area. There, sat his wife, unattended as the color steeped in her pulled-back hair, fingers and toes in mid-process of soaking.

Cassandra saw him approach out of the corner of her eye. He leaned close to her ear and whispered something which turned her blood cold. He then left her sitting there.

Two hours later, Gregory sat in his office at the house and waited for his wife.

I called Sandy back shortly after Gregory abruptly left. She answered on the first ring.

"I was about to call the cops," she said. "What happened?"

"I had a surprise guest. Gregory dropped by to say hello."

"What did he want?" she asked.

"Well, that's still up in the air other than to gather some intel and perhaps let me know he knows I'm watching him. We used to get that all the time while doing surveillance on bad guys in Chicago. They'd come out, wave right at the camera, sometimes using just one finger to do it. I think Gregory was giving me the one-finger shaka today."

"That's kinda ballsy, don't you think?" Sandy asked.

"Well, I think that was the biggest thing he accomplished. Although he nearly caught me with my pants down," I conceded.

"I hope you mean figuratively, not literally," she said with a laugh. "I've always told you not to leave the door open when you attend to business."

I rolled my eyes and wondered if Sandy could hear me doing it like I could hear her.

"No, figuratively. I had all the journal pages scattered on piles on the dining room table and he walked right on in while I was on the lanai talking to you."

"I heard you holler 'come on in'," she said. "You didn't know it was him?"

"I thought it was my upstairs neighbor. We've hung out a bit since I got here and I thought it was him dropping by. Imagine my surprise to see Gregory standing ten feet from his own journal pages."

"How did you manage to keep him from seeing the documents?"

"I'm not sure I did, now." As I thought about it, he had easily been close enough to be able to identify the pages just from the way they looked. "The writing and blocking of the pages is so unique, Sandy, that the more I think about it, he might have recognized them just from the appearance without knowing exactly what I had."

"Well, you know I can read papers upside down on your desk from nearly that far away," Sandy said with pride. "Don't let your guard down, Otto. I'd lock up those papers."

"I've already got them scanned into my computer and I've put them onto the office server as encrypted files into the case record," I reported.

"I know," she said.

"You know?"

"Yeah, of course, Otto."

"How could you read them? I encrypted them."

"Don't you remember who gave you the encryption program and who administers our office computer system?" She laughed. "You piqued my interest by mentioning the existence of the journal pages and you know what happens when you pique my interest." She paused. "Are you mad at me?"

"No, Sandy," I said. "I'm not angry with you. So?"

"So?"

"So what do you think we're dealing with here? A simple cheater or something more?"

"Well, when you hear what just came to me from the Orange County Sheriff's Office here in Orlando, I think you're going to be thinking the same thing I am. That's we're dealing with something more than a simple cheater here."

"I can hardly wait. Go ahead."

"I'm sending you files to your email, but we have a similar situation with Michelle Wirtz in Orlando that we do with Jessi Bollenbeck in Augusta. Michelle Wirtz turned up missing shortly after her divorce case concluded."

"How long ago?" I asked, opening my computer and launching my email program.

"She was reported missing ten years ago. Before you ask, the ex-husband had an airtight alibi."

I scanned the email and opened the attached files, which were very similar to those provided by the Augusta P.D. The Missing Persons poster again showed a smiling, young and attractive brunette and said she was last seen jogging from her home on the outskirts of Orlando.

"I see she was last seen jogging from her home," I said. "Who saw her? Obviously, I haven't had a chance to read the reports."

"Neighbor across the street. She and Michelle had known each other for several years, so she was very familiar. They also had a statement from people who remember seeing her in the nearby park after they were given a description of what she had worn out of the house."

"That all sounds vaguely familiar, that scenario," I said.

"I know. It reminds me very much of that case in Oregon just before Christmas a few years back. That did turn out to be the husband. He's cooling his heels in a six-by-eight now until he assumes room temperature."

"That's it. He said he went pheasant hunting, left her home alone, came home eight hours later and she was gone. Poof," I said. "Seemingly into thin air. They had reports from neighbors and people along a nearby walking path that the wife had been seen out walking after he left home, as I recall."

"Yeah, but they found a body in that case. Nobody has seen or heard from Michelle since she went out running. Just like with Jessi, it's as if Michelle just vanished off the face of the earth."

"They have alligators in Orlando, don't they?"

"What are you suggesting, Otto? That a gator snatched her out of the park and that's why she's not been seen?"

"I doubt it would be the first time," I said defensively.

"I'm starting to wonder if Gregory's ex-girlfriends just have really bad luck after the affair ends," Sandy said.

"You think our boy had something to do with both these disappearances?" I asked. "That would be a stretch, wouldn't it?"

"About as much as your gator snatch theory, Otto."

"That's not a theory of mine, Sandy, in Florida it's a possibility. Hell, in Florida gators have become so tamed by the presence of man, people have found them inside their homes after the critters have crawled through doggy doors. That aside, my theory is that these disappearances are tied somehow to the alleged affairs and to either Gregory and or Cassie."

"Cassie?" Sandy asked.

I could hear in her voice that she hadn't even contemplated that possibility which didn't necessarily surprise me. Sandy thinks like a lawyer, not a cop. I think like a cop.

"You have to remember that as I cop, I always ruled everyone in until I could rule them out, not the other way around."

"So you're willing to consider Cassie had a hand in the disappearances?"

I thought about that for a minute. It had been three decades since I had known Cassie. That's a long time in a person's evolution when you're talking going from the age of fifteen to forty-five. I had already caught her in at least one lie of substance over the last week since she walked back into my life. She was being more than selective in providing us with information. On the other hand, I had met and spoken to Gregory and there's definitely something out of plumb in his rigging. They both have access to almost limitless resources, so even if neither of them were guilty of directly causing the disappearances of two women - that we are aware of thus far - then they certainly could have had it done for them.

"As of right now, Sandy, I am ruling nothing out. Including happenstance. Everybody involved is a person of interest, except of course you and me."

"Happenstance?" she said. "I thought you didn't believe in coincidences."

"I don't," I replied. "I do, however, give a certain amount of credence to happenstance."

"Whatever, Otto," she said with a chuckle. "As for ruling people out, you can eliminate me for sure. I'm not always sure about you."

"Cute. Real cute. So, where are you off to next? Des Moines or Cheyenne?"

"Neither," she said. "I almost forgot to tell you. I've had a lead on this Janet Hopkins woman. You know, the one marked 'recent' and 'Canada'?"

"Yeah, I remember."

"Well, after you hung up to have your heart-to-heart male bonding with Gregory, I had time to do some research into the goings on in the land of snow and ice, and guess what?"

"Not in the mood for twenty questions, Sandy. Spill it."

"Guess who just had a missing person's report filed on them? Janet Hopkins. Guess how recent?

"Sandy..."

"The report was filed on Monday. She's been missing since returning from a trip to Hawaii."

"Maui?" I asked.

"The information I have from the Montreal Missing Persons website is that she was in Hawaii. It didn't go into specifics and you called before I was able to ring them up for further information."

"Are you telling me that Janet Hopkins could very well have been right here on Maui within the past week? That she was reported missing on Monday? Three days ago?"

"That's what I'm telling you, Otto. I emailed you the link to the Missing Persons page for Janet Hopkins. There's a problem, however. She doesn't fit the profile. Janet Hopkins is blonde."

I found the email and clicked the link. There, nearly identical from the others I had viewed today, was a photo of a beautiful, young, smiling woman on a Missing Person's poster. Only this woman had bobbed, strawberry blonde hair.

"I see it, Sandy," I said. "I'm looking at the digital poster now." There was something else Sandy had said just a moment ago which caught my subconscious. Something in the journal pages I had read now nearly a dozen times. "Sandy, what did you say a few moments ago? About research in Canada? Yeah, that's it, you said something about doing some research into the goings on..."

"Um, the goings on, what?" she said. I could hear her thinking. "Oh, yeah, in the land of snow and ice, is that it?"

"Yeah, I said, something about snow and ice." I grabbed my computer bag and retrieved the papers I had stuffed in there when Gregory showed up. "There's a journal entry talking about cold. It was all about cold. Ice and snow are cold. The pages which were different from the others. Different in appearance, I mean."

"Oh, my God," Sandy said. "Yes, I remember it. It was short, only a couple of paragraphs, and it was written with a different script and on different paper, more like legal paper with a margin line, but it seemed obsessed with the 'embracing cold'."

I found the page I was looking for. Reading the passage in a vacuum had meant nothing to me, but in the context of a missing woman from Canada with strawberry blonde hair, it was chilling. Pun not intended.

"The old adage is snow on the roof, fire in the hearth, or something to that effect. Whoever penned that axiom had never met the ice queen or experienced her deep, embracing cold. She appeared as an opportunity, and given the unseasonable frost which gripped my heart, I accepted the challenge of change. It is said sometimes change breeds contempt, and that is certainly what this interaction did.

Her heart was frozen, unwilling to thaw regardless of the level or type of heat offered it. In the end, I returned her to her domain of cold and darkness, however, even that gift to the heart of the ice queen was greeted with cold contempt. Perhaps it was merely a function of the shortness of time which prevented the defrosting of her heart. She was guilty nonetheless. A perversion of womanhood. Whatever her problems were, the experience has retaught me the lessons of the comforting warmth of sameness. This was a mistake I will never make again."

"Well, that seals the question," Sandy said.

"Which question?"

"Where to next? In the morning, I'll double check those records requests I have out to law enforcement in Des Moines and Cheyenne, and add the information that we may be looking for a missing person case because I think we're seeing a pattern here. When I can, I'm headed for Montreal. It's the hottest lead we have."

"I agree, Sandy. Get some rest and I'll talk to you tomorrow."

"Goodnight, Otto. Please watch your back."

"No worries, Sandy."

I hung up and thought about calling Cassie and confronting her with what we had learned. I still wanted to see her reaction, face-to-face, however, because this was fairly important stuff. After all, it could also be a risk to Cassie's safety should our suspicions of Gregory's involvement in the cases of two or perhaps three missing women, especially given his unusual drop in today. On the other hand, she was his wife and had specifically told me she could handle him. I flipped open my phone, sat there looking at the number on the display. I closed it almost immediately and laid it on the table. I decided there would be time to talk to Cassie once we knew a little bit more.

Cassie endured the rest of her spa session. Her planned day was ruined, that much was a given. Of course Gregory knew where to find her because she always came to the Four Seasons for a spa day, but he had no idea why she had really come to the hotel today. She was certain he had no idea who was waiting for her in a suite upstairs and how she had intended to muss up the hair which was now being so carefully coiffed and sprayed, or how she had selected the nail polish color because it would look so hot raking across Dan's tanned body, or how she had asked special attention be paid to her feet and toes because Dan liked them soft and supple. All that was over for today.

Gregory's words echoed in her head. As she sat through the final combing and spritzing and buffing and polishing, she thought about how to handle what he had told her. She was certain she could talk him through it. She could calm him down. It would be all right, she told herself. After all, she had done it before, years ago, after that Chicago thing. He hadn't even been certain if she had lost it anywhere it could turn up and be connected, yet he refused to let it go. For weeks he would bring it up. For weeks she paid the price. Slowly, over time, she had been able to work him away from his obsessing. She could do it again.

Finally, they were done. Cassie popped out of the chair, took the moment to admire herself in the mirrors, then reached carefully into her purse and tipped the staff.

"You girls are miracle workers," she said with a smile.

"It's easy when we've got the palette that you provide us to work with, Mrs. Thomason," her hairdresser replied. "You're a beautiful woman, we just make you a little better."

Cassie loved the ego fluffing the staff at the Four Seasons provided. She also knew they were the best at what they did on the island or they wouldn't be here. Over the years she'd also heard how they talked after the client had tipped and exited. Cattiness knows now bounds. She smiled at the hairdresser and walked away.

In the elevator on the way up to Dan's suite, Cassie could feel her body responding to his proximity. She craved him like she had never craved anyone and the closer she moved to his presence the less she worried about Gregory's words. Dan was her obsession, and she had never felt that way about anyone, ever. She was certain of that. She loved him. She was certain of that, too.

Once this thing with Gregory concluded, and she hoped it would wrap up just as she had planned, she and Dan would have a beautiful life together. She was as certain of that as she was of her own name. Cassie closed her eyes, used the moments for imagining. She wanted what she wanted, and for her entire life Cassie got what Cassie wanted.

The paneled doors opened with a muted ding, and she exited, turned down the hallway and found the room with ease. She could have been blindfolded and she could have found their room. Always the same room, and she loved it. It was their place. She put her hand up to the door. She could sense him in there, waiting for her, wanting her as much as she was wanting him. The passion within her flowed freely and it saddened her that her desire would not be quenched today. She knocked softly. When Dan opened the door, his body was bare save the towel wrapped around his waist. Or maybe she could be quenched, she thought, for a little while anyway.

"You're a little over dressed, aren't you?" she teased.

He reached for her hand, gently pulled her in. The door closed behind her and he pushed her up against it, his body pinning her firmly. She responded naturally, reaching for him, pulling him even closer. Their eyes met, their mouths met. Her passion overflowed as his hands moved over her body; the power of his desire was obvious, even through the towel which she then let fall to the floor.

She grabbed for him, found him fuller and harder than she thought any man could ever be. She knew there would be no talking, no words of reluctance or time, just their two bodies, their two hearts, their two souls taking from and giving to each other freely. It was a blur. Her head spun. He hadn't taken her with such animal desire for a long time and she loved it. She had called his name over and over, told him she loved him, held him close and pulled him even deeper within her. At the moment of his release he had looked her in the eyes and his hands had pinned hers to the bed, their fingers intertwined just as were their bodies, their hearts, their souls, their futures.

He lay on his back resting after it was over. He had one leg bent at the knee. She nuzzled against him, her leg over his other, and he pulled her close. It was cool in the room, yet they both were drenched in sweat. She could hear his heart as it slowly resumed its normal rhythm. Cassie felt safe and loved in his arms. She knew they would be together forever. He would never hurt her, or abuse her, or betray her. She knew that all.

A few moments later, she felt as if she knew nothing.

"Baby, we've got a problem," he said.

"With us there are no problems," she said. She moved against him, purred softly at the exhilaration of his skin against hers.

"I'm serious, baby." He pulled away slightly, reached into the drawer of the bedside table.

Cassie sat up, watched him pull out a small envelope from the drawer.

"I found these slipped under my door this morning," he lied, and then he handed her the package.

Cassie opened it, looked inside and then turned it over, spilling a dozen photographs onto the rumpled sheets. She recognized the setting immediately: Kipahulu Point, the fence, the church, Sunday last. She turned the others over one by one until all twelve screamed the proclamation of her stupidity at her. For the second time today, her blood ran cold.

"You say you found these this morning? That someone had slipped them under the door?" she asked him.

"Yes," he lied again. "I have no idea when they were delivered, just sometime between the time I went to sleep last night and the time I got up this morning."

She stared at the photos and wondered if Gregory was involved or if they had come from an independent source. She found no note within the envelope.

"No note?" she asked him. "Nothing? Just the photos?"

"Nothing, baby," he said. He had wanted to put a note in with the photos, but Bev had overruled him. She had said, at this point it would be a bad idea to give Cassandra anything to pick at. In the end, he had agreed with Bev's logic. If they gave Cassie a loose thread to pull, it wouldn't be long before she'd unravel the entire scheme. "Just the envelope and photos."

Cassie sat naked and cross-legged on the bed. Her face revealed she was deep in thought, weighing all the possibilities. As Dan watched her, he better understood the brilliance of Bev's position. He could see Cassie was considering everything at the same time, all the possibilities, all the eventualities, even every endgame, and was totally incapable of focusing on any single aspect of the problem. She was in overload. Bev had said if they kept her off balance, it would be easier for them to get from her just about anything they wanted. Dan squelched a smile as he watched her sitting there, while he painted a look of deep concern on his face.

"Who do you think would be behind this?" he asked her. "Do you think Gregory could be onto us?" As he played this out, he knew why Bev had been so excited. It was a game, and one where they held all the cards.

Cassie put her fingers to her mouth, but resisted the urge to damage her new nails by biting them like she did when she would grow nervous as a child.

"I'm not certain," she said. "He has been acting a little off lately, well, a little off for him, which is a lot off for most people." She stifled a little laugh. "It could be coming from any number of directions. The positive is, if everything comes off according to my plan, it won't matter one whit. This will all be moot in a few days."

"Are you that certain?" he asked. He understood the basics of her plan, but not all the details. "Do you think Gregory will just give up that easily?"

"Give up?" she replied. "No, I don't expect he'll give up at all. That's exactly why I staffed the team the way I did."

"You mean this private dick from New Orleans?"

"Yes, Willy will never let me down," she said.

"As I recall, he already did, all those years ago," he asserted.

"That was childhood, darling," she said. Cassie looked at him, then unexpectedly leaned forward on her knees, fell against his chest and kissed him. "That's exactly why he'll never let me down again."

Dan wondered how she could be so certain. He hoped she hadn't started sleeping with this private dick. He may not love the woman who just kissed him and now looked affectionately at him, but he hated the thought of someone else having her while he was having her. That just wasn't right.

She got out of bed, padded to the bathroom, returned a couple minutes later fully dressed. Not that she had much to put on, as Dan had just discovered, no bra, no panties, just a light dress in patterned shades of red.

He watched her scoop up the photos and stuff them back into the envelope. No matter, he knew, there were plenty more to be printed with just a mouse click or two. She retrieved her purse from the floor by the door, placed the envelope inside and came to kiss him.

"Don't look so concerned, my love," she said. "Let me handle everything."

"I am putty in your hands, baby," he said. "As for the rest, it's your game. I'm just the lowly court jester vying for your heart."

"My heart you already have," she said, putting her fingertips to his cheek. "In a few days, you'll have everything else as well."

He smiled and kissed the palm of her hand.

"I'll be in touch," she said as she broke the physical connection and headed toward the door. "I've got a crazy king to deal with."

He watched her blow him a kiss as she opened the door. He made a play at catching it. Then she was gone, and the door closed again.

Dan reached for his phone and called Bev.

"How did it go?" she asked.

"Just as you said it would," he told her. "Are you coming back? I think the queen has left the building for a while."

"I'll be right up. I was just getting some sun on the beach."

"The beach? You commoner," he teased.

"Look who's talking. Is there anything more common than a usurper in your little palace charade?" There was a hint of venom in her last remark.

Dan blew it off.

"Only the commoners," he laughed. "See you in a bit."

"Take a shower," she said. Then she clicked off.

Cassie handed the parking ticket to the valet and he jogged off to retrieve her car. A few minutes later, he pulled up in the little red BMW convertible. She tipped him, got in, noticed he watched her legs as she pulled them inside, dropped the top and sped out toward the main drive.

When she turned left onto Wailea Alanui, she pulled out her phone and dialed Willy's cell number. Before the call connected, she clicked off and tossed the phone onto the passenger seat next to her purse. She had a better idea. The envelope with the photos stuck out slightly and buffeted in the wind. She tucked it in more securely. It would not be good were it to blow out onto the road.

When she reached the entrance to the Palms at Wailea, she pulled through the gate and drove straight in toward the front desk area in the community building. She left the car idling in the circular drive in the shadow of a large tree and walked into the reception area.

A young woman in a full-length, muted green floral dress and wearing a brass-colored name tag greeted her and Cassie asked to see the manager. A moment later, a tall, thin man walked out from the back and introduced himself as the manager for the resort company. His shirt matched the woman's dress and he also had a name tag. She motioned him to the side, pulled the envelope from her purse, added a note inside, sealed it, and wrote Willy's room number on the front. She added an instruction on the front and then handed the package to the manager.

"Three days," she said. "Deliver this in three days. Not before, understand?"

She handed him a hundred dollar bill which he first rejected but then accepted following a gentle prod.

"I'll see to it personally," he said.

"Release it to nobody before that time," she said. "Except me, should I be back here before then."

"Understood, ma'am," he said. "Your name?"

"You'll recognize me, won't you?"

He looked her over.

"Of course, but we do see many people here. A name would help. Just for me, you understand." He glanced over to the desk. The clerk was engaged in some sort of bookkeeping activity and not paying attention to them.

"Okay, it's Sandy, Sandy Beach," she said.

"Thank you, Ms. Beach," he said. "You can count on me."

"I already am," Cassie said, turning to leave.

She rounded the corner and walked out to her car. The manager tapped the envelope on his hand a couple of times. Photos he thought with a smile. Then he headed behind the desk and back toward his office.

"Sandy Beach, that's a good one," the clerk said as he passed behind her.

"Mind your business, Sheila," he warned. As he walked into his office he smiled and then said to himself, "Worst fake name I've ever heard."

Cassie pulled out of the gate, made the left, then a right on Kilohana and drove up to the traffic light at the Pi'ilani. Another left and she accelerated onto the highway for the first leg of the trip toward home. She exhaled deeply. All her displayed confidence and bravado aside, she only knew one thing for certain at that moment: Gregory was waiting for her at home.

Chapter Sixteen

Marcy again sat at the kitchen table with Belle. She had spent the night in one of the spare bedrooms at Belle's insistence. This morning, Marcy and Belle were sharing a light breakfast of coffee, melon, toast and jam. To Marcy's delight, Belle had orange marmalade to offer. She relayed the story of how she loved the tart topping and how much Janet hated it. Belle smiled and patted her hand, then sat down across from her.

"Tamra had a difficult night," Belle said. "I don't know how that poor girl goes on." She looked up toward the ceiling. "It's the Hand of God, that's all I can figure."

"I never was much of a believer," Marcy said. "However, something, or someone is guiding and strengthening me right now. Whatever that force may be, it's honest and loving and it led me to you good people."

Belle looked across her toast toward Marcy.

"It's the Hand of God, my dear." She smiled. "He gave you to us yesterday. He does indeed work in mysterious ways. In addition to guiding you, He delivered you here to bring a smile to an old woman, and returned a sense of purpose to an old man."

A knock came to the door and Belle hollered an invitation to come in.

"Speaking of whom," she said.

Marcy could hear the measured steps of Thomas coming down the hallway accompanied by the clicking of Isabella's nails on the hardwood floor.

"Good morning, good morning," he said as he entered the room. He patted Marcy on the top of her head. "How do you feel this morning, honey?"

"Uplifted is the best word I can come up with."

Thomas smiled and pulled out a chair. He turned down coffee and food, informing Belle he and Isabella had enjoyed their breakfast hours ago at home.

"Good morning, Isabella," Marcy said. The dog jumped into her lap and tried to give her a kiss.

"Isabella, you behave," Thomas mock scolded.

The dog settled down, laid in Marcy's lap and put her snout on Marcy's knee.

"She normally doesn't take to strangers, but she sure likes you, Marcy."

"She's a good dog," Marcy said. "I wanted to thank you for yesterday as well, Thomas. You both have been so kind."

"Gotcha kind of thinking differently about us Vermont folks, eh?" He patted her hand again. "Glad to do it, Marcy. So, all rested, are you ready for a little intrigue today?" There was a twinkle in his eye.

Marcy looked to him and then to Belle. Belle gave her a smile and a little surreptitious wink.

"I believe my whole week has been a little bit if intrigue," she said. "I'm looking for some answers."

Thomas leaned forward conspiratorially. His eyes moved to Belle and then back to Marcy.

"I've got it all figured," he said. "Last night I thought about who we're going to have to deal with over there at the airport, and while I am still owed many favors by lots of folks, sometimes they forget. So, we have to be a little clever. I hope you won't mind playing the role of my great-great-granddaughter."

Marcy smile at him.

"Not at all, Gramps," she said.

Thomas smiled at her. Belle sat back and folded her arms and watched the two conspirators work out their plan.

"Now," he continued. "Even though most of the folks over there at the airlines are local, they've got faceless corporate bosses over in Chicago and Dallas and Atlanta who don't give a damn about favors and friendship and the like, so we're gonna have to massage them a little bit."

"I'm all for a little massaging," Marcy said. "How do you want to play it?"

"Well, here's how I've got it figured," he said, and then he went on to lay it all out for her.

Marcy listened intently while he explained how things would work while scratching Isabella behind the ears. Fifteen minutes later, the unlikely duo of amateur sleuths was on their way to the airport.

Sandy was up early, way too early to call William. She cursed the time difference of six hours now that she was on Eastern time, jumped in the shower and then headed downstairs for the motel's deluxe continental breakfast.

Orlando, being a tourist city meant guests from all over the world came to stay, and along with serving up fresh waffles and not-so-fresh reconstituted orange juice - Sandy somehow found that last part a bit ironic - the hotel offered a wide assortment of newspapers from around the country. For some reason, Sandy picked up the San Francisco Chronicle for her morning reading.

After wading through the heavy world and national news pages, she turned to the lighter fare offered in the Arts & Entertainment section. According to the know-it-all reviewers, the summer movie selections were pretty much all stinko, and the much ballyhooed arrival of the Bolshoi Ballet Company apparently fell flat, footed, that is. She smiled at the pun and was about to put the section away and go back to her room when a full-page color ad caught her eye.

'The McCormick Galleries is proud to announce the premier exhibition of a new multimedia talent, Miss Jennifer Shea of Molokai, Hawaii.' From the page, staring out at her was a younger version of the woman who had started this whole chase a week ago. Sandy stared at the photo; the eyes, the facial features, the smile, even the hair style to a point, all told her this was a likeness of a younger Cassie, but the text belied that conclusion by stating it was an artist known as Jennifer Shea. Of Molokai.

Sandy fought to remember the geography of the Hawaiian Islands from years ago when she had been to Oahu. While she couldn't be certain, she thought Molokai was near Maui. She folded the paper, stuck it under her arm and headed back to her room.

Time zones be damned, she said to herself and then she pulled out her phone and called William.

"Otto, it's me," she said. Sorry to wake you, but I found Jennifer Shea. She's alive and well and living, get this, on Molokai." She rolled her eyes at the phone and responded to his question. "It's an island, I think right next to Maui."

Cassie woke with a start. She sensed she wasn't where she ought to be and when she tried to move there was a metallic clinking at the foot of the bed. She opened her eyes but it was pitch black and she couldn't see a thing. She tried to sit up but her head started spinning and she fell back down to the bed.

"I wouldn't try that again, my dear," came the voice in the dark.

Then he turned on a light on the table next to where he was sitting and the sensation of a thousand suns shooting into her eyes knocked her flat. Cassie threw an arm over her eyes to further shield them from the pain.

Her mouth felt like it was stuffed with cotton. She heard motion across the room and then felt something touch her lips. She recoiled and then the voice spoke again.

"It's water, don't sit up, drink through the straw," the voice said. "Come on, sweetie, you know the drill."

She sipped on the water. When she tried to take it too fast he pinched off the flow, reminded her to go slowly. He released the pinch and she drank again, slower. The water was cool, sweet, refreshing. She felt the cotton melting from her mouth.

"Why?" she said, her voice a near-silent rasp.

"Why what?" the voice in the dark said.

"Why are you doing this?" Her voice was a little stronger.

He removed the straw from her reach. When she removed her arm from her eyes she shrieked in pain.

"Please," she begged. "Please, turn off the light."

Cassie heard the click and then slowly moved her arm from her face. There was no searing pain in her eyes anymore. The room was cool, nearly silent save the low hum of air conditioning equipment moving the air.

When she tried to move again, every joint in her body protested. Her ankle throbbed, she felt the manacle chafing against her skin. It seemed her only option at the moment was to lay still, try to get some rest. She knew the anesthetic he used would dissipate in her system within twelve hours. She heard him settle back into the chair in the corner.

"How long?" she asked.

"I can't see my watch in the dark anymore," he said. "If I had to guess I would say nine hours, give or take."

"Why are you doing this, Gregory?"

"Do you realize how many times I have been asked that very question? Of course you do. Because you were there, every time. You watched each of them go through exactly what you just went through. The disorientation, the pain, the fear. How does it feel, Cassandra? Tell me how it feels. I want to know."

"Give me the keys and the needle and I'll show you how it feels," she said through gritted teeth.

"Good," he said. "You're going to fight. I like the fight. I loathed the ones that simply gave up. The fighters lived. The others died." He laughed. "Well, in the end, they all died, but you know what I mean. Death is a condition of the mind, Cassandra."

"How far are you going to take this?" she asked. Gregory had given her lessons before, just never this real.

"All the way, my dear," he said as he rose from the chair. "You rest now. We'll talk later."

She heard him unlock the door. A slice of light swept in and she recoiled. He closed the door again, she heard the locks falling closed.

As Gregory walked across the lava tube from Cassandra's block house to the central control room and workshop he repeated the line, "All the way."

Marcy and Thomas lingered in the airport restaurant. As they came through for coffee or breaks or lunch, they'd chat informally with the ramp workers and ticket agents employed by United Express, American Eagle, Continental Express, Delta Connection and USAir Express, the main players at the airport. They also caught up with several of the car rental clerks. While many of these folks were too new to remember Thomas' work as the Airport Manager, some still did and that helped loosen the normally cautious tongues of the others.

From the information Marcy had developed back in Montreal with Kevin's assistance, they knew the person who was traveling under the name of Tamra Sommers had flown into Burlington last Saturday on United Express connecting through Chicago O'Hare International Airport. They had no idea if she changed identities and flew out under another name, rented a car and drove someplace, or just disappeared into the countryside. Whomever had pulled Tamra's name out of the air could certainly be local, she concluded. There was a whole deck of possibilities, but as morning turned to afternoon, they were narrowing the cards down nicely.

So far, an agent for United Express was able to confirm the ticket in the name of Tamra Sommers from Chicago was indeed used. She did come into Burlington last Saturday afternoon. That was good news, because had the woman disappeared into O'Hare they may never be able to track her down. At lunch, two ramp workers with United Express confirmed they recognized the photos of the woman.

Also at lunch, the station manager for United Express stopped by the table and quietly told Thomas he'd do anything he could to help. Thomas informed Marcy after the man had left that Thomas had saved the man's career about fifteen years ago when he was a gate agent and never reported a security violation because it had not gone anywhere serious. 'It's just what we do for each other in small towns', he told Marcy.

It was in the mid-afternoon that they caught their biggest break on what happened after the woman arrived in Burlington when a shift change took place for American Eagle and the p.m. shift agents stopped in for a cup of coffee. They had been told by the a.m. shift about the informal inquiry taking place in the restaurant, so they came right to the table after they spotted Thomas and Marcy.

"Well, Thomas, it's been a long time," said the elder of the pair.

His name tag read Phil and Thomas later related to Marcy that he had always wanted to be an airline pilot. Thomas and Phil went back to the mid-80s when Phil would hang around the airport as a kid. Thomas would see him standing at the fence line watching airplanes and had taken him under his wing, so to speak. He had given Phil the kid his first job around the airport doing minor maintenance work, painting, and the like during the summer months. At the end of the summer, Thomas had arranged for Phil to take his first flight lessons at the local fixed base operator. Sadly, a heart arrhythmia had ended Phil's dream of flying professionally, but he's been part of aviation's ground side for years.

"Why, Phil, how long has it been?" Thomas replied. "At least a couple of years, eh?"

"Time does fly, doesn't it?" Phil said. "By the way, this is Emma." He introduced the young redheaded woman standing with him. "She's not from here, but transferred from our station in Traverse City, Michigan when her husband got a new job in town."

"Pleasure to meet you, Emma," Thomas said. "Is Phil treating you right?"

"Yes, he is," she said. "Everyone has been great."

"Traverse City, Michigan," Thomas said. "That's cherry country, isn't it?"

"Why, yes, it is," Emma said with a smile.

"I love cherries," he said. "Can you two sit for a minute?"

They took chairs across the table.

"This is my great-great-granddaughter, Marcy," he said.

They exchanged hellos.

"It turns out Marcy has had a friend go missing in Montreal where she lives now, and her path ironically led her here."

Thomas gave them the same sketchy details he had given everyone else so far today.

"I didn't know you had any relatives in Montreal, Thomas," Phil said. "As a matter of fact, I didn't know either of your two boys ever had children."

Thomas gave him a crooked smile which Phil returned.

"There's a lot you don't know about this old coot," he said. He leaned toward Phil and beckoned him come close with a single gnarled finger. Phil leaned forward. "You've most likely have forgotten many things, Phil, like that time I found you with those Playboy magazines in the fuel truck. Don't be a putz, this is important."

They both laughed and sat back. Thomas eyed him.

"Of course," Phil said. "I remember now. Bobby's grandchild."

"I knew you'd remember," Thomas said. "Anyway, we're trying to track down this woman. We know she arrived here on United Express from Chicago last Saturday. After that, we lost her."

Marcy passed over the photos of the woman. They both looked them over.

"I don't remember her," Phil said.

"Me either," Emma said. "Sorry."

Thomas noticed that Emma kept looking at the photos. Phil passed his set back to Marcy. Thomas sat watching Emma and nudged Marcy in under the table.

"What is it, Emma?" Thomas asked.

"There's something familiar," Emma said, her face showing deep thought. "Do you have an extra copy of this photo, Marcy, one I can mark on a bit?"

"Go ahead and use that one if you like," Marcy said. "I've got extras."

"Just a sec," Emma said, and she disappeared out of the restaurant. A few minutes later she returned with some pencils and markers in a little box. She set the box down, tossed open the lid and placed the photo on the table where she could work on it. "I was an art major in college," she told the group. "Decided eating was better than starving, so I took a day job. I have always loved drawing and painting people more than anything. My instructors said I had an eye for it."

The three watched silently as Emma went to work on the photo. She masked the clothes and hair carefully with markers which matched the background, then started drawing them back, differently. The transformation was fascinating to watch. As they all looked on, Emma finished and then looked at each of them to find the same look of utter disbelief staring back at her from each of their faces.

"Now I'm positive of it," Emma said. Their eyes began to blink, and she noticed Phil slowly nodding in silent confirmation. Emma grabbed another of the photos of the woman traveling as Tamra Sommers and then held it and the recreated image side by side. "This woman may have flown in, but..." she declared, laying that image face down on the table and holding the other for them all to see. "This man flew out."

"That's right," Phil said. "I remember him. He went out on our last flight to Dallas last Saturday. No luggage."

Marcy was shellshocked. Thomas grinned widely, patted Marcy on the shoulder and then sat back and folded his arms in a muted show of victory.

"Was Dallas his final destination?" Marcy asked.

"Yes," Phil and Emma said at the same time.

"By the time he would have arrived in Dallas, there wouldn't have been many places for him to go out to anyway, but I recall he was only going as far as Dallas."

"Does this help?" Emma asked Marcy, who was obviously deep in thought.

"Oh, very much so," Marcy said. She picked up the Emma's drawing. "Is there someplace we can get some color copies of this made, Emma?"

"Sure," Emma said. "Come to the ticket counter and we'll run some off in the back."

"I'll see if we can pull a name from the manifest and then see if this guy shows up going somewhere after Dallas," Phil added.

The four rose from the table; before leaving, Thomas dropped a pair of twenties at the counter for the waitress who had kept them in coffee and things all day. The three younger people walked ahead to the American Eagle ticket counter. Thomas pulled up the rear still wearing his grin.

Emma disappeared into the back room with the drawing. Phil logged on to the Sabre terminal and pulled up the manifest from last Saturday evening's Dallas flight. There were forty-six names, twenty-nine male adults. He then looked at the bag check information for the flight. Of the twenty-nine male adults, only six had not checked any luggage.

Marcy stood patiently at the counter. She looked around and saw Thomas at the United Express counter speaking to the station manager.

A moment later, Emma poked her head out of the back and asked if Marcy had an email address and a cell phone number. Marcy gave them to her and then asked why. Emma told her she had scanned the photo into an electronic document format and would email it to Marcy and send it along to her phone. All Marcy could do was smile. She knew if she tried to speak at this point, she just may lose it. She thought of the events of the last twenty-four hours and then looked down at Thomas. Then she remembered

Belle's words about how she had given an old man a new purpose, and she did cry.

Phil saw Marcy's tears and handed her a few Kleenex from behind the counter.

"Don't cry, Marcy," he said. "The hard part's done. It's all downhill from here." He looked down the counters toward Thomas. "You're lucky you've got a good friend there."

"That's my gramps," she said. She watched Thomas finish up his conversation, shake the man's hand and then make his way down to her. He put his arm around her shoulder. She could feel his frailty when he pulled her close.

"I told you these were good people here," he said. "Dry your eyes, sweetie. This is a happy time."

Marcy did as she was told. She felt her phone vibrate in her pocket and removed it to watch the image file transfer into memory. Emma came out of the back about the same time with a handful of color copies of the drawing. She handed them across to Marcy.

"There you go, Marcy," Emma said. "I kept a couple of copies myself should we need them for some reason. I hope that's okay."

"Whatever you need, Emma," Marcy said to her. "I can't thank you enough for what you've done for me."

"Just glad I could help," Emma said. She gave Marcy a knowing smile. Then she went over and looked over Phil's shoulder. "Whatcha got?"

Phil briefed her on what he had found. He kept pulling things up. Occasionally, the old dot-matrix printer would zip out a handful of lines. He looked up and noted some people were arriving in line for the four o'clock to JFK. He nodded to Emma.

"Can you take care of them, Emma? Just send any printing to the back office, I don't know how much I'll wind up with here and don't want it to get mixed up."

"No problem, Phil," she said, nodding to the first person in line. "Oh, the JFK inbound is in-range. Ramp knows, but one of us will have to get up to the gate in about ten minutes. Also, SOC sent out a notice that with this weather front moving in down south, things could get messy tonight."

Phil nodded and kept typing, chasing records and printing snippets he thought important.

Five minutes later, Phil zipped the reports from the printer and held them low behind the counter. He pulled Thomas and Marcy to the far end and spoke in a hushed tone.

"This is all I can get you right now. According to the records, of the twenty-nine males on that flight, only six did not check any luggage as I recall our man did not." He surreptitiously handed over the folded papers. "Please do not open this here. Do it at home. I hope you understand how both against company policy and illegal this is, but family is family. The six names are there, along with any home address information we have on them. As you will see when you look through the paperwork, two live in the Dallas/Fort Worth area, one lives in Austin and caught a late flight home that night out of DFW. Of the other three, two we have nothing further as far as travel goes, but they live in the Burlington area and I can assume they were going to Dallas for some reason, and the last one did not provide any address information but he went out to Honolulu on the morning nonstop flight on Sunday."

"Honolulu?" Marcy said. "Our man went to Hawaii? Sunday morning?"

"If we assume that this was our man, then yes." Phil looked at his watch and caught Emma's glance at the same time. "I'm sorry, but I have to go to the gate." He eyed the paperwork in Marcy's hand. "Go look through that information and let me know if you need anything else."

"How can I ever thank you?" asked Marcy.

"No thanks necessary, Marcy," he said. He looked at Thomas and winked. "The bill was prepaid years ago." He shook their hands and disappeared into the back area.

Emma was processing the line of passengers. They waved at her and headed for the door. She waved and smiled and mouthed, 'Good Luck' to Marcy. Marcy mouthed 'Thank You' back and she and Thomas walked slowly for the exit.

"Well, that was a good day's work," Thomas said as they hit the sunshine. "I could use one of Belle's special lemonades. How about you?"

"Sounds like a great idea, Gramps," Marcy said. "Let's go see if we can nail down this bastard."

While she drove back to Belle's, Marcy kept thinking of the six people who could have a connection to Janet's disappearance. She also wondered about the Hawaii coincidence. Did this thing track all the way back to Maui? While she felt closer to the truth than she had since this all began, with each step forward she was losing the last glimmers of hope that she'd find Janet alive and well.

Out of the corner of her eye, she saw Thomas was still grinning. Marcy remembered Belle's words of this morning. 'The Hand of God', she thought.

Sandy booked a flight to Montreal through New York on American before leaving her hotel around noon. She'd be in Montreal early in the evening, given good weather and on-time flights, which was currently not a good bet given the radar pictures she had seen on the news in the lobby. A large line of thunderstorms stretching from the Canadian border to north Carolina was making its way east nearing western Pennsylvania and Sandy knew how screwed up airline stuff could get on the east coast when weather moved in.

On the ride to the airport, she again phoned William and further discussed the morning's revelation that Jennifer Shea was so close at hand. William said he had checked transportation options to Molokai and the best he was going to be able to do was the morning ferry out of Lahaina. He said he had also arranged for a rental car at the ferry dock and obtained a home address for Miss Shea.

According to real property records, the home had been purchased for cash - one-point-six million to be exact - approximately one year ago and the registered owner was one Jennifer Shea. He had also been able to track her back to Chicago where she had been working in an art gallery on Michigan Avenue and before that to College Station, Texas where she had grown up. He informed Sandy that Jennifer Shea's parents had died in a house fire a little over a year ago. It was unclear where she would have been able to raise the one-point-six million dollars other than from life or other insurance payments to buy the house on Molokai, but William suspected he knew where that trail would eventually lead and Sandy concurred.

When they discussed the photograph in the San Francisco Chronicle, which William had found online, they both agreed it had only served to confirm that the woman pictured and identified as the Molokai artist Jennifer Shea was indeed the one Jennifer Shea in the world they were looking for. It would be a highly unlikely event if she weren't, given whom she so greatly resembled. Sandy and William had bantered about alternate possibilities as to Jennifer's connection to the case, because while she certainly fit Gregory's type, it was way too creepy to consider she had been one of his mistresses.

The only other news William had for Sandy was that reaching Cassie by cell phone had been impossible. No, he hadn't tried her yesterday after she called him en route to her spa appointments, but this morning had yielded nothing but immediate pick ups by voice mail. Given it was still early on Maui and he wouldn't be going to Molokai until tomorrow morning, he told Sandy he'd perhaps do some covert surveillance of Cassie's home if he still was unable to reach her this afternoon.

Sandy had little more for him since yesterday, although she expressed the opinion they would most likely be confronted with more missing women in Des Moines and Cheyenne once the police reports came back. She reminded William to make sure he kept Willie and Sam close at hand, especially if he was going anywhere near Gregory. He had confirmed to her that he already was. That gave her a little extra comfort when they disconnected.

Sandy doodled in her notebook on the flight north out of sunny - and hot and humid - central Florida. Even the airplane had been overheated at the gate, but she was able to upgrade to First Class and that left her just a little less cranky than she would have been wedged into a coach seat.

Finally, as they climbed above the building cumulus puffs, the cabin cooled down to a more comfortable level and she ordered a club soda from the flight attendant with a sense of humor whose name tag identified her as 'O Miss'.

"What's with the circles?" O Miss asked her as she set down the glass of club soda, complete with a wedge of lime, on a napkin placed on the arm rest beverage area between Sandy and the open window seat.

"They're called Venn diagrams, and they're used for visualizing conditional logic statements."

Noting the quizzical look on the face of O Miss, Sandy turned a page and drew a circle and labeled it 'All Flight Attendants', then she drew a smaller circle which connected in a small segment and labeled that one 'People With a Sense of Humor' and inside the intersecting lenticular-shaped slice she placed an X and labeled that 'O Miss'. See, that's you and using logical arguments of 'if yes, then' and 'if no, then' we can identify you as both a flight attendant and a member of people with a sense of humor. Where those two circles intersect we call the flight attendants who have a sense of humor in this example.

"How do you know I have a sense of humor?" O Miss asked, her quizzical look now even more quizzical.

Sandy pointed to her name tag.

"From that," she said. "O Miss on your name tag."

"But that's my name, Olivia Miss," she said. "I don't get it." She walked forward to the galley shaking her head.

Sandy made a mental note to remember to tell that one during the next girls night out, then she turned the page back over and continued with her logic statements and diagrams.

When she felt she had exercised every possible logical option, there was still one circle which remained unconnected to any of the others and that involved the journal pages which dealt with the woman from Chicago identified as being spotted on south Kihei Road wearing the teal blue bikini.

Sandy tapped her pen on the circle and asked herself a compound question under her breath, 'Who is this woman and how many more are there?'

I was becoming increasingly convinced there was something here besides a cheating husband case, and since Cassie had stated unequivocally that she didn't believe in coincidences, I was feeling my role here was not one. Sandy's words to me played back repeatedly as I sat and pondered the situation in which I found myself.

Cassie's refusal or inability to answer her phone had become more than disconcerting. The last I had spoken to her was yesterday morning. A quick check with the Four Seasons using a fake name of a Maui Police Officer and an affected accent only confirmed that she had indeed been there yesterday for her appointments. Even the phony officialdom could not get them to give any further details.

Heading to Molokai to visit the only known living and available woman thus far on the list was going to have to wait until tomorrow, so I sat and wondered what else I could do. I turned on one of the 24-hour news stations on the television, was promptly reminded that we were all still doomed, and then turned off the TV.

I picked up the black-and-white printed version of the photo of Jennifer Shea and compared it to the digitized color announcement ad from the San Francisco Chronicle from which I had printed the blow up. I marveled at the physical resemblance between Jennifer Shea and a younger Cassie. I guessed the Shea woman's age to be between twenty-five and thirty, something I was able to later confirm with some graduation records from College Station, Texas.

When I was sufficiently bored, I decided to make a trip to the Four Seasons Hotel and see if any of the staff could be induced to talk about anything unusual which may have happened during Cassie's appointments yesterday. It was a long shot, but, like I said, I was sufficiently bored.

The drive took less than five minutes, the parking was free save the ten bucks to the valet, and the staff at both the spa and the Orchid Salon, where I learned Cassie had spent most of her time yesterday, were equally well schooled on the privacy of their guests as had been the woman on the phone earlier. As I waited for the elevator to take me back to the main level, a woman in salon uniform came and stood next to me. On the ride up one floor she told me that she had been doing the manicure on Mrs. Thomason yesterday and that near the end of her session a man had come in, whispered something in Mrs. Thomason's ear which appeared to cause her some distress, and then left. After I gave a quick description of Mr. Thomason, the woman confirmed it was indeed Gregory who had come to the salon. Considering the woman's recollection, it must have been shortly after he left my condo. Considering *my* recollection of the conversation Gregory and I had shared yesterday, especially the part as he left asking the rhetorical question of 'Why I would be so interested in his life?', I was becoming increasingly concerned about Cassie's safety and well-being.

I jogged through the lobby - as best as I can jog - and slapped the ticket and ten bucks into the valet's palm. I saw the Jeep still in the circular drive, so I told him that I'd just take it from there. He called out when I was about fifteen feet past, I looked and he tossed me the keys. Ten-seconds later, I was out on the road starting the long trip to the island's south shore. I double checked my 'operations duffel' was in the back seat and then looked at the time on the dashboard. I knew I'd be out there way before sunset, which was not necessarily the way I wanted it for surveilling Gregory's property, but I'd have a couple hours of driving to come up with a plan.

Alex finally had been able to get Jennifer to talk late yesterday afternoon and they were still talking at midnight. It seemed when the girl's floodgates finally opened they had a full season of rainwater stored up behind them. He learned things he hadn't heard before - from her or from Gregory - and this morning he awoke to discover his conscience was bothering him.

He had heard her early this morning going into the studio and had fought the urge to go see what she was doing. Instead, he lay in bed, the ceiling fan moving the cool air about the room and he watched the morning's small waves rolling in. Alex recalled many of the more serious things he'd done wrong in his life, and there were many things he hated recalling, but this betrayal of Jennifer kept coming back as the worst of the worst.

At first, it had been a way to make money from Gregory. It had been easy. Run into the girl at the MACC and strike up a conversation. Grow that conversation into a friendship and earn more money. Keep tabs on her and report back to his benefactor and another stack of cash would arrive. He had seen nothing wrong with it when it all started, but as he got to know her, he also came to genuinely like her. Who wouldn't like Jennifer? She was a truly wonderful person with very few flaws. Other than she's far too trusting, that was. Alex hoped for a wry smile out of that irony, but even that was hard to come by when his conscience was nagging at him.

He debated on whether to report all the information he had learned last night to Gregory. In the end, however, the debate was not if, but whether he'd do it today or someday down the road when he could milk a bigger payout from him. He had no idea that at that very moment Gregory was watching both he and Jennifer in living color and complete with sound. What Alex also didn't know was that Gregory had already heard every word and seen every action that occurred last evening.

In his office in the home, high above the lava tube, Gregory watched the segments showing different views of the Molokai home on his flat screen. He narrowed the view to two segments - each taking up one half of the large screen - one of Jennifer in the studio and one of Alex in his bedroom. He contemplated the things he heard last evening and measured them against the lack of a phone call from Alex.

Gregory zoomed in on Alex's face and read indecision within him. 'So that explains the lack of a call,' he said softly to himself. 'He's growing fonder of her than of the cash, and more afraid of hurting the girl than of disappointing me,' he added. Silly boy, he thought, and he wondered if Alex was becoming more of a liability than an asset.

A red light flashed on the upper right corner of his display and Gregory tapped in some commands on his keyboard to change the view. It was kind of like picture-in-picture in effect, Alex and Jennifer went off to the upper left and a night vision view of Cassandra sitting up on her bed took up a larger portion of the screen. Gregory tapped a few more keys and the lights came on in Cassandra's cell. The night vision camera flared and then a second later a normal camera view replaced it on the screen. Cassandra was shielding her eyes and cursing.

"God, she can swear like a sailor with the clap," he said with a laugh.

He turned off the monitor with a remote and slid the keyboard back into the desk. Pushing the chair away, he stood and walked to the bookcase, opened the hidden door and began his descent into the lava tube. As he descended, he began to whistle.

Chapter Seventeen

As the drug wore off, Cassie discovered four things: she was naked, she was shackled to the bed, yet able to move fully about the room, and she had never been so frightened in her life.

Once before, Gregory had given her a glimpse of this experience. He had told her that he wanted her to feel what the others had felt, and on certain levels it excited her to do so. When she would travel back to their homes to use the return flight coupons and provide those who would come looking with evidence the missing had indeed come home from their trip, she would take on a piece of these women's life. She would see their home, she would respond to their name, she would become them for that brief period. Cassie felt walking in their shoes, so to speak, had enriched her life in so many ways.

This time, however, the confinement was different. This time, it had not been discussed in advance. This time, there were external factors at play, things she had done to covertly undermine Gregory and, of course, her plans for the future with Dan. As she lay in the bed, her mind slowly clearing, she thought through all the possible ways she could have screwed up, trying to pinpoint where she could have given Gregory advanced warning of her plans. The trip to the lava tube and the loss of her slipper - and subsequent recovery by Gregory - last Saturday was indeed a key event. After all, it had been Sunday morning when he had loosened her brake line.

Her eyes went wide at that moment. My God, she thought, there were six vehicles in the garage that morning and he had picked the correct one she would take on the trip to the church. How had he known? She had arranged on her cell phone to meet Dan that day, and she couldn't remember if she had told him that she would be taking the Jeep. Though she could have. There was still an anesthetic fog lingering in parts of her brain. Some recent memories were just not clear. Was her phone bugged? Her room? At this point, Cassie decided should she get out of here, she would assume Gregory would know her every step, her every conversation.

What did he know of William's role? Did Gregory know she had gone to New Orleans? As hard as she had worked to cover her tracks, paying cash for airline flights and the hotel, traveling under assumed names, leaving her cell phone in Dallas while forwarding calls to a throw away Dan had picked up at Wal-Mart or some such place. Could he have tracked her to New Orleans? Could he know what she and Dan had discussed? Certainly he could not know the things she hasn't told anyone. As good as Gregory may be at watching and learning, there was no way he could get inside her head. Was there?

She heard the locks open in the door. Gregory had opted for electronic locks over mechanical ones, so she knew he was there, manipulating the keypad. The locks, she also knew, would fail in the locked position if there were a power failure to the units. So he had to be out there preparing to come in. She readied herself, sat up in the bed, pulled the sheet above her breasts, not in modesty, but in the hopes of not angering him. She had seen it before when women had not adopted the proper level of modesty during his early visits. She ran her fingers through her hair, wiped her face with her hands. She was prepared as she could be, yet she still jumped when the door came open.

"Good afternoon, my dear," he said, his lips curling over a faked smile. "How did you rest? I wanted to give you some extra time to become more of yourself. I did use a little extra dose on you. As you know, the anesthetic is weight variable, and I think you've chunked up a bit lately. Must be all that good living." He grinned at her, walked to the chair and sat down.

She watched him carefully, judged his face, his words, his movements. She knew him better than anyone could, but even she was sometimes surprised by him. She could not let that happen. She could not be caught unaware again. Dealing with Gregory when he had you in his sights, she knew, was the most dangerous activity a human being could undertake. She wanted to use every advantage, every bit of her knowledge of him to survive this.

"I'm the same weight as when you married me," she said.

He smiled.

"Yes, indeed. Then you realize I always liked a little meat on the bone. More cushion for the pushin', as they say, eh?" He laughed.

"Is that why you're doing this, Gregory?" she challenged. "Because you think I've grown soft and fat?"

Cassie knew he hated surrender more than anything in people. He could not, would not tolerate it. When he saw someone giving up - not the mere act of giving in to him, no that was different - but giving up, surrendering as his mother had that day at the lake, it enraged him more than anything else under God's Creation and made him even more dangerous and worse still, unpredictable. So, for as long as it took, she needed to not only be strong, but to challenge him.

His favorite movie character was the British colonel in the *Bridge Over The River Kwai*. 'Dumb bastard', he would say when watching the film, but then he'd add, 'Balls like a cast iron bull, though'. The colonel never gave up, never gave in, and that's what Cassie knew she would have to do if she ever wanted to see the sun again.

Gregory glared at her. Then he sat back and crossed his legs, laid his hands on his lap.

"We both know why I've done this, my love," he said. "The goal here, however, is not for me to tell you, but for you to explain it to me."

Cassie took a passively confrontational tact, just like the colonel when the prisoners first arrived at the camp. Cassie smiled to herself when she thought the colonel must have been the inspiration for the 'Just say NO' campaign.

"If we both know the reasons, then this whole exercise is a waste of time. What purpose would it serve for either of us then to tell the other?"

"You asked, my sweet. You wanted to know why I was doing this to you, and my answer was that you already did know. So I've answered your question. I've already told you that your task was that you will tell me. That's your key out of this room."

Work on the bridge, Cassie thought. Your key to life, is work on the bridge. He was baiting her.

"Officers don't do manual labor, Gregory. I'm not going to tell you a goddamn thing."

He smiled at her. A knowing smile, and a bit less malevolent than a moment before. He wagged a finger at her showing slight amusement at her attempt to beguile him. Then, an instant later, like a shadow's fall with the approach of a terrible storm, his face changed. She recognized this face too, and her heart froze.

He rose up slowly.

She could feel the terror seize her whole body.

He approached her, his eyes locked into hers.

With all her strength, she pasted a mask of resistance onto her face. She knew what was coming, and this was just the beginning of the storm. Inside her mind, Cassie found a place of solace and comfort; she retreated to the storm cellar she had kept for herself for decades.

She felt his hands upon her. She knew physical resistance was futile. Gregory knew where to apply the pressure, how to apply it, and how much to apply to inflict the greatest pain. Inside her storm cellar, Cassie could hear him beating against the door like hurricane force winds. She knew her body was enduring immense physical pain, but she also knew it was not the type of pain which would result in permanent injury; and she knew she was safe so long as he didn't breach her door.

In her mind, she sat on the floor of the storm cellar with her back braced against the door. She could feel the blows to the door, but it held. Time passed. How much, she wasn't certain. Something was changing. Slowly, the room became smaller, the circle of darkness grew tighter around her and she knew her body was succumbing to the pain and she would soon pass out. She envisioned herself pushing back against the door, bracing herself so she would not fall away from it in the coming darkness. Then there was nothing but blackness. No sound, no wind, no force against the door. Just blackness, and she knew in that silent blackness she could rest, for now. The next storm would come, but there would be warning.

I approached the south shore of the island on the upper road, which then turned east and descended along the mountain closer to the ocean. It was the King's Highway, the Pi'ilani, named for its builder, the ancient Maui ruler Pi'ilani who united the island two hundred and fifty years before the coming of Kamehameha. I read that in a tour book last night before I went to bed.

Anyway, I was considering my options on how to surveil Cassie's home and whether a covert or overt approach was the best plan. Then I remembered Keoki and how the man spent his days observing the property. I also considered Gregory's counter-surveillance capabilities included both off-property as well as on-property. I would have to approach the area sans Jeep, on foot. Even on foot, I would have to approach either after dark or by stealth. My gaze went up the mountain, at the rugged terrain where a klutz like myself was certain to twist an ankle at the minimum.

Awaiting the fall of darkness and then walking up the bad gravel road was looking like a much better idea.

So, I found a small roadway which lead to a flat, grassed plateau toward the sea cliffs, and drove in. The land was obviously used for grazing cattle, but was vacant at the time and I hoped would remain so. Let's just say, never trust a cow and leave it at that. About two hundred yards from the black lava precipice, I found a stand of short trees which would serve to hide the Jeep from anyone passing on the roadway above. I pulled in, shut off the motor, opened the windows to allow the breeze to blow through the car and used the time to go through the contents of my duffel bag. From the sun's angle, I calculated about a four hour wait for darkness.

Sandy's trip north turned into a true adventure when the storm front clobbered the east coast. First the flight from Orlando was delayed on the ground for an hour and then advised it would be held for another hour offshore of New York while JFK and the other area airports dealt flights clearance to land one at a time like so many cards from a well-shuffled deck. As her plane circled in the relatively clear air over the Atlantic, she could see the line of dark clouds closing on the water's edge and knew she'd not enjoy the bumpy trek back toward JFK when their card was eventually dealt.

She now regretted her decision to take the earlier flight up the east coast rather than the later routing which would have taken her on United through Chicago and well behind this weather system. Besides, she really wasn't a big fan of American Airlines, or it's regional operation American Eagle, especially since she overheard a crew talking one day and adapting the familiar 'something special in the air' catchphrase to 'something scary in the air' and laughing. Oh well, she thought, can't change horses now, and she cinched her seatbelt just a little tighter.

As it turned out, getting into JFK was easier than getting out. By five p.m., the rush had begun and flights headed east began canceling all over the country. By seven p.m., the front had stalled at the seashore and began hammering away at every major airport along the coast from Bangor, Maine to Wilmington, north Carolina, causing long lists of outbound flights to cancel as well. By nine p.m., about the time Sandy decided to give up the ghost and book the morning flight out to Montreal as a standby, all the hotels nearby were filled up. So, as she settled into a row of seats along a wall in a relatively quiet gate area, making her bed from half a dozen blankets she had swiped from the plane on the way in just in case, she called William to tell him she'd be delayed in hitting the Janet Hopkins trail.

"Hey, Sandy, how's Montreal?" William asked as his greeting.

"Not sure, Otto, I'm stuck at JFK on a row of seats with pilfered blankets as my bed for the night. The weather stalled on the coast and everything in and out of anywhere here is canceled until morning. What's happening there? Any emails from Des Moines or Cheyenne PD?"

"Not as of when I headed out early this afternoon," he said. "Right now, I'm sitting in my Jeep under a group of keawe trees about five miles from Cassie's house waiting for sundown to go do some recon work."

"Still no word from Cassie?" she asked.

"Nothing," he reported. "I even stopped and used a pay phone in case she was avoiding me for some reason."

Sandy found that a little odd, but given everything else that the woman had done, not entirely out of character. She didn't pass that assessment on to William.

"The plan is to go over to Molokai in the morning on the ferry and touch base with Jennifer Shea?" Sandy remembered the stories about Molokai being a not-so-friendly place for strangers from when she had been in the islands years ago. She wondered if it had changed, but experience told her it probably had not. "By the way, the natives on Molokai have a reputation for being suspicious, sometimes even hostile, toward visitors, Otto.   Especially haole visitors. Just an FYI when you go over there. Don't expect them to be anything but."

"Are you worried about me, Sandy?"

"Nah," she lied.   "I just don't want you starting some sort of international incident."

"Ah, last I heard, Hawaii is still part of the good old U.S. of A., honey," he jabbed.

"I'm talking about between you and a group of Molokai warriors," she jabbed back.   "I don't think they ever did this kind of stuff, but I'd hate to one day find your shrunken head on a pencil in a gift shop."

"I don't think I'd like that much myself," William said with a chuckle.   "Don't worry, Sandy, I'll take care of myself and I'll be good as well."

"So, what's the plan for you?" he asked.   "Going out tomorrow morning?"

"Yeah, I'm on standby for the first flight out of JFK to Montreal in the morning. Talking to the gate agents, who are quite frazzled by all this as you can imagine, I was told that because things are so screwed up all over by this storm I should have no trouble getting a seat because the whole system, oh what's the word they used, yeah, ah, resets."

"Have you located where this Janet Hopkins lives?" William asked.

"Yeah, an area of town called Le Village, known for a large population of gays and lesbians."

"Wow, our boy is really off the reservation on this one, isn't he? Blonde and a lesbian."

"I didn't say she was a lesbian, just the area is known for a large gay population, just like certain areas in New York and San Francisco."

"Well, chances are good you're going find that to be the case. I have to wonder why our boy may have taken such a leap from type. I'm no FBI profiler, but that action would seem to indicate some kind of stressor has taken place in his life."

"You've been watching too many *Criminal Minds* reruns," she said. "Next you'll be telling me that you think Gregory Thomason is some kind of criminal genius responsible for disappearances all over north America."

After she spoke the words out loud, Sandy wondered if that idea was too far fetched. He had plenty of means. From the journal pages he purportedly wrote, he definitely has some issues. From what William has reported, the guy is oddly confrontational and aggressive.

"Don't tell me that very thought hasn't crossed your mind in the last twenty-four hours, Sandy. I know you better than that."

"Oh, it's crossed it, I'm just not putting all the dots together to the point of starting to proceed on that assumption at this point, but since you're in the line of fire, I'm kinda glad *you* are. It will make you be more careful."

"Let's just say Willie and Sam are enjoying full employment right now," William advised.

"So what's your plan for tonight?" Sandy asked, hoping he wasn't going to tell her that he was going to go into the house looking for Cassie.

"When it gets dark, I'm going to head over and see this Keoki fellow. He hates Gregory, has less antipathy for Cassie, and has a house which overlooks the property."

"Okay, and then what?"

"Depends on what he's seen since yesterday. That damn house is so soundproof you can't even hear the wind howling outside or a helicopter land right next to it when you're in there. It's also a counter-surveillance nightmare. I scoped out at least two penetration alarm systems, know that there's state-of-the-art audio and video recording equipment throughout the house and property, and there's even ground sensors around the perimeter to notify him if anyone sets foot inside the fence. Nobody is slipping in unnoticed unless he's left the back gate open, and that back gate is a vicious little body of water the locals call the 'I'll end you ha ha' channel and you know I'm no fan of being in the water."

After William spoke the words, he wondered just what he *would* do tonight. The place was covertly impenetrable as he just told Sandy. Anybody setting foot near the property risked being detected immediately, if not sooner.

"Please be careful, Otto," she pleaded. "Do you think it's time to bring in the police?"

"And tell them what, exactly? That we have stumbled across a couple of missing persons cases going back twenty years which are allegedly linked to one of the country's richest men?"

"A current missing person's case and a potentially missing wife," she reminded him. "No, I'm not suggesting you call in the Cavalry just yet, I'm just wondering if it's time to expand your relationship with that deputy chief you met the other day. Give him a status report so somebody besides me knows what we've been uncovering."

That made some sense to William, especially when he took a moment to consider her words.

"That could be a very good idea, Sandy," he said. "Thanks for putting up with me."

"You're my partner, Otto, what else can I do?"

"I'll talk to you in the morning," he said before clicking off. "Have a good night in JFK."

"You stay out of the water," she said. "Call me anytime if something comes up *before* you go in guns a-blazin'."

They both nervously laughed at that one, mainly because they each knew it could very well happen that way.

Marcy, Thomas, and Belle sat in the front room, the parlor, Belle had called it. They sipped lemonade after returning from the airport, and once the clock had passed five o'clock, Thomas asked Belle, if he could spike his up a little bit. He brought out a little flask, offered each of the ladies a touch of the old country, and then poured a little golden brown liquid into each of their glasses. Isabella snoozed under the coffee table on the large, rag rug.

Marcy took a sip of the blend, coughed and asked which exactly was the old country to which he referred?

"Why Scotland, my dear," he said. "The Parish of Campsie, in Stirlingshire to be exact. That's the origin of my Clan."

"And the spike?" she asked, still a bit raspy. "What do you call that, rocket fuel?"

Marcy watched Belle take a sip and smile.

"Why no, dear, although it most likely could serve that purpose well," he said. "This is twelve-year-old single malt Scottish Whiskey, 'uisge beatha' (he pronounced it oosh-ga beh-huh), which translated from the original Gaelic is the *Water of Life*."

"It goes wonderfully with my lemonade," Belle quipped. "Thank you, Thomas."

"My pleasure, Belle," he said. "I have tried the thirty-year-old vintage and found it too hot even for me." He winked at Marcy then said to Belle: "Can you imagine that, Belle, one-third my vintage and too hot to handle?"

"Settle down, old man," Belle said. "Just because this young lady has reinvigorated your oats with this investigation, doesn't mean you've got any need to look to go sowing them."

They all settled into a good laugh. Marcy looked at the two elders and felt genuine love for each of them even though before yesterday they had been total strangers. They reminded her that there was indeed good in the world.

"Speaking of this investigation," Thomas began and then took a long draw of lemonade and single-malt. "I've been thinking of the next step and think I have it."

"I thought I'd book a flight to Dallas and see if I could do the same thing we did here today," Marcy said. "That's where the trail goes."

Thomas shook his head emphatically, and Marcy saw so did Belle.

"No, I think that would be wrong," Thomas said. "That's headquarters area and these airline types get closed mouthed when you get closer to HQ. It's not like rekindling old friendships out here in the boonies. No, I think you'd find nothing but dead ends in Dallas, honey."

"I agree with Thomas, Marcy," Belle chimed. "You two got lucky up here today. That luck won't follow you down there."

"So, what do you think I should do, Thomas?" Marcy asked.

Thomas drained his glass. Marcy thought it interesting that during the entire hour they'd been sitting in the parlor, he'd barely touched the lemonade, now in the few minutes since he had spiked it up, he had downed a whole serving. Marcy wondered if his earlier sipping was just making room in the glass for the whiskey. Thomas refilled from the iced pitcher and spiked up a second glass for himself. Each of the ladies waved off any more just yet.

"What I think we should do, Marcy, is look up the boy who used to cut my lawn, Chuck."

"The boy who cut your lawn?" Marcy asked.

"I think that's a brilliant idea, Thomas," Belle said.

Marcy looked from Thomas to Belle and back again.

"See, Chuck is in his middle fifties now," Thomas explained. "He's the manager of the Vermont Department of Motor Vehicles office here in Burlington. He used to cut my lawn when he was a kid."

Marcy laughed.

"When am I going to learn I should hold my questions until you are done telling the story?" she asked. "It would save so much time."

"I hope you learn soon," Thomas said. "Time isn't on my side anymore."

That thought made Marcy sad and she looked hard with soft eyes at Thomas as he continued.

"We have an artist's sketch of this guy, we have a handful of names, and with Chuck we have access to the DMV databases across the country. Tomorrow morning, you and I are going to go down and see Chuck and ask that he pull up some driver records and if we get a photo match, you know exactly where your next stop will be and exactly who you will be looking for. I only wish I could be there when you confront this rat."

"Is there anyplace in this city that you don't have friends, Thomas?" Marcy asked.

"Not many," Belle said.

"Oh, in ninety years I am certain I've made an enemy or three along the way, too. The lucky thing is that the Good Lord has let me outlive most of those."

Thomas finished his second glass of spiked lemonade.

"Isabella," he said. The dog jumped to her feet and shook off the sleep. "Time to go home. I'm very tired tonight and I need to get some rest."

"I'll walk you home, Thomas," Marcy said. She got up and helped Thomas to his feet. She grabbed Isabella's leash and hooked up the dog.

"Good evening, Belle," he said. "Thank you for the lemonade."

"Thank you for the spike," she said. She watched them leave and thought about the good that had come to town with that young girl. Belle hoped that Marcy would leave with more inside herself than she had come with as well.

Thomas was walking a little slower than normal on the way home, Marcy thought. It seemed Isabella felt so as well, since she was pulling at the leash, trying to speed him up. Marcy attributed it to the alcohol combined with a big day and his ninety year old frailty. She held onto his arm and enjoyed the last of the day. To the southeast, an odd greenish gray sky indicated a huge thunderstorm moving through. They had heard the thunder earlier, but it had remained dry in Burlington.

"My wife and I used to walk this neighborhood almost every evening," Thomas said. "I still walk it, but I have missed the feeling of having a lovely, charming woman on my arm when I do it. Thank you, Marcy."

"Oh, Thomas, I have so enjoyed meeting you," she said. "You've done so much to help me. How can I ever repay your kindness?"

"You already have, my dear," he said.

Isabella stopped to pee at a tree. Then they continued.

"What was your wife's name, Thomas?"

"Excuse me, honey," he said a moment later. "My mind was wandering off."

"Your wife's name, Thomas. What was it?"

"Angela," he said. "That's Latin for 'angel', although technically, it means 'messenger', but derives from the same word as angel, so most people take it to mean 'Messenger from God'."

"That's beautiful," she said. "Marcy is short for Marcella, and I think that's Latin for 'destined to grow old alone'. At least that's what I thought before I met Janet."

"Cervantes wrote in *Don Quixote* of Marcella, that she was probably 'the most beautiful creature ever sent into the world'. Did you know that?"

"Yes, but do you know the rest of the story? I do, because I read *Don Quixote* in high school and chose the Marcella character on whom to do a report for my senior English class. She was a rich, beautiful orphan who left behind her wealth for a life herding sheep. Marcella was reputed to be kind and modest and she charmed everyone, but refused to accept the advances of all suitors, and from that, she was assumed to be cruel in matters of the heart. She is blamed for the death of Chrysostom after she refuses his advances, claiming her beauty is a gift from heaven and therefore she must remain chaste. On Chrysostom's tombstone, his fellow shepherds wrote: 'From Chrysostom's fate, learn to abhor Marcella, that common enemy of man, whose beauty and cruelty are both in the extreme'. So I've got that going for me."

Thomas appeared to be deep in thought. They arrived at his gate. He opened the gate and let Isabella off the leash and into the yard. She ran around happily, found a squirrel hiding in the corner and chased it up a tree. They both watched the chase.

"Marcy, I am so glad I had the chance to meet you," he said. "You embody everything good about the fictional Marcella, and nothing of the bad. Regardless of what you may eventually discover about Janet's fate, you will love again. Even if you wind up alone at the end of your life, like me, well, you'll have all those memories to keep you company, and all that wisdom so you may have the chance to pass a bit of it along to someone who may not even be born yet. Life is for living and loving and experiencing, young lady, and that is just what you will do."

He gave her a hug and then scuffed through the gate.

"Pick me up at nine in the morning and we'll go over to see Chuck," he said. "I'm tired tonight and I'd appreciate the ride in the morning. Remember, while God may place obstacles in our path, he sometimes puts a gem on the side of the road."

"I'll be here," she said. "Good night, Thomas. Thank you." She ran up and gave him a big hug and a kiss on the cheek. When she looked into his eyes, she saw how truly tired he was.

She walked back toward Belle's house and thought about what he had said to her. The sun was getting low in the west and the air had turned cooler with the addition of a breeze from the northwest. The leaves rustled overhead in the wind.

She looked back toward Thomas' house and smiled.

As the sun neared its final drop into the Pacific, I started the Jeep and pulled back out to the main road. The next five miles took me nearly twenty minutes to navigate without lights and by the time I found the little inset adjacent to a cattle guard, it was totally dark. I backed the Jeep into the small area off the road and taking a hint from the tourist book, grabbed the only thing of value, my duffel, and began the walk up the roadway toward Keoki's property.

I turned up the drive and then paused to give him the chance to see it was me. I silently prayed that Keoki didn't shoot trespassers first to ask questions later and continued up the drive toward the ramshackle house. As I got closer, I could see him sitting on the porch, a cooler, full of beer, I assumed, on the floor at his side.

"Ah, Malihini, I see you come," Keoki said to me as I approached the porch.

"I'm glad your night vision is better than mine," I said.

"I still see good in da dark. I know dat you."

"Mind if I pull up a step," I asked.

"Sit, Malihini," he said. "You want beer?"

"I'd love one," I said. I opened the cooler and took out a can. I offered him one.

"I got beer," he said. "What in da bag, Malihini?"

"Some things to use to spy on your neighbor," I said.

I asked him what had been going on across the road.

"He come home, she come home," Keoki said. "I no see her no more."

"I haven't been able to contact Cassie, since yesterday morning," I told him.

"Like I say, she come home, I no see her no more."

"When did she come home?" I asked.

"Yesterday, later. Still light."

From this vantage point on Keoki's porch, about three hundred feet above the Thomason's house, one could see the entire estate, except for the areas of the first floor lanai shadowed by the second floor lanais. No wonder it bugged the hell out of Gregory that all Keoki seemed to do all day was sit on his porch, drink beer and watch his property.

I popped the top on the beer, drank a healthy draw. I had neglected to bring a bottle of water along today, so the last few hours had made me fairly dry. Opening the duffel, I pulled out the night vision goggles and put them on before powering them up. I looked over Cassie's house and property. It was like looking at things during the day, only with greenish glow to everything. I switched to infrared illumination and took another look around. I pulled them off and let Keoki take a look. A big grin took over his face.

Next I pulled out the parabolic dish listening device and put on the head phones. I pointed the dish at various locations on the house, the laser tracker providing a red dot where the dish was aimed. I doubted I'd pick anything up but background noise of the ocean waves, but at this range, I might not even hear that. The unit was only effective to about four-hundred-fifty feet under most circumstances. Given the sound proofing of the house, the only possible reflection could come from the vibrations of the glass panes. I targeted each window on the mountain side of the home but heard absolutely nothing. From my inspection of the windows on the inside, I expected nothing more. The thermopane windows were quadruple glazed. In order for sound waves to bounce through they'd have to be fairly intense, and after all, we had missed the sound of a helicopter landing two hundred feet away.

Keoki looked curious, so I explained the system to him. He popped another beer and I accepted a second as well. I told him why it didn't work on the glass.

"Use on da door glass," he said. "Dat just da regular kine."

The front door glass? I pointed the laser onto the sidelight on the front door. There was a muffled sound. I adjusted the controls on the antenna, moved the laser to various points on the glass to find the sweet spot. There it was, a man's voice. One sided conversation. Calm. It sounded like one side of a phone call. From this distance, I couldn't quite make out any words, just tones of speech.

I pulled out a cellular phone scanner and turned it on, hoping the call was not on a wired line. The lights flashed across the front panel and then locked on a channel, then a second. Since the scanner had limited range, and we were in the boonies, I anticipated we'd pick up Gregory's call fairly quickly. I was right. Catching Gregory's frequency was only half the equation. Because cell phones allow for simultaneous conversation, they're considered full-duplex equipment and that means one frequency for talking and one for listening. The cellular towers assign the frequencies and high tech digital equipment manages the calls. It's more than I desire to understand. All I care is that the listening device can capture the current technology and how that all works I leave to the experts.

I tied in a digital recording device and put on the headphones. Out of the corner of my eye, I saw Keoki was mesmerized. I listened in on what sounded to be the end of the conversation.

"Well, you just stay there a few more days," said the voice which I identified as Gregory.

"I've got plans this weekend, Gregory," the other voice said. A male voice. Younger, Caucasian, I judged.

"I don't give a shit about your plans," Gregory said. "I want you there."

"So long as you make it worth my while, I guess I can do that."

"All right, call me tomorrow."

"Ciao."

The call was gone.

I left the system set up and scanning just in case Gregory made another call. Many times, people make several calls in a row, a lesson I'd learned one time when I had turned off the equipment when the subject had concluded his call only to miss the next one. That's embarrassing when you're sitting in the office of an attorney who has the phone records and you have a transcript of a call to the subject's brother but miss the next one to his alleged mistress.

"So many things, brah," Keoki said. "You need all dat?"

"They're the tools of the trade today, Keoki. Years ago, all a private detective needed was a pair of eyes, a notebook and a comfortable pair of shoes. Times have changed."

I thought while the electronics monitored things for a bit, I'd talk to Keoki about the property, the construction, the things he's seen over the years. Knowing Gregory was inside and given the counter-surveillance stuff I saw, not to mention the stuff I didn't see, meant that sneaking into the place tonight was too risky. All I could hope for was an intercepted cell phone call by Cassie to confirm she was there and all right. To test the system, I pulled out my cell and dialed her number. The system went directly to voicemail, but my scanner immediately picked up both sides of the transmission. I hung up before leaving a message.

"So, Keoki, you've spent your entire life on this property?" I asked.

"I live here my whole life," he said. "I go off da aina tree time. One go to my cousin wedding Big Island. One go New Orleans wit my son. One time Las Vegas. No odda reason to leave."

"How did you like Las Vegas," I asked.

"So many people, so many noise," he said. "I no want go back. My son, he like dat place. Dawta too. They no more of this aina, they like you now, they Malihini."

I saw his eyes tear. It must have tore him apart to close this tiny stage to them so he could open up the whole of the world to them. He knew this life was dying, unsustainable. The only hope for the kids these days was to get off the islands, get to the mainland, while the haoles and other outsiders buy up the island and try to make it their own. I had only been here a few days, but I was beginning to understand the legacy of this land to its people. Like the American Indian, Hawaiians have seen their land stolen by crafty Europeans since Captain Cook first came in the mid-18th century. From what I have read, it was ironically the Christian missionaries who raped the islands more than the profiteers.

"You did right by your keiki, Keoki," I said.

"You tink so, Malihini?" he said.

I think for some reason my opinion really mattered to him.

"I do," I said.

"When I a boy, we know every part of this ahupua'a, and that one, and that one, and on and on. One ohana, one ahupua'a." He pointed each way. "I know da ohana all dis aina."

"The families, the landowners?"

"Dat right. I know all. Now different. All changed."

He pointed at his house, then down toward Cassie's home.

"Dat not right, brah. Dis all a kane need. Not dat." He shook his head. Then popped another beer, tossed me another.

"You said that the land, the ahupua'a gave every family all they needed, from the sea to the mountaintop. Those cliffs are so steep, how did your family get to the sea without scaling the rocks or going down the shore, across someone else's ahupua'a?"

He looked at me for a minute and then nodded understanding.

"Da tube, brah, take you makai. To da watah."

"The tube?"

He pointed to the ground made a line from the porch to the ocean.

"You mean a tunnel?"

"Yeah, da tube go from da watah, into da mauna, da mountain."

"How do you get to the tunnel?" I asked.

"Two places, one up here, one down there." He pointed above his house and then down toward Cassie's place. "But dat one down there under dat house now. No more can."

"How big is this tunnel? The tube?"

"Big enough. Small here, big down there. Even you can walk inside. My father keep his canoe inside."

"About where was the entry down there?"

"On dat side, by da end."

He pointed toward the east wing, about where Gregory's office was located.

"When he build dat house, he put a cap on da spot to go to da tube."

"A cap?"

I assumed Keoki meant he concreted the opening, but why do that? Just move the house and pour the foundation on solid lava. If the tube is at or near sea level on that end, that's a hundred feet or more of opening to fill up. Who would do that? Even Gregory wouldn't throw money down a hole, literally, like that.

"Yeah, a hat wit a door, lotta men work in da tube for lotta day."

What was he telling me? That Gregory may have incorporated access to the tunnel into the house design? That he may have installed an access down to sea level from inside the house? Inside his office area? When I was in there with Cassie, I saw no concrete cap or hat. No openings other than the office door. Maybe it was hidden. In the bookcases like in some bad horror flick, or my office bar?

"Do you think Gregory built things down in the tunnel? That he made it connect to the surface inside the house?"

"Yeah, brah, whatchu tink I tell you?"

The third beer was beginning to affect me. I wondered how Keoki could sit here all day and drink without falling down flat on his face by sunset.

"Have you ever gone down into the tube to see what Gregory may have built down there? You can still get down there through the other opening behind the house, right?"

"No me no go. No can no more. Too old. So I sit here and watch dat asshole." He displayed an evil grin.

I could understand why he enjoyed getting under Gregory's skin. It was starting to get a little late, I had a bit of a buzz and a long way on bad, dark roads to drive home. In addition, I had a ferry to catch in the morning on the other side of the island. I reached into the duffel and pulled out a prepaid cell phone. I turned it on and made sure it registered with the network.

"I'd like to give you this phone, Keoki," I said. "You know how to use a cell phone?"

"You tink I stupid? I can use a phone."

"No, I don't think you're stupid.   My cell phone number is programmed in using the number two on the speed dial.   Hold down the number two key until you hear a long beep and it will call my phone." I showed him how to do it.   "Can you call me if Gregory or Cassie show up outside or leave the property?   I need to get inside that house when he's not there.   I'm worried about Cassie."

"I can do dat, one ting," he said.

"One thing? You mean one condition?"

"Yeah, one ting."

I reached for my wallet.

"No, next time you come, you bring Keoki beer."

"Deal," I said.   I packed up my gear into the duffel.   I reached out to shake his hand, and after a two or three changes in grips he let it go.

Two hours later, I was back in my condo, eating a Whopper and fries I picked up in Kahului.   When that was gone, I took a Prilosec, set the alarm, and went to sleep.

"Wake up, sweetie," Gregory said.   "Cassandra, we need to talk."

Cassandra rolled over in the bed.   Her insides ached and she stifled a moan when she rolled over to look at him.   This time she could see him in the dark.   She winced an instant later when the lights came on full intensity.   Gregory was wearing sunglasses.   She had seen this routine before, as well.   She hadn't eaten in a day, she estimated, yet she felt the urge to throw up.

In Gregory's hand was a small, black device the size of a policeman's flashlight.   She knew it was one of his cattle prods.   Non-lethal, but quite painful on naked skin.   It would leave two small pinpricks in her flesh from the electrodes.   In two or three days, they would be blistered.   She began to shiver, but stared defiantly into his sunglasses.

"Really, Gregory?" she said.   "The cattle prod now?   What are you, a broken record?"

She saw the insult hit him, but he was the one holding the cattle prod. She wondered if it was a good idea to arouse his wrath; there was a subtle difference between holding strong and antagonizing your captor.   She also realized that attempted seduction would not work here either.   She resolved to enduring this session's program and retreated again to her storm shelter. She bolted the door and curled up in a ball in the corner.

"Why are we here, Cassandra?" he said.

Inside her shelter, the words were muffled. She did not answer. An instant later, she heard the snap of the spark. In her mind she saw the door bulge inward, yet it held. Then again, and again, and again. Before each spark, she heard the muffled question. Each time it was spoken, it came through a little clearer. The last time it was spoken, it was as if he were screaming it through the door. She knew he never raised his voice during these sessions, and that meant he was close to breaking through. In her mind, she curled tighter and then came the final snap. In her shelter, the snap had the same sound as a thunderclap. She gritted her teeth.

"You know why we're here just as well as I do, Gregory," she said. She was breathing heavily from the mental exertion and physical pain which was just now surging to her brain from spots all over her body.

The lights went off and she opened her eyes enough to watch him leave. When he opened the door, she could see it was night outside. After he closed the door, she went to the sink and dampened a washcloth with cold water. She dabbed at the spots. She knew there would be twenty, but found only nineteen spots on her body.

When she turned on her side to sleep, she winced. Her fingers moved to the source of the new pain, and she found the twentieth spot in the middle of her left cheek, halfway between her ear and mouth. She could not remember him ever using a cattle prod on any of their faces. Perhaps that was retribution for the broken record remark. She would indeed remember that for next time. Eventually, she drifted off to sleep. The nightmares followed soon after.

Chapter Eighteen

Marcy was up at sunrise. She padded down the hall to Tamra's room. The nurse was there, reading a magazine in the chair at Tamra's bedside. Marcy stopped at the door, the nurse looked up and smiled.

"It's okay to come in," she said. "Tamra's sleeping."

Marcy approached the bedside. Tamra's body was contorted, her muscles in a permanent state of tension. She had watched the therapists working on her yesterday and could not imagine the pain the girl would feel if she were not unconscious most of the time. Marcy wondered what the girl felt, what she thought. Was she still inside there, or had God allowed her to escape her worldly existence to some place where she was whole and alive and not confined to this bed? Marcy prayed that was so, then she thought how she had come to think of the reality of a God in just a couple of days after so many years of denying. She prayed Tamra was not locked inside a body which had abandoned her with full knowledge of everything that went on around her. The pain alone would drive a person to madness, she imagined.

Marcy bent close to the girl's ear and whispered to her. She straightened up and patted Tamra's hand. She stroked her hair. When Marcy turned to leave, she saw Belle standing in the doorway.

"You're up early this morning, dear," Belle said.

"Couldn't sleep anymore," Marcy replied. "I feel rested and ready for the day, whatever it is that this day becomes."

"Would you like something to eat?" Belle asked. "I could make some eggs and toast. We still have some of that marmalade you like."

"No thank you," Marcy replied. "I think I'll take a quick shower and then go surprise Thomas and Isabella by taking them to a restaurant for breakfast. Would you like to come with us?"

"I would enjoy that, dear," Belle said. "It's been quite a while since someone has invited me to breakfast."

Marcy went and took a shower, and Belle got ready to go as well. Half an hour later, they met downstairs and went out into the morning. The coolness of the evening had already changed to a promise of a sweltering, humid new day. According to the weather reporter this morning, the storm system which had paralyzed much of the east coast yesterday had moved out over the Atlantic and was being replaced by another rapidly advancing low pressure system from the midwest. Moisture and heat were being funneled up between the two fronts from the Gulf of Mexico all the way up into Newfoundland.

A minute later, Marcy pulled the car up in front of Thomas' house. She left Belle in the car with the air conditioning running and walked up to the front door. She rang the bell. Then knocked. She could hear Isabella inside barking. Marcy walked back to the car. Belle rolled down her window.

"I can hear Isabella barking in there, but Thomas isn't coming to the door," Marcy reported. "He wouldn't have gone out without Isabella, would he?"

"Thomas takes Isabella everywhere, dear," Belle said. "He wouldn't leave her alone in the house at this time of day." A look crossed Belle's face, but was gone before Marcy could identify it. "Perhaps he's involved in his morning constitutional, my dear. Let's give him a few minutes."

Marcy got back in the car. It was cool inside and outside it was becoming uncomfortable already. She realized it was going to be all the scorcher of a day they were predicting.

"Do you think he's still sleeping, Belle?" Marcy asked.

"Thomas Kincaid hasn't slept past sunrise in sixty years," she replied. "He's more reliable as to the dawn than any rooster could be."

Several minutes passed.

"Go back to the door, dear," Belle suggested. "Give the bell another ring or two."

Marcy again approached the door and rang the bell. She could hear it was working. Again Isabella was behind the door, barking. A moment later, Marcy felt a hand on the small of her back and she turned to see Belle standing behind her. Marcy looked into Belle's eyes. What she saw caused her to become afraid.

"It's okay, dear," Belle reassured. "Try the door."

Marcy opened the screen door, then tried the knob on the inside door. It turned freely. It was unlocked. She turned and looked at Belle again.

"We old timers in Vermont don't lock our doors, dear. That's normal."

As the door opened, Isabella barked one more time and then recognized Belle and Marcy and her tail began to wag.

"Thomas, it's Belle and Marcy," Belle called. "We're coming in."

At Belle's urging, Marcy stepped inside. The house was cool and dark and silent. Thomas did not answer back. Marcy felt a foreboding. She stopped inside the door.

"Would you like to wait here, dear?" Belle asked. "I can go through the house myself."

Marcy felt a sting coming to her eyes. Her stomach was doing flips and her hands were shaking. Yet she knew she had to do this.

"No, I'll go too," she said.

She and Belle moved through the house together. Isabella trailed behind. At Thomas' bedroom door, Isabella sat down, refused to enter the room.

They found him in his bed, the bed he had shared with his Angela for sixty-seven years. He was dressed in his pajamas, and lying on his back under the covers. His slippers were alongside the bed. His eyes were closed. His face was peaceful. He was cool to the touch.

Sandy was up at sunrise as well. She hadn't slept much during the night, what with worrying about people walking off with her stuff and the constant need to shift position on the most uncomfortable place she had ever slept. She walked to the Starbucks and bought a Grande and a muffin. Then she headed to the gate from which the Departures board reported the first flight to Montreal was leaving.

Sandy checked in with the agent, who looked at her like, 'What, did you sleep at the airport last night?'.

"Yes, I did sleep at the airport last night," Sandy said.

The agent flushed, and continued typing into the system.

"You're in luck, Ms. Langdon, with the weather mess last evening, the passenger load this morning is relatively light. I can give you a complimentary upgrade to First Class for all your trouble."

"That would be great," Sandy said.

She took the boarding pass from the agent and moved to a seat near the windows to eat her muffin and drink her coffee. When that was done, she found the nearest restroom and cleaned herself up. By the time she arrived back at the gate area, the flight was ready to board. She walked down the jetway and took her seat. Before the flight pushed back from the gate, she was asleep.

When she awoke, the plane was touching down in Montreal. She stretched in her seat; she felt a thousand times better than when she had boarded. At the gate, Sandy retrieved her carry on and computer bag out of the overhead and walked up the jetway. She could feel it was going to be a scorcher in Montreal.

After processing through Immigration and Customs, Sandy walked out to the taxi stand. She gave the address to the driver and twenty minutes later stood on the sidewalk in front of Janet Hopkins' apartment building. The cabbie had agreed to wait for her.

Sandy first rang the buzzer for the apartment listed as Janet's, just in case someone was staying there. When there was no response, Sandy buzzed the Manager's unit. She looked at her watch. It was a little past nine thirty. She pushed the buzzer again.

"Yeah?" came the raspy voice of an irritated woman through the cheap intercom speaker. "Who is it?"

Sandy identified herself to the woman who told her to come in and go to the basement workshop where she'd find the manager, her husband, Ernie. Silently, Sandy thanked God she wouldn't have to face the irritable old bat. She pulled open the door when the buzzer sounded and then walked downstairs in search of Ernie.

She found him in a work area fiddling with a section of pipe in a vise. When he saw her he smiled. Sandy saw in his eyes a man who was obviously not well treated by his wife and readily welcomed the smile of a friendly female.

"Ernie, and I apologize for being so informal, but I don't know your last name. Your wife buzzed me in and told me you'd be down here, but she and I were not properly introduced."

"Ernie is just fine, ah, Miss..."

"I'm sorry, my name is Sandy, Sandy Langdon." She extended her hand. "Please call me Sandy."

Ernie showed her his hands were not clean enough for shaking a lady's hand. Sandy lowered hers to her side, giving him a smile instead.

"What can I do for you, Sandy? We've got no current vacancies, although there may be one coming in the next month or so."

"I'm not here to rent an apartment, Ernie. I'm an investigator from New Orleans and I'm here inquiring into the disappearance of Janet Hopkins."

A cloud of sadness passed over Ernie's face. He shook his head.

Sandy handed him a business card. He took it and read it while obviously collecting his thoughts.

"I liked Janet," he said. "I like Marcy, too, eh. I'm not sure if Marcy will take over the apartment if Janet doesn't come back."

"I'm sorry," Sandy said. "Marcy?"

"Marcy is Janet's, ah, friend," Ernie said uncomfortably. "Girlfriend, you know."

Sandy made a mental note.

"Do you know Marcy's last name? I'd really like to talk to her."

"I think her name is Simon. See she's not on the lease, but she stayed over a fair amount, right."

"Is she staying over now?" Sandy asked. "I buzzed the apartment before yours but nobody answered."

"No, Marcy left a couple of days ago. She said she had some information on Janet and went to follow the lead."

"Do you know what kind of lead, Ernie? It's quite important if you could tell me."

Ernie told her what he knew, which to Sandy was quite a bit for a building manager. To her it seemed the man enjoyed talking to an attractive woman who paid him some courtesy and respect. She pulled out her pad and made notes as he spoke.

"Do you have a cell number for Marcy?" she asked.

Ernie reached into his back pocket and handed her a folded piece of paper. Sandy unfolded it to find a photo of a brunette woman walking from the apartment building. She recognized the photo as being from a street surveillance camera from the digital date/time and data stamp in the lower right corner. Under the photo was contact information for Marcy Simon, including her cell phone number. Sandy took down the information and then thought the document itself may be of help to her.

"May I keep this, Ernie?"

He thought for a moment and then nodded. Sandy tucked the paper into her notebook. When she felt he had relayed all he could remember and she could think of no new questions, Sandy asked if she could possibly see the apartment.

"That could be a problem, Sandy. Canada is very strict about tenants' rights, eh?"

"Your tenant is officially a Missing Person, Ernie. I'm looking for her. I'm on Janet's side here." She smiled at him. "Please, Ernie, this could be important."

He thought about it a moment or two. She continued to smile and finally she saw him nod and then he led her up to Janet's apartment. When he opened the door, he put a finger to his lips signaling her to please be quiet with his wife next door. She returned the signal with a nod. Sandy was beginning to think he was more afraid of his wife than of Canadian rental authorities.

Sandy moved about the apartment. It was small, what she'd call an efficiency unit, so it didn't take long. On the dresser was a photograph of two women. She recognized Janet from the Missing Person's site. She picked up the photo and whispered to Ernie if the other woman was Marcy. He nodded. She set down the photo and took a couple of digital pictures of it. She leaned a bit closer and whispered into Ernie's ear if the photo was representative of what Marcy looked like now. He nodded. She figured the physical closeness would buy her another few minutes of looking around.

Sandy intentionally bumped the mouse of the computer on the desk, and a few seconds later the screen came to life. She opened a few drawers in the desk. Ernie was starting to shift from foot to foot nervously. She was running out of time. She opened another drawer in the desk. On top were a number of photos, papers, and a DVD marked transit surveillance footage and dated last Saturday. Sandy peeked over her shoulder. Ernie was watching her.

Suddenly there was a racket in the hallway as a family came down the stairs. A beach ball bounced down and into the open entryway. Ernie turned to look, and that's when Sandy snatched the papers, photos and DVD from the drawer and slipped them into her notebook. By the time Ernie turned back toward her, Sandy was standing up, looking out the window and the desk drawers were all closed.

She figured her welcome was quickly running out, so she thanked Ernie, walked to the door and out into the hallway. Ernie locked the door to Janet's apartment and escorted Sandy to the street. Once outside the apartment building, Sandy asked if she could call him if she had any questions. He nodded, and then gave her his cell phone number. He held the door to her cab for her. She thanked him again and got inside. He closed the door. The cab drove away from the curb.

"Back to the airport, please," she told the driver.

Sandy pulled the papers and photos from her notebook and started to go through them. She knew there wouldn't be time to go through the DVD on the drive, so she decided to save that for the airport lounge. After that, she'd decide which direction she would be headed next.

Marcy sat on the front stoop, scratching Isabella's ears as the dog lay next to her. The funeral home had just removed Thomas' body from the house and the Coroner stood inside with Belle completing his paperwork. It was a simple case of an old man passing in his sleep, he had told them.

She heard the door being closed behind her and the Coroner walked past down the steps. He patted her shoulder as he went by. Isabella lifted her head and watched him go. Belle followed him out and sat down next to Marcy.

"I've called his sons and they will be here this afternoon to take care of things. Bobby, his youngest, told me Thomas had expressed his wish that he be cremated, his ashes placed into Angela's urn and then that they be buried together in the family plot without fanfare or ceremony."

"What now, Belle?" Marcy asked.

"What do you mean, dear?"

"What do I do now?"

Marcy felt empty inside. Lost.

"Now, you and I and this old dog are going to get into your car and drive down to see Chuck. We're going to get you that information to send you on your way and then you're going to follow that trail, just like you would have done had Thomas still been here."

Marcy looked at Belle but didn't say anything.

"Don't you dare go feeling sorry for Thomas Kincaid. He had a very full life. In the last two days, I saw more spark in that man since he lost Angela. You brought something into his life at the most important of times, when a person faces his end. He left this life not as a lonely old man pining away for his wife, but with a smile on his face and a song in his heart, and you helped put them there. The last two days reminded him that he wasn't just an old man without any purpose anymore just waiting to die. He was waiting for you. It was God's Hand."

Marcy remembered his words of yesterday afternoon about the obstacles in one's path and the gems sometimes found on the side of the road. Her eyes were again stinging and Belle wrapped an arm around Marcy.

"Are you ready to go, dear?" Belle asked. "Time's a wasting."

"You bet, Belle," she said. "Are you ready to go, Isabella?"

The dog looked up at her then popped to her feet and ran to the gate and circled. The pair of women followed. At the car, with Isabella and Belle inside, Marcy took one last look at the house that had been Thomas' home for his entire ninety years of life. She wanted to remember it always.

They drove to see Chuck.

After the introductions, Chuck brought Marcy and Belle into his office. He closed the door. Isabella sat on Belle's lap. Normally, government offices don't allow non-service animals inside, but this was Burlington and it was Thomas Kincaid's dog. They are also not normally open on Saturday's, but again, this was Burlington.

Marcy provided Chuck with the names she had from the airline. The first two names were local to Vermont and Chuck pulled up their DMV records. He swiveled the screen toward Marcy and clicked through both records. She could easily tell neither was the man in Emma's drawing.

"Okay, so Texas for three others, you said?" Chuck asked.

"That's right. Two in the Dallas area and one from Austin," Marcy said.

"You know just a few years ago we couldn't do this connecting into other state's DMV records, but with all this identity theft stuff and people obtaining government-issued ID's left and right and then skipping before the paperwork went through the systems, well, it's one thing lawmakers did right." He tapped on the keyboard, navigated screens. "Of course, that's only my humble opinion. I'm certain there are plenty of folks out there who see Big Brother around every corner these days."

"The laws are somewhat different in Canada," Marcy told him. "In some ways, it's better, in some ways worse."

"Oh, I didn't know you were from Canada. Where about?"

Marcy explained to him what was behind the inquiry, not that he had asked. When he heard the request had come through Thomas, he had gone right to work, without questioning why. Now, he was even more motivated after hearing Marcy's story.

"Okay, here we go," Chuck said, and again swiveled the screen toward Marcy.

She shook her head with each record. The man wasn't from Texas.

"One to go," Chuck said. "Let's check out the aloha state."

"I'm not even sure that's where this Alexander Hale is from," Marcy said. "All I know is that's where he went. He didn't provide an address to the airline, so he could be from anywhere."

Chuck was logging into the Hawaii DMV records and entered the name, 'Alexander Hale' and just for grins, 'Alex Hale'. One record came up under the formal name of Alexander. He pivoted the screen.

"That's him," Marcy exclaimed. She showed the drawing to Chuck. Belle was nodding.

"I think we found your man, Marcy," Chuck said. "Alexander David Hale, Lahaina, Hawaii. Five feet seven inches tall, one hundred forty pounds, brown hair, green eyes, corrective lenses required for driving. Let's see what else we can find."

Chuck logged into another database.

"See, the state of Hawaii, like most states these days, use a person's Social Security number as an identifier. Many folks aren't happy about it, but most people don't give it another thought that with that little nine-digit number, almost everything can be discovered about an individual. Bank accounts, criminal records, medical information, loans, credit cards, you name it. Take a look."

Marcy came around the desk this time and there before her on the computer screen was the life history of Alexander David Hale. There was information regarding two arrests for lewd behavior, one DUI conviction in Maryland five years ago and a short list of moving violations in several states, a schedule of insurance claims, some medical information, state licensing data, credit information. It went on and on. Marcy was shocked there was this much information cataloged to his Social Security number which could be so easily accessed.

"Could you print this out for me?" she asked. "And the DMV record with his photo?"

Chuck rocked back in his chair, thought about it. He eyed Belle, then Marcy. Belle nodded to him.

"Sure," he said. "What the hell. Just if anyone asks, you don't remember where you got it. Okay?"

"Where am I? I'm a stranger in this land, and a bit confused," Marcy joked.

Several minutes later, the trio left the DMV office and walked back to Marcy's rental car.

"Well, I guess you'll be leaving us," Belle said.

"When I can," Marcy replied. "I have to follow the trail. For Janet, and for Thomas."

They drove back to Belle's house and Marcy went onto the internet to try to find flights to Hawaii. Alex's driver's license record showed him as living on Maui, in Lahaina. He must have caught an inter-island flight home after arriving in Honolulu, Marcy thought. She found she'd be able to get out on any of the carriers this afternoon and get part of the way and then pick up in the morning, or she could book on American, Delta, or United out of Burlington in the morning and go all the way tomorrow. Marcy decided it was time to leave, so she booked online with United as far as Denver today. In the morning, she'd catch the nonstop flight out of there directly to Kahului, Maui, arriving in the early afternoon.

She booked a rental car online, and found a hotel in a place called Ka'anapali on the west side of the island, just north of Lahaina, according to the website. She could think of nothing else to be done online, so she logged off, closed her laptop and went to find Belle.

Marcy found her in Tamra's room, reading softly to the girl from an old, leather-bound book. Belle spotted Marcy at the doorway and stopped reading. She pulled a satin marker into place and closed the book.

"I do this every afternoon for about an hour," Belle said. "This month it's One Thousand and One Arabian Nights."

"I've come to thank you for everything you've done, Belle," Marcy said.

"So you're leaving today?"

"I have booked a flight as far as Denver today, then on to Maui in the morning. I'll be there tomorrow afternoon. I'm leaving now."

Belle started to get up. Marcy touched her shoulder and asked her to please stay with her granddaughter. Marcy again walked over to the bedside and whispered into Tamra's ear. She kissed the girl's forehead and smoothed her hair. Then she went and bent over by Belle and gave her a hug.

"Good luck to you, and Janet, Marcy. God go with you both."

"Good bye, Belle. Thank you, for everything."

On the way out the door, she scratched Isabella's ears.

Marcy tossed her bags into the car and retraced her steps back to the airport. As she passed by Thomas' house she didn't look. She already had its image burned into her happier memory. She waved to Emma at the American Eagle ticket counter and then felt a little bad because she had booked on United. When she saw Emma was free, she stopped by to explain the developments. Word had already spread at the airport about Thomas, Emma told her. As for using another carrier, Emma confided she sometimes did too.

An hour later, Marcy was sitting in a regional jet headed for Chicago to catch her connection to Denver.

Sandy called me while I was driving to Lahaina to catch the ferry to Molokai. She filled me in on the developments in Montreal. From Janet Hopkins' apartment, Sandy had removed a number of documents, photos and a DVD which she said contained clips of surveillance video which focused on Janet and an unidentified brunette woman.

She had a contact phone number for Janet's significant other, a Marcy Simon. Sandy had snapped a photo of a photo of the pair and had emailed it to me but I told her I hadn't seen it yet. She had also scanned the documents and emailed the video snippets as well.

She mentioned there was a desktop computer up and running in the apartment, but she had been unable to access it with the building manager hovering. Apparently, this manager, an Ernie somebody, was a bit hen-pecked and appreciated a good looking woman's attention, so I asked Sandy if it made any sense to go back and try to get a peek at the computer. She said she'd think on it a bit, but first since some the video surveillance had obviously come from the airport in Montreal that she wanted to check in with the chief of security. She had already called the office and was told that he was out to lunch and would be back shortly.

I wheeled the Jeep into a parking spot at the Lahaina harbor, paid for parking, asked Sandy to please stay out of a Canadian jail, disconnected, and then walked down to the ferry dock.

The ferry was boarding as I arrived. The boat was about one-hundred feet long and looked seaworthy enough, but I am no fan of either boats or water. I showed them the online ticket receipt and climbed aboard. I found a seat inside the cabin area, after helping myself to a bit of fruit they had to offer and grabbing a can of Coke which cost four dollars.

Several minutes later, we pushed away from the dock and navigated the short distance out of the small harbor area toward the open channel. The internet site advised the trip would take about an hour and a half, and that's just what the Captain said over the loudspeaker. As the water started splashing the windows and we bumped up against a repetitive wave flow, I began to hope both the website and the Captain were overstating the time. The sooner the better as far as this passenger was concerned.

To take my mind off of drowning, I pulled out the papers and reviewed the information on Molokai, Jennifer Shea's house, the car rental reservation, anything that kept me from looking outside. By the end of the ninety minutes, I was reading the ingredients in Coke. Phosphoric acid? Really?

Finally, we docked in Kaunakakai, on the south shore about the middle of the island. It's the largest city on Molokai and has a population of under three thousand people. The problem, as I saw it, was the dock was located on what they call Pier Island, nineteen hundred feet offshore. A roadway connected the dock to the island.

When I stepped off the boat, I saw a gentleman from my rental car company holding a sign with my name on it. Considering the fact that he was out on the pier, and had obviously driven the car out there along that road, I estimated my chances of getting to shore without getting wet were better than fifty-fifty, so I got in and let him drive me to solid land.

After some paperwork, I drove off in an older and slightly worn Jeep Cherokee. I started off heading west on highway 460 toward the town of Maunaloa. Before getting there, I veered off to the north and headed to the west shore. I had been told that once I saw the signs to the Papohaku Beach Park, I'd be getting close.

Surprisingly, I only had to turn around twice after missing the turn I wanted, and forty minutes after leaving the rental car place, I arrived at the drive to Jennifer Shea's house. The home was large, by island and even mainland standards, but much smaller than Cassie's place, and appeared to be all contained on one floor. To the north stretched Papohaku Beach, to the south a craggy, black, lava shoreline. From the looks of it, there were other lots in this parcel of land, but not many had been developed.

I drove the Jeep onto the private drive, pulled up under a large portico built of stone and timbers, parked and shut off the engine. I always pause in the vehicle for a minute or two in a situation like this, so the occupants of the house can become aware of me, and sometimes to give them time to get the wrong idea.

The door opened as I was about to get out of the Jeep. A smallish man stood there looking at me like I had just landed from another planet. Apparently, they don't get much traffic out this way.

"Hey," I said, affecting a generic Texas accent. "I'm John Portman, Houston, Texas, and I'm looking for Miss Jennifer Shea. I saw she was going to be having an exhibition of her art in San Francisco in a couple of weeks and since I was in the islands this week and I'm unfortunately going to be in Hong Kong during her show, I thought I'd drop by. I got directions, don't ask me how, or the person who gave them to me said he'd have to kill me, but couldn't find a number to call. Most likely you folks just use cell phones. That makes sense. You know, I've seen some of her previews online and really like her real life work, so, um, is she perhaps here?"

He looked like he had been steamrolled. Which, is exactly what I hoped for when I used the John Portman persona. Chatty Texan. Sober as a judge. Some would say my alter-ego. I always envision Jim Rockford when I'm channeling Portman.

"Ah, yeah, she's here," he said, a little overwhelmed, but he recovered quickly. "Would you like to come in, Mr. Portman?"

I moved through the doorway like a west Texas wind - whatever that means - and stuck out my hand to the little feller.

"Please, I'd be mighty obliged if you just call me John," I said.

He shook my hand. A limp, feminine grip in my big paw. I tried not to hurt him. I dropped my shoes at the door.

"Okay, John. I'm Alex, a friend of Jennifer's," he said and lead the way inside. "Jennifer's been in her studio since sun up this morning working on a new piece, so I'll announce you, if you don't mind."

He offered me a place to sit in a central great room. I told him I'd stretch my legs around the room if he didn't mind. He didn't. I watched him disappear down the hall to the left and enter a room toward the end of the wing. I heard the door close. Doing what I said I'd be doing just in case anyone was watching, I wandered around the great room, peeked outside at the view and generally took in a lay of the land.

"She'd be happy to see you, John," he said.

Man, he was quiet. I never heard him coming. I walked toward the studio wing of the house and Alex directed me down to the last door on the right. Since there were no doors on the left, I kinda figured it would be on the right, but perhaps he didn't want me walking straight out because there was a door on the end of the hall.

I knocked lightly on the open door and then walked in and met Jennifer Shea. She was beautiful with sparkling brown eyes, possessed a shapely, feminine body with long legs and small feet. Her toenails were painted bright red while her fingernails were bare and smeared with acrylic paint. Her chestnut hair was held back in a pony tail with a yellow elastic band. She was Cassie in her twenties, although the information we had put her at thirty this year. Had I to guess, she must have thought I was staring at her like she had just landed from another planet.

"Jennifer Shea," she said.   "Don't worry about the paint, whatever is still there is dry." She wiped her hand on an apron, and extended it to me.

I took her hand and shook it. Her grip was firm and confident, much stronger than the little guy's had been.

"John Portman, ma'am," I said. "It's such a pleasure to meet you. Thank you for taking the time to greet a new fan of your work." I noted over her shoulder a painting with a mother and young child at the shoreline. I pointed and walked past her. "Now that's what I'm talking about. You capture real life better than anyone I have ever seen."

"Why, thank you, Mr. Portman."

"I told that Alex to just call me John and that invite certainly applies to you, little lady."

"All right, John, so long as we're all on a first name basis. Call me Jennifer."

She gave me a tour of her hanging work, including the interesting transpositional landscape in acrylics she was working on, said many items had already been crated for shipping to the show in San Francisco, and then said she was jut about to take a break and asked if I'd like something to drink.

We walked down the hall to the great room. She offered iced tea and I accepted. Alex was nowhere to be seen. She then asked if I wanted to sit outside by the pool. Frankly, it would be hard for any man to resist following Jennifer Shea anywhere, so I told her where she led I'd follow. We moved outside and took places at the table under a green and white striped umbrella.   The chairs were remarkably comfortable and I said so. The wind had started to pick up. I was learning it was a daily cycle on the islands. The umbrella was flapping noisily, so we spoke up a little louder than normal.

"Lovely place you have here, Jennifer," I said. "A long way from east Texas."

"Have you ever been there?" she asked.

"Where?" I asked. Oh-oh, I thought.

"east Texas?"

"Why, I was born and raised in Houston, darlin'," I said in a last ditch effort to maintain the cover.

I watched a huge smile show up on her face.

"John, if that is your name, regardless of what you have heard in high school lore, you can't fool a girl from east Texas." She looked at me like it would be okay to tell her the truth. She sipped her tea and waited.

So I did. I explained to her that the affectation had been a last minute decision and done to mainly throw Alex off balance. I told her who I was, where I was from and most of why I was there. Yeah, I said, most. She took it all in and didn't seem phased by any part of the story. As to her involvement on the list, I explained that there had been some disappearances which went back years and I was mainly there to make sure she was still safe and well. I told her that we tracked her down through the art gallery ad, otherwise we may still be trying to identify her. I left out the name of my client, and her husband, but I took it from her facial expression that she may have guessed. Finally, I told her there were holes which I could to fill in if she wanted. When I was done, I sipped my tea. And waited.

It didn't take long.

"Mr. Langdon, I appreciate your efforts," she said. "I truly do. As you can see, I am safe and well. I have never had an affair with any married men, nor do I intend to. My benefactor is a wealthy man who, I learned recently, had some connection years ago to my bio-mom. While he hasn't said it in so many words, I assume he took me under his wing because of that connection. See, I was adopted when I was born and have never met my bio-mom or bio-dad. My adoptive parents, Bruce and Elisa Shea were my mom and dad. They passed away in a house fire a little over a year ago. Shortly after, I met my benefactor while working in an art gallery in Chicago and he offered me this house, his financial assistance, and help to build my career as an artist. He has never crossed any unethical lines or done anything which could be construed as being out of context to the relationship I describe. It was during the trip home from San Francisco recently that he told me about my bio-mom and frankly, I think it embarrassed him to admit there was even that hint of an ulterior motive. He went out of his way to assure me it was my artistic talent which drew him to me."

She had filled in a number of holes. Combined with what I already knew, and added to the simple observations I made, I had a fairly well-paved road laid out in front of me. There was one big question which lingered: Why would Cassie put Jennifer's name on the list of potential mistresses? Could it be that she didn't know this younger version of herself even existed so close to her world?

Whatever the answer to that question, it was up to Cassie to decide how to continue. I quickly decided it was not my job to broach the subject of her bio-mom to Jennifer. Whatever I had intended to learn by visiting with Ms. Shea, I had accomplished, and more. So, I drank the rest of my iced tea and prepared to leave.

"I apologize again for the ruse, Jennifer," I said. "Your hospitality and understanding are truly appreciated. I really do like your art, by the way."

"Well, obviously you have an eye for talented artists, so hopefully your trip wasn't a total waste of your time," she said. "By the way, no apologies needed. Alex is a good friend and a good soul, but he can be excessively protective. Your ruse, as you called it, was most likely just what was needed to get in to see me today."

"I'd better get back to the ferry," I said. "I think I've taken up enough of your time."

We walked out to the Jeep. Alex was still MIA, so I asked Jennifer to keep my secret. She agreed it was probably best. I slipped her my business card and asked that if anything unusual developed she give me a call. She agreed to that as well. Finally, I asked her if she ever wanted to meet her bio-mom. She admitted that it had been increasingly on her mind since her benefactor had told her the connection, but she still hadn't made the final decision. Nothing for nothing, but I told her that whatever decision she made, it would be the right decision for her.

I drove back to the harbor.

After he heard the Jeep roll out the drive, Alex placed a call to Gregory to report that some fast-talking Texan by the name of John Portman had stopped by out of the blue wanting to see Jennifer. He transmitted the entire line laid out by William's alter ego.

Gregory pulled up the cameras at the Molokai house but saw nobody but Jennifer walking into her studio and Alex sitting in his room. The outside cameras showed no vehicle under the portico.

"Why didn't you call me immediately?" Gregory scolded.

"Because I took a shower and when I got out, he was gone," replied Alex. "How was I supposed to know it was so important?"

Gregory hung up the phone. Alex was getting on his nerves. He watched as Alex figured out the line was dead, flipped the phone the bird, tossed it onto the bed and then walked back into his bathroom.

Gregory let loose a derisive snort and then pulled up the stored footage from the Molokai house. He watched the old Jeep pull under the portico and saw Alex open the door. As he watched William Langdon get out of the Jeep and walk into the house, he felt his blood coming to a boil. He slammed his fist into the desk and even though it was not yet time for the next session, descended into the lava tube.

Chapter Nineteen

Sandy finally reached the Montreal airport's head of security in the mid-afternoon. Kevin Bastian agreed to meet with her only after she mentioned Janet Hopkins and Marcy Simon. She could hear concern in his voice, but when she told him that she was from the United States that concern seemed to dissipate a bit. At least that's the way Sandy heard it in the conversation and it made her suspect Kevin was the source of much, if not all, of the video clips she found in Janet's apartment.

She was surprised when she saw him. He was a diminutive man, shorter than her by about two inches. She also noted that he carried himself with confidence, displayed an easy smile and returned a strong handshake. She handed him a business card. Sandy had determined from their phone conversation to approach this in a strict business manner and give him as little information as possible. She certainly could not tell him she had stolen the DVD and other papers from Janet's desk.

"Mr. Bastian," she said. "I am honored you have seen fit to see me."

"Not at all, Ms. Langdon," he replied. "We work closely with investigative agencies, both governmental and private."

He looked over her card. Handed her one of his.

"You mentioned this had something to do with a Janet Hopkins and Marcy Simon," he said. "I want you to know that they are both acquaintances of mine and I am certain you already know that Janet Hopkins has been missing for nearly a week now. Anything you and

I can do together to help bring her home will be welcome on both the professional and personal fronts."

"That's our goal, Mr. Bastian, to help. We are not interested in interfering with, or, God forbid, impeding any official investigation."

"Have you spoken to Marcy Simon?" he asked.

"No, I have not. I only obtained her information several hours ago and I know she is traveling and doing her own investigation. I have no interest in drawing her attention from that trail unnecessarily. However, we also have investigative resources in place in this case."

"And your client?" he asked.

"Confidential," she replied. "However, I can tell you that our client is unrelated to Janet Hopkins and only seeks to speak with her regarding a civil matter, should she be missing of her own volition."

"From what little I know, Janet has not gone missing voluntarily. For any reason."

Enough for the volleying, Sandy thought. Time to serve the ace.

"We have information regarding certain video surveillance which may exist and which may show both the arrival in Montreal of Janet Hopkins last week early Saturday and the departure from Montreal of a woman of interest later that morning."

Kevin maintained a poker face, but Sandy had seen people crack on the witness stand and in depositions, and she saw something pass through Kevin's mind which confirmed what she suspected.

"Is that so," he said. "You came upon this knowledge how?"

"It really does not matter how, but suffice it to say we do know this material exists."

He thought for a moment. An expression of resigned resolve came to his face.

"Let's cut the crap, shall we, Ms. Langdon? Do you have a copy of the DVD I gave to Marcy? I don't care where you got it or how you got it, all I want to know is can you help in finding Janet."

"Yes, we have it. Frankly, Mr. Bastian, we don't care how Marcy got it or who gave it to her or whether it was legal or not, our only goal is to locate a happy and healthy Janet Hopkins and bring her home."

"Then we're both on the same page. What else can I do to help you?"

"Where is Marcy headed?"

"Burlington, Vermont.   To find a woman named Tamra Sommers. That's the last I heard from her."

"Who is this Tamra Sommers?"

"That's the name we found for the woman of interest."

"What's the fastest way to Burlington?"

"Rent a car and drive. It's about one-hundred-fifty kilometers, a little more than ninety miles. Take you less than two hours to get there."

She closed up her notebook and stuffed it into her computer bag.

"Don't you think you want to put Marcy into the loop?" he asked.

"I'm thinking Marcy is already ahead of the loop. I don't want to slow her down."

She offered her hand to him and he shook it.

"Please feel free to call me should something come up," Sandy said. "Please, don't tell Marcy someone is following behind her. I think her eyes should be looking forward, not over her shoulder."

He appeared to consider that last statement.

"I think you're right.   I'll maintain the confidence unless something drastically changes."

"Okay, now which way to the rental cars?"

"I'll walk you," he said.

Twenty minutes later, Sandy was driving out of Montreal, headed south for Vermont.

The lights came on and the locks disengaged at the same instant. Cassie jumped and covered her eyes. This was way too soon, she thought. In an instant he was inside the room and he left the door open behind him.

"Who the fuck is William Langdon and what is he doing in my life?" he screamed at her.

"I told you, Gregory, an old friend whom I ran into several days ago."

"Don't fucking lie to me, Cassandra or I'll kill you before you draw your next breath."

She could see his face was flushed, the arteries in his neck were pulsating heavily, and his fists were clenched. This was genuine rage. It was not part of the process. Her mind raced. She wondered what the hell had happened to precipitate this questioning. She knew the other day that William had annoyed him at the house, and Gregory had told her that he stopped in at William's condo to shake him up a bit, but he had remained in control when he had told her. What had changed, she thought. Whatever it was, she decided that deflection was the best course of action to save her from his wrath.

"I would not lie to you, Gregory," she soothed. "You know you can trust me implicitly. Whatever William is doing to you has nothing to do with me."

He stared at her. She could sense his tension ease a bit. At least his rage toward her was ebbing. Her heart was pounding in her chest.

He pointed a finger in her direction and when he spoke, it was in a tone she had heard before and she knew what he said was not a mere threat; he would make it happen.

"The next time I see that son of a bitch William Langdon, I swear on my mother's grave that I am going to kill him."

He turned and walked out. He slammed the door, hard, and she jumped in reaction. She heard the locks close and then the lights went out. Cassie sat in the dark, covered only by the sheet and even though it was not too cool in the room, she began to shake. It was the first time she truly thought she might fail.

I called Sandy from the ferry on the way back to Maui. I was surprised to hear she had left Montreal by car and was closing in on Burlington, Vermont. We each filled in the other on the recent developments and then her trip into maple syrup country all made perfect sense. I wasn't sure it would be a good idea for her to run into Marcy Simon, but there wasn't any reason to worry about it, I told her. We were now making up the script as we moved along.

There were too many ears on the ferry to go into too much of a discussion of specifics about where things stood, but we agreed to speak before the end of the day, Sandy's time, and thoroughly review where we were at.

After hanging up with Sandy, I considered giving Keoki a call to see if anything was happening and then thought better about it knowing if something had happened at the property, he would have called.

I bought another four dollar Coke and took a seat toward the center of the boat. The ride was a bit choppier than it had been this morning. Rather than focus on the waves and water - and the odds I would drown on this crossing - I sat and closed my eyes and reviewed the case. In terms of finding evidence of adulterous behavior by Gregory, we were running pretty much at zero. Cassie hadn't been totally honest with me and that had made me conclude the real motive of her hiring us was still her little secret. I was beginning to get annoyed.

Jennifer Shea had been totally believable regarding her relationship with Gregory even though she never once mentioned his name. Gregory obviously knew of the connection between Cassie and Jennifer. Why else would he be so generous to a total stranger?

Cassie has a baby. She gives it up for adoption, finishes school and goes on with her life. A married couple in Texas adopts the baby girl who grows up to be Jennifer Shea. Somehow Gregory finds out about the child, tracks the family down and then what, takes the woman under his wing? Jennifer said he came into her life about a year ago, shortly after the accidental death of her parents in a house fire. Could all that have been some sort of set up? Could Gregory have had something to do with the fire? Did Cassie know Jennifer was on Molokai? Is that how Jennifer Shea ended up on the list of potential mistresses?

If Cassie knew about Jennifer's presence so close at hand, and did know she was her child, why would she want me to find Jennifer as a potential mistress? If Cassie did not know who Jennifer was, then perhaps she just wanted me to find out the truth of the situation for her. Maybe she really did believe Jennifer was a mistress to Gregory.

What about the missing persons? How did they go missing? Can they be traced back to Gregory and if not, how did they wind up on Cassie's list and how is it the journal passages seemingly lined up with these particular women? My cop sense told me that Gregory Thomason was most likely involved in the disappearances, but I can't quite figure how he did it and I sure as hell can't prove it. Sure, he had the means a million times over, but what would his motive be? To keep them quiet? He had more than enough money to pay them off. There would be no reason to risk a prison term just to muzzle a woman who polished your knob for a while, especially given the amateurish construction of this so-called prenuptial agreement.

That leads to the question of the timing in the execution of the agreement. Who would draft and sign a prenup five years into the marriage? Was there a predicating factor? Since Cassie would theoretically benefit from the document more than Gregory ever could, did she hold something over his head then? If so, what was it?

My head was beginning to throb with all the unanswered questions. It seems the more we dug around here, the more duplicity we uncovered and the only thing we harvested was a bumper crop of more questions. Then there was the biggest question of all: Do we have anything here that the cops should know about?

The next thing I knew, the boat bumped the dock and I was startled back to reality. I grabbed my Coke and disembarked with the rest of the passengers. Before I went back to Kihei, I walked up the block to the ice cream store I had seen this morning and bought a dish of white chocolate macadamia. Having mentioned it to Gregory the other day had given me a craving. I walked across the street and sat in the shade of a huge banyan tree to eat the ice cream and consider what to do next.

Sandy drove into the small town of Burlington about the same time Marcy departed for Chicago, the coincidence unbeknownst to either woman. En route, Sandy had obtained an address for Tamra Sommers and driving directions off the highway to the home.

As she drove up and parked in front of the house, Sandy wasn't certain what to expect and had no plan on how to play it, so she decided the best thing to do would be to drop any pretext and just be friendly, non-threatening, and as honest as possible. She was just asking questions to follow up on a case. She checked her hair and makeup in the rear view mirror and stepped out of the car. The change from the air conditioned vehicle to the hot and muggy weather hit her, but she pasted a smile on her face and walked up to the door and knocked.

A few moments later, a grandmotherly figure in a summer house dress and antique hairstyle responded to the knocking. She was accompanied by a small brown dog which yipped and yapped at Sandy until the woman told her it was all right. Apparently the dog's name was Isabella.

"Yes?" the woman said. She flashed Sandy a wary smile.

"Hello," Sandy began, returning the smile. "I really hate to bother you but I'm a looking for Tamra Sommers."

"Tamra?" the old woman repeated. "May I ask who you are, dear, and why you wish to see my granddaughter?"

Sandy began to explain who she was and why she was at the door asking to see the woman's granddaughter. Midway through the explanation, the old woman asked if Sandy would like to come in out of the heat and Sandy was grateful for the invitation inside. The elderly woman led Sandy to the kitchen, offered her a glass of water which Sandy accepted and then she finished the story.

"Are you a friend of Marcy, dear?" the old woman asked.

Sandy considered the question a moment and decided quickly it would do no good to lie.

"No, in truth, Marcy and I have never met. We are working for the same goal, though, and that is to find Janet Hopkins." Sandy saw the woman did not seem fully convinced so she added: "We are working for a client and Marcy is working for personal reasons, but my firm is dedicated to getting to the bottom of this just as much as Marcy is."

Sandy sipped her water and waited. The woman stood up, pulled a dog biscuit from a bag on the counter and gave it to Isabella. She came back to the table and sat down again. Sandy realized the chore gave the woman a moment to come to a decision.

The old woman, who Sandy now learned was named Belle, then told in great detail the story of the last two days and how Marcy had left just this afternoon on a flight to follow a lead. Belle talked of Thomas Kincaid, the investigation Marcy and he had conducted, the help from Chuck this morning, and finally the story of Tamra's accident. When she finished, Belle took Sandy upstairs to see the girl.

They returned to the kitchen a few minutes later. Sandy asked Belle if she could ask her some questions and take some notes. Belle nodded and Sandy pulled out her notebook. She stuffed the papers from Janet's desk into the side flap and flipped pages on the tablet to a new sheet. When she looked up, Sandy noticed Belle was looking toward the photos Sandy had tucked away. Sandy pulled them out and laid them on the vinyl tablecloth.

"Have you seen these before, Belle?" Sandy asked. Sandy felt it best to show Belle she was being totally honest with her, and besides, if they were the same ones Marcy had used, all the better to reinforce the working toward the same goals theme.

"Of course, dear," Belle said as she shifted through the several pages of photos. "Marcy had the same exact ones."

Belle smiled like the Cheshire Cat as she looked at one of the photos of the woman of interest, the brunette who left the apartment building after Janet had come home.

"What is it, Belle?" Sandy asked. She was certain now the old woman was holding back some details. "Something you forgot to tell me?"

"Well, yes, dear," Belle said with a hint of apology in her voice. "I did hold a thing or two back, just in case you were not who you said you were."

Sandy waited, her pen poised above the tablet.

"You see this photo here?" Belle said tapping with her finger.

Sandy noted Belle was pointing to the full face shot of the brunette, obviously taken in the Metro train. It was the best identifiable photo they had of the woman.

Sandy nodded.

"Well, it's one of the things I omitted before, and I apologize for not being fully honest, but you understand, don't you?"

Sandy nodded again.

"Of course, Bell, perfectly understandable."

"This isn't a woman, you know," Belle said.

"It's not?"

Sandy wondered if the woman was a little senile. This was clearly a photograph of a woman.

"No, dear, it's a man."

Belle took in the look on her face and laughed as Sandy picked up the photo and held it close to pick up details.

"It struck us with a bit of surprise as well," Belle said. "Thomas had said he'd run into a few of those types while on shore leave when he was with the Navy during the Second World War, but not a single one of them had ever looked so good."

Sandy studied the photos, looked for telltales like an Adams Apple, the size of the hands, the hair on the arms, the size and shape of the feet.   Nothing.   This was one feminine man, if Belle was correct.

"His name is something Hardy, no, Hale, Mr. Hale," Belle added. "Lives in Hawaii."

My cellphone rang during the drive back to the condo. The plan was to check my email from Sandy and then pick up some beer and drive over to sit with Keoki and stare at Cassie's house hoping either she'd show or Gregory would decide to decamp for a while.   I realized both were long shots, but I was beginning to get really worried about Cassie and short of going up to the door and knocking, I was running out of ideas.

I fished the phone from my pocket and found a very excited Sandy on the other end of the line.

"Otto, you're not going to believe this," she said instead of hello. "Have you seen my emails of the Montreal stuff yet?"

"No, I'm about fifteen minutes away from the condo right now, but the plan is to go through your stuff right away."

"Do that, and then give me a call.   I've got something that's going to blow you away."

"Where are you now?" I asked.   I realized asking for the information now would be fruitless. Sandy obviously wanted me to be looking at something before she spilled it.

"Sitting in my rental car outside of Tamra Sommers' grandmother's house."

I told Sandy I'd get back to her shortly.   She told me she was headed to a motel recommended by some woman named Belle, whom I assumed was the grandmother.   We clicked off, and I accelerated a little around the big curve just before the Kealia pond, which was expansive, but dry as a bone.

Fourteen minutes later, I walked into the condo. First I made a comfort stop, and then I grabbed a Coke from the fridge. Finally, I opened my laptop and pulled down the email. Along with a number from Sandy, most of which contained large video files, there was one from the Cheyenne PD, and one from the Des Moines Police Department. I opened those first, skimmed through the email and the attachments and found mostly what I had suspected.

Tammy Boeldt of Cheyenne, Wyoming went missing from her place of employment on the first day back at work following her vacation nine years ago and hasn't been seen since. Her car was found parked in the lot before the start of her shift, but no Tammy.

The physical description fit the profile, good looking, brunette, twenty-five, five-foot-six, one hundred twenty pounds, brown eyes. The photo on the Missing Person's flyer was just the final proof that our guy was sticking to his taste. Cheyenne PD included the cold case file with few redactions.

Des Moines confirmed that Randi Janzen was a still an open Missing Person's case from four years ago. She had been reported missing by her parents after they had been called by her employer, Northwest Airlines. According to the report, Randi had been scheduled for a three-day trip and failed to show. After leaving numerous messages on her cell and home phones, the airline had called her emergency number and raised her parents in Council Bluffs, Iowa a week later.

Police checked her apartment and found her uniform laid out on the bed, her bag packed for what appeared to be a work trip, and employee travel tickets to Minneapolis for the commute to the scheduled trip made out in her purse. It was like she was all ready to go and then simply vanished.

I.D. photos showed an attractive brunette with shoulder length hair and brown eyes. The police report contained the physical description from DMV records. Five-eight, one-thirty-five, no corrective lenses. Randi, too, fit the profile. I wondered how many more we'd uncover and how we could tie them to Gregory. Hell, even if most of these women *were* on the same island as our boy, it didn't connect them beyond some cryptic scribblings in a diary which we didn't even know for certain he had authored. The link was so tenuous as it stood that a first year law student could get Gregory off. We needed more.

I went through Sandy's photos and information from Montreal. Then I called her.

"I'm going through things," I said. "Did you see the stuff from Cheyenne and Des Moines?"

"Yeah, going through that now," she reported. "Like deja vu all over again as Yogi Berra used to say. What do you think is going on?"

"I've got some ideas, Sandy, but for now I want to keep them to myself and let you also draw conclusions without me influencing your thinking. I'm certain we're going to come to the same endpoint."

"I'm having trouble tying it all back to our boy," she said. "I'm also really having trouble with the 'Why you?' question."

"So what's this information you think is going to blow me away?" I asked.

"Pull up the scan number 0722939 and take a look at the woman."

I located the file and put it up full-screen. It was a full face shot of the woman of interest from Montreal. I told Sandy I had it.

"Attractive lady, eh?" she said.

"Yeah, real pretty. Much more our guy's type than Janet Hopkins. Except for the gorgeous green eyes, that is."

"It's a dude."

I didn't think I heard her right, so in my best etiquette I asked her to kindly repeat what she had just said.

"Huh?"

"Otto, it's a guy in drag," she said. Last name, Hale. H-A-L-E. I don't have a first name."

"Who told you this was a guy?" I asked. I zoomed around the picture and then opened others in sequence which showed body shots and looked for clues leading to the conclusion this person was an XY and not a XX. I didn't see it.

"Belle said some agent who was an art major in college worked at the airport and looked at the photo of the woman and redid it into a guy."

"Belle is Tamra Sommers' grandmother?"

"Yeah, and friend of Thomas Kincaid, now deceased."

"The paint with light guy is dead?" I asked incredulously.

"No, a different Thomas Kincaid."

"Why don't you just start from the beginning and bring me up to speed? It'll save time, I think."

Sandy went through the Burlington chapter of the story from beginning to end, including the sad tales of Tamra Sommers and Thomas Kincaid. I listened, took a few notes, but kept returning to the photo of the stunning brunette. The more I looked, the more it haunted me. There was something familiar about it, but I couldn't put my finger on it.

When she had finished, I had a few more questions. Sandy had some of the answers; others were obviously destined to remain questions for a while longer.

At this point, Sandy was going to stay overnight in Burlington and then decide where to go next, if anywhere. I packed up my computer, made sure I had that little cellular internet device Sandy had given me before I left New Orleans and headed out. In the parking lot, I ran into Steve from upstairs.

"Hey, remember the other night during the All Star game when you were talking about this place you're watching and the intruder stuff they had on the perimeter of the property?"

I looked at him and wondered where this was going, but still answered yes. He continued.

"Well, I happened to be chatting with an old buddy of mine online the other day, and he has a son who's a Navy Seal. Long story short, his son tells him about how they sometimes defeat strong perimeter defenses in assaults. You do like the Germans did during World War II with the French Maginot Line, you go around. Or in the case of a full perimeter defense, you drop in behind the lines. Simple. They can't shoot at you if you're behind them, right?"

"Parachute, Steve?"

"Yeah, avoid the defenses."

"Thanks, I'll keep it in mind," I said. "Hey, where can I buy a bunch of beer cheap?"

"Planning a party?" he asked.

"No, paying a debt," I replied.

"Kihei Liquors, just off Kihei Road on the opposite end of the building from the Cafe O'Lei. It's where the locals go."

I thanked him again, tossed my duffel and computer bag into the car and drove out the gate.

"Parachute in, simple," I said to myself with a chuckle. "Yeah, right." Then something else he said struck me: 'Go around...'

Marcy arrived in Denver and took a courtesy shuttle to a motel as near the airport as possible. Once checked into her room, she scoped out some businesses in the yellow pages and then called a cab to take her around to run some errands. She had a few things to buy before flying out to Maui in the morning.

Her first stop was local Wal-Mart where she picked up a small backpack, duct tape, and some quarter-inch nylon rope, and some other things. Next stop was a police supply store where she picked up a set of handcuffs and a couple items she hoped would make it through security. Finally, she stopped at an Office Max and picked up a digital recorder, remote microphone, and some extra batteries.

On the way back to the motel, she persuaded the driver to pull into the Popeye's Chicken drive through where she bought a meal for herself and one for him. In her room a short time later, she ate, and then packed the items in her bag she knew she'd have to check in the morning. She figured that unless Ray Charles was working the x-ray machine at security, there would be no way she got through with that stuff in her carry on.

An hour later, she tried to get some sleep.

Just as she was dozing off, her cell phone rang. She didn't recognize the number in the caller I.D., but she answered it anyway.

"Marcy, it's Belle, dear," came the voice. "I hope it's not too late by you."

"Of course not, Belle, so good to hear your voice. Is everything all right?"

"Oh, I do hope so, dear. You see, there was a woman who showed up at the house after you left today. A very nice woman by the name of, oh now where's her card again, yes, here it is, Sandy Langdon of William Langdon Investigations of New Orleans."

"Okay," Marcy said, wondering where this was coming from and where it was going.

"Well, she said they had been hired by a client whom she refused to name to help find Janet. Since she had the same photos as you do, I thought you were working with her, so I gave her much of the information you had turned up here in Burlington. Much of it, but not all of it."

"You say this woman, this Sandy person..."

"Langdon, dear, Sandy Langdon."

"Okay, this Sandy Langdon works for a private detective agency from New Orleans and showed you the same photos that I have from the surveillance tapes?"

"They certainly appeared to be the same, dear," Belle said. "Oh my, I hope I didn't do anything wrong. I was sitting here thinking about it after she left, and she seemed so nice, so concerned, and she knew so much about Janet. I was hoping she could help. I do hope I didn't do anything wrong," she repeated.

"I'm certain you did nothing wrong, Belle. Please don't worry yourself about it." Marcy thought about who may have hired a private detective and why did they go all the way to New Orleans to do it? Janet's parents? They're from Calgary. She had no immediate answers for any of the questions. "I do appreciate you letting me know, Belle."

Marcy asked Belle to read the business card information to her and she copied it all down. After again assuring Belle she had done nothing wrong, they hung up and then she opened her laptop and went online. Yes, there was indeed a William Langdon Investigations firm in New Orleans and it appeared to be staffed by a husband and wife team. Marcy looked at the photos of the Langdon's and Belle was correct, Sandy did look like a nice lady.

Marcy thought about trying to get back to sleep but knew it would be pointless. Her mind was buzzing and she debated the urge to call Sandy Langdon's cell phone and ask her directly what was going on, what her involvement was. How did she get the same photos? Had she spoken to Kevin? Who was her client? She ultimately decided it really didn't matter, that was looking back and she needed to be looking forward. Tomorrow was a big day.

The first order of business upon arriving in Maui would be to find Alexander David Hale of Lahaina. Her plan was to then get him alone and do whatever she needed to do to find out what happened to Janet. To accomplish that, she didn't need another set of eyes too close. For now, Marcy concluded the further behind her Sandy Langdon was, the better.

I drove through Kahului and connected to the upper road which took me toward Kula and Ulapalakua and then to Keoki's place. Two cases of beer rode along in the back seat. My operations duffel was on the floor in front of the passenger seat. I wore long pants this afternoon and that meant both Willie and Sam were where they should be.

Passing Oprah's place, I made a call to the cell phone I had given Keoki. He answered on the first ring and said all was quiet at Cassie's house. He reported that he'd neither seen them outside the house nor had either of them left the property, unless, he said, they may have left while he was sleeping, but he doubted that. He said he'd have heard any vehicles. I believed him.

Since there was daylight left, and would still be by the time I got out there, Keoki had me describe the area where I had waited out the sun yesterday and said to park the Jeep there and he'd come get me in his car. Having not seen a car on his property, I asked him if he was sure that would work. He said it would. I believed him again.

Forty minutes later, I was pulling into the cow pasture. I parked the car under the same trees, grabbed my duffel, opened the back door and pulled out the cases of beer. I heard a diesel engine and the sound of tires. I peered out of the trees thinking I'd find a curious rancher, only to see Keoki sitting behind the wheel of a relatively new midnight blue Mercedes.

He popped the trunk from the driver's seat and I put the duffel and beer inside, then I climbed into the rear seat at his direction.

"You lay down until we in," he said. "Dat way, he no can see."

I did as instructed. On the five mile drive back to his place, Keoki explained he had saved a little of the money he got from Gregory and Cassie for the land and had bought the car. He drove the road slowly, carefully avoiding the worst of the potholes, treating the Mercedes like his seventh keiki. Eventually, we pulled up his driveway and around back of the house into a brand new garage which can't be seen from the road.

"Okay, Malihini, you get out now, go in da house, stay inside. I put da beer on ice, sit outside alone till dark," he said.

I followed him inside his small house, which was as ramshackle inside as it was out, save the plasma television hung on one wall and if not for that television, I thought I would rather live in the garage with the Mercedes. He brushed off an old wooden chair for me and I took a seat near a window, refused a beer, and then watched him go outside, bury a number of cans deep into the ice chest, crack one and take up his regular station.

The rest of the afternoon passed into evening without any movement at the Thomason place. In the darkened house, I pulled out the parabolic mic and tried for another pick up noise from within the house. Nothing. The cellular scanner flashed and flashed, locked once on conversation by locals talking so fast and clipped that I couldn't pick out a word. Keoki laughed as they spoke.

"Paca lolo," he said with a snort. He took a long drink to drain the last of the beer, crushed the can and pulled another. "Maui wowie, marijuana," he translated for me.

That was the limit of our excitement until shortly after the sun was gone. From our vantage point on the mountain, the summer sun had passed behind the mountain an hour earlier, but we knew it had sunk into the ocean when the darkness came to replace the shadow.

At a little past seven fifteen, one of the garage doors opened on the house, a light came on and one person entered the driver's seat of the yellow Corvette Gregory had driven to my condo a couple of days ago. I searched for the night vision goggles, turned on the infrared mode and could make out only one form inside the car. When the engine started, it heated quickly and flashed the infrared, so I switched back to normal night vision and watched as Gregory drove up and out the driveway. He made the left turn onto the main road and drove off much faster than Keoki had navigated it. From the straight line of the tail lights, I doubted Gregory took much notice of the potholes.

I walked out onto the porch, the change of temperature was noticeable and I wiped my arm across my brow. The house had been stifling, even near the open windows.

"You tink of going in, brah?" Keoki asked.

"That's what I'm thinking, Keoki," I replied. "Any ideas?"

"Crooks break in, Malihini, I tink you walk right in da front door."

"That's what I was thinking."

I pulled out my cell and tried Cassie's number. No answer, right to voice mail which meant the phone was either off or out of range. Next I changed into a black coverall and pulled on a black cotton stocking cap which covered my head and face. Keoki watched as I grabbed some things from the duffel and after I slipped on a black Velcro belt, stuck some of the items onto it. I looked like a middle aged, slightly paunchy ninja. For some reason, Keoki must have thought so to because he stifled a laugh.

Double checking that my phone was set to vibrate, I told Keoki to call me with his cell phone if he spotted Gregory coming back to the house. I set off across the road and approached the gate. I pulled the radio frequency repeater - essentially a fancy garage door opener which could also capture codes - off my belt and aimed it at the control box. The gate opened. When Cassie had opened the gate for me the other day, I captured the gate code with the unit, not knowing if it may come in handy. It did.

Before setting foot onto the property, I assumed Gregory would have used laser trip lines inside the gate, not wanting to waste the trembler system on a road. I pulled a small canister from the Velcro belt and blew smoke inside along the ground. Three lines glowed red across the drive, near the gate. Stepping over each one, I fogged again and saw no more, so I turned around, aimed my control and closed the gate. I walked to the house in the center of the roadway. As I approached, I fogged toward the front door and found no more laser trips.

I slipped on a pair of black nitrile gloves. Should Gregory discover that I had been inside, I didn't want to leave anything tangible for the police to find. There was no doubt in my mind that Gregory would know it was me who had come, but there would be nothing but trouble for me if I left prints or surveillance photos of my smiling face behind in places I shouldn't have been, hence, the mask and gloves.

Knowing that often the simplest answer is the correct one, I put my hand to the door handle and tried the thumb latch. It opened. Apparently Gregory was confident enough in his perimeter security to not lock the house. Of course, there was another possibility and that was this was one giant mousetrap and yours truly was a two hundred sixty pound mouse just about to walk right into it. I could see the wall-mounted alarm panel inside the doorway showed only a steady green light and after fogging along the floor and finding no lasers, I walked in and closed the door.

The house, thankfully, was comfortably cool, even in my getup. I pulled out a flashlight and moved the beam around the entry hallway. Slowly, I made my way down to the rotunda and decided the best place to begin would be Cassie's master suite. I walked quietly up the stairs and headed first down the east wing. There were some low wattage lights shining from somewhere, just enough to keep me from running into walls, but before I entered each room in turn, I used my flashlight to search all the corners and closets. Finally, I reached Cassie's master suite and opened the door. Empty. The sinks, tub, and shower were bone dry.

I repeated the search pattern down the west wing toward Gregory's master suite. Again, empty, but his bathroom had been recently used. The shower was wet. Only one damp towel hung on the rack.

I walked downstairs, searched the rotunda, and then the west wing toward the kitchen and garage. Inside the garage, I found five vehicles, including the little red BMW convertible Cassie said she was driving on Thursday morning, the last time I talked to her. I looked into each car, popped each trunk. Nothing. My search of the house had been slow, methodical. I checked my cellphone for the time and noted I had been inside the gate for exactly one hour at that point.

Finally, I moved down the first floor east wing. I made certain if a door was open, I left it open. If it was closed, I re-closed it. Nothing. The last possibility in the whole house was Gregory's office. I knelt down at the hallway table, as I had seen Cassie doing by pure feel, but used my flashlight to find the little nook which held the key, slipped it free and then used it to unlock Gregory's office door. I walked inside, left the key in the lock and closed the door.

I used the flashlight to search the bookcases for any evidence of a hidden panel which would reveal the concrete hat Keoki had described covering the entrance to the lava tube. I found no seams out of place, no evidence of any wear marks, nothing to indicate a part of the wall moved. I checked the floor. Nothing. I flipped back the corners of the area rugs. If it was here, I certainly couldn't find it.

Turning my attention to the desk, I saw that the top was completely clear, save a remote control for the television on the far wall. I opened the center drawer and found a keyboard, but could find no computer to which it was connected. Upon further checking, there were no wires at all to the keyboard, meaning it either operated by way of radio signal or infrared connection. I decided to leave it alone.

I checked all the other drawers, found them open and when I rifled the contents, saw nothing but routine papers and documents. Even Gregory Thomason, it seemed, kept the registration cards and operating manuals for his stuff. Lastly, I pushed the chair out of the way and crawled under the desk. I shone the light on the perimeter of the panel I had seen open that day I followed Cassie in after our lunch. The quality of the craftsmanship was superb, and had I not seen the panel open I never would have believed it did.

I pushed on corners, center, center and a corner, tried every conceivable combination of pushes, touches, and manipulations that I could think of yet the panel refused to yield itself. I laid down under the desk, shone my light into places that I couldn't get to sitting there, and then I saw it, a tiny scratch on one edge of the side panel just below the kick plate trim piece. I used one finger and pushed the trim piece down and the door popped open. I opened it all the way and revealed the contents of the compartment.

Inside, I found the two large red leather bound journals in one of the sections and two old cigar boxes behind a handful of legal pads in another. I pulled one journal out of place and opened it. The same precise writing filled the pages. I estimated the book held two hundred pages, meaning a total of four hundred sides for writing and this journal was filled to the last page. The first entry was dated twenty-two years ago and dealt with his mommy drowning, and the last page dated seven years ago.

I removed the other journal and opened it to the first page, found the same date seven years ago. A satin bookmark was inserted approximately one-third of the way back. The problem with these pages, as with the others Cassie had copied for me, was there was nothing incriminating, just vague references and musings. The remainder of the pages in the second journal were empty.

My cell vibrated in my pocket and a jolt of adrenaline rushed through my body. I pulled the phone from my pocket and saw the call was indeed coming from the phone I had given Keoki. I answered the call.

"Hey, Malihini, he come back."

"Where is he now?" I asked.

"I see light coming, helicopter. I use da goggles, it him."

I thanked him and told him I was on my way out. Then I clicked off.

Obviously Gregory had gone to the airport and swapped out the Corvette for the chopper. Thankfully, I thought, that was good and bad. Good because I could most likely get out the way I came using the drive, especially if I timed it right, and bad, because he would be here very shortly. I had a decision to make, and very little time to make it. My middle age heart was beating out of my chest and the sweating had returned.

I pulled a black mesh bag from my belt, put the journals inside and then grabbed both cigar boxes and put them inside as well. Lastly, I grabbed the two other boxes and legal pads and tucked them inside as well. I'd go through everything at my condo and then get them back here sometime. Maybe.

"Well, if he finds the journals are gone is he going to be any more pissed that the cigar boxes and the others things are gone too?" I said out loud. "Probably not."

I pushed the panel closed, rolled out from under the desk, pulled out the bag, replaced the chair and headed for the door. I twisted the knob and nothing happened. It moved, but the latch didn't slide back. Oh my God, I thought. I reached for Willie, just in case I needed the firepower. My heart was pounding, my body was sweating, I jostled the knob, gripped it harder and twisted it both ways, nothing. I pulled out my flashlight, shined it on the knob area, wondering if the door required a key to exit as well as enter, then I spotted a small, ridged slider. I slid it to the right and turned the knob. The door opened freely and I was out.

I made one more risky move, I hollered for Cassie and then paused to listen carefully. I yelled her name again. Nothing. I closed the office door, made sure it was locked, removed the key and replaced it in the nook under the table and made my way to the front door. I looked through the sidelight to make sure I wasn't going to open it in Gregory's face. All was dark outside. I opened the door. I could hear the approaching helicopter but could not see it anywhere in the western sky. The rhythmic beating of the main rotor blades echoed off the mountain, the noise seemed to be coming from every direction.

I walked out into the night and suddenly the chopper appeared out of nowhere around the corner of the east wing. The noise was incredible. It's searchlight cut a swath across the drive and toward the front door. I jumped back inside and slammed the door closed just ahead of the light. I watched in horror as the helicopter moved up the drive, following it's light right to Keoki's porch. Then I witnessed one of the most incredible sights. Keoki sat there, a beer in his hand. As the searchlight focused on him, he lifted his free hand and threw Gregory a one finger salute. I had no trouble mistaking that from a shaka, even at this distance.

The helicopter banked away and lined up with the helipad off the west wing. I made my break for the drive and didn't look back until I got near the three lasers. I turned, watched the chopper settle, it's back to me. I fogged the lasers, stepped carefully over them, used my remote to operate the gate and was off the property and across the roadway crouched down behind a large chunk of lava rock before the chopper's engine had wound down. I made sure the gate was closed and watched as Gregory walked from the helicopter and entered the side door to the garage.

My heart was beginning to slow to a normal beat. I pulled off the cotton mask which felt like it was about to suffocate me, put it into my pocket, picked up the bag and walked up to Keoki's porch to take a seat on his steps and a beer from his cooler.

Chapter Twenty

Cassie sat on the edge of her bed eating the banana she found inside her room when she awoke. The wrapped sandwich which had also been there she put inside the small refrigerator for later. She had wrapped her sheet around her body like a sarong, and it made her feel much less vulnerable than being naked. After Gregory's outburst, she had done considerable thinking about how to retake control of the situation, and the sarong was a first step.

Gregory had also unmasked the small window in the door and she could now have a bit of a view around the lava tube. What she was able to see was limited, but at least she could judge the time of day by the amount of natural light flowing in from the seaside opening.

She finished the banana and walked the peel to the garbage can in the corner by the little sink. She rinsed her hands and splashed some water on her face and then after doing some stretches, she padded to the door and peered outside. From the light, she judged it to be early morning; but which day? Had she been in here three days or only two? Two, she decided. She had come home after seeing Dan on Thursday and then awoke sometime that night down here, still groggy from the needle. Hours later had come the physical pressure session, that could have been early Friday morning. Then came the cattle prod, that must have been late Friday night or early Saturday morning. He had come to yell at her about Willy and that had to be Saturday afternoon. Now it was nearing dawn. So this could be Sunday? This is the third day then, she thought.

Other than dropping off some food and unmasking the door's window, Gregory had not been in to see her since he came to rant about William. At first, she had been horrified by his anger, but then after considering the entirety of the situation she now felt it was exactly how she wanted him: blinded with rage toward William. Yes, she thought as she looked through the glass, Gregory's anger is perfectly directed.

She walked back and sat on the edge of the bed and looked up at the cameras in two of the corners on the ceiling. Cassie wondered if Gregory was watching her right now. Did it matter? Her mind was refocused on her plan. She understood now she could make it work just as before, perhaps even with more certainty of outcome than had Gregory not taken this drastic step of putting her down here. Timing, she thought. It would all come down to timing.

First though, she needed a shower.

Gregory watched her pacing and then coming to sit on the bed again. He wondered how she could be so calm. By now, most of them were breaking down, getting weaker, coming closer to just giving up. Cassie appeared to be getting stronger. Oh, she had stumbled early on, mainly from the disorientation and shock of the situation, he thought, but for some reason she had rebounded. Well, it will be interesting when he incorporated the next step, he thought.

He watched her strip off the bed sheet sarong and step into the shower enclosure. Her body was still magnificent, strong, lithe, shapely. He enjoyed watching her move. He always had. It would be one of the things about her he would surely miss. Somehow, that made him sad. He switched off the monitor and walked over to the desk. He thought about writing his observations into a special section about Cassie in his journal. He hadn't written about her in years. Gregory pulled out the desk chair and sat down. His mind was racing through thoughts, and then he laughed when he realized the irony of the situation. Who would transcribe his notes into his journal after Cassie was gone? He enjoyed the exactness of her handwriting, the precision with which she filled each line evenly without crowding or expanding the lettering. Perhaps he could get her to do it for him in her cell. He would enjoy reading and rereading his words about her written in her own hand. Having her write the words, unknowing of her fate, would make a fitting epitaph for the soon-to-be late Cassandra Thomason.

He pulled out a new pad of paper from the drawer and began to write excitedly.

"Teddy, it's been a long time," Sandy said to him as he hugged her at the gate.

"You look terrific, honey, and you feel good too."

"Now, Teddy, behave," she joked. "You don't want me to have to tell the Big Dog you made a pass at his ex-wife, do you?"

He let her go, not because of the jab, but because the hug had been long enough between old friends.

"Speaking of the devil, what the hell is he doing in Hawaii and how does your case have anything to do with a missing person investigation in Chicago from fifteen years ago?"

Teddy grabbed her carryon bag from her tow and put his arm around her shoulders. She put her free arm around his waist. They walked through the terminal toward the street. Sandy did look great, he thought, but that was merely the shell of a very special woman. One of a kind. William was one stupid son of a bitch to let her get away. Teddy had told him that on several occasions.

"You probably got the same story I did on the phone in the middle of the night, Teddy," Sandy told him. "We're working a case which purportedly relates to the terms of a prenuptial agreement between two very wealthy people and we're collecting information to assist one side proving adultery against the other."

"You're running not into mistresses, but are five for five missing persons so far, going back as far as twenty years ago and as recently as this girl from Canada?" he said. "That's most of what the Big Dog told me. In addition, there are some kind of journals which describe the women, how the perp met them, stuff like that, and your client gave you the names of six women total, one of whom you've found alive and well on another island. He's been able to connect details on the five missing women, but there's no entry for this woman you've found alive, yet. The other pages your client originally gave him describe a woman from Chicago whom the perp met fifteen years ago, and he wants us to see if we can help connect those dots."

"That's about it, Teddy," she said.

"About it, hell," he said. "If we locate this case and it connects to your perp in the islands, I don't care how rich he is, Chicago is going to want him."

Sandy let that go unanswered.

They walked past the ticket counters and out onto the upper roadway where cabs usually dumped departing passengers and bags before circling around to the lower level for new fares coming out of baggage claim. He walked her toward his unmarked Crown Victoria parked along the curb at the far end.

"Hey, TSA," Teddy yelled at the young guy in a traffic vest looking into the Crown Vic's windshield and talking on his radio. He showed the kid his badge and I.D. and told him the car was parked there on police business.

"You can't park here," the kid said.

"Bullshit, I can't," Teddy said, coming chest-to-chest with the Fed, well, more like Teddy's chest to the kid's chin. "Who says I can't park here on police business?"

The kid's face turned red. His eyes went to Sandy, saw nothing but an understanding smile before he summoned forth a bit of regulatory courage.

"Federal regulations," he said, taking a step backward. "I think you should know this is against the new Homeland Security rules and I'm a Federal Agent."

"This is still Chicago, you little shit," Teddy said in his menacing voice. "Why don't you go feel up grandma to see if she's packing anything in her diaper."

Then Teddy walked right through the TSA puke and tossed Sandy's bag into the back seat, opened the door for her, admired her legs as she got in, and then walked around and got in. He flipped off the kid and pulled into traffic.

"You were kind of hard on him, weren't you?" Sandy asked as they made their way back out to the main roads. "He was just doing his job, Teddy."

"Aw, frickin' TSA," he said. "They think they own the joint now, throw their weight around every chance they get. A year ago they were minimum wage refugees from fast food restaurants, now they're flunkies with a federal badge, and it's gone to their head. It's just good to kick 'em back once in a while. Keeps 'em awake."

"William talks to some of the old guys now and again. They tell him things aren't like they used to be. They all use the phrase, 'back in the day' as a common lament," she said.

"They got that right, Sandy," Teddy said with a hint of resignation in his voice. "I just am biding my time until retirement. Then I might go buy that piece of that bar in the Cayman's the Big Dog gave up to marry you."

"I think sometimes he wishes he was still back there, alone," she said.

"Are you kidding me, Sandy? That guy thinks the sun rises and sets with you. He's told me so."

"If he did, then maybe he could have controlled himself a little better, don't you think?" she said. "I mean, Vanessa Lafontaine, two olives on toothpicks, for Christ's sake."

"Well, you know the Big Dog, always a sucker for olives and toothpicks," he joked.

"Not funny, Teddy," Sandy said. She looked out the window as they cruised toward the city on the Kennedy expressway. The Sears Tower glistened in the midday sun.

"Sorry, Sandy," he said. "Sometimes I forget myself."

"Don't worry about it, Teddy. It just still stings."

Teddy mentally kicked himself the rest of the way downtown. Someday, he promised himself, he'd get that verbal filter installed like his third wife had told him he needed.

I had my iPod cranked and was killing my hearing with the screamed lyrics of 'she's a bad, bad girlfriend' when Steve and Shelly showed up at my door. They dropped off the case of Coke and box of brown sugar Pop Tarts I had asked they pick up when they went to Safeway this morning. I was out of caffeine and sugar and just didn't want to stop going through Gregory's collection of 'I'm a sick, sick bastard' stuff. A night of no sleep had me changing the words during the song, making me wonder which of us was sicker. One more look across my table and that question was answered. I needed a break, so I asked my neighbors in for a while.

I put the Coke into the fridge, got a glass with ice and poured the contents of a can in to do a quick chill. I pulled a twin-pack of Pop Tarts from the box and zipped open the bag. Steve and Shelly said they were fine when I offered to share, so I stood at the kitchen counter and had my breakfast. There are few things I'm compulsive about - depending, of course, who you ask - but eating Pop Tarts is one. I break them in half, then each half in half again, and repeat, eating one-eighth of each tart in each bite. I think if I ever just took bites from a whole Pop Tart, my eyes would fall out, so I do it the same way I did since I was a kid and my grandma bought the cheaper store brand Toaster Tarts, or whatever. It's how I control my tart, I guess.

Steve and Shelly were perusing the assortment of items strewn across my dining room table. Each cigar box had held about three dozen small manila envelopes about three inches by five inches, each was marked with a number. Inside each envelope, I found what I call stuff, the FBI profilers may call it trophies, and Gregory may just call it treasures. Whatever it was called, it was a collection of things which had not belonged to Gregory. Each envelope had been sealed and I had carefully used a razor knife to split the adhesive. While handling everything I had taken last night, I had worn blue nitrile gloves, figuring I'd put it all back before I called the cops, so they could find it cleanly. When Gregory went down for whatever it was he has done, I didn't want evidence tossed because of me.

There was one item which was not in any envelope in one of the cigar boxes, the one with numbers one through thirty-six. Since all the envelopes had been sealed and there was no matching item in any of the others, I don't think it had fallen out. For some reason, it had been placed in there on its own. It was that single item which caught Shelly's eye. She pointed to it, I told her not to touch it without a glove and she stopped her hand.

"That looks like one of ours," she said. "From Na Hoku."

"Oh yeah?" I said. "This is all stuff from my investigation. Please don't mess it up, it all has to go back where it came from."

"I wasn't going to touch anything," she said. "I just wanted to see that earring. It's different from our standard version, bigger, and has a larger diamond."

Always interested in knowing something about a unique piece of evidence, I walked over to the table and handed her a blue glove. She slipped it on like a pro, something most people have a hard time doing. I gave her a look.

"I used to work in the medical field," she said.

She picked up the earring, turned it over. She moved to the window and manipulated it in the sunshine, concentrating on the diamond in the center.

"Well, it is one of ours, but it's special order, for sure," Shelly said.

"Special order?" I asked. "How can you tell it's yours and that it's special order?"

Over the next couple of minutes, Shelly gave me a lesson in Jewelry 101. She turned the earring over and showed me the jeweler's mark which indicated Na Hoku had made it, then showed me the 'PT950' stamp which meant it was made of ninety-five percent platinum. She said they normally made these earrings only in 14k yellow and 14k white gold. Platinum would be special order. She also said the standard casting was smaller, maybe by fifty percent. This had to come from a special mold, she said, again indicating a custom order, and considerable extra cost.

After that, she showed me the diamond, and even without a loupe I could see what she was talking about. She said they normally offer G or H color with SI1 quality. I asked and she explained what that meant: near colorless with easily spottable inclusions under the loupe, the fifth quality grade down from Flawless. This diamond was totally colorless and flashed in the sunlight like none I had ever seen before, outside of Cassie's engagement ring. It was as flawless and perfectly cut stone as ever I had seen. She repeated that the piece had to be special order because she's never seen them in this size, material, and with this size and quality of diamond.

I held the earring in my hand, flipped it over. I already had digital photos of it, but I positioned it to take close ups of the marks she had identified. I asked her what they called the item.

"We call those our plumeria earrings," Shelly said. "Timeless, and we own the patent on this design."

"Would you have a list of people who special ordered it?"

"Of course, but given the size, the fact it's in platinum, and the diamond, I would bet the list will be very short, maybe just one person."

"Can you get me the list?" I asked.

Shelly thought about it a moment, then said she'd do what she could.

Marcy's flight had started its descent into Maui. She could feel herself growing increasingly anxious with every mile put behind them. As she looked out the window into the white glare, her foot was bouncing and she was having a hard time sitting still. So much was she agitated and animated on the flight, that the person originally sitting next to her had moved to another seat several hours ago.

She had memorized the maps of Lahaina and Ka'anapali, played the confrontation scenario over and over in her head a hundred times. Marcy could be an intimidating presence, she knew. Her deep green eyes flashed when she was angered, and at five-foot-ten, one hundred eighty pounds, she was physically large for a woman. It wasn't fat she carried, but rather her paternal heritage's large frame and musculature. Her spiked platinum blonde hair also contributed to the menacing mirage that was Marcy. She had relied upon the look her entire life, never having to prove her toughness physically. Yet. She wondered if she could rise to the occasion if Alexander David Hale put up a fight. After all, when she had just come close to an imagined confrontation with Tamra Sommers, she had turned into a pile of Jell-O on the side of the road. This was different though, she thought. Then she looked at the photograph of her and Janet taken at the lake earlier this summer and she knew that she could do whatever it would take to find the truth.

The captain made the announcement they'd be landing in about fifteen minutes. Marcy put her stuff away, she wanted to be out of the airplane quickly to beat the crowd to the rental car outlet. She had studied the airport diagram as well to make her exit expeditiously.

Marcy felt she was as well prepared as she could be for whatever would come her way in the next hours. She closed her eyes, breathed deeply and tried to relax.

Sandy and Teddy sat in his office at the 1st District headquarters on south State Street. He brought her a cup of coffee. She tried it just to be polite, then discretely slid the cup a safe distance across the desk.

She removed her laptop from its case and opened the file of the journal pages which discussed the woman from Chicago. Teddy read the document, asked if he could have a printed copy. Sandy again ignored his question and laid out the parameters they needed to search. Teddy caught the sidestep and decided to just move forward. He knew that he'd be able to get a copy from the Big Dog. Sandy may have been an old friend too, but she was also a lawyer and Teddy knew lawyers sometimes had intermittent hearing.

Fortunately Chicago had done a little more digitizing of old records and case details than had the smaller cities Sandy had visited. The numbers of people who go missing in Chicago each year was staggering, nearly 20,000 last year alone, about 400 each week, Teddy told her, although she remembered the immense scope of the numbers from years ago. The figures Teddy quoted are up about fifty percent over the last fifteen years.

In Chicago, like everywhere across the U.S., a vast majority are runaways, and less than half, almost 8,000 last year, were adults. Teddy told her something she already knew, that not many resources are given to missing adults much of the time, because they aren't really missing, just gone. Sandy understood that sometimes adults run away too.

When there is no overt evidence a crime having been committed, the resources put toward the search for a missing adult are quite minimal beyond placing that person's name, information, and photograph into a file. These days, with the internet, cases can get wider attention than years ago, but even now these listings are often hard to find and search using only descriptives like height, weight, hair color, etc.

Teddy punched in some search parameters for fifteen years ago and came up with some disheartening numbers: 10,924 total missing, 3,743 adults over 17, 1,655 women, 898 Caucasian women. After Sandy provided a bit more information, he narrowed the search parameters to Caucasian females between the age of 20 and 40. 546 Caucasian females still fit.

"The client's anniversary is August 17, try a month either side of that," Sandy suggested.

"Anniversary?" Teddy asked.

Sandy gave him a 'don't ask' look and he updated the search parameters. Thankfully, the time between July 17 and September 17 was a lighter-than-average time for women going missing that year. The results were down to 42.

"Can you search by physical description?" Sandy asked.

"No can do, Sandy," Teddy said. "The legislators didn't give us that kind of money. We're lucky we got as much in as we did."

"Okay, can we see the files here or do we have to go down and dig out paper someplace?"

"We can read some documents here, but once we narrow it down, we're going to be digging through paper files at HQ over on 35th and Michigan," he said. "Since today is Sunday, we're going to be doing it tomorrow. Us flatfoots may work 24/7/365, but records clerks have a cushy 9 to 5, Monday through Friday type job."

Over the next three hours, they pulled up what they could on each of the 42 possibles, rejecting some out of hand, marking some as possibles, and picking out a few favorites. Since reports listed what the reporting person gave for a description of the missing woman, which as to height and weight could be grossly misjudged, it could only be corrected once the officers received some more reliable data like DMV records and those details were in the stored files. Even then, they both understood, sometimes women lie about height and weight on their driver's license.

Sandy knew Gregory's type included brunettes, but given the most recent anomaly, they didn't reject based on hair color. She knew he preferred women between five-foot-six and five-foot-eight, but also didn't reject records based on height if it was close. Finally, they knew he preferred relatively fit women, and from the journal pages this woman had been exceptional, so they did reject any woman who was reported to be above two hundred pounds. That single rejection criterion resulted in shrinking the list down to 19 possibles. Thank God for midwest obesity, Sandy thought.

Teddy printed a list of the possibles. He also sent an email over to a records clerk he knew well asking that they be given some priority in the morning and providing her with a list of the case numbers of interest. Then, since they could do nothing further on a late Sunday afternoon, he asked Sandy out to dinner. She consented, but only if he let her take him. He agreed and suggested a little chain restaurant just up the block.

"Are you kidding me?" Sandy asked. "Do you really think William would let me get away with that? How does Lawry's sound?"

"Can I use the siren and lights?" he joked.

"You're the detective, detective," she said, laughing.

Gregory completed a draft of his segment for Cassandra. He hoped he could persuade her to transcribe the words into his journal for him. It would make the perfect bookend for the record of his life. When he reread the words he had written, he felt proud. What a woman she was. People reading his words a thousand years from now will understand his Cassandra and how she had disappointed him. Of course, once they understood how she had failed him, they'd then be able to fully understand and condone his actions. A man, after all, must be able to trust his woman. If he cannot trust her, like his father obviously could not trust his mother, then there was no point.

Over twenty years of marriage - twenty-one coming up next month, he remembered - Gregory had never dishonored his vow to remain faithful to Cassandra. Sadly, he knew, she could not make the same claim. Well, she could make the claim, but he knew differently. While he had personally witnessed his mother's indiscretion one day, he wanted to hear the words out of Cassandra's mouth. He wanted her to admit her failing, and then he would make her surrender all. He sat back in his chair and smirked at the irony. Just as his mother had betrayed his father, and paid for her dishonor with her life, so had his wife done the same, and so will Cassandra suffer the same fate. First, however, he had quite the surprise for his wandering bride, and he would unveil it during her surrendering.

Gregory felt hungry. He went to the kitchen to make himself something for lunch: a salmon filet, blackened, potato salad, and a glass of limeade. For dessert, he decided on a dish of sherbet. He walked the tray into the office and turned on the monitor to watch Cassie. In what he considered yet another noble act on his part, he decided after he had finished his lunch, he'd recreate the meal for her. She would enjoy that. She didn't deserve it, he thought, but she'd enjoy it. Even Colonel Saito had offered Colonel Nicholson dinner during the attempt to break the man in the *Bridge Over The River Kwai*, he thought.

Marcy drove the highway to Lahaina. Curving around an elevated lookout, she took momentary note of the beauty of the sea and islands beyond, then quickly brought her attention back to the road. She had decided to change her plans and not go check into her hotel before beginning to track down Alexander David Hale. She hated even thinking his name, her brain spitting it out in disgust. So, she'd stop in Lahaina first, go by the property he shared and see if she could find him.

At the stoplight under the shadow of the old sugar mill, she turned right and drove up the mountain. She found each road in turn, matching letter for letter the street names in the directions on her paper to the signs on the street corners. She knew she'd never be able to pronounce them should she need to ask for directions, so she drove with extreme caution. She watched for house numbers once she located the proper street, drove slowly, but found it difficult to find any consistency in the location or style of the numbers on the houses. Many did not have any numbers displayed at all and the mailboxes were haphazardly located and stacked. It appeared to Marcy after a while that these people enjoyed not being found easily.

Fortunately, Google Map provided aerial views of the property so she could see what it looked like before she found it. The property she was seeking had several buildings on it, a main house and two smaller, separate units which the locals called an *ohana*. From what Marcy had read on the flight, ohana is Hawaiian for family and these smaller cottages on the properties were originally built to house relatives just like some people on the mainland had a mother-in-law room or wing built onto their house, but over the years these ohanas were increasingly being used for income to the landowner by renting them to strangers.

Marcy spotted the location of the property and drove past slowly, turned around in the cul de sac and drove by again, then she pulled to the curb and parked behind a a couple of motorized scooters. She grabbed her backpack, put the buck knife and sheath into her waistband, pulled the keys from the ignition and got out of the car. She wore what she had traveled in, jeans, T-shirt, walking shoes. When she left the plane, she added some plastic framed, wraparound sunglasses. Standing on the street, she drew a deep breath and was amazed she felt absolutely none of the nervous trepidation she had felt in Burlington. All she felt now was the physical buzzing of confident resolve.

With the backpack slung over one shoulder, she walked down the street toward the property. Her eyes moved behind the lenses of her sunglasses which at various angles looked either yellow or blue or some combination of the two.   She thought they gave her a menacing look, but she mainly had bought them because they effectively hid her eyes while not being too dark for wearing indoors. She didn't want her quarry to see, and possibly misjudge her eyes.

Most of the properties in the neighborhood had either rock walls or heavy vegetation bordering along the street. The fencing opened only for access to the driveway and the owners of the property where Alexander David Hale lived matched the neighborhood's penchant for privacy.   She came around a high hedge and turned into the driveway.   Marcy walked with the same confidence she felt inside. Observers, were there any, would call it a purposeful walk, the gait of someone who had been there before, of someone who belonged and knew where she was going.   It was not the tentative walk of a stranger to the area.   Marcy consciously worked toward achieving that affect and hoped it carried forth the desired effect.

Two vehicles were parked haphazardly in the driveway.   Marcy knew from the DMV Records of Title Chuck had pulled for her that neither parked there matched the type registered to Alex Hale, but she double checked the license numbers from memory just to be certain.   Neither matched the tag number assigned to his car. Undaunted, she continued her walk to the main house door. As she approached, she could hear music coming through the screen door from inside.

Marcy knocked firmly.   She heard some movement and voices inside and a moment later a tall, fit, tanned male in his early twenties and wearing only board shorts appeared behind the screen. Had he been in Montreal, and much more pale, he could have been the double of the officer who had taken the missing persons report from her. She saw he had an easy smile which she assumed came from an unburdened youthfulness and he pushed the door open to ask what she needed.

"I'm looking for Alexander Hale," she said.

"Alex?" he replied. "Alex isn't here." His eyes narrowed a bit, revealing to Marcy the cautious look of someone who distrusted authority figures and didn't want to be thought of as a rat, so the next words out of his mouth were not a surprise to her. "You a friend of his?"

"Years ago," she said. "I'm here on holiday and thought I'd drop in to see him."

The reply seemed to relax him a bit.   He pointed a thumb toward the building off to the right.

"He's in the ohana," he said.

Marcy was about to thank him and walk over to the small unit to the right rear of the main house.

"He's not home," the man added before she could say anything.

"Do you know when he'll be back?" she asked.

He moved his back to the door post and scratched up against it.

"Nah," he said.   "He comes and goes a lot."

"Do you know where I could find him?   I'm only going to be here for a few days and I'd really like to connect."

"You got his digits?" he asked.

"No, it's been too long, I don't have his cell number."

"I don't either," he chuckled.   "Just thought I'd ask."

He scratched against the door post.   Unsatisfied, he turned his back to her.

"Do you mind?" he asked.   "Center, about halfway up."

Marcy obliged and scratched his back.   He gave out a satisfied sigh.   She stopped before he got all worked up.

"Ah, thanks, babe," he said.   "See, he went to visit that artist chick friend of his on Molokai a few days ago.   Flew over on a helicopter she paid for.   Great work if you can get it.   Of course, his train doesn't run on that track, you know what I mean?"

She got the hint.

"Do you know who this woman would be?" she asked.

"Ah, Jenny something," he said, his eyes searching his brain. "She's some kind of painter.   Of course, in Hawaii who isn't some kind of artist, right?"

She gave him a tightlipped smile in response.

"Do you have a last name?   Where she might live?   Any phone number?"

"I don't even have *his* cell, so why would I have hers?" he asked rhetorically.   "He told me she had this cool place on the west shore, right on the beach."   His eyes appeared to be looking into his brain while he thought.   "I think her last name is something like May, or Day, no wait, Shea."   He nodded.   "Yeah, that's it, Jenny Shea."

"How does one get to Molokai?" she asked.

"Lotta ways," he said.   "Plane, chopper, boat, I even heard of a guy who used a paddle board."   He chuckled again.   "That would be the long, hard way. Nope, easiest way would be the ferry. Leaves right from the dock down there. I think they make two runs a day."

Marcy looked down the mountain toward the ocean where he was pointing. From where they stood, she could make out the harbor. She pointed to it to confirm and asked him if that's the harbor the ferry left from. He hadn't finished responding when she jogged off the property, around the hedge and up the street to her car. She tossed the backpack on the front seat and tore down the mountain to the harbor.

Marcy found a parking space which had a thirty-minute time limit but put the rental car there anyway. She grabbed the back pack and asked everyone she ran into where the ferry to Molokai was and finally someone told her it was just about to leave and pointed out toward the boat. She ran down the pier hollering just as they were about to remove the gangplank. A female crew member pulled her aboard. The boat lines were released and the ferry moved out. Marcy paid the cash for a ticket; she also gave her a handsome tip.

Ninety minutes later, the ferry docked on Molokai and Marcy met the rental car guy from the company which the crew member had suggested during the trip across the channel. She had been able to locate an address on the internet for a Jennifer Shea on Molokai and the rental agent provided her with directions.

"Her art must really be something," the guy said. "You're the second person in two days to come to see her. I had a guy yesterday morning who went out there, too."

Marcy thanked him and then drove out, throwing a bit of gravel before the tires bit on asphalt. She floored it down the road. As she drove she wondered if the person who had been there the day before had been a coincidence, a real art fan. She thought of the woman from the New Orleans P.I. firm whom Belle had called about last night. Marcy remembered the website showed two people, a woman and a man, both named Langdon. How could he have been here yesterday morning looking for Alexander Hale when his partner only discovered the man's partial identity late yesterday afternoon? If it was the male Langdon, she thought, could he have been tracking Jennifer Shea and not Alexander Hale? Was there some kind of connection between the two of them and Janet? Marcy checked her rearview mirror and again floored the Jeep on the narrow road.

She found the house easily, without making any wrong turns. It was like she was drawn there. She moved through the open gate, slowly onto the drive, and parked under the some scraggly looking trees a distance from the house. She pulled her knapsack from the car and then walked down the side of the drive to the house.

During the drive over, she had decided to play it like both Jennifer and Alex were involved in Janet's disappearance. That would be the safe play, she concluded. The problem would be controlling and overpowering two people without a gun. She had considered going in stealthy, but without knowing the layout of the house, and not having the time to surveil it, she decided finally a friendly, frontal approach would provide her the most expeditious, if not safest, alternative.

With her backpack slung over her shoulder, she knocked at the front door. No answer. She tried the latch and found it open. Apparently people on Molokai don't lock their doors either, she thought. It brought to mind Belle and Thomas and she drew strength from the memory. Marcy entered quietly, she walked down the short hallway to a large open area. It was empty, she surveyed the kitchen, then walked over to the patio doors and peered outside. She didn't see a soul. The house had two wings, she saw, and she picked the one going off to the left first. Each of the doors down that wing was closed, she listened at each and heard nothing. As she progressed, she detected music coming from one of the rooms.

She pulled the buck knife from its sheath and opened the blade, which locked into place. It was small, only about a four-inch blade, but it was vicious looking, pointy with a slight curve, thick and serrated on the back side half way up to the handle. The handle felt good in her hand and she had already decided she would use the weapon if she had to. She had seen a television special about guns in homes and the experts all agreed that for a gun in the home to be effective the owner had to already be of the mindset to use the weapon if he or she pulled it on an intruder. Even though Marcy was the intruder here, and held a knife, she had already made the determination to use the weapon, if necessary.

She moved to the door of the room with the music. She put her ear to the door. Classical, she didn't recognize the tune or composer. Marcy opened the door slowly, looked around what appeared to be an art studio. The music spilled into the hallway and Marcy glanced back down the hall before quickly stepping inside and quietly closing the door behind her. She hoped Jennifer liked to work alone. Taking one of them at a time in separate rooms would be the easiest way, she knew. She moved around the small wall sections hung with art. Most of it was good, she thought. The woman obviously had enough talent to afford this house, Marcy concluded, so why would it be a surprise that her art was good?

She stepped from behind a wall and saw Jennifer standing with her back to where Marcy stood, she was cleaning a brush with a rag and considering an incomplete landscape. Marcy took a step and her sneaker squeaked on the tile floor. The woman turned and the smiling face flashed to a mask of alarm when she saw the knife in Mary's hand. Marcy put her finger over her mouth signaling the woman to be quiet, then moved quickly, held the knife forward menacingly and grabbed the woman's arm. She had the advantage of surprise and size, but when she turned the woman around, Marcy felt a wiry strength which she instinctively knew was to be avoided.

Marcy ordered Jennifer to the floor; she firmly pushed the point of the knife to the woman's back. Jennifer complied and Marcy put a knee into the middle of her back while opening the backpack. She pulled out the roll of duct tape, tore a section and applied it to the woman's mouth while saying in a controlled voice that she had no desire to hurt Jennifer, if she cooperated. Jennifer's eyes showed fear, but not panic. Marcy took that as a good sign Jennifer would not do something stupid.

She ordered Jennifer to put her hands behind her back, put the knife between her teeth and then wrapped duct tape around the woman's wrists. To keep her from working the binding, Marcy also wrapped Jennifer's elbows with tape. Marcy pulled her onto her butt and looked into her eyes.

"Where's Alexander?" she said, holding the knife under Jennifer's chin.

Jennifer tried to speak but the tape prevented it. Marcy told her if she screamed she'd be dead before the sound got out of the room, and asked if she understood that. Jennifer nodded. Marcy pulled the tape loose from one side gently, she had no reason to hurt the woman at this point, and asked again. Jennifer told her the last time she knew, he had gone to his room to take nap and described which room that would be. Marcy replaced the tape, turned the woman over, taped her ankles and left her with a warning. Jennifer again nodded her understanding.

When she heard her captor leave the room, Jennifer tested the bindings and found them more than secure. She quickly concluded she'd have to see where this was going, but the intruder's focus had been on Alex.

Marcy moved back into the hallway, found the door Jennifer had identified would lead into Alex's room, and tried the knob. It was unlocked - naturally - and she opened it as quietly as possible. The instant she saw him lying on his back on the bed, she knew he was the one. She had to fight the urge to rush in, jump on his tiny chest and push the knife under his chin until his eyes bulged in fear and pain. Marcy swallowed the sour bile which had rushed to the back of her throat and crept inside. Once she was close, she was on him in a flash. He thrashed against the surprise awakening for a moment, until he felt the point of the knife drawing blood under his chin and heard the woman's commands.

She soon had him cuffed and slapped a piece of duct tape across his mouth. She asked him if there was anyone else in the house - the same question she had asked Jennifer - and told him if she found out he lied to her she would cut off his manhood and he'd discover the joy of sucking *his own* dick for eternity. He gave the same response as Jennifer had. Marcy knew then they were alone in the house.

Marcy walked him out to the great room, taped each of his ankles to the legs of a chair then wrapped several bindings around his torso and the back of the chair as well. She brandished the knife in his face and gave him an unmistakable look to stay put. He nodded. She turned and went back down the hall to collect Jennifer. On the way, Marcy considered that it may be best to question them individually, but she needed to be able to watch them both so efficacy would suffer for exigency.

As he watched her move out of the room and down the hall, Alex searched his mind for where he'd seen her before, and he knew he had. Recently. She had a bit of a tan, but not enough to be local. It had to have been off the island. Then it occurred to him. Montreal. In the apartment. The photographs on the dresser and desk. He struggled against the tape, found it unyielding. Inside his head he screamed a question.

"How did that fucking dyke find me?"

Chapter Twenty-One

Gregory sat in the chair in the corner of her cell and watched Cassandra finish her late lunch. She had been hungry all right, and thanked him. He felt good about this gesture of kindness and made a note to add it to his writings for future generations to read of his humanity even to those who had betrayed their honor and vow to him.

As he studied her, he wondered when would be the best time to bring down the journal so she could memorialize his words to her. Perhaps tomorrow, he decided, after he finished drafting the appendix. He watched as she drained her glass of limeade; he knew she preferred lemonade, but sometimes criminals had to take what was offered them.

Cassandra sat on the edge of the bed and finished the meal he had brought. She watched him across the room, watching her. He wore a self-satisfied smirk and for some reason that really pissed her off. She drank the limeade - disgusting stuff - and took note of the mirth in his eyes as she did. He knew she hated limeade. That pissed her off too. While he was watching her drink, she palmed the fork off the tray and secreted it under her pillow. It was their kitchen standard, high quality stainless steel, weighty and solid to the feel.

She replaced the glass onto the tray and began to rise to take it all to the little table. She decided her next action was worth the risk. Today was the third day since she had dropped the envelope with the photos at the front desk of the Palms condominiums where Willy was staying. He should be seeing them this afternoon, and her note. It was time to light Gregory's fuse and she laughed inside that he had given her the match by bringing this meal.

As she started to stand, she saw Gregory rising out of his chair. He held his palm out at her signaling that she should stay where she was. This would be easier, she thought. She sat back down, waited for him to come to her. As he bent over to pick up the tray, she struck. Her fist wrapped around the handle of the fork and she pulled it from under the pillow with lightning speed. He saw it coming out of the corner of his eye but was powerless to stop it with both hands on the tray. Cassandra plunged the fork into his chest, she felt it pierce muscle and hit bone. Gregory recoiled and let loose an animalistic scream. He pulled away so quickly that she lost her grip on the fork and it remained embedded in his chest, his shirt growing a red stain around the sunken tines.

He stood there, his composure regained in amazing time, and she saw him smile. He pointed to the fork, left it where it was and looked her in the eye.

"You fucking bitch," he said through his teeth. "This is going to cost you."

"It's already cost me, you sick fuck," she said. "Yes, since we're both already aware of why I am here, the answer is yes. Yes, I am fucking William."

She saw the rage rebuild within him and she wondered how much of it she would have to endure, so she prepared to retreat to her mind's storm cellar.

With the fork still in his chest, he gripped the tray and walked out with it. He closed the door and the locks engaged automatically. She ran to the window and watched him move across the tube to the walkway.

"I guess that's that," she said under her breath. "I'd hate to be Willy the next time Gregory sees him." She looked toward the seaside opening and gauged the sunlight. Soon, she thought. Soon.

Gregory arrived back at his office, walked though to the kitchen. He placed the tray on the counter and then went to the bathroom. There, he removed the fork while channeling the pain into the William Langdon account for storage until he needed to draw upon it. He removed his shirt, inspected the stain and the holes and then tossed it into the garbage can. He opened the medicine cabinet and found the hydrogen peroxide. Spreading the wound, he poured the liquid over the area and into the tine holes. The pain that action produced went into the interest column of William's account.

After bandaging the wound with gauze and tape, he grabbed another shirt from his closet and then went to his office. He sat on the leather couch and turned on the monitor. He watched Cassandra move about her cell nervously. Pacing was how she bled off nervous energy, he knew. Thinking of the next step, he tuned into the surveillance at the Molokai house and flipped through the camera locations. He found Jennifer and Alex sitting together in the great room. His brow furrowed as he looked on and his brain fought to tell him something was not right. He zoomed in and then someone crossed into the screen. Now who the hell is there, he thought. When the screen cleared he saw the pair were restrained with silver tape. Jennifer's mouth was taped as well, but Alex was talking. A tall woman with spiked, blonde hair and wearing sunglasses stood over him with a knife. He turned up the volume and listened for a minute, then he jumped to his feet.

Gregory pulled the gun case from the shelf in his office, opened it and noted the weapon was there and all the ammo slots were full. He walked quickly down the hallway, out of the house, to the helicopter and started it up. He saw Keoki watching from the porch of his house. He lifted off, flew low over his neighbor's place and headed northwest toward Molokai. The navigational computer confirmed he'd be at the house in twenty-one minutes.

Keoki used the cell phone to call William and let him know that Gregory had just left, alone, in the helicopter. The old Hawaiian added that his neighbor appeared to be more annoyed than normal.

I took the call from Keoki, thanked him for the information and then clicked off. There was no need for me to try to make it out to Cassie's place, mainly because there was no way I could know that Gregory would not be back before I made the drive, and secondarily because the information I was able to pull from his house yesterday had definitely shifted the game.

Whatever Cassie was doing here, it was far beyond what she had told me. The prenup was a joke, and the women whose names she had provided had all been missing for years. She obviously had wanted me to know this information, but now I was more interested in what she was holding back. I looked over the items spread across my dining room table. For some reason I kept coming back to that single earring and wondered what role it played in all this.

While there was more than enough information that Gregory had known all these women, and scores more over the decades, there was still nothing but speculation which tied him to their disappearances. Crimes, if they were crimes, were scattered over jurisdictions in as many as twenty-three states. The former cop in me knew there wasn't enough solid evidence of criminal activity for any agency to be particularly interested at this point. Much of what I had wasn't even evidence, but more speculation and interpretation. I'd be laughed out of any single precinct house with this.

Then, I thought about the FBI. After all, if all my speculation played out true, there was kidnapping and interstate operation at the very least and those *were* under the Fibbies' purview. However, to get the Feds to even open a file took months and I knew Cassie didn't have that kind of time left. Even if I was able to get someone to raid the house, I had already been through it all and she wasn't there. Plus, all the evidence in the case was currently scattered across my dining room table and had been illegally obtained. With everything thrown out of court, there was no chance of convicting Gregory of anything but being a creep, and if he didn't speak, maybe not even that.

So I sat on my hands. The hardest thing for me to do. I needed more before calling in anyone, and I needed to get this stuff back into Gregory's desk so the investigative agency could discover it legally. The how and the when were just going to take some planning, so I went to the fridge and as I stood looking in, wished I had bought more beer. I grabbed a Coke instead and started back through Gregory's menagerie one more time.

Gregory kept the helicopter below five hundred feet to stay out of the approach corridor for the airport and eliminating the possibility of any official record of his trip. He pushed the airspeed to redline and watched the time to destination click off. On the seat next to him lay the gray leather gun case.

Before leaving the house, he had heard the gist of the questions the woman was asking Alex. In over twenty years, this was the first time someone had tracked his scheme. Mostly, the friends, family, and even the cops had never looked beyond the locality from which the women had gone missing. Even though he couldn't know Alex's thoughts, Gregory ironically repeated a version of his question to himself: 'Who is this dyke and how did she find Alex?'.

Jennifer watched the female intruder pace the floor and listened as she fired questions at Alex. She had no idea what the woman was talking about, but intuition told her Alex did. Intuition also told her Alex was stalling. What intuition didn't tell her was why he'd do that.

Marcy pulled Emma's drawing from her backpack and showed it to Alex. He stared at it, didn't react.

"Kind of like looking in the mirror, isn't it?" she mocked. "Now quit the denials and tell me what you were doing at my friend Janet Hopkins' apartment building last Saturday morning."

"Some drawing you had made of me puts me in, where was it, Toronto a week ago?" he said. "I don't know what you are smoking lady, but I haven't been off the islands in months."

"Wrong answer again," Marcy snarled. She poked the point of the knife into his chest enough to draw a bit of blood. She pulled the printout of his travel itinerary from Burlington and showed it to him. Again, he didn't react. "What about this?"

"So where was I lady, Toronto or Vermont?" he mocked. "Make up your mind."

Marcy's eyes flared behind the glasses.

"Montreal, goddammit," she screamed at him. "Montreal, not Toronto."

She had been at this for nearly half an hour and he refused to admit anything even though she had proof in black and white. She was beginning to run out of ideas beyond the infliction of severe physical pain, but wanted to avoid torture, if possible. What if he passed out, she thought. Then what?

She turned to look at Jennifer and a black thought entered her heart. Marcy had already asked the artist questions and felt Jennifer was being totally honest with her. She had no knowledge or involvement in Janet's disappearance. Marcy was convinced the woman was innocent, just a victim of happenstance.

Yet, Alex was giving her nothing. She looked from Alex to Jennifer and back to Alex. The five or six spots where she had lightly punctured his bare chest were dripping blood but were obviously not dangerous to his health. With all the adrenaline which must be pumping through his veins Marcy doubted he even felt the wounds. She returned to the black thought.

"I'm going to give you one last chance to tell me the truth," she said. "I need you to tell me what I want to know, and you will." She looked toward Jennifer, pushed her sunglasses to the top of her head so he could now see her eyes. She hardened her stare and pointed the knife toward Jennifer. Her voice reflected the evilness of the black thought. "I don't need her."

Marcy walked behind Jennifer, grabbed a handful of hair and pulled her head back with one hand. She put the blade under Jennifer's left ear. Jennifer's eyes showed panic now. Her mouth worked against the duct tape, so it was her eyes which silently implored Alex to tell the woman what she wanted to know. Marcy felt sick to her stomach. She had taken a step from which she could not retreat and she prayed to God in that moment that Alex would not force her hand.

For his part, Alex stared coldly. No emotion, no fear. Both women saw the same thing at the same time and while they held different roles in the current stand off, each of them wondered what the hell Alex was playing at.

Finally, he started to speak, and each of the women slightly relaxed, but only for an instant.

"You can do whatever you want, bitch," he said softly and slowly. "I don't give a fuck what you do to her, and then you can suck my big fat dick."

Marcy was furious he would sacrifice his friend like this, but she had no choice but to follow through or nothing she threatened going forward would matter. She remembered Thomas' words about accepting the truth about whatever she would find happened to Janet. She had known in her brain that Janet was most likely gone forever, but until that instant had refused to believe it in her heart. That instant of realization now provided her the resolve she needed to do it whatever it took.

Jennifer felt the pressure of the blade relax for a moment as Marcy repositioned her grip, and then an instant later winced as she felt it push deeper into her flesh and begin to move. Her mind screamed at the pain, then as her heart pounded in her chest she felt reality begin to fade.

In the next instant, everything seemed to freeze as their collective attention was directed toward the front door which flew open and Gregory moved down the hallway pointing a gun directly at the center of Marcy's chest. A laser pinpointed exactly where the projectile would hit. He spoke no words.

Jennifer watched his finger tense on the trigger and then heard a whoosh sound like a movie silencer followed by the thud sound of the projectile hitting Marcy's chest. Marcy dropped to the floor a moment later like a sack of potatoes. The knife fell into Jennifer's lap.

Jennifer did not notice the blood running down her neck from the wound Marcy had begun to inflict. Her mind was racing a million different directions as she saw Gregory move to a position directly in front of Alex.

"About fucking time you got here," Alex said.

Jennifer watched as Gregory stood about ten feet from Alex. His back was to her and she could not see his eyes. A moment later she saw Alex's eyes flare and he started to struggle impotently against the restraints just before Gregory raised his arm and fired twice. Jennifer saw the two darts hit into his chest. Alex's head fell forward a few moments later. She stared in horror as his chest began rising and falling in a rapid rhythm and then fell and did not rise again.

Then Gregory turned to her. He must have seen the questions and emotions rushing across her face because for the first time since coming in, he spoke.

"I'm very sorry to have to do this, my dear," he said.

She looked into his eyes and they were sad but resigned. She fought against the tape and her silenced mouth begged him not to, but he fired a single dart into her chest. The room swirled, then went unfocused, and an instant later total blackness engulfed her.

Gregory inspected the wound on Jennifer's neck. He walked to the bathroom and retrieved the first aid kit. The cut was deep, but not life threatening in the area the woman had started to slice. A half inch more, however, and she would have hit the left carotid artery and Jennifer's death would have been unstoppable. The bitch had been going to do it, he thought. Just the act of Jennifer's head falling forward had already sealed the wound, but he cleaned the area and then applied gauze and a bandage anyway.

He then laid out the unidentified attacker on the floor so she could breathe properly. He didn't want her dying until he knew who she was and how she had tracked Alex. Next, he cut the tape from Jennifer and laid her on the couch. He searched the woman's backpack and found no identification. Then he went out to the Jeep he had seen parked under some trees up the drive and found a purse, and inside a Canadian passport. 'Marcy Simon of Montreal. Interesting', he said out loud. He found the rental contract on top of the visor and inspected it. Then he drove the Jeep out to the main road and pulled into the parking lot for the public beach access. He found a spot in the lot off to the side and just off the road to make it look like the vehicle had coasted in. He popped the hood. With Marcy's knife, he scraped an ignition wire bare, spread some dirt on it to make it appear like an aged abrasion, then tested the engine. It cranked, but didn't fire.

He retrieved all of Marcy's personal stuff from the vehicle but left the rental agreement inside on the passenger seat. On the walk back to the house, he used Marcy's cell phone to call the rental agency to report the vehicle had broken down, and gave the location. Knowing Molokai and the tenor of its residents fairly well, he gave the rental agency about a fifty-fifty shot of recovering the vehicle before somebody burned it out.

When he arrived back at the house, he double checked Alex and confirmed he was indeed dead. One dart would deliver enough fast acting anesthetic to knock him out for eight or nine hours, but he had been reasonably certain that two would overpower his respiratory system and kill him. He had been right.

He checked on the women and found them both sleeping soundly. Gregory pondered the situation. He had three boats left. Each would hold one woman. There was no chance of doubling up to include Alex's corpse. Then he had an idea and went down to the workout room and brought back two fifty pound free weights. He grabbed the nylon rope he had found in Marcy's backpack.

Over the next half hour, he trussed Alex's body with the nylon rope and then lugged the two weights out to the helicopter. He attached a doubled length of rope to the weights which he had laid on the ground. Next, he dragged Alex's body out of the house and placed him into the right front seat of the helicopter. He wrapped the lap belt around him and then took the rope connected to the weights and tied them into to the ropes around the body. His plan was to fly Alex out to sea north of the island after dark with the weights hanging free outside of the chopper. At the proper location, he'd engage the autopilot and then open the door, unlatch the lap belt and push the body out. He was certain he could do that easily enough from the left seat. The weights would hold the body down long enough for the predators and scavengers of the sea to do their job.

Next, he went inside, got something to drink and stood watching the women. He used a paper towel to wipe the sweat from his head. He checked the clock and saw he had about half an hour before sunset. The timing would be perfect. First he moved Jennifer into the back of the helicopter and laid her across the seats. Marcy Simon he put on the floor in the back.

He went through the house one last time and made sure to remove Alex's personal items. He put a twenty pound weight into the bag and after locking the house and setting the alarm tossed the bag into the helicopter. He'd send it to Davy Jones' Locker along with its owner.

Just after sunset, he started the helicopter and flew north of the island about five miles. With the autopilot flying along at a slow speed at just over one hundred feet off the water, he unlatched his seatbelt and slid over to reach the opposite door. He could feel the hundred pounds of dead weight swinging on the ropes like a pair of pendulums which were adding forces with which he, and now the autopilot had to contend. Gregory wasted no time pushing Alex out the door. He dropped like a stone and sank the same way. Next, he tossed out the duffel. Gregory secured the door and slid back to his seat. He turned the helicopter back to the south, flew over Molokai at five hundred feet and then set course for home.

Half an hour later he set the chopper down on the helipad. He knew Keoki was watching, so he went into the house by himself. He'd bring the women in during the night after that asshole up the hill went to bed.

I decided to repack the envelopes and put them back into the cigar boxes. I had catalogued every item, photographed each one, and had made photocopies of the journals and legal pads at the Office Max in Kahului this afternoon and then scanned those into my computer. Every bit of the collection was now photographically documented, catalogued, and saved in digital files which had been uploaded to the office server. An email advised Sandy they were all there. So, since little could be gained by physically handling the items which could not be accomplished by looking through the stored digital photographic records, I had made the decision to pack it all away.

The chore was accomplished just after dark and I was exhausted. I had been up for thirty-six straight hours, fueled by sugar and Coke, and a bad pizza delivered from a place which had no business making pizzas. How I craved a good old, greasy, Pizza Village pie.

My phone rang and I picked it up from the table and I walked down the hall to the bedroom. It was Keoki, reporting that Gregory had just returned. I checked the clock on my computer which read a few minutes after eight p.m. As it turned out, I could have made it out there and gone in again for about an hour, but I had no desire to repeat last night's close call. I thanked Keoki and asked him to let me know if anything else developed. He asked when I come out again that I bring more beer. I promised I would. I left my clothes where they fell and hit the sheets.

A few minutes later, I was dead asleep.

Chapter Twenty-Two

Cassie awoke to find her window masked again. From the way she felt, she assumed it was early Monday morning, possibly just before sunrise. Today, she told herself, it will happen today.

Sandy and Teddy arrived at the records repository just after nine on Monday morning. After a little schmoozing, a rotund, pleasant, records clerk lead them to a large table surrounded by row upon row of towering racks containing many decades of boxed police records somewhere deep in the bowels of the building. On the way down, they were admonished to not go searching the stacks of stored files on their own. They each obediently took a chair and waited.

"Records clerks can be fanatical about maintaining order in the system," Teddy told Sandy. "They're a little like librarians that way. If you ever want to see a librarian freak out - and I'm talking a true librarian, not just someone who happens to work in a library - start moving books around the shelves and then stand back."

"We had one like that in our law library at the firm," Sandy said. "Woe be the attorney or law clerk who dared tread within her domain to remove or return a book to the shelf."

They shared a little laugh and then engaged in some small talk. Most of the catching up had been done at dinner the night before, as had bringing Teddy fully up to speed on the investigation, without mentioning names or privileged client information, of course, so until the files started coming they were down to chit chat. Sandy enjoyed spending time with Teddy, but her mind was four thousand miles away with William. She had called him after returning from dinner last night and he sounded tired and frustrated.

From her perspective, to William, what had started off as a fun and interesting reconnection to his youth had turned into a huge, convoluted mess. She was feeling a bit helpless, along with holding the misguided belief she was partly responsible for his frustrations. Every rock she overturned only muddied the water and lead to another twist, or another dead end. Add to that his growing concern there was something massively criminal going on inside that house, and the fact their client had obviously lied to them from the outset and was now missing, or at least incommunicado, and his frustration was understandable. William was a doer, he solved problems for people, yet every step he took in this case only sank him deeper into an engulfing mire.

While William had still rejected the idea, at least outwardly, Sandy believed it was Cassandra who was manipulating the entire situation for some unknown purpose. Sandy had disliked the woman from the instant she watched her slither into the office. A woman can tell a lot about another woman that a man will either be unable or unwilling to see, she knew.

The first several files arrived at the table and she and Teddy began to go through them in order. Sandy checked each case number against the list they had printed yesterday. The folders were relatively sparse for case files, but what could be expected with missing persons cases where no evidence existed of a crime? Sandy took notes on her laptop and Teddy made photocopies of anything interesting or unusual in the files. Sandy immediately scanned the documents into the case file on her computer. Neither was certain what they were looking for, but Sandy was convinced they'd know it when they saw it.

Then something struck her like a bolt of lightning. Sandy looked into the case file, found what she was looking for and then pulled out her cell phone. No service.

"You're not going to get cell service in here," Teddy said. "Beepers or pagers either. It's why we call this place *The Tomb*. It's a great place to hide out for a while and think."

"I need to make a call, though, Teddy," she said. "Something just hit me and I never thought any more of it."

Teddy directed her to a phone mounted on a nearby column, gave her his I.D. number to enter into the system and told her how to navigate to an outside line. Only bureaucrats would come up with a series of hoops like this just to make a call, she thought, but she figured that's what we pay bureaucrats to do.

The call rang through finally and while she waited for him to pick up Sandy prayed he still had the case file handy to research her question. The phone rang six, seven, eight times...

"Cheyenne Police Department, Sergeant George speaking."

"Yes, Sergeant George, this is Sandy Langdon calling. You remember we spoke about the Tammy Boeldt missing person case a few days ago?"

"Certainly, I remember, Ms. Langdon," he said. "How can I help you today."

"Well, first I wanted to thank you for getting back to us so quickly, and I wanted to ask you about the information you sent over."

He accepted the thanks and waited for the question.

"The report stated Tammy had been reported missing from her workplace, that her vehicle had been found in the parking lot but she had failed to report to work upon returning from vacation."

"That's correct, as I recall," he said.

"Well, can you find in the file where she had been vacationing?"

"I've got the file right here," he said. "Let me look."

Sandy waited patiently, but suspected she already knew the answer.

"According to a follow up report," he said. "Hawaii."

"Is it any more specific, does it say which island," she asked.

"Which island?"

"Yes, Hawaii is really eight islands, six of which are tourist destinations." She went on to list them. "Does the report state which island? Oahu, that's where Honolulu is, Kauai, Lanai, Maui, the Big..."

"Yeah, here it is, she went to Maui."

Sandy thanked him again and made three other calls. She was able to get one more response, the other three would need to call her back. Then she placed a call to Ernie in Montreal.

"Ernie," she said. "It's Sandy Langdon. Yes, I'm fine, thank you. Listen, Ernie, do you know where Janet had been before she disappeared?"

Sandy's eyes got larger. She thanked him again and hung up the phone. Teddy noted her excitement when she sat down.

"What is it?" he asked.

"The common thread," she said. "I have answers for all but one woman, but three of the five disappeared immediately upon, or shortly after returning from vacation." She looked him in the eye. "Get this, on Maui."

"They all disappeared from their home towns," Teddy said. "That means they traveled home and then went missing. These days with these TSA pricks and enhanced security, you just can't fly on someone else's ticket, you need a photo I.D. which matches the name on the ticket."

"I.D.'s are faked all the time, Teddy," Sandy retorted. "You've seen it enough in your career."

Teddy sat back in his chair and thought about possible scenarios.

"Okay, given this isn't just one big coincidence, and there is a link to Maui, that means one of two scenarios to me: One, the perp followed them home and kidnapped them from their homes, work parking lots, shopping malls, etc., which would mean a record of the perp's travel somewhere; or, two, they never came back at all, they were snatched on Maui and someone else traveled back home, put their stuff away, used their car and abandoned it someplace it would be found and traced back."

Teddy shook his head.

"All without being seen?" he said rhetorically.

"You forget the woman from Montreal, Teddy," Sandy reminded. "We had video surveillance of our girl, a blonde, coming back, but an hour later a brunette leaves the apartment building? A woman none of the neighbors recognized or knew? Then she travels nearly two thousand miles by way of Chicago to move geographically less than one hundred miles, arrives in Burlington, Vermont as a woman but leaves as a man?"

"We could be dealing with a serial here, one with means," Teddy observed. He paused. "One possessing the ability to pass as a woman."

"All these women fit a physical type, Teddy. Five feet six to five feet eight, one hundred twenty to one hundred forty pounds, brown hair, except for our latest victim, and between twenty-five and thirty-five. One guy fitting that physical description, or close to it could easily pull this off."

"We're talking cases that go back twenty years, and that's what we know, and still this guy is passing for a woman in the mid-twenties to mid-thirties?" Teddy shook his head. He looked skeptical. "That doesn't make sense to me, Sandy. I'll tell you why."

"I'm listening," she said.

Teddy pushed back on his chair so it balanced on the back two legs. He put his hands behind his head.

"Statistics show that these types of perpetrators are white males, generally loner types, and between the ages of twenty and forty, or so. After that, they either get caught, die off, or just fade away as the testosterone level drops off. This guy has been doing this for at least twenty years, and nobody's gotten a whiff of him in all that time?"

"What if he started in his twenties, and now he's in his forties?" she offered. "He could still pass, with a big hat, heavy make-up, glasses. I've seen some of these boys dressing like women in Vegas shows, and occasionally wandering The Quarter during Mardi Gras, and sometimes it's hard to tell. Remember that BTK surfaced, dropped out, resurfaced, for over twenty-five years before they finally nailed his sick ass. He hunted in his own home town, for God's sake. Think of the numbers of women who anonymously flow through Hawaii every year, over twenty years."

"Yeah, but most of them go with someone. People go to Hawaii on their honeymoons, for weddings, group stuff."

"They also go for seminars, as did Janet Hopkins, they go with tours, and women are traveling alone more and more these days, even to places like Hawaii," she said.

"I guess," Teddy replied, still thinking. Then he rocked forward in his chair, put his elbows on the table and spoke in a low tone to her. "Sandy, we're friends and we all go way back, but this needs to be said. You haven't told me who your client is, and how this person may be related to someone you suspect of doing these things, but if we find this woman from Chicago and she ties in, I'm going to want it all. This can't remain a private matter when there could be so many hurting families in so many places out there."

Sandy didn't hesitate.

"Teddy, you have my word that if we can tie this missing Chicago woman to this case of ours, the Big Dog and I will give you everything we have got.   Frankly, all we have right now is happenstance and speculation and as a lawyer I can tell you that won't cut it with any prosecutor or grand jury anywhere.   We'll get the proof, and when we do, you're first on the list to get it."

They went back to work pouring over the files.   By noon, they had gone through ten, half of the possible case files, with a fine tooth comb.   While they waited for the other files to be pulled, they went out and walked to a nearby deli to grab a sandwich.   Sandy called William from her cell as they sat outside to eat and took in some fresh air.

Somehow, my exhausted body had been able to persuade my brain to shut down last night so the entire me could recover from being up for thirty-six straight hours.   I awoke on Monday to another brilliant sunrise and blue skies, and I felt rested and as fresh as the morning.

Around seven thirty, as I stood looking down the greenway to the ocean, a view I was growing accustomed to enjoying, my cell phone buzzed and chirped out Sandy's special tone.   I walked to the table, now blessedly uncluttered of Gregory's crap, and picked it up.

"Good morning, Sandy," I said.

"Hey, Otto, you sound a heck of a lot better this morning."

"I got some rest last night.   It seems the best cure for insomnia is physical exhaustion after nearly getting caught in another person's house."

"Maybe you could market that," Sandy joked.   "Of course, our society would just rather take a pill."

"Yeah, I know.   Anyway, what are you and Teddy finding today?"

Sandy filled me in on what they had found, or rather what they had not found this morning in the Chicago case files and then, in typical Sandy fashion, she dropped the bombshell.

"So, you're telling me that three of five women on the list had just returned from Maui when they disappeared?" I asked.

"Yep.   I suspect we're going to hear the same thing from Des Moines, frankly."

"The first one, Jessi Bollenbeck, she hadn't been to Maui, she had been in New York," I said.

"Yeah, but that was twenty years ago, Otto," Sandy shot back. "Our boy wasn't in Maui twenty years ago. He moved to Maui just under sixteen years ago. Twenty years ago, he was living in New York."

"That's right," I said. "So if we're correct, he has been doing this for more than the time he's been on Maui?"

"Oh, my God," Sandy said. "Otto, look in your briefing book. Something just hit me."

I found the Operation Puppy Love binder.

"What?"

"In Gregory's summary, I remember something about a teacher who went missing after an alleged affair was revealed between her and Gregory."

I found the page.

"Yeah, here it is. At Abbotsford Military Academy, a woman teacher went missing after an alleged affair had been discovered between them during his junior year in high school. He was seventeen and the woman has never turned up for questioning."

"Can it go back that far?" she asked. "Thirty-three years?"

"That would put him past BTK in longevity," I said. I thought about what we were suggesting. "Come on, Sandy, don't you think we're making some leaps here?"

She was silent for a time, and then came back.

"Maybe," she said. "It gives us something to go further with, though."

"I think we've got enough on our plates," I told her. "I'll look at the journals again and see what I find after his opening mommy discussion just as soon as I can. Perhaps he talks about teacher obsessions, although I don't recall it from my earlier reviews.."

"Good enough, Otto."

"Now, what do you and Teddy think the Maui connection is here?"

We bounced the current theoretical scenarios back and forth and settled on three which appeared the most probable. Sandy reported Teddy felt we were looking at only two, so I felt good our three included Teddy's two. Viewing each objectively, they all had promise, but they also all had holes. When one looked at Cassie's original story about this being a divorce case with what we now know is a worthless prenuptial agreement, a scenario which I no longer believed, and added in what we have learned, I was beginning to get that sick feeling in my stomach that usually came when I had been played. Perhaps Sandy had been right all along, but I didn't tell her that. At least not yet.

A knock came at the door. I told Sandy to hold on and went to answer the knock. A short Asian woman in maid's garb with her hair dyed the color of carrots handed me an envelope. She apologized, saying that it was to have been delivered last night, but the night clerk had not received an answer when she had knocked. I said it was all right and that I had most likely been asleep.

I turned the envelope in my hand. It was sealed and there was a handwritten instruction on the front to deliver it to me three days from the date it was dropped off. It was dated last Thursday afternoon. Yesterday would have been three days.

Putting the phone on speaker with Sandy still on the line, I set it onto the table and then slid my finger along the flap to open the envelope. I pulled out half a dozen photographs and a folded piece of paper. I dropped the entire contents onto the table.

"Somebody sending you love letters, Otto?" Sandy asked.

I picked up each photo one by one. Each showed Cassie and a tall, younger man I didn't recognize in a verdant setting. Having seen these type of photographs before, and having taken these kind many times myself, I would attest there was some level of intimacy between the pair, but how much could be debated. Photos may replace one thousand words, but I know enough about the trade to understand sometimes those words are woven into lies. In one photo the two were seated on a bench, holding hands; in two others they were embracing. It appeared the prints had been created on a home photo printer as there were no lab markings on the back side.

I described what I was seeing in the photos to Sandy, told her I'd scan and email them to her later. Then I picked up the folded sheet of paper and opened it. The handwriting was the same as on the outside of the envelope: a vaguely familiar chirography which was really a cross between printing and script. I skimmed the note before reading it to Sandy. At the bottom was a flowing signature, 'Cassie'.

"Willy: These photographs were delivered to me today at The Four Seasons. I am assuming Gregory is behind them. Do not believe what you see. I am

concerned Gregory is moving to circumvent our efforts and I am going home to meet with him. If you receive this, please come for me. Do not be fooled, I will be there. Cassie P.S. Do not involve the police. Trust me."

When I finished, Sandy was silent for a moment. I assume she transcribed the words as I read them and then was rereading them.

"Come for me?" she asked. "What the heck do you think that means?"

"I'm assuming it means exactly what it says. I have not been able to reach her since Thursday morning, so I have to assume Gregory has done something with her, and I need to help her."

"Don't be a fool, Otto," she said. "This woman has been playing games since she first called to see you. Remember I told you I didn't trust her. Now, we all suspect her husband is involved in the disappearances, and most likely the deaths, of at least five women, because we followed the half-assed breadcrumb trail she gave us and now you're thinking of running off to the castle to rescue the poor damsel locked away in the dungeon? You were all over that house the other night, and found no sign of her."

"The Cassie I know would not play me. Sure, she hasn't been totally honest about all this, but I'm certain she has her reasons. She warned me that Gregory was dangerous, and this note proves it."

"For all we know, she's drawing you into a trap," she said. "I will say it again, I don't trust her, and regardless what her note or your heart says, neither should you."

"I'll consider that, Sandy," I said.

"Meaning you're going to do what you are going to do," she replied. "You know, Otto, I've heard those words before and you have lived to regret speaking them."

"I'm still here," I said. "Don't worry, I can take care of myself." Then I lied to her: "Let me give this some thought."

"I assume there is nothing more to be said. We're going to go back and get through the rest of the files. Just promise me before you do anything stupid you'll talk to me."

"All right, mother, I promise," I lied again, but there are some lies you tell so someone who loves you won't worry, even though you know they will.

Gregory moved down into the lava tube at sunrise. Each of the three cells was now occupied. He had not wanted it to work out this way, but since these were the cards he had been dealt, he'd go all in and play the hand.

He had masked off Cassandra's window during the night when he brought Jennifer down and placed her in the middle cell. No sense allowing Cassandra see her daughter before he was ready to spring the surprise. Like her mother, Jennifer was tethered to the bed with a manacle around one ankle. Unlike her mother, he had left Jennifer clothed.

The other one, this interloper from Canada named Marcy Simon, he thought, would be dealt with first. He didn't really need to break her, he had concluded overnight, but he knew how he could. She was also the only one who could be really dangerous, Cassandra's incident with the fork aside, so he had left Marcy handcuffed in addition to the manacle tether on her ankle. He also had no interest in stripping her bare. She wasn't going to be at the party that long.

Gregory had watched each of the women as he ate breakfast in his office before he came down. Now, standing in the little workshop area down in the lava tube, he turned on the monitors and then hit the lights in all three cells.

"Show Time," he said out loud.

When the lights came on full intensity he saw Cassandra shielded her eyes, Jennifer rolled over, and the dyke struggled to sit up on the edge of the bed. Jennifer and Marcy should be mostly recovered from the effects of the anesthetic by now, he knew, but they'd still be thirsty. The two new arrivals had much longer to recover than had Cassandra and had also received a lesser dose, so he knew they'd be less affected by the light and be less disoriented.

He had brought down some oranges and bananas for Cassandra. He walked out of the workshop with the bag of fruit, opened the small portal in Cassandra's door and dropped it in. He slammed the cover and latched it.

Next, he moved to the middle cell and opened the door. He brought with him a jug of water and a straw. Jennifer turned to look at him when the door opened. He moved inside and left the door ajar. He approached Jennifer and offered her the water. She stared at him. He knew she would be thirsty, but he also knew she was confused and may not trust him anymore. He took a long drink from the straw and re-offered it to her. She grabbed the jug and sucked water voraciously. He advised her to take it slow or nausea would be the result and he was certain she didn't want to spend such a big day with her head hanging in the toilet.

"Why are you doing this, Gregory?" she asked, her voice raspy.

"Believe me Jennifer, I didn't want it to go this way, but other people forced my hand," he said with genuine remorse in his voice. "My goal was to provide you with the opportunity to meet and get to know your bio-mom and for her to get to know you. She's here, by the way, but she does not yet know you are."

"Where is here, Gregory?" she asked, her voice a little stronger and clearer.

"Here is my home, my dear," he said and looked around. "Well, near my home."

"Why did you hurt Alex?"

"I didn't hurt him. He felt nothing more than you did, a pinprick and then moments later a deep slumber."

"You shot him twice. I saw you. I watched his breathing stop," she nearly shouted the accusation. She rubbed her head with both hands. "Did I dream it?"

Gregory turned his back to her and pondered the proper response. He had no desire to traumatize the girl any more than he already had, but neither did he wish to coddle her.

"Alex betrayed you," he said. "He was an evildoer who won't be missed. You should not lament his passing."

Jennifer looked at him so hard he felt her eyes piercing his soul, if there were such a thing. When she spoke the venom dripped from her words.

"Then what does that make you?"

"I am what I always have been, my dear. Nothing more, nothing less. Save your final judgment for when you know the entire story. Like your paintings, you cannot know the full effect of this work until you can contemplate every detail."

He placed a bag containing some fruit, a sandwich, a small container of ibuprofen, and a couple bottles of Gatorade to help her body recover more quickly from the draining effects of the anesthetic at the foot of her bed.

"You'll find almost everything you need to feel better in that little cabinet and this bag," he said, pointing to each. "No luxuries, you understand, but the basic essentials." He turned to leave and then over his shoulder added: "Not that your stay will be too long, but hopefully it will not be too uncomfortable."

He left her cell and closed the door. She heard the locks tumble into place, yet still stumbled forward and tested it. She could hear him moving outside but could not see anything but a muted shadow slide across her masked window.

Emotionally and physically exhausted, her body aching from head to toe, she turned her back to the door and slowly crumbled to the ground into a seated fetal position. She closed her eyes against the tears which still managed to seep through, locked her arms around her legs and began to rock slowly back and forth while her mind screamed, 'Why is this happening?'.

Gregory moved next to the other end cell, the one closest to the water. He removed a corner of the masking from the window and peered inside. It had been minutes since he had seen the dyke trying to sit up in the bed and he didn't want any surprises from this one. He didn't bring this one food, or water, or anything else which would make her feel a bit more comfortable. This one had interfered, ruined his finely tuned plan. Gregory's fists balled together as he thought of all the damage her arrival had wrought. He almost regretted that he had not sent her to the bottom right away like he had Alex, and then he fought back the thought of simply opening the door and beating her to death with his bare hands. No, this one deserved the full treatment for her crimes against him; and he was resolved to giving her every taste of his wrath.

He opened the door and observed her sitting on the edge of the bed, her large, bony feet flat on the concrete floor, her arms secured behind her body by the very handcuffs she had brought with her and had placed on Alex. Her body was hunched forward and her head was bowed in the pain of a dry recovery to the anesthetic. She turned her head slowly to look at him. The hatred in her reddened eyes tried to burn through him, but he deflected the venom and simply returned a smile.

"Your papers say your name is Marcy Simon and that you're visiting us from Montreal, Canada," he said, as he stood in the doorway, safely beyond the reach of the tether should she decide to throw her Amazonian body at him. He realized she wasn't really all that large, just a bit bigger than the women he surrounded himself with. From what he heard on the surveillance of the Molokai house, quite a bit less of a lady.

"Go fuck yourself, asshole," she spit out at him in a rasp that was barely audible. "Give me an opening and I'll wring your skinny neck until your eyes pop out of your filthy head."

Gregory realized each word caused her severe pain without the help of water to replenish her ravaged body. He was frankly impressed with the level of hatred she was able to harness against the pain.

"Now, is that any way to speak to your host?" he mocked. "I had intended to treat you so very well during what will be your, sorry to say it, brief stay." He wagged a finger at her. "You have no idea the trouble your showing up here has caused me."

She merely glared at him, then turned her face toward the floor. He watched her with the curiosity of a child. She had both challenged him and surrendered to him in the span of a few moments. Not to matter, he thought to himself, but he decided to make a mental note for later mention in her section of his journal.

"I take it you traveled here in search of news of your friend, Janet Hopkins," he said, not admitting to her that he already knew this from watching her interrogation of Alex. "Did you know that Janet occupied this very cell?"

Marcy turned her face to him. Even in the relative coolness of the cell, he saw her face was sweating, slowly seeping more precious moisture from her already depleted body.

"Yes, she did," he said. "She surrendered on that very spot where you are right now. On that very bed."

Gregory could see her eyes gauging the length of the manacle chain, considering the reach she could add with her body, and the distance which now separated him from her. He smiled.

"Go ahead and try," he said in a teasing tone. "You will find your attempt will fall to right about here." He scuffed an imaginary line onto the concrete with the toe of his shoe. "Go ahead, make my day." He smiled at the pun.

He was the only one to find it clever. Yet Marcy made no attempt to confirm his estimation. She refused to give him anything, but what she could not know is that she had already given him everything he needed with just the one look.

"I have a little surprise for you," he said. "A gift. A prize for doing something nobody has been able to do in over three decades." He looked off into space. "My goodness, has it been that long?"

He shook his head, tossing off the thoughts of the past.

Marcy watched him. He reached inside his pocket and pulled out a small remote control, pushed a button and a flat screen television mounted to the wall came to power, followed by a few short screen flashes, and then a digital video played showing what she recognized as this cell but with Janet lying on the bed. Marcy saw Janet's arms were free, but her foot was similarly manacled to the bed. She was naked. To Marcy it appeared that Janet was rousing from a deep sleep. Suddenly, there was a slice of light which moved across the lowly lit room and she watched in horror as Gregory moved in with a jug of something and wanted her drink from it. Janet had originally refused, but he took a drink and then she did as well. Gregory pressed another button on the remote and sound came along with the video.

"Where am I?" came Janet's first words with a deep rasp.

Marcy watched as Janet looked at Gregory.

"You're the man from the banquet. What do you want from me?" Her voice grew stronger with each sip of the liquid from the jug.

"I want nothing from you but everything," Gregory said to her.

He pushed a button on the remote and the image froze on the screen.

"See?" he asked Marcy. "She was right here, and you know, she did give me everything."

Marcy's stomach flipped and she felt the bile build. She lurched toward the toilet, a reaction rather than a courtesy to her host, and tried to vomit forth anything she could from her empty stomach. She managed nothing but the mucus-like bile. Her insides cramped from the effort. She stood with great difficulty and then turned on a faucet after maneuvering her bound hands around the sink. Gregory watched in amusement as she bowed her head under the flowing faucet and took a drink, then immediately vomited the water back out.

She heard him laugh.

"Salt water," he said. "Normally the flow is fresh water, but sometimes I like to switch it up for my favored guests."

Marcy looked at him with burning eyes as saliva dripped down her chin. He finished his thought to her.

"You, Marcy Simon, of Montreal, Canada, are definitely one of my favorite favored guests." His grin was wrought of pure hatred and evil.

He backed out of the doorway, left her kneeling there on the floor, soiled and crying.

"You get your rest," he said. "Believe it or not, you've got a big day ahead of you. As for me, I've got some preparations to accomplish."

He closed the door and the locks tumbled into place. The lights went off and the room was back to being almost totally darkened. Only the frozen screen image of Janet's plaintiff face obviously searching out her captor's intent but looking almost directly into the camera remained. Marcy sobbed with anger, and sadness, and finally fear.

Chapter Twenty-Three

Sandy and Teddy walked back into the records building. While they made their way into The Tomb after lunch, she relayed the conversation with William, again, being careful to redact any mention of the client's identity. He listened intently, as any friend would, given the story Sandy was telling.

"Sounds to me like the Big Dog is gonna go in hot on this one," he said. "I see no other option for him at this point."

"I'm coming to the same conclusion, Teddy," she said. "Why is it nobody can control Mr. William Langdon?"

"He's always been a slow boiler, Sandy, you know that. He's not rash in his decision making. His problem has always been *after* he makes the decision and lights the fuse. Once he lights that fuse, it's best to be very far away from the unstoppable explosion that's coming."

"Is that what happened in the warehouse?" Sandy asked.

Teddy looked at her. His eyes told her what his words would not. He knew that while lawyers sometimes had intermittent hearing, cops sometimes had lapses of speech.

"Honey, nobody knows exactly what went down in that warehouse that night, except for William Langdon."

William had never given her all the details of what had lead up to, and occurred that night, although much of the story was in the public domain and she had done her research. She filled in the gaps with lawyer's logic, much like a defense attorney does when they suspect a guilty client, and the totality of the story she assembled was of the character Teddy just described: a lit fuse leading to an inevitable and unstoppable explosion.

Sandy sat at the table with the remaining missing person's files and considered those words.   There had been more than enough in the public record about the warehouse gun battle for anyone looking to come to a similar conclusion.   She wondered if Cassie had seen the same information, and concluded that William was capable of being a cold blooded killer.   Was that why she had gone out of her way to track him down and hire him?   Was this all just a manipulation to get him to light a fuse?   A fuse which this time lead to a powder keg wedged firmly in the ass of Gregory Thomason?

She did not share those last thoughts with Teddy. He was, after all, still a sworn law enforcement officer, no matter how good and old a friend he was to William and her.   She was beginning to really worry about William, but rather than focus on those concerns regarding events unfolding over four thousand miles away and upon which she had no control, Sandy immersed herself in the last of the files.

On the way to Cassie's house a metaphor Sandy used during our last conversation suddenly jumped out at me. I doubt she even knew what she had implied when the words fell out of her mouth - and neither did I at the time - but as I drove along the upper road they came into focus as if someone had written them in huge letters on the side of the mountain using neon pink paint.   Her metaphor of me 'running off to the castle to rescue the poor damsel locked away in the dungeon' had been incredibly, if accidentally, insightful.

My heart beat faster at the thought and I must have stepped harder on the accelerator because over the next rise I nearly flipped the Jeep while taking a blind turn too fast.   That little adventure caused an adrenalin rush which pumped up my heartbeat a little faster, and unlike many times in my life, I accepted the lesson as a warning and slowed the Jeep down.

"That's it," I said to myself. "The dungeon. He's got her in the lava tube."

I called Sandy's cell to pass on the revelation and thank her for the idea, however, the call went immediately to voicemail and I had to leave the message. I guessed she and Teddy must have been back in the records vault without cell service.

This time I didn't bother with hiding my vehicle down the road and instead drove directly into Keoki's yard. I did, however, pull around to the back of the house, uphill of the garage. Keoki shot me the shaka as I drove by the front porch. I hoped he didn't break my balls about forgetting to bring him more beer.

As I walked around the house, he greeted me with a smile and my new Hawaiian name. He also busted my balls about forgetting to bring him more beer.

"Ah, Malihini, what you no bring Keoki beer? After all I do for you?"

I apologized about forgetting the beer and promised I'd bring even more next time. He reported to me that there's been no activity in or around the house since last night when Gregory returned after dark in the helicopter. I told him what I suspected and he took it in and let it ruminate a bit.

"You know, dat make sense. Where else he have her? Plenty room down there," he said.

I explained how I had searched for the hat or cap or whatever he had called it the other night which he reported was located toward the end of the east wing of the house. He watched me carefully as I described Gregory's office being on that end of the house, and then nodded.

"Nalonalo ala," he said and saw me looking at him quizzically. "Mean hidden trail, Malihini. He hide in da walls."

"I looked and couldn't find it," I told him. "If the ala is indeed nalonalo, then he nalonalo'd it damn well."

Now it was Keoki's turn to look quizzical.

"I got mine dough, Brah," he said and nodded up the mountain. "He no can take dat from Keoki. He not know it even there." A big grin came across his face. "So, if she down there, and he down there, you sure surprise the shit out of him you come from da back. I like see dat, but me elemakule; old, Malihini, I too old go down dat hole. But, I tell you how."

While I sat with him, Keoki explained the climb into the lava tube from the upper entry. Apparently the lower entry was much more steep, high and dangerous than the upper entry. He laughed and said that was why he and his friends used to take that one when they were keiki instead of the safer upper hole his father told them to use. It had been a sign of warrior bravery to him and his friends. I liked the thought of a less steep, less high, less dangerous entry into the lava tube.

A few minutes later, we climbed off the porch and walked the old pathway toward the upper entry located above his house and garage. On the way past the Jeep, I grabbed a flashlight, a pair of handcuffs. The flashlight, I held in my hand, the cuffs I slipped into my waistband in back next to Willie. I could feel Sam snuggly attached just above my left ankle.

At the hole, which more closely resembled a rough, irregular, vertical gash in the rocky side of the mountain, I shined my light down the opening and could see the passage wove back and forth just like Keoki had described. I wondered to myself who was the first person to decide this looked like a good place to go explore. Then again, somebody had to be the first to look at a lobster and think, 'Yeah, this looks like something I'd like to eat'. I let the thought pass. As Keoki would say, 'It no mattah'.

Just before descending from the light into the darkness, I asked Keoki to call the police if I didn't return in three hours. I also told him there was a bag of evidence in my Jeep, the things he saw me remove from the house the other night. I asked that he not touch them. He agreed to both issues. Then, I then went into the earth.

Gregory checked over one of the remaining three boats. He didn't want to run the engine dry, so he hooked the electrical system up to a small AC to DC converter and confirmed the operation of all the controls and cameras. Everything was as he expected it to be, in perfect operational order. Next, he unfastened the hatch cover over the occupant area and placed it off to the side.

With everything ready, he turned and looked toward Marcy's cell. He usually waited for nightfall to launch the boats so there would be less chance of them being spotted in the channel, but he wanted to be shed of that bitch as soon as possible. There was just one more thing he wanted to show her before putting her aboard.

As he walked back to his workshop, he heard a commotion coming from up the lava tube. In the darkness, far beyond his area, he heard a tumbling noise, then a loud echo down the tube followed by total silence. He grabbed a flashlight from a rack above his bench, walked into the center of the tube and shone it into the darkness. He listened intently, but there was no more sound.

Gregory thought of walking up to find the source of the noise, but dismissed that thought just as quickly. Each time he had made the trek before all he had found was a pile of rocks which had come loose from somewhere above. He returned to his workroom, replaced the flashlight in the rack, put the remote control back into his pocket and then grabbed the dart gun and loaded it with a low-dose round. The low-dose round was not enough to knock the dyke out, but more than enough to render her docile. He just hoped the lift worked and he didn't have to lug her fat ass into the boat.

Gregory approached the door to Marcy's cell. Again he peeked through the masking to make certain she was not lurking near the end of her tether. She was sitting on the edge of the bed staring at the monitor. For a fleeting instant he felt sorry for her, but then he quickly reforged his anger. Opening the door caught her a bit off-guard and he smiled as she jumped.

"Now what, asshole?" she said, her voice slowly recovering on its own. "You'll be one sorry eunuch if you pull what I can only assume is one sad excuse for manhood on me, because I'll rip it off and feed it to you."

He stood there and shook his head, a whimsical look on his face.

"Do you really think this has anything to do with sex, Marcy? Would it surprise you if I told you I have never been unfaithful to my wife?"

"Lucky her," she spat.

"No, this is about something much larger than sex; something I have neither the time nor the desire to explain to the likes of you. Your lifestyle is an abomination. What would you know about sex, or love for that matter? Did you really think you were in love with this Janet person?"

She didn't answer him. She refused to grant him the satisfaction of any information or commentary in response to his inquiries. Instead she stared him down, which did make him a bit uncomfortable, so he moved things along.

"Please, watch the screen, Marcy." He pointed toward the television. "You've been given a glimpse of Janet in my possession, but now I thought I'd show you her final moments."

Marcy's eyes flared and she felt a knife sink into her heart. It no longer remained a question. Janet was gone. Part of her wished she was dead too, but then a moment later something flowed into her which she could only describe as a divine infusion. She thought of Thomas and Belle's words about having the strength to bear witness to and accept whatever had been Janet's fate. Marcy sat up straight and looked at the screen. She was ready for the images to be burned into her soul.

Gregory pushed a button on his remote and the still shot of Janet was replaced by video which showed her lying on her stomach in an enclosed area, her hands and feet bound by duct tape. The camera panned back and forth over her then settled upon her face. Marcy had seen this look before, the time they did a boat tour of Niagara Falls and Janet got seasick. The audio revealed her moaning, and the sound of an engine running in the distance. Suddenly there was a loud pop, followed shortly thereafter by a second. The sound of the motor stopped.

Marcy watched in horror as Janet began thrashing about in the confined space. Janet's eyes then changed from confusion to fear to panic in the matter of a few seconds. Then Marcy saw it, water was rising in the compartment, slowly at first, then more quickly. Janet held her head as high above the rising water as she could but it soon overwhelmed her. Marcy saw Janet struggling, splashing, thrashing, fighting the battle for her life. Then, she watched as Janet stopped moving and her eyes went dull. Marcy hung her head. Gregory watched her, an evil grin on his face.

"Now, my dear," he said.

Marcy heard his voice as if standing in opposite ends of a long tunnel filled with cotton. It was distant and muffled, the words made no sense, as if they had been spoken in some alien language.

"Now, my dear," he repeated more loudly. "It's time for you to join your dear departed Janet. It's time for you to pay for your abomination against nature."

Marcy slowly turned her face to him.

"Who are you to judge? Who are you to condemn me, or Janet, or any of the others you must have had through here? You know nothing of love or life or happiness. You are dead inside." She saw there was no emotion on his face, no reaction to her words. "There is a special place in hell for people like you."

"Are you finished?" he asked.

Marcy did not respond. She saw him raise the dart pistol toward her and she reflexively recoiled.

"Not to worry, my dear Marcy," he said as he pulled the trigger. "This won't put you to sleep so you don't have to worry about missing any of the fun, but it will make you less dangerous while I entomb you."

Marcy jolted from the impact of the dart in her side, felt the heat of the puncture and then another hotter sensation as the medicine seeped into her body. Moments later, the world began to spin slowly and then everything went out of focus. Out of the blackness, she could feel his hands upon her but she was powerless to resist. Images formed and then dissolved just as rapidly. The next conscious image she had was of her body positioned on her belly inside a compartment like she had just seen on the television. She rocked against the restraints, felt the panic of a lifetime of claustrophobia seize her mind.

If this was the easy entry, I would have hated to even attempt the steeper, higher, and more dangerous one. I estimated I had been making my way down for fifteen or twenty minutes. About ten minutes earlier, I had placed my foot onto what looked like a sound shelf when it let loose and sent rocks down into the darkness. I waited in the darkened silence for my heartbeat to return to normal and wondered if Gregory had heard anything down in the tube. If he was down there, that was.

Keoki told me he and his friends could descend to the tube in about half an hour when they were kids. I estimated that it would take me almost double that at my age. When I had asked him how I would know when I was finally in the main lava tube, he had laughed and said 'Just watch dat last step, Malihini, it a doozy.'

Any light filtering in from above had quickly evaporated in the pitch black crags as I descended, so I was increasingly using my flashlight. The last thing I wanted, however, was Gregory being able to see the movement of light spilling out into tube.

So I'd carefully illuminate an area, make a few steps of descent, and repeat the process. Occasionally, I'd rest, and listen for any noises reflecting through the tube. There were areas where the walls would close in and I'd have to squeeze down like toothpaste being dropped onto an unseen brush and then other areas where the walls would open up and you could fit a VW microbus inside. So it went, my journey into the center of the earth, well, sorta.

Gregory secured the latches on the compartment, sealing Marcy inside the boat. She had given him no resistance after the dart delivered its medicine, but from the thrashing she was now doing inside there, he realized he had gotten her in just in time. He knocked on the cover and she just fought harder against her restraints. Gregory smiled to himself. Even if she were able to break free of the cuffs and duct tape, there was nowhere for her to go. The compartment was securely sealed from the outside.

He rolled the cart toward the opening of the lava tube. The channel beyond was remarkably calm. The blue sky allowed for nearly unlimited visibility. He assumed he would be able to see all the way to the Big Island from the house. As he approached the edge of the concrete floor at the start of the rocky beach, Marcy went quiet. She must have worn her little self out, he thought and he lowered the ramp which would help him slide the boat out onto the loose, smooth rocks. As many times as he'd done this, he still had no better solution for this part of the journey. It was just muscling the boat downhill to the water, but it was becoming increasingly physically exhausting each time.

He slid the boat off the cart and it thumped against the rocks. Marcy started up again with her bouncing around. He knocked on the cover and asked if she'd please just go quietly into that good night. He doubted she heard him, and if she did, he doubted she'd think it clever. He pulled the boat across the rocks in a lurching motion, each pull put him two or three feet closer to the surf, which today was just slowly ebbing onto shore.

He looked to the cart for the radio control and cursed to himself. He made another couple of pulls and then took a rest and headed back to the workshop to grab the controller. As he made his way he swore he saw a flash of light deep inside the tube. He stood and watched for a repeat of the flash, but saw nothing and then continued into the workshop. Once inside, he checked the monitor on both Cassandra and Jennifer. Jennifer appeared to be sleeping, but Cassandra was sitting on her bed with her back against the wall. Her legs straight out and her ankles crossed. She rested her hands on her lap.

"Looks like she's waiting on a damn bus," Gregory said out loud. He repositioned the camera. The bag of fruit laid where it had fallen. He shrugged, picked up the controller from the desk, and walked back out to the ocean.

The last step was indeed a doozy and I nearly fell fifteen feet to a very irregular surface. I caught myself, but the flashlight fell to the floor. Fortunately, the rubber cover muffled the sound, but as it hit, the flashlight went on for an instant and then thankfully went off. After I made my way to the floor, I found the flashlight, turned my back to the other end of the tube, hooded the light and turned it on, or tried to at least. It was a goner, but I tucked it into my waistband nonetheless. Carefully, I moved toward the light on the far end of the tube. My eyes had adjusted to the dark during the descent, and the shadows cast by the distant sunlight helped me move along without twisting an ankle.

I was sweaty and my muscles ached. I was thirsty. That descent had been the biggest workout this body had seen in a while. Maybe I'd start listening to Sandy's nagging about me moving out of my chair occasionally. She thought taking a walk together was a way of getting fresh air, some exercise, and conversation all rolled into one little activity we could do over the lunch hour. I told her I valued my lunch hours more than strapping on walking shoes and heading outside into the heat and humidity of New Orleans. So, she suggested we do it after work. I told her that lately I valued my happy hours more than lunch. She hadn't been amused.

As I got closer to the light, I could hear some activity and see a person moving around. The built-up area was incredible as I came upon it. Farther down the tube toward the water sat three separate block structures about the size of a small room along the east wall. Closer to where I stood, and situated more toward the center of the tube sat a larger concrete block structure. Equipment of various configurations hummed quietly near each of the buildings.

Before the buildings, the first structure I laid my hands on was a stairway with rubber covered ramps and lights which snaked its way from the floor and disappeared up inside what I concluded must be the lower opening exiting somewhere behind the walls of Gregory's office. That meant I was now standing more or less directly under Gregory's office. I wondered what Keoki would make of all this and then I saw Gregory come out of the bigger block house in the center carrying a white box about the size of a portable radio and walking toward the ocean. A small boat sat out on the rocks. Two more just like it rested on carts along the wall just oceanside of the smaller blockhouses.

Gregory had his back to me as he walked out toward the ocean. I moved quickly to the back of the center block house, peered around the corner to make certain he was still not looking in my direction, then slid around the corner and hugged the wall while I inched along the side. Turning the last corner, I was inside a moment later. I watched from the doorway of the larger blockhouse as Gregory hung the small box on the cart and then walked to the boat. I then took a moment or two to look around inside.

The room was a combination workshop, storage area and electronics complex. Servers, switches, routers, monitors, and DVR equipment were all hooked into a complex arrangement. It was cool inside, obviously climate controlled. That's what the running equipment must do, I concluded. In the center of the room was a desk with half a dozen monitors. I walked around behind the desk and that's what sent me running back out into the tube. Gregory was dragging the boat to the water, just about to move around to the back for the final push into the channel when I ran up and drew down on him with Willie.

"Don't you move you son of a bitch or I'll send you to hell a little early," I said.

He turned slowly and glared at me. His eyes were calculating something and for a moment I thought he may just eat a bullet in exchange for getting the boat pushed into the channel. Now, looking down the barrel of a high caliber, semiautomatic weapon is a rush nobody wants to repeat. Believe me, I know. Gregory didn't react beyond staring at me. I ordered him to move away from the boat and get down on the rocks. He moved slowly up the side of the boat toward the stern. I repeated the command.

"This is the ultimate test, William," he said with a sneer. "The moment when our mettle is tested. Oh, I know you have shot and killed men before, hell, I read you even killed a woman once. So I know you're quite capable of pulling that trigger."

"Gregory, get on the ground now," I repeated.

"Or what, *private* detective?" he said, the word 'private' spit from his lips in an intentional slur. He now stood about five feet away, holding on to the port stern corner of the boat. I heard some rustling coming from inside the vessel. My eyes moved to the coffin-sized hatch cover which was securely dogged down and realized someone was inside the small craft. In that momentary window of inattention I gave him, he moved.

The first kick came faster than I could react and caught me just under the ribs on my left side. I winced, felt the air leave my lungs and my body buckled. I know my finger tensed on the trigger, but before I could manage to apply the three pounds of pull required to fire the weapon, he had pushed himself off the corner of the boat and caught me with both feet square in the chest sending me stumbling backwards on the loose rock. As I went down the gun fired wild. Gregory did not retreat from the shot, but rather he advanced, and was on me before I could re-aim my pistol.

I had hit the ground hard, my head bounced off the loosely piled rock. My eyes went unfocused and I got off another unaimed shot which went wide. His next kick hit my right arm like a speeding freight train slamming into a semi-truck stalled on the crossing and my bones buckled. Willie went flying into the rocks and a third impotent shot rang out. Then, the last kick hit me in the side of the head and the world went black.

Gregory picked up the gun from the rock pile. He pointed it at William's head and began to apply pressure to the trigger. Then, he relaxed his finger and tucked the gun into the back of his waistband. He saw William's right forearm laying at a painfully grotesque angle and smiled. Marcy was shuffling around inside the boat, hollering and making a hell of a racket. He thought of pulling the gun again and pumping three or four rounds into the compartment just to shut her up, but quickly overruled that idea as well.

"So many assholes, so little time," he said to himself.

He pulled the unconscious William across the rocks and onto the empty boat cart. He walked the cart into the lava tube and stopped it outside of Cassandra's cell door. After punching in the door code, and hearing the door unlock, he pulled it open. Cassandra was still sitting casually on her bed. When she saw Gregory, she pulled her legs up reflexively and stared at him.

Gregory moved out of the doorway and dragged William from the cart, onto the floor and into Cassandra's cell. He left him spread out on the floor, winked at Cassandra and then exited, closing the door behind him.

He crossed to the workshop room. As he walked, he began to softly whistle an old tune.

Cassie's first thought, as always, was for herself. *Oh my God* were the first words to materialize in her mind. In the instant that the images became real, she knew everything had fallen apart with Willy lying there and Gregory walking away. Her plan had failed. Then, she thought of something her old minister would tell the congregation, mainly to motivate those who'd sit on their hands and do nothing while they waited for God's Plan to reveal itself, and that was: 'God helps those who help themselves'.

"I hope so," she said to nobody.

She jumped off the bed and moved to William's side. He was unconscious but when she moved his right arm he moaned in pain. When she looked at his arm, it was quite obvious both bones were broken. Cassie felt the arm, went to the bed and began tearing the bottom sheet into strips. She then grabbed a couple of magazines which Gregory had brought her yesterday afternoon. She did the best she could aligning the arm, pulling on William's wrist to extend the flesh until she felt the bones come back together. She then wrapped the magazines around his lower arm and tied them with the strips of sheet. It was the best she could do, but after the initial shock of seeing him wore off she wondered if it would really matter now anyway. She considered the thought and then continued to do what she could. Ironically, though Cassie had for years refused to believe in coincidences, she knew now she had to start believing in miracles.

She pulled him into a sitting position, then bound his broken arm across his body with more strips of sheet. Next, she wet some of the remaining sheet and applied the cool compress to the growing knob on the side of his head. She wiped his face and then reapplied the compress. After a few minutes, he started to come around.

Sandy and Teddy emerged from the records hall late in the afternoon. When they hit the sidewalk, cell service returned and Sandy's phone buzzed indicating she had a waiting voicemail. She checked the missed call screen and saw the message had come from

William less than an hour after she had spoken to him at lunch. She called to retrieve the voicemail.

"William," she said to Teddy.

He nodded to her, then walked a short distance down the sidewalk and lit a cigarette. Teddy watched Sandy as her face morphed from neutral to angry. He thought 'Oh boy', then snuffed out the butt on the sidewalk and walked over to her to see what had caused her such concern.

"What did our boy do now?" he asked, trying to calm her a bit.

"It was something I said as a joke earlier," she said. "I chastised him about thinking he was rushing in to rescue the damsel locked in the dungeon. That made him think her husband has got her stashed away in something called a lava tube which runs under the house. William said he was going to climb down this crack in the mountain and find her."

"I told you our boy was gonna go in hot," Teddy said with a knowing grin coming over his face.

Sandy looked at her watch and compared it to the time the message had come in. She hit the speed dial button for William's cell but it went immediately to voicemail.

Next she dialed the phone number of the prepaid he carried with him. It rang several times before it was answered.

"Dis Keoki," the voice said. "Who dat?"

She wondered for an instant if the person on the other end of the line was speaking some foreign language, but then realized this was the old Hawaiian who lived across from Cassie and Gregory whom William had spoke of.

"Keoki, this is Sandy Langdon, William's partner."

"Oh, yeah, he tell me about you."

"Is he there, Keoki?"

"Malihini in da tube by now. Gone one hour, little more."

"Did he leave you with any instructions?"

"Tree hour, call da cops."

Sandy thanked the man and clicked off after telling him she'd call back if anything should change. She also asked him to call her or have William call her if anything happens on that end. Teddy was standing there, waiting, looking at her. The situation was changing rapidly, she knew, and to contend with obviously not fully understanding the process of 'going in hot', she dragged Teddy to the Starbucks on the corner and told him everything she had been holding back. She then listened to his advice.

"Remember in the old western movies, when the cavalry was said to arrive just in the nick of time?" Teddy asked.

Sandy nodded.

"Well, that's the point here, Sandy. The cavalry needs to show up over there, but they had best do it just in the nick of time. Too early and an opportunity can be forever lost, and that leads to perps who walk out of court with a shit eating grin on their face. Too late, and we find dead cops face down in an alley. That's why it's called the nick of time, Honey. There's nobody better at judging when that is than the Big Dog."

"What if this time he's wrong?" she asked.

"Hasn't he ever told you to never doubt the Big Dog?" he asked back. "There's a good reason for that."

Gregory took some time to consider his options. He sat in the workshop and looked at the screens on the desk. He shook his head as he watched Jennifer sleep. How could she just sleep, he wondered. Cassandra was nursing her knight in shining armor and it appeared he was starting to come around.

"Betcha have a hell of a headache, buddy," Gregory said to the screen. "It'll make that arm seem like a sliver by comparison." He laughed out loud.

The bitch in the boat had worn herself down again and she was quiet. Not that it mattered. There wasn't a soul on earth who could hear her unless they were standing right next to the boat. As he thought about it, he really owed the bitch for drawing William's attention and giving him the opening to kick the crap out of him. Too bad he couldn't do something pleasant for her as a reward, he thought, an evil grin retaking his face.

It was obvious to him that the arrival of William on the scene meant more people on the outside knew now where to look. He wondered how long he had before the cops came out of the dark just like the big dummy had.

Gregory had much to consider, and not much time in which to do it. His plans were coming increasingly undone, even his back up plan was dissolving into nothingness. He could feel the rage building inside him.

I heard her voice as if coming to me through a tunnel. My eyes refused to focus. I shifted my body and pain shot from my right arm and ribs. I had taken blows before, but never delivered with such speed and ferocity. Gregory would not get another chance, that much I promised myself. I moved my left leg, began to reach for Sam with my left hand when I felt Cassie's hand on mine.

"He's watching," she whispered in my ear. "It's still there." She patted my leg confirming the 'it' to which she referred.

"How long?" I asked, meaning how long had I been out.

"About ten minutes since he brought you in here. I don't know how long he had you outside."

"Neither do I," I joked. "You were right, Cassie. He is a very dangerous man."

My head was slowly beginning to defog. Things were becoming more clear, my vision was coming back. The headache was the worst I had ever experienced, but I knew that too would pass in time. The very fact that things were getting better, rather than worse over time told me there was nothing medically serious going on under my thick skull.

"Cassie, what is this place down here?" I asked her. I knew he was watching, assumed from her first whisper that he was listening too, but what did it matter if I asked these questions?

"All I've seen of it is this cell," she said. "I came home last Thursday afternoon and the next thing I remember I awoke chained to this bed." That part, at least was true. "Did you get my note?"

"This morning," I told her. "Cassie, the pictures?"

She had included six in the envelope. She did not tell me how many had been there when they had been delivered to her.

"Stupid," she said. "A friend only. Not to worry."

She patted my hand, took it in hers and kissed it, and although I didn't realize it, her eyes looked not at me, but directly into a camera when she did it.

"I think someone wanted to blackmail me with Gregory and this had been some kind of opening shot. There had been no demand, no note, no threat, just the photos."

"We'll deal with that later," I told her. If there is a later, I thought to myself. "So you haven't seen the operation he has down here?"

"That's the second time you've used those words. Down here. What do you mean down here?"

"We're in a lava tube which runs under the house. A natural cave created when the island was an active volcano. This one runs from the ocean back into the mountain," I explained. "There apparently are two entries from above, one behind Keoki's house which is how I got in, and one under Gregory's office in the house."

"Oh my God," she said. "I had no idea." She looked around the cell. "We're in a cave?"

My head throbbed, seemingly with every word, every thought. It started to zap my strength. We could talk about the details later, I decided, since Cassie obviously could not, or would not provide further intelligence or insight.

"We'll talk about all that later," I said. If there is a later, I again thought to myself. I am a realist. I have never understood the viewpoints of the eternal optimist or the perpetual pessimist. I see things the way they are and work to solve the problem, not waste time painting it white or black. My next words to Cassie were spoken in a whisper. "I don't know if or when we'll get a chance to make a move, but be ready to react to what I do when it comes."

"Yes, my darling," she said out loud. "Later. You rest now."

Cassie got up and rinsed the compress. She came back and placed it on my head. It felt cool again. She also brought a cup with water in it and four ibuprofen tablets. She placed the pills in my left hand and held the cup for me.

"These are ibuprofen," she said. "Gregory gives them to help with the aftereffects of the sodium thiopental anesthetic he uses. I took some, so I know they are safe."

I looked at her and considered her words. While the verbiage and detail she just used struck me as odd, I would deal with that later. I looked into my hand. The pills certainly looked like the generic form of ibuprofen, so I popped them and she followed with the water. I drank more than what was necessary to down the pills. Along with everything else, I was still thirsty from the exertion during the descent. With every passing moment, I was becoming increasingly lucent. My eyes seemed sensitive to the lights that were on in the room, but my vision had started to clear.

"Did you know there are two other women down here?" I asked her. I wanted to know what else she would give up, inadvertently or not, like the name of the anesthesia Gregory used.

"What?" she said. "Two other women? Who are they?" Looking into her eyes told me this part of what I told her was truly new information to her.

"There are a total of three cells down here, plus another larger block house which looks like a combination workshop and media center, and a series of ramps which I can only assume lead up to a hidden entry into Gregory's office."

"The other two cells each contain another woman?"

"That's right." I said, not going into details about the boat at this point. Thankfully, the pills were already giving some relief to the pain in both my head and my arm. "Who they are, I don't know. One is a blonde with spiked hair. The other I could not see clearly as she was mostly covered up, lying on her stomach and apparently sleeping."

"What is he doing?" she said. "Why is he doing this?"

"If you don't know, then I certainly don't know," I replied.

Gregory had made some decisions. He walked out to the ocean and launched the boat containing Marcy out into the channel. He set the autopilot to take it out to the coordinates he had set into the equipment and tied in the explosives to operate automatically when the boat arrived and the motor stopped. If luck played any role, he thought, the boat would settle very close to the one which took Janet to the bottom. That was his favor he decided Marcy deserved for helping him deal with William. He smiled as he watched the small craft head out.

Next, he moved another boat close to Cassandra's cell. He checked it over, removed the hatch and then walked to her cell door. He carried the tranquilizer gun loaded with two low-dose darts in his hand. He still had William's semiautomatic tucked into the back of his waistband if worse came to worse, but he felt William deserved the full experience. Gregory had never used a real gun in any of this over the years and had never liked handling firearms, but somehow, having this pistol tucked into the small of his back made him feel like a real badass.

He opened the door to Cassandra's cell.

I saw a swaggering Gregory when the door next opened to the cell. He stood in the doorway a moment, then raised his arm. I could tell he held some sort of CO2 powered air gun, most likely a tranquilizer pistol. Cassie recoiled slightly, seemed to try to use me as a shield. I used her movement to cover my pulling my left ankle closer to my reach.

"We were just talking, Greg," I said with the last of my bravado. I saw his eyes flash with anger, then watched as a grin came to his mouth.

"I heard," he said. He looked at Cassie. "I heard it all."

"Even the whispers?" I asked. "Those were kinda private."

"Ah, a smart ass to the end, eh?" he said to me. Then to Cassie: "How do you like your shining knight now, my dear?"

She didn't respond, huddled herself further behind my bulky body.

He glared at me. I kept my eyes locked with his. My left hand inched toward my left ankle. My mind considered the timing since he already had a weapon drawn and aimed, yet I was thankful it was not Willie. With Willie, I would be dead before Sam came clear of the ankle holster. With a tranquilizer gun, I stood a chance even if he got a dart away. Had I looked, I would have noticed the little red dot of light in the middle of my chest.

"Last words between lovers are not of my concern," he said. "The judgement alone has already sealed your fates."

"Lovers?" I asked. "Cassie and I were never lovers. What gave you that idea Greg?"

His eyes moved from me to Cassie and I used his distraction the same way he had used mine earlier. My left hand found the holster and in a flash my thumb released the trigger strap and I pulled Sam and fired four quick shots roughly aimed at the center of his chest. I felt something hit my body and Gregory fell backward out the door. Cassie screamed. I could see he wasn't moving once he hit the ground.

I asked Cassie to help me up and as I rose to my feet with her assistance, I looked down and saw a dart sticking into one of the magazines wrapping my broken right arm. I pulled it free, looked at it, and then tossed it to the ground. The needle was short and I felt no effects of anesthetic, so I assumed it had not penetrated the temporary splint. With Sam pointed toward Gregory's chest, I exited the cell and walked up to his body. He was spread eagle on his back, four holes in his chest. I saw no respiration, heard no noises, yet decided not to risk setting Sam down to check for a pulse. That's Hollywood stuff anyway. Gregory's eyes told me nobody was home anymore.

Cassie walked as close up behind me as her tether would allow. I told her there was a cuff key on the Swiss Army knife key fob in my pocket. She found it and unlocked her ankle. She came out of the cell and looked down at her dead husband.

'He did it', she thought. It was over. Miracles do happen. She looked down at Gregory. His eyes were vacant and his face registered the bud of a look of surprise that would never fully bloom. She felt incredible satisfaction. However, it was not the time for celebration, she thought. That would come later and with Dan, not Willy, at her side.

It was almost surreal. The plan she had conceived, gestated, birthed, and then set out on its own had worked perfectly. Gregory was dead, she was free, and she was free and clear.

"Let's free the other women," I said, then I looked down the tube and saw the boat on the shore was gone. "The boat. It's gone."

"What boat?" Cassie said. "I see two boats." She pointed to the two boats left in the tube.

"No, the boat that he was about to launch when I confronted him. There was a woman in there."

Cassie's eyes registered something then quickly shaded the thought. I wondered what the hell that meant. I tucked Sam into my waistband in back and walked to the workshop. I moved around to the backside of the desk with Cassie following behind and I pointed to the monitor which showed the woman with the spiked blonde hair gently bouncing in a closed compartment. She was obviously in the channel. Her eyes showed no fear, but rather a combination of resignation and apprehension. Whatever fate she thought awaited her, or Gregory had promised her, she had obviously accepted it.

I studied the monitors. The other woman was still sleeping on her stomach, the sheet pulled almost over her head. She could wait,

I determined. My mind raced and prioritized a To Do list. The first thing was to get that boat, and the blonde woman, back here. I realized Gregory wouldn't just send these women out in these boats. Eventually, they would be found. He was sending them out and sinking them. That was the only answer. If the bayous and backwaters of the Gulf could hide Louisiana mob secrets, this channel could certainly hide those of the late Gregory Thomason.

"Do you know anything about this equipment?" I asked Cassie and then decided I wanted to add some consequences to her next answer. "A woman's life is at stake, so please tell me if you do."

"I can barely take digital pictures," she said, a look of incredulity on her face.

I stared at her. Her response was a dodge, not really a lie, and did not address my question, but I'd deal with that later.

Taking a seat in the desk chair, I saw a small two small tags on the upper right of the monitor which showed the woman: 'Autopilot ON COORD' and 'EXP ARMED COORD'. Lying on the corner of the desk was the little control box I had seen Gregory carry out by the boat earlier. There were a series of buttons and switches and two toggles like you'd find in a remote controlled model boat or airplane box. I'd seen kids running the things in Audubon Park during the summer.

"Well, how hard can it be?" I asked myself more than Cassie.

She moved behind me watched a moment, then walked to the corner of the room, opened a small refrigerator and returned with two cans of Coke. She popped the top on one and set it down in front of me. I looked at her for a moment, then went back to studying the controller.

I made an executive decision, flipped one of the switches and looked on the monitor. The EXP ARMED COORD notation was gone. Well, that's one problem solved, I thought. Then I pushed buttons one at a time, but nothing seemed to happen until I pushed the blue one in the center of four directional buttons and a menu appeared on screen. I tried the directional buttons and was able to navigate through the various menus like a TV remote.

When I reached a screen labeled 'NAV', I carefully read through the options and then used the directional buttons to navigate to the line I wanted. I pushed the blue button and the line of text highlighted. On the screen the 'Autopilot ON COORD' changed to

'Autopilot ON RET'. I'm no genius, but I immediately thought that I had solved problem number two. Now it was just a matter of waiting for the boat to return, if that's truly what I had just instructed it to do.

"Look at that," Cassie pointed to the lower right on the screen. "That changed when you hit blue button."

She pointed to what appeared to be a countdown timer. I remembered seeing it counting down from around forty-five minutes, it was now counting down from twenty and change. I told Cassie to look around for a length of rope that we could use to pull the boat onto shore. She went rummaging around. The woman in the center cell rolled over and I saw for the first time who it was.

What the hell was Jennifer Shea doing here?

Chapter Twenty-Four

Sandy and Teddy finished their coffee, and their heart-to-heart. She walked out into late July afternoon while Teddy went 'to see a man about a horse'. Why guys have such a hard time saying they need to use the restroom, is a mystery which will perhaps forever elude her understanding, she thought.

A thunderstorm had drenched the city while they were in the Starbuck's and had left the air cooler than it had been. She looked to the east and watched the storm continue to flash and rumble out over Lake Michigan as it blew toward the state with the same name. Sandy offered a silent prayer that the storm William was facing in Maui would also pass, leaving him safe and sound.

I watched the counter tick down under five minutes and then walked out to the end of the tube. Cassie followed. Somewhere she had found a pair of flip-flops which oddly seemed to complete the bed sheet sarong outfit. As I looked out into the channel, searching for the first glimpse of what I hoped to see, I thought about the meeting which was to come.

That was an item or two down my mental To Do list, so I decided we'd take that particular issue as it came up. My eyes shot daggers of searing pain into my brain and sought to hide from the light, but I forced them to keep searching. I told Cassie to watch as well. I hoped the boat would come close enough for us to get a rope on it and pull it ashore. With one bad arm, I wasn't going to be much use if someone had to go swimming for it.

"There!" Cassie exclaimed and pointed off to the left.

Sure enough, the boat was returning and appeared to be headed straight for the beach. Could we possibly be this lucky, I asked myself. With each passing second, the boat moved closer and closer. Finally, it reached a spot about twenty feet from the beach and the motor shut off. Had I been back in the workshop looking at the monitor, I would see the clock had reset and begun a two minute countdown. I wasn't, so I didn't.

Cassie and I moved to the shoreline. I was amazed to see how fast the bottom sloped away into darkness. I was about to ask her for the rope when I turned and saw Cassie fashioning a loop and then take a throwing stance. She missed the first time, and the second. The third time proved the proverbial charm and the loop captured a small knob at the front of the boat. Together we pulled the boat up to the shore. There was no way we could shift the weight uphill out of the water, so Cassie pulled herself onto the deck and moved to the hatch cover. She opened the dogs and then struggled with the cover. I held the line with one hand.

Finally, Cassie lifted the cover off and tossed it into the ocean. She reached down and helped the blonde woman onto the deck. She was obviously weak, her limbs rubbery, but she recovered quickly and just as obviously wanted to spend no more time on the boat. Her hands were cuffed, but we'd deal with that once she came ashore which she did with Cassie's help a few seconds later. Together we moved back into the tube where the woman sat on the concrete floor. Cassie pulled the cuff key from my pocket again and moments later the blonde was free of the cuffs. She threw them into the ocean with a look of disgust on her face.

Suddenly, there was a dull thud, followed quickly by a second. We all startled and looked toward the boat which a few moments later slipped away from the shore and then slowly sank.

"Hmm, I thought had I fixed that," I said.

I took a seat next to the blonde woman on the floor.

"I guess you'd be Marcy Simon," I said. "Forgive me if I don't offer a handshake. "I'm..."

"William Langdon," she said. "I've seen your photograph on your website."

I introduced Cassie to Marcy and then remembered the To Do list wasn't done. We walked back into the lava tube and Marcy stopped to look at Gregory's body. I hoped she didn't freak and attack the corpse. It wouldn't be the first time I had to pull a family member from the perp, but I just wasn't feeling up to it right about now. Thankfully, a few moments later she turned her back on him and walked away.

"Do you know the combination which opens the door?" I asked Cassie.

"How would I know?" she said with a touch of irritation.

"*Any* ideas?" I asked. "Most people reuse number patterns so they have less to remember. Birthdays, anniversaries, etc."

Cassie walked to the locked center cell door and pushed some numbers. She made a show of trying Greg's birthday, then hers, then their anniversary, then even the date they met, in various formats. I watched as she plugged one in, got a red light and tried another. Nothing. She tried another number pattern and the light went green and we heard the locks tumble open.

She pulled the door open and we looked inside. The lights were off and it was fairly dark inside. The woman in the bed roused and looked out the door. Cassie went in and used my cuff key to release the woman's ankle.

"Come on out," Cassie said. "It's all over. You're safe."

As I watched Jennifer roll out of bed and test rubbery legs, I asked Cassie what the final number was.

"The date his mother died, zero-nine-zero-six," she said.

Marcy had come up to stand behind us.

As Jennifer emerged into the light, I made the introduction which was only necessary for purposes of names. The recognition by mother and daughter, even after thirty years, was instantaneous. Jennifer moved first, and then Cassie pulled the girl into her arms.

I stood back with Marcy and explained what was going on. I also told her that I was certain Jennifer had nothing to do with Janet's disappearance. She told me she believed that and then what Gregory had told her and how Alex had played into the story.

"Alex is Mr. Hale?" I asked, stunned.

"Was," Marcy said. "From what that piece of shit lying there told me, Alexander David Hale sleeps with the fishes."

From what I could tell, everyone had a few different pieces of the puzzle which needed to be put together to complete the story. As I looked at Cassie, however, I felt even with everything being told by Marcy, Jennifer and myself, there would still be pieces missing.

"I think it's time we go up and call the cops," I said.

With Cassie leading the way, the four of us ascended the ramps to the hat Keoki had described. Cassie opened the door, then pushed against what appeared to be just the right place on the wall and a moment later we walked into Gregory's office. I looked closely at the section of book case which served as a hidden doorway.

Missing pieces indeed, I thought to myself.

Cassie said she was going to take the other women up to her room so they could all shower and change. I told them that even though it really shouldn't matter to the investigation, it would be prudent to put their current clothing into separate bags. They stopped by the kitchen pantry and grabbed some garbage bags, then went by the fridge and pulled a weirdly shaped bottle Cassie said was vodka from the freezer. I said it probably wasn't a good idea to do too much drinking before the police arrived. What Marcy and Cassie said the police could do to themselves I didn't think was anatomically possible. The trio disappeared upstairs and I began making calls.

My first call went to Sandy. When she heard my voice, she started to cry, then laugh. I asked her why. She told me what Teddy had said about the cavalry arriving just in the nick of time and trusting the Big Dog, and I understood. I gave her a brief rundown and told her I'd call her later. She said she was going to be on a flight in the morning and before I could protest, she was gone.

I called Keoki and told him that he didn't need to call the cops, that I'd take care of it. He reminded me it hadn't been three hours yet, so no worries. I gave him the news about Gregory and he sounded genuinely sorry to receive it. For some reason, he said he'd say a prayer for Gregory's soul. I guess you never can tell.

Last, I pulled out my wallet and found the card for Deputy Chief Tom Ishikawa. I dialed his direct number. He answered on the second ring.

"Tom," I said. "It's Will Langdon, the P.I. from New Orleans."

"Yeah, Will," he said. "Don't tell me you shot somebody."

"As a matter of fact, I did."

"I take it from your tone, the person is no longer with us," he said.

"I've seen dead before, Tom, and he's definitely it."

I related an outline of the story to him and asked that he send his people. He said he would come himself, but the squads would most likely beat him to the scene. He said he'd have them merely secure the property until he arrived with his team of detectives. He also said the coroner may arrive before he did too, and if he did, I should keep him in the house.

You see, Tom, like cops everywhere regardless of rank, have no jurisdiction over the coroner, even when the deceased became that way as the result of criminal activity. When I asked how I could keep the coroner away from the body, Tom said I should ask him about fishing, then he hung up.

With the cops on the way, I sat down in the rotunda living room area on the soft leather couch. I could really have used a shot or three of bourbon, but thought it better to talk to Tom and his crew completely sober. Besides, I knew I had an appointment with a doc in my near future and I thought he'd not give me high marks for drinking after a head injury with LOC, loss of consciousness.

I recalled that the journals, keepsakes and other items were still in my Jeep up on Keoki's property and thought about how to handle those things now that the situation had played itself out. Considering the amount of recorded information Gregory had obviously kept, I doubted there would be much problem in closing most, if not all, of the related missing person's cases without the police needing the journals and keepsakes. Besides, there was going to be no prosecution of the late Gregory Thomason, so no defense lawyers would be calling for the suppression of any evidence I may have.

Considering my growing suspicions, I concluded it may just be best if the stuff from under the desk stayed in my possession for now. I was glad I hadn't told Cassie I had them in the aftermath of things going down in the lava tube.

As I sat there, my body began to wind down from the massive adrenaline burst which had driven me from the time I started to descend into the mountain. I tried to fight the exhaustion and returning pain by mentally reviewing the events of the past two weeks, but with each passing moment my eyelids were staying closed longer than they were open and before I knew it, I had fallen asleep.

Cassie and Jennifer looked at each other across the seating area in her room. Jennifer had passed on the vodka, and instead sipped a can of Coke. Marcy was in the shower, and Cassie had found some clothes which would fit in her closet and laid them out on the bed. Cassie had to stop Marcy from taking the bottle into the shower, although, she thought, after what the woman had just gone through, who could blame her?

Words were coming hard, and even with the vodka providing a bit of lubrication she hadn't felt in twelve years of sobriety, Cassie was finding talking to her daughter difficult. As a result the two were spending the time together mainly alone in their own thoughts. Jennifer was indeed a beautiful young woman, Cassie thought, and as Dan had said, a younger version of herself. She had an easy smile and a warm, welcoming personality which Cassie attributed wholly to her adoptive parents and the values they had instilled in the girl.

Over the years, Cassie had thought often of the baby girl she had never even held. According to the terms of the papers she had signed, the child had been removed from the delivery room almost before Cassie had heard her first breaths expressed as cries of surprise at the new world. She had remembered those cries, and the slicing of her heart that each had delivered. Yet it had been the best thing for Jennifer.

'Jennifer', Cassie thought, a lovely name for a girl, but so common, and certainly not one she would have given her. Not that she had allowed herself the indulgence of playing that game of testing names for the unborn child as it grew within her. That exercise was reserved for married couples, for legitimate couplings which resulted in God's gift of a child, not for teenaged sluts who allowed their stepfather into their bed. Rape, she had told Willy, but it had been anything but.

However, as the years went by, and as the images in dreams of a faceless young woman became more frequent, Cassie had eventually given in and thought of the girl as Felicity, which comes from the Latin meaning 'happy' and is one of what people call the 'virtue' names, like Chastity and Faith.

Cassie's mother had believed the child to be William's after finding out Cassie was pregnant, and had pushed for the adoption. Her brothers and sisters had never known anything of the baby; instead they were told the same story the rest of the world who asked about Cassie was told, that the sudden move had hit her hard and she had gone to stay with a relative in Baton Rouge for the summer. It was a cliched rouse, and it had worked with her siblings, none of whom had ever questioned her, though Cassie was certain everyone else had at least strong suspicions. When she returned in the fall to resume her family and school life, everything returned to normal, and Jennifer had apparently become a newfound joy to a couple from Texas.

Marcy emerged from the bathroom wrapped in a towel, grabbed another shot of vodka and the clothes on the bed and exited again. When she came out a few minutes later, she was dressed and a little tipsy. She took a seat on the small couch next to Jennifer. An uncomfortableness was rapidly replacing the camaraderie of a shared escape, so Jennifer rose in silence to go and shower, which left Marcy and Cassie alone.

"Good idea, the vodka," Marcy said to Cassie. She poured another shot and looked at her host over the glass as it went down. "By the way, thanks for the clothes, too."

"No thanks necessary," Cassie said. "I'm so very sorry for all this. I cannot even find the words to express my condolences. It's all beyond my understanding."

Marcy watched her closely as she spoke.

"You don't have any reason to apologize just because you were married to that asshole," Marcy said. "Hell, he had you locked up down there too and had another boat all ready to go outside your cell. He was going to send you to the bottom just like me." In the back of her mind, Marcy wondered how the woman could not know what had been going on, obviously for years, but since Cassie did help fish her out of the channel, she decided she couldn't be too judgmental. "Besides, I know you had nothing to do with Janet's disappearance or murder. That sick son of a bitch showed me video he made of my sweet Janet in captivity and more as she died in another of his fucking boats." She grabbed another shot of vodka and slugged it down. "Screw him, I hope he enjoys taking it up the ass for eternity."

"I am certain Gregory is not enjoying anything about where he is right now," Cassie said. "Wherever that is, his location and treatment in the next life now falls under God's purview." She hoped that would shut the woman up on that subject. "You know, if you wish, you are free to stay here after the police are finished with us. Just let me know if you need anything done for you and I'll arrange for it."

"I guess money solves a multitude of problems, eh?" Marcy said, the vodka definitely affecting her verbal filter. "No, when the cops are done with me, I'm getting a ride to the airport and leaving this frigging rock forever." One more shot of vodka. "Thanks anyway."

Jennifer returned from the shower, dressed in a colorful, lightweight cotton dress borrowed from her mother. She was beautiful even without a touch of make-up and even though her hair was still wet. Cassie knew that it would dry naturally as gorgeous as if it had been salon styled. She had always been the same way. Cassie was finding that she enjoyed watching her daughter move, it was like watching herself at that age. She had a brief thought that her pride might be a bit narcissistic, but then pushed the judgment aside.

Jennifer excused herself from the room as her mother went into the bathroom next. She left Marcy sitting alone with the rapidly draining vodka bottle and walked downstairs. She found William sleeping on the big white leather couch in the rotunda and sat down next to him with her Coke, pulled her feet up underneath her, covered them with the dress and looked out at the channel.

I must have sensed a presence because I awoke to find Jennifer seated on the far end of the couch, looking fresh and beautiful in a floral dress. I smiled as I noticed she had pulled her feet up under herself and arranged the dress to cover them, just like her mother would do. Looking at Jennifer was indeed like looking at a younger Cassie, a fact I had discovered a couple of days ago on Molokai when she turned around to greet me in her studio.

"Hey," I said. "Where'd you get the Coke?"

"In the kitchen," she said. "I'll get you one."

I watched her get up and walk out of the room and was amazed at her easy, confident demeanor after such a traumatic event. I've seen many people in very stressful situations over the years, but very few possessed the comportment displayed by Jennifer Shea. It must be something in the genes, I thought. The other possibility, of course, was that an emotional crash would follow down the road. As she returned with two fresh cans of Coke, handed me one and I saw the clarity in her eyes, I was betting she'd be just fine after all this was over. Perhaps I was just hoping.

"A lot to take in," I said. "Two days ago you were a burgeoning new artist preparing for your first big show..." I let the words trail off. "I'm sorry, I guess the blow to my head has made me less tactful than my ex-wife says I am normally."

She smiled at me as she resumed her previous spot and positioning on the couch.

"Don't fret about it, Mr. Langdon," she said. "I am the same person I was two days ago when you met me. I still am a burgeoning new artist and I am assuming nothing will change about the upcoming show." Her eyes moved toward the upstairs. "As for the rest, I told you the other day my parents were Bruce and Elisa Shea of College Station, Texas. Biology aside, the woman upstairs is a stranger. I am glad to have met her after all these years - although I would have wished for very different circumstances - and from what she has told me about her decision to give me up, I understand and hold no grudges; but apart from genetics, there is nothing between us other than our shared external appearance. That's both fleeting and shallow."

I sipped the Coke and nodded at her observations. They were deeper than one would expect from a thirty year old woman, especially given the last twenty-four hours of her life, but I wasn't at all surprised when she spoke them because Jennifer Shea had impressed me from the instant I had met her.

"This whole thing with Gregory, the set up," I said. "You've got to feel betrayed, uncertain."

"Are you trying to psychoanalyze me, Mr. Langdon?" she asked, her eyes searching for any clues to my motivation.

"Perhaps I am just wanting to make sure you're going to be all right, Jennifer."

"Oh, I'll be better than all right, Mr. Langdon. As we say in east Texas, you can bet your last dollar on this horse."

"Because it's you, I'll place that bet," I said with a smile.

There was a loud, solid series of knocks delivered onto the front door which echoed into the living area and could only come from a cop. I heard Cassie and Marcy moving down the stairs. Marcy walked into the living area and took a seat on the other end of the couch. I heard the voices of official greeting as Cassie responded to the door. The sound of rubber soles on marble tile preceded the group of detectives lead by Tom Ishikawa and an older gentlemen I immediately took as the coroner. Tom made the introductions on his end, I made them for myself and the ladies.

"You didn't tell me anyone was hurt besides the deceased," Tom said, looking at my head and arm. "You need an ambulance?"

"No, but I'd appreciate a lift to the docs when we're all done," I said, minimizing my injuries and masking the rapidly returning pain with ex-cop-to-cop bravado.

"We can do that," he said. "Let's get down to business."

With those words, a flurry of hands produced a flurry of notebooks and mini-recorders.

"You want to separate us?" I asked Tom.

"From what you told me on the phone, Will, you each have different perspectives and information all going to the same subject, so perhaps it's best we save some time and just put the story together as a group. Then, we'll go down to the lava tube and take a look."

It made sense to me. Tom was doing this the smart way. There was little of contention regarding the crimes and who had committed them, so getting the statements put together into a single story and then going down and seeing the results and other evidence would be the way I would have played it as well.

Of course, I had to turn Sam over to them for ballistics testing. I explained Willie was most likely either on Gregory's person or he had stashed it someplace after kicking the crap out of me. I think making that admission in front of fellow cops was more painful than the injuries I had suffered in the beating.

Over the next couple of hours, we were questioned and each of us took turns filling in holes in the story. What emerged, in this ex-cop's humble opinion, was a fairly complete picture into *how* it all happened. What lacked was a clear explanation as to *why*. Sure, there were some of the things Gregory had said to Marcy and me, but Jennifer was totally clueless on that aspect of the story, and I observed that Cassie was especially quiet; and so did Tom, I noticed.

Once things concluded upstairs, Tom, two detectives, the Coroner and his team, a couple of CSI techs, and a pair of uniforms followed me down into the lava tube. The women asked if they could stay topside and Tom thought that would be a good idea. Two detectives and two uniforms stayed up there with them.

I knew this whole thing was going to lead to thousands of man hours spent sorting it all out and getting information to various jurisdictions on missing persons who may have been connected to Gregory's actions over the years. Tom and I discussed some of that during the descent on the walkway. As we went down, I could tell the Coroner's team was none too happy about the thought of lugging Gregory's sick ass out of here. Were I to take a bet on *that* action, I would suspect dragging him out the end of the tube to feed the sharks would be the winning bet.

Once down in the tube, I could read the looks of surprise on everyone's face. Outside of the pages of a fictional Alex Cross thriller, a set up like this would be unheard of. Most serial killers possessed far less imagination and the means to carry it all out. Tom told me there had never been a case of a true serial killer operating in Maui County. I guess there's a first time for everything.

I guided them through everything that had happened from the time I entered the tube. I showed them where access from Keoki's property entered and I could tell when the Coroner's boys saw that way out they were seriously psyched about the walkway thing.

The Coroner concluded Gregory was most likely dead before hitting the ground and I shared a look with the other cops which communicated to one another how we wished the bastard had not gotten out that easily. There was no evidence outside of the boat which had obviously gone to the bottom, pulling the rope in with it. Tom told me that if they wanted to see it, they'd fish it out, but most likely it would remain at the bottom of the channel.

"I wonder how many he put out there," Tom said as we looked out over the darkening water.

The sun was going down, throwing long shadows from the cliffs above.

"I think you'll get a fairly complete count based on his digital storage," I said. "From what Marcy told me he showed her, I think some of what your people witness will bring more than a few nightmares."

Tom turned and looked back up the tube. I watched his gaze move over everything: the two boats sat on their carts, the three cells stood open, techs loaded up boxes of DVDs and other loose evidence from the workshop, the place where Gregory had fallen could be identified only by the marked outline on the concrete. Yeah, they really still do that.   Gregory's underground resembled some highly organized military operation, yet it was all the creation not of a large group of people dedicated to the protection of their fellow citizens, but rather of one sick individual for the sole purpose of terrorizing and disposing of women he judged unfit to live, and all because they possessed a physical similarity to his mother.

I watched Tom shake his head. I'm with you on that one, buddy, I thought.

"You ready to see the doc?" he asked.

"More than ready, Tom," I said.

"I'll take you. Make sure you get out of there quickly, though. Maui Memorial has a nasty reputation of killing you if they keep you too long."

I looked at him, told him I hated going to the doc ever since that time when I had turned forty and the doctor had violated me and then never called me the next day, and that I hoped he was joking about the hospital.

"No joke, brah," he said with a laugh at my expense.

We started up the lava tube together.

Chapter Twenty-Five

Marcy stopped by the hospital to see me the following morning, beginning the day's mini-parade of people into room 413.

Last evening, she had hitched a ride back to Lahaina with one of the uniforms, found her car had been towed, and had spent the night at a hotel in Ka'anapali. Earlier this morning, the tow company delivered the rental car to her, compliments of Tom Ishikawa.

She had come by to thank me again, she said. I told her there were no thanks needed, I was only sorry we hadn't been here a couple of weeks earlier to save Janet. Those were hollow words, I knew, but they were the best I could do. She seemed to accept the sentiment they conveyed, and that was all I could expect.

"Where are you headed, Marcy?" I asked.

"I'm going back to Canada, but with a stop first in Vermont," she said. "I've got some things to do for Janet up in Montreal, and a few things to do for me in Burlington."

"I heard about Tamra and Belle and Thomas and Isabella from Sandy," I said. "She'll be here this afternoon, by the way. I know she'd like to meet you."

"I'm flying out this morning," she said. "I'd like to meet her too, but I have to get off this rock and never look back."

She had tears in her eyes and I took her hand in my one good one. I told her that she could call us any time for any reason. She said she would remember that, but for some reason I felt this was the last we'd hear from her. She gave me a hug. As she walked out of the room, even though I had never even heard her name before a couple of days ago, I missed her already.

The doc stopped in and said when Sandy got there he'd let me go. My head CT had come out normal and I was showing no signs of a lingering concussion, he said, so as long as I had someone to stay with me over the next 24 hours, I could go with his blessing. After Tom's warning, I was grateful to be getting out. The doc did say the swelling had made setting my arm difficult, and admonished me not to wait six hours before seeking medical attention with a broken bone next time. I promised him, if there was a next time, I'd be more cognizant of the time.

He asked when I thought Sandy would be by. I told him and he looked a little pained. I asked why and he said that the surf was up on the north shore and he was hoping to catch some wave time. I didn't tell him what I was thinking next.

Tom stopped by with one of the detectives from yesterday. I apologized for not remembering his name, and when he repeated it to me today, I understood why I couldn't remember it. Heck, I couldn't even repeat it.

They had been going through the digital recordings and had thus far catalogued thirty-four different women. A couple of identification hits had come back already, but it was going to be a long process. We all understood without saying it that there would be some victims who would never be identified, especially those going back further in time.

I asked that if they came across a woman from Chicago, possibly wearing a teal blue bikini and going back about fifteen years ago that they contact me. Tom asked how I would know such details and I told him not to ask. He said he'd honor the first request, but if there was something he should know that the second one would go out the window. For now he trusted me, he said.

He left two envelopes with me, one contained Willie and one held Sam. They had released them back to me as a courtesy since departmental protocols would have held them for a long, long time. I thanked him for the courtesy.

Toward the end of their visit, Tom asked the detective to wait outside. Then, he confided to me his one concern over the whole matter and I told him my suspicions as well. We discussed the possibilities and solutions. I told him I'd call him once I got out and that I'd obviously do anything I could to help.

Jennifer came about lunch time. She brought me a chicken salad sandwich and Caesar salad from a nearby bakery deli and I gladly pushed away the tasteless brown soup, purple taro roll, apple sauce, and lime Jell-O the hospital kitchen had sent up. I was beginning to think Tom meant they killed you with the food in this place.

She sat on the edge of the bed and told me she had been in touch with the McCormick Gallery in San Francisco this morning and John McCormick confirmed the show was still a go. He had asked why she even wondered and she had told him. I can't even imagine what the poor man was thinking as she laid it all out to him, but I have to give him credit for sticking with her. She asked if I would come to the show and I told her that I'd do my best.

For most of her visit, we both avoided broaching the subject of her mother, or as she called Cassie, her bio-mom. Finally, she told me that Mrs. Thomason had asked if she would like to stay with her at the house, but she had declined. I told her I understood perfectly, and then asked if she was going to go back to Molokai. Jennifer told me she had come to love the place, but thought the memories would be overwhelming, so she was going to sell it and move back to College Station. She believed being closer to home would be good for her art, and for her soul. Not that it was any of my business, but I couldn't fault her logic.

Jennifer hugged me too before leaving. She told me she was on the American Airlines flight this afternoon to Dallas and then on to College Station. I asked and she told me that Mr. McCormick was going to send a crew to pack up the rest of her art and ship it to the mainland for the show. The realtor she found would do the same with her personal effects when the house sold. Again, this young lady totally impressed me.

I thought I would love for Sandy to meet Jennifer Shea. I believed with everything I was that Sandy would enjoy meeting her.

Sandy arrived on United's direct flight from Chicago in the mid-afternoon. I was dozing in the bed, the combination of the aftereffects of yesterday's excitement and pain medication. She gave me the biggest hug of the day, and there was something in it that told me she never wanted to let me go.

"That was the best hug I've had all day," I said.

"That one was from Teddy," she replied. "You'll get mine a little later after I tell you how angry I am at you for, as Teddy put it, going in hot after you promised me."

I smiled. Leave it to Teddy to stoke the fire, I thought. I was far too weary to fence with Sandy, so I apologized, reminded her that it did result in at least one life saved, and promised that I'd never do it again, unless it was necessary.

Satisfied, or at least mollified, Sandy gave me her hug and it was far, far, far better than the one Teddy had sent along. She smelled great, even after nine hours on an airliner and she looked even better. The combination made me wish I had two good arms.

I was surprised to see my Jeep waiting out front of the hospital. Sandy told me a detective had met her flight at the gate and had brought her my Jeep. Apparently, this Tom Ishikawa liked me, she said. I asked her to drive and as we pulled out, I noted that both my duffel and the mesh bag with the journals and keepsakes and other items was right where I had left them. Had they gone through things, they were good at putting them back perfectly, and in all my years in law enforcement I had never met anyone that good. So I assumed my little withholding of evidence was still my secret alone.

We arrived back at my condo. Steve and Shelly were coming home from the beach and after a few words to explain my physical condition, I introduced them to Sandy. They told us they had some steaks and fresh corn on the cob for dinner and asked if we'd like to join them. It sounded good to me, so I told them we'd be up for sunset. I gave Sandy the quick tour and we went back out and brought in the stuff from the Jeep. She rolled her bag into the master bedroom.

"That's the master," I said.

"I figured it was," she replied.

"I guess I can sleep in the guest room."

"Why?" she asked.

In the morning, I sat in bed with Sandy at my side and we watched the effects as the morning light clawed its way over the mountain top behind us. I had seen this play of morning light several times since I arrived on the island, but it had never been so beautiful.

Sandy nestled against my chest and my left arm wrapped around her. We could hear the morning birds, including those annoying francolins, through the closed windows and doors, but the show was the morning light, and the flickers in Sandy's eyes every time she looked at me.

The ocean awoke as a deep azure, the palms perfection in green and brown, the grass dewy and cool. Shadows grew and then retreated as the sun drew higher in the sky. Apart from the woman next to me, it was the most beautiful thing under heaven to me.

"What's for breakfast?" she asked.

"You're hungry after that huge meal last night?"

"I'm famished," she said, her finger tracing through my chest hair.

"I heard there's a little place right down the hill on the beach," I told her, my fingers gently stroking the middle of her back.

"How long do they serve breakfast?" she asked as she moved a little closer and let her tracings expand just enough.

"Long enough," I said.

Later, when the shadows were as short as they could get, she jumped out of bed and pulled down the covers on me.

"Now I'm really famished," she said. "Come jump in the shower with me and let's get something to eat."

I pointed to my cast and told her she would have to help me wash up. Well, one thing led to another and, ah, we made it to the Five Palms for a late lunch.

After lunch, we came back to the condo and sat down with Sandy's missing person information from Chicago. While I really didn't feel much like re-immersing myself into that mess just yet, I thought I owed it to people who may have been wondering what happened to their loved one for the last fifteen years.

Sandy and Teddy had culled the nineteen possibles down to six probables. All six matched the late Gregory Thomason's type, and three had returned from vacations before disappearing, but the reports did not mention exactly when and where. I paged through the files while Sandy put on a bikini and went out on the lanai to catch a few early afternoon rays. Yeah, I was distracted a moment or two and my mind wandered a bit.

I had yet to discuss my ongoing concerns about the case with Sandy. It's not that we hadn't had our share of talking opportunities over the last twenty hours, but Cassie had not been the first thought on my mind during those times. While she may have made a brief appearance during one of our non-talking times, that bit of information I take to the grave.

Tom and I were on the same page with our suspicions, however, we were coming at it from two different directions. I had some information which he didn't have and the way Cassie had made her way around the lava tube and the walkway up to Gregory's office had just been the final straws for me.

Then I saw it.

"Sandy," I called. "Come in here please."

"What?" she said, placing her hand on my shoulder and looking at what I was holding.

"Why did you print this photo and why is it in *this* case file?"

"That photo came in *this* case file. That's a photocopy."

I reached into the bag with the journals and keepsakes and pulled out one of the cigar boxes, rummaged through it, and then removed the other box and found what I was looking for.

"This is the earring I photographed and put into *our* case file."

"That may be," she said, grabbing the photo of the plumeria earring from my hand. "This photo is of a plumeria earring found at the home of Cynthia Andrews. From the report, it was not matched with its mate in the home."

"Please go upstairs and see if Shelly is there. Bring her down if she is."

"What is it?"

"Please, just bring her down here." I took back the earring from her hand and held it up. "Unless I'm way off base, I believe this is the mate."

Sandy left and returned alone a minute later.

"She's there. She'll be right down."

"Sandy, were there other pictures of this in the file? Especially of the back?"

"No, but there was a description. I recall it discussed some markings on the back."

I searched the papers until I found it. I read the description of the makers mark and material identification. Just then, Shelly walked in.

"Shelly, did you get me the information on this?" I asked, holding the earring up to her.

"Yeah, but after you told us the story last night over dinner, I thought the point was moot," she said. "What difference would it make now that the earrings were ordered by Gregory Thomason for his wife on their fifth anniversary fifteen years ago? Didn't you already know that?"

"Are you certain?" I asked. "It's important."

"Ninety-nine percent positive," she said. "The only way to make it one hundred percent is to look at the diamond serial number on the girdle."

"The what?" I asked.

"Most diamonds, especially the better quality ones, going back about twenty years have a security feature. A unique serial number laser etched on the girdle."

"How can you see this number?"

"Jeweler's loupe should do it," she said. "I've got one upstairs."

I sent Shelly up to get the loupe and asked Sandy to call Teddy to see if he could get anyone to see if the earring in Chicago had been taken into evidence. Teddy told her it was kind of late, but he'd call around. I asked for the phone and then I told him the report pages I had didn't mention whether it had been collected or left with the family and that it was really important. He told me he'd call me back just as quickly as he could track someone down.

Shelly returned with the loupe and Sandy wrote down the number. A call to the Na Hoku offices confirmed the earring in the cigar box was one of the pair Gregory had ordered and picked up, obviously from the journal entry, the same day he also picked up the woman from Chicago in the teal blue bikini. As of today, that woman had a name: Cynthia Andrews.

I slid out the photo of her from the file. She was indeed beautiful, just as the journal described her. Her eyes sparkled when she smiled. It pissed me off that her life had been cut short by that piece of shit, but what made me even angrier at that moment was that he got out of it in such a relatively painless way. What he deserved, he may now be receiving in the afterlife, as Marcy had expressed, but the world was due a debt by him and he left still owing the house.

A half hour later, my cell rang with Teddy on the other end. He said he had raised someone at the evidence room and the earring had indeed been collected. He had it pulled and then taken up to the CSI lab where they used a microscope to check for the serial number on the diamond's girdle and indeed found one. He read me the number and I wrote it down. I told him I owed him one and he said I owed him a big one.

I showed the number from Chicago to Shelly and she looked on her note. The earring found at the home of Cynthia Andrews was the other one ordered and delivered to Gregory Thomason. Cassie had been at the house in Chicago and lost an earring. I was certain that was why Gregory had put the other one into his keepsake box. It was Gregory's insurance policy which now put Cassie smack in the middle of these murders.

My heart sank as the reality of what this all meant struck home. I thanked Shelly for her help and then asked that she keep this all to herself until further word from me or the police. Yeah, I told her, you can tell Steve. Sandy walked her back upstairs.

When Sandy came back, I was on the phone with Tom Ishikawa. I gave him the lowdown and suggested a plan. He told me to sit tight, that he'd send a patrol car for Sandy and I and would meet us. He said the patrol car could get us to Kahului faster than we could drive ourselves, but then I thought a couple of steps ahead and told him why it would be best if the squad acted as a lead for our Jeep. He agreed.

I told Sandy to get dressed and dialed the prepaid phone I had left with Keoki. When he answered, I asked if there was anything going on at the house. He responded that he thought it was all over but yes, he was still watching from his porch. He said the cops were there again this morning but had left a couple of hours ago with another trunk load of boxes. Then he said that a car had arrived yesterday afternoon with two men in it. One had flown off in the helicopter and the other had not yet left the house because the car still was parked in the driveway. I asked if he had ever seen the men before, and all he could confirm is that he knew the one who retrieved the chopper was the regular helicopter pilot who flew when Gregory did not. The other one he described as haole, tall, tanned, with short brown hair. I assumed it was the man in the purported blackmail photos. Keoki said the car was Gregory's yellow Corvette.

Sandy came out of the bedroom about the same time the squad car arrived in the parking lot. I waved out the window to the officer, grabbed my duffel and the bag with the journals, the keepsakes, and two other boxes. I asked Sandy to grab the her laptop and the Chicago files and we loaded into the Jeep and took off in hot pursuit of our lead car which left the complex with lights and siren going - 'Code Three' as they used to say on *Adam 12* - with Sandy at the wheel of our Jeep.

We drove to an intersection in Kahului. Waiting there for us was an unmarked Chevrolet Caprice driven by Tom Ishikawa and carrying the same detective he had been with at the hospital yesterday. Tom swapped out of the unmarked car and got into the Jeep with Sandy and myself. The convoy, lead by the marked squad with us in the middle and the rear brought up by the unmarked cruiser headed up the mountain to the upper road with lights and sirens going. I estimated this would be my fastest trip to Cassie's house. I checked my cell phone, it was three o'clock in the afternoon.

Cassie snuggled against Dan in her bed, in her house. It was the first time they had ever been together there. She laid her head on his chest, slid one leg over his, moved one hand over his body. He had brought out the chopper pilot to fly the helicopter back to the hangar yesterday afternoon and had stayed overnight. She thought about waking up with him this morning and she moved even closer to him.

"I can't believe it all worked out just as I planned, Dan," she said to him. "I told you when the time came he would do it. Although being held down there by Gregory hadn't exactly been part of my vision."

"I have to hand it to you, baby," he said, his right hand moving up and down her side. "You played every card perfectly." He thought of Bev and how she had become irate after hearing of Gregory's death which meant the end of their blackmail plan. She had cursed Dan when he told her he was going to see Cassie and may not be around for a few days. By the time he had walked out of her apartment in Kahului, he was already formulating a new plan for his future. Perhaps, he had thought, marrying Cassie would not be such a bad deal after all. He was certain he could keep Bev on the side.

"You know," Cassie said, pulling herself free and propping her head on one hand. "It was truly fun to egg Gregory on at the end. I told him I was fucking Willy, which I knew would infuriate him enough to force Willy to fight for his life when the two faced each other. Putting Willy in the position to fight or die would ensure he did exactly what I anticipated he'd do anyway. That part had been a modification to the plan, but it sure as hell worked." She laughed. "As a matter of fact, it almost worked too well. I almost peed in my sheet sarong when I watched Gregory drag an unconscious Willy into my cell. I had no idea Willy carried a second gun until I accidentally brushed against it when I was nursing his arm and head. You should have seen Gregory's eyes when those shots rang out. Hell, my ears are still ringing from the sound that gun made in that little room."

"You're amazing, babe," Dan said. "I wouldn't want to stumble onto your bad side."

Cassie tossed her head, throwing her hair over her shoulder. Her eyes turned deadly serious.

"Just don't ever fuck me," she said and then she laughed. "I mean, you should always fuck me, just never fuck me over. You know what I mean."

Cassie rolled onto her back and stretched under the covers. She really was feeling on the top of the world. She even thought of sending Willy another fifty-thousand dollars as a bonus. She'd tell the accountants it could be classified as a charitable deduction: Services rendered in the betterment of the human race, or something like that.

Her cell phone vibrated on the nightstand. She picked it up and looked at the caller I.D.

"Willy," she said, answering the call with a flirtatious lilt in her voice. "How are you feeling? Did they let you out of that awful hospital yet? I really meant to visit you, but with all the comings and goings here, there just hasn't been time, my darling. I hope you understand."

Dan watched as she listened. He saw her face morph from saucy and sassy to serious and concerned. Cassie clicked off and set the phone down. She rolled herself to the edge of the bed, sat with her feet on the floor and her back to him.

"What is it, babe?" he asked. Dan reached over and stroked her back.

"He's on his way out here," she said. "He thinks there may be a problem."

"What problem?"

"He wants to see me." Cassie got up and walked to the shower without another word.

I closed my phone and smiled at Sandy.

"How did she sound?" Tom asked.

"A little concerned at the end there," I said. "She was never one to like unpleasant surprises, and she's got a ginormous one coming around the corner."

Tom radioed the squad car and told the uniform to cut the siren. He also told the officer that he wanted him to drop off before we got close. I described the pull off spot I had found and he thought that would work perfectly. He passed that information along to the squad and unmarked and told them that we'd all stop in there and swap out the cars again.

"Take a look at this," Tom said to us and he handed me a file folder of photocopied pages. "We recovered this on a pad of paper from Mr. Thomason's office desk drawer."

I read the documents and it was perfectly clear to me after having read the journals that Gregory was writing a descriptive about his wife. He had obviously planned it for insertion into the journals, perhaps as Cassie's memorial because I had no doubt he would have killed her in that second boat had I not shot him dead. I explained my conclusions to Tom. He looked at me with some irritation because before this moment he hadn't even heard about the journals. I told him they were in the bag, along with a couple of cigar boxes of keepsakes. I held back on telling him about the other items in the two black lacquer boxes, for now. Frankly, when he'd learned I'd withheld the journals, cigar boxes and legal pads from him on Monday he was a little pissed at me. I couldn't blame him, really, and I explained I had my reasons. He shot me an irritated look and let it drop.

A few minutes later, we arrived at the pull off and all three cars drove down into the pasture and parked by the trees. I called Keoki and he said nothing had changed at the house and that he'd be here in a few minutes. We all exited the cars and formed a little huddle. As Sandy got out of the Jeep, she apparently saw the envelope with the photos for the first time because she brought it out asking what it was. I explained it was the envelope which had come when she was talking to me on the phone, you know, I said, 'the match which had lit the fuse on Monday and sent me into the lava tube to rescue the previously described damsel in distress'. Sandy shot me an irritated look.

There was something in Sandy's face that only I saw as we planned the strategy for the upcoming confrontation I would have with Cassie. My mind skipped backward two weeks to when this had all began as we talked. While many of the cases I had worked over the years had taken an unanticipated turn at the end, this one had been awarded the Magilla Gorilla of surprise endings. I chuckled to myself about how this was going to close out the only open chapter of my life in an unusual way.

"Strangest life I've ever known," I said under my breath.

"What?" asked Tom.

"Nothing," I said.

I suggested that Sandy and Tom ride back with Keoki and set up the parabolic sound equipment and long range video camera in the window behind the porch on his house. I would drive the Jeep onto the property about fifteen minutes later with the detective hiding in the back seat. He could provide armed backup should something go drastically wrong since I would not be carrying. Cassie would definitely want to give me a hug greeting and I didn't want her to think I was either wired or armed. I needed her totally relaxed if this was going to work. Tom confirmed they had portables with them which would allow him to be in communication with the detective.

Once inside the house, I would quietly confide to Cassie that I suspected the police had bugged the place and get her to walk outside to talk. I would then lead her onto the lawn west of the house for a direct line of sight for the recording equipment. That's when I would set the trap for her.

Tom asked if the sound recording equipment would indeed work at that distance. I explained we would be at the far end of the range, but with the weather today, a breeze out of the south directly up the mountain would help. I also said I thought we didn't have any other options. He thought a moment and then concurred.

I hadn't seen Sandy digging in the bag for the journals but I definitely heard her exclamation. We all did.

"Jesus," she said. "Have you noticed this?"

She walked a journal over to us, held Cassie's note over the page, and dropped another bombshell: The words of the journal may have been Gregory's, but the handwriting in them was Cassie's. She pointed out some of the telltales that she based that conclusion upon and said the best people to truly judge were at the FBI. It was yet another nail in Cassie's metaphorical coffin, but we all agreed that we still needed more to seal down the lid securely. Getting Cassie to admit to me what role she had played was the more we needed. To get that admission, I was going to have to play my role at Oscar level, because, as I told the group, Cassie may be riding high right now, but she's not stupid. She had expressed that fact to me quite forcefully, after all.

Keoki drove into the pasture in his Mercedes. I gave him a brief summary of what we needed and he agreed to continue to help. We loaded up the Mercedes with the equipment. I took the bag of journals and keepsakes with me, along with the file on the Andrews woman. The earring from the cigar box went into my pocket. The other two boxes I had removed from Gregory's desk the other night I pushed under the Jeep's rear seat. Sandy gave me a kiss for luck then got into the back seat of Keoki's car. I pulled out my cell phone and told Tom I'd give him a fifteen minute head start and then I'd head out.

The three of them drove off and I noted the time again on my cell phone. The three of us left behind made some small talk. I looked out over the channel and noted it was such a different day than the last time I was here. Monday was warm, bright, and sunny without a hint of breeze which left the air so clean and clear that you could damn near see all the way across the channel. The water had been almost millpond calm. Today, by contrast, was dreary, overcast, with a breeze directly off the water which had the channel churned up into whitecaps. A wall of gray mist hung offshore and rose to blend seamlessly with the overcast which shed sheets of clouds inland all the way to the mountaintop. The irony of the change was not lost on me.

I thought of the Cassie I had known so many years ago and wondered what had happened to her in the intervening decades which had made her capable of doing the things she had obviously done. In my mind, to participate in the murders of so many women over the decades, even if that participation had been ancillary to the acts carried out by her husband, required the woman be a monster.

How could I have missed it? Was she that good at hiding her true personality or was I just blinded to it by the glare of the past or the polishing she did of my ego? Sandy had sensed the true Cassie and had tried to warn me, but I had let my heart overrule my brain. I had wanted Cassie to be the same. How many other people believed only what they saw through rose colored glasses when looking into their pasts, I wondered. Class reunions were filled with them, I concluded.

"Time to go," the detective said, bringing me back from my thoughts.

I nodded and he huddled down into the Jeep's back seat, covered himself with a gray blanket from the trunk of the squad. I tossed the bag onto the passenger seat and then got in behind the wheel. On the drive down the bad unpaved road, I hardened myself to the task at hand. I set aside the soft memories and replaced them with the images of the women who had been the victims of what had become the most horrifying case of my career, both in and out of law enforcement. By the time I parked next to the yellow Corvette on the driveway and stood there with that black mesh bag in my hand, I had fully prepared myself. When I saw Cassie open the door, however, a smile on her face and her eyes bright enough to cut through the approaching mist, my heart still skipped a beat.

I approached her. She hugged me, being careful of my cast, but then patted me like mobsters often did when meeting other mobsters so they knew if the other person was wired or carrying. She invited me in and led me to the rotunda.

"Care to sit?" she said. "How are you feeling, Willy?" Her eyes sparkled and grabbed at my imagination.

Then my resolve softened and part of me wanted to grab her around the waist and pull her to myself and say into her ear that I needed her to tell me all my conclusions were wrong, that she had nothing whatever to do with this mess. I wanted to look into her eyes and see the truth, not the truth of my head, but the truth of my heart where even now she was still Cassie Yeats. I wanted to tell her no matter what I still was in love with her. It's what I wanted to do.

That was not what I did.

Instead I followed the plan. I did pull her close, but what I whispered was not a plea for her to proclaim her innocence, but rather a warning that I suspected the police had left bugs inside the house and that I needed to discuss some sensitive information with her and that we should go outside to do it.

When she pulled back and I did look into her eyes, I didn't see the confusion of the innocent, but rather the concern of the guilty. At that instant, I felt a revulsion fill my heart and soul where memories of Cassie Yeats had lived for thirty years, and in that moment there were no more hidden pockets of softness inside me for this woman.

She walked me out the side door of the garage, and I lead her to a spot in direct line with Keoki's window, across the grass at the edge of the precipice, the waves crashing against pitch black lava far below.

"All this mystery, Willy," she said, a smile still on her face, her voice playful, coquettish. "Have you seen too many bad movies? What is this all about? What's in the bag?"

"I've figured it all out, Cassandra," I said. My eyes cut into her, then released her as I looked out over the channel. "What kind of fool do you think I am?" My eyes returned to her.

"Honey, what are you talking about?" she said. She took a step toward me. "I love you."

I took a step backward. In a flash I saw her eyes harden, then instantly soften. Oh, she was so good. Out of the corner of my eye, I saw a male figure clad in only white boxers standing behind one of the glass lanai doors to her bedroom.

"Honey, what's in the bag," she asked again.

"Gregory's journals," I said. "And his cigar boxes."

"What?" It was she who now took a step backward.

"I grabbed them Saturday night, when I first came looking for you. From the hiding spot you so conveniently left open that day we had lunch together and I followed you into Gregory's office."

"So?" she said with an air of defiant resignation. "The rantings of a depraved individual, who you killed, remember?"

"Oh, I do remember, Cassandra, quite well," I said. "I will remember it every day of my life."

"It's over," she said. "Case closed."

"Not quite," I said. "The evidence in this bag leads beyond Gregory. The journals may contain the rantings of a depraved individual, as you say, but you transcribed them onto the pages."

"You're guessing," she spat. "The writings look nothing like my handwriting."

"Oh, you're very wrong there, Cassie. You did a good job of hiding it, but the telltales are easily detectible by experts. If I can see it just from comparing these to your little note you left for me, think what the FBI can do."

"So what if I did rewrite his scribblings?" she challenged. "You're the only one who has seen them." She pointed to the bag and gestured over the cliff. "Throw them away and all this is washed clean."

"The keepsakes too?" I asked. "In the cigar boxes. All those little envelopes of items collected from all those women?"

"Those too," she said without a hint of remorse. "Throw them to the sea. Then we can pick up where we lost each other so long ago. We can have a second chance at happiness."

I set the bag down, slid my hand into my pocket and brought out the earring.

"And this?" I said. "Toss this away as well?"

"Where did you find that?" she asked, her eyes ticking back and forth like a Felix the Cat clock in hyper speed as she thought about her next lie.

"Inside one of the cigar boxes. Gregory must have kept it as his ace in the hole."

"An earring?" She was playing incredulous now. "How is that an ace in the hole?"

"Because I found the mate," I said, pulling out the photo of the earring found in Cynthia Andrews' house in Chicago. "You lost it when you went back there to set up a woman's disappearance. Cynthia Andrews, that was her name, in case you've forgotten. This was in the house. One half of your present from Gregory for your fifth wedding anniversary."

Her eyes lingered on the photograph, just like suspects did in the interview room when they needed a moment to concoct another lie. When she looked up at me, she didn't lie.

"So that's where that went," she said dismissively. "But so what, they sell thousands of pairs of those every year in the islands. Common as coconuts here."

"Not made of platinum, with one karat flawless diamonds, each marked with serial numbers recorded by the jeweler," I said. "Na Hoku's records matched them to Gregory's special order."

She said nothing. Her eyes moved from the photo to me. It's right about now that suspects took the Fifth and requested a lawyer. However, we weren't in an interview room, and Cassandra still felt safe, not cornered.

"What's this about, Willy? Money?"

"No, Cassandra, it's not about money." I chuckled. "I just want to understand before I throw this all into the ocean and we move forward, together."

I saw her eyes brighten. I had given her an exit and if Sandy and Tom were recording, this was where the payoff would come.

"Of course, my darling," she said, reclaiming that step toward me. "How very foolish of me to think anything but honorable motives could come from the man I have always loved."

Her eyes looked deeply into mine. Were I to let her in, she could still capture my soul.

"Just help me understand, Cassandra," I baited. "Then, I'll make all this go away, for us." I gestured to the bag.

I turned my eyes out to sea. I couldn't bear looking into her eyes. She wasn't in there anymore. The girl who could light up my world was dead and gone, replaced by this sad, corrupted soul. Then she began to explain, her words spoken in a flat, emotionless voice, as I stared into the formless mist.

"Gregory didn't just see his mother die when he was seven years old, he let her die. He was an excellent swimmer, even at that age, and could have saved her easily, but instead he stood on the dock and watched the transition as she at first fought for her life, then slowly gave up. The surrender he witnessed, both excited and fascinated him.

"Through the years he sought to recapture that feeling. He didn't get any sexual satisfaction from it, understand, he never even touched any of these women inappropriately. His fidelity to me was unblemished to the day he died.

"That was very important to him, fidelity to one's vows. See, his mother had violated hers to his father, and Gregory had witnessed the naked gropings between his mother and a man who worked at the house, and that had angered him. So when his mother fell into distress in that lake, Gregory felt it was God's way of testing her, and she failed. The penalty was the surrender of her life. That's what underpinned everything he did thereafter."

"You helped him?" I asked. "Why? Didn't you see the insanity in that whole vision?"

"At first, but then I witnessed it myself. The fear, the resignation, the final surrender to death itself. The actions of their executioner justified by the very sins they had committed and admitted to in those cells, and before we came here, in other places of less efficiency but with the same results. The offenses to God Himself that they admitted to. You saw it in the eyes of that Marcy woman. You saw her eyes just as I did on that monitor before we brought her back. Didn't that fascinate you? That conscious surrendering of control?"

"I saw someone beyond fear," I said. "Someone who needed our help, and we helped her." I silently wondered if Cassandra had become as sick and delusional as her husband had been.

"You did not get the chance to see the finality of it, Willy. Perhaps had you witnessed the end of her, you would have been transformed like I had been, like Gregory had been. That is why I reset the explosives. I wanted you to be able to see."

"You did that?" I asked. "But you rescued her from the boat."

"What could I do?" she said. "I had wanted you to witness her final moments, but things didn't work out."

She dismissed it with the wave of her hand.

"How did you two carry this all off, Cassandra? All these years and not a hint of suspicion on either of you."

"It was brilliant, Willy. Gregory's plan." I could see her face light with excitement out of the corner of my eye. "Gregory would spot a woman, alone, without ties on the island, or wherever we were, one who fit his vision of his mother. You realize his mother was very physically similar to me. We would invite the woman to the house, or simply whisk her away. Then, he'd simply make her vanish. Over time in the cell, she would admit her sins to Gregory.

He had many methods of bringing them to the truth. Some would give up quickly, others took a while. Always, though, he would obtain information from them regarding who they were, where they lived, when they were returning home. So many details. Sometimes it would make my head swim, but he would remember it all. When they were to return home, I would assume their identity and travel back on their ticket."

"What about the identification? Even if they all looked similar in type to you, there was huge risk if you merely used their identification to travel."

She rolled her eyes at me.

"I'm a little surprised at your naivete, Willy. Phony IDs are a dime a dozen, and Gregory had many dimes. So I would travel back, use the ticket, take suspicion off the island, and enter their life. I'd unpack, rummage things around, sleep in their bed, eat their food, and then I'd simply make them disappear. I'd leave their car in the parking lot at a store or at their work. Sometimes, like with that Andrews woman, I'd just jog away and eventually someone would come looking. They'd always discover that the person had returned from vacation or conference or whatever, and then the cops would look around the hometowns for what happened, never thinking to trace it back this far because, after all, the tickets had been used. Government-certified by identification checks." She laughed. "You can't get better than government-certified."

Her eyes had taken on a distant look. I think she was dissociating, speaking about it with such clinical detachment.

"Then I'd fly back in my own name, or another fake name with a different ID. In, out, gone. Nobody would be any the wiser."

"With Janet Hopkins, it wasn't so perfect," I said.

"That's because Gregory used that fruitcake from Lahaina, Alex somebody, and he screwed up. I understand from Jennifer that he's dead. That Gregory killed him for screwing up. I had nothing to do with that event. I was in Dallas visiting my stepfather, and coming to see you." She put her hand to my face, then snatched it back when she saw it did not soften me.

"Yeah, and why did you come to see me?" I asked. "Why me?"

"That's the best part. Because of who you are, Willy. I had seen your name in the papers, as I told you, with this warehouse thing and how people were labeling you a vigilante cop. Then it all went away.

Zap. Nothing more on it. I remembered. You were a man who would do what had to be done. I knew when I brought you here, you would see the wrong in what Gregory had done and kill him for me. If you didn't, Gregory would see the wrong in us, you and me, and try to kill you first. I always had faith that you would prevail. You're my knight in shining armor, Willy, you always have been."

"You didn't want to get away from Gregory to come to me, did you?" I motioned up to her bedroom window and the watching man.

She turned and looked up to the window. Her eyes lowered to the ground. She turned back to me, but didn't look up.

"Oh, you know about Dan," she said. "I'm sorry, my love, but he was the catalyst. He's our pilot, and I fell for him." Her eyes came up to mine. "That's before there was a you and me, an *us* again. Before you were fully back in my life."

"Yeah, but he's the one standing in your bedroom in his boxers, sweetie."

She looked up at him again. I saw a flicker of a smile before she extinguished it.

"Hmm."

That was all she said.

"So you came to me to be your executioner? Why?"

"Like I said, I fell for Dan and, of course, that's wrong because I'm a married woman. As I told you, that's before you were back in my life and I discovered what I really wanted. So, yes, I initially created the plan to get away, to be with Dan."

"Why not just leave Gregory?"

"Why, darling, one just doesn't leave a man like Gregory."

"You mean you couldn't leave your serial murderer husband alive and free out there to track you down one night and give you the submarine treatment?"

"Exactly! Now you see it. I set up the entire ruse to get you here and mix you in with Gregory. One way or another, with various lies to him, and you, my darling, I'm so sorry, the two of you would invariably come to a confrontation and final resolution. Brilliant, don't you think?"

"He put you in the cell, and he may have killed you. Was that part of your plan?"

"Oh, that was an unforeseen circumstance, to be sure." She touched a pair of fingers to the healing blisters on her cheek. "It did work out just fine, though. It's why I left you the note and asked them to deliver it to you on Sunday." Her face adopted a small look of disappointment. "Of course, when you didn't come on that day, I did get a little concerned."

She delivered the last with a small pout, mock scolding me.

"They delivered your envelope a day late," I said.

"Oh. Well, it all worked out in the end."

"How many were there, Cassandra?"

"Women brought to atone? I don't know. Sixty? Seventy? I didn't keep count. Gregory used to say, 'The compulsion is like a black hole, a total absence of light and pulling at me with the crushing force of infinite gravity. It's relentless, powerful, mysterious, compelling, dangerous, consuming and satisfying all at the same moment. I am powerless against it'. So whenever he felt the need or an opportunity presented itself. I didn't care."

"How could you be so cold, Cassandra?"

Before she could answer, out of the corner of my eye, I spotted the detective jogging across the lawn, his gun drawn. Apparently Tom had heard enough and had called an end to it all, ordering his man in to make an official arrest. Up on the hill, I saw Tom and Sandy out on the porch with Keoki. Cassandra followed my gaze, turned to see the detective coming and then looked frantically back at me. Her eyes conveyed the emotions her mouth could not. I bent down to pick up the bag at my feet. It was over. When I looked up, her rage at my betrayal had boiled over and she found her voice.

"You bastard," she screamed, and in that instant lunged at me.

Her hands landed squarely in the middle of my chest with a force which belied our size difference. As I reacted, my feet slipped on the damp grass and I went down onto my back. I reached out for her, but an instant later she was gone from my grasp. As if in slow motion, I saw her momentum carry her over me.

The man in his boxers ran out onto the lanai and began screaming something I could neither hear nor comprehend. The detective reached me a moment later and pulled me to my feet, he had seen what I had not. He asked if I was all right and I nodded. I looked around for Cassandra and then I followed his gaze and saw her, lying motionless on the rocks below. The waves spilled over her body. She was gone. I fell to my knees. And I cried, not for the corrupted woman Cassandra Yeats-Thomason, but for Cassie Yeats, the girl I had known, and loved, and lost all those years ago.

In the distance, I heard the approaching siren of the squad car. As my gaze left her and moved out over the channel, a curtain of mist began to drift slowly onto the shore, swallowing first Cassie, then me.

A few moments later, Sandy was there beside me. She dropped to her knees. She held me.

Eventually, she took me home.